The Cycle of Fire

THE CYCLE OF FIRE

Stormwarden

Keeper of the Keys

Shadowfane

JANNY WURTS

HarperPrism

A Division of HarperCollins*Publishers*

CONTENTS

Morbrith Gairé's
o Main o Corlin
Redwater
Seitforest
Dunmoreland
Furlains
Mearren Ard

Hallowild

Imrill Kand

The Buttons

Keithland

Kendia

Free Isles Alliance

N

Tierl Enneth

Islamere

Landfast

Innishari

Corine Sea

Harborside Skane's Edge

Westisle

Isle of the Vaere

Northsea

Wrecker's Bay

Cover's Warren

Felwaithe

Kierkforest

Murieton

Canyon Lake

Riftwater

Eastplain

Cliffhaven

Kisburn

Royal Palace

Mainstrait

Elrinfaer Tower

Merk's Point

Terin Sea

Elrinfaer

Telshire

Cael's Falls

Mhored Kara

Veshforest

Stormwarden

Book One of the
Cycle of Fire

For my parents

ACKNOWLEDGMENTS

With special thanks to those painters within the field of fantasy and science fiction illustration whose advice and encouragement contributed to my career as an artist. And for those special friends who provided my "home away from home" in New York.

Prologue

Written in the records of the Vaere is the tale of the binding of the Mharg-demons at Elrinfaer by the wizard of wind and wave, Anskiere. He was helped in his task by Ivain, master of fire and earth, for the skills of a single sorcerer were insufficient to subdue so formidable a foe. But at the moment of crisis, when the peril of the Mharg-demons was greatest, legend holds that Ivain betrayed his companion out of jealousy.

Yet, Anskiere survived and the Mharg-demons were bound. The major wards are sealed still by Anskiere's powers. And though neither Ivain nor Anskiere ever spoke of the dissent which arose between them on a lonely isle at Northsea, so potent was the magic in the words spoken by Anskiere to his betrayer, sailors who have visited the rocky spread of beach claim the winds there repeat them to this day.

> *Your offense against me is pardoned but not forgotten. This geas I lay upon you: should I call, you, Ivain, shall answer, and complete a deed of my choice, even to the end of your days. And should you die, my will shall pass to your eldest son, and to his son's sons after him, until the debt is paid.*

On a nearby ledge, battered by tide, lies a stone with an inscription believed to be Ivain's reply.

> *Summon me, sorcerer, and know sorrow. Be sure I will leave nothing of value for your use, even should my offspring inherit.*

CHAPTER I

Stormwarden

The fisher folk clustered in a tight knot before the cottage door. Wind off the sea tugged their home-woven trousers into untidy wrinkles, making the cloth look awkwardly sewn. One man, tougher, uglier, and more sunburned than the rest, finally knocked loudly and stepped back, frowning.

The door opened. Dull pewter light from a lowering sky touched a figure in shadow beyond.

"Anskiri?" The fisherman's tone was rough, aggressively pitched to cover embarrassment.

"I am Anskiere." A quiet voice restored the name's foreign inflection. "Has there been trouble?" With the dignity associated with great power, the Stormwarden of Imrill Kand stepped over the threshold, a thin, straight man with sculpted features and harsh gray eyes. Sea wind whipped white hair about shoulders clothed simply in wool.

"Ye're wanted, sorcerer, at Adin's Landing."

"Then there has been trouble, yes?" Anskiere's light eyes flicked over the men confronting him. No one answered, and no one met his glance. The breezes fanned the fishermen's weathered cheeks, and their sea boots scuffed over pebbled stone and marsh grass. Their large, twine-callused hands stayed jammed in the pockets of oilskin jackets.

The Stormwarden's gaze dropped. He laid a slim capable hand on the door frame, careful to move slowly, without threat. "I will come. Give me a minute to bank the fire."

Anskiere stepped inside. A low mutter arose at his back, and someone spat. If the sorcerer noticed, he gave no sign. The distant sigh of the breakers filled the interval until his return. A gray cloak banded with black hooded his silver head, and in his hand he carried a knotted satchel of dyed leather. Somehow he had guessed his summons might be permanent. No one from Imrill Kand had seen either satchel or cloak since the sorcerer's arrival five winters past.

A tear in the clouds spilled sunlight like gilt over the shore flats. Anskiere paused. His eyes swept across the rocky spit of land he had chosen as home and fixed on the ocean's horizon. The fishermen stirred uneasily, but a long interval passed before Anskiere recalled his attention from the sea. He barred the cottage door.

"I am ready." He moved among them, his landsman's stride sharply delineated from the rolling gait of the fishermen. Through the long walk over the tor, he did not speak, and never once did he look back.

Angled like a gull's nest against the cliff overlooking the harbor, Adin's Landing was visible to the Stormwarden and his escort long ahead of arrival. Towering over the familiar jumble of shacks, stacked salt barrels, and drying fish nets was a black crosshatch of rigging; five warships rode at anchor. A sixth was warped to the fishers' wharf. The town streets, normally empty at noon, seethed with activity, clotted here and there by dark masses of men-at-arms.

Anskiere paused at the tor's crest and pushed his hood back. "King's men?" A gust of wind hissed through the grass at his feet, perhaps summoned by him as warning of his first stir of anger. But his voice remained gentle. "Is this why you called me?"

The ugly man clenched his hands. "Anskiere, don't ask!" He gestured impatiently down the trail.

The sorcerer remained motionless.

"Mordan, he has a right to know." The other's outburst sounded anguished and reluctant. "Five years he has served as Stormwarden, and not a life lost to the sea. He deserves an answer at least."

Mordan's lips tightened and his eyes flinched away from the sorcerer. "We cannot shelter you!"

"I did not ask shelter." Anskiere sought the one who had spoken in his behalf, and found he knew him, though the boy had grown nearly to manhood. "Tell me, Emien."

The young man flinched unhappily at the mention of his name.

"Emien, why do King's ships and King's men trouble with Imrill Kand?"

Emien drew a shaking breath and stared at hands already deeply scarred by hours of hauling twine. "Stormwarden, a Constable waits at the Fisherman's Barrel with a writ sealed by the King."

Anskiere contemplated the sky's edge. "And?"

"Kordane's Blessed Fires!" Emien's blasphemy was laced with tears. "Warden, they call you murderer. They tell of a storm that arose from the sea and tore villages, boats, and cattle from the shore of Tierl Enneth. Your doing, they said." The boy faltered. "Warden, they say you watched, drunk with laughter, as the people screamed and drowned. And they carry with them a staff marked with the device you wore when you first arrived here."

"A falcon ringed with a triple circle," Anskiere said softly. "I know it well. Thank you, Emien."

The boy stepped back, startled into fear at the sorcerer's acceptance. The penalty for malign sorcery was death by fire. "Then it's true?"

"We all have enemies." Anskiere stepped firmly onto the trail, and around him, the wind dwindled to ominous stillness.

Market square lay under a haze of dust churned up by milling feet. The entire village had gathered to see their Stormwarden accused. Taciturn, a unit of the King's Guard patrolled the streets off Rat's Alley. Foot lancers clogged the lanes between the merchants' stalls, and before the steps of the Fisherman's Barrel Inn a dais constructed of boarding planks and pickling vats held a brocaded row of officials.

"We've brought him!" Mordan shouted above the confusion.

"Be still." Anskiere bestowed a glare dark and troubled as a hurricane. "I'll go willingly, or not at all."

"Just so ye go." Mordan fell back, bristling with unease. Anskiere slipped past. Though his storm-gray cloak stood out stark as a whitecap amid a sea of russets and browns, no one noticed him until he stood before the dais. A gap widened in the crowd, leaving him isolated in a circle of dust as he set his satchel down.

"If you have asked for me, I am Anskiere." His pale, cold eyes rested on the officials.

The villagers murmured and reluctantly quieted as a plump man in scarlet leaned forward, porcine features crinkled with calculation. "I am the Constable of the King's Justice." He paused. "You have been accused of murder, Anshiri." A syrupy western accent mangled the name. "Over four thousand deaths were recorded at Tierl Enneth."

A gasp arose from the villagers, cut off as the Constable sighed and laced ringed fingers under his chin. "Have you anything to say?"

Anskiere lifted hands capable of driving sea and sky into fury. The crowd watched as though mesmerized by a snake. Yet neither wind nor wave stirred in response to the sorcerer's gesture. Gray cloth slipped back, exposing slim veined wrists, and Anskiere's reply fell softly as rain.

"I am guilty, Eminence."

Stunned, the onlookers stood rooted, unable to believe the Stormwarden who had protected their fishing fleet from ruin would meekly surrender his powers. Anskiere stayed motionless, arms outstretched. He did not look like a murderer. All of Imrill Kand had trusted and loved him. Their betrayal was ugly to watch.

The Constable nodded. "Take him."

Men-at-arms closed at his command, pinioning the accused's shoulders with mailed fists. Three black-robed sorcerers rose from the dais, one to shackle the offered wrists with fetters woven of enchantment. The others fashioned a net of wardspells to bind Anskiere's mastery of wind, wave, and weather, and sensing security in his helplessness, the crowd roused sluggishly to anger. As people surged toward the dais, the foot lancers squared off and formed a cordon, jostled by aggressive hands. Anskiere spoke once, mildly. One of the men-at-arms struck him. His hood fell back, spilling silver hair. When he lifted his face, blood ran from his mouth.

"Kill the murderer!" someone shouted. The mob howled approval. Kicked, cuffed, and shoved until he stumbled, Anskiere was herded across the square. Thick as swarming insects, the King's Guard bundled him away from the crowd, across the fishers' wharf, and onto the decks of their ship. His light head soon vanished into the depths of the hold.

The crowd screamed and stamped, and dust eddied. Striped with shadow cast by a damp fish net, Emien bent and shook the shoulder of a small girl who lay weeping in the dirt. "Taen, please."

The child tossed back black hair, her cheeks lined with tracks of tears. "Why did they take him? Why?"

"He killed people. Taen, get up. Crying won't help." Emien caught his sister's hand and tugged. "You'll be kicked or stepped on if you stay here."

Taen shook her head. "Stormwarden *saved* lives. He saved me." She curled wet fingers tightly around her brother's wrist and pulled herself awkwardly to her feet. With one ankle twisted beyond all help of a healer's skills, she limped piteously. "The fat man lied."

Emien frowned, sickened by the child's naïvete. "Did Anskiere lie also? He *said* he killed people. Could you count the mackerel in *Dacsen's* hold yesterday? That many died, Taen."

The child's mouth puckered. She refused to answer.

Her brother sighed, lifted her into his arms, and pressed through the villagers who jammed the square. Taen was unlikely to accept the sorcerer's act as evil. Anskiere had stilled the worst gale in memory to bring a healer from the mainland when an accident with a loading winch had crushed her leg. Since that hour, the girl had idolized him. The Stormwarden had visited often during her convalescence, a still, tall presence at her bedside. Taen had done little but hold his hand. Uncomfortably Emien recalled his uncle's embarrassed words of gratitude, and the long, tortuous hikes across the island with the fish and the firewood they could not spare. But his mother had insisted, though the Stormwarden had asked for nothing.

A sharp kick caught Emien squarely in the kneecap. The past forgotten, he gasped, bent and yelled through lips whitened with pain. "Taen!"

Despite his reprimand, his sister squirmed free of his hold and darted into the crowd. Emien swore. When Taen wished, she could move like a rabbit. Angrily he pursued, but the closely packed bodies thwarted his efforts. A fishwife cursed him. Flushed beneath his tan, Emien sat on a nail keg and rubbed his sore leg. The brat could get herself home for supper.

But night fell without her return. Too late Emien thought of the dark ship which had sailed from the fishers' wharf that afternoon, to anchor beyond the headland.

"I'll find her," he promised, wounded by his mother's tears. He took a sack of biscuit from the pantry shelf and let himself out onto the puddled brick of Rat's Alley.

The moon curved like sail needle over the water at the harbor's edge. Emien cast off the mooring of his cousin's sloop *Dacsen,* fear coiled in his gut.

"Taen, I'll kill you," he said bitterly, and wept as he hauled on the halyard. Tanbark canvas flapped sullenly up the mast. Emien abruptly wished he could kill the Stormwarden instead, for stealing the child's trust.

The black ship *Crow* rolled mildly at her anchorage, tugged by the rhythmic swell off the barrier reefs. Gimbaled oil lamps swung in the tight confines of her aft cabin, fanning splayed shadows across the curly head and fat shoulders of the Constable where he sat at the chart table. He had shed his scarlet finery in favor of a dressing robe of white silk and he reeked of drink.

"You disappointed the Guard Sergeant," he said. "He expected the villagers to fight for you, and he wanted to bash heads. How very clever of you to plead guilty, Anshiri. Blessed Fires! Instead he had to protect you from them." The Constable crashed his cup, empty, onto the chart locker. He stroked his stomach. "The Sergeant cursed you for that."

A fainter gleam of white stirred in the dimness beside the bulkhead, accompanied by the clink of enchanted fetters. "But I am guilty, Eminence." Anskiere spoke with dry irony. "Had I not spared your mistress's life, Tierl Enneth would not have drowned at her hand."

The fat man chuckled. "Tathagres richly enjoyed your performance, you know. It was entertaining to hear you confess in her place, just to spare an islet of shit-stinking fisher folk. Or were you truly eager to escape their gull-splattered rock?"

Anskiere sat with his head bent. The oil lamp carved deep shadows under his eyes and tinted his skin as yellow as an old painting.

"I forgot." The Constable belched. "You love fish stench and poverty and, oh yes, a boy whose sister has a twisted leg. Tell me, was he good?"

"Innocent as you are foul." Anskiere spoke softly, but his glance held warning. "Why mention the boy?"

The Constable smiled and bellowed for more wine. He licked wet lips, and his hands stilled on his belly. "Ah, it was touching, Anshiri. The forecastle watch caught the boy climbing the anchor cable. He claimed his sister had stowed away, for love of you, and he came to fetch her home in a fish-reeking little boat. He was angry. I believe he hates you."

The Constable's chuckle was clipped by Anskiere's query.

"What? The girl?" The official blinked, then sobered. "We searched, of course, but didn't find her. Perhaps she fell overboard." Planks creaked under his bulk as he leaned forward, slitted eyes intent on the prisoner's face. His features oozed into another smile. "You lied, Anshiri. You said Tathagres had no means to force your will. But I think now that she does."

*   *   *

Taen woke to her brother's sudden shout.

"No!" His words carried clearly to her hiding place in the ship's galley. "I beg you! Without *Dacsen*, my mother and cousins will starve."

Emien's protest was answered by the drawl of a deckhand. "Cap'n said cut her adrift, boy." Laughter followed.

Taen shivered. The chilly rims of cooking pots gouged her back as she pressed her face against a crack in the planking to see out. Torches flickered amidships, casting sultry light over the naked shoulders of the sailors. Black armor gleamed in their midst. Taen saw her brother hoisted in the grip of a foot lancer. The boy struggled as a rigging knife flashed in a sailor's hand. A rope parted under its edge, and the whispered flop of *Dacsen's* sails silenced as wind swung her bow out of the dark ship's shadow.

"That was unjust." Emien's desperation turned sullen with anger. "I've done no wrong."

The foot lancer shook him. In the pot locker, Taen flinched, and her fingers twisted in the cloth of her shift.

"Cap'n don't like flotsam dragglin' aft." The sailor sheathed his knife and nodded toward the open hatch grating. "An' he won't have shore rats messin' his deck, neither. You'll go below."

Helplessly Taen watched the foot lancers drag her brother away. The sailors clustered round the hatch, grinning at Emien's curses; aft, the deck was deserted. Taen bit her lip, hesitant. Earlier she had seen the Constable push Anskiere through a companionway left unguarded. Abruptly resolved, the girl crept from the cranny which had sheltered her and slipped from the galley, the drag of her lame foot masked by the slap of wavelets against the hull. She paused, trembling, by the mainmast. Torches moved up forward. A deckhand said something coarse, and a splatter of laughter followed. The white crash of breakers on the reef to starboard was joined by a hollow scream of splintering plank.

Taen blinked back tears. *Dacsen* had struck. Through wet eyes she saw sailors crowding the forecastle rail to watch the sea pound the small sloop to wreckage. With a restraint beyond her years, Taen seized her opportunity while their backs were turned. She crossed the open deck into the dark gloom of the quarterdeck.

The latch lifted soundlessly in her hands. Beyond lay a narrow passage lit dimly by the glow which spilled from the open door of the mate's cabin. Taen heard voices arguing within. She peered through, and saw the two sorcerers who had bound Anskiere's power leaning over the mate's berth. Bright against the woolen blanket lay a staff capped with a looped interlace of brass and counterweighted at the base. Beside it rested Anskiere's leather satchel.

"Fool!" The sorcerer robed in red gestured with thin splayed fingers at the man in the braid. "You may know your way about a ship, *Captain.* You know nothing of craft. Anskiere's staff is harmless."

The captain moved to interrupt. Fast as a cat, the sorcerer in black hooked his sleeve. "Believe him, Captain. That staff was discharged by Tathagres herself. How else could she have raised the sea and ruined Tierl Enneth? You don't believe the power was her own, do you?"

"Fires, no." The captain fretted uncomfortably and tugged his clothing free. "But I'll certainly have mutiny, a bloody one, unless you can convince my crew that Anskiere can work no vengeance."

"That should not prove difficult." The sorcerer in red caught the satchel with a veined hand, and in the doorway Taen shrank from his smile. "An enchanter separated from his staff seldom goes undefended. Anskiere will not differ." The sorcerer loosened the knots of the pouch, upended it, and spilled its contents with a rustle onto the blanket.

Taen strained for a glimpse of what lay between the men.

"Feathers!" The captain reached out contemptuously, and found his wrist captured in a bony grip.

"Don't touch. Would you ruin us?" Disgustedly, the sorcerer released the captain. "Each of those feathers is a weather ward, set by Anskiere against need. You look upon enough force to level Imrill Kand, Captain."

The dark sorcerer lifted a slim brown quill from the pile. Taen recognized the wing feather of a shearwater. She watched with stony eyes as the sorcerer tossed it lightly into the air.

As the feather drifted downward into a spin, it became to the eye a blur ringed suddenly by a halo of blue-violet light. From its center sprang the sleek, elegant form of the bird itself, wings extended for flight. Damp salt wind arose from nowhere, tossing the lamp on its hook. Shadows danced crazily.

The red sorcerer clapped a hand to his belt. A dagger flashed in his fist. He struck like a snake. The bird was wrenched from midair and tumbled limp to the deck, blood jumping in bright beads across the oiled wood. The bird quivered once, and the breeze died with it.

Taen shivered in a grip of nausea. The red sorcerer wiped the knife on his sleeve while the dark sorcerer picked another feather from the bed. Before long the hem of his robe hung splattered with scarlet. A pile of winged corpses grew at his feet, and blood ran with the roll of the ship. At each bird's death there was a fleeting scent of spring rain, or a touch of mellow summer sun, and more than once the harsh cold edge of the gales of autumn. At last, sickened beyond tolerance, Taen stumbled past the door. Preoccupied with their slaughter, the men within did not notice.

Beyond the chart room door, Taen heard the wet bubbly snores of the Constable. The lamp had burned low. Her eyes adjusted slowly to the gloom. Past the chart table and the Constable's slumped bulk, Anskiere sat with his head resting on crossed arms. Enchanted fetters shone like coals through tangled hair, and his robe was dusty and creased.

Taen stepped through the door. At the faint scrape of her lame foot,

Anskiere roused, opened eyes flat as slate, and saw her in the doorway. He beckoned, and the chime of his bonds masked her clumsy run as she flung herself into his arms.

"The soldiers took Emien, and *Daesen* wrecked on the reef." Her whisper caught as a sob wrenched her throat.

"I know, little one." Anskiere held her grief-racked body close.

Taen gripped his sleeve urgently. "Warden, the sorcerers are killing your birds. I saw them."

"Hush, child. They've not taken the one that matters most." Anskiere flicked a tear from the girl's chin. "Can I trust her to your care?"

Taen nodded. She watched gravely as the Stormwarden made a rip in the seam of his hood lining. He drew forth a tawny feather barred with black and laid it in her palm.

The girl turned the quill over in her hands. The shape was thin, keen as a knife, and the markings unfamiliar. Anskiere touched her shoulder. Reluctantly she looked up.

"Taen, listen carefully. Go on deck and loose the feather on the wind."

The girl nodded. "On the wind," she repeated, and started at the sudden tramp of feet beyond the door. Fast as a rat, she scuttled into the shadow of the chart table. The Constable snored on above her head, oblivious.

Men entered; the captain and both sorcerers. Bloodstreaked hands seized Anskiere and hauled him upright, leaving Taen with a view of his feet.

"Where is it?" The red sorcerer's voice was shrill.

Anskiere's reply held arctic calm. "Be specific, Hearvin." Somebody slapped him.

The black sorcerer advanced. His robe left smears on the deck. "You have a stormfalcon among your collection, yes? It was not in the satchel."

"You'll not find her."

"Won't we?" The black sorcerer laughed. Taen shivered with gooseflesh at the sound, and gripped the feather tightly against her chest.

"Search him."

Cloth tore and Anskiere staggered. Taen cowered against the Constable's boots as the sorcerers ripped Anskiere's cloak and robe to rags. Near the table's edge, mangled wool fell to the deck, marked across with bloody fingerprints.

"It isn't on him," said the captain anxiously. "What shall I tell the crew?"

The red sorcerer whirled crossly. "Tell them nothing, fool!" Taen heard a squeal of hinges as he yanked open the chart room door. "Confine the Stormwarden under guard, and keep him from the boy."

The stamp of feet dwindled down the passage, underscored by the glassy clink of Anskiere's fetters. Taen shivered with the aftermath of terror, and against her, the Constable twitched like a dog in his sleep. The smell of sweat and spilled wine, and the impact of all she had witnessed, suddenly wrung Taen with dizziness. She left the shelter of the table and bolted through the open door. With the feather clamped in whitened fingers, she turned starboard, clumsily dragging her twisted foot up the companionway which led to the quarterdeck.

A sailor lounged topside, one elbow hooked over the binnacle. Taen saw his silhouette against the spoked curve of the wheel, and dodged just as the sailor spotted her.

"You!" He dove and missed. His knuckles barked against hatchboards. Taen skinned past and ran for the taffrail.

"Fires!" the sailor cursed. At her heels Taen heard a scuffle of movement as he untangled himself from the binnacle.

Torches moved amidships. At the edge of her vision, Taen saw the black outline of a foot lancer's helm above the companionway stair. Driven and desperate, she flung herself upward against the beaded wood of the rail. Hard hands caught her, yanked her back. She flailed wildly, balance lost, and the sea breeze snatched the feather from her fingers. It skimmed upward out of reach.

Taen felt herself shaken till her teeth rattled. Through blurred eyes she watched Anskiere's feather whirl away on the wind. It shimmered, exploded with a snap into a tawny falcon marked with black. Violet and blue against the stars, a heavy triple halo of light circled its outstretched wings. Taen smelled lightning on the air. The man above her swore, and below, a crowd began to gather in the ship's waist.

"Stormfalcon!" a sailor cried. His companions shouted maledictions, threaded through with Anskiere's name, as the bird overhead took flight. Wind gusted, screaming, through the rigging. Half quenched by spray blown off the reef, the torches streamed ragged tails of smoke.

Smothered by the cloth of her captor's sleeve, Taen heard someone yell for a bow. But the falcon vanished into the night long before one could be brought. The sergeant rounded angrily on the girl held pinioned by the deckhand.

"Is that the brat the boy came looking for? I'll whip the blazes out of her. She's caused us a skinful of trouble!"

But the voice of the black sorcerer cut like a whip through the confusion. *"Leave the child be."*

Startled stillness fell; the wind had died, leaving the mournful rush of the swells etched against silence. The onlookers shifted hastily out of the sorcerer's path as he approached the sergeant who held Taen in his arms.

"The harm is done." The sorcerer's voice was as brittle as shells. "The stormfalcon is already flown. The girl, I'm told, is valued by Anskiere. Give her to me. He will soon be forced to recall his bird."

Taen was passed like a bundle of goods to the sorcerer. The touch of his bony wrists, crisscrossed still with bloodstains, caused her at last to be sick.

"Fires!" The sergeant laughed. "Take her with my blessing."

"Go and tell Tathagres what has passed," said the sorcerer, and the sergeant's mirth died off as though choked.

Below decks, a guard twisted a key in a heavy padlock. With a creak of rusted hinges, a door opened into a darkness filled with the sour smell of mildewed canvas. The black sorcerer pushed forwrard and swore with impatience. Nervously, the boatswain on his heels lifted the lantern higher; light flickered over a bunched mass of folded sails and the gaunt outline of a man chained to a ring in the bulkhead. A deckhand's cotton replaced the captive's ruined robe and the gleam of enchanted fetters on his wrists was buried under baggy cuffs.

The black sorcerer studied Anskiere with contempt. "I've brought you a gift." He threw back a fold of his robe and set Taen abruptly on her feet.

The girl stumbled into Anskiere's shirt and clung. The Stormwarden locked his hands over her quivering back.

The black sorcerer smiled. "Stormwarden, you are betrayed." He added sweetly, "Earlier you claimed you would rather burn for the murders at Tierl Enneth than bargain with Tathagres. But for the child's sake perhaps you will reconsider."

Anskiere did not speak. Presently, muttered oaths and a scuffle beyond the doorway heralded a new arrival as two sailors brought Emien, trussed and struggling, between them. The black sorcerer stepped aside to avoid being jostled. Given a clear view of the sailroom, the boy caught sight of his sister, then the Stormwarden sheltering her.

"Taen!" His outcry held despair mingled with anger. "Taen, why did you come here?"

When the girl failed to respond, her brother spat at the Stormwarden's feet. One of the sailors laughed.

"Do you find hatred amusing?" said a new voice from the darkness behind.

The sailor who had laughed gasped and fell silent, eyes widened with fear.

"Or did I arrive too late to share some jest?" Preceded by a faint sparkle of amethyst, a tall, slender woman stepped into view. Silver-blond hair feathered around a face of extraordinary beauty; beneath a masculine browline her eyes were thickly lashed and violet as the jewels which trimmed her cloak at collar and hem.

The black sorcerer bowed. "Tathagres."

The woman slipped past the boatswain's lantern and entered. She placed an elegant hand upon the bulkhead, leaned on it, and bent a bright gaze upon the Stormwarden and the girl he sheltered.

"You are brought low, Anskiere of Elrinfaer." Her accent was meticulously perfect.

The Stormwarden cradled Taen against his chest. "Not so low."

"No? You'll do the King's bidding." Tathagres fingered the hilt of the dagger at her waist, serene as a marble carving. "Stormwarden, recall your falcon."

Anskiere answered with grave courtesy. "The bird is beyond my present powers." He lifted his hands from Taen's shift, and cotton sleeves tumbled back, unveiling the sultry glow of fetters. "Dare you free me? I'll recall her then."

Tathagres' fingers flinched into a fist around the dagger hilt. The skin of her neck and cheeks paled delicately. "You presume far too much. Do you think your stormfalcon concerns me? She is insignificant, and you are less. If you value that little girl's life, you'll go to Cliffhaven and ward weather for the Kielmark, by royal decree."

Anskiere stirred. Gently, he covered Taen's head with crossed palms. Her black hair streaked his knuckles like ink as he spoke. "Do you threaten?"

"Have you never heard a child scream?" said Tathagres. "You shall, I promise."

Behind her, Emien struggled violently; the sailors cuffed him until he subsided. Tathagres resumed as though no disturbance had occurred. "Aren't you interested enough to ask why?"

Yet Anskiere showed less regard for the royal intentions concerning the Kielmark, who ruled an empire of outlaws, than for the girl beneath his hands.

Irritated by his silence, Tathagres straightened and folded her arms. "The King promises you legal pardon for Tierl Enneth."

Without moving, Anskiere said, "Providing I free the frostwargs," and at Tathagres' startled intake of breath added, "the Constable couldn't resist telling me that the King desires their release so he can break the Free Isles' alliance. What did he offer for your help? Wealth, or the Kielmark's power?"

Tathagres stiffened. A flush suffused her cheeks, yet only triumph colored her reply. "Nothing so slight, Cloud-shifter. I asked for the Keys to Elrinfaer Tower itself."

At that, Anskiere looked up, still as the calm before a terrible storm. His fingers tightened over Taen's ears. "Be warned, Tathagres. The King will never command my actions, even should children be made to suffer."

Which was more than Emien could stomach. He lunged against the sailors' hold, thin face twisted with horror. "Kordane's Fires consume you, sorcerer!"

Tathagres met the boy's outburst with disinterested eyes. "Be still."

Emien quieted as though slapped. He glared sullenly as Tathagres tilted her head. Her hair glittered like frost against her gem-collared throat where the pulse beat visibly, giving an impression of vulnerability. Unaware his emotions had become her weapon, Emien was moved by a powerful urge to protect her. He swallowed, and his hands relaxed against the sailors' grip. Tathagres smiled.

"Boy," she said huskily. "Should your Stormwarden refuse the King's command, will you help me break him?"

It was Anskiere's fault Taen had endangered herself. Anskiere's fault the sloop was lost. As the son of generations of fishermen, the offense was beyond pardon. He spat on his palm, then raised his fist to his forehead. "By my oath." His voice grew passionate with hatred as he met Tathagres' glance. "Misfortune and the Sea's curse claim me should I swear falsely."

"So be it." Tathagres signaled the deckhands who held the boy. "He has sworn service to me. Free him."

The men's hands fell away. Emien shivered and rubbed reddened arms, eyes fixed on his mistress. "I think," he said, then hesitated. "I think you are the most beautiful lady I have ever known."

And Taen suddenly comprehended her brother's change of alliance. "You shame your father!" she shouted. Anskiere's touch soothed her.

Emien lifted his chin with scorn. "He'll kill you, sister."

But Taen turned her face away, into the Stormwarden's shoulder, and refused to move. The boatswain pulled her, screaming, from his arms.

"Let me have charge of her." Emien raised his voice over her cries. "I'll make her understand."

But Tathagres only gestured to the boatswain. "Lock the girl in the hold."

Believing she tested his loyalty, Emien made no protest, though the brave new oath he had sworn ached in him like a burden. He waited while Tathagres and her entourage left the sailroom. As the torch was carried past, light cast an ugly distorted profile of his face against the bulkhead. Emien hid his eyes. The sting of his raw wrists reminded him of the shackles which still prisoned Anskiere, and he longed for the simple awe he had known for the Stormwarden of his childhood. Shamed, he lingered, expecting sharp rebuke for the rebuttal of his upbringing on Imrill Kand.

But Anskiere offered no reprimand. Neither did he plead. When he spoke at last, his words held sad and terrible understanding.

"The waters of the world are deep. Chart your course with care, Marl's son."

And Emien realized he had already been weak. "Murderer," Emien whispered. "Sister-killer." Driven by feelings beyond his understanding, he banged the door shut, leaving darkness.

CHAPTER II

Cliffhaven

The wind, which usually blew from the west in summer, dwindled until the sails hung limp from the yards. *Crow* wallowed over oil-sleek swells, her gear slatting and banging aloft until Emien wished he had been born deaf. The deckhands cursed. The captain grew sullen and silent and watched Tathagres' sorcerers with distrust. No one mentioned the storm-falcon. No one dared. Yet archers were stationed in the crosstrees with orders to watch for her return.

Emien paused for a drink at the scuttlebutt, but bitter water did nothing to ease the knot in the pit of his stomach. All his life he had lived by the sea; in the oppressive, unnatural calm he read warning of a savage storm. He squinted uneasily at the horizon. No quiver of air stirred. The ocean lay smooth as pewter. Day after day the sun rose and blazed like a lamp overhead until the sky seemed to have forgotten clouds, and the oakum seams between planks softened and blistered underfoot.

"Deck there!" the mate's shout roused the sailhands who idled in the few patches of shade. "Turn out both watches to shorten sail. The captain's called for oars."

Emien joined the crew at the ratlines with trepidation. Uncovered oarports could become a hazard in open waters. A sudden squall could drive the waves high enough to let in the sea. Yet the risk seemed less than the prospect of lying motionless at the mercy of the storm every soul on board believed Anskiere's falcon would unleash. And though Emien had not seen Tathagres since the night he had sworn her service, her impatience could be felt the length and beam of the galleass.

Yet even under the strong pull of her oarsmen, three more days passed before the lookout sighted land. The moment the call came from aloft, Emien joined the crowd at the rails, unable to contain his curiosity. All his life, he had heard tales of the stronghold of the pirates; this would be the first time he set eyes on it.

Cliffhaven jutted upward from the sea, black as flint against the sky. The slate roofs of a village glinted between jagged outcrops of rock, and above them, like a battered crown, lay the battlements of the Kielmark's fortress. Emien shivered. No man had ever challenged the Kielmark's sovereignty and won. If the tales were true, beneath the galleass' keel lay the bones of scores of ships his fleet had sunk to the bottom. Here even Tathagres was obliged to move with caution.

Crow entered the harbor beneath a white flag of neutrality. No royal ensign flew from her mizzenmast. On deck, her hands worked quickly, and without chanteys, aware their vessel would receive questionable welcome if she lingered.

Emien helped the sailors sway out the longboat which would carry Anskiere ashore. Beyond the rail, the sun threw a blazing reflection upon waters glazed with calm. Emien licked sweat from his lips and felt strangely chilled. Never had he seen such weather, not in fourteen years of fishing. The sooner the Stormwarden was offboard the better.

Blocks squealed overhead and the boat struck with a smack, scattering ripples. Emien made fast his slackened line and glanced toward the companionway just as Anskiere was brought on deck. Two sorcerers stood guard at his side and fetters still gleamed on his wrists, but there all semblance of captivity ended. Emien gasped. Anskiere stood newly clad in indigo velvet adorned with gold. He carried both staff and cloak, and his silver hair lay trimmed neatly against his collar.

Surprised by such finery, Emien knew resentment. "They treat him better than he deserves."

A nearby soldier spat and shook his head. "No, they condemn him. Anskiere wore those same robes when Tierl Enneth was destroyed."

Emien blinked perspiration from his lashes. "He looks like a king's son."

The soldier grinned outright. "You didn't know? He *is* a king's son."

Unsure if he was being gulled, Emien fell silent, brows puckered into a scowl. If his ignorant upbringing on Imrill Kand amused people, one day he would find means to end their laughter. Resolved and bitter, he gripped the taffrail while Anskiere descended the side battens and stepped into the boat. Both sorcerers went with him. Hooded like vultures under ebony cowls, they settled in the stern seat.

Emien cast off the line, and felt a hand on his back. At his shoulder, Tathagres called out.

"Stormwarden!"

Startled by her voice, Emien turned, still frowning. Her scent enveloped him, and his ears rang with the fine jingle of gold as she leaned past him over the rail.

"Anskiere, remember the King's will." Tathagres closed her fingers over Emien's wrist in warning.

Below, the oarsmen threaded their looms, and the boat rocked slightly in the glassy calm. At last Anskiere looked up.

Tathagres' grip tightened. Her nails dug into Emien's flesh. "Lest you be tempted, remember those you have left in my care."

Anskiere's gaze shifted to include Emien, and lingered. The boy broke into sweat despite Tathagres' presence. Chills prickled his skin, for that searching look seemed to weigh the balance of his very soul.

"Mistress," said the Stormwarden, "should you gain entry to Elrinfaer, you will be doomed."

Tathagres tossed her hair, and ornaments and amethysts flashed in the sunlight. "Your threats mean nothing. If I win access to the seat of your powers, Cloud-shifter, the ruin shall be yours."

Anskiere ran lean fingers over his staff. "Your plan is flawed. Elrinfaer does not, nor ever did, contain the foundation of my power. For that you must search elsewhere."

"If the Keys of Elrinfaer fail me, I will," Tathagres replied. She released Emien and addressed the captain briskly. "Deliver the Stormwarden to the Kielmark. We sail the moment he is ashore."

The oarsmen leaned into their stroke, and the longboat sheared out of *Crow*'s shadow, water curling at her bow. But Emien did not linger to watch Anskiere's departure. He left his place at the rail and bowed before Tathagres.

"Lady, with the Stormwarden gone, will you permit me to fetch my sister from the hold?"

"The girl is a hostage, and valuable." Tathagres studied the boy's face as though assessing the set of his jaw. Suddenly she smiled. "You may visit her. But wait until the longboat returns, and *Crow* is back underway."

Speechless with gratitude, Emien bowed again. When he rose, Tathagres had gone, and shouted orders from the captain dispersed the crowd at the rails. Yet despite the bustle of activity, the interval before the longboat arrived passed slowly. Emien paced from the rail to hatch grating, consumed by impatience. The moment the deckhands threaded pins into the capstan, he bolted for the hold.

He stood, blinking in darkness, and the clank of chain through the hawse reverberated painfully in his ears as the anchor rose from the seabed.

"Taen?"

Light flickered overhead. A guardsman descended with a lantern. Emien picked out the dim outlines of baled cargo, and the flash of reflection from a pan of water. A rat raised luminous eyes and darted away from a lump of sourdough biscuit nearby.

Emien shivered. "Taen?" The sight of abandoned food left an uneasy feeling in the pit of his stomach. Raised plainly, the girl was not one to waste. Nothing moved in the shadows. Emien glanced up at the guard. "She's not here."

"Impossible." The man wheezed, stepped off the bottom rung, and swung the lantern onto a hook in the beam overhead. With a final clang the anchor settled and the echoes faded.

"She didn't eat." Emien's voice sounded loud in the sudden stillness.

"No?" The guard glanced at the bread and sighed. "She's probably hiding. But she won't have gotten far. Her hands were tied."

"Not any more." Emien bent, pulled a frayed bit of line from the sharpened twist of wire which bound a wool bale. The strands were stained dark with blood.

The guard gestured impatiently. "Well, search for her, then!"

Emien stumbled into blackness, nostrils revolted by the smell of bilge and the rotted odor of damp and brandy casks. He tried not to think about the rats. "Taen?"

His call dissolved into silence, overlaid by the bump of oars being threaded overhead. And though he searched the hold with frantic care, he found no trace of his sister. The guard left reluctantly to inform Tathagres.

Soldiers were sent to assist. For an hour, the hold resonated with men's curses and the squeal of startled rats. But they found nothing. Desolate, Emien wiped his brow with a grimy wrist and sat on a sack of barley flour. Helpless anger overcame him. If harm had come to Taen, the Stormwarden would be made to pay dearly.

"The girl could not have escaped," said Tathagres clearly from above. "If she's hiding, hunger and thirst will drive her out in good time. Until then let the vermin keep her company."

Beyond the shops and houses which crowded against the wharves of Cliffhaven, a stair seamed the face of a rocky, scrubstrewn cliffside. The walls of the Kielmark's fortifications crowned the crest, black and sheer above the twisted limbs of almond trees. While Crow rowed from the outer harbor, Anskiere climbed the stair.

The bindings had been stuck from his wrists, and noon shadow pooled beneath the gold-trimmed hem of his robe. He used his former staff as a walking stick. The metal tip clinked sourly against risers so ancient that grasses had pried footholds between the cracked marble. Summer's sun had bleached their jointed stems pale as the bones of fairy folk; and like bones, they crunched under the bootsoles of the two sorcerers sent as escorts.

"You will ask directly for audience with the Kielmark," reminded the one on the Stormwarden's left.

Anskiere said nothing. Except for the rasp of crickets, the hillside seemed deserted and the town beneath lay dormant. Yet none were deceived by the stillness. Renowned for vigilance, the Kielmark's guards had surely noticed them the moment Crow's longboat reached shore; as strangers, their presence would be challenged.

Anskiere paused on the landing below the gate, staff hooked in the crook of his elbow. The cloak on his forearm hung without a ripple in the still air.

"Well?" The sorcerer on his right gestured impatiently. "Move on."

But Anskiere refused to be hurried. That moment, the rocks beside the stair seemed to erupt with movement, and the three found themselves surrounded by armed men with spears held leveled in a hostile ring.

"State your business," said the largest soldier briskly. His tanned body was clad in little but leather armor. He carried no device. Only the well-kept steel of his buckles and blade, and the alert edge to his voice, bespoke disciplined authority.

Anskiere answered calmly. "Your weapons are not needed. I wish only words with the Kielmark."

The guard captain studied the Stormwarden with unfriendliness, but he lowered his spear. "By what right do you claim audience, stranger? The Kielmark dislikes intruders. Why should he honor you?"

Before Anskiere could reply, one of the sorcerers pushed forward. As one the weapons lifted to his chest.

"Slowly," the captain warned. "Your life is cheap here."

Livid under his hood, the sorcerer placed a finger upon the steel edge closest to his throat. "Take care. Do you know whom you threaten? You point your toys at Anskiere of Elrinfaer, once Stormwarden at Tierl Enneth."

The captain sucked in his breath. Sudden sweat spangled his knuckles, and his bearded face went a shade paler.

Anskiere smiled ruefully. "To me, your weapon is no toy. I bleed as readily as any other man."

The captain withdrew his spear, jabbed the butt ringingly onto stone. "Are you . . ." He jerked his head at the elaborate gold borders which patterned the blue robe at cuffs and hem, eyes narrowed with wariness.

"I am Anskiere, once of Elrinfaer, come to speak with your master. Will you tell him?"

The captain turned on his heel without another word. Hedged by skeptical men-at-arms, the two sorcerers in black exchanged quiet sighs of relief. It seemed Anskiere intended to see the Kielmark willingly. Even with his arcane powers bound and the children from Imrill Kand as hostage, the Stormwarden made an unpredictable charge. The mortal strength he still possessed could yet make their task difficult.

The sorcerers waited nervously in the heat while the looped metal at the head of the staff cast angular lines of shadow across the Stormwarden's face. They watched as he stared at the horizon, and his very stillness fueled their unease.

"The weather doesn't seem to bother him," one sorcerer whispered to his colleague in the language of their craft. "He almost seems part of it."

"Impossible." The other blotted his brow with his sleeve. "He can originate nothing with a spent staff, and the major bindings hold."

"Stormfalcon . . ."

"Nonsense. She never returned."

A spear flashed in the nervous grip of a guard, checking the discussion abruptly. The tense interval which followed passed uninterrupted until the captain's return.

He emerged in haste from the gatehouse, whitened beneath his tan and dripping sweat. "Put up your weapons."

The men complied with alacrity. To Anskiere, the captain said, "The Kielmark will see you at once."

Stormwarden and escort resumed their ascent of the stair, accompanied by the dry slap of sandaled feet; the men-at-arms moved with them.

For this the captain shrugged in taut apology. "The men must come along. No one has ever entered the Kielmark's presence armed. With you he makes an exception."

Anskiere paused beneath the stone arches of the gatehouse. "I would surrender my staff, should the Kielmark ask," he said, but his offer did not reassure.

The captain's manner became sharply guarded. "He's not such a fool." Any man with experience knew the touch of a sorcerer's staff caused death. The captain's face reddened in memory of the Kielmark's curt order: "A sorcerer at Cliffhaven is just as dangerous to my interests as one standing in my presence, with one difference. Here I can watch his hands. Bring him in directly."

The Kielmark waited beneath the arches of a great vaulted hall. There the richness of Anskiere's robes did not seem misplaced, for the chamber was ornamented, walls and floor, with the plunder of uncounted ships. Gilt, pearl inlay and jewels adorned everything, from tapestries to rare wood furnishings; the Stormwarden and his escort approached the dais across a costly expanse of carpet.

Except for a single seated man, the chamber was empty. The Kielmark chose to meet them alone. Tathagres' sorcerers were not beguiled. Their sharp eyes missed nothing. Amid the cluttered display of wealth, they discovered a mind geared toward violence: the great hall of the Kielmark was arrayed in strategic expectation of attack, its glitter a trap for any man fool enough to challenge the Lord of Cliffhaven.

Seated in a chair draped with leopard hides, the Kielmark returned the scrutiny of his visitors in icy detachment. Except for the tap of a single nervous finger, he seemed unimpressed, even bored by the fact Anskiere's name was linked with four thousand deaths. Outlaws came to Cliffhaven to serve or they died there, for the King of Renegades tolerated no disloyalty, and his judgment was swift.

And strangely, the sovereign who reigned in such gaudy splendor was himself the note that jarred, the piece which did not fit. As the sorcerers drew near, they saw, and redoubled their wariness. Beyond a torque set with rubies, the Kielmark wore plain leather armor like his men. But there, comparison ended, for his frame was stupendously muscled, and his brow reflected intelligence untempered by gentleness. Dark hair shadowed eyes blue and intent as a wolf's. The man had all the stillness of a weapon confident of its killing edge.

The sorcerers glanced at Anskiere, and found him calm. Untouched by the tension which ringed him, he stopped before the dais and waited for the Kielmark to speak.

"Why have you come here?" The sudden question was an open challenge.

The Stormwarden answered quietly. "I plead sanctuary."

"*Sanctuary!*" The Kielmark closed massive fists over the arms of his chair. His eyes narrowed. "Sanctuary," he repeated, and his gaze moved over the blue robes and gold embroidery which made the request seem like mockery. "So. You present yourself as supplicant. Yet you do not bow."

The sorcerers struggled to conceal rising apprehension. The interview had not opened in accordance with Tathagres' plan. And subtly Anskiere extended his appeal. He raised the heavy staff from his shoulder, laid it flat on the dais stair, and stepped back, empty hands relaxed at his sides.

"I do not bow."

The statement met silence cold as death. Shocked by the symbol of a sorcerer's powers relinquished, the men-at-arms all but stopped breathing. But the staff on the stair roused nothing but calculation on the Kielmark's florid face. His attention shifted to the sorcerers, and in their bland lack of reaction found discrepancy. His lips tightened. "Warden, your colleagues seem strangely unimpressed by your gesture."

Anskiere shrugged. "These?"

The sorcerers shifted uneasily as his simple gesture framed them.

"They are none of mine, Eminence," said Anskiere softly.

The Kielmark sat suddenly forward, brows arched upward. "*Not yours?* Then why are they here?"

Anskiere met his glare. "Let them speak for themselves."

"Ah," said the Kielmark. He settled back, keenly interested, and laced his knuckles through his beard. Almost inaudibly, he said, "What have you brought us, Sorcerer?"

The Stormwarden made no effort to answer. The sorcerers, also, chose silence. For a lengthy interval, nothing moved in the chamber but the flies which threaded circles through the single square of sunlight on the floor.

"What happened at Tierl Enneth?" said the Kielmark. His manner was guarded, and his voice dangerously curt.

Anskiere stayed utterly still, but something in his attitude seemed suddenly defensive. Although at Cliffhaven his reply would be judged with no thought for morality, he answered carefully. "I was betrayed."

The Kielmark blinked like a cat. "Only that? Nothing more?" When he received no answer, he tried again. "Were you responsible?"

Anskiere bent his head, and his long, expressive fingers clenched at his sides. "Yes."

A murmur stirred the ranks of men-at-arms, silenced by the Kielmark's glare. Tathagres' sorcerers fidgeted restlessly, disquieted by the turn the interview had taken. Anskiere's request for sanctuary had initiated an exchange whose outcome could not be controlled. And with lowered spears at their back, they dared not intervene.

The Kielmark shifted in this chair, muscles relaxed beneath his swarthy skin. "I accept that," he said, and abruptly reached a decision. "You are welcome to what safety Cliffhaven can provide, if you will ward the weather in return."

Anskiere looked up. "There are limits to both." Without explaining how severely his powers were curtailed, he added, "I will do all I can."

The Kielmark nodded, rubies flashing at his neck. "I understand. You may take back your staff. Now what would you suggest I do with the two who came with you?"

"Nothing, Eminence." Anskiere retrieved the staff and straightened with an expression of bland amusement. "For them I claim sole responsibility."

One sorcerer hissed in astonishment. The other whirled, openly affronted by Anskiere's presumptuous boldness. And on the dais, the Kielmark awarded their shattered composure a sharp bellow of laughter. "So. The hyenas have not forgotten their spots," he observed. He sobered in the space of a second, strong fingers twined in the leopard fur. "I will allow you their fate, Stormwarden, but with one difference. I mistrust the intentions of anyone who claims no convictions, be they sorcerers or men. I wish this pair gone from Cliffhaven in three days' time."

The sorcerers settled in smug satisfaction. The Kielmark had cornered Anskiere neatly; with his powers bound and the lives of two children at risk, he could never complete such a promise. Eager as hounds on fresh scent, the sorcerers waited for Anskiere to confess his helplessness, and appeal to the Kielmark's mercy.

But to their surprise, Anskiere executed the bow he had refused the Kielmark earlier. "Lordship, I give my word." No gap was discernible in his assurance, but his gesture carried the haunted quality of a man who has just signed a pact with death.

Confident Anskiere's lie would ruin him, the sorcerers stepped back in anticipation of dismissal. But the Kielmark gestured and the men-at-arms raised weapons, stopping their hasty retreat.

"Wait."

Without moving from his chair, the Kielmark stretched and caught a sword from its peg on the wall behind him. The basket hilt glittered in the sunlight as he extended the weapon to Anskiere. "You may have need of this."

A startled twitch of one sorcerer's cheek immediately justified his impulsive action. And when Anskiere reached to grasp the hilt, his sleeve fell back to expose a livid line where a fetter had recently circled his wrist.

Shaken by such blatant evidence of abuse, the Kielmark tugged gently on the sword as Anskiere's hand closed over the grip. He spoke barely above a whisper. "Come here."

Anskiere mounted the steps.

The Kielmark bent close, so no other could hear. "I see I did not misjudge, old friend." He inclined his head toward the sorcerers who waited, rigid with annoyance. "Could they ruin you?"

The Stormwarden drew a long breath. Through the weapon held commonly between them, the Kielmark noted fine tremors of tension

Anskiere's robes had concealed until now. Yet the Stormwarden's eyes were untroubled when he spoke. "I think not."

"Your difficulties are beyond me. I have no choice but to trust you." The Kielmark's huge wrist flexed, twisting the sword against Anskiere's palm. With greater clarity, he said, "Then you can rid us of this accursed heat?"

Anskiere smiled. "That would require violent methods, Eminence."

Below the dais, the sorcerers twitched as though vexed.

"Koridan's Fires," swore the Kielmark, and he chuckled. "Your puppets seem displeased. Be violent, then, Cloud-shifter, with my blessing. After that we'll talk again." And he released the sword with a broad wave of dismissal.

Escorted only by sorcerers, Anskiere left the Kielmark's fortress without delay. Once past the gatehouse, urgency left him. He paused on the terrace at the head of the stair and began an intent inspection of the harbor. The view was creased with heatwaves. Below, the town reawakened; he could hear the crack of shutters as shopkeepers opened their stalls. The ocean lay flat as burnished metal, and the air smelled like an oven. Anskiere shifted his grip on the staff.

The sorcerers watched his restlessness with impatience of their own. Apparently Anskiere did not find what he sought so keenly. And although the Kielmark had granted him freedom of Cliffhaven, he passed up the shade and refreshment of a tavern. He left the stair. Careless of his velvet finery, he set off into the scrub on what seemed to be a goat track.

Like shadows, the sorcerers followed. By custom of sanctuary, they would use no force to stop him, except in defiance of the Kielmark's law. The sword added inconvenience to nuisance. Anskiere's acceptance of mortal steel reflected an independent turn of mind they dared ignore no longer.

The hillside offered wretched footing. The taller sorcerer stumbled on a loose rock. Brush clawed his clothing. "Fires!" he swore, and grabbed his companion for balance. Awkward as the maneuver appeared, it was timed to allow Anskiere to pass beyond earshot. The sorcerer spoke softly in the ear of his comrade. "Tathagres misjudged him."

The other sorcerer considered, a frown on his face. "Perhaps. But Anskiere seems to have chosen isolation. If so, we have him secure. The Kielmark's edict of sanctuary will be little help to him in the hills."

"Didn't you notice?" The first sorcerer gestured angrily and strained to maintain a prudently lowered voice. "The Kielmark *knew* him. And asking sanctuary instead of service was a master stroke. Anskiere will have a reason." Briskly, he started forward.

His companion hustled to keep up. "I'd thought of that." A thorn branch snagged his sleeve. He yanked clear. Sweat trickled at his brow, and his soft boots were unsuited to hiking. Yet the Stormwarden showed no sign of slackening pace. Well ahead of his escort he began to ascend a defile. He moved easily, despite the difficult terrain.

The sorcerers pursued, unable to guess his purpose.

"He could be bluffing."

"You're a fool to think so. And Tathagres is a fool to wish the wards on Elrinfaer Tower broken. I don't think the Stormwarden lied when he said the foundation of his powers lay elsewhere."

The second sorcerer stopped midstride; disturbed pebbles clattered down the hillside, rousing thin spurts of dust. He said quickly, "What is Elrinfaer to you?"

The first sorcerer shrugged. "A pile of granite, no more. But if the frostwargs are not released on schedule, the Free Isles will not fall." He glared at his companion, breathing hard. "Hearvin was misinformed. *Never* has Anskiere of Elrinfaer been known to use guile. He's not bluffing. The stormfalcon will return. Mark me. Then we'll have trouble."

The other sorcerer pondered this, then glanced at the Stormwarden, who stood outlined in sky at the crest of the rise, staring out to sea yet again.

The sorcerer signed. "Very well," he said. "We'll separate. You follow Anskiere. Challenge his intentions. Then watch him carefully."

"And you?"

"I will proceed to the cave of the frostwargs. If Anskiere breaks our control, I can rearrange the wards which bind him. His own release shall rouse the frostwargs. They will break from sleep in a rage, and ravage Cliffhaven, with Anskiere alone to blame." A smile creased the sorcerer's face, revealing broken teeth. "After Tierl Enneth, do you suppose the Kielmark would forgive him?"

The other sorcerer smiled also. "Anskiere is guileless. He would loose the frostwargs himself rather than ruin an ally." With the smile still on his lips, he left to follow the Stormwarden.

Above the fortress, the climb steepened and the goat track faded, lost among jagged outcrops of shale. Anskiere toiled upward. Weather-rotted stone crumbled loose under his boots and bounced in flat arcs down the slope.

Chafed by sweat-drenched robes, the sorcerer tripped and stumbled on the Stormwarden's heels, pelted by pebbles from above. He cursed the land, the suffocating heat, and the wizard he guarded, but he followed with the diligence of a madman. When Anskiere at last reached the summit, he was only half a pace behind, and not much wiser than he had been earlier. Anskiere's intentions were still obscure, though the sorcerer had sifted possibilities until his head ached from thought.

On the crest of the crag the Stormwarden paused. He leaned on his staff and bent a searching gaze toward the far horizon, his features expressionless. At his side, the sorcerer looked also, but saw nothing in the scenery to warrant such close attention. The afternoon was spent. Below, a spread of hills quivered in the heat haze. A gull flapped above a pale stretch of sand, and the beach plums and dune grasses lay still, untouched by a ripple of breeze. The bleached vault of the sky hung empty and at the edge of the sea, like massive bruises, lay the headlands of Mainstrait, key to the Kielmark's power; for every ship which passed the strait to trade with the eastern kingdoms, Cliffhaven exacted tribute. Yet no vessel moved in the dense calm.

To the sorcerer, the earth's own vitality seemed locked behind the Stormwarden's silence. The thought was irrational. Irked at himself, the sorcerer said, "You cannot keep your promise to the Kielmark."

Anskiere stared out over Mainstrait, utterly still.

"Well?" The sorcerer spoke sharply. "Do you believe yourself capable of warding weather?"

Anskiere glanced briefly at his adversary, and his reply held no rancor. "No."

"Then what have you gained, Cloud-shifter, except enmity in the one inhabited place left open to your presence?"

Anskiere regarded the ocean as though searching for something lost. He did not speak. And that quiet lack of response unsettled his escort as nothing had before. The sorcerer longed to lay rough hands on his charge, and shatter the stillness which clothed him. In a tone stripped by malice he said, "What bard will sing of you, with the blood of Tierl Enneth on your hands?"

"What bard would have liberty to sing, should the Free Isles' Alliance be broken?" Anskiere removed his attention from the sea to the sorcerer. "Hear me," he said softly. "Not once did I promise to free the frostwargs."

Tathagres' henchman reddened beneath that steady gaze. "Beware. The little girl will be made to suffer for your treason."

Anskiere laughed. *Treason?* Against whom? Tathagres?"

"Against the Kielmark, Cloud-shifter. And against your sovereign lord, the King of Kisburn."

Anskiere gestured impatiently. "I am no vassal of Kisburn's, to be called to heel like a dog. His ambitions will ruin him without any help from me."

"What of the Kielmark?" The sorcerer reached out, and delicately plucked a tern's feather from a cranny in the rocks. "If you defy my liege and the frostwargs are not freed by your hand, recovery of your power will rouse them to riot. To alter the weather, you must bring about destruction upon Cliffhaven. Your promise is now linked to your demise."

"So is your threat." Anskiere stood straight as an ash spear. Dying sunlight glanced through the interlaced metal which capped his staff, unaltered by any trace of resonant force. Yet his assurance seemed complete as he said, "Dare you tell your mistress?"

"Dare I?" The black sorcerer stiffened, and the quill crumpled like a flower petal between his fingers. "Tathagres is the King of Kisburn's tool. As you are." And he released the feather, letting it drift, broken, to the ground.

Anskiere caught it as it fell. He turned its mangled length over in his hands, then slowly smoothed it straight. Without another word, he set off down the slope toward the sea.

The pace he set was recklessly fast. Angrily the sorcerer followed. If Anskiere would not be ruled, his will would be broken by force, however distasteful the method. The sorcerer plunged down an embankment, flailing his arms for balance as the footing crumbled under him. Over a rattle of pebbles he said, "You have until dawn. After that, I have no choice but to inform Tathagres. When the child cries out in agony perhaps you will reconsider."

Anskiere's knuckles whitened against the wood of his staff. But that was the only sign he heard the words at all.

CHAPTER III

Tempest

Fuzzed by heat haze, night fell over Cliffhaven, and a reddened quarter moon dangled above Mainstrait, mirrored by ocean unmarred by waves or current. At the crest of a bluff overlooking the beach, Anskiere waited on a cluster of rocks, his staff against his shoulder. He had stood watch since sunset. Close by, the black sorcerer sat among the dune grass, irritably keeping his vigil. The heat had not lifted. The surrounding land seemed poisoned, throttled by a hush which silenced summer's chorus of crickets. Even the gnats were absent.

The sorcerer blotted his sweating face, nagged by the feeling that the simplest of motions somehow violated the unnatural quiet. He shifted uncomfortably to ease cramped limbs. Grasses pricked through his robe, making him itch, and his flesh ached for rest and for the meals he had neglected. Yet while Anskiere remained on the rocks, the sorcerer had no choice but to stay with him.

The moon set well after midnight. Overhead, the stars wheeled with imperceptible slowness until dawn at last paled the sky above the mountains.

The sorcerer stirred stiffly. He shook the dew from his robe as day brightened around him. "Stormwarden," he said. "Give me your decision. Will you consent to the royal command, or shall the village girl be made to suffer?"

Anskiere raised his head and closely studied his adversary. "I chose on the night I left Imrill Kand." He smiled, and a slight cat's paw of breeze stirred his hair.

Wind. The weather was changing. The sorcerer noticed a chill against his skin, and his stomach knotted with apprehension. A second puff stirred the cloth around his knees. Uncomfortably, he felt as though something stalked him from behind. He whirled, and that moment discovered how Anskiere had manipulated him.

Low in the northwest, a black anvil of cloud rolled above the crags of Cliffhaven; nightlong, Anskiere had directed his attention to the east, a ruse of such simplicity it had not been challenged. The sorcerer had never thought to watch his back. Appalled by his error, he licked whitened lips and tried not to overreact.

"Stormfalcon," he said accusingly. "This shouldn't be possible. What object could possibly key the bird's return? Your powers were bound well before her release, and Tathagres had you stripped of everything you brought from Imrill Kand, even your clothes."

A gust slammed down from the north, flattening the dune grass. Anskiere's cloak streamed like a flag. He raised the staff, and the sorcerer understood with a jolt. *The staff itself had been the object of the falcon's homing,* a provision set up well in advance of Anskiere's imprisonment; and a risk no responsible adept could justify. That power of such magnitude should be linked to an object possessed by an enemy was unthinkable. Yet Anskiere had dared.

The gale rattled through the beach plums, wrenching off dead leaves. With only seconds to act, the sorcerer sprang at the Stormwarden. Anskiere gave ground. Steel chimed from his scabbard, and he blocked his attacker's rush with the Kielmark's weapon.

The sorcerer checked, and escaped with a torn sleeve. His wrist trickled blood, penalty of an instinctive reflex to ward off the blade which thrust at his heart.

"Fires consume you!" he shouted. "Do you think steel can save you?" And quivering with outrage at the insult, for his prowess went well beyond mortal weapons, he raised both arms and began to shape a spell which would bring Anskiere to his knees.

Light arched between his fingers as the binding took form. But sword in hand, Anskiere paid the spell little heed. His face stayed set like a rock beneath tumbled hair. Suddenly he whistled and lifted the staff.

The sorcerer tensed with the spell only half complete, and at the edge of vision glimpsed a black-and-yellow shape which knifed the air like a scimitar, haloed in blue-violet light. He spun around, saw the stormfalcon rise, feathers parted by wind, her target Anskiere's staff. The sorcerer altered tactics to suit. He snatched up his knife, and with a word redirected his spell. The light he had conjured arced with a snap and joined with the blade in his hand. He then flung the knife at the falcon.

Anskiere shouted. His sword fell, ringing onto stone, as the knife flashed toward the bird's soft breast. She cried shrilly. The sorcerer laughed in triumph. Desperately the stormfalcon banked, talons upraised. And the halo of force around her suddenly split into the brilliant triple aura of a defense ward.

The knife struck a starred pulse of light. Energy whined on the wind. The sorcerer's laughter changed pitch, transformed to a scream of terror. Unbelievably, the falcon carried all the safeguards of the power Anskiere had once invested in his staff. It was reckless folly, all the more unbelievable after what had gone before, that an adept should ever bind such force into a form a stranger could trigger. Incredibly, Anskiere had done so.

Trapped by miscalculation, the sorcerer saw his enchanted knife tumble, charred, to the ground. Before he could invoke a countermeasure, the terrible power his attack had released ripped across the spell which linked him with his weapon, and tossed him limp to the ground.

*   *   *

Anskiere steadied the staff as the falcon alighted. Her aura transferred with a crackle of sound, restored to its rightful center amid the interlaced metal. He could not damp the force, which was wasteful. Although shielded by the resonance of his own conjuring, the Stormwarden could direct none of the energy. One enemy now lay dead, but the sorcerer who remained still held sway over his powers.

Anskiere coaxed the falcon to his wrist. He had to recover his weather sense and quickly, for linked inextricably to the falcon's presence was the fiercest tempest ever to rage across the northeast latitudes. Already the sky churned, blackened by clouds. The ocean tossed, ripped into spume, and waves crashed against the shore, hurling fountainheads of spray. Storm and tide would shortly break with unmanageable violence over Cliffhaven. Gripping his staff for balance, Anskiere hoped the Kielmark had heeded the warning he had tried to deliver; any ship caught beyond sheltered waters would be pounded by nature's most merciless fury. Until Tathagres' remaining sorcerer could be found and dispatched, Anskiere was helpless to save them; and the sorcerer certainly would be found in the worst possible location. Anskiere jabbed his staff into the earth, and bent his steps toward the cave of the frostwargs.

The storm struck with the violence of a crazed man's nightmare. Daylight lay smothered under sooty combers of cloud. Rain mixed with hail battered Cliffhaven with a rattle like enemy bowfire. In the town the street lanterns were quenched by the torrent, and folk huddled around darkened dripping chimneys and shivered as the wind tore the slate from their roofs.

The gale raged across the headland, screaming through the rocks above the cave which imprisoned the frostwargs. Although the entrance was narrow, the tunnel plunged steeply downward, doubling back upon itself; the walls carved the gusts into a hollow dirgelike wail. Far down, beneath the level of the seabed, the passage opened into a stone cavern. Even there, the storm caused drafts which rippled the robe of Tathagres' remaining sorcerer and teased his upraised torch until it guttered and hissed in complaint.

Even underground he felt the stormfalcon's return. He also knew his companion was dead, since the spell which confined Anskiere's powers had partially linked their awareness. Rather than pause for mourning, the sorcerer who survived plotted vengeance with the neatness of a spider spinning its web. He lifted the torch higher, and at last discovered what he came to find.

Close to a century before, the Firelord Ivain had employed his command of flame and earth to fashion a prison for the frostwargs. In the flickering spill of light, the King's sorcerer saw a circular pit incised into the cavern floor. He made his way cautiously to the brink. The torch revealed no bottom. Below lay darkness so thick it bewildered the senses.

A man who gazed too long into those depths could became dizzied by vertigo and fall headlong to his death. The sorcerer did not look down. Instead he jammed the torch in a niche. The draft extinguished the flame. He made no move to restore it. Rigid with concentration, he drew upon his craft, and soon a small blaze of illumination arose between his fingers.

He bent, anchored the light at the edge of the drop with a word of mastery. Reflections glazed the sweat on his brow as he stepped back, then loosed the spell with a gesture.

The spark drifted across the abyss, scribing a thin, violet line across the deep. The sorcerer rounded the pit. He fielded the spell as it reached the far side, and flicked it out, leaving the glow of its passage bridged like a needle across the expanse. The sorcerer stepped widdershins to the side. Another spell flashed in his hands. Presently a second line crossed the pit. Patiently, the sorcerer moved again, creating a third, then a fourth line, until the mouth of the frostwargs' prison lay masked in meshes of light. Restless currents of air sighed around his head as he stood back, gazing contentedly upon his handiwork.

Far beneath the starred eye of his spell slept the frostwargs. At one time, the sorcerer knew, the creatures had roamed the lands above, ravaging forests and farmlands from the first chill of autumn until spring. Come summer, they burrowed into the ground to sleep until the cold returned to color the leaves. In Landfast's records, the sorcerer had read accounts of wasted acres and dismembered settlements; from Hearvin, who trained him, he learned the secret of the frostwargs' confinement. The arrangement was so simple that he laughed.

Temperature change keyed the frostwargs' awakening, and warm weather kept them comatose. Ivain, who was both Earthmaster and Fire-lord, had merely sunk a shaft for them below reach of winter's cold, where the air stayed constant from season to season. In the years since their entombment, the creatures had never roused.

The sorcerer smoothed his robes, congratulating himself for clever-ness. He stood at the brink of the pit and let his consciousness conjoin with the horrors who slumbered below. Their dreams were restless. Aware they had been cheated of their seasonal rampage, the frostwargs emanated viciousness like lust. Their eight-legged forms twitched, claws clicking against stone; spiked tails thrashed, and between hornlike mandibles slim tongues flickered in memory of the taste of blood and torn earth. Stirred by the creatures' subconscious desires, the sorcerer shivered in anticipa-tion. For the passage of years had unbalanced the rhythm of the frost-wargs' slumber; any shift in the air would disrupt their fragile dreams. Warmth, instead of further prolonging hibernation, would stir them to ungovernable rage.

Delicately the sorcerer disengaged his contact. With the finesse of a man courting a reluctant lover, he summoned forth the framework of the wards which locked Anskiere's powers. They flamed across his mind's eye, a maze of convoluted force, once sealed into a structure Anskiere could not break. But now the death of one of its creators had spoiled the symmetry. Gapped interstices and torn angles showed where the spell was vulnerable. This the sorcerer changed.

He balanced the breaks with a linkage to the net woven across the pit. The principle was artlessly simple; should Anskiere attempt to exploit the advantage he had gained by murdering Tathagres' warden, his aggression would transfer to the web and dissipate into the pit as heat. The plot made the sorcerer smile.

"Try to escape," he mocked, wishing his adversary were present. "Just try. Your efforts will free none but the frostwargs." And his smile dissolved into laughter until the grotto bounced with echoes. Confident of the trap he had wrought, the sorcerer groped among the rocks for his torch. Once it was lit, he started up the shaft.

The weight of sodden velvet bowed Anskiere's shoulders like mail as he traversed the cliffs where Ivain had secured the frostwargs. He had discarded the cloak long since. Knotted in a sling of rags torn from the lining, his staff glowed at his back. The stormfalcon circled above, held by the geas of homing even as the storm was bound still to her flight path. Anskiere toiled over rocks glazed by rain, beleaguered by gales his own hand had once controlled; the sensitive instincts which enabled him to bend weather into harmony with his will were absent. Unaccustomed to the hostility of the elements, Anskiere felt like an artist gone blind in the midst of a masterpiece. The predicament might have hurt less had his adversaries not captured the children.

A breaker smoked over the reef, needling Anskiere with spray. His skin had long since gone numb. Shivering, he crossed a narrow ledge, unable to gauge when the storm would peak, or estimate the high tide mark. The waves were still building. Foam smothered another almost under his boot, and spindrift stung his eyes. The ledge was certainly unsafe.

Ivain had designed the frostwargs' prison above reefs which slashed the tides into boiling currents of whitewater; waves threatened to dash Anskiere like flotsam from the path. Forced to give ground time after time, still, when the water receded, the Stormwarden always pressed on. He had no choice but to cross at once, before the storm rendered the ledge impassable.

But progress was painfully slow. Morning was nearly spent when Anskiere began the final approach to the cave. Tormented by the conviction that his enemy had used the delay to his disadvantage, the Stormwarden began the ascent of the final precipice. There, with the cave entrance an arm's reach overhead, he heard the sea rise at his back.

Anskiere leaped, grabbed a handhold. The foaming maw of the breaker thundered into his shoulders, slammed him against rock. Water pummeled the breath from his lungs, dragged cruelly at his limbs. Grimly he clung.

His palms tore on the stones. His body slipped slowly seaward. The surf would kill him, bash him over and over against the coral until his flesh was a mangled rag. Tathagres would laugh, and Taen . . .

Anskiere grimaced, consumed by the need to survive. He gathered himself, driven by the roar of another larger wave. With a heave that taxed every sinew in his frame, Anskiere clawed his way through the tumble of receding water. He rolled, gasping and disheveled, into the shaft.

Pebbles scored his skin. The staff clanged against close stone walls and wedged in a fissure. Caught by the sling, Anskiere tumbled onto a mild incline. He lay prone, blinking salt from his eyes, content at first to be still. But the chill soon made him shiver. Bruised, abraded, and wrenched in every joint, the Stormwarden rose to his feet. Outside the gale battered the cliff face, blocking his retreat; and below, if his assessment was correct, an enemy awaited his plans to ruin him.

Anskiere shook the water from his hair, spat out the taste of salt. He reached for his staff. Sodden knots loosened reluctantly under his fingers as he freed the wood from the sling. The sea had inflamed the marks on his wrists, but their sting was overlaid by the sharper memory of Taen's fists clamped in his shirt. Distressed, he started down the shaft, scattering droplets from his robe. Now he was glad the dead sorcerer's aggression had kindled the wards in his staff, for their bright radiance lit his way like a beacon.

The path was smooth at first. Deeper, Anskiere recalled, tunnels twisted with angles and buttresses of slagged stone. Below, the prison fashioned for the frostwargs was as black and tangled as the character of its creator.

Ivain had originally melted the rock with wizardry of fire, but the acrid smell Anskiere remembered from the shaft's forming had faded long since, replaced by musty odors of roots, earth, and moist granite. Except for the echo of his own steps the cave was silent. Bats sought other roosts than the arched ceilings overhead, and wildlife avoided the place, instinctively shunning the evil which hibernated below. The Stormwarden rounded a bend, and the terrain under his boots roughened. Beneath stretched a series of terraces hedged with crystals like swords. Here amid the dazzle of refracted light a misstep could cripple the unwary trespasser. Anskiere trod carefully, unsurprised to discover human bones tumbled among the cave's bewitching beauty. The Ivain he knew had always been careless, even disdainful of life. Uneasy, the Stormwarden proceeded with every sense alert for danger. The din of the storm receded above, dampened by baffles of stone; far ahead, a polished vein of agate threw back a reflection the color of blood.

The Stormwarden noted, and froze. Cloaked in the frosty gleam of his staff, he looked closer, and saw the crimson flicker brighten slowly into orange. He identified flamelight as its source. Someone with a torch must be ascending the shaft from below and presumably no one had interest in the frostwargs except Tathagres' henchman.

Fenced by the razor edges of thousands of crystals, Anskiere was in a poor position for confrontation. The staff could not be quenched to glean any cover from darkness, and by now the brilliance of the wards might have warned the enemy sorcerer he was not alone in the shaft. Before the sorcerer caught him, Anskiere chose retreat, hoping to reach the narrow place where the corridor crooked, barely a hundred paces higher. Anguished by thoughts of a small child's tears, he hurried, and barely felt the sting of a crystal against his calf, or the blood which welled above the top of his boot.

"Why run?" said a voice from below. "By now the tide will have sealed off the entrance."

Anskiere leaped the last tiers of crystals and whirled, panting, beneath the curve of the upper tunnel. Outside the radiance of the staff lay darkness. The sorcerer had not rounded the corner below; he possibly had yet to notice the wards stood complete, a piece of luck Anskiere had wished for but dared not assume. He seated himself on an outcrop just past the place where the tunnel narrowed. The staff's confined aura bathed him in a raw light. Under similar circumstances, Anskiere recalled, Ivain would have smiled.

Slowly the orange glow in the distance brightened and acquired the harsh edges of open flame. Light danced up from below, trapped in the hearts of the faery forest of crystals.

"Fires!" swore the sorcerer. He had at last sighted the wards. Picking his next steps with care, he said, "So that's how you killed Omer." And he paused and cursed for a minute and a half.

Ivain perhaps would have chuckled. Positioned at the mouth of the tunnel, Anskiere derived little satisfaction from his enemy's predicament. Blocked by solid stone, the sorcerer could not force the Stormwarden out of the shaft without direct contact with a staff whose aura was instantly fatal to anyone unattuned to its forces.

"You can't win," said the sorcerer. He raised his torch, haloed by a haze of reflections. "The staff will eventually burn itself out."

Anskiere did not state the obvious, that well before it dimmed the staff could be reduced to safer levels if only his powers were freed. Aware he was protected, he waited for his enemy to reveal whatever plot had drawn him into the cave.

The sorcerer stopped. He threw back his hood, exposing features polished like a skull's. "The girl will suffer well for this."

"Can you contact Tathagres through rock, then?" Anskiere said mildly. But his voice missed its usual note.

"Fires!" The sorcerer gestured angrily. "That ward won't block me forever. I'm not fond of patience. Perhaps we could settle things more quickly."

Anskiere did not reply.

The sorcerer impaled his torch on a crystal and gazed upward, his attitude one of regret. "I think you should be taught a lesson, Cloud-shifter."

He lifted his hands, and light blossomed, firing the crystals into a thousand pinpoint reflections. The cavern blazed, suddenly lit by a pattern delineated in the air. Spread before him, Anskiere saw the spell which confined his powers revealed in geometric splendor. And his trained eye noted, like sour notes in a counterpoint, the gaps one sorcerer's death had torn through the structure, weakening it.

The display was a blatant invitation to challenge; and also a fully baited trap. Anskiere's hand jerked once against the wood of his staff. Without weather sense, or magic, he could not explore the dangers any resistance might unleash. He rose slowly, burdened by responsibility for the children from Imrill Kand whose loyalties brought them to share his fate. Bound, he could not save them. Free, he had a chance, if a slim one, to counteract the threat his aggression would spring. The marred pattern taunted him. One sorcerer had underestimated him; he had no choice but hope that the second had done the same, "By the Vaere," he murmured. "Let me be right."

"Won't you bid for your powers?" the sorcerer urged. He pitched his confidence to antagonize.

Anskiere gathered his will and calmly thrust his consciousness into the spell which spread like a web across the dark. He thought he heard laughter in the moment before his mind caught in the strands. But whether the sound arose from the sorcerer or from an older memory of Ivain, he could not tell. Power snared his awareness like birdlime; fierce opposition blocked all effort to fathom the forces aligned against his inner control. Anskiere never hesitated. The forces which held him were flawed. Poised on that knowledge, he condensed his consciousness to a pinpoint and darted through a gap. The move triggered a sharp blaze of heat. The trap had sprung. Anskiere had no choice but discover the sorcerer's intent swiftly, and try to unbalance his enemy through brash action. Since the threat had been left linked through each break in the spell, Anskiere embraced the pattern's entirety and rammed thoughts like hot needles across every weakness he encountered. Then he withdrew.

Aware once more of the cold illumination from his staff, he shivered, gripped by the distinct impression he had raised a holocaust. Seconds later, when a high, keening wail arose from the bowels of the tunnel, he understood why. The dead sorcerer's threat had been a real one.

"Fires," the Stormwarden said softly. "Between us we've roused the frostwargs." And where Ivain would have laughed outright, he felt only terrible calm.

Below, his enemy stirred from a pose of taut concentration, and the spell's bright pattern faded. Though pleased by the success of his plot, Anskiere's lack of response startled him. Only the insane would linger to face a frostwarg. The sorcerer masked uncertainty with scorn. "Fool. You've accomplished nothing but Tathagres' bidding after all."

A second ululation issued from below, reverberating eerily through the cave. A faint click of claws followed. Anskiere sat down on his rock. "I see that."

The rattle of horny carapaces echoed up the shaft; the frostwargs scuttled wildly toward freedom. They moved with horrifying speed, Anskiere recalled. He watched his antagonist's face turn pale, triumph transformed to dismay. The only available exit was still blocked by the aura of an active staff.

The sorcerer snatched up his torch. "I'll not set you free. You must flee. You have no other alternative."

The staff burned steady as a brand in Anskiere's hands. He did not move.

The scrabble of the frostwargs drew nearer. Their frenzied whistles rose, braided into a shrill crescendo of harmonics. A crystal shattered into slivers.

The sorcerer started forward, careless of sharpened edges under his boots. "Fly! Is your memory gone? No ward can stop a frostwarg."

"I hadn't forgotten." Anskiere stood solidly in the tunnel.

The sorcerer checked. His mouth opened, speechless, and his hands fluttered in an imploring gesture he already guessed was futile. The Stormwarden evidently intended to meet the frostwargs, and die.

Furious, the sorcerer shouted over the rising clatter of claws. "You have lost, Cloud-shifter! The frostwargs are released, and no Firelord remains to control them. The Free Isles will fall, and Cliffhaven also." He spat. "You're a suicide, unmanned by a child's tears and a mother-clinger's principles. Were you worthy of your training, you'd not lie down for death."

"Have I?" said Anskiere.

A ringing clash underscored his words. Armored by heavy shells, the frostwargs spilled the lower bend in the shaft. Mustard and black by torchlight, mottled bodies hurtled over the bottom rung of crystals, tumbling them like glass. The sorcerer clanged down, saw a row of glowing purple eyes, and horny mandibles glistened with curved spikes. Nimble as centipedes, the frostwargs swarmed through the cavern, arched tails rattling behind.

The sorcerer gasped. He dropped his torch, whirled and fled. A crystal bit like a blade into his calf. He fell. Terror overwhelmed him and he screamed aloud. In the corridor above, Anskiere felt the barriers imposed on his powers suddenly dissolve.

His mind rang, no longer numb to the energies thrown off by the staff; and reawakened weather sense deluged his inner vision with information governing the storm which raged topside. Freed, Anskiere seized control. Without pausing to watch the sorcerer's demise, he quenched the staff's aura and ran. Only seconds remained before the frostwargs tired of the corpse and tasted his scent.

Daylight glimmered ahead. Too far ahead; Anskiere knew he could not reach the cave mouth. He stopped. From his sleeve he pulled the tiny feather Tathagres' sorcerer had used to taunt him. The quill glowed blue in his hand as he tossed it into the air.

"Fly," he said, and placed his will upon it.

The feather shimmered into light. From its center flew a living tern, fragile and white as porcelain in the darkness. The bird darted on spread wings for the opening above. The moment it cleared the cave, Anskiere plunged his awareness into the raging heart of the storm. The tempest answered. Wind shrieked like a chorus of hags, funneling down the shaft. Anskiere shouted, conscious of the frostwargs' whistles at his back. The gale struck. His clothing tore, flogged into tatters. Hair lashed his face. Flattened against the tunnel wall, Anskiere drew breath and called the rain.

Water cascaded into the cave, a wrathful, rampaging torrent. It bounded from rock to rock like a demented animal, capped by slavering jaws of foam. Anskiere spoke, even as the water blinded him, and the temperature dropped at his command. Spray fell, rattling, transformed to pellets of ice. Anskiere spoke again, and the cold intensified. Waterfalls froze, arrested in midflight, and the current which curled over his knees crystallized, locking his boots in a grip of iron. Yet the Stormwarden did not relent. He drove the temperature down, and down again, until the stone snapped and sang, shackled by bands of frost. Ivain's tunnel became choked by a glassy, impenetrable bastion against which the frostwargs' razor claws scraped in vain. Sealed in by a solid mass of ice, they howled and gnashed their mandibles.

Above, enmeshed in the effects of his own defenses, Anskiere heard their enraged cries, and where Ivain might have cursed in self-reproach, he smiled. As the ice encased his limbs, he engaged the last of his resources.

Past the blocked mouth of the cave, the stormfalcon lifted barred wings and exploded into flight. Rising swiftly on the wind, she circled and turned eastward, away from Mainstrait, for the staff no longer ruled her homing. In her wake fluttered a tern whose form contained a ward of safety for a certain small girl. And lastly, locked living in a tomb of ice, Anskiere invoked the geas he had placed upon Ivain at the time of betrayal. The act was born of desperation, for, better than any, Anskiere knew his only hope of release lay in a Firelord's skills. And between the crisp crackle of frost and the shrieks of the frostwargs, he thought he heard someone speak.

"Truly, now I have triumphed," mocked a well-remembered voice, and the laughter which followed seemed to last a long time. . . .

Exhausted by wind and rain, a guard captain banged at the entrance of the Kielmark's study. The door opened. He entered and saluted, dripping water.

Surrounded by his staff, the Kielmark straightened from a table draped with charts. Wet hair lay plastered against his cheekbones and the skin of both hands was abraded from shortening docklines against the gale.

"Well?" he said sharply.

"The storm is lifting." The captain leaned wearily against the wall. "The wind has dropped forty knots in an hour and the tower watch reports visibility to Mainstrait."

"By Kor." The Kielmark sat heavily in a chair, uncharacteristically withdrawn for a commander who had lost six moored vessels to the tide, and whose domain sustained an untallied toll of damages. "The Cloud-shifter kept his word then."

Relaxed by his apparent unconcern, the men burst into excited talk.

The Kielmark's great fist slammed into the charts. "Fires! Are we as impressionable as fresh maids? I want this entire island surveyed by night-fall and a list of losses, wounded, and dead, accurate to the last drowned hen. Am I clear?"

As the captain moved toward the door, the Kielmark's voice pursued them. "I don't want one of you back until your report is complete. And send a company to me at the south wharf warehouse. I'm going to clear it of tribute for use as a mercy shelter. Direct the homeless there."

Despite the severity of the Kielmark's orders, scarely an hour passed before a rider clattered to a halt at the dockside with a dispatch. Summoned from the warehouse, the Lord of Cliffhaven heard the message and after a moment of silence dismissed the courier with savage discourtesy. The remainder of the afternoon passed without incident. By sunset each of the captains had reported, and were excused from duty with the praise they had earned. Only after the last one left did the Kielmark's attention return to the earlier message. He saddled a horse and set off across the twilit dunes toward the island's northern headlands.

The heavy clouds had parted. A star shone against the cobalt of the zenith, and angered, storm-whipped surf slammed beaches tumbled and darkened with sea wrack. The Kielmark reined his horse beside the bluffs overlooking the sea. Wind brushed his hair, his cloak, and the stiff mane of his mount. In silence, alone, the Lord of Cliffhaven beheld the phenomenon the courier had described, and confirmed every word to be true.

Spread before him, in high summer, stood a cliff ridged with ice. Gulls wheeled and called above perches silvered with frozen cascades. They did not alight.

The Kielmark shivered, gripped abruptly by intuition. Bitterness tight-ened his throat. Since Ivain Firelord's death, no sorcerer remained who could achieve Anskiere's release. "Old friend," he said to the air. "You spared us. Could you not also spare yourself?"

He sat in the saddle and waited. No answer came. But long after dark, when he turned his horse to leave, the wind ruffled his hair like a brother.

CHAPTER IV

Summons

Far north of Cliffhaven, in the copychamber of Morbrith Keep, a scribe's apprentice suddenly shivered. Though summer sunlight beat strongly across the trestle where he sat hunched over parchment and open books, Jaric was cold. His pen felt clumsy as a stick in fingers gone peculiarly numb. The boy hugged ink-stained hands close to his body and thought wistfully of the woolens packed into chests lined with cedar.

"Jaric!" Master Iveg rose from his desk and padded stiffly across the library. Stooped as an old bear, his shadow fell across the parchment Jaric had been lettering. "Are you dreaming again, boy?"

The master's tone was not unkindly. Yet Jaric flinched, and his thin frame shuddered afresh with chills. Immediately the master's manner changed from gruffness to concern.

"Jaric? By Kor, if you spent the copper I gave you on drink or women, I'll have you branded misfit."

Had he felt better, Jaric would have smiled. Unwatered wine made him fall asleep; and the coarsest trollop in Stal's Tavern invariably treated him with matronly kindness. Although he was nearly seventeen, he had the build of a sickly child.

Master Iveg leaned over his assistant, nearsightedly squinting. At length, he clicked his tongue. "Are you ill, then?"

Jaric blinked, suddenly dizzy. "Maybe." Through blurred vision he tried to read the line he had been inking, and saw his pen had dripped on the parchment. The blotch annoyed him. Unskilled at athletic pursuits, his sole passion was neat copy.

Iveg sighed. As Master Archivist to a busy court, he was reluctant to spare his most diligent pupil even for an hour. But the boy was obviously unwell. Long since resigned to his apprentice's delicate constitution, Iveg pushed a book away from Jaric's stained fingers and said, "Go outside. Sit in the sun for awhile. Perhaps a break and some fresh air will clear your head."

Jaric rose obediently. Careful not to trip, he caught the doorframe with evident unsteadiness. Aware the boy resented coddling, Iveg stayed by the copy table, his droopy hound's features lined with worry. "If you want, I'll send for a healer."

Jaric shook his head. "No need. I feel a little faint, that's all." And he passed quickly into the hall, fearful if he delayed longer his legs might fail him.

His boots echoed unexpectedly on stone. The carpets had been rolled aside, and a serving maid knelt industriously beside a bucket brimming with suds. She peered into Jaric's face as he approached.

"You going ta puke?" She gestured, and her sodden brush spattered soap against his shins. "If so, go elsewhere, d'ya mind?"

Jaric eyed the plump flesh which quivered beneath her blouse and said nothing. Dizzy though he was, nothing ailed his stomach. Accustomed to taunts, he crossed the puddle left by her scrubbing and marked unsteady footprints the length of the corridor.

"Kor," yelled the woman at his back. "Ya messed my clean floor with yer blighty feet, ya daisy."

With a grimace, Jaric caught the latch of the postern. The woman's insults failed to provoke. He was wise enough to understand she intended no malice. The fact he was small and awkward with weapons did not make him any less a scholar; if some women felt his dark eyes and fine hands should have been paired with more manly attributes, he refused to cloud what gifts he did possess with bitterness over his shortcomings. All the same, he longed to slam the door as he let himself out. Yet even so slight a rejoinder proved beyond his strength.

Shaken by sudden vertigo, Jaric barely managed to avoid being struck by the heavy iron-bossed panel as it swung shut. He stumbled down the steps into sunlight. The apothecary's herb gardens were snugly tucked in a courtyard between the outer battlements and the west keep. Jaric often came there in times of trouble. Today light-headedness transformed the gravel paths into a shimmer of glare, and the close high walls buckled crazily before his eyes. He felt inexplicably menaced. The rich scent of poppies seemed to choke him. Disoriented, Jaric sat gasping on the bottom stair. Sun-warmed stone shocked his flesh like a brand, yet he continued to shake with chills. He frowned. Lank mouse-colored hair fringed his wrists as he rested his head in his hands. *What was the matter with him?*

His cheeks tingled. The sage brush by his knee rippled as though stirred by current. Then his vision blurred and slid sickeningly into darkness.

Afraid he might faint, Jaric chafed his arms, unaware his nails gouged flesh. Though immersed in the heat of midsummer noon, cold clamped like a fist in his chest. He could not breathe. Trapped in a morass of confusion, he felt a compulsion rise up to smother his will. Desperate with panic, he resisted.

"Mercy!" The plea emerged as a pinched croak. Aware the force he wrestled was another's, Jaric tried again. *"Let me be. I am blameless!"*

But no quarter was granted. The alien power gained intensity, stripping away his identity like flame-seared wax. Words died on his tongue. He felt himself falling, not into the familiar fragrance of sage leaves, but into icy, limitless space. Another reality flooded his inward eye, carved into ruthless focus. Like a scene viewed through a ship's glass, Jaric saw a promontory exposed to a thunderous clamor of surf. A vibrant red-headed man crouched against the rocks. His face contorted with hatred toward a second man, a gale-whipped figure with silver hair and ragged blood-stained clothes. Had Jaric been able to move, he would have shivered. But the image held him frozen as the second stranger raised his head. His features were as battered as the rest of him, yet he spoke with inhuman calm. And his words tore into Jaric with the fury of the wind, shackling his spirit bondage as absolute as death.

Your offense against me is pardoned but not forgotten. This geas I lay upon you: should I call, you, Ivain, shall answer, and complete a deed of my choice, even to the end of your days. And should you die, my will shall pass to your eldest son, and to his son's sons after him, until the debt is paid . . .

"No!" Jaric shouted.

But, inexhaustible as the elements, the stranger's powers sealed him within ringing nets of force. Terrified, Jaric knew if he yielded, that other will would consume him. His entire existence would plunge into change. Ill-prepared for the world beyond Master Iveg's study, he took refuge deep within his mind, where no light, no sound, and no sensation could reach him. Sprawled across the stair by the apothecary's herb garden, Jaric lay as though dead.

The night *Crow* made rendezvous, the King of Kisburn's war fleet lay becalmed fifty leagues from Islamere, easternmost archipelago under the Alliance's charter. Tathagres at last granted the crew reprieve from the blistering pace she had demanded since leaving Cliffhaven, and *Crow's* company rested gratefully. Crusted with the dried sweat of exertion, the rowers slept beside oar-ports left unsealed in the heat. The helmsman drowsed against the binnacle with the wheel clamped in the friction brake as the galleass drifted under the limp billows of her staysails. She scribed barely an eddy in the smooth face of the sea.

Curled in a berth in the forecastle, Emien lay awake, eyes fixed sullenly on the hammocks of his crewmates. Each morning he visited the hold, but Taen had not answered his call; two days without water or food should by now have driven her from hiding. Miserably, Emien recalled his promise to bring her safely home. He could send his mother and cousins the silver he earned to pay for the wreck of *Dacsen*, yet even Tathagres' largest ame-thyst could not atone for the loss of a sister. Emien stirred restlessly. Although the sorcerer Hearvin had recently forbidden him to enter the hold, he decided to try one last time. With no guards present, surely he could coax Taen to come out.

Emien rose grimly. He would lie, even bribe his sister with promises of Anskiere's release. Once she was found he would make her understand; the Stormwarden would be forgotten.

Emien's bare feet made no sound as he slipped through the rows of sleepers in their hammocks. The running lamps at bow and stern cross-hatched the decks with shadow. Beyond the rail, the lights of the fleet were scattered like fireflies beneath a sky featureless and black as a pit. But Emien did not notice the absence of stars. Intent upon stealth, he slipped down the companionway. The sailor on watch lounged by the port capstan, cleaning his nails with a marlinspike. He raised no alarm as the boy crept past the galley and lowered himself through the hatch which led to the oar deck.

Emien descended the ladder, progress masked by the noisy snores of a slave. Dizzied by the odor of confined humanity, the boy waited for some-one to raise an outcry. But the officer on duty had his back turned and the lantern guttered on its hook, nearly out of oil; the sooty flame barely glimmered through the glass. Emien groped in the gloom, caught the slidebolt which secured the lower hatch. He spat on the metal, careful to work the bolt gently before drawing the pin. The hinges smelled of grease. Sweating, Emien raised the grating, eyes clenched shut. But the hatch opened soundlessly. Damp sour air wafted from the hold.

Sails ruffled topside; *Crow* shuddered and nosed a ripple in the sea as Emien swung himself onto the ladder. But he had no chance to notice the fact that the terrible calm had ended.

Something scraped overhead, followed by a flurry of sound. Emien froze just as a white object plummeted from the beams of the oar deck. He waited, breath locked in fear. But the disturbance was caused by a bird. Feathers brushed past his cheek. Emien recoiled bruisingly into the ladder.

Though the hold was a cavern of darkness, he saw the creature clearly. Traced by a faint halo of blue-white light, it drifted on slender wings. Emien felt blood leap in his veins. The bird was surely Anskiere's. Certain it had come for Taen, the boy hooked an elbow over a rung. No longer concerned with silence, he snatched the dagger from his belt, clamped the blade in his teeth, and hurled himself downward.

That moment, wind arose over the sea like a howl of outrage. Someone shouted topside. The sails jibed, then crashed back onto starboard tack with a bang that rattled the chainplates. Over-canvassed, *Crow* rolled vio-lently on her side. Emien was tossed backward into the ladder. The fall spared him; a crate overbalanced and tumbled across the deck where he had stood a moment before. It crashed heavily into the timbers between the galleass' ribs.

Emien heard a sickening splinter of wood. Water fountained through the breach. Above decks, another gust shrieked through the rigging. The headsails flogged and thundered taut, and stressed lines whined as *Crow* heeled, oar-ports pressed remorselessly to the waterline. Mired by the broad yards of her staysails, the galleass began to drink the sea.

Emien grabbed the ladder and took the knife from his teeth. "Taen!" His shout blended horribly with the screams of oarsmen chained helplessly to their benches. Emien heard a mounting roar. Water dashed like a spillway into the bilge. Across the bulk of stacked cargo, he saw the tern alight with a flutter on the rim of a cask.

The ship lurched. Emien knew fear. If the galleass pitched any further, her ballast would shift. Iron bars would tumble like battering rams, slivering the contents of the hold to wreckage. Desperate, Emien shouted again. "Taen!"

A snap sounded aloft, followed by the whipcrack report of torn canvas. Emien swore with relief. A bolt rope had broken. One sail, at least, would spill the murderous burden of wind which held the vessel pinned. Emien clung to the ladder as the galleass ponderously answered the helm. Water sloshed. *Crow* began to head up.

Emien peered across the hold. The tern still perched on the cask, wings outstretched for balance as the ship slowly righted. The halo shone like ghostlight on frail black-tipped feathers. Carefully Emien gauged the distance and aimed the knife.

Abruptly the aura around the bird brightened to a hard-edged ring of force. Emien tensed to throw. The tern cocked its head and regarded him with a bright unwinking eye. All at once the bird seemed to contain everything he had loved and left behind on Imrill Kand. Arrested by a sense of poignant loss, the boy hesitated. He forgot his hatred of Anskiere. His impulse to murder withered before a beauty so clean it made him ache.

Emien's hand trembled. The weapon suddenly burdened his arm past bearing. He longed to cast the steel aside to follow the bird toward a destiny that rang bright as music in his ears. But the memory of his oath to Tathagres left echoes which spoiled the harmony.

Slapped by the waves of a roused sea, *Crow* rounded into the wind. Water sloshed coldly over Emien's ankles. He felt nothing. Oblivious to the shouts of the officers and the stormridden chaos aloft, the boy stood torn by indecision, his mind wrung by promises of laughter and life, and his cheeks drenched with tears. He did not see the lanternlight which struck down from above. Neither did he notice the sorcerer who descended the ladder, robes the red of new blood in the flamelight.

"Boy!" Hearvin's voice was curt with annoyance. "Boy!"

Emien did not budge. Shadow flickered across his face. Absorbed by the tern, he let his hand loosen. The knife dropped into the bilge with a splash. "Taen?" Bemused as a dreamer, Emien stepped forward.

Hearvin sprang from the ladder and grabbed the boy's wrist. "Idiot! Are you mad?"

He jerked Emien back. The boy stumbled clumsily. Hearvin yanked him around, and the lantern lit the shining streaks of tears on a face unnaturally fixed in tranquillity. The sorcerer understood the cause. Anskiere had engaged the power he had recovered, and tried to form a geas to summon the children. Hearvin's fingers knotted savagely in the boy's sleeve. The girl was still missing, but apparently the attempt had found the boy susceptible; Tathagres was going to be distinctly displeased.

"Kor's Fires!" Hearvin slung the lantern on a peg and traced his hands swiftly before the boy's eyes. A symbol glowed in the air where it passed. The sorcerer muttered a counterspell; the glyph flashed scarlet and faded. Emien blinked. He shuddered, and his peaceful expression crumpled into horror as the illusion which called him dissolved into a nightmare of storm-tossed darkness. He drew breath and cried out.

Hearvin shook him. "Forget Imrill Kand! Forget your family! Your loyalty belongs to Tathagres, and she has summoned you."

Wind screeched above his words. *Crow* heaved awkwardly, dragged into another roll by the swirling gallons which flooded her hold. Emien staggered and shrugged free of Hearvin's grip. The deck tilted. Steel rattled and clanged overhead as terrified rowers struggled to tear free of their chains. Their panic might prevent the seamen from sealing the oar-ports, Emien thought dully. *Crow* was in peril of sinking. Strangely, he did not care.

Hearvin caught the lantern from its hook, and the hold fell into darkness, loud with the enclosed splash of the bilge. "I forbade you to come down here." He started up the ladder. "Why did you?"

Emien followed, sullenly silent. Just before he reached the hatch, he glanced back, but could not recall what had drawn him to leave his berth in the forecastle. Hearvin noted the boy's confusion with satisfaction. The spell of binding he had crafted was sufficient; Anskiere's meddling would trouble Emien no further.

The sorcerer did not perceive the tern which perched on the rim of a certain brandy cask in the depths of the hold. The binding he had used to secure Emien had also blinded the boy to its presence, since the shimmer of the bird's aura was invisible to hostile eyes. The one child Anskiere's ward still guarded would not be sought until she was delivered to safety.

Caught by a rising wave, *Crow* pitched, and the wheel clattered with a rattle like old bones as her helmsman strove to hold her bow to windward. Although Tathagres was land bred, she braved the quarterdeck on braced feet, white hair lashed into tangles by the gale. The cling of sodden velvet shamelessly accentuated her femininity; but the captain who confronted her had little appetite, no matter how alluring her curves. His gesture of protest withered under her scornful regard, and his mouth gaped speechlessly open.

Tathagres laughed. The oath she uttered belied her delicacy, as did the command which followed. "Slaughter them, then, but get those oar-ports *closed*." Her violet eyes narrowed angrily. "They're only slaves. If they drown, they'll be just as dead. So will we all, if you don't act quickly."

A gust slammed into the spanker, which men still labored to furl. The captain lost his balance. Testily, he grabbed a stay, and barely missed jostling Tathagres. He began a plea for temperance. "Lady—"

The woman returned no threats. Yet the captain felt a quiver in his knees. "I'll see it done," he said quickly, though he had intended different words. Reduced to subservience on his own vessel, he hastened toward the companionway and almost collided with Hearvin, who had just arrived topside with the boy.

Tathagres transferred her displeasure to the sorcerer. "By the Great Fall," she exclaimed fiercely. "You owe me an explanation, Hearvin. Anskiere's possessions were scuttled, you said. How in Kor's Name could that stormfalcon get a homing fix on us?"

A wave smacked *Crow* onto her beam ends. The quartermaster wrestled the helm, and Tathagres slammed into the rail, knocked breathless. As Hearvin fetched up beside her, she noticed that Emien seemed strangely passive in the sorcerer's grip. She began at once to comment, but Hearvin interrupted.

"I did tell you. At the time I knew of no means by which the stormfalcon could track anything other than its original key of return." He regarded the woman without apprehension. "I also counseled caution, which you unwisely ignored. My two colleagues are dead."

Tathagres flung her head back, drenched by spray as *Crow* wallowed, lee rails awash in the waist. The galleass recovered sluggishly. An officer shouted frantic orders; the deckhands abandoned the spanker and slashed the halyards. But not even the pandemonium and canting decks disrupted Tathagres' obsession.

"Anskiere? Has he defied me?"

Hearvin's mouth twitched. "He has escaped. At what cost, I cannot guess. But this much I promise: the frostwargs are roused, but not free, and the stormfalcon circles Kisburn's fleet. Your plans are balked."

"Not balked." Tathagres released the rail as the galleass swung level. "Never that. We have the boy." She detailed two deckhands to ready *Crow's* pinnace for launch, intending to sail directly and confront Anskiere at Cliffhaven.

Hearvin watched her until rain fell in sheets and quenched the stern lantern. Familiar with her temper, he had prudently avoided telling Tathagres how close she had come to losing the boy. Neither did he mention the fact that he guessed the pinnace would not make landfall at the Kielmark's isle. *Crow* quivered, battered by ever steepening waves. The wind skirled like demonsong through her masts. Hearvin heard its violence, and was not fooled. Unlike his dead companions, he did not underestimate the threat Anskiere's falcon had unleashed. The Free Isles might condemn the Stormwarden whose powers had leveled Tierl Enneth; but Anskiere's loyalty would never change. Kisburn's warships would be smashed like toys.

The gale worsened. Towering whitecaps tumbled across the galleass' decks, sweeping gear and human life into the sea with equal abandon. The effort to launch the pinnace soon became a struggle for survival. Awash up to her oar deck, *Crow* plowed clumsily into the waves, unresponsive to the helm. Despite the efforts of her crew, the galleass could not be saved. Hoarsely, the captain ordered the longboats unlashed. But no man would board until the King's officers were away in the pinnace. Beaten and tired the captain left the quartermaster at the helm and sought Tathagres.

Thigh-deep in the foam-laced flood of the waist, *Crow's* best seamen labored with the pinnace. The sea sucked and thudded, and the mast traced dizzy circles against the sky. The captain found Tathagres with her sorcerer, clinging to the companionway rail. He touched her shoulder even as the pinnace jerked, freed at last from her cradle. Tathagres returned a slitted glare of annoyance.

The captain was too pressured to be cowed. "Get to the boat. If the seamen panic, I cannot ensure your safety."

A gust shivered the rigging, and something gave way aloft, streaming a snarl of lines to leeward. Tathagres' reply was obliterated by a sailhand's shout and the booming crash of a fallen yard. She made no move toward the pinnace.

Hearvin caught her arm. "Go at once."

Tathagres resisted. "Where is the Constable?"

Exasperated, the captain shouted warning. "You'll lose your chance!" He pointed forward.

A great sea reared above the galleass' bows. For an instant, a bowsprit rose, a glistening spear aimed at a sky which smoked with spindrift. Then the wave broke, avalanching water across the forecastle. A thunderous cascade of foam spun the pinnace in the waist. The seamen strove to hold her but the sea unravelled their grip like crochetwork. The boat struck the rail. Beaded wood exploded into wind-borne fragments. The next wave would likely tear the pinnace loose, empty of passengers.

"Go!" Hearvin thrust Tathagres and the boy headlong down the companionway. Moving hard on their heels, he shouted, "It's too late for the Constable!"

The sea swirled up to receive them. Belted chest-high by cold water, Tathagres stumbled. A seaman caught her. The deck tilted; he lost his balance and shoved her roughly into the arms of another man. Tathagres was lifted and dumped rudely onto the floorboards of the pinnace.

The next wave struck. Spray geysered overhead. Kicked by bare feet as the seamen tumbled into the boat, Tathagres had no chance to struggle upright. The pinnace slewed. Water bashed and hissed under the keel, and a gust tore the shouts of the seamen into unintelligible scraps. Then with a bump that knocked Tathagres against a thwart, the pinnace broke free.

"I have the boy," cried Hearvin from the stern.

A sailor lost his footing and fell, clutching desperately to the gunwale. The boat rolled under his weight and threatened to capsize. Another seaman pulped the man's knuckles with an oar. His screams were quickly lost astern as the pinnace lifted like a chip over storm-maddened crests. The seamen fought her steady. They bent over the oars. Spray slashed their backs and washed stinging runnels into their eyes. If the pinnace broached, even once, all her passengers would drown.

Tathagres pushed her hands against the boards, and curtly demanded the heading. Hearvin explained that the storm drove them southwest, toward Innishari and the lower reaches of the Alliance. Cliffhaven lay in the opposite direction, and until the weather improved, the pinnace could hold no better course. Tathagres accepted the reverse with steely practicality. She reviewed her assets, beginning with the boy from Imrill Kand who sat in the stern, an oddly wooden expression on his face.

Tathagres studied him carefully. A fisherman's son whose past actions had been impulsively, even violently, brash, would never sit passive while his boat was endangered by heavy seas.

"Emien," she said sharply.

The boy responded as though drugged. Tathagres frowned. "Hearvin." Reprimand edged her voice. "You've placed a stay-spell on the boy. Why?"

The sorcerer leaned with the motion of the pinnace, his hood pulled over his head and his features in shadow. "You'd have lost him to Anskiere, had I not. The falcon's return forestalled any chance to involve you."

"*What!*" Tathagres stiffened. She struck the seat with her fist, and gold jangled through the rush of the gale. "Do you tell me Anskiere sent a summoning aboard *Crow,* and you saw fit not to inform me? Koridan's Fires! *I'd like to see you flayed.* Because of your misjudgment, that foolish little girl will probably survive." She stared crossly over waters wracked by spume. "We won't recover her now, that's certain."

Hearvin said nothing. What he thought could not be guessed as Tathagres spun back to face him, her wet hair twisted into snake locks.

"It *is* a stay-spell?" She paused only for Hearvin's affirmation. "Then release him. I want the boy aware his sister's death was caused by that cloud-shifter's stormfalcon. Convince him, if he asks, that Taen perished in the hold of the galleass."

Hearvin obediently traced a pass in the air before the boy. A symbol glimmered red, framed briefly by the black surge of a wave before the sorcerer snapped his fingers. The glyph faded. Emien blinked, started, and his blankly disoriented expression transformed into a desperate survey of the pinnace's passengers.

Tathagres awaited her opening. With narrowed, predator's eyes, she absorbed every nuance of the boy's expression as he realized his sister was absent. He did not speak. But his body convulsed with a savage flare of rage.

Plotting for the future, Tathagres sought a way to exploit that anger; and in the seawater sloshing under her knees, found inspiration. She yanked a bucket from the pinnace's locker and thrust it between the boy's hands. "Bail," she urged softly. "Your life, and mine, depends upon keeping this craft seaworthy."

Emien seized the handles with a grip that blanched his knuckles, his eyes already hardened. He would live, Tathagres saw, expressly to avenge his sister. She smiled in the darkness. The boy was tough as sword steel and charged like a thunderhead with passion. Under her guidance he would become a magnificent weapon. Settled by the thought, Tathagres leaned against a thwart and shut her eyes.

Of the survivors of the pinnace, Emien alone searched astern for a glimpse of the vessel left behind. *Crow* reeled in her death throes. Thrashed like flotsam, she listed in the spume, the corpses of her slaves streaming from the oar ports. As Emien watched, rain alone wet his cheeks. Once, he would have wept for the sister he had lost. Now his grief was eclipsed by hatred so pure it burned his very soul. If he lived, Anskiere would die. Mechanically, Emien continued to bail.

The abandoned galleass settled slowly to her deep water grave. No living man remained to observe as, tickled by a trail of bubbles from the hold, a brandy cask rose like a cork to the surface. Perched precariously on the rim, a tern spread wings haloed by the blaze of an enchanter's craft. Though gusts hammered the surrounding waves into a churning millrace of foam, the cask bobbed gently, girdled by calm only one sorcerer could command. Dry inside, Taen slept. Anskiere's ward drew her scathelessly through the gale-ravaged wreckage of Kisburn's fleet and westward into the open sea.

CHAPTER V

Ivain's Heir

In the close heat of evening Jaric lay limp on his cot in the loft above Morbrith Keep's smithy. Although more than one healer plied him with remedies, he had not regained consciousness since he had fallen senseless in the apothecary's herb garden two days past. Sightless as an icon beneath his blankets, he did not respond to the flare of light beneath the dormer by his head; nor did he stir as the tramp of booted feet shook the ladder which led to the loft. Far beyond reach of physical senses, the scribe's apprentice remained unaware his illness had earned him the attention of the Master Healer, and oddly, the Earl of Morbrith himself.

A liveried servant raised a lantern over the cot, revealing a profile now sharp-edged and sunken. Flamelight accentuated the boy's bloodless lips, and the fingers splayed on the coverlet seemed as fragile as the fluted shells washed in by the tide.

"He seems dead," said the Earl. Emeralds flashed as he bent and lifted Jaric's wrist. The limb was icy, and slender as a maid's in the man's calloused grip. The Earl swallowed, moved to pity for the boy. Raised by the Smith's Guild, Jaric had proved too slight for the forges; he had been forced to repay the cost of his fostering on a copyist's wages. The Earl chafed the boy's skin, startled to discover blisters. He turned the hand he held to the light. "Did you see this?"

The Master Healer clicked his tongue. "Severe sunburn," he said gruffly. "The boy lay unprotected for several hours before anyone noticed him. The other side of his face is marked also. Except for that, he shows no trace of injury. I found no bruises, and if he's sick, his symptoms match no affliction I have ever known. I tell you, Lord, I believe him stricken by sorcery."

The Earl smoothed Jaric's arm on the blanket. He settled on his heels, remembering Kerain, the smith's son, who had hung for murdering his betrothed. Under oath at his trial, Kerain had sworn he had done nothing except prevent the girl from slaughtering her newborn child. The young man claimed to have snatched the infant from under her knife, and she had promptly turned the blade against herself. The earl winced in recollection. Condemned to the scaffold, Kerain had voiced his death wish; he claimed the orphaned baby as his own. Morbrith Keep's archives recorded the boy child as Kerainson Jaric, assigned as ward of the Smith's Guild. Sixteen years later, the Earl studied the delicate features of that same boy, now certain the burly, black-haired Kerain had not been the father. If Jaric was a sorcerer's get, his mother's attempt at murder became plausible; a wizard's heir inherited the enemies of his sire, and terrible misfortune often befell those who surrounded him.

The Earl blotted sweat from his temples. Had he guessed the truth at the trial, he would have spared Kerain, and put the child to the sword instead. But hindsight was useless. The present offered options considerably less favorable. Unhappily, the Earl made his decision.

"I want the boy moved to the sanctuary tower behind Koridan's Shrine."

The healer gasped, startled. "That's not wise." The tower lay outside the walls, on the other side of the summerfair. The crowded alleys beyond the gates were no place to be carrying a sick boy after dark. "Jaric's condition is most serious, my Lord."

The Earl straightened angrily. "You'll move that boy quickly and without any fuss. I'll send guardsmen to help. Am I clear?"

"Very." The healer bowed with evident distress. "But you risk the boy's life."

Pressured by concern he had no wish to explain, the Earl said nothing. What healer could understand that this boy might be better dead? For should Jaric prove to be other than Kerain's get, the consequences might threaten all of Morbrith.

Jaric never felt the hands which lifted his blanket-wrapped body from the cot above the smithy. Fretful from worry, the Master Healer oversaw the guardsmen as they hefted the boy down the ladder. More guards waited below. Even with the doors open, the forge was stifling with the smoky heat of banked embers. Yet Jaric stayed chill to the touch, and his eyes glinted, pupils widened and black in the glare of the lamps.

"Kor," said one guardsman. "He's cold as fish. You sure he's not dead?" Watched uneasily by his companions, he lowered the boy onto a litter.

"If he were dead, none of us would be missing sleep," snapped the healer. He snatched up his satchel of remedies and stalked out of the forge. The men-at-arms followed more slowly with the boy.

"Damned summerfair's no place to go with a litter," muttered the guardsman in the lead. His complaint was just. The nomads who gathered on Morbrith Heath each solstice were clannish and temperamental; though merchants bartered goods with them during the day, no townsman lingered outside the keep walls after dark. To cross the festival with a helpless boy was to invite violence; but no Morbrith man dared gainsay the High Earl's command.

In the shadowed security of the gatehouse, the guardsmen checked their weapons. The valley below was patterned like patchwork with wagons, colored lights, and the flimsy wooden booths of the summerfair. Shouts and laughter and the scraping notes of fiddles blended raucously on the night air. The guardsmen formed up. With the healer and the boy sheltered inside a ring of mailed bodies, they set out.

From the moment the gates clanged shut, the crowd enveloped the small party like the surge of a breaker. The guards struggled to maintain position, aware steel would be little deterrent should they encounter trouble. Jaric never stirred, though he was shoved, fingered, and jostled by painted clansmen who reeked of sweat and spirits. He knew nothing of the noise, the discomfort, or the dust as the Earl's men-at-arms labored to clear a path through the closely packed revelers. By the time they reached the far boundary of the summerfair the men were tired, white with the strain of handling clansmen who were drunk, and often quick to draw knives.

As the noise and lights fell behind, the healer permitted a short pause by the river at the edge of the heath. The men rested the litter on the stone buttresses of the bridge. In the wind-tossed light of the lantern, the boy's eyes seemed as glazed as a corpse's. One guardsman whispered apprehensively and another disguised a shiver by dusting the grit out of his tunic.

"He sure looks dead."

The healer overheard. He jammed his hat over his ears until his hair stuck out in bristles, and gestured toward the summerfair. "Want to go back? No? Then he's alive and that's the end of it."

The men moved reluctantly forward. The path to the sanctuary tower laced between a stand of pines, dim and gray by starlight. The healer lifted Jaric's wrists from the blankets. The boy's pulse was erratic, and much too fast. If Jaric was going to die, let it happen in the High Lord's presence, the healer thought vindictively. He urged the men to increase their pace.

The land rose sharply, eroded into gullies made treacherous by roots and loose shale. The lantern swung, and cast bewildering shadows over the footing which steadily worsened. The guardsmen stumbled and swore until exertion robbed them of breath. The trail steepened. Jaric jounced on his litter, raked by branches and bruised against rocks. The poles which bore his weight dragged against the scrub, and weaponry clanked. Night birds startled into flight almost under the guardsmen's boots as they toiled through narrow clefts of rock.

Finally lights glimmered ahead and the spire of the sanctuary tower reared in silhouette against a starry arch of sky. The men quickened pace, anxious to reach the stone-paved security of Koridan's Shrine.

Just before the gates a figure on horseback cut them off.

Certain that he faced an outlaw, the healer started back and slammed painfully into a litter pole. The men-at-arms reached for weapons.

"Desist at once!" commanded the Earl of Morbrith, his voice overlaid by the dissonant ring of steel. "Fires!"

He dismounted irritably. His horse sidled, oddly noiseless; its hooves and bit had been muffled in flannel, and it smelled of sweat. The Earl had brought no escort, and his cloak, tunic, and the harness of his mount were bare of ornaments. Whatever his intentions, he had taken care to travel without attracting notice.

"How is the boy?"

The healer framed his reply with resentment. "He lives, but barely." His insolence was ignored.

The Earl lifted lathered reins from the horse's neck, and offered no explanation for his appearance. He turned immediately with instructions to his guardsmen. "Remain here. Let no man enter the shrine." His tone softened. "You've done well. The flask of wine in my saddlebag may be shared among you, but keep the celebration quiet. I want no priests awakened before I return."

The Earl tossed his reins to the guard captain. Then he bent over the litter, gathered Jaric in his arms and started for the gates. The healer moved after, determined to protect his charge; through thirty years of practice, he had never known the Lord of Morbrith to behave so callously.

The Earl paused and blocked his path. "Your services are no longer needed," he said coldly.

The healer's muscles knotted with outrage. "You're unaware of the risks. Would you sanction murder? I'll stay only if you swear no harm will come to the boy."

The Earl answered in a tone of ringing authority. "I'll swear to nothing. Consider yourself excused, or I'll have the guards tie you like a felon."

"You've gone mad." The healer groped for words to argue, and lamely shook his head. "Stark mad."

The Earl said nothing. Unwilling to linger under the healer's accusing stare, he spun on his heel and bore Kerainson Jaric out of the circle of lamplight.

The healer watched with a leaden sense of foreboding. The haste, the secrecy, and the Earl's curt manner were reasons enough to fear for Jaric's safety. The boy had no family but the Smith's Guild; who would ask questions on his behalf should he fail to return? Spurred by self-righteous concern, the healer decided to follow.

The Earl had proceeded in the direction of the sanctuary tower, but darkness, rocky footing, and the need for silence hampered the healer's progress. By the time his eyes had adjusted to the dark, his quarry had already reached the postern of the tower. The Earl was no longer alone. The healer saw a tall figure muffled in gray standing beside him. From the shadow of its cloak hood gleamed lidless orange eyes, too widely spaced to be human and with pupils slotted like a serpent's.

The healer gasped. Sweat sprang along his spine and his hat seemed suddenly too tight against his brow. The creature he beheld was surely of demonkind, a Llondian empath; its presence within shrine grounds became a breach of natural law. The healer strove to quell his fear, without success.

Surely as tide, the Earl intended to investigate Jaric's affliction through contact with the accursed being's mind. Such practice was unthinkable, heresy beyond the pardon of any decent man.

Without pausing to review consequences, the healer ran forward, hands interlocked in a gesture to ward off evil. "I cannot sanction this!" he shouted.

The pair ahead froze and looked back. Startled, the Llondel whistled and ducked into the arched doorway of the tower. Its eyes shone like coals in the dark.

"Be still, you fool." The Earl shifted the unconscious boy against his shoulder and faced the healer with an expression of rage. "Waken the priests, and I'll see you burn with me. If a member of my household is struck down by a sorcerer, I'll know who, and why, no matter what methods are required. I'll not endanger all of Morbrith for the sake of a single boy."

"This is irresponsible." Trembling, the healer considered the powers of the Llondelei, and the accounts of humans driven mad from their effects. "Have you no thought for your guardsmen? They lie well within range of Llondel's imaging, and you left them without warning."

The Earl stood stiffly as the wind tumbled Jaric's hair against his collar. "You're wrong," he said at last. "The wine is drugged. The men-at-arms will sleep soundly until dawn. Either accompany us or go back and share the flask with them."

But the healer held his ground. "What of the priests in the shrine?"

"That was less easily arranged." The Earl sighed. "But I can promise they will suffer no ill effects from this night's work."

The Llondel glanced around, orange eyes ablaze with unfriendliness. It copied the healer's earlier gesture with seamed, six-fingered hands, and stalked after the Earl. The healer straightened his hat and watched as its dusky cloak blended into the dark. For all his concern, this time he was unable to proceed.

The Earl waited, circled by the intricate mosaic work which patterned the anteroom of the sanctuary tower. The Llondel barred the door, its movements liquidly graceful.

"I'm sorry," the Earl said softly, aware the being he addressed could follow his emotion, if not his words. "Few of my kind understand."

The Llondel trilled a treble seventh. It touched the Earl's shoulder, trilled again, and extended long arms toward the boy.

Muscles aching, the Earl surrendered Jaric's weight with a grateful sigh. Moments like this always made him wonder why Kordane's Law held all demons alike. Most types were dangerous, it was true; the Llondelei were no exception. But their empathic sensitivity made them gentle, even retiring, and they spun harmful images only when threatened. The Earl of Morbrith started up the stair, knowing stone walls made the Llondel ill at ease. Yet the creature had come without hesitation earlier when he had relayed the plight of the boy.

'*Sorcerer*,' the Earl thought, and recognized the mind-touch of the Llondel by the way the concept formed; the creature must have picked up his inner reflection. It stopped on the stair, shifted Jaric's limp form into the crook of one elbow, and repeated the healer's gesture to ward off evil. '*Must*,' it sent urgently, then consolidated its disjointed attempt at communication into a single image.

And the Earl frowned, for the concept the demon pressed against his awareness implied the evil to be averted constituted danger to the *sender* of Jaric's affliction. Exasperated, he sighed. The Llondel was surely mistaken.

'*No*.' Orange eyes flashed up out of the gloom. '*Not wrong*.' Frustrated with word symbol images, the Llondel stamped a clawed foot on the stairway, bitterly offended.

"I'm sorry." The Earl was desperate to know the cause of Jaric's distress. He pushed open the door at the head of the landing and held the carved panel wide. "Humans have difficulty believing what they cannot see. Will you show us?"

Light flooded from the chamber beyond, illuminating a gray-brown alien face. The creature hesitated. Crescent nostrils quivered, and its bone-slim fingers tightened on the blanket-wrapped boy.

"We need your help," the Earl coaxed softly.

The Llondel returned a sour chirp. It moved forward, but not, the Earl understood, for the sake of Morbrith. As the demon crossed the threshold, he again received the impression of a sorcerer endangered; but this time he held his opinion. He closed and barred the door, and a voice called querulously from the shadows.

"You took eternity to get here."

"I know." The Earl bent and stuffed a length of felt into the crack beneath the door. "I had to wait for the guardsmen. Would you want to cross the summerfair with a litter?"

A grunt answered him. The Earl straightened and regarded the wizened countenance of Morbrith's Master Seer by the light of the cresset which blazed in an iron bracket close by.

The old man glared back, chin jutted outward from a nest of untrimmed hair. His mouth pursed deeply with displeasure. "Better that than the saddle at my age. You'd never, were you seventy. My bones ache."

But spry movements belied his complaint as he rose and shuttered the chamber's single window. The Llondel seated itself in the center of the floor with Jaric cradled in its lap. Then it fixed its sultry gaze upon the Earl and pointed to the cresset.

'*End the light*,' it sent.

The Lord of Morbrith lifted the torch and plunged it into a water bucket beneath. The chamber went dark with a crackling hiss of steam. The man settled himself beside the seer, and waited as the last airborn spark flurried and died, leaving blackness punctured by two burning red-gold lamps which were the Llondel's eyes.

Suddenly uneasy, the Earl clamped damp palms on his sleeves. "You will reveal to us the sender of this boy's affliction," he said to the Llondel. "No harm will come to any human here."

The eyes vanished, eclipsed by the cloak hood as the Llondel bowed its head. No image arose in reply, and no sound intruded but faintly labored wheezes from the seer. But as the Earl strained to see form in the darkness, a spark of yellow appeared suspended in the air. It flared brighter, acquiring the flowing edges of live flame, then widened into a ghostly wheel of fire which shed no light on any of the surrounding objects. The apparition sent a thrill of fear down the Earl's spine. The Llondel and the boy appeared to have vanished.

Through a gut-deep hollow of dread, the man understood that he gazed directly upon Jaric's nightmare, and he longed suddenly to be out-doors, surrounded by summer's chorus of crickets. But door and window were barred, and every chink battened with felt. The Llondel's empathic imaging smothered the Earl's wish, pitched his awareness through the spinning heart of the flame, into the boy's mind. . . .

. . . Fog, wind, and the icy sting of spray. Surf hammered into rocks scant yards below the ledge where Jaric huddled, arms clasped tightly around his knees. The elements battered his unprotected body with cruel force. Though soaked and chilled, he did not care. His face remained hidden behind hands as rigid as carved ivory, even when he sensed he was no longer alone. The sorcerer from his earlier vision stepped out of the mist and paused on the ledge, before him. But Jaric did not look up.

"I call you, Firelord's Son." The sorcerer gazed down at the boy. The wind tossed his silver hair, his staff glowed with a brilliant aura of power, and the air tingled with the resonance of terrible forces held in check.

Yet Jaric made no move. If he acknowledged the sorcerer's existence, he might forfeit control of his destiny forever. His will would be crushed, scattered like the ashes of the dead, and he would lose all that was dear to him.

"In the name of Anskiere you are summoned," said the sorcerer, and he raised the staff over the stiff figure of the boy.

Jaric felt the power around him shift, align like a spear to pierce his innermost self. Dread locked his limbs. His thoughts raced, and some-thing, no, someone jabbed him with the realization that he would die, should he continue to reject the fate the sorcerer had decreed for him. But Jaric ignored the warning. Heedless as the moth which flies into candleflame, he chose oblivion; and was blocked. Two slit-pupiled eyes appeared, etched like coals against his retinas.

Jaric screamed. His own eyes were closed. Yet hotly as Kor's Fires, the demonic gaze trapped him. His mind was possessed by a nightmare vision of shame and guilt and the horrid certainty that his denial would eventually condemn his entire race. "Let me be!" shouted Jaric. But the eyes melted into smoke, replaced by an image of Master Iveg chained amid a blazing pyre of books while demon forms danced in silhouette. Their shapes were black as ink, pooling into darkness. Jaric found himself thrust into the streets of Morbrith Keep, a torch clutched in sweating hands; and the bleached skeletons of dead men snapped like sticks under his feet as he walked. Then out of the shadowed sockets of a skull, the demon's red eyes reappeared and focused accusingly upon him.

'You alone can prevent this.'

He cried aloud in denial, but his heart betrayed him. He could never let Morbrith be destroyed.

The demon's dream rippled like fabric and left him.

Beaten to his knees, Jaric looked up at last, beheld the weather mage who had called him. He had no spirit left to resist. Empty of passion, he stared into features troubled as storm sea. Just then the staff descended in a blistering arc of light.

It struck with a blast of energy. Gale wind screamed. The sea rose, towered into boiling crests which broke over the ledge with a roar. Foam-laced tons of water hurled Jaric from his perch.

He shouted in panic as he tumbled over and over. Then darkness drowned him in yet another dream. Ice snapped and sang like harpstrings in his ears, overlaid by the cries of creatures imprisoned, yet lusting hotly for blood and killing. Jaric shivered, shaken by the knowledge that those cries would echo for centuries yet to come were nothing done. Then an arching flare of sunlight struck his face. He squinted, saw a cliff armored with prisms of ice. Waves boomed beneath, splintered into diamond drops of spray and the wind crooned in a minor key. Tragedy had occurred here, Jaric understood, and he knew unconsolable grief. Tears traced his cheeks. Then the scene upended, replaced by the stinging prod of Anskiere's geas. Direction aligned like a compass within his mind; he knew he must travel southeast. The sorcerer's command intensified, became a compulsion no protest could deny.

Then Jaric knew only darkness, threaded by a far-off echo of voices. Fuzzily, he attempted to orient himself. His eyes seemed clotted with shadow and his limbs weighed like lead. Confused by the return of his senses, Jaric stirred in the Llondel's embrace, then sighed and lifted his head. An elderly man with rumpled hair lifted a freshly lit torch from a bracket in the wall. Jaric recognized the Master Seer of Morbrith but the chamber was unfamiliar, decidedly not part of the castle. The walls were strangely polished and incised with geometrical carvings. Jaric blinked, confused, and the voice which droned in his ears slowly resolved into speech.

". . . Must be Ivain Firelord's son," said the seer in a tone of misgiving. No sorcerer's name was more feared, except that of Anskiere, who had leveled Tierl Enneth; and Anskiere himself had called the boy into thrall.

"Kor's Blessed Fires!" The Earl leaned sharply forward, clenched both hands into fists, and crossed his wrists in a gesture to avert malign sorcery.

Jaric felt someone's arms tighten around him. He looked up, startled by the creature who held him, surely a demon with hideous glowing eyes. The boy gasped in fear. *This was the sender of images who had forced his submission to Anskiere.*

He appealed at once to the Earl. "Have mercy. My Lord, I beg you. Have the demon release me."

But the Earl acted as though Jaric had never spoken. He stared at the Llondel, his expression like iron in the torchlight. When he spoke, his reply was for the demon alone. "I'm sorry. I cannot permit the boy to live."

The Llondel hissed. Paralyzed with terror, Jaric saw the Earl draw his knife. The seer shouted, and dropped the torch. Flame streaked as it tumbled to the floor. Amid a mad whirl of shadows, Jaric saw a blade flash, quickly eclipsed by the Llondel's body. The creature rolled, bearing Jaric with it. The boy heard a thump, felt the quiver as steel struck flesh. He knew no pain. The Llondel had taken the thrust intended for him just below the shoulder.

The Earl cursed. Jaric gasped as the demon's good arm tightened around him. His face was crushed into cloth which smelled of sweetgrass. He struggled but could not break loose. The Llondel lifted him, fumbled the door open, and dragged him into the landing beyond. Jounced and half suffocated by blood-soaked fabric, Jaric fought to tear free. But the Llondel bundled him toward the stairway with a grip like wire. Jaric panicked. He wrenched against this captor, pulled clear long enough to manage a glance behind.

The Earl had not pursued. He crouched, bloodied to the elbow, over the sprawled body of a boy with pale hair. With a jolt, Jaric recognized himself. The handle of the knife stuck through the blankets, piercing his heart.

Jaric screamed. The Llondel yanked him forward, sent him crashing down the stairs. Stone risers bruised his bare heels. They were solid, *real,* as the corpse in the room could not be.

'*Image,*' assured the demon, picking up his distress. It jabbed him between the shoulder blades with a spurred palm, driving him downward. '*I show your kind what would happen should they kill you.*'

Jaric tripped, caught the railing to prevent himself from falling. "Why do you care?" His voice cracked with emotion. Already he could feel Anskiere's geas tug at his mind, urging him southeast with the wretched persistence of a headache.

Calmly the Llondel framed a reply. '*I act for the sorcerer.*' A steel crossguard gleamed beyond the curve of the cloak hood; the Earl's knife was embedded still in the demon's back. Jaric felt his skin crawl. Surely the creature was in agony. A man had wounded it, yet it stood patiently, its luminous gaze unpleasantly dispassionate.

"You're hurt." Jaric pointed to the weapon, wrung by revulsion. "Why should you suffer for the sorcerer who massacred all of Tierl Enneth?"

The demon hissed in anger. It grabbed the boy's wrist, tore him away from the railing, then spun him, reeling downward. *'Fool,'* it sent. *'Tierl Enneth fell at Tathagres' hand. And now, in ignorance, she seeks to free the Mharg-spawn as well.'*

But fear and trauma, and the ache of Anskiere's geas, had driven Jaric far beyond rational understanding. Half blinded by tears, he stumbled across the anteroom and struck the door with such force the breath slammed from his lungs. The Llondel arrived just behind him. Spurs clicked like dice against metal as it raised the bolt. The portal swung, pitching Jaric headlong into the night. He fell, tumbling over and over, clawed by weedstalks and dew-drenched grass. But the Llondel permitted no respite. It jabbed an image into his mind. Flat on his back, Jaric saw the stars obliterated by a clearly focused scene outside the gates of Koridan's Shrine. Six of the Earl's guardsmen lay asleep in the scrub. A horse browsed in their midst, saddled, bridled, and equipped with a sword in a sheath beneath the stirrup.

'Now go,' sent the Llondel. *'Take the animal and flee, for your own kind will surely take your life.'*

Cornered by Anskiere's geas and the Earl's intent to murder, Jaric had no other option. Horses intimidated him. A sword in his hands was so much dead weight. Yet with a throat tight with grief, he rose to his feet and ran.

The Llondel watched him go with burning eyes. Satisfied the boy would not turn back, it clutched its hurt shoulder and sank slowly to the floor. There it lay still. Warm blood pooled, darkening the mosaic in a widening puddle. Aware its wound was mortal, the Llondian shunned communication with its own kind. Instead it clung to consciousness, spent its last strength spinning thought-forms; and images bloomed like opium dreams in the minds of the humans in the chamber above.

In the baleful flicker of torchlight, the Earl watched the blood he believed to be Jaric's drip down his wrists. Prisoned by the Llondel's imaging, he felt as if the knife he just used for murder had also severed the threads of natural progression. Chaos remained. Violence echoed on the air with the dissonance of a snapped harpstring, and the stains on his hands darkened, dried, and blew away as dust. A woman's face appeared, circled by braided coils of hair the color of frost. She was lovely beyond description, but behind amethyst eyes shone an inhuman lust for power. The Earl felt his stomach tighten in recognition of evil. The image shifted, showed the woman kneeling while the occupant of a jeweled throne handed her a cube of black stone which contained Keys to a sorcerer's ward. A smile touched her lips; and the Llondel's vision of the future shattered into nightmare.

The woman rose, *uncontested because Jaric had died of a knife thrust,* and armies marched. Towns blazed like festival lanterns, and corpses bloated in the parched soil of ruined fields. The woman laughed. The cube in her hand went molten, blazed whitely, and became a wheel of fire. A sorcerer's defenses burst with a white-hot snap of energy and winds rose, smashing maddened waves upon a desolate stretch of shoreline. Nearby a tower of granite tumbled and fell. Demonkind spewed forth, hideous beyond any the Earl had ever known. Fanged, taloned, and patterned with iridescent scales, they swept skyward with a thunder of membranous wings. Where they passed, their breath withered flesh, curdled the fruit on the trees, and left the stripped veins of leaves blowing like cobwebs in the breeze. The earth rotted and knew no spring. The oceans spewed up dead fish. And at Morbrith Keep the streets lay reeking with a tangle of human remains.

"No!" the Earl's scream tore from his throat in near physical agony, but the images kept coming. He saw a forest dell tangled with the white flowering vine which often grew on gravesites. There a black-haired fisherman's daughter dragged a silvery object which contained a wardspell to stay the escaped demons. But she was slain, cut down by a brother's sword, and soldiers turned the box's powers against their own kind. The snow-haired woman whispered praise, and her voice became the croak of ravens feasting on dead flesh.

Weeping now, the Earl beheld a headland scabbed with dirtied drifts of ice. A ragged band of survivors set fire to stacked logs, while other men chipped through the resulting slush with swords and shovels. They hoped to release a weather mage believed to be trapped inside, for legend held his powers might subdue the horrors which blighted the land. But where the sorcerer had been, they discovered bones wrapped loosely in a bundle of rags. Exhausted from their labor, the men abandoned the place in despair; and through a rift in the ice, a quavering whistle echoed across the lonely face of the sea. The snow-haired woman laughed. And the Earl saw his civilization plunge into a well of darkness, all for the murder of a Morbrith boy in the sanctuary tower at midsummer.

"No! Koridan's Fires, *no!*" With his throat still raw from screaming, the Earl opened his eyes. Daylight spilled brightly through the casement. The seer crouched trembling in the sunlight, his white head familiarly rumpled. No bloodied corpse marred the floor.

The Earl buried his face in his hands. *He had only dreamed the boy's death.* But the Llondel's prescient images left a deep and lingering warning of danger. Preoccupied, the Earl did not notice the rich blue robes of the men who arrived in the doorway until after the Archpriest had addressed him.

"My Lord, it is unavoidable. You must be tried for heresy."

The Earl swore tiredly and leaned back against the wall. He did not immediately respond. The seer watched him in naked alarm, but said nothing.

The priest mistook his silence for regret. "Perhaps you may not burn for the crime. Your men claim the knife which killed the Llondian demon is your Lordship's. If you can prove you dealt the death blow, you may be judged more leniently."

From the doorway, the healer broke in with vindictive satisfaction. "Jaric has escaped. He stole your horse."

"Don't pursue him," the Earl said quickly. He stared down at the floor, stung to a flurry of thought. Jaric must not be stopped. He added in a hoarse whisper, "The horse was a gift."

The Earl did not resist as the priests drew him to his feet and placed fetters on his wrists. His own dilemma seemed of small importance beside the warning of the Llondel's death image. For it appeared the fate of Morbrith rested on the shoulders of a small sickly apprentice whose sole talent was penmanship.

"Kor protect him," muttered the seer, and the priests, misinterpreting, bowed their heads in earnest prayer for the man they had taken into custody.

CHAPTER VI

Gaire's Main

The gale set loose by Anskiere's stormfalcon raged across the southwest latitudes and finally spent itself, leaving skies whipped with cirrus and air scoured clean by rain. Emien woke in the pinnace to a cold fair morning. Bruised after days of battling maddened elements, he raised himself from the floorboards. Bilgewater dripped from his sleeves as he stretched and rubbed salt-crusted eyes. The pinnace wallowed through the troughs, her helm lashed and her oarsmen sprawled in exhausted slumber across their benches; but the craft's other two occupants seemed strangely unaffected by fatigue. Hearvin and Tathagres sat near the stern, involved in conversation.

Emien gripped the gunwale. Seasoned fisherman though he was, his palms had blistered at the oar; waterlogged skin had since split into sores. Yet the boy noticed no sting, obsessed as he was with his desire for vengeance. Of those on board only Tathagres hated Anskiere as he did. She had promised the Stormwarden's demise, and for that the boy had sworn an oath no fisherman's son would betray. Though weary and starved, his first thought was for his mistress.

Emien stood cautiously. Dehydration had left him lightheaded, and the roll of the pinnace made movement without a handhold impossible. Unsatisfied with the boat's performance, he ran a critical eye over the canvas set since the storm relented. The mainsheet needed easing, and the headsail drove the bow down because the halyard was too slack. Instinctively, Emien started to adjust lines.

The sound of raised voices carried clearly from the stern as he worked. Hearvin and Tathagres openly argued, and Emien paused to listen.

". . . Failed to accomplish your purpose," Hearvin said bluntly. He sat as he always did, straight as chiseled wood against the curve of the swells.

Tathagres responded inaudibly but her gesture bespoke annoyance.

"What else have you achieved?" Hearvin jabbed a hand into the wet folds of his cloak. "Your liege expected the release of the frostwargs and a Stormwarden on Cliffhaven who would subvert the Kielmark's sovereignty. Thus far you have delivered two dead sorcerers, a smashed war fleet, and a boy you would have lost had I not intervened."

Absently Emien reached for the mainsheet. Although a gust masked Tathagres' reply, her expression became haughtily angry.

Hearvin stiffened, no longer impassive. "And I say you've meddled enough!"

This time Tathagres' voice cut cleanly across the white hiss of spray. "Do you challenge me? How dare you! You fear the Stormwarden, that much is evident. And you speak of the Kielmark as more than a mortal man, which proves your judgment is dim as an itinerant conjurer's. I'm disappointed. Kisburn promised me better."

Hearvin jerked a fist from his robe and made a pass in the air, as if he thought to retaliate with sorcery. Concerned for his mistress, Emien cleated the line in his hand and hastened aft. But Tathagres met the sorcerer's threat with a scornful laugh.

Hearvin abruptly recovered control. "I warn you, Lady. Don't underestimate me as you did Anskiere." The sorcerer stopped, forced to brace himself as a wave lifted the stern.

The pinnace lurched. Emien stumbled noisily against a thwart. Hearvin started around. The wind snatched his hood, unveiling pinched cheeks and an expression of annoyance. Tathagres seemed to welcome the interruption. She tilted her head and smiled sweetly at the fisherman's son from Imrill Kand.

"Boy, were you taught navigation?" She raked tangled hair from her brow and smiled with girlish appeal. "Do you know enough to sail this boat to land?"

Close up, Emien saw the marks Anskiere's storm had inflicted on the mistress he had chosen. Her fair complexion was chapped from salt water and sun, and weariness had printed circles dark as bruises beneath her eyes. Emien swallowed, momentarily overcome by the urge to protect her beauty from further ruin. Embarrassed by his flushed skin and knotted muscles, the boy answered self-consciously.

"My Lady need not have worried. I took sights last night while the polestar was visible. The isles of Innishari could be reached in a fortnight with good wind. If Kor grants us rainfall for water, I could get you there safely."

Tathagres tumbled the bracelets on her wrists with elegant fingers and bestowed a vindictive glance upon Hearvin. "Then let us sail directly. At Innishari we can engage a trader bound for Cliffhaven. Have you any more objections? Do tell me. I'm certain Emien would welcome the entertainment."

She waited, poised like a cat toying with helpless prey. But the sorcerer refused to be baited.

He raised his hood over his head, apparently content to let the quarrel lapse. Only Emien glimpsed wary anger in the sorcerer's eyes before shadow obscured it. The boy distrusted Hearvin's intentions, but he was canny enough to keep silent. He could serve Tathagres best if the sorcerer remained unsuspecting; and dedicated less to intrigue than to practicality, he applied himself to the task of sailing the pinnace to Innishari.

His responsibility was not slight. The following days would bring hardship enough to tax the endurance of the toughest man on board. Tathagres' slim build left her perishable as a woodland flower. Without nourishment she would be first to weaken.

Brooding, Emien considered his priorities. The pinnace held course decently enough with the tiller lashed, but her heading would be more accurate if the helm were manned. With the self-reliance gained while fishing aboard *Dacsen,* the boy began to strip the rope from the whipstaff. The knots were barely loosened when he noticed Tathagres watching him, her lips curved with disdain.

Emien frowned. "Does my Lady disapprove?"

Tathagres braced herself against the gunwale, aware the backdrop of empty sky accentuated her femininity. "I gave you the charge of the pinnace. Does a captain stand watch like a common seaman?" Carefully judging her interval, she raised violet eyes and regarded the boy from Imrill Kand.

Caught staring, Emien reddened. Shamed by an adolescent rush of desire and stung by scorn from the woman who inspired it, he responded awkwardly. "Is that what you wish?" He abandoned the lashing, charged with frustration he dared not express. "If I establish watches among the seamen, I'll require a log to maintain dead reckoning." He did not belabor the fact he could not write.

Tathagres neatly eliminated the need. "Then Hearvin will act as your secretary."

Nervously Emien glanced at the sorcerer. But Hearvin made no protest; left no course but one which did not defeat his pride, the boy licked dry lips and faced his mistress.

"Well?" prompted Tathagres.

Balked by conflicting emotions, Emien could not answer. He turned on his heel and made his way forward. He did not see Tathagres' smile of approval when his reluctance transformed into rage. He jabbed the nearest seaman awake with his toe, and anger lent him authority beyond his years.

"You! Take the helm, and steer southwest."

The sailhand stumbled to his feet, too startled to protest. Emien felt the power of command surge through him, sweeter than fine wine and far more intoxicating. Never again would he grovel as an ignorant fisherman before his betters. In time, he too would be master. Tathagres would see she had chosen well by asking him into her service.

Emien braced his legs against the roll of the pinnace, brow drawn into a scowl. "You will stand watch until noon. I will send a man to relieve you."

Accustomed to discipline, the seaman obeyed. And on a reckless wave of daring, the boy decided to explore the limits of his discovery. He turned aft and bowed respectfully to Tathagres.

"My Lady, for the good of the vessel, I require the jewelry you use to fasten your cloak."

Tathagres stared at him with a calculating expression. Sweat sprang along Emien's temples. Yet he did not tremble or back down, and at length, Tathagres unpinned the two gold brooches. She handed them over to Emien and asked no explanation.

The exchange was not lost upon the seaman at the helm. As the boy made his final bow and moved forward, he viewed Emien with fresh respect. The boy's confidence swelled. He felt himself a man for the first time since the accident with the net which had caused his father's death. On Imrill Kand, he had been called bungler, a child bereft of common sense and shamefully slow to learn. Now he knew otherwise. With his chin lifted haughtily, Emien cupped the brooches in his torn palms, and chose a place where he could work and still keep an eye on the helmsman.

Hearvin watched as, skillfully, the boy began to twist the jewelry into lures and hooks to catch fish. "Well, at least there's a chance we won't starve, even if our meals are dearly bought," the sorcerer commented. He leaned back against the gunwale and blandly faced Tathagres. "That boy learns remarkably fast. Perhaps too fast."

Tathagres said nothing. Her attention seemed absorbed by the flash of the gold between Emien's fingers. But the thoughts reflected in her amethyst eyes had a hungry quality which left the sorcerer uneasy.

Just past noon on the day following his flight from the sanctuary tower, Jaric rode into the village of Gaire's Main. Both nose and throat were gritty with dust. The insides of his knees were raw from the saddle, and his ankles bruised repeatedly against the stirrups, which dangled too long from his feet. Jaric had not paused to shorten the leathers. Though his flight had taken him through several settlements, he dared not stop, even to water his horse, in any town subject to the Earl's authority.

But Gaire's Main lay outside the borders of Morbrith. The site had once been sacred to the tribes who gathered for the summerfair, but now only the name remained as a reminder of less civilized times. Jaric reined his mount down a lane lined by sleepy cottages, whitewashed and neatly roofed with thatch. The horse stumbled with exhaustion. Lather dripped from the rags used to muffle the bit. The animal's sides heaved, each breath labored, and the low-pitched clink at each stride made Jaric suspect a loose shoe. If he did not find a smith, he risked laming the horse. Travel afoot frightened him more than Morbrith's retribution; with no mount, he would be helpless.

Jaric rounded a crook in the lane. Ahead, a wide crossroad sliced Gaire's Main into quarters; there also lay the spring where the tribes had once held rites. But the traditional ringstones of slate had been pulled down for shingles. A brick trough replaced them, and the run-off trickled into a chain of muddy puddles presently foraged by tame ducks, and a sow tended by a boy with a stick. They too stared at the strange rider who entered the square.

The horse sensed water and raised its head. Jaric gave it rein. Children rushed out to run beside his stirrup and their excited chatter made his head ring. A woman with a bucket paused in a doorway to point. As the horse plodded tiredly across the square, Jaric felt as though all the folk of Gaire's Main had stopped their work to watch him.

He was too weary to care. The horse splashed through a puddle, scattering fowl. The sow raised herself from her wallow with a grunt, as Jaric dropped the reins and permitted his mount to thrust its muzzle into the trough.

"Why, the rider is barefoot!" exclaimed the pig-boy, and the other children giggled.

Jaric sighed. They seemed enviably carefree. Any other time, he would have been cheered by the laughter of children; but now Anskiere's geas throbbed like a wound in his chest, and he had no inclination to smile. Beyond the spring lay a tall, sprawling structure with a shingled roof. A board hung on chains from the gables. Faded letters identified the building as a tavern, but the sign was unnecessary; Gaire's Main offered little else but peasant cottages. Jaric knew from keeping accounts that the folk traveled to Morbrith for goods. He could not recall whether the village boasted a smith. He would have to inquire.

The horse snorted loudly, and resumed drinking. Summoned by the noise, a weathered man in dusty coveralls emerged from the wings which held the stables. His hair was white and his cheeks sunburned. He braced sinewy arms on the lip of the trough, and regarded Jaric suspiciously.

"Ridden all night, have you?" His voice was rusty, with an inflection as quaint as the town. "What brings you to Gaire's Main?"

Jaric reddened. A ragged woman shambled out of the stables and joined the old man. Ancient and gnarled as treebark, she peered at Jaric with eyes turned pearly white by cataracts. Assuredly she was blind; yet she stared as though she were sighted. Jaric shivered with apprehension. Resigned to the fact the entire village was listening, he answered in the cultured accents learned at court.

His voice came out hoarse, as though he had forgotten the use of it. "No doubt you think me childish. I wagered my cousin that I could ride fifty leagues in my nightshirt and still defend my honor without weapons. The contest was made in drunken folly. Do you wonder, now I'm sober, that I chose to ride at night?"

Intrigued, the children clustered closer. The ragged woman pinned him with eyes like fish roe, and the man stared pointedly at Jaric's soft hands and blistered knees. He grimaced in contempt.

"Your horse needs a shoe," he said carefully. "Shall I see to it?"

Jaric nodded, his throat too tight for speech. The folk had not believed his lie, but apparently no one present chose to question it. Relieved, he slid from the saddle, but to his dismay, his knees buckled the instant his feet struck ground. The pain of tortured muscles made him gasp.

The beggar woman caught his shoulder with gnarled hands and steadied him. Her grip felt like ice. Jaric flinched, startled by the chill. Through a wave of dizziness, he saw she was wizened and small, and clothed not in rags but in knotted leather skins like the hill tribe's dress. Not every inhabitant of Gaire's Main was civilized; with a jolt, Jaric recognized what he had been too tired to notice earlier: the woman could only be the Lady of the Well. Blinded by ritual as a maiden and dedicated to oracular vision, she would tend the shrine until death, though the place had probably changed much since she was a girl. She smelled of the byre. Nevertheless, she deserved respect. The boy drew breath to offer thanks.

But his words were blurred by a cry as eldritch as the mystery which surrounded the spring. Jaric's spine prickled horribly. Darkness arose in him, and his senses reeled.

"Fire!" said the woman clearly. "I see thee a man, ringed with the living fire. The ravens of discord fly at thy heels."

She added more in the tongue of the clans. But Jaric heard none of her warning. Lost in a rushing tide of faintness, he collapsed, and even his slight weight was too great for the Lady. She staggered against the stable master, who caught the boy in his arms.

Shaken by the upsurge of the old powers, the stablemaster lifted a pale, uncertain face to the blind priestess. For years she had been senile and helpless, little more than a beggarwoman who slept in his hayloft. "What shall I do with this boy?"

The woman blinked, relapsed into the blankness of advanced age. But her reply was lucid. "Do all that is needful for him, as well as his mount. You'll find silver in his saddlebag. Take what fee you earn, and set him on his way. He must not be delayed." She subsided into muttering. The children who had lingered to observe scattered suddenly and ran.

Alone by the spring, the stablemaster left the gelding with its reins trailing. The animal had been ridden to exhaustion; it would not stray while he carried the young master inside to the innkeeper's wife.

Jaric revived, coughing, to the sharp taste of plum brandy. He swallowed, stinging the membranes of his throat, and opened his eyes. A plump middle-aged woman with blowsy hair bent over him. When she touched the flask to his lips for a second draught, he shook his head, momentarily unable to speak.

"What's wrong? Can't you hold a man's drink?" The woman set the flask on a trestle by her elbow. Out of habit, she wiped damp hands on her skirt, her manner softened by the matronly kindness Jaric's frailty invariably inspired. "You'll stay scrawny, lad, if you don't learn to handle your liquor."

Jaric sighed and wished the advice was true. In the copy-chamber his delicate stature had been no disadvantage. But alone on the road, he was unable to avoid the fact that he was unfit to survive the regions of his own culture. For the first time, the thought shamed him. He could not meet the woman's eyes.

"Drink the rest if you can," she urged gently. "I'll send my daughter Kencie out with a meal."

She passed through the doorway to the kitchen with the comfortable self-possession accumulated through years of hospitality. Jaric studied his surroundings uneasily. He sat in an armchair built of plain wood which was dwarfed by an immense stone fireplace. No logs burned, but a tallow candle on the table illuminated a beamed ceiling, whitewashed walls, and trestles and benches well-polished with use. Except for a man whittling by the tap, the common room was deserted. For all the notice the elder gave the boy, he might have been deaf.

Presently Kencie appeared with a tray of food. Large-boned, blond and close to Jaric's age, she set her burden on the table, and regarded the boy with curiosity. Startled by her likeness to her mother, Jaric stared back.

"Quit gawking and eat." Kencie rubbed knuckles still damp with dishwater on her apron. Her cheeks dimpled faintly with disdain. "By your looks you need to. Got wrists so thin I'd suspect you'd have trouble lifting a fork."

Jaric plucked a roll from the tray and bit into it, as though to blunt the taste of bitterness. Accustomed as he was to taunts from the women at Morbrith, Kencie's comments cut him; her brisk observation granted no respect, even for a stranger who shared the inn's hospitality. Jaric tasted the stew, and even in Kencie's presence could not keep his hand steady.

Hoping to soften her contempt, he said, "The food is quite good." But exhaustion left him barely able to eat.

Kencie shrugged. "You look half dead. I'll wrap what you can't finish. You can take it in your saddlebag." She wrinkled her nose and smiled. "At least they can't make me polish your boots."

Her banter appeared friendly. But as she swept the floor beneath the trestles, Jaric caught her staring when she thought he would not notice, and once, from the corner of his eye, he saw her raise crossed fists in the sign to avert evil sorcery. Plainly, the wise woman's prophecy had marked him; the townsfolk of Gaire's Main treated him well because they wished to be rid of him. Unhappiness raised a lump in Jaric's throat. How could he possibly manage, without Morbrith's walls and the sanctuary of the library? Kencie's teasing made Anskiere's geas seem bleak and hopeless as exile. Caught by fresh terror, Jaric felt his stomach clench.

He set the spoon aside, afraid he would drop it, afraid Kencie would notice his weakness and laugh anew. Jaric shoved his hands into his lap to hide their trembling. "I can't finish any more," he said desperately.

Kencie propped her broom against the bar. "Come along, then. Mother asked me to show you to the front room."

Jaric stumbled to his feet. "You're very kind."

"No. You're paying." Kencie fetched a candle from her apron pocket and touched the wick to the one already alight on the trestle. "Mother saw you carried only silver. She said she'd charge you half, since the Lady spoke for you. But you can't stay more than a night."

Relieved to discover the Earl's saddlebags had at least contained coins, Jaric limped stiffly toward the stair. The villagers need not have worried. Hounded by the sorcerer's geas, he doubted he could linger in Gaire's Main an hour longer than necessary.

Jaric slept dreamlessly through the afternoon. Fully clothed and dusty from travel, he lay crumpled across the bed exactly as he had fallen when Kencie closed the door to his chamber. He never stirred, even at sundown when the innkeeper's wife brought him hot water to wash. She left the steaming basin on the stand by the window, and quietly departed, convinced the boy would rest until morning. Left to himself, he might have; but the sorcerer whose summons had claimed him seemed to permit no allowance for weakness. Jaric was jabbed out of sleep by restlessness which brought him fully and instantly awake.

The room was dark. Beyond the window, the moon drifted, yellowed as old ivory above the hills. Though a full hour remained before dawn, Jaric could not stay in bed. The geas goaded his muscles into aching knots of tension. His skin tingled as if the very air might scald him if he stayed still any longer.

Jaric rose, groped blindly for candle and striker. He bashed his wrist into the basin. Water slopped over the side, wetting his fingers, but its coolness did nothing to ease the discomfort which increased steadily with each passing minute. Jaric endured only long enough to rinse his face, and bolted for the door.

Movement brought respite. Shivering with relief, Jaric hurried down the corridor. He would have to find his horse quickly and settle his account with the inn before uncertainty and the cruel effects of the geas overwhelmed him.

The common room was deserted. Outside, Kencie leaned over the spring with a yoke and two buckets, drawing water for the kitchen. As the main door to the inn swung open, she glanced up, surprised by the sight of Jaric on the steps.

"Leaving?" She set her burden down and approached him, careful to avoid the puddles which gleamed in dull silver patches on the ground. "You're early. The stablemaster isn't up yet."

Irked that she should regard him as helpless, Jaric said, "I can saddle my own mount."

Kencie shrugged, her face a blurred oval in the predawn mist. "Very well. If you wait, I'll fetch your saddlebags. The rest of your horse's gear is in the tackroom, just beyond the ladder to the loft."

But Jaric could not stay still. The compulsion set upon him would relent for nothing, far less courtesy, and while Kencie retrieved her buckets, the boy hurried on into the stables.

He located the tackroom by touch in the dark; his was the only saddle and bridle on the rack. Aroused by the noise, the Earl's black gelding lifted its head, the blaze on its muzzle visible in the gloom of the aisle beyond. Jaric dragged the tack to the stall, reminded by the damp straw under his soles that his feet were bare. His hands shook with nerves as he caught the horse's halter.

The gelding shied. Leather burned the boy's palms, and the clang of the tether ring startled pigeons from the loft. Driven by necessity Jaric tried the singsong words he had heard in the forges since childhood; yet where his efforts then had failed, this animal responded. Its eye stopped rolling; taut muscles relaxed and the blazed head lowered, nostrils widened in a soft inquisitive snort.

Jaric slipped the bridle over the broad forehead with unpracticed clumsiness, but the horse seemed not to mind. The saddle, with scabbard and sword attached, proved too bulky for the boy to lift above his shoulder. He had to clamber onto the manger just to reach the gelding's back. Kencie returned as he hauled the girths tight and jumped down. Unaware he had stopped trembling, Jaric led the horse from the stall. Kencie buckled the saddlebags in place, covering his silence with a spate of chatter.

"Mother charged you one silver for bed and board. The stablemaster took a half-silver for grain and resetting your horse's shoe. Five and one remain in the purse in the left pocket. I put food in the right, with your cloak." She stepped back to discover Jaric inspecting the near hind hoof of his mount. "Is the shoe set to your satisfaction?"

Jaric released the gelding's fetlock and straightened. "It will pass." His words masked irritation. The work was poorly done. At the tender age of four, the exacting standards of his guardians had been drummed into his head; but without enough muscle to wield the hammer, the boy could do nothing now but regret the stablemaster's ineptness. He caught the bridle and led the horse from the stable, careful not to look back lest his toes get crushed by steel-shod hooves.

The time had come to mount and ride. Kencie hovered uncertainly to one side as the horse splashed through the puddles by the spring. Jaric set his foot in the stirrup while the animal drank.

"Wait," Kencie blurted. She whirled and ran into the tavern.

Jaric paused, and suffered the first tingling warning of the geas for the sake of her request. He braced himself to resist, but Kencie was gone no more than a moment.

She emerged through the entrance to the courtyard, clutching a pair of boots. Fine double-stitched leather was well cut, and trimmed with coral beadwork and fur.

"Here." Kencie pushed the boots into Jaric's arms. "These are yours. Their owner died of fever while lodging at our tavern. Rich clothes don't suit anyone in Gaire's Main. Wager or not, you can't continue to go barefoot."

Jaric reddened, embarrassed by the transparency of his lie, and the vulnerable need behind it. Ashamed before Kencie's generosity, he bent quickly to try on her gift, before she noticed and thought him ungracious.

The boots were ludicrously large. Inches of extra cuff flapped around calves thin as twigs. Jaric bit his lip and stood up. "I'll think of you with thanks at every step." He smiled gravely and granted Kencie the courtesy due Morbrith's court ladies. "May your inn and its patrons prosper well."

He hastened to mount, and the horse sidled, spoiling the grace of his gesture. Kencie caught the bridle, steadied the gelding until Jaric had gained the saddle. As he gathered the reins, she looked up at his face, into sensitive dark eyes, and an expression pathetic with fear.

"You're so small," she said softly, and instantly regretted the words.

Jaric stiffened. Kencie had given the boots because she was sorry for him. Rage tore through him. He had asked for nothing. Anonymity and a scholar's position in a library had contented him perfectly. At a stroke of fate, a sorcerer's geas and a priestess' prophecy had plundered his self-worth, transformed him into an object of pity; now he was dependent upon charity every bit as much as the lame who begged in the gutter.

In taut-lipped silence, he jerked the gelding free of Kencie's hand. With a jab of his heels he sent it thundering out of Gaire's Main on the south road.

Behind him, Kencie rubbed skinned fingers on her apron, sick at heart for the blow she had dealt his pride. Strange, she thought; if not for Jaric's wretched skinniness, she might have admired more than his courage. The hoofbeats faded slowly in the distance. With stoic practicality, Kencie recalled her neglected chores. But as she walked toward the inn, the ancient priestess of the Well shuffled out of the barn and blocked her path.

The woman scratched her belly through a rip in the skins which clothed her, then lifted blind eyes to the lane where Jaric and the horse had vanished only minutes earlier.

"Do ye know?" The hag caught Kencie's sleeve. "The boy won't walk twenty paces in that pair of boots."

The girl's breath caught. She shoved the priestess rudely aside and fled into the kitchen; and not even her mother could coax her to explain why she looked so pale.

The Earl's gelding stretched into a gallop and the rooftops of Gaire's Main soon disappeared behind the curve of the hills. Tilled farmland gave way to thorny scrub and the heat of Jaric's anger ebbed, leaving loneliness. Ahead the road wound through a wide valley, mist-clothed and deserted. Rendered in shades of charcoal under a pearly sky, the land framed him with solitude. Everything he valued lay behind him. The boy shortened rein to slow the gelding's pace, but the animal proved unexpectedly spirited; it flattened its ears and leaned sullenly on the bit. Jaric felt its stride lengthen until mane whipped his wrists and the earth became a blur under its hooves.

The frightened boy cursed and dragged at the reins until his shoulders ached. The animal had already been ridden hard the night he had stolen it. Now, after rest and grain, the gelding was too strong for him; until it had spent its first fresh energy, Jaric could not hope to control it. Weeping tears of frustration, he clung to the mane and prayed the brute would keep to the road.

Distance unwound like clock chain to the rhythm of the horse's gallop. Its hooves struck with a pure and solid ring, raising tiny puffs of dust. The breeze flung mane and tail and Jaric's light hair like a rough caress. Beneath knees that stung with sores, the boy felt the healthy thrust of the shoulder muscles; the animal enjoyed its resilience, and the run through the cool morning became not a threat but a celebration of its own being. Jaric discovered harmony in the beast's simple pleasure; his panic transformed to wild exhilaration. He relaxed his grip on the reins. The horse stretched its neck and went faster.

When the sun's edge sliced above the horizon, Jaric's cheeks were flushed with excitement. He felt more at ease in the saddle than ever before, and as though attuned to the change in its rider, the gelding gradually slowed. With a shake of its head, it dropped to a trot. And struck by disappointment, Jaric lost his nerve.

He pulled the horse down to a walk, happiness marred by the unchanged fact that his body was no match for a spirited mount. The thrill he had tasted now added edge to his misery. With a tearing pang of sorrow, he understood that Morbrith's library could no longer shelter his frailty, or his innocence. For the first time, he felt imprisoned by his physical limitations, and the grief of that recognition branded his soul.

CHAPTER VII

Crossroads

The road became crowded as the sun rose higher. By mid-morning, Jaric rode through dusty clouds raised by herds of livestock being driven to market. Buffeted by sheep and cows, and forced aside by the fast passage of the post riders, he strove to calm his restive mount. The gelding jigged nervously, ears pricked and neck muscles taut as cable beneath a sheen of sweat. Jaric's back and shoulders ached without letup. Long before noon, the joints in his elbows and wrists developed the shooting pains of stressed tendons. Yet exhausted as he was, the sorcerer's summons granted him no quarter; he must continue, it seemed, until he collapsed.

At length the dirt track from Gaire's Main merged with the stone highway which paralleled the Redwater River to Corlin Town. Here caravans congested the route; the rumble of ox wagons and the ceaseless shouts of drovers made Jaric's head swim. His eyes and nostrils became irritated with grit. The reins skinned his hands to the point where he feared to dismount. Should the horse shy in the tumult, he could never keep hold of the bridle; neither could he reach the food Kencie had packed in his saddlebag. Jaric hunched miserably over the gelding's mane and hoped enough silver remained in the Earl's purse to pay for a bath and a night's lodging in Corlin.

The afternoon wore on. The teamsters joked and grew boisterous in anticipation of the women their pay would buy when they reached the taverns. Encouraged, Jaric glanced ahead. Thin as pen strokes on parchment, the spires of Corlin notched the horizon to the east. Below lay the valley where the barge ferry crossed the Redwater; the road resumed on the other side, shining like ribbon against the dark border of Seitforest. Jaric counted clusters of pack animals and wagons on the near bank. At least four caravans awaited the barge. He wondered whether he could get across before sundown. By night, Corlin's guardsmen closed the gates to protect against the bands of outlaws who plied the trade routes for plunder. Alone and unskilled with arms, Jaric made easy prey for such robbers. Apprehensively, he eased the gelding into a trot.

The gait aggravated his discomfort. Dazed by fatigue, and with his thoughts flickering on the hazy borders of delirium, Jaric failed at first to notice the sting of Anskiere's geas. He crested the hill where the road swung north to meet the ferry, and was suddenly jabbed by an irrational urge to turn down a footpath which branched to the right. He resisted.

To abandon the security of a well-traveled route invited disaster. Jaric turned the gelding's head firmly toward the ferry and rammed his heels into its flanks. The horse sprang into a run.

Yet even survival held no sway over the geas which had claimed his destiny. The instant Jaric drew abreast of the footpath, a vortex of force erupted under the gelding's hooves. Wind arose, and a rushing prison of air whirled around horse and rider, forbidding them to pass. The animal scrambled in terror and reared. Blinded by whipping mane, the boy fought to stay astride.

Energy slashed into Jaric's mind. He cried out as the sight of ferry and road splintered, replaced by a vision of ice cliffs mauled by the endless crash of storm breakers; the air smelled of damp and dune grass, and the sour cries of gulls haunted the sky overhead. Threaded through the melancholy of that place, Jaric sensed the call which summoned him would relent only when he reached that desolate shore; that the blood debt of Ivain had fallen upon his puny shoulders made not the slightest difference. Anskiere's command would stand, whether the boy's suffering brought the wrath of Koridan's Fires, or his life became forfeit. Jaric would go, or be driven haplessly as a leaf in the gales of autumn.

The fabric of the dream parted, leaving Jaric shakily clinging to the saddle. His mount quivered under him, paralyzed with fright. The boy stroked its neck mechanically, while the scent of the sea faded, overlaid by the tang of dust. The turnoff snaked like bleached cord across the meadows which flanked the Redwater, then lost itself in the gloomy fringes of Seitforest. For a rebellious moment Jaric refused to move. A gust fanned in warning through the weeds beneath the gelding's legs. Anskiere's powers never slept. The boy sighed. With beaten resignation, he gathered the reins and pulled the horse's head southeast, away from the ferry and safety. Jaric's face bore the weary stamp of hopelessness, for the geas led him to ruin with all the finality of a calf marked for slaughter.

The horse quieted once the road fell behind. Jaric tried not to look back at the towers of Corlin. Reddened by the lowering sun, the grass tips glistened as if dipped in blood. All too soon the meadowlands ended, and the trail led him into Seitforest.

The slanting rays of sunset dappled the forest with light; ancient as time, oaks and beeches rose over delicate carpets of ferns. Moss-streaked trunks rose up on either side, massive as the pillars of a king's hall, and the backlit foliage between glowed like lanterns at summerfair. Yet Jaric rode numbed with dread. For all of its bewitching magnificence, Seitforest was renowned as the domain of the lawless; none but the desperate rode its twisted trails without torches and an army of stout retainers. The vast wood seemed to swallow Jaric's presence, and even his horse's hoofbeats were deadened by musty drifts of leaf mold.

In the rosy pallor of the afterglow, a forester clad in dyed leather stepped from a thicket. Ebony hair streaked with white tumbled over the fellow's shoulders. A full game bag hung at his hip, and the bird snares which dangled from his belt swung gently as he paused to stare at the boy on the horse.

"Boy," the forester called softly. "You'd best turn back. Camp beside the ferry, if you'll take a stranger's advice. If you must travel this way, at least wait until you can join someone with a company of men-at-arms. Those who ride alone fare badly hereabouts."

Jaric made no effort to reply. Tortured by the memory of Kencie's pity, he chose not to pause and explain his plight. As he passed, the forester shrugged and ducked back into the undergrowth. Jaric gripped the reins tightly and restrained an urge to call him back.

The trail wound deeper into the wood. Shadows lengthened, until the evening star pricked like a fairy jewel through the leaves. Jaric traversed a chain of open glades, each more serene than the last. But all of nature's loveliness failed to ease the boy's unrest. In the gloom of twilight, the lawless of Seitforest overtook him.

Warned by a furtive rustle in the foliage, he reached for the Earl's sword. The weapon was heavy. Jaric needed both hands to lift it. Even before the blade cleared the scabbard, a man leapt from the brush, gauntleted hands stretched to seize the bridle. The gelding shied and smashed sideways through a clump of bracken. Tossed against the animal's neck, Jaric tugged the sword free. He slammed his heels into the horse in a desperate attempt to ride his attacker down. The man shouted angrily and dodged aside.

The gelding plunged on across the clearing, its reins flying loose. Over the sharpened edge of the sword, Jaric saw more outlaws run from the trees. Several carried clubs. They blocked his escape. Alarmed by their rush, the horse swerved. Its iron-shod hooves slashed through a stand of saplings. Branches whipped, clattering across the swordblade. Jaric fought to keep his seat. Suddenly the bridle snagged on a dead bough. Jerked short, the gelding staggered onto its haunches. Jaric heard a grunt of human exertion. Tough fingers grabbed his collar. He swung the sword. Steel clashed with the metal-bossed wood of a club. The shock stung Jaric to the shoulders and broke his grip.

The blade fell, slithered through undergrowth, and stabbed deeply into the earth. The outlaw yanked the boy from the saddle. Jaric tumbled, his cheek raked cruelly by the rings sewn on his assailant's jerkin. He landed with a thump in the bracken. Torn fronds framed a glimpse of a scarred face, and the rising silhouette of a club.

"No! Please! Have mercy!" Jaric raised his forearm to ward off the blow. Fenced by the rapid, trampling thud of hooves, he heard laughter. The club descended and struck. Bones snapped like sticks. Jaric screamed in agony. With a savage whistle of air, the club fell again. Jaric rolled, and caught a glancing blow on the head. His skull seemed to explode into fire, and he fell into darkness.

* * *

The moon shone high overhead when the forester reached the clearing to check the last of his snares. He paused, warned by the stillness that something was amiss. Where night-thrushes normally flourished, he heard only crickets, and by the path fronds of bracken dangled, crushed and torn on their stems. Attuned more deeply to the wood than his fellow men, the forester stooped and studied the ground. There he uncovered a tale of violence; soft moss had been gouged by the hooves of a frightened horse. The predator too left his mark; the forester traced the heelprint of a man's boot. Touched by a deep anger, his fingers clenched into a fist. Hurriedly, he followed the tracks down a swath of lacerated vegetation, and there found the robber's prey. A boy sprawled face down on a bed of leaves, his naked limbs veined like marble with blood.

Very likely the child was dead. Such tragedies were common in Seitforest. The forester sighed, grieved such brutality had overcome one so small and helpless.

"I warned you, didn't I, lad?" the man said aloud, and around him the crickets fell silent.

But when he touched him, he discovered the child was alive, and several years older than he had first assumed. Gently, the forester explored the boy's injuries. One arm was cleanly broken; a dark congested swelling and a gash remained from a severe blow to the head. The wound would require a poultice. The forester draped the boy with his cloak of marten skins, and cursing the folly of youth, drew his knife and cut a straight sapling for splints. If this boy recovered, he swore by Kor's fires to teach him how to defend himself.

Fine curtains of mist and rain turned the night into ink. Water beaded on the pinnace's seats, and the sails flopped, disturbed by the swell, and teased by uncertain wind. Drenched after five hours at the helm, Emien drew a deep breath. The warm earthy scent he had noticed a moment ago was now unmistakable. Seventeen days had passed since Tathagres appointed him command of the pinnace, and after a second gale and two spells of calm, an unknown islet lay ahead.

The wind veered south. Emien adjusted course, and the mainsheet slapped with a rattle of blocks. Landfall could hardly have occurred at a worse time, he thought sourly. Since the weather had closed in, the watches sailed on compass heading, visibility reduced to a few yards; no stars had shone for several days. By dead reckoning, Emien calculated the Isles of Innishari must be nine leagues distant. But swift currents might have set the boat off course, and here, where archipelagoes strung like beads across the Corine Sea and submerged reefs frequently clawed the waters into combers, an exact position was a necessity.

The breeze slackened. Again Emien caught the cloying smell of vegetation and sand. The shoreline was dangerously near. In the darkness he could see nothing, not even the white ruffles of foam spread by the bow wave; an attempt to beach the pinnace might well spill them all onto the razor fangs of a coral head. Presently, over the squeal of tackle, Emien heard the thunder of the surf off the bowsprit.

Gooseflesh prickled his arms. He might have left his decision too late. The pinnace was almost on top of the island. Emien bit his lip, agonized by responsibility. Drained by exposure, the sailors would rouse too slowly if left to themselves. No leeway remained for mistakes; and Emien knew he could never endure Tathagres' scorn should he fail to bring the pinnace in safely.

He undid the knotted cord which bound his breeches to his waist, then brought it whistling down on the nearest seaman's back. "All hands awake! Second watch, man the oars!"

The pinnace's occupants surged into action. Emien caught the man he had struck, shoved him into the sternsheet. "Take the helm, you, and head up. Into the wind and hold her there."

While the boat swung, Emien pushed his way forward, shouting instructions to shorten sail.

"Boy!" Tathagres called imperiously out of the dark. "What's amiss?"

Emien answered curtly. "Land. Much too close, and on a bad heading. We drop anchor, or risk our lives. The pinnace can't beach on a strange shore at night with safety."

The crash of breakers was unmistakable. Now even an inexperienced ear could detect the suck and boom of undertow dragging over rock. As he bent over the lashing which secured the anchor, Emien felt the bow lift, tossed as the swell rolled over the shoals and peaked into knife-edged crests which immediately preceded a breaking wave.

The boy shouted, frantic with recognition. "Out oars!" They had only seconds left. His blisters tore as he jerked the knots. The cord gave with a slither. "Row! Get lively, you bastards! Row! Or by Kor we'll swim!"

Emien knelt, clutching anchor chain in both hands as the oars rumbled out and bit raggedly into the sea. The pinnace jerked, shoved by the forces of loom and wave. Emien shouted an order. The oarsmen swung the pinnace starboard. A crest slapped her thwart as she turned, and a fringe of spray shot over the gunwale. The craft lay perilously close to broaching.

Yet Emien held steady. Fevered as he was, he made himself wait. On a bottom of rock or coral, the anchor would not hold unless he allowed plenty of scope. This close, the pinnace would be aground by the time the line came taut; breakers would smash her planking in seconds. But patience became torment, with the taint of earth thick on the breeze. Emien gripped the chain. Rusted links bit into his hands as the oarsmen steadied, synchronized, and the squeal of leathers against the rowlocks blended into rhythmic stroke. The pinnace made tortuous headway. Emien listened intently over the slap of the halyards and loosened canvas. The mutter of surf fell slowly astern. Now his judgment was critical; if the anchor did not grab on the first try, the oarsmen must have stamina remaining to pull the pinnace clear once again.

Emien gritted his teeth. The men were worn, sun-blistered, and starved. Exhaustion would overtake them swiftly, and the over-laden pinnace could easily become unmanageable. With a whisper of appeal to the spirits of the deep, he let the anchor go. Chain clanked, dissonant as death bells. Emien strung the line through his hands though it burned him, counting the knots which slipped across his palms. Two fathoms, three, four; at five the rope slackened. The anchor struck bottom.

"Reverse stroke!" Emien payed out more line, made swift allowance for the depth, current, and consistency of the bottom, then made the rope fast to a cleat. Stressed plies moaned taut as the pinnace swung, pulled short on her tether. Yet Emien knew better than to count the danger past; whether the hook would hold without dragging would be close to impossible to determine with no visible landmark.

Wearily Emien ordered the oars run in. He dismissed the helmsman and the sail crew and permitted the remaining hands to rest at their benches. Then he seated himself beside the lashed bar of the tiller to stand anchor watch. Through the long hours before dawn, he waited in the misty dark, listening to the waves, tuned to the texture of the swell which jostled the hull. Sound and sensation alone would warn whether the pinnace drifted into the shoals which lay only yards from her rudder.

The rain stopped. By sunrise the mist lifted, streaming scarves of rose and gold across skies like mother of pearl. Curled against the stern, Emien hugged his cloak close to his body. A chill prickled the length of his back as daylight brightened, revealing the contours of the land mass so narrowly evaded during the night. The island rose from the sea like a behemoth, ribbed with cliffs and terraced ledges and shadowed by crags which seemed to comb the roof of heaven. Waterfalls unreeled down rocks flecked like ice with flocks of perched gulls. Below, where crescent beaches met the incoming tide, all image of serenity was spoiled. The sea between pinnace and shoreline was slashed into spray by the jagged knuckles of a reef. Emien rummaged in the stern locker for a ship's glass. He surveyed the boiling rush of breakers, horrified to discover how closely the pinnace had skirted disaster in the dark. Carefully as he searched, he saw no safe route to land.

He turned and studied the seaward horizon with the glass. The mist had dispersed, leaving the humped blue outlines of several surrounding islands visible to the southwest. Emien checked his charts, snapped the glass closed, and rose to consult Tathagres.

He found her propped against the mainmast. Her hair was snarled from water and wind, and beneath the tattered shoulders of her blouse the fine skin he had once admired was sunblistered and cracked. Even closed, her eyes were hollowed with dark circles of exhaustion. Emien hesitated, reluctant to rouse her. A moment later he was grateful for his temerity.

Tathagres spoke without moving. "Boy? If you have something to tell me, speak."

Emien flinched, too startled to note her derisive tone. "Lady, we are anchored off the northeast shore of Skane's Edge. Innishari lies seventeen leagues due north, against an unfavorable wind."

Tathagres' lids flicked open, violet eyes narrowed with annoyance. She said nothing, but her silence struck the boy like a breath of cold.

Emien stiffened, knuckles balanced against the brass bands of the ship's glass. No longer the simple fisherman's boy who had left Imrill Kand, he did not tremble, nor did his uncertainty show. "Lady, I would not trouble you without reason. The casks are empty. Badly as the crewmen need water, I hesitate to consider a landing here. If you would step aft, you'll see the risks."

He offered his hand and helped her rise. Weather and starvation had not robbed Tathagres of grace. She moved like a panther, the slender lines of muscle and bone accentuated all the more by her leanness. Embarrassed to discover he could not repress a thrill of desire, Emien let her go ahead. The deckhands also followed her with eyes like hungry dogs. The boy felt a hot stab of jealousy. That moment, he wished Tathagres would command him to sail to Innishari with the casks still empty. Let the sailors row until they shriveled in the heat, Emien thought, unaware that a scant week past he would never have dared to regard his mistress possessively.

Tathagres paused in the stern, a hand poised on the backstay for balance. She regarded the shores of Skane's Edge with a strange and ruthless intensity. Emien chose a place at her side. Absorbed by the tumble of waves over the reefs, he soon forgot his quarrel with the deckhands. The breeze had freshened out of the north, and sunlight jeweled the spume like sequined lace. Yet to a sailor such beauty clothed murderous hazard; between wind and rocks, no safe landing was possible on this beach. Emien knew he had no choice but to sail on and seek a more favorable harbor. The weight of that conclusion oppressed him. That the oarsmen must suffer fresh hardship now filled him with revulsion; the risk of losing even a single life became not sacrifice but intolerable waste.

Disturbed by his conscience, Emien stared at his hands as if the cracked and blistered skin held answer to the dilemma of command. "Lady," he began. Tathagres turned her face toward him, and he looked up, at first unable to believe what he saw.

His mistress wore an expression of joy. Her eyes glittered with a challenge fiercer than any lust. "You will land the pinnace at once," she said firmly.

Emien's jaw dropped. Fear choked the breath in his throat.

"You heard." Tathagres leaned close and spoke directly into his ear. Though she wore no scent, her proximity unnerved him. "Are you fit to command, or do you yield your will like a nursemaid for the lives of the scum who serve you?"

Emien's jaw clenched. Tathagres mocked him; after Anskiere's storm, she viewed his handling of the pinnace as nothing more than sport to amuse her. Now, like a cat grown bored with teasing a mouse, she sought to slaughter the pride he had gained at the cost of his own sister's life. The jest, at such a price, was too bitter to contemplate.

Emien drew breath, heated by deadly anger. "Lady," he said tersely, "you shall have your landing." And consumed by bitterness which admit-

ted neither regret nor compassion, he yanked the knotted cord from
his waist. He strode forward, oblivious to the fact another observed his
actions even more keenly than his mistress.

Hunched like a great scavenger bird in the bow, Hearvin sat with
his hood thrown back, bald head exposed to the sky. In stiff-lipped silence,
he watched Emien drive the sailhands to the benches with the lash. Wind
eddied the sound, lending the crack of the cord across flesh an unreal
quality, distant and dreamlike as the spool pictures the sorcerer had viewed
long ago during Koridan's Grand Ceremony at Landfast. To compel the
deckhands' obedience, the boy inspired them to fear him more than death
by drowning; the result was disturbingly brutal. Hearvin watched with
stony eyes, until Tathagres arrived and perched herself at his side, her
cheeks flushed with unnatural exuberance.

"You set that boy up to fail," the sorcerer accused drily.

By the mast, Emien cuffed a recalcitrant oarsman. Wind tossed his
black hair like a horse's mane, baring wild eyes and contorted lips. He had
channeled his frustrated tangle of passions into violence, and the effect
was successful. With curses and wild anger, the boy bullied the crew into
submission. Tathagres noted their subservience with satisfaction.

"Why?" said Hearvin softly. "No amount of cruelty will keep this craft
clear of the reef. That boy has given you loyalty already. What will you
gain by breaking him?"

Delicately Tathagres peeled a torn thumbnail with her teeth. "If he
fails me now, won't he extend himself to greater lengths to regain my
favor?" She smiled, dropped her hand and suddenly sobered. "His loyalty
is not enough. For the purpose I have in mind I need his soul as well.
Then I will have the weapon to bring Anskiere to his knees."

If Hearvin replied, his words were buried by the rumble as the men
threaded oars onto the rowlocks.

Emien barely waited until the action was complete. "Stroke!" He
slashed the nearest back for emphasis, then raced to the bow. Hearvin
moved aside as the boy uncleated the anchor line. Close up, the boy reeked
of sweat, and his skin radiated a feverish heat. The line whipped free.
Emien hauled, adding his weight to the efforts of the oarsmen. The pinnace eased ahead. Chain clanked and the anchor splashed clear of the sea.
Emien bent to secure it, shouting orders over his shoulder. The starboard
oarsmen reversed stroke. The pinnace swung. Her bowsprit dipped, grace-
fully as a maid's curtsy, and pointed toward the forbidding shores of
Skane's Edge.

"Forward, stroke!" Emien dashed aft and ripped the tiller loose.
Braced against the plunging deck, he dragged the helm, brought the bow
around to the place he had selected. Ahead the water rushed in a dark,
angry vee, fenced by gateposts of rock. Emien would have to steer the
pinnace through the gap like a raft on rapids. He grimaced, aware of the
difficulties. The men must row faster than the current or he would lose
steerage; too fast, and the craft would plunge her bow into a trough and

pitchpole. The rocks rushed closer. Waves peaked, crashed, and creamed white off the bow as the pinnace closed with the reef. Surf bashed the keel. Vibrations stung Emien's hands as the rudder slammed against the pins. The sounds of human struggle became obliterated by the thunder of the foam. Drenched by spray, Emien flung hair from his face and wrestled the tiller straight. The gap yawned like jaws off the bow.

"Ship oars!" His shout sounded plaintive as a lost child's. Somehow the men heard.

A wave crashed to port. The pinnace yawed. Emien hauled on the helm. Though the muscles of his shoulders and arms burned with strain, he dragged the pinnace straight. Through salt-splashed eyes, he saw a seaman fumble an oar.

Emien shouted, too late. Rock already loomed above them, a buttress of barnacle-studded granite. The oar struck. Jarred against the rowlock, it smashed the man's ribcage. His scream sawed through the hiss of the foam. The pinnace slewed sideways and punched into the stone. Planking slivered; the gunwale burst with an agonizing crack. Emien dropped the helm. He leapt over the benches, caught Tathagres just as a comber burst like an avalanche over the thwart. Water bashed them overboard. In the last frantic instant before the sea swept Emien under, he clamped his hand in Tathagres' shirt. Then he was tumbled downward. Dark angry waters closed above his head.

Emien struggled to swim. Tossed over and over, he kicked and tried to break free of the current's icy grip. Although Tathagres' thrashing hampered him, he clung tightly to her clothing. He had failed to save Taen; now, with the pinnace wrecked and everything lost except his sworn oath of loyalty, the boy was determined to see his mistress safely ashore.

Water swirled, plunging him deeper. Pressure crackled his eardrums, and his lungs ached. Emien fought, driven by desperate need for air. Suddenly his shoulder scuffed packed sand. The bottom was shoaling. Relieved to find the current had swept him toward land, the boy pushed away the kelp which twined about his body. He caught Tathagres' hair. She had stopped struggling; fearful she might have lost consciousness, Emien twisted, dug his feet into the sea bottom, and shoved off for the surface.

Something sharp grazed his wrist. Stung by unexpected pain, Emien let go. Without warning, Tathagres yanked at the hand still twined in her shirt, forced the boy to release her. Emien broke water, dizzied and starved for air. Foam-webbed water slapped his cheek. In the second before the next wave rolled him under, he glimpsed a reddened gash in the muscle of his lower arm. The wound itself was unmistakable; *Tathagres had knifed him to free herself.*

Stunned, Emien mistimed his stroke. The breaker which bore him shoreward surged, lifted, and broke. Current pummeled his flesh, dragging him like a rag doll across the shapened edges of coral. Clothing and skin tore from his body. Choking, bleeding, and bruised beyond rational thought, Emien sensed the turbulence shift; the wave was ebbing. He flung

his good hand down, instinctively sought the bottom. His fingers scrabbled through weed and loose shells, then caught on a rock. He clung until
the greedy suck of the undertow relented.

Emien released and kicked hard. His head broke water. He managed a
quick breath before the crash of the next comber overtook him. Tossed
like a chip in a maelstrom, he was flung head over heels. This time, his
knee struck bottom before the wave receded. He stroked with his arms,
dragged himself forward, and managed at last to gain the shallows. Around
him, the water thinned into a lacy sheet, and slid seaward with a throaty
chuckle of sound. Emien crawled, gasping, and collapsed on the damp sand
of Skane's Edge. His throat stung. Blood traced patterns across cheek,
shoulder, and arm. The flash of wet shells and mica stabbed into his eyes.
He closed his lids. Left faint by the sweet rush of air into his lungs, he
lay prone, and the boom of the surf masked the sound of footsteps.

He did not notice Tathagres' presence until he opened his eyes. She
leaned over him, hair coiled like sodden silk around her collar. Her tunic
dripped in his face as she fingered the ornamental dagger Emien had often
noticed in the sheath at her belt. Her face seemed neutral.

But when she spoke, her words were edged with anger. "Boy, I will
warn you no more after this. No matter what the circumstances, you will
never again lay hands upon me without my express command. Should you
repeat your late indiscretion, you will suffer far more than a cut as a
penalty. *Am I clear?*"

Emien coughed, sickened by the taste of blood on his lips. His arm
throbbed, and every inch of abraded skin stung with the fury of the lash.
Yet his physical hurts were slight compared with the deeper wound in his
spirit. Sprawled where he had fallen on the sand, he voiced an apology. As
Tathagres turned on her heel and left, tears mingled with the brine on his
face. Once, as a child, he had accidentally fouled a fishnet; his father went
over the side to correct the mistake, became tangled, and drowned. Then,
Emien had been too small to understand what was happening. Now old
enough to act responsibly toward those he loved, he had first failed his
sister, then suffered a rejection no reason could console. Motionless on
the beach of Skane's Edge, Emien wept for the last time in his life. Hence-
forth his tears would flow from the eyes of others, he resolved; and the
overly sensitive emotions which had always made him vulnerable hardened
into a knot of aggressive self-interest never to be released.

The sorcerer Hearvin viewed the scene from an outcrop above the
shore, drenched robes flapping in the breeze. His eyes narrowed into slits
against the glare as he regarded the boy from Imrill Kand.

"You've misjudged," he said softly, and though Tathagres was not present, she heard. "I fear this time you've scarred the boy too deeply. Who
will pay the price?"

Hearvin waited, but Tathagres sent no answer. And because he also was
chilled and weary from the sea, he was careless and did not pursue the
matter further.

CHAPTER VIII

Skane's Edge

Of the seven sailhands who manned the pinnace from the foundering of the galleass *Crow* only four reached the beaches of Skane's Edge alive. Followed by Hearvin and Tathagres, the survivors chose a dell beside a pool of deep, clear water, refreshed themselves, then slept off the exhaustion of their ordeal.

Emien did not join them. Instead he sought a place farther downstream where willows overhung banks edged by spear-straight ranks of cattails. The brook ran shallow and clean over a bed of rounded stones. Emien knelt and drank deeply. He found the water sweeter than the brackish wells he had known on Imrill Kand, but the improvement brought him no pleasure. Surrounded by the mournful trill of marsh thrushes, he bathed without hurry, rinsed the salt crust from his hair and clothes, and bound his cut forearm with strips torn from his shirt. He was bone tired. His eyes stung with sleeplessness, yet he felt no inclination to rest. Tathagres' hostility had disrupted his confidence, confused his thoughts till they circled in his mind like a pack of dogs balked by conflicting scents. Emien possessed no understanding, only bitterness, and he longed for the harsh life of Imrill Kand intensely. But Taen's death forever barred his return.

Troubled by cherished memories of the beaches where he had scavenged shells as a child, Emien twisted the last strip of bandage into place and tightened the knot with his teeth. The cut beneath was not deep, yet it stung without surcease. A ragged line of blood quickly soaked three layers of linen. The color reminded Emien of the marks his lash had left on the backs of the sailors. On Imrill Kand, brutality of any kind had revolted him; yet the unpleasantness had barely crossed his mind aboard the pinnace. Even now he felt no regret. He had struck the seamen not to punish but to ensure the unquestioning obedience necessary for efficient seamanship.

Inwardly aching, Emien leaned back against the trunk of the nearest willow. The thrushes over his head hopped to higher branches, nervously silent, while he rubbed at his bandaged arm. Emien could not have guessed Tathagres would swim the dangerous shores of Skane's Edge with such ease. Absorbed by his command, he had done nothing but overlook her self-confidence. That was no transgression. His desire to protect her had been right, justifiably human, as her reaction had not been.

A jay scolded on the far bank. Lost in contemplation, Emien traced a finger over his wound. Tathagres had intended no lasting harm; the gash was shallow, running parallel to the muscle fibre, where it would least impair movement. She had *said* she gave him warning, exactly as he had used his lash for laggardliness; *but his sailors were not lazy.* Emien stiffened, chilled by sudden revelation. What if, *like him,* Tathagres had cut to shape him for her own purpose?

Emien drove explosively to his feet. The marsh thrushes startled into flight and vanished with a whir of brown feathers. The stream sounded louder in their absence; yet Emien heard only the recollection of Anskiere's words the last time he had seen Taen alive.

"The waters of the world are deep. Chart your course with care, Marl's son." The Stormwarden had spoken confidently, as if he already knew how roughly the boy he addressed might be used. The advice galled for its patronizing smugness. Emien knew fierce rage. He kicked a stone in a short hard arc toward the stream. It struck shallows with a splash, and fish fled like shadows for cover. But the boy saw only the face of the sorcerer who had angered him. The willows trailed closely about his shoulders, hedging him like the meshes of a destiny he did not want. Near to panic, Emien spun on his heel and crashed through the brush to the beach.

Bathed in afternoon light, the cove was a snowy crescent flecked with the chipped crystal glitter of shells. Soothed by the open sea, Emien could almost forget the painful snarl his life had become. He walked along the tidemark and searched for the smooth fist-sized stones he preferred for hunting rabbits. The meadows of Skane's Edge were uncommonly lush. From the size of the droppings in the grass, the boy guessed the animals were plentiful and plump; easy prey if he chose good cover. And on Imrill Kand, stalking rabbits with throwing stones had been his favorite escape from chores which he now understood were the thankless inheritance of poverty. He had been right to leave; he only needed space to regroup shattered dreams.

Tathagres had taught him to question the oath of loyalty sworn on *Crow*'s decks. On Skane's Edge the boy might be subject to her will; but the Free Isles numbered more than the souls of Imrill Kand, and the empire beyond was vast. Emien resolved to learn from his mistress's methods, then strike off on his own. With or without her, he would exact the price of his sister's death from Anskiere.

Emien bent and scooped a speckled stone from the sand. He tossed it from hand to hand, testing its balance and weighing choices. His oath did not set limits on ambition. Nothing prevented him from playing Tathagres' plots for his own stakes. Emien slipped the stone in his pocket and presently forgot he had ever missed the village of his birth.

The cliffs of Skane's Edge gleamed like hammered bronze in the afterglow of sunset and lengthened shadows tangled beneath the boughs in the wood where Emien ran. He stumbled across a gully. Pebbles scattered beneath his feet, fell soundlessly into moss. The boy recovered his balance, then hurried on, anxious to locate Tathagres before dark. He had lingered in the hills far later than he had intended, but the time was not spent fruitlessly; two rabbits dangled from his belt, each killed by flawless aim. Emien fingered the single stone left in his pocket, regretful the daylight had faded too soon to make use of it. Two coneys would hardly feed seven people; but even these were scant use if he failed to reach the lowlands before night hid the landmarks.

Twilight deepened over the forest. Accustomed to ocean and the open tors of Imrill Kand, Emien felt uncomfortably hemmed in. Silver beeches leaned on either side, roots knuckled like miser's fists in rotted mats of leaves. Twigs clawed his clothing and foliage smothered the sky. No star shone through to guide the boy and the light had all but failed. With an unpleasant chill, Emien realized he might be forced to spend the night alone in the wilds. Even Tathagres' haughty company seemed preferable.

But presently a gleam of firelight twinkled through the branches ahead. The rabbits bumped limply against Emien's legs as he increased pace. His shirtsleeve snagged on a thorn, but the boy plunged on, drawn by the familiar smell of wood-smoke and comforted by thoughts of fresh meat.

Yet as Emien neared the campsite, he noticed the crickets seemed eerily silent. Over the limpid spill of the stream, he heard Tathagres' voice raised in anger. Cautious of her temper, the boy crouched in the bush to listen.

Tathagres spoke, and the tone of her voice made his skin prickle. "Your sovereign appointed you to my service. You'll go where I command. Fool. Did you think I would return to Kisburn empty-handed?"

Her rebuke was directed toward Hearvin. Certain the sorcerer's secretive silences boded ill for Tathagres, the boy crept closer. He hid behind a thicket and peered anxiously through the leaves. Hearvin stood with his back turned, a hooded silhouette against the firelight. Though his reply to Tathagres held no emotion, Emien sensed threat underlying, subtle and low as a scraped harpstring. Already the exchange had evolved well beyond the simple quarrel he had overheard on the pinnace.

"But the King did not send me." Hearvin's sleeve flapped about his bony wrist as he gestured conversationally. "His Grace of Kisburn granted you the service of both his grand conjurers, and in ignorance you lost them their lives. One was my apprentice. He was a slow learner, true enough, but he died meanly, for greed. What can you answer for him?"

Tathagres advanced, taut as a stalking leopard. Gold gleamed at her throat. "*I* lost their lives? For a lackey that's a presumptuous accusation! Kisburn wishes the frostwargs loosed. I desire the Keys to Elrinfaer. Tell me, what is *your* interest? Or do you claim no ambition other than charity? I don't believe you have no alliance at all with the King."

Hearvin did not trouble himself with a denial. His manner seemed unruffled, yet Emien suspected that fury burned like acid beneath his placid exterior.

"I came because of Tierl Enneth," the sorcerer said unexpectedly. This time his voice showed an edge.

Tathagres interrupted. "I'm amused. Do be more explicit."

"That's unnecessary." Hearvin moved. Emien flinched, braced for violence, but the sorcerer only clasped his hands behind his back. "Why belabor the obvious? I've seen enough. You wish the source of Anskiere's power for your own twisted passions. The King's will was simple convenience, and his resources your playthings. From the start, you were unfit to command any of the lives placed at your disposal. I swore no oath to Kisburn. But for reasons of my own I see fit to protect the royal reputation. You shall not return to Cliffhaven. The Kielmark will be subdued by other means, and I forbid you the Keys to Elrinfaer." He lowered his voice, until Emien had to strain to hear. "Seek elsewhere, Merya. I have tested your mettle and found it wanting."

The name made Tathagres pause. The flush drained from her cheeks, and her eyes widened, startled. But the gap in her poise lasted only a second. The viperish look she bestowed on Hearvin sent chills down Emien's spine. She would never accept the sorcerer's authority, he observed. And threatened, suddenly, by the fact that his own face was entangled with hers, the boy dug in his pocket and closed his fingers over the cool rounded surface of his last throwing stone.

"You speak quite nicely," said Tathagres to Hearvin. "Tell me, can you act?"

She baited him, Emien saw. But the sorcerer also knew guile. He pushed the black cloth of his hood back over his shoulders, and his crown gleamed in the firelight, lending him an air of elderly vulnerability.

"Be warned, woman. I will challenge. If that happens, you'll be sorry for it."

Tathagres sobered instantly. "You meddle. Were you trained by the Vaere? If not, your threats are wasted. I shall return to Cliffhaven. Prevent me at your peril."

Hearvin bowed his head, his stance gone strangely rigid. "You will be stopped."

White light flared at the sorcerer's feet. Emien cringed, fearful of the spell. On Imrill Kand, Anskiere had always known when others watched his work covertly. But Hearvin remained oblivious and Tathagres seemed absorbed, intent as a hawk covering prey. She lifted her hands, touched the golden torque at her throat.

"I regret this," she said. But nothing of remorse showed in her expression. "You might have worked with me and been rewarded." She tilted her chin, then spoke a word to focus her defenses. Sparks crackled across her flexed wrists and caught like frost in her hair.

Hearvin waited, motionless. From hiding in the thicket, Emien saw a second spell flicker to life between the sorcerer's fingers, this one harsh and red, a needle-sharp geometric of light. Since Hearvin's hands stayed clenched behind his back, Tathagres was unaware of any additional threat. Emien dared not warn her; Hearvin would count the boy's life cheaply in this contest of wills. Miserably afraid, the boy huddled deeper into the thicket. He could not so much as call out, even for his mistress' sake.

Tathagres lifted her hands from the neckband and a golden haze of illumination quivered in the air above her palms. Poised like a quartz figurine, she pitched the energy at the sorcerer who opposed her.

Light met light with a tortured shriek of sound. Blinded by the flash, Emien buried his face in his hands. The night air shivered with the harmonics, as if tempered steel struck glass which would not shatter. Over the din, Emien heard Tathagres' shout of surprise. He forced himself to look. Through a glare of unbearable brilliance, he saw Hearvin had loosed his second spell; Tathagres struggled like a fly in a web of shimmering strands. She reached for her necklace. But Hearvin riposted with a curt gesture of his hand. The spell snapped into a spindle, symmetrically scribed as a crystal's matrix. Trapped, Tathagres renewed her attack. The energy she summoned backlashed, and an agonized scream escaped her throat. Emien panicked.

Ruled by terror, he ripped the stone from his pocket and flung it at the sorcerer.

His throw struck true. Hearvin swayed and slowly crumpled, blood on his temple. The spell which imprisoned Tathagres unraveled into smoke. But Emien saw nothing. Sorcery clove his awareness, sudden and bright as lightning, and he pitched downward into deepest unconsciousness.

Emien wakened gradually, his mouth foul with the acrid taste of ash. Water dripped down his neck, and someone shook his shoulder urgently.

"Emien?"

Gentle fingers traced his cheek. The boy stirred, fuzzily aware Tathagres leaned over him, her hands still damp from the stream.

"Emien?"

Her tone of voice might have moved the boy to joy under other circumstances. But with his head aching and his senses confused with dizziness, just opening his eyes was an effort. Speech became more than he could manage.

"Boy, you did well," Tathagres said, her manner more kindly than ever he might have imagined. "Had you not struck Hearvin, I could not have won free so easily."

Emien blinked. Briefly he wondered whether she could have escaped the red spell at all without help. Memory returned with the precise clarity of an etching; Emien recalled the conflict, the stone, and blood on Hearvin's face. In his mind he felt the soft limp fur of the rabbits when he recovered them, still warm, from the grass. Yet this time his prey had been human; revulsion tore through him. He battled a sudden urge to be sick.

Tathagres held him, her touch gentle against his brow. As if she understood his distress, she spoke again, concern in her violet eyes. "You did right, Emien. By your oath of service you had no other choice." Her fingers lingered on his cheek. "You shall accompany me to Cliffhaven. After we deal with Anskiere, we will return to Kisburn. My liege will be told of your courage in defending me. He is no mean King. You shall be well rewarded."

Distressed by the warmth of her praise and unable to escape the sting of his conscience, Emien tensed under her hands. Raised in bitter hardship, he had been taught to treasure life. Appalled to discover how easily he had struck a man with intent to harm, he searched the delicate planes of Tathagres' face with his eyes. She held his gaze. Emien studied her amethyst eyes, all shadows and depth, and complex as weather to fathom. *How alike we are,* he realized, and shrank at the thought. He drew an aching breath. Speech came at last, with difficulty.

"Hearvin," he whispered. "What happened?"

"He is dead." Tathagres shifted, settled herself in the leaves at Emien's side. Her fine hands went loose in her lap. "You killed him cleanly. Kor's Divine Fires, how fortunate you chose a rock! Had you thrown a knife, or any other object crafted as a weapon, the defense ward which grazed you would certainly have taken your life. But a stone could not be traced except by direction. Hearvin was caught off guard. He died instantly."

Emien turned aside, rejecting her approval. Though Tathagres intended comfort, her words wrought only remorse. He had killed. Neither logic nor circumstances would alter the wretched truth; the act was beyond pardon. The details revolted him. The boy gasped, desperately needing to weep. But no tears flowed, and a spasm of nausea wracked him.

Tathagres caught his shoulders firmly. Emien felt the warmth of sorcery in her touch. His retching eased, then stilled, and a queer dreamlike peace flowed over his jangled nerves. Yet not even drowsiness could blunt his need to acknowledge the consequence of his deed. In a voice gone dry and bleak, he said, "That was murder." The word ached in his throat.

Tathagres bent close and sighed. White hair brushed his face, while her eyes gazed down, lovely as jewels, and for once clear of intrigue. "By the Alliance's charter, yes, you committed murder. But you serve me, Emien. I am subject to none but the King. By Crown Law, Hearvin was a traitor. You shall never come to trial, I swear it. And the sailors will never talk. They shall be sold to the galleys and we will use the silver to buy passage to Cliffhaven." She paused and traced Emien's brow with her fingertips. Her touch brought weariness and his lashes drooped.

"Sleep now." Tathagres' voice softened, blended into distance like rain over leaves. The boy sank into slumber.

"We begin our vengeance against Anskiere tomorrow morning."

Emien slept. Dreams rose and burst in his mind like bubbles from a well's black depths; he saw sun, and sky, and the swells which rose green and mild off the coast of Imrill Kand. His hands were smaller, younger, less callused, and he struggled with a child's strength to stow the soggy brown twine of a net.

"No! Emien, not like that!" Drawn out of memory, his father's voice rebuked him, gruff and annoyed, yet still filled with love. But in the dream, as on the day during his tenth summer, the warning came too late. The net tumbled overboard.

The child started, pulled his hand back, but not fast enough. A coil snared his wrist, whipped taut, and jerked his arm across the gunwale. Wood skinned his elbow. Emien cried out in pain. Yanked off balance, he lunged awkwardly, but failed to recover the snarl of weights before they tripped overboard and splashed into the sea. The drag on his arm increased. Emien braced his weight, tried frantically to tug free. But the twine tightened, hauling him inexorably after the net. He slipped on the floorboards, bashed his side against the thwart. Crying now from hurt and fear, he saw his father lean over him and slash once with the fishing knife which hung always at his hip. The twine fell away, swallowed by the sea.

Emien tumbled limply against his father's chest. Though the man's huge hands cradled him the boy could not stop weeping.

"There, son," soothed his father, impossibly close and warm; his comfort was only an illusion born of troubled sleep. Though the boy stirred restlessly, the dream continued, brutal for its clarity; for Emien yearned to erase this moment from memory. The burden it had left upon his heart was unbearable.

Familiar fingers ruffled his hair. "Little harm is done, child. You're too young for Evertt's work, I know. When he gets well, the net can be replaced. Dry your tears. The weather will soak me well enough without you adding to it, see? I think a squall is coming."

Emien looked up, saw the clouds which rolled like ink across the windward horizon. He sniffed and rubbed his chin on the grimy cuff of his tunic, old enough to understand the loss of a net was no slight misfortune. Illness had kept Evertt ashore for nearly a fortnight and the coppers were nearly all spent. His mother and small sister might go hungry until his father brought in a catch. And now under the threat of storm the sloop's sail must be shortened. Already the loose canvas slapped and banged against the sheets. Emien made a valiant effort to master himself.

His father squeezed his shoulder and smiled. "Good boy. Take the helm, could you? I'll not be long with the sails."

Emien moved aft, rubbing skinned wrists with fingers still stinging from the twine. He perched on the wide sternseat while his father uncleated the main halyard. Gear rattled aloft. The mainsail billowed, nearly ready for reefing, and the boy curled small hands over the tiller. A gust hissed out of the north, raking his hair and clothes. Canvas smacked taut, and the sloop heeled steeply. Spray boiled over the lee rail, ragged as frayed silk. Emien tried to steer, but strangely the helm would not respond.

"Head up!" his father shouted, impatient, for the boat yawed on an unsafe heading.

The boy pitched the sum of his strength against the wooden shaft. He strained until his muscles ached, but the rudder had fouled, caught in the twisted coils of the net recently lost overboard. With tiller stuck fast, the sloop reeled, sails thrashing thunder aloft. Tossed by rising crests, she bucked under cloud-darkened skies.

Emien's father abandoned the reefing. Slapped by fresh gusts, the sloop's patched canvas flogged with a fury no man could subdue; short of slashing the halyards, the choices left were few. Huddled miserably in the stern, Emien watched his father through a moment of agonized indecision. Green as he was, the boy understood; cut the sails down, and without steering, the boat would be abandoned to the violence of the squall. An unlucky wave might broach her, and everything would be lost. But if the rudder were cleared first, the sails could be brought safely under control. The net might be recovered as well. Emien saw his father assess the waves, the wind, and the oncoming weather with experienced eyes. Then he reached for a spare line and knotted it securely around his waist. The older, dreaming boy wished desperately to cry out, to freeze that moment in time and reverse its fatal outcome. His father would dive only to drown, entangled by the nets as the storm's contrary winds jibbed the rudderless sloop again and again and again.

Yet the nightmare granted no respite. With cruel clarity Emien watched his father spring over the gunwale, never to surface. The boy screamed, jerked the unresponsive tiller until his palms blistered and split. Blind, bestial panic overturned his reason as the boom and thunder of the squall savaged the ocean. Rain fell in whipping sheets. Winds keened through the rigging, unravelling the whitecaps into driving veils of spindrift. Buffeted by the elements and trapped in stormridden meshes of horror, Emien lost all sense of continuity. The sloop's crude, hand-hewn timbers smoothed under his fists, transformed to the slim lines of *Crow*'s pinnace. Emien leaned over one thwart, nails gouged deep into vanished spruce. Showered by blown spray, he strained to reach a brandy cask which bobbed just out of reach in a trough.

He licked salty lips, shouted. "Taen!"

The cask and his sister's fate were somehow entangled. But Emien's need was not great enough to abandon the pinnace and follow her. In the desperation of his dream, he snatched up an oar and stretched outward, trying to hook the cask and draw it to the boat. But a white tern appeared out of the mist. Ringed by the harsh aura of a sorcerer's craft, the bird dove at his face. Blinding light burst upon Emien's retinas. Then someone gripped his shoulders and shook him painfully. The brilliance vanished, muffled in darkness.

"Emien?"

The boy woke with a start. He blinked, momentarily disoriented.

Tathagres bent over him, her white hair enhanced by the pearly glow of dawn.

"You must get up," urged his mistress. "We travel at daybreak."

Emien braced himself awkwardly on one elbow. "I dreamed." He paused to steady the shake in his voice. "I saw my sister Taen floating in a brandy cask after the wreck of the *Crow*. She was under a spell by Anskiere. Could this be so, Lady? Should she be alive I—"

"No," Tathagres interrupted. "You saw nothing but a nightmare."

She released the boy and turned her face away. "Rise at once, Emien. If we're to cross the heights of Skane's Edge before nightfall, we'll require an early start. And I would prefer dinner and a bed in a tavern."

Emien clambered stiffly to his feet, too preoccupied to observe the glint of speculation in his mistress's eyes. He banished all memory of the dream, forgetting in his grief his island heritage, that any vision he had experienced could hold more truth than any word of Tathagres'.

Far south of Skane's Edge and well beyond the farthest archipelago under the Alliance's charter, the cask which had sheltered Taen since the wreck of the King's war fleet at last neared its destination. It rolled gently, unmolested by the surf which broke and creamed whitely over the coast of an islet never marked on any chart. Drawn safely to the shallows by Anskiere's geas, the cask grounded with scarcely a bump. The tern perched on the rim stretched slender wings, and a wavelet arose, curling under its tail feathers. The cask lifted on the crest, and was propelled shoreward, and the water receded, chuckling over dampened sand, its burden delivered to firm soil.

None came to greet the Stormwarden's protege upon her arrival. Breezes rustled through serried tufts of dune grass, and tossed the boughs of cedars whose majestic growth had never known the bite of an axeblade, nor any other abuse of man's invention. The tern hopped to the sand, head cocked to one side. It pecked at the barnacles which crusted the side of the cask. Taen stirred within, roused from her enchanted sleep.

The Stormwarden's spell released her gradually. Protective as a mother's embrace, the warmth which cradled her limbs faded gently away. Wakened by the light which leaked through the bunghole in the top of the barrel, Taen stretched. Though she recalled taking refuge in the cask while Tathagres held her captive in *Crow*'s dank hold, she felt no fear. She heard the boom of surf muffled by the staves, and the solid stillness of the land beneath reassured her.

Taen shifted into a crouch. The bunghole let in a cloud-flecked view of sky, and the smells of tide wrack and cedar. Intently she listened, yet heard no sound but waves and the shrill cries of sand swallows; as far as she could tell, the beach outside was deserted. The girl hammered her fists against the top of the barrel. Barnacles grated, then yielded their grip on the seams. Sunlight flared through a crack and the weathered boards loosened and fell aside.

Blinking against the glare, Taen stood upright and clung to the rim of the barrel. Except that her shift was speckled with mildew, she seemed little the worse for her journey by sea. Anskiere had delivered her from Tathagres' hands, she was certain; her acceptance of his stewardship went deeper than childish faith. In a manner which had disturbed the villagers on Imrill Kand, Taen often perceived things no youngster should have known. She was fey, her peers had accused in whispers. Their taunts had quickly taught her to value silence. Graced by recognition that the Stormwarden had not taken her destiny in hand without reason, Taen braced her elbows against the raw ends of the staves and gazed about.

A tern pecked the sand in the barrel's shadow, but there all sense of the ordinary ended. The islet was as beautiful as a dreamer's paradise, uncanny in its perfection. Daylight shone with transcendent clarity upon beaches bejeweled with crystal reflections. Taen raised her eyes to the spear-tipped ranks of the cedars beyond and felt her skin prickle with uneasiness. She had landed on a northeast shore. Raised where life was tyrannized by the moods of weather and sea, she knew the fury of storms from that quarter. Yet if the trees on this shoreline had ever known the brunt of a winter gale, they suffered no damage. Their symmetry was faultless. The place where they grew seemed possessed by a presence older than man's origins, brooding, silent, and eerily sentient.

Taen's fingers tightened on the barrel staves. She intruded upon territory tenanted by powers which resented mortal trespass; this she understood by the same intuition which had shown her Anskiere's innocence the day Imrill Kand had betrayed him. Now as then she did not strangle her gift with logic as her brother would have done. Though to set foot on this beach was to challenge the isle's strange guardians, Taen swung her good leg over the rim of the barrel and leapt down. The Stormwarden had chosen this site. Confident of his wisdom, Taen was unafraid.

Her movement startled the tern into flight. Light exploded from its wingtips, blue-white and blinding. The energy which bound its form unravelled, whining like a dead man's shade as it fled into the air. Overhead the sand swallows wheeled and dove for cover.

Taen landed, stumbling to her knees in warm sand. A feather drifted where the tern had vanished. Sorry the creature had left, the girl caught the quill in her fingers as it fell. Someone had crumpled it once; the delicate spine was creased again and again along its snowy length. The resonant violence of the act tingled through Taen's awareness; pressured by a sudden urge to weep, she buried her face in her hands. Imrill Kand lay uncounted leagues distant. Reft of all security, the girl longed to be released from the fate Anskiere had bequeathed her. Yet tears were a useless indulgence. Inured to hardship, Taen drew upon the resilience of spirit which had seen her through Tathagres' threats and the horrors of the *Crow*'s pestilent hold.

On Imrill Kand, she had felt inadequate, a clumsy child with a lame leg unfit for work on a fishing boat's deck. Forced to remain ashore, she had resented her place with the pregnant women, the arthritic and the elderly. Here at least she could escape the widows in their musty wool skirts who had scolded her often for hasty stitches and girlish pranks; here she did not have to sit silent and straight on a hard wooden chair, knotting tedious acres of netting. No longer must she endure while the gossip of her elders veiled sorrows which Taen sensed but dared never to mention. Steadied by peace she only knew when she was solitary, the girl uncovered her face and discovered her inner sense had erred. She was no longer alone.

CHAPTER IX

The Vaere

Taen blinked, unable to believe her eyes. On the sand before her strode a man little taller than a grown person's thigh. Clothed in a fawn-colored tunic and dark brown hose tucked neatly into the cuffs of his deerskin boots, he walked with a step as fluid as quicksilver. He stopped abruptly before Taen. Beads, feathers, and tingy brass bells dangled from thongs stitched to his sleeves; their jingle reminded the girl of the chimes which hung from the eaves of the houses on Imrill Kand for luck against unfavorable winds.

The little man planted his feet. Black-eyed, bearded, and wizened as a walnut, he folded his arms and regarded her with an intensity made disturbing by the fact her inner awareness detected nothing of his existence. Always she sensed when others were near.

"Who are you?" Taen demanded, irritable rather than bold.

The creature stiffened with a thin jangle of bells. He ignored the girl's question. "You trespass. That's trouble. No mortal sets foot here who does not suffer penalty."

"What?" Taen tossed her head, and a black snarl of hair tumbled across her brow. "I was sent here by Anskiere."

"Surely so. Anskiere is the only mortal on Keithland soil capable of the feat. But this changes nothing." The little man drummed his fingers rapidly against his sleeve. Taen noticed his feathers remained oddly unruffled, though brisk wind blew off the sea.

Uncertainty made her curt. "What do you mean? I don't know what land *this* is, far less any place called Keithland."

"Those lands inhabited by men were named Keithland by your forebears." Suddenly very still, the man smiled in grim irony. "You have landed on the isle of the Vaere."

Taen tucked her heels under her shift, sat, and gasped. Had she dared she would have sworn like a fishwife. According to stories told by sailors, the Vaere were perilous, fey, and fond of tricks; few people believed they existed outside of fable. Confronted by a being which showed no resonant trace of humanity, Taen chose to believe. If the tales held true, the Vaere were guardians of forbidden knowledge and also the bane of demonkind; the unlucky mortal who encountered them invariably vanished without a trace, or returned unnaturally aged and sometimes afflicted with madness.

For all their perilous wisdom, rumor claimed the Vaere had one weakness; the man who discovered what it was could bring about their ruin.

Stubbornly insistent, Taen rubbed sweat from her palms. "The Stormwarden delivered me here for a reason."

The Vaere disappeared. Astonished, Taen scrambled to her feet. She stared at the empty place where the creature had stood but an instant earlier.

"Did he so?" replied a voice at her back.

Taen whirled, discovered the Vaere behind her, now seated comfortably on the rim of the brandy cask.

Bells clashed softly as he leapt down. "There was a purpose? Well then, we shall find it."

"Find it?" Annoyed by the Vaere's oblique behavior, Taen scuffed the sand with her foot. "But I don't know how. Anskiere never told me."

The Vaere laughed, and his bells released a shimmering tinkle of sound. "Nonetheless we shall find it. But you must come with me."

Taen stepped back, reluctant to leave the beach. She knew little of Vaerish sorceries, except that they frightened her. The thought of following this peculiar creature to an unknown destination made her distinctly uneasy.

The Vaere sensed her hesitation at once. "I cannot permit you to stay here. Come as my guest or go as my captive, which do you choose?"

Taen swallowed and discovered her mouth was suddenly dry. "I'll come."

The Vaere clapped his hands with a merry shiver of bells. "You are a most unusual child. If Anskiere sent you here, perhaps he chose rightly."

But Taen felt less confident of the Stormwarden's guidance than she ever had previously. As she faced the dark loom of the cedars, she considered changing her mind.

"No. You mustn't." The Vaere stamped his foot with a dissonant jangle. Taen heard an angry whine. Energy suffused the air around her body; her skin prickled, then burned, as though stung repeatedly by hornets. With a startled cry of pain, she stumbled forward. The pain ceased at once.

"Don't lag," the Vaere admonished. He shook his finger at her, and knotted the end of his beard with the other hand. "You must abide by your choice, for the wardspells which guard this place are not forgiving."

The Vaere skipped ahead. Very near to panic, Taen followed up the steep face of a dune. Slipping and sliding as dry sand loosened under her weight, she noticed with foreboding that the Vaere left no footprints. But she had no chance to wonder why. The creature vanished the moment he reached the crest of the dune.

Taen scrambled after, saw her guide reappear at the edge of the wood. Quick as a deer, he darted between the trees. Taen broke into an ungainly run to keep up. She flailed down the slope, then crashed into the cedars on the far side. The wood was dark, a matted interlace of trunks and branches unbroken by any path. Dead sticks clawed at her and her shift snagged on a briar. Yet the Vaere moved without a rustle through the same undergrowth, a faint jangle of bells the only sign of his presence. Taen pursued. All sense of direction forsook her. Sweat pasted her hair against her neck and her game leg ached without respite. Yet the Vaere kept going. The sound of his bells drew the girl onward like the fabled sea sprites whose songs were said to lure unlucky mariners to their doom.

She ran on, through forest so dense daylight seemed to have been forgotten. Finally Taen saw a gleam through the branches ahead of her. She stopped, panting, at the edge of a clearing surrounded by oak trees grown lofty and regal with age. Grass grew beneath, fresh as the growth of early spring, and tiny flowers spangled the turf. No sun shone, only a changeless, silvery glow, like the deep twilight of midsummer.

Before her lay the heart of Vaerish mystery, beside which her own mortality seemed brief and shadowy as a dream. Time held no meaning in this place, and nature's laws seemed usurped by another less malleable power. No frost would blight the blossoms here; nor had winter burdened the limbs of the evergreens with snow for countless centuries of seasons. Taen balked at the clearing's edge, trembling. To step forward was to yield herself to the magic of the Vaere, and no mortal who did so could escape the consequences.

The little man reappeared, seated on a low stone in the grass. A soft glimmer of light haloed his slim form. His beads clinked as sweetly as the wind-borne chime of the goat bells Taen recalled from Imrill Kand as he reached into his pocket and drew forth a carved briar pipe. He struck no flame. But when he puffed upon the stem, smoke twined in lazy patterns around his cheeks. He crossed his legs, blew a wobbly chain of rings into the air, and regarded Taen with sharp black eyes. All urgency seemed to have left him.

"Once a Prince of Elrinfaer paused where you stand now." The Vaere's tone was not unkindly. He blew smoke and continued. "The boy had been delivered here by a mage of great power, who promised he had the potential talent to ward weather."

"Anskiere," Taen said softly.

The Vaere nodded, drew deeply on his pipe, and released three more smoke rings in rapid succession. "Yes, Anskiere. Child, many seek, but few of your kind ever find this place. Fewer still receive the training that only the Vaere can offer. None leave without forfeit. Knowledge, like every thing of power, brings about change. If Anskiere sent you, he did so knowingly. Better you choose with a willing heart, as he did, though he renounced both crown and inheritance, with no more assurance than the faith he held for his mentor."

Taen bit her lip, uncertain how to reply. And in the instant she demurred, the Vaere vanished, leaving only spent smoke rings to mark the fact he had been there at all.

Taen twisted her hands in the limp cloth of her shift. The early brash courage which had first prompted her to follow Anskiere dissolved, leaving her desolate. There could be no turning back. She thought of her brother, recalled how Emien had met adversity with rage and hatred; how Tathagres easily had turned that anger to her own advantage. Taen wondered whether the Stormwarden would use her loyalty in the same manner. If she followed the sorcerer's guidance her choice might later set her against her own kin. But any other alternative was impossible to contemplate. Burdened by sorrow and a heavy sense of loss, the girl chose the way of the Vaere. She stepped into the clearing, unaware the powers which guarded that place had keenly observed her struggle.

Nothing happened. Partially reassured, Taen moved with increased confidence. Worn by the pain in her bad ankle, she perched on the same stone the Vaere had used and waited.

Silence surrounded her like a wall; the wood sheltered no wildlife, and the leaves remained still as stone in the half-lit splendor of the grove. The fragrance of the flowers lay heavy on the air and the light never altered, blurring any concept of time. Shortly the girl's head nodded drowsily. Instinct warned her not to rest in this place. She struggled to keep her eyes open, but soon, weariness overcame her. Lulled by well-being, she stretched out on the soft ground.

Snared by the magic of the Vaere, she fell dreamlessly asleep as many another mortal had before her. Presently an alien vibration invaded the clearing. A circular crack sliced through the turf where she lay. Blue light spilled through the gap, jarringly bright against the rough dark of the oaks. Slowly, hydraulic machinery beneath lowered the platform of soil where Taen slept, conveying her below the ground. A specialized array of robots bundled her limp form into the silvery, ovoid shell of a life-support capsule which once had furnished the flight deck of an interstellar probe ship. When her body was sealed inside, the lift rose and settled flush with the outside grass. No trace remained to betray the fact that a high-tech installation lay concealed beneath the island.

Busy as metallic insects, servo-mechanisms completed cable hook-up with the capsule, that the girl within could dream in concert with the Vaere. Though her stay might extend for years, she would never discover the nature of the entity which analyzed, nurtured, and trained her. For the electronic intelligence known as the Vaere never disclosed itself to men. Several life forms remained who yet sought vengeance against the descendents of the crew who once had manned the star probe *Corinne Dane*. The Vaere took every possible precaution that those known as demons never discovered how desperately vulnerable was the primary power which guarded mankind's survival. The hope of their star-born forebears must never be lost, that one day this band of castaways could be reunited with their own kind.

* * *

Well-versed in the lore of herbs, the forester, Telemark, tended Jaric's injuries with gentle hands and a mind better schooled than most in the art of healing. Yet four full days after the assault by the brigands of Seit-forest, the boy had still not regained consciousness. Pale against the coarse wool of the coverlet he tossed, sweating, troubled by delirious nightmares.

Concerned by the lack of progress, Telemark prepared a poultice of ladybush leaves in a kettle and hung it from the bracket above the hearth to steep. If the boy did not waken soon, he would not survive. The forester removed the bandage which bound the cut on Jaric's head. With careful fingers, he explored the extent of the damage. For the third time, he encountered inflammation and swelling, but no broken bone; the wound itself was healing cleanly. The boy's hair would hide the scar.

Telemark sighed in frustration and tossed clean dressings into the pot above the fire. The contents hissed and steam arose, pungent with the scent of ladybush leaves. They would act as a potent astringent, but their virtue was beyond question. If the blow had caused swelling inside the boy's skull, increased circulation to the area could do little else but good. And time now was of the essence.

Telemark lifted the pot from the flames and set it on the settle while the poultice cooled. He regarded the boy on the bed with faded, weather-creased eyes, and wondered anew what desperate purpose had driven one so helpless to attempt passage through Seitforest alone. The lawless who ranged the wood were numerous enough that none of the high-born from Corlin would hunt there. Telemark preferred the isolation; game was more plentiful as a result. But this child, who in his ravings had named himself Kerainson Jaric, was obviously unused to the outdoors. His slight build was more delicate than that of a pampered maid. Yet he had more courage than many men twice his size.

With a regretful shake of his head, Telemark tested the poultice and hastily withdrew a burned finger. He reached for a linen cloth to dry his knuckles, and looked up in time to see Jaric stir on the bed. The forester rose instantly to his feet. The boy raised an arm to his face. The man caught his slim wrist and firmly prevented Jaric from disturbing the uncovered wound in his scalp.

"Steady, boy. Steady. You've suffered quite a bash on the head. The healing won't be helped by touching it."

Jaric protested. His eyelids quivered and flicked open. Telemark swore with relief. With his free hand, the forester caught the oil lamp from its peg and lowered it to the small table by the bedside. The boy's pupils contracted sluggishly under the increased light, and his expression remained blankly confused. He twisted against Telemark's hold, distressed and lost in delirium. But he was conscious at last, which was an improvement. Lucid or not, he could at least swallow broth, and chances were good he would recover his self-awareness.

Once Telemark had served as healer to the Duke of Corlin's mercenaries; he had seen enough head injuries to know that recovery could often be painfully slow. A man might temporarily lose his wits, and Kor knew this boy had been dealt a nasty buffet. With hope in his heart, the forester wrung out the fresh bandages and expertly dressed the boy's wound. Jaric lay limp as he worked, brown eyes fixed and sightless. For many days, Telemark saw little improvement in the boy's condition.

But years in the forest had taught him patience. Where another man might have lost heart and placed the lad with Koridan's initiates in Corlin, the forester continued to care for the boy himself. When Jaric recovered his full strength, he would leave, Telemark held little doubt; any purpose which drove a man into Seitforest alone could never be slight.

The settlement of Harborside on Skane's Edge was small and ill-accustomed to strangers, far less ones who arrived sunblistered and barefoot in the town square at dusk. But after a night's rest, a bath, and a fine tavern meal, the townsfolk stopped whispering when Emien's back was turned. Tathagres sought passage off the island the next morning. A merchant brig headed for the ports beyond Mainstrait rode at anchor off the breakwater. Since the vessel was obliged to pay the Kielmark's tribute before passing the straits, passengers bound for Cliffhaven required no change in course. Yet the captain looked askance at anyone who wished business with that fortress of renegades. Tathagres' request met stubborn resistance.

"They're pirates, every one of them a detriment to honest trade," objected the captain.

A bribe quickly overcame his distaste, though Emien felt his fee was preposterously greedy; twelve coin-weights gold apiece would have imported a prize mare from Dunmorelands. But unless they wished to wait for another ship, the brig was their only option.

The ship weighed anchor when the tide ebbed. If Emien regretted the four sailhands traded to the harbormaster for the gold to pay their passage, he did not dwell on the thought. The familiar roll of a ship's deck underfoot buoyed his spirits, and before the ridges of Skane's Edge had slipped below the horizon he asked the captain for work. The brig sailed shorthanded. He owned nothing but the clothes on his back, and these were sadly tattered; come winter, he had no desire to rely on Tathagres for silvers to buy a cloak and a good pair of boots.

Four weeks of labor in the rigging fleshed out Emien's starved frame, and the sound sleep of exhaustion gradually eased his harried nerves. Happiest when his mind was absorbed with the simple tasks of seamanship, the boy brooded little. By the time the black battlements of Cliffhaven hove into sight to the northeast, he wished the voyage had not ended so quickly.

The mate bawled out orders to furl sail. Emien swung himself aloft with an oddly reluctant heart. As the anchor cleaved the blue waters of the harbor, the boy felt as if his contentment sank with it. The last time he had viewed these shores, Taen had been alive and no burden of murder weighted his conscience. Now his desire for revenge against Anskiere was complicated by an insatiable yearning for power.

The mate shouted and the deck crew swayed a longboat out. An officer waited to escort the strongbox containing the Kielmark's tribute ashore. Emien slung himself off the mizzen yard and descended the ratlines, certain Tathagres would summon him.

But the longboat departed with no word from her. Puzzled, Emien sought his mistress. He knocked at the door of her cabin, half fearful she would turn him away with his question unanswered. But she greeted him pleasantly, and after one glance at his expression, volunteered her intentions without his needing to ask.

"Go to the captain. Release yourself from service and collect what coin you've earned. Then report back to me. We shall go ashore after sundown, for I've no desire to involve myself with the Kielmark. If we are to succeed against Anskiere, our plans must be carefully laid."

The sun was low in the west by the time Emien returned. Busy with other complaints, the captain had been slow to attend the details of his dismissal and the brig's purser was unavailable until the water barrels and stores were replenished. But silver in his pocket made the boy feel less vulnerable, should his mistress be displeased by his delay.

Emien arrived at her cabin breathless. Tathagres admitted him without complaint, a preoccupied expression on her face. Her earlier garb was replaced by tunic and hose of unrelieved black. Except for the gold torque, she had stripped herself of jewelry, and her bright hair was knotted under a scarf at the nape of her neck.

"I have clothing for you." She waved absently in the direction of the berth. "See whether it fits."

Emien squeezed past, overwhelmingly aware of her in the tight confines of the cabin. Set on edge by his involuntary response, he forced himself to concentrate on the items laid out on the berth. Spread on the mattress were two cloaks, a tunic, and a pair of hose. The garments seemed right. Reluctant to undress before Tathagres, Emien looked up, but the intensity of her mood robbed him of all protest. In silence he turned his back and peeled off his ragged shirt.

"The clothes fit," he announced after an interval. He swung around, boyishly embarrassed, but his mistress paid no heed. She sat before the cabin's small writing desk with her hands clenched in her lap.

Emien took an uncertain step toward her. "Tathagres? The tunic fits just fine."

But his mistress remained unresponsive as a stone statue. Disturbed, the boy moved closer. He peered over her shoulder, and saw that sorcery engaged her attention. Hair prickled on the back of his neck and his hands clenched reflexively into fists. On the desk lay what appeared to be a feather. But closer scrutiny yielded another view superimposed over the first. Above the scarred surface of the desktop, Emien viewed the living image of a cliff side bound by tiered prisms of ice. Gulls wheeled above the heights, their cries faint and plaintive above the boom of the breakers which smoked spray across a shoreline of jagged rocks.

Emien gasped and started back, bruising his elbow painfully against the bulkhead. Tathagres roused at the noise. Absorbed by her own thoughts, she sat silently while Emien rubbed his arm. When she did speak, her words seemed intended for someone else.

"What has he *done*?" Perplexed, she shook her head, then focused on Emien, as though aware of him for the first time. "We shall find out, I suppose, when we get ashore. Do the clothes fit?"

The boy nodded, decidedly ill at ease. Seldom had he seen Tathagres unsure of herself. Yet if her confidence was shaken she rallied swiftly.

"Boy, to all appearances, Anskiere has set a seal of ice across the mouth of the cavern which imprisons the frostwargs. All attempts to trace his location end at that same barrier. I am certain he cannot have left Cliff-haven. But finding him may prove more difficult than I expected. We must be cautious." She laced her fingers together so tightly the knuckles turned white. "Should we fall into the Kielmark's hands, reveal nothing. The man may be formidably powerful but he cannot deter me. If you keep your silence, you shall be safe."

Tathagres looked up, and the lack of emotion in her violet eyes chilled the marrow of Emien's bones. "But should you betray my trust, you'll wish your mother had never lived to give you birth."

"If Anskiere escapes, I should feel just as miserable," the boy replied hotly.

"That is well." Tathagres stretched like a cat in her chair and smiled. "Then we agree perfectly. Meet me by the starboard davit at nightfall. The captain has agreed to leave us the brig's pinnace."

Familiar with the captain's fussy temperament, Emien dared not guess how that had been accomplished. As he opened the cabin door, he regretted he had not been witness to the arrangements; no doubt his companions in the forecastle would have given their shirts to know.

Tathagres laughed. In that uncanny manner which always unsettled Emien, she answered as if he had spoken his thought aloud. "I won the craft at cards, boy, but Kor wouldn't have sanctioned my technique. When we reach court, I'll teach you, if you remember to ask."

But the friendliness in her offer embarrassed the boy, and he hurried off without answering.

Taen awoke believing she still lay in the grove, amid the oaks. Unaware a machine had taken her into custody, and unable to distinguish the fact that all she experienced since was a dream inspired by advanced technology, she sat up. The Vaere stood on the stone by her elbow. He regarded her in silence and smoke from his pipe twined patterns in the air around his wizened face.

Taen stretched, her mood somewhat cranky. She had worried herself ragged for no apparent reason, and memory of her recent discomfort rankled. "Nothing happened," she accused the creature beside her.

"I beg your pardon." The Vaere stiffened, accompanied by a dissonance of beads and bells. "Quite a bit happened. You were judged, and my kind decided what will be done with your future. Take care, mortal. You are ignorant."

Nettled by the Vaere's superiority, Taen tilted her chin at an angle her brother would have found all too familiar. "I have a *name*."

"But few manners," the Vaere observed. "I am called Tamlin. I trained Anskiere, and before him the one you call Ivain Firelord. You were sent here because you possess the rare gift of empathy; you share the emotions and feelings of your own kind."

Taen drew breath to interrupt, but Tamlin waved her silent. "You must learn to listen, child. There are demons abroad who would take your life, for your talent threatens their secrets. Without defenses, some among your own kind would stone you, or worse; and lacking control of your gift, since birth you've suffered the unwanted miseries of others who happened into your presence. But the Vaere would change that."

Tamlin leapt off his rock and gestured expansively with his pipe. "These are troubled times. Certain demons have bound mortals to their cause, to the sorrow and destruction of mankind. Did you hear of Tierl Enneth?"

Taen bit her lip and realized the Vaere referred obliquely to Tathagres, whose obsessive desire to usurp Anskiere's powers could be explained no other way.

"Just so," said Tamlin. "Anskiere is the only defender left, since Ivain Firelord's death." The Vaere paused and chewed reflectively on his pipe stem. "Now more than ever before a channel is needed to sound the minds of men. You will provide that link, Taen."

The girl shivered and drew her knees up to her chin. The most powerful sorcerers in Keithland were trained by the Vaere. Nothing of her upbringing on Imrill Kand had prepared her for Tamlin's proposal. As a cripple and a child who had known adult problems at an unnaturally tender age, she felt small and helpless, a mere cipher in the age-long struggle between demonkind and man.

Tamlin blew a large smoke ring, and his bells tinkled as softly as rain onto glass. "You have great heart for one so small," he said gently. "And though you will pay a heavy price for your learning, the damage to your leg will be mended. When you go, your body will have aged fully seven years, though far less time will have passed in your absence. But never again will you limp, and the dreams and aspirations of all mankind will be within your dominion. Because of you, there may be peace for the next generation."

And though she found hope and much cause for joy in the words of the Vaere, Taen bent her head and wept for the first time since leaving home on Imrill Kand. If Tathagres allied herself with demons, then Emien trod the very path of evil; unless he came to his senses, he would someday meet his sister as an enemy.

CHAPTER X

Prison of the Frostwargs

The overcast of afternoon broke at sunset. By dark, when the sailors launched the pinnace, Cliffhaven lay like sculpted ebony against a dusky sapphire sky. From the rendezvous point by the starboard davit, Emien studied the view with a fisherman's eye for weather, more irritated than pleased by the change. Clear skies would not favor a concealed landing on a northerly shore.

Chosen for silence and deadly skill with weapons, the Kielmark's sentries would kill for far less cause than trespass. Emien tugged his cloak closer about his shoulders. He distrusted the brash exhilaration which invariably possessed Tathagres in the face of danger. After the disaster of Skane's Edge, the boy hesitated to suggest a change of course. Doubtless the woman would drive him straight at the Kielmark's front gates, should he mention prudence at the wrong moment. Beside his mistress, the sentries were the more predictable risk.

"Are you ready, boy?"

Surprised out of reflection, Emien started. Tathagres paused at his side, her expression brittle as porcelain and her mood black as the cloth which bound her hair. She lifted a hand unfamiliarly bare of ornament and pointed to the pinnace below. "They're anxious to cast us off."

She swung herself over the railing without waiting for assistance. Cautious of her temper, Emien followed her down the side battens and into the cockpit of the pinnace.

He did not speak until she had settled herself on the stern seat. "If the Kielmark stations guards on his northwest shore, they'll see us when we land." The boy indicated the last clouds which drifted, underlit and pale as knotted fleece above the island. "Moon's rising, and this tub carries bleached canvas. We'll stand out like silver in a coal heap."

"Why not row?" Tathagres pitched her tone to wound. "Or don't you trust me to manage the guards?"

Emien banged open the sail locker without answering. With a bucket like the pinnace, the Kielmark needed no guards on his northwest shore. Lacking four stout hands to man the benches, her oars were useless sticks, and for a craft built as heavy as scrap iron she was clumsily rigged as well.

Emien guessed by her lines she would be cursed with a lee helm. The crossing to Cliffhaven promised agony enough without Tathagres baiting him.

Emien dragged a ratty headsail out of the locker and discovered five hanks torn off. He swore then in earnest, for baggy canvas meant the pinnace would point like a lumbering bitch. Bilgewater lapped at his boots, warning of leaks in the hull. Radiating anger, Emien stamped forward to find the jib halyard. If Tathagres had lost even a single coin in her cursed game of cards, the captain had claimed the winning stake after all.

Tathagres leaned against a thwart and watched the boy fuss with the tackle. "Once ashore you can scuttle this boat if you wish. We won't be needing it again."

"For sure?" Poised with halyard in hand, Emien laughed, his spirits partially restored. "Let it be rocks then, big ones, right through these worm-ridden planks." He did not add that on a lee shore in the dead of night, the rocks might complete their task before the time appointed. At least after Skane's Edge he knew Tathagres could swim.

A stiff breeze blew out of the north and the sails cracked and flogged aloft as Emien made the last lines fast. Later, the clear weather would bring calm; anxious to reach shore while the conditions held fair, the boy cast off promptly. He sheeted in main and jib and the pinnace drew clear of the brig, her lee rail well down and her wake a gurgle of bubbles astern.

The crossing to Cliffhaven began smoothly, marked by the slap of reefpoints in the wind, and the occasional squeal of blocks as Emien adjusted a sail. Absorbed by her own thoughts, Tathagres made no conversation, and busy with the wayward roll of the pinnace, Emien made no effort to draw her out. He maintained his heading, guided by the cold glitter of the polestar, until a rising moon rendered the waves in ink and silver and the island fortress reared up off the bow, notched and black against the horizon.

As the pinnace drew nearer, Emien saw the white glitter of ice partially veiled by mist. Breakers crashed beneath, their thunderous impact warning of submerged reefs; spume jetted skyward, then subsided into foam with a hiss like a hag's cauldron, making any landing there impossible. Yet after Skane's Edge, Emien dared not meddle with Tathagres' intent. Grimly he held his course, helm gripped in sweaty hands, until the bowsprit thrust against current lit like fairy lace in the moonlight.

"We'll land there." Tathagres' voice was barely audible above the boom of the surf.

Emien looked where she pointed. A thin crescent of sand gleamed just east of the cliffs. Though hedged by wreaths of white water, the beach seemed free of obstructions. Properly handled, the pinnace might barely thread through, but timing was critical. Emien hauled in the sheets, shoved the helm down, and let the craft jibe. Wind slammed the sails onto the other tack. Unmindful of the line which burned through his palms, he let the jib run free. The pinnace slewed. Then a wave lifted her stern, and the boat careened shoreward with all the grace of a rock shot from a catapult.

Something moved overhead. Emien glanced up. A spear drove past the mast and thumped with a rattle of splinters into the sternseat inches from his knee.

Emien sprang to his feet.

"Hold course!" Tathagres leaned over the gunwale. Poised like a figurehead against the baroque swirl of foam, she raised her hand to the gold band at her throat and invoked a spell. A bright interlace of lines shot through her fingers.

Dread sent chills through the pit of Emien's stomach. Although he knew Tathagres conjured in defense, her sorceries brought no comfort. Her mastery only forced recognition of the depths of his ignorance. Shamed and furious, Emien steadied the pinnace against the heave of the breakers and loosed the mainsheet. Lines smoked through tackle, and the sails banged overhead. Deafened by the report of soaked canvas, the boy dragged the helm amidships, just as a crest flung the bow skyward. Spray flew, carved into sheets by the rail. Then the craft grounded with a crunch that rattled every plank in the hull. Emien abandoned the tiller and leapt overboard just as a second spear arched overhead, aimed with killing accuracy.

Thigh deep in the flood of the breakers, the boy flung himself against the pinnace. The spear hissed down. Tathagres shouted and a flash of red ripped the air. Barely shy of its mark, the weapon exploded with a snap and a shower of sparks. Then the drag of the undertow flung the pinnace sideways. The next wave would broach her, despite Emien's efforts. He called warning to his mistress.

Tathagres gathered herself and jumped lightly as a cat from the gunwale. She landed without mishap in the surf, just as the pinnace tore free of the boy's grip. Sand grated hoarsely across planking. Then the boat capsized, and the crest of the following wave cascaded over her starboard thwart. Emien watched as the sea boomed and broke, smashing the craft to a snarl of slivered wood.

At his side, Tathagres pulled the cloth from her hair, her mood brittle and dangerous. "Get ashore!" She shoved the scarf roughly into Emien's hands.

The boy flinched as if wakened from nightmare. In the moment his eyes met hers, he caught a glimpse of runes glowing red against the gold band which adorned her throat. Then Tathagres turned away, in haste to reach the land. Emien plunged after, hands knotted painfully in cloth which smelled of ozone. Waves mauled the pinnace's planking like bones at his back. He shivered and bit his lip. There could be no escape by sea now. Wary of his own vulnerability, the boy slogged through the shallows toward a shore defended by hostile men-at-arms. He cursed the fact that he had no sword, nor any training with weapons.

Tathagres walked ahead as if the water was the finest of silken carpets under her feet. Contemptuous of the spears and defended only by sorcery, she paused while Emien caught up, her arrogant air of confidence a challenge no attacker could resist. And yet no weapons fell.

Breathlessly Emien drew alongside. Close at hand, the sheer height and mass of the frozen cliffs overwhelmed him. Yet he repressed his uneasiness as Tathagres leaned close and spoke in his ear. "Stay behind me, no matter what happens. You must not come forward until I have finished with the guards. Disobey me at your peril, for if you stray, I cannot protect you. None who cross my path shall live. Am I clear?"

Chilled and mute, Emien nodded. Gripped by indefinable foreboding, he watched his mistress stride boldly shoreward. She reached dry sand unchallenged, tossed her cloak to the ground, and left it in a heap at her feet. Her hair blew free, and burnished like pearl by moonlight, her skin gleamed against the deeper shadow of the land beyond. In morbid fascination, Emien saw his mistress lift her head and touch the band at her throat with her hands.

Mist arose, translucent as smoke from lit shavings. It twined around her, interlaced like gossamer in the moonlight until her slender body seemed clothed, not in black wool, but some garb out of faery, all shimmer and cling and no substance. The ivory curve of her shoulders, breasts, and hips caught the eyes of the concealed guardsmen, and held them helplessly enthralled. Emien felt as if a great weight crushed his chest. He struggled to breathe. Though the spell was not designed to doom him, still his body flushed and sweated and ached. Numbed by the chill water about his ankles, he beheld the vision of lust his mistress wove to doom the guardsmen, and even as his flesh yearned to possess her, his spirit cried out for reprieve; Tathagres' cruelty knew no bounds. In her hands, man's admiration for woman became a weapon to slay, a terrible tool to implement her powers. When the first guard tumbled from his niche in the rocks, Emien bunched his fingers into fists. Tears spilled down his cheeks. He watched helplessly while a second man fell headlong to the sand below the cliffs.

The sentry's body twitched on the sand and settled finally, grotesque and still as statuary in the moonlight. Nothing moved on the beach but the tireless roll of the surf. Emien roused. Shuddering as if the frosts of winter clenched his bones, he started forward and stumbled to his knees in brine.

But Tathagres was not finished conjuring. She lifted arms pale as bone against the rise of the dunes, and softly, too softly for natural hearing, whispered an incantation. The words pierced Emien's ears like a needle sharpened by longing; loneliness opened like a wound within him, until the woman posed on the shoreline framed his sole hope of redemption. But the song Tathagres sang was not shaped for him. Agonized by her rejection, Emien cried out, tasting salt. Only the bitter reflection of his own inadequacy made him hesitate. Her music became discord in his ears.

No portion of his being could bend it to harmony, and the pain of that recognition was more than his spirit could endure.

Emien crouched like a beast in the surf, at first unaware that a third guardsman emerged from the scrub, his fingers clamped around a drawn sword and his eyes dark hollows of desire.

Tathagres arched her body, arms extended in welcome. Drawn by her movement, Emien looked up, saw a stranger approach her with the confidence of a lover. The man's muscles quivered under his leather tunic, and his breath came in labored gasps. He reached out and touched her bared shoulder, and the rapture in his face poisoned Emien with jealousy.

Tathagres bent her head, murmured something into the hollow of the guardsman's throat. His fingers shifted, releasing the sword. It fell and struck rock with a sour clank. The man took no heed of his fallen weapon; discipline forgotten, he smiled as Tathagres melted into his embrace and knotted her hands with fevered passion in the hair which spilled over his collar. The man whispered hoarsely. His arms tightened around her slim shoulders. Driven by lust no human could deny, he sought her lips, kissed her deeply and long. Around him the very air quivered as her spell closed over his heart.

Crazed by frustration, Emien hammered his fists against his thighs. He wept as though his heart would break, oblivious to the waves which broke behind him, sending foam swirling and splashing around his boots. Blinded by tears, he saw nothing as the guardsman's arms quivered and tumbled loose. Only when the man's knees buckled did Emien recognize the snare Tathagres had set to destroy the last of the Kielmark's sentries. Her victim swayed and spilled onto the sand. He sprawled dead in the moonlight; incoming tide lapped at his outflung hands. Horror jolted Emien free of passion. He trembled while Tathagres retrieved the abandoned sword, and her laughter sickened him to the core of his being.

The air crackled, scoured by a brief rain of sparks as the spell dispersed around her. Emien choked, doubled over with nausea. He jabbed his hands to the wrists in icy water, coughing and miserable, until Tathagres arrived at his side.

When his equilibrium did not immediately return, she plucked insistently at his cloak. "I've brought you a gift."

Emien raised his head, discovered the dead guardsman's sword posed above her outstretched hand like a needle etched in light. Though earlier he had craved a blade of his own, the offering appalled him, made him feel less than human. Still he accepted the weapon with unemotional practicality. Tathagres' tricks had eliminated the guards from the beach; but if anyone reported to the Kielmark at the time the pinnace was sighted, their present safety was not secure.

Tathagres snapped as if she heard his thought, "You worry like a pregnant heiress. Get ashore. We have a task before us."

Stung by her scorn, Emien surged to his feet. With his hands clenched tightly around the sword hilt, he sloshed through the shallows. Ahead of him, Tathagres stepped over the guardsman's corpse with barely a pause. Unable to match her callousness, Emien glanced down. Lifeless eyes stared skyward, as if a reason for mortal betrayal lay scribed in the depths of the heavens; the hands lay helpless and open, denied any vengeance for a death which held no honor. Emien regretted the fact that he had lingered. To recognize the guardsman's anguish and not act was to share the inhumanity of the crime.

Shamed by the cowardice, he moved on without stopping to recover the sword sheath and buckler from the body. With the steel naked in his hand, he hastened across the strand, and for one reckless instant longed to bury the blade to the crossguard in his mistress's back. Fear alone stayed his hand. For the guardsman's death, not even hatred of Anskiere could relieve his tortured conscience, and troubled by fresh guilt, the boy hurried into the shadow of the escarpment.

The ice cliffs towered above, terraced against the dark sky. There Tathagres halted and peered upward.

"Wait," she commanded, and set her hands to the gold band at her throat.

Emien leaned against a rough shoulder of rock. Huddled in the wet wool, he propped the sword near at hand and blew on his knuckles while Tathagres cast magic about her like a net. Soft violet light haloed her form, then widened like a corona until it thinned to invisibility. Emien felt a tingle of heat fan his flesh. From the hollow by the dunes, a nightbird startled into flight with a soft whir of wings. Its melancholy calls faded in the darkness, and the warmth of the spell fled with it. The ice radiated cold like the deepest heart of winter. Chilled by more than frost, Emien sifted through the noises of the night, listening for the faint telltale chime of metal which might herald the arrival of a patrol. Should the Kielmark's guards encounter them now, the cliffs would block any chance of escape.

But no men-at-arms arrived. Presently Tathagres stirred. She lifted her head. The magic she had cast forth dispelled with a snap, and for a second the wind wafted the acrid smell of brimstone toward the waiting boy.

Tathagres turned from the cliff. Her brows knitted with frustration, and the gesture she directed upward delineated vivid anger. "The Stormwarden is there, *inside*, and certainly trapped." She chewed her lip, irritated by the discovery. "Boy, fetch my cloak from the beach. I wish to know more, but I cannot risk a deep trance here. This place is dangerously exposed. We must climb higher."

Sullen and silent, Emien collected his sword; at least his mistress had spared a moment to consider caution. The moon hung dead overhead. Shadow spread like soot beneath Emien's boots as he walked back to the water's edge. Ebbing waves had ribbed channels the breadth of the beach. Tathagres' cloak still lay at the edge of the tide mark. Wise enough not to leave unnecessary evidence for the Kielmark's patrols, Emien retrieved the garment and dragged the hem over the tracks marked by his passing. Although the dead guardsmen lay exposed, already stiff, and blatant as a scream of warning to any arriving scout, corpses were more than the boy could bear to handle alone. His weakness made him fretful. Guards would certainly come. Tathagres' confidence made her careless to a fault.

But he mentioned nothing of his uncertainty when he returned the cloak to Tathagres. With a brief nod, she pulled it over her shoulders and tucked her hair out of sight beneath the hood. Then, without asking whether Emien would follow, she began her ascent of the cliff.

The boy set foot in her tracks, his heart hardened like ice in his chest. The sword dragged at his wrist, forcing him to grip with his free hand to steady himself. Cold burned his flesh, bitter as venom, and his boots slipped treacherously, as if apparently solid footing were an illusion born of the powers which bound the ice, hostile to intrusion and dangerous to scale. Emien toiled upward grimly. The memory of Taen in the Stormwarden's arms robbed any threat from a fall; and three dead guardsmen on the beach below diminished the meaning of all else. Now he might feel insignificant as a leaf tossed before the winds of a storm; but one day he vowed his fate would no longer be commanded by the whims of enchanters.

The black wool of Tathagres' cloak veiled her features from view. Emien could not see the smile of cruel satisfaction which curved her perfect mouth. Absorbed by the perils of the climb and dizzied by the sweep of the waves over the rocks below, he never suspected his anger awaited her purpose, volatile as tinder to her hand. By the time Tathagres halted beneath a natural overhand of rock, the expression she presented to the boy was concerned, even friendly.

"We shall pause here," she announced. "The trance I must employ to trace the Stormwarden's presence may last several hours. If you stand guard, do you think you can stay awake?"

"If I sleep I'd freeze." Emien hauled himself onto the ledge beside her, weary and displeased by the place. The terrain was rough, buffeted by wind, and framed by an archway of frozen cascades. Anyone arriving below would sight them easily. Yet the boy offered no complaint, for here where the cold rose like blight from the bared bones of the rock, he would at last know Anskiere's fate.

Tathagres settled herself cross-legged at the juncture of the ledge and the ice. She braced her back against a buttress of stone, touched her necklace with her fingertips, and closed her eyes. This time Emien saw no flare of light. Her spell of summoning took effect with a thin whine of sound, and a tracery like engraving flickered across the band at her throat. The characters glared red against the band's polished surface. Consumed by curiosity, the boy edged nearer.

Careful not to disturb her concentration, he leaned close and examined the ornament which controlled Tathagres' spells. Wrought as a seamless ring, the metal was as thick as his forefinger, and deadly plain when not in use. But now while Tathagres engaged her powers to tap the depths of Anskiere's sorcery, runes blazed, etched in light across the surface of the gold. Emien could not read. But he had seen trader's lists often enough to recognize a scribe's hand; the writing on the band described no human letters. With a sharp chill of foreboding, Emien drew back.

Once on Imrill Kand, a severe storm had washed a bit of wreckage ashore beside the rotted pilings of the fisher's wharf. Emien had been there when the child who found it burned his fingers to the bone trying to pick it up. The object had borne markings similar to those on Tathagres' gold collar. Anskiere had destroyed the artifact the instant he saw it, claiming it bore runes of power no human should know. No villager on Imrill Kand questioned the sorcerer's wisdom; plainly the object was crafted by demons. And though Emien had repudiated all belief in Anskiere's doings, the possibility Tathagres' magic might be founded by the works of Kordane's Accursed had never before entered his mind.

Troubled, he seated himself on a shelf of rock, balanced the sword blade across his knees, and regarded his mistress. Her angry violet eyes were closed. Moonlight rendered her form in silver, lovely as the icon Emien recalled from the shrine by Kordane's Bridge. From the smooth skin of cheek and brow to the finely sculpted wrists resting in her lap, her pose seemed the image of peace and perfection. Wrung breathless by an unexpected rush of desire, Emien clamped his fist on the pommel of his weapon. Surely Anskiere was wrong. Not all demons were evil. Perilous, surely; in ignorance, the child of Imrill Kand had touched their formidable powers and been harmed. But Tathagres controlled similar forces as effortlessly as breathing.

Emien perched his chin on his knuckles, teeth clenched against the cold. Any enemy of Anskiere's was an ally to his cause, a hand to lend impetus toward vengeance for Taen's death. Why should he be troubled to know the source of Tathagres' powers? But the bleak mood which accompanied his discovery persisted.

Emien stared morosely over the sea but saw no horizon. Images of the guardsman's fatal embrace returned and haunted him. Wind pried at his clothing, sharp with the coming frosts of autumn, and the breath of the ice pierced the very marrow of his bones. Poisoned by the knowledge of his own mortality, Emien dreamed hungrily of power. His thoughts dwelt deeply and long upon Tathagres' gold necklace as the moon wheeled across the sky to its setting. If somehow he came to possess such an object, he could be secure from the meddling of men and sorcerers forever after.

Fog moved in at sunrise. It beaded Emien's cloak and lashes and sword hilt with droplets, and coiled like wraiths over the ice cliffs; surf boomed and echoed invisibly off the rocks, eerily amplified. As the first gulls took flight over Cliffhaven, Tathagres stirred from her trance. In the half-lit gloom while night yielded to daylight, Emien saw her eyelids tremble and open. She stretched, showing no trace of stiffness, a secretive, self-satisfied expression on her face.

Chilled and disgruntled, the boy waited for her to speak. Finally, after seven weary weeks and an unpleasant night-long vigil, he would learn what befell the Stormwarden whose meddling had stolen Taen's loyalty and whose tempest had taken her life. Bitter as spoiled wine, Emien thumbed the bare edge of the blade on his knees. When Tathagres at last met his gaze, he barely curbed an outright demand for the result of her search of the ice cliffs.

His tension appeared to amuse her, which annoyed Emien further. With his knuckles whitened against the chased steel of the crossguard, he glared in furious silence. Like a coquettish high court lady, Tathagres tossed her fine white hair and laughed.

Emien sprang halfway to his feet in a moment of wild anger. Then he realized her caprice was caused not by him, but by Anskiere. Unable to restrain his own fierce smile, he settled back.

"Anskiere is a fool," Tathagres said softly. Above her shoulders the mist swirled like smoke over the blocky spine of the ridge, and for a second weak sunlight struck through, striking gold highlights against the ice. Paler than usual and obviously cold, Tathagres rearranged her cloak over her shoulders. "When the frostwargs wakened, the Stormwarden sealed them behind a wall of ice. But he could not free himself. The ice imprisoned him as well."

Emien raised the sword, saluting her triumph. "Then the Stormwarden is dead."

Tathagres tilted her head, gazed in speculation through the thinning veils of mist. Her reply held dreamlike tranquillity. "He's alive but in stasis, a trance so deep he lies a hair's breadth from death. He cannot last indefinitely in such a state. He believes he will be saved."

Emien lowered the sword, black brows gathered into a frown. He began a vehement protest, but Tathagres stopped him sharply, violet eyes widened with murderous intent. Her expression froze the breath in Emien's chest and he clenched his teeth to keep from quivering like a terrified child.

"The Stormwarden has unleashed his curse upon Ivain Firelord." Tathagres shaped her words with harsh, incredulous fury. "He trusts a geas and a stripling boy to spare him from the frostwargs' ferocity." She laughed again, but her mirth sounded forced, as if some inner plan had been thwarted.

Cued by a leap of intuition, Emien said quickly, "You can't touch him." The thought sparkled resentment.

"I can't touch him, true." Tathagres leaned forward, dangerously rapt. "I don't *need* to reach him. His fate is sealed already, with no help from me. Look, I'll show you."

She reached out and caught the sword. Emien relinquished the weapon, reluctant, yet also determined to share her discovery. He crouched, braced on one fist, while Tathagres turned the blade point downward and scratched a triangle into the ice between her knees.

She rested the tip of the sword on the apex, then touched the worn pommel to the gold band above her collar.

"Ivain's heir is a half-wit weakling." Her lip curled in scorn. "See for yourself."

The lines scored in the ice blazed with sudden violent light, followed by scorching heat as the sorcery took hold. Ragged drifts of steam rose and mingled with the mist. Emien braced his body, mistrustful of the sorcery, yet unable to tear himself away. Before his eyes the ice melted and an image from a place far distant reformed on its surface. Inside a neat, single-room cabin, a boy sat propped in a wicker chair. His body was half buried under woolen blankets, though sunlight spilled warmly through the open window beside him. Framed by a straggle of mouse-colored hair, his features were blanched by ill health and the fingers resting across his knees were fragile as spring twigs. He appeared asleep. On closer examination, Emien noticed the boy's eyes were open but vacant, as though bereft of intelligence. Yet even as Emien watched, the brown eyes lifted. For the space of an instant, the boy in the cabin seemed to focus directly upon him.

Touched by foreboding, Emien flinched and flung back. "Kordane's Fires, who is he?"

Tathagres withdrew the blade with a coarse scrape. The image spattered into sparks. She regarded Emien with a strangely guarded expression and said, "Who? He is named Kerainson Jaric, and he is Ivain Firelord's heir. But he will never survive to rescue Anskiere, even if he did possess a constitution sturdy enough to achieve his father's prowess. The initiation process, the Cycle of Fire, itself engenders madness; Ivain suffered as much. His heir is already damaged, a half-wit, couldn't you see? The Vaere would never accept him for training, and without the skills of the father, Anskiere is doomed."

Emien sucked fresh air into his lungs. Harmless as Kerainson Jaric appeared, something about his presence touched off an instinct of warning. Born and raised a fisherman, Emien preferred never to ignore hunches, however illogical they appeared. Yet his island superstitions seemed foolish beside Tathagres' worldly sophistication.

Embarrassed by his premonition, Emien accepted the sword from Tathagres' hand. An equally heavy weight seemed to settle on his heart. For at last he correctly interpreted the cause of Tathagres' brittle temper; with the frostwargs confined and the Stormwarden beyond reach of her command, she could not claim the Keys of Elrinfaer from her King. The setback galled her. Judging her pique, Emien guessed the powers of her neck band were still no match for the forces which bound the frostwargs behind their bastion of ice. Anskiere had bested her in this contest of wills, even if he had forfeited his own life in the accomplishment.

Unwilling to relinquish his passion for vengeance, Emien searched his mistress for signs of defeat; if she gave up after all he had suffered, he would strike her, though he died for impertinence. But the violet eyes which met his gaze still burned with determination.

"Your Stormwarden, if he survives long enough, shall certainly pay for his tempest." Tathagres' mouth thinned with sovereign cruelty. "The ice cannot protect him forever, this much I promise."

Suddenly Tathagres stiffened. Emien heard a horse stamp and snort somewhere below. Alarmed, he searched the thinning mist, hands clenched on the sword hilt. Hazy sunlight illuminated the beach. Fog still clung to the cliffs, but not for much longer. Within seconds the ledge would be visible to the patrol which approached from below. Emien prayed the bodies of the murdered guards would pass unnoticed.

That moment a man shouted in horrified discovery. Harness jingled and hooves pounded across wet sand. Another man hailed from the ridge above, followed abruptly by the din of an armed company dismounting.

Emien licked dry lips. "We're surrounded," he whispered frantically. Lifting his sword, he ducked beneath the ridge of ice, prepared to defend their position as best he could.

But Tathagres seized his wrist and jerked him painfully to her side. "No. Stay by me." Her nails dug like claws into his forearm. "I am going to tap the powers of Anskiere's geas, use them to pull us out of here. Unless they have archers we are safe."

Trembling, helpless, and diminished once again by Tathagres' superior powers, Emien wrestled to contain his panic. Sweat slicked his back. Clinging to mangled pride, he stood rigid in Tathagres' hold, while she touched her free hand to her collar and began an invocation. The last billow of mist drifted clear of the ice. Plainly visible on the strand below, an armored knot of men clustered around the corpse Tathagres had kissed to his death. Even as Emien estimated their number, the dark captain in their midst glanced up and stared straight at them.

CHAPTER XI

Backlash

"There!" shouted the Kielmark. He raised a muscled arm and pointed at the intruders. Cloaked in black like scavenger crows, a woman and a boy with a sword stood on a ledge of rock seventy yards above the beach. Who they were and what purpose had brought them to Cliffhaven made no difference. Three guardsmen lay dead, most likely of poison; for that crime, they would never receive pardon.

With blue eyes narrowed to slits of anger, the Lord of Cliffhaven commanded his men-at-arms. "You." His gesture singled out a horseman on the fringes. "Ride to the east station and bring back archers." The man appointed wheeled his mount, spurred at once to a gallop. The Kielmark raised his voice over drumroll of retreating hooves. "The rest of you cordon that cliff. Cut off every possibility of escape. When the bowmen arrive, you will close in and take the boy and the woman alive."

The men broke ranks with alacrity, aware their performance might later be reviewed to the last critical detail. But this once, the Kielmark's concern lay elsewhere. Tense as a caged lion, he paced the tide mark, stooping now and again to examine scattered fragments of planking which once had been a boat. The keel and a few ribs were intact, enough to determine the craft's dimensions. The Kielmark planted his foot on the wreckage, and with thumbs hooked in his sword belt, regarded the corpses sprawled upon the beach. After a moment he spat in the sand and swore with a violence few men ever witnessed and lived to describe.

The boat, an aged, ungainly rig, at least explained why last night's watch had ignored his most urgent directive, that every person who trespassed on Cliffhaven be reported on sight. Probably the three had shirked duty on the assumption such a clumsy craft should carry equally harmless passengers. The mistake had killed them. That much was simple justice, the Kielmark reflected, and he fingered the pommel of his sword in temperamental fury. Though spared the nuisance of three hangings for disobedience, he still confronted the consequence the dead men's negligence had wrought.

The woman and the boy remained on the ledge, pinned in position by the relentless efficiency of the guardsmen. The base of the ice cliffs lay ringed by a glittering half circle of weapons and a full score more men waited on horseback, prepared to ride down any attempted escape through the lines. The presentation was perfect, each man alert at his post with his spear held angled and ready for instant action. Yet the Kielmark scratched his bearded jaw, distinctly unsettled. Where other commanders might disdain to pitch sixty men-at-arms against an unarmed woman and a boy, the King of Renegades acted without a second's hesitation. He deployed his finest company precisely because his trespassers seemed so contemptibly vulnerable.

With the wily patience of the desert wolf, the Kielmark studied the two who had dared trespass his domain. The boy evidently knew no swordplay, he gripped his weapon like a simple stick. The Kielmark dismissed him as terrified and ordinary, turning eyes cold and bleak as glacial ice upon the silver-haired woman who stood at the boy's side. A less careful man might have wasted precious minutes in appreciation of her strikingly beautiful form. The Lord of Cliffhaven searched only for inconsistency which might lend him advantage; and the woman's utter lack of concern jarred him like a sour note in counterpoint. Anyone confronted by sixty men-at-arms could be expected to show distress, but the only tension visible about this woman was in the hand she held clenched at her throat.

Revelation struck the Kielmark between one stride and the next. Arrogance on that scale accompanied none but an enchanter's power; if the woman had slain last night's watch with sorcery, even an armed company could well prove no match for her. Fearful for the lives under his command, the Kielmark sprinted up the beach. Whoever the woman was, she came for Anskiere, but not as his ally; any friend of the Stormwarden's would never have done murder.

"Back!" shouted the Kielmark. He waved his arm at the cliff. "Withdraw from the ice."

The troop captain glanced around, stupidly surprised. Irate, the Kielmark shouted again with an edge to his tone no officer under him dared disobey. *"Pull those men back!"*

White with alarm, the captain barked an order. The formation coalesced, initiated an orderly retreat. And the Kielmark cursed and regarded the woman once again, his great corded fist clenched in frustration around the hilt of his sword.

The jangle of weapons and linkmail echoed and bounded off the ice, threaded through by the rapid beat of hooves. Riders approached, the archers the Kielmark had sent for earlier. He spun to meet them, planted his massive frame squarely in their path. To avoid riding him down, the lead horseman reined back from a gallop with a violence that yanked his rawboned mount onto its haunches. The animal scrambled down the steep side of the dune, and sand showered over the Kielmark's leather leggings as it plunged to a halt scarcely a yard away. The Kielmark sprang forward, snatched the bow from the scabbard at the saddlebow. He grabbed for an arrow while the two score archers summoned from the east station thundered to a standstill around him. Without pause for explanation, the Kielmark shouldered clear of the press, bent the bow, raised it to the woman on the ledge. He aimed for the triangle of bare flesh framed by her black wool collar, and the drift of her fine silver hair.

His target made no move in defense. Her lips parted with amusement, and she laughed aloud at the notched threat of the arrow. A gust eddied her cloak hem. The Kielmark released. His shaft hissed skyward, described a flawless arc across the morning sky. The woman's smile dissolved. She lifted her hand. The arrow deflected, cracked harmlessly into rock, and rebounded in slivers.

"Sorcery!" shouted the captain. "She's a witch!" He raised crossed wrists in the traditional sign against evil, just as the woman touched both hands to the gold which encircled her neck.

Her gesture overturned the elements. Air howled suddenly overhead, as if a dragon had appeared out of legend and inhaled a piece of sky. With a crackle like tearing fabric, the woman and boy vanished as if they had never existed, transferred elsewhere by forces wrenched from the framework of Anskiere's geas. The Kielmark cursed with savage eloquence and flung down the bow.

Backlash struck an instant later as the powers the woman tapped to execute her escape ripped all else out of equilibrium.

Wind screamed off the sea, whined over cliff and dune and beach head. Sucked into a whirling tornado of force, the gale spiraled across the ice cliffs, bashing men and horses from their feet and uprooting trees like twigs. Hammered to his knees, blinded by a maelstrom of driven sand, the Kielmark buried his face in his hands. Somewhere to his right a horse thrashed and a wounded man screamed in agony; but the sounds seemed strangely overpowered. A second later the Kielmark divined the reason. Driven to towering heights by the wind, breakers raged shoreward, crests frayed into spindrift. Icy spray dashed the Kielmark's cheek, proof his shores were presently being ravaged by forces none but a weather mage could subdue. Every man ordered to duty beneath the ice cliffs stood in peril of drowning.

Determined to prevent losses, the Kielmark tore off the sash which bound his tunic and flung it over his face to protect his eyes. The gale harried the cloth, snapped it out of his fingers as he tried to tie a knot. He struggled, too stubborn to quit. At last, protected by his makeshift blindfold, he leaned into the wind and gained his feet.

Weather harried his every movement. Stung by flying sand and deafened by the rage of the elements, the Kielmark battled for each step gained; the effort taxed even his great strength. Never in memory had Cliffhaven's shores been beset by so violent a gale. Aware the entire island might be affected, the Kielmark forged ahead, possessed by outrage. He swore. There would be survivors; but the inevitable waste of men and resources galled him without end.

Laboring into the wind, he blundered into a man's wrist. Encouraged to find at least one of his guardsmen alive, the Kielmark guided the man's fingers to his belt. The wind screamed like a torture victim in his ears, making any word of encouragement impossible. The Kielmark granted the man a moment to steady himself, then plowed forward and sought after another. Soon he had gathered a small band of survivors. The stronger ones lent their efforts to his, and gradually the group gained on the storm and pulled back, away from the rampaging seas and into the scanty shelter of the dunes.

Even there, gale wind shrieked and buffeted their shoulders, sharp and punitive as a lash. Braced on widely planted feet, the Kielmark panted for breath. He tugged the cloth from his eyes. Six of his finest fighting men crouched in the lee of the rocks, battered and bleeding and half beaten with exhaustion. One of the horse archers had fallen on his quiver when thrown from the saddle; the broken shaft of an arrow protruded from an ugly wound in his thigh. Close to seventy of Cliffhaven's finest men still struggled for their lives, all for a woman's meddling and a guard captain's failure at duty. Now all of Cliffhaven stood endangered. The Kielmark's great hands knotted into fists and his lip curled in a manner which sent chills down the spines of the men who clustered round him. But his voice and actions remained controlled, after the manner of a wolf stalked by mastiffs.

He touched the arm of the man who stood nearest, and even his shout could barely be heard above the din. "Fetch others. Form a chain. And make sure you place the wounded well up on high ground."

The man nodded, rallied gamely to the task. And concerned for the rest of his island demesne, the Kielmark left the hollow with no more delay. Belabored by the elements, he clambered over rocks and thorny scrub to higher ground. There the scope of the destruction the woman's sorcery had unleashed across Cliffhaven became awesomely apparent. Wind roared in from all points of the compass. The Kielmark was now certain Anskiere's powers had been usurped to complete the woman's transfer to safety. A mass of air had rushed elsewhere upon her departure, and the sharp drop in pressure made it plain a gale would follow, fiercer than any tempest. A towering line of squalls spanned the horizon as far as the eye could see. The speed of the storm's approach defied all credibility. Throughout a lifetime of collecting tales, only once had the Kielmark ever heard such weather described, and then by a gouty old salt who claimed to have survived the drowning of Tierl Enneth. Impossibly, a similar horror beset Cliffhaven.

The Kielmark rejected the inertia of despair. He crashed like a bull through the thornbrakes, and by luck stumbled across a loose horse. He caught the bridle, vaulted astride without touching the stirrup, then slashed the reins on the animal's flank again and again, until its white hide quivered, flecked scarlet. Sped by pain and panic, the animal galloped mindlessly. The Kielmark shouted like a madman and urged it still faster.

Except for a few scattered steadings, Cliffhaven's population lived

mostly on high ground. But several families of refugees left homeless by
Anskiere's earlier tempest sheltered yet in the warehouses by the dockside;
if the sea rose, they would perish. Racing the closing storm as if Kor's
Accursed howled at his heels, the Kielmark drove the horse beyond safe
limits. He would arrive in time to save his own, he swore by his very life.
And he vowed also, for each death and every injury accrued beneath the
ice cliffs that morning, the next man, child, or woman who dared set foot
on Cliffhaven in the name of Anskiere of Elrinfaer would be put to the
sword.

The axeblade whistled through the air and bit cleanly into the center
of the old beech stump by the cabin door. Warmed by exertion, Telemark
the forester leaned against the woodpile and paused to rake the hair back
from his face. The air carried the first piquant chill of autumn, and true
to habit, the ground before the woodshed held an untidy jumble of logs
to be split before the coming winter. But unlike other years, the pile inside
already stood waist high; with an invalid boy under his roof, Telemark
took no risk of running short of fuel. His canny forestbred instincts
warned that the coming season would be harsh, even for the lands north
of the Furlains. Snowfall would be heavy and deep, and wood scarce; but
cold weather enhanced the pelts. He could expect good trapping.

Telemark reached once again for the axe, and froze with his fist on the
handle. The brushpheasant in the south thicket had stopped calling.
Attuned like a musician to the natural rhythm of the woods, the forester
listened and swept a glance across the sky to see if a hawk flew overhead.
Noisily the brushpheasant took wing, an odd trait for a species whose best
defense was camouflage and stillness. That moment Telemark heard the
sound which had startled it into flight.

A high keening gust of air rushed down on the clearing from the
southeast, bending the treetops like ripe wheat and wrenching off a whirlwind of twigs and leaves and dead branches. The disturbance resembled
no weather pattern Telemark had ever known, and even as his hair prickled
with alarm he dropped the axe and sprinted for the cabin.

The force overtook him before he reached the doorway. Wind struck
with the impact of a battle hammer. Slammed between the shoulders by
the brunt of its violence, Telemark missed stride, tumbled into a rolling
fall which fetched him hard against the stone stoop. Bruised, frightened,
and half stunned, he groaned and struggled to rise while pelted by a malicious shower of sticks and torn leaves. And above his head, the wind
smashed headlong into the door. Leather hinges rent like paper and the
latch burst into a fountainhead of sparks. Horrified by recognition, Telemark saw his dwelling assaulted by the powers of sorcery.

Frantic with concern for Jaric, the forester caught hold of the doorframe and dragged himself across the threshold. There he confronted a
scene which tore him to the heart. Wind raged like a demon's curse

through the cabin's tight confines. Bottles of rare herbs tumbled from the shelves, seasons of careful collecting spoiled in an instant. Tools pinwheeled from their hooks and the polished copper pots from the pantry clattered across the floor, splintering all in their path to wreckage. A meticulous man by nature, Telemark winced and looked beyond the immediate destruction for the boy. The wicker chair lay overturned by the hearth, its stuffed pillows strewn dangerously close to the flames. Jaric sprawled on the floorboards nearby and the blankets which once had covered him flapped like bats across the floor by his side.

Telemark clutched the doorjamb to steady himself. Splintered wood jabbed his palms as the wind buffeted his frame, but the first violence of the assault appeared to be waning. Even as the forester noticed the change, the sorcery set against him dwindled and abruptly died. Ripped from table and shelves and hooks, the belongings he had acquired through long years of solitude lay scattered and smashed in the corners. A pan lid described a drunken circle across the floor, its metallic ring like a shout against sudden silence. Shaking with reaction, Telemark kicked the object to a stop. Then he fell back against the breached security of his wall, and blinked back tears of anger.

Wise to the ways of the world beyond his wood, the forester considered his desecrated home, and knew that the damage resulted from a backlash of power. Somewhere two sorcerers stood in conflict, and a deflection in equilibrium between them had brought ruin through his door because the boy he sheltered was somehow involved. Telemark twisted his hands in his sleeves, pained by the inevitable; no safety existed for Jaric here. Whoever the boy on his hearthstone was, he had enemies beyond the capabilities of any forester, even one who had once served mercenaries in the Duke's army. The decision weighted heavily on Telemark's heart. Yet he dared not keep the boy longer; with sorcerers involved, the peril was too great to shoulder in solitude.

Beyond the door the brushpheasant called, returned to its thicket. Assured the immediate danger was past, Telemark crossed the littered floor and stooped at Jaric's side. Though deeply unconscious, the boy seemed physically undamaged; time would determine whether anything else was amiss. With the stiff-lipped expression he assumed when commanded to snare songbirds for the Duke's menagerie, Telemark gathered the boy off the floor.

With unsteady hands he laid Jaric on the cot in the corner, then paced restlessly to the window. Except for a mangled drift of branches by the shed, the forest stood unchanged, its green depths a balm to the eye after the pathetic wreckage inside the cabin. The shadows slanted only slightly; if he hurried, he could be across by sunset. The town gates closed promptly at nightfall. Much as the forester cared for Jaric, the sooner the boy was placed in the care of Kor's initiates in Corlin, the better his own peace of mind. Without pausing to sort the ruins of his home, Telemark belted on his sword, slung bow and quiver across his wide shoulders, and bundled his charge into a blanket. Then he lifted Jaric in his arms, picked his way around the slivered door, and turned his steps toward Corlin.

The hollow where the path joined the main trail through Seitforest seemed oddly dark for midday. Telemark frowned, hesitated, and shifted Jaric's weight higher on his shoulder. Something was amiss. Overhead the sky was cloudless, but the light which filtered down through the crowns of the oaks seemed strangely murky. The trees themselves stood hushed, undisturbed even by the busy rustle of squirrels in a place where the acorns lay abundant as beach pebbles among the leaves.

Telemark halted at the edge of a thicket, every sense alert. Leftwards, behind a heavy stand of brush, he heard a footfall stealthy enough that even a wild creature might overlook so slight a sound. He laid Jaric at his feet, and with swift, sure fingers, strung his bow. Then he drew his sword and ran it point first into the moss, with the hilt ready to his hand. And he waited.

No common footpad lurked behind the trees. A human would make more noise, perhaps startle the birds and cause the squirrels to scold from the branches; but no disturbance of man's making could explain the eerie dimmed light. Even as Telemark sought the cause the gloom deepened, as if the very stuff of darkness clotted upon the air. Slowly, cautiously, the forester eased an arrow from his quiver. The familiar grip of the bow felt clammy to his palm as he knocked shaft to string and bent the weapon to full draw. Again he waited, motionless, his muscled arms steady as old knotted wood, and his aim on the brush as unerring as if he stalked the shy satin-deer. But with chill certainty, Telemark knew he hunted no animal.

As the shadow darkened around him, he heard a slight sound, nothing more than the sigh of a brushed leaf. And a pair of eyes gleamed ahead, orange as live coals, and as deadly. Telemark swung the bow fractionally. He brought his arrow to bear, knowing his doom was upon him; for the creature he opposed was of demonkind, a Llondian empath whose defenses no mortal could withstand.

Before Telemark could release, a thought image ripped into his mind, words shot through with a white-hot blaze of agony. 'Mortal, *place the weapon down*.'

The forester resisted, quivering. Cold sweat beaded his forehead and his streaked hair clung damply to his temples. For the sake of the boy at his feet, he loosed his cramped fingers from the string. The bow sang, transformed by Llondian influence to a note of pure sorrow. The arrow hissed into the brush. In the instant the demon's whistle of anger clove his ears, Telemark saw his shaft rattle through the branches and cleanly miss. Llondian eyes looked up in scarlet accusation. And its anger transformed unbearably into an image sharpened to wound its attacker.

Telemark screamed. He saw the greenery of Seitforest withered, the stately, familiar trees riven from the earth. Blackened roots jabbed at the sky like accusing fingers, and across the vale beyond the Redwater, Corlin Town smoked and blazed; all for an arrow carelessly loosed upon a creature who intended no harm.

There the image ceased. Abruptly released, the forester returned to himself with the echoes of his own cry of pain still ringing in his ears. He straightened, shaking, and saw the cloaked figure of the Llondel poised in the gloom before him. Baleful orange eyes regarded him, and a good deal less steadily Telemark stared back.

"What do you want?" he asked hoarsely, and risked a glance at Jaric. The boy appeared unharmed. But only a hole remained where the sword had rested in the ground. The Llondian took no risks.

'Never you take the young fire-bearer to the blue-cloaks,' the demon sent.

"What?" Telemark spread his hands, palms upward, to show he did not understand.

The Llondel lifted a finger slim and gray as a lichened twig. It pointed to Jaric. *'Never you take,'* and an image of uprooted trees and the smell of burning overlaid the words, sharply defined warning of the demon's powers.

The forester stepped back, unable to contain the desperate cornered fear a songbird knows when the snare closes over its neck. What was he to do with a boy who was shadowed by the meddling of sorcerers, if not leave him with the initiates at Kordane's Sanctuary? To keep Jaric was to risk his death; yet the Llondel's intent was clear. Telemark felt a sensation of well-being brush his mind, plainly an attempt at reassurance. But no man dared trust a demon.

Burdened by a poignant sense of helplessness, Telemark shook his head. "I'm sorry," he said firmly. "I cannot keep the boy. He requires better care and security than I can provide."

The Llondel trilled a treble fifth and moved suddenly, lifting the missing sword from the dusky folds of its cloak. It offered the weapon to the forester, hilt first, with a hiss of aggrieved affront. *'Leave, then.'*

Telemark hesitated, unsure of the creature's intent, afraid if he reached for the weapon he would again be made to suffer.

The demon jabbed the pommel impatiently at his chest. *'Man-fool,'* it sent. *'You take.'*

Careful to move without threat, the forester raised his hand to the sword. But the instant his flesh touched the grip, demon images clove his mind like the sheared edge of an axeblade, and swept away all semblance of identity.

Telemark saw the forest through alien eyes, but the trees, the sky, and the dusky humid smell of vegetation in his nostrils, were like nothing he had ever known. The wood was a place of dim violet shadows. Long trailing tendrils of leaves arched overhead, dappled by reddish light, and strange animals whistled from the thickets. Yet the vision held no ambiguity of meaning; Telemark understood he beheld the Llondel's home, a place inconceivably removed from Keithland soil.

Suddenly the alien forest was slashed by an aching flare of brilliance. A shrill scream of sound ripped away the image of trees, and Telemark's eyes were seared by the blistering glory of Kordane's Fires as they had shone before the Great Fall. But to the Llondel, the Fires brought not salvation but captivity, exile, and suffering. Shackled by the demon's imaging, Telemark saw the Fires arc like heated steel across the velvet depths of the heavens, then plunge earthward, never to rise again.

His sight went dark. Beset by pain, he breathed air which ached his lungs, dry and thin and cold after that of his home forest. One with the first Llondelei of Keithland, he crawled forth from the wreckage of an engine which lay smashed in the snow of a hillside. The image spun, wavered, blurred encompassing generations of Llondian history. Pinned by an onslaught of incomprehensible realities, Telemark tasted insanity, hopelessness, and a longing for the purple twilit shadow of a homeworld believed lost. His heart ached with a measure of sorrow unknown to the heritage of man. Tears coursed down his cheeks. Just when it seemed the demon would break him upon a wheel of sheer despair, the image shifted.

A man appeared, etched against the darkness. And bound to the Llondel's intent, Telemark beheld the silver hair and the stern sad features of the Stormwarden of Elrinfaer; but the sorcerer's wrists were fettered and his powers dumb, and for that reason darkness closed over the world, never to be lifted. Savaged by an agony of loss, the forester cried out. And his scream drew fire.

Swept under by a red-gold flood of flame, Telemark flung his hands across his face, but the blaze consumed his fingers, and his vision was not spared. The conflagration raged and spun, fanning outward into a wheel of light. At the center stood a man whose hair streamed over raggedly clothed shoulders like a spill of raw gold. With a jolt of startled awe, Telemark recognized the fine dark eyes of Kerainson Jaric; and the Llondel's image ceased.

Released, Telemark opened tear-soaked lashes and discovered he sat in the wooden chair in his own cabin. His bow and his sword lay at his feet. Shivering with reaction, and half stunned by disbelief, he glanced about and saw that his belongings had been straightened up, each item returned to its place; the smashed jars of herbs stood restored on the shelves, the glass miraculously repaired. Except for the charred ruin of the latch, the backlash, and the Llondel's intervention, it might all have been a dream. . . .

Still caught in wonder, Telemark rose stiffly to his feet, and at his movement, Jaric stirred on the cot in the corner. The forester crossed to the boy's side in time to see the brown eyes open, restored to true awareness for the first time since the injury. Telemark stared down at the boy upon the bed with a mixture of awe and trepidation and tenderness. For incomprehensible as much of the Llondel's imaging had been, a portion of its message was plain; with the Stormwarden of Elrinfaer entrapped, this boy represented the final hope of the Llondelei to end the exile which began at the time of the Great Fall. Never would the demons permit Jaric to fall into the hands of the priests.

Haunted by the mystery of the fire image, Telemark watched the boy's recovery carefully, uncertain what to expect. But Jaric's initial reaction seemed entirely ordinary.

Confronted by the strange confines of the cabin, his hands tightened on the blanket and his pale brow creased in confusion as if seeking the reassurance of something familiar. Quickly Telemark caught the boy's hand.

"Easy," he said softly. "You've had a tough time since I took you in. Can you tell me how you feel?"

The words did nothing to reassure. Jaric's frown deepened, and he seemed to struggle for speech. At last in a thin frightened voice, he admitted, "I can't remember who I am."

CHAPTER XII

Protégé

Telemark gave Jaric's hand a squeeze of reassurance and reflected that the aftereffects of a head injury could occasionally prove merciful. This boy had ridden into Seitforest harried by powers no mortal could support with grace; he would recover his health more easily without recollection of his immediate past.

"Don't fret." The forester tugged the blanket free of the boy's tense fingers. "You suffered a terrible blow to the head, but time and rest will set everything right, even your memory."

Jaric twisted his head on the pillow. "But I don't even know my name." His gaze quartered the cabin again, as if he searched for something lost. "How did I get here?"

Telemark sighed. "Your name, which you mentioned when delirious with fever, is Kerainson Jaric. And I picked you up off the ground in Seitforest after you were assaulted by bandits. They robbed you of everything, even your clothes, which effectively eliminates any further clues. Since no one seems to have searched for you since, I suggest you winter with me while you recover. You'll be as safe here as anywhere else, and I could use help with the traplines."

Jaric bit his lip, eyes widening to encompass the neat rows of snares which hung from pegs on the far wall. "But I know nothing," he said softly. The admission seemed wrung from the depths of his heart, and the anguish reflected on his features moved the forester to pity.

Telemark framed the boy's face between his palms. "Don't worry. I'll teach you. And in our spare time, you'll study swordplay. That way, when you recall who you are, you'll not get your skull cracked again at the hands of the lawless."

Jaric's expression eased. Encouraged by the response Telemark winked, and was rewarded for the first time by a smile.

For Telemark the following days became a time of discovery and revelation, after so many weeks of caring for a comatose invalid. Though weak and unsure of himself, Jaric applied himself to life with a feverish sense of determination. Watching him re-weave the laces of an old snowshoe, the forester sensed the boy lived in fear of incompetence. The harsh leather of the thongs cut into the delicate skin of his fingers, but Jaric persisted until his face became pinched with fatigue. Still he showed no sign of quitting until the task was complete.

Telemark laid the pack strap he was mending across his chairback and crossed the cabin to the boy's side. "No need to finish the whole task today." He ran his fingers over the weave, and found the firm, careful execution of a job well-handled. "You've done fine."

Jaric looked up, eyes dark with uncertainty. He said nothing, but plainer than speech his expression revealed his distrust of the praise. The boy would finish with the snowshoe though the thongs wore his fingers raw, Telemark observed. With a small sigh of frustration, he let his patient be.

Hours later, when Jaric knotted the last thong in place, Telemark was startled by the sweet smile of satisfaction which lit the boy's face. And it occurred to the forester that for Jaric, who had no recognizable past, the accomplishment represented a major victory.

Oblivious to the fact she actually slept in a capsule deep beneath the isle of the Vaere, Taen dreamed she sat cross-legged in the changeless silvery twilight of the clearing. Tamlin stood opposite her, pipe clenched between his teeth. His red-brown whiskers framed a thoughtful expression.

"I'm thinking you're ready," he said softly, and for the first time Taen could recall, his feathers and his bells were stilled.

She tilted her chin impishly and grinned at him. "You mean you're finally tired of hearing me describe how much that old fisherman dreams about the tavern girl at the docks?" Under the Vaere's tutelage, her skills had grown and refined, and recently, as an exercise, Tamlin made her spend tedious hours tracking the mind of a crotchety fish trapper who sailed just north of the island checking his lines. She *was* getting better, and increased confidence gave her leeway enough to tease.

But levity was wasted effort with the Vaere. "How many pairs of socks does the fellow own? Can you tell?" Tamlin bit down on his pipe and puffed furiously, frowning at his charge.

Taen wrinkled her nose in distaste. "Socks?" With a resigned sigh, she closed her eyes and cast her mind outward, awareness spread like a net across the lifeless face of the sea. At first she felt nothing.

"You're overriding the subject," said Tamlin sharply. "Stay annoyed with me, and even if you manage to locate the old man, you'll alter his frame of reference. Perhaps at that you're not ready at all."

Although Taen had not the slightest idea what she was supposed to be ready for, she curbed her irritation and concentrated on emptying her mind. Her sense of self gradually receded, replaced by a passive quality of waiting timeless as the magic which bound the clearing. Presently, like the tentative flicker of the first star at twilight, she felt the old man's consciousness brush against her awareness. Bent over a reeking bucket of fish bait, his thoughts preoccupied by daydreams of the tavern wench's ample bustline, his mind interested Taen about as much as old woolens in need of darning. But she persisted, threading cleanly through the man's surface awareness in pursuit of his collection of footwear.

The information she discovered startled her to the point where she burst into honest laughter. Opening her eyes, she glared at Tamlin, who maddeningly vanished at once. But by now she was accustomed to his vagaries.

"You knew," she accused the spot where he had stood a moment earlier.

A smoke ring appeared, wavering in the air, and an instant later, Tamlin materialized beneath, frowning in agitation. "Knew what?"

Taen twisted a stray lock of hair between her fingers. "Knew about the socks," she said, and grinned. "The old crow doesn't *have* any. He goes barefoot."

"True enough." Tamlin folded his arms with a rattle of beads. "But that's no excuse for carelessness." And he left her with the image of the fisherman, who scratched his gray head with fingers still slimy from the fish bait, and puzzled to fathom why the tavern girl's fair bosom suddenly reminded him of socks.

"You must practice," said Tamlin, and the sudden curtness in his tone cut Taen's amusement short. The flush left by laughter drained slowly from her cheeks. Her blue eyes turned serious.

"Not the fisherman," she pleaded.

Tamlin paced, his bells a jingling counterpoint to his impatience. "No. You've grown beyond that. I rather thought you should try something more demanding." He stopped short, and sharply considered her. "Your short-range skills are quite satisfactory. It's time to try you over distance. Close relations often make the easiest subjects to start. How would you feel if I asked you to dream-read the members of your immediate family?"

Taen glanced up, transformed by excitement. Although she had dedicated herself heart and mind to the training offered her by the Vaere, the satisfaction gained through her progress had been marred by constant worry for the mother she had left on Imrill Kand. And Emien, when she had last parted from him, had been troubled and desperate with worry for her.

"Your skills are ready," said Tamlin. "But there are perils. I leave the choice up to you."

But the chance to look in on those she loved, and perhaps reassure them of her well-being, attracted Taen beyond caution. "I would try now," she said steadily.

Tamlin shifted his pipe between his teeth and puffed on it, considering her answer. Then he nodded, blew a smoke ring, and vanished, obviously well pleased with his charge.

Taen sat down in the grass, trembling in anticipation. Ever since she had learned her gifts could be controlled, she had longed to contact her home. Now with permission granted she felt strangely apprehensive. What if she discovered all was not well? Yet before the lonely yearning in her heart even fear held no power to sway her. Proud of her place as one chosen by the Vaere, she closed her eyes and began the primary exercises to prepare her mind for her craft.

In recalling Imrill Kand, the first thing Taen remembered was the dusky smell of the peat. Even in summer, fires burned in the smokehouses, curing herring against the long, lean months when boats could be locked in the harbor by winter's storms. Guided by that memory, Taen felt the darkness within her mind shift and part before the reality of another place. Though the deep shadow of evening lay over the isle, she knew her dream-sense had brought her home.

Poised on her gift like a hawk on an air current, Taen hovered over Imrill Kand, startled to find the keen chill of autumn in the air. Lulled by the magic of the Vaere, she had forgotten that seasons would continue in her absence, and the discovery disturbed her. She would return one day, perhaps; but all she knew would be changed. And like a small girl caught in a nightmare, she fled to the house off Rat's Alley for comfort and protection.

Her mother dozed in the wooden rocker by the hearth, sheltered still by the brother who had taken her in since the death of her husband. Beloved work-worn hands lay cradled in her apron, and a familiar curl had strayed form the pins which secured her hair; Taen noticed new lines around eyes already heavily wrinkled by hardship and loss. But the women of Imrill Kand were inured to life's deprivations; Leri Marl's widow had endured her personal tragedies without yielding to despair.

Suddenly uncertain of her control, Taen reached out, tentatively opened contact with her mother's mind. But delicate as her first touch was, she was noticed. The woman's eyes quivered open, blue, but faded now by the first traces of cataracts. Her seamed lips parted into a smile of welcome which changed almost at once to laughter.

"Taen?" Her mother blinked, spilling sudden tears of welcome. Secure in her island heritage, she never thought to question when the sight was upon her; and no vision ever brought more joy than the assurance of her daughter's well-being. "You are safe, I see, Fires be thanked for that." She paused and smiled again, unabashed by the moisture on her cheeks. "Have you seen Emien? I worry about your brother. He was always brash, and quick to resent what he could not change. I fear he bears the Stormwarden no love, child. And that sets sorrow upon me, for Anskiere was like a father to you both."

Taen hesitated, reluctant to share what little she knew of Emien. And mercifully her mother mistook her silence for impatience. "Go, child. Seek your brother. Tell him he is missed, and that *Dacsen* is needed at home."

But the sloop was lost, cast onto the reefs by orders of a King's man now dead. If the wreckage had failed to wash ashore, Taen could not bear to break the news. Burdened by a sense of her own responsibility, she withdrew from her mother's presence and flung herself headlong into a search for her brother, as if by finding him she could negate the betrayal of his upbringing and the sorrow that knowledge might cause the folk who raised him.

Darkness closed like a tunnel about her. Suffocated by the sensations of distance and cold, Taen struggled to regain control of her gift. Unlike the old fisherman, Emien's mind was hard and bright, a fierce turmoil of emotional conflicts; the pattern was closer to her than any other. No matter how remote her brother had grown, Taen was determined to find him. She steadied herself with a memory of his face, black hair spilled untidily across his brow, his eyes shadowed and wary since the day the accident had claimed their father's life. And light suddenly exploded into existence around her, as if the association opened a connection between them.

Centered by the powers of her gift, Taen found herself looking down on the torchlit arcade of a palace courtyard. Two men circled over the patterned brick beyond the archway, stripped to the waist, and armed with practice foils. In a fast-paced exchange of swordplay, the larger man lunged. His blade clanged against his opponent's guard. The smaller fellow grunted and recovered.

"Mind your footwork, boy," said the larger man, and with a start of surprise, Taen recognized her brother as his partner.

Annoyed by the correction and unaware of his sister's presence, Emien riposted. Linked by her dream-sense, Taen shared her brother's bitter satisfaction as he hammered blows upon his tutor's weapon. The pace increased. Flamelight gleamed on sweat-slicked shoulders as the fighters wove across the courtyard, graceful as dancers in the rhythms of parry and riposte. The sparring was intended for practice, an exercise to develop sharper skills. But merged with her brother's mind, Taen realized Emien fought for much higher stakes, as if the outcome of this simple match held capacity to poison his future. Wrapped in a black web of passion, he fenced as if his teacher were an enemy.

Steel rang upon crossguard with a sharp, angry clamor. Both men gasped for breath. Absorbed by the fiery play of light on the foils, each teased and feinted, seeking an opening in his opponent's guard. And drugged on the wine of her brother's hatred, Taen almost missed the raised hand as his instructor signaled the end of the bout. For one ragged, flickering instant, it seemed Emien would not desist. Then he lowered his foil, and rubbed his damp forehead with the back of his wrist.

His instructor regarded him intently, then collected the practice weapon. "You're getting quite good. With work, you have the potential to be very good indeed. Now get some rest. I'll meet you again tomorrow."

Emien watched the swordmaster depart with narrowed eyes. The praise was a string of meaningless words in his ears. Still oblivious to Taen's presence, he crossed the courtyard and retrieved his shirt and tunic from a bench. Sewn of soft scarlet material, the garments were bordered with black and gold threadwork, with laces at cuff and neck caught by jewelled hooks. Amazed by his finery, Taen shivered as the sweat chilled on her brother's body. He had risen high since they had parted on the decks of *Crow*. And somehow, somewhere, along with his bettered station, he had acquired a hunger for power no training at weapons could assuage.

Numbed by his strangeness, Taen did little but follow as Emien entered the palace. He made his way down a series of ornately decorated corridors and entered a carpeted antechamber. A pair of men-at-arms guarded the doorway beyond. Emien nodded in greeting and crossed inside, blinking in the sudden glare of candles.

The room's furnishings represented more wealth than Taen could have imagined in one place; but after three weeks of life in King Kisburn's court, Emien barely noticed the rare wood, the patterned rugs, or the fine wool tapestries which covered the walls by the casements. He paused with his tunic and shirt draped over his forearm, embarrassed to discover the chamber was not empty.

A richly dressed official stood by the hearth, engaged in animated conversation with a woman clad in ermine and amethysts. Fine gold wires bound her snowy hair and the bracelets on her slender wrists chimed as sweetly as Tamlin's bells as she lifted her head and acknowledged the boy's presence. The official faltered and fell silent, plump cheeks quivering with irritation.

Emien bowed smoothly, as if accustomed to court manners all his life. The easy grace of the movement left Taen uneasy, and worse, the face of the official seemed strangely cloaked in shadow, as if something about his complexion did not agree with the light.

If Emien perceived anything unusual about the person of the official, he chose not to be bothered. "Tathagres, my Lord Sholl, I beg to be excused. Had I guessed the council would end early, I'd have chosen a different route."

Tathagres waved him impatiently past. Painfully conscious of her beauty, Emien proceeded to the suite of rooms which served as his own apartment. There he tossed the rich tunic carelessly over a stuffed chair, summoned servants, and called querulously for bath water. Appalled by the ease with which he had shed his upbringing on Imrill Kand, Taen watched Emien berate the servants for clumsiness and savagely banish them from his presence. Soured by the exchange, he finished his washing in solitude, then poured himself wine and sprawled, exhausted, across the rich coverlet of his bed.

He did not immediately sleep, but lay staring with widened eyes at the single candle left alight on the nightstand. Rest came with difficulty, Taen sensed, and troubled by the unhappy changes court life had wrought in her brother, she decided to engage her gift and bring him comfort. Poised like a dream on the edge of Emien's awareness, Taen gathered her powers into tight focus and spread a blanket of peace over his thoughts. She led him back to his beginnings on Imrill Kand. Enfolded in the soft scent of peat and the sigh of sea wind through the chimes on the rooftree above the loft where he slept during childhood, Emien relaxed. Disarmed by the gentleness of her sending, he slipped into sleep.

Oblivious to the fact that his thoughts were influenced by another, he imagined he stood with his sister on a grassy hillside above the village. Summer breezes fanned her black hair across her cheeks and the gray wool of her shift blew loosely about her while the small brown goats left their grazing and nosed her hands, begging for grain. Taen tangled her fingers in their rough coats, a smile of joy on her face. Watching her, Emien could almost forget her lameness and the innocent vulnerability which had permitted her to believe Anskiere's lies; but now she was dead, drowned in a storm like his father. Never again would she play with the goats in the meadows of Imrill Kand.

Though her memory held nothing but tragedy, in the dream she would not stop smiling. Through the window of her gift, she regarded her brother with eyes of clearest blue and said, "But, Emien, I am alive."

Emien tossed on the bed, struggled to free himself from a torment he now recognized as nightmare. Taen had died; Imrill Kand was forever barred to him. Fevered and sweating, he fought the vision of his sister, insistent in his hatred of Anskiere. The dream would not release him; he could not make himself waken.

"Emien, no." Taen's voice battered against his isolation, seductive with compassion. "I survived the storm when *Crow* foundered. The Stormwarden protected me. I am with you now, can't you see? Oh, why must you believe Tathagres' lies? Don't you know she uses you?"

But her words failed to soothe. The kindness Taen intended brought Emien nothing but anguish, poisoned as he was by his own guilt. For if his sister had been preserved at the Stormwarden's hand, every act he had committed in the cause of her vengeance became evil beyond question.

He tossed on the bed, sobbing aloud with misery. "You're *dead*," he accused, and when the image of his sister's presence failed to leave him, his voice went ugly with rage. "Leave me!"

"But why?" Taen searched his face, her light eyes suddenly flooded with tears. "What could make you turn against the Stormwarden who once protected you? Did you believe the Constable, that he murdered the folk of Tierl Enneth? Emien, Anskiere was innocent. *I can show you.*"

Confident of his trust, Taen gathered her skills, assembled dream images to prove to her brother how her gift had enabled her to know beyond question that Anskiere had not caused the drowning of helpless people. She touched her brother's mind with truth, utterly unprepared for the fact that her message brought him nothing but guilt.

Emien's voice split into a raw scream of denial. "No!" Condemned beyond pardon by the vision she wove, he lashed back, set the poisoned dregs of his own warped reason against his sister in attempt to restore the dignity he had lost when he first accepted Tathagres as mistress.

The dream link reversed itself. Caught in the meshes of her brother's passion, Taen felt herself tossed headlong into clouded skies and the savage, storm-whipped seas of a gale. To the battered, emotionally torn mind of her brother, this tempest seemed more than a natural contest of elements. A squall had taken the life of his father. Hammered by thunderous, foam-laced swells, *Crow* had foundered, and above the demented howl of the gusts Emien heard once again the screams of drowning slaves and the cries of his lost sister; and with the pinnace's tiller clenched once more in his blistered hands, he watched, helpless, as the seas stripped the lives of the survivors with passionless cruelty. Soon scarcely a handful remained. Always the sea lurked at his back, a tireless, insatiable enemy. Humbled over and over again by its might, and by the powers of the sorcerer who controlled it, Emien wept in frustration.

Inflamed by the need to retaliate, he raced down a rocky beach on the isle of Cliffhaven. Drawn along by the dream link, Taen felt the icy air ache in his lungs with each breath, through his ears heard the crash as the breakers creamed white against the shore and the shrill calling of gulls. Ahead, cliffs rose like a wall against the sky, lofty stone tiers encased in crystalline sheets of ice. The raw cold of a sorcerer's enchantment reddened Emien's skin, but he felt no discomfort; beyond that bastion of frost lay his enemy, and his obsession for vengeance permitted no rest. He would pierce Anskiere's defenses though he broke his hands trying, and with a separate thrill of horror, Taen realized the glassy abutments of ice imprisoned the Stormwarden who once had protected her from harm.

She tried to break free, to wrest control of the dream from her brother's maddened grasp. She had to know more concerning the Stormwarden's fate. But Emien's hatred was too strong to resist, and her presence itself threatened his existence. Even as Taen reached to manipulate the fabric of his image, her brother drew the sword from the sheath at his side and lifted it high overhead, point poised for a killing blow.

"No!" Taen fell back, spread-eagled against the ice, unable to believe he would strike. "Would you murder your own sister? Emien!"

But the words failed to deter him. Emien seemed not to see her at all, and with a pang of awful horror Taen realized the fury which drove him was directed solely at the Stormwarden of Elrinfaer. Emien would drive the sword home, and never notice she stood in his path.

Just as his wrist tensed to engage the downstroke, a shout rang out down the beach. Hooves thundered like war drums over the sand. Emien whirled and saw one of the Kielmark's mounted patrols bearing down on him at a gallop. Steel sang through the air as he twisted, white-faced and frightened. But before he could ready himself for defense, a force like white-hot magma closed over him, and he felt himself ripped into transfer by the powers of Tathagres' neckband.

The dream link carried Taen along with him. Even with her senses overwhelmed by the rush of strange forces, she heard her brother scream aloud in terror, for the memory of his transfer from Cliffhaven to the palace of Kisburn's court recurred to him only in nightmare. Ripped away from the solid ground beneath the ice cliffs, he felt himself suspended as before, in a place where darkness reigned. The air he breathed held the metallic tang of a blacksmith's forge, and dizzied by its heat, his grip upon his own self-awareness wavered. As if torchlit against a backdrop of dark, Emien beheld beings whose features contained no trace of humanity. While the forces of the transfer held him locked and helpless, the black-skinned, red-eyed visages of Kor's Accursed leered down upon him from a high dais of stone.

Trapped in his frame of reference, Taen also noticed the demons. Powerless to intervene, she stood by as they conferred among themselves, weighing the poison in her brother's soul. And with a horror as great as Emien's own, the girl watched one of the demons rise and point, and pronounce her brother's name as one chosen.

Revulsion tore through her. The dream link unraveled under a lightning burst of negative force, and flung across distance by an explosion of emotional rejection, Taen shivered and woke in the dell on the Isle of the Vaere. Sheltered once more within the grove, she huddled with her arms clenched around her knees. The place seemed less than secure. Taen glanced about her with dream-haunted eyes. Although the link with Emien stood severed, she sensed the resonant echo of her brother's screams as he woke from nightmare on the silken coverlet of his bed in Kisburn's palace.

Never in Taen's darkest imagination had she guessed her brother might stand in such peril, even when fear and anger had sometimes made him cruel. Troubled, she hesitated to confide her findings to the Vaere. Though quick in his perceptions, Tamlin could often be dispassionate concerning events beyond his island sanctuary. If Emien was to be helped, he would require the care and the compassion of one who understood his difficult nature; one who knew, as his family did, that he had never been able to forgive himself the error which tangled the net and began the inexorable string of circumstances which resulted in his father's death.

Alone with her dilemma and confined to the Isle of the Vaere, Taen knew only one on all of Keithland capable enough to restore her brother's trust. Without pausing to ask Tamlin's permission, she gathered the battered remains of her dream-sense around her, and launched her awareness in search of Anskiere of Elrinfaer.

Fragile as fine silk thread, her probe unreeled across the void. Though the Stormwarden's mind had largely stayed closed to her, Taen recalled every nuance of his presence. She searched for the constant rhythm of surf against the beaches of home; the wild, keening song of the first north wind of autumn, and the sure power of the solstice tides; Anskiere was all that and more, changeless as the renewal discovered each year in the gentle showers of spring. Confident the Stormwarden would recognize her, Taen strengthened her sending and presently located a thin glimmer of daylight. Hurrying now, eager to reach her goal, Taen rushed through the gap, into a reality far distant.

She was greeted first by the solid boom of breakers and the sigh of breezes combing windswept heights. A moment later, the darkness parted around her, and her dream-sense ached in the glare of sunlight thrown off the sheer, impenetrable heights of the same ice cliffs she had encountered in Emien's dream. The sight dismayed her. Pierced by the plaintive cries of the gulls, Taen felt daunted by unanswerable sorrow. She surveyed that desolate vista, unwilling to believe her search would end here, in a place of deserted wilds. With the care Tamlin had taught her, Taen focused her dream-sense and sounded the place for traces of life, or any clue which might reveal the Stormwarden's presence.

Almost at once the resonance of Anskiere's power surged through the gate she had opened in her mind. Constant and strong as storm tide, the warding forces he had set forth in that place sang across the channels of Taen's sensitivity. Reassured of his presence, the girl gathered herself and turned her dream-reader's skills to tap the ward's source.

Darkness met her, deep and vast as night, and seemingly solid as a wall. Taen gasped, unable to orient herself. She delved deeper, sought to thrust the suffocating blackness aside and reach the Stormwarden's aware-ness. But her meager skills would not answer in that place; the shadow refused to part. Tossed about like a moth in a downdraft, Taen floundered and struggled to reorient. But the wards restricted her, making progress impossible.

Taen persisted. Cold savaged her flesh, cut deep into her bones until it seemed her very thoughts would freeze in place. Her dream-sense labored, suddenly burdened by an overwhelming weight of earth and ice overhead. Taen persevered, striving to fathom the hidden center of the wardspell, but it was not Anskiere she found. High and thin with distance, she caught the whistling echo of a cry. Strange creatures lay imprisoned beneath. The eerie harmonics of their wailing chilled Taen even more than the terrible cold, for the sound touched her dream-sense with a feeling of lust and killing beyond the capacity of violence to assuage. Held fast by Anskiere's wardenship, the creatures she sensed could not win through to freedom; but here, at the vortex of his powers, where she should have encountered the Stormwarden's living presence, Taen found silence and frost and the impenetrable stillness of ages.

Discouraged at last she withdrew, returned to awareness of her own body. But the grove of the Vaere seemed strangely comfortless after her sojourn, its unbreakable quiet a constraint upon her ears. Grieved for the fate of her brother and distressed by the loss and the loneliness created by the Stormwarden's absence, Taen bent her head and wept. With her face buried within her crossed arms and her shoulders shaking with misery, she did not notice the thin chime of bells as Tamlin appeared at her side.

He seated himself on the rock by her feet, his forehead creased by a frown. "I warned there might be risks, child." He paused to puff on his pipe. Blue smoke rose and braided on the air currents around his hair, untouched by any hint of a breeze. "Now, why not tell me what troubles you so."

Taen lifted her head, embarrassed by the tears on her cheeks. She dried her face with her sleeve while Tamlin waited with his thumbs hooked in his pockets, his beads and his bells strangely silent in the silvery twilight of the clearing. Slowly, carefully, Taen described what she had experienced of her brother. Her phrases were clumsy and halting, but Tamlin did not interrupt. With bearded lips thinned with concentration, he puffed furiously on his pipe, now and again touching Taen's mind directly to gain a detail left out.

Her tears began again as she described the plight of Anskiere, but she hardly noticed. Tamlin's eyes became piercing and his pipe hung forgotten between his teeth. Yet he spoke no word until she lapsed, faltering, into silence, her tale complete.

"You bring me sad tidings, Reader of Dreams." Tamlin sighed. He raked stubby fingers through his beard and twirled the pipe stem thoughtfully between his hands. At last he stirred, and regretfully studied the tear-stained face of his charge.

"The demons of Keithland grow overly bold, I think. Mankind must not be left defenseless. If the Stormwarden of Elrinfaer is no longer active, your training and your skills become a matter of urgent importance." Tamlin paused as if weighted by an impossible quandary. "After I have held council on the issue, the Free Isles must be warned of the danger. For if I read the matter correctly, the demons prepare an assault against Landfast. There are records there, in Kordane's shrine, which must never leave the care of humanity."

He did not add, as he could have, that much of the burden of mankind's defense might fall on the slender shoulders of the girl who stood before him. Soon, of necessity, she must confront the supreme test of her abilities.

CHAPTER XIII

Cycle of Dreams

Lights flickered like a fixed swarm of fireflies across the console in the underground installation which housed the Vaere. If some of the panels stayed dark, the autologic and memory banks which once had served the star probe *Corinne Dane* still functioned to capacity. But charged with responsibility for mankind's survival, the computer itself had evolved in a manner her builders never conceived.

The Vaere turned the intricate mathematical functions once employed for stellar navigation toward probability equations. Taen's encounter with her brother showed evidence of a demon's plot against mankind. The Vaere required more data. But with the Firelord dead and the clan priestesses fallen into disrepute, many sources of intelligence had lapsed. Anskiere knew enough to assess the implications of Taen's dream. Yet her failure to find him at the vortex of his own wardspell created complications; the Vaere itself could not penetrate those defenses.

All sophisticated mechanical practicality, the Vaere pursued alternatives, then mathematically simulated the consequences. The numbers turned up negative with persistent regularity. Had the Vaere been human, it would have cursed in frustration. Being a machine, it tallied assets, and considered a fresh approach. The Stormwarden of Elrinfaer could be reached, but only at considerable risk.

In an ocean trench beneath the polar ice cap lay Sathid, the crystals which founded Anskiere's powers. The Vaere could generate sonic interference and rouse the crystals; Anskiere would know at once he was needed. But if, as Taen's dream suggested, he had somehow become incapacitated, the crystals would discover his weakness; they might rise up against him. The Sathid were alien biotes which augmented the psychic abilities of a host; when bonded with an intelligent being, the crystals acquired sentience, and an insatiable lust for dominance. Agitated lights raced across the console as the Vaere ran yet another set of probabilities. *Should the Sathid attempt rebellion, how much of Anskiere's resources could be diverted without risking a reversal of control?* Past events offered basis for analysis.

An access circuit closed in the memory banks and the Vaere reran the profile of Anskiere's reactions when he first bonded with the Sathid matrixes. He had subjugated the first crystal without undue hardship. The graphs mapping his physical and psychic responses rose in clean, even lines, then tapered back to normal. But the second graph differed. Decades later, the Vaere surveyed a struggle whose outcome was by no means guaranteed. Controlled, the double bond yielded an exponential increase in power. But failure inevitably created a monster possessed by alien passions; Anskiere opted for a Stormwarden's mastery with full knowledge he would succeed, or be killed instantly by the Vaere who had trained him.

His stress rose in steep, jagged lines, spiked high into the danger zone as the new Sathid linked with the first. Both matrixes combined to battle the sorcerer's will. Plunged into torment, Anskiere had held his ground, and eventually battered the two Sathid into quiescence.

The Vaere juggled facts with electronic accuracy. Should the Sathid rise up with Anskiere in difficulty, the most optimistic calculation showed his chances were slight; and if he had raised wards at Cliffhaven to confine frostwargs, he would certainly fail.

Balked by improbable odds, the Vaere abandoned the idea of contacting Anskiere. With no Firelord left to restrain the frostwargs, the Stormwarden was no option. With every alternative exhausted, the Vaere considered Taen, whose empathic abilities held such promise, but whose training was far from complete. Linked with a Sathid matrix, the girl's sensitivity would increase to the point where she could tap any human mind of Keithland for information. Every nuance of the demons' plot would be immediately attainable. The girl was young, untried, and as yet barely able to command her gift. But she was also extraordinarily brave.

Reluctantly the Vaere ran a third set of equations. Lacking her mentor's years of training and preparation, did the girl possess enough resilience to master the bonding process on her own? Her personality profile was still sketchy; the Vaere had not mapped her tolerance to stress. But extrapolations based on her past history yielded figures which offered a slim possibility of success.

Never in Keithland's history had the Vaere been forced to make this crucial a decision on such scanty data. The stakes were inflexibly severe; should Taen fail to withstand the rigors of a Sathid bonding, if she once lost control to the matrix, she could not be permitted to survive. Yet logic offered no better course of action.

The lights on the control panels flickered red as the Vaere entered sequence after sequence of probability figures. If the demons' plan was to be thwarted, Taen must master the Sathid matrix, and achieve the full potential of her gift. Programmed to protect humanity, the Vaere could only ensure her ordeal was handled with optimum chance of success.

The girl rested dreamlessly in her capsule while the Vaere finalized its rigorous analysis. A day later, after pursuing each alternative, it concluded that Taen's self-confidence would become seriously impaired were she to be given last minute instruction. Knowledge of the bonding process would be no help to her.

The Vaere surveyed her vital signs, ran a final check on her health. Unlike Anskiere and Ivain, this child must experience the ardors of bonding ignorant and untrained. If she survived to gain her mastery, she would be physically changed, for the Sathid took seven years to mature. But by applying the principles of the star-drive directly to her capsule, the Vaere would create a time anomaly; she would emerge at the age of seventeen, but Keithland's continuum would have advanced only days by contrast. Once the parameters of the time envelope were set, the girl would be physically isolated from Keithland's reality. No longer could the Vaere intervene in her behalf.

Taen lay peacefully in her capsule, her ebony hair, red lips, and pale skin like the sleeping beauty in the tale from old earth. She felt no pain as the needle pierced her flesh. The Vaere injected a solution containing an alien entity into the vein in her arm; when the Sathid evolved enough to challenge, it would strike when Taen was most vulnerable. In time, the girl would battle her psychic nemesis.

The Sathid spread swiftly through Taen's body. Triggered by warmth and the presence of life, it germinated and groped, instinctively as a new-born child, for awareness of its new host. Impressed by Taen's own character, the Sathid began patterning itself to mesh with her mind. The sensitive psychic empathy of her gift opened like a gateway to her inner-most self. Guided by the Sathid's need to explore, Taen began to dream of her past.

Time meant nothing to the matrix. From the moment of birth to the first acquisition of language, it experienced the girl's memories, analyzing even the most trifling details. Through her memories, it learned to walk, to speak, and to reason. Sharing a stolen tart in the alley behind the bakeshop it discovered duplicity, and from her first lie it gained cunning. Taen dreamed on, at first unaware a foreign entity inhabited her awareness.

Carried back to the age of two, she sat in her mother's lap, playing with shells, while the gusts of an afternoon squall battered the window panes and rain fell in hissing sheets down the chimney. Taen concentrated single-mindedly on her game, uneasy in the strange surroundings of her cousins' house. But Uncle Evertt tossed in his cot, sick with a fever. Her mother tended him while Emien and their father were off fishing in the sloop.

Thunder rumbled overhead, shaking the floor with its violence. The girl cowered against her mother's breast, small fists clenched around her shells. Suddenly, horribly, she had difficulty breathing. Taen choked, red-faced, and struggled not to cry; she had promised to be quiet, and let Uncle Evertt sleep. But the air seemed thick as syrup in her lungs. A sharp, tearing pain gripped her chest. Taen felt dizzy. Tears traced silently down her cheeks and soaked into the neck of her wool shift. And alerted by the quiver in her daughter's body, her mother lifted her up.

"Child, what in Kor's Fires ails you?" She peered anxiously at her daughter's face.

Yet Taen knew no words to explain what her mind envisioned, that her father struggled for his life, entangled in a net under the sloop's dark keel. Too young to comprehend his death, she laid her head against her mother's shoulder and wept. And the Sathid, sensing discord in her life, probed deeper.

Three days later, the townsfolk brought Emien home. Taen heard the scrape of boots on the brick sill of the kitchen door. Men spoke in hushed voices in the next room, and suddenly her mother cried aloud in anguish. Alarmed, Taen peeked around the door, her rag doll forgotten in her arms. She saw Emien standing among strangers, still clad in his oilskins. Her brother's clothing dripped seawater, and he stared with unresponsive eyes at the floor while the men talked.

"We found him adrift beyond the reef," said the tall man to her mother. "The sloop took some damage in the storm, but repairs can be made. The shipwright offered his services for nothing."

Taen saw her mother straighten in her chair. "And Marl? What happened to Marl?"

The stranger shrugged, ill at ease. "Can't say, mistress. Old sharks fair ruined the remains. Your boy knows. But he won't talk."

"Emien?" Marl's widow turned tear-streaked eyes upon her son and opened her arms wide to receive him. But the boy flinched back and refused to meet her gaze. Aware something serious was amiss, Taen ducked out of sight behind the door. She fled the house, crowded as it was with strangers, and sought refuge in the shed behind the goat barn, where the dusty darkness and fragrant piles of hay hid her distress. She lay still. Miserable and alone, she listened between the clink of windchimes and the mournful notes of the pigeons for the boisterous voice of her father returning home. But she heard only the shouts of the village boys sent out to search for her. She would not answer, however frantic their concern. Well after sundown, when the wind blew cold off the harbor and the inn's faded signboard creaked like an old man's rocker above deserted village streets, Taen returned to the house.

The strange men had gone. But her mother's grief tore into Taen's young mind, feeding her nightmares of ruined hope, and that night her Uncle Evertt started shouting. The Sathid looked on, intrigued, while she cowered behind the linen chest with both ears muffled by winter blankets. Yet even through the wool, the girl heard the relentless slap of her uncle's belt, and Emien's cries of pain. Assaulted through the window of her gift by violence, anger, and misunderstanding, she pressed the blankets more tightly over her face; but the shouting seemed never to end. Punishment only made Emien sullen. Weeks passed. He never spoke of the storm. Only Taen, whose strange perception permitted understanding of her brother's mind, knew he had not been at fault for the loss of his father's life. She was too young to explain. And since Emien also was a sensitive child, the damage quickly became permanent. Nothing would ever amend Emien's distrust of his uncle.

Evertt seemed not to care. He shouldered the additional burden of providing for his brother's family with an islander's dour fatalism. Along with her young cousins, Taen learned to be silent when her uncle returned from the docks, and to stay clear of his boot when rough weather confined the fleet to anchorage. Evertt had always been a brooding, reclusive man; but after Marl's death he spoke little and smiled less. Each of the children tried incessantly to please him, but nothing Emien ever did was acceptable.

Emien stayed aloof from the village boys. Taen, through the rare insight of her gift, became the only person on Imrill Kand to bridge his isolation, until Anskiere came.

The Stormwarden had a way with the boy. Where the villagers saw recalcitrance, the sorcerer looked deeper and recognized loneliness and need. He delighted in Emien's company. After a time, the boy began to tag at the Stormwarden's heels.

Influenced by the Sathid's prompting, Taen dreamed of the year she turned seven. Though still too small to accompany her brother on his jaunts with the sorcerer, she recalled how Anskiere called the wild shearwaters in from the open sea, or dissolved the overcast to bring sunshine. Slowly Emien learned to laugh again, though never in his uncle's presence. His confidence grew in Anskiere's shadow, until at last he managed to tell of the storm, and the accident which had taken the life of his father. The village forgave him. Yet Emien never fully regained his self-confidence.

On a stormy day the spring she turned eight, Taen ran down to the docks to meet the fishing fleet. As silent observer, the Sathid absorbed the pattern of her dream as she threaded her way breathlessly through the alleys behind market square. Wind tore at her cloak. It rattled the loose boards in the fish stalls and tumbled broken sticks and bits of loose refuse across the rain-sleek cobbles. Taen skipped through the gap in the drying racks, salted by wind-blown spray. Today her brother would return home, after close to three weeks' absence.

Taen slowed to a walk as she reached the shore. Exposed to the full brunt of the gale, the storm slashed across the face of the sea, fraying the wave crests into white tendrils of spindrift. Waves smashed hungrily across the breakwater, thudding into the docks with malicious force; the old tarred pilings shook with the impact.

Taen surveyed the soaked planks with trepidation. The weather had worsened since morning. Anxious to locate the fleet, she squinted against the spray and intently surveyed the harbor. Several small boats jounced and yawed at their moorings, the greenish copper of their bottom paint showing like a drunken maid's petticoats. Buried under tattered layers of cloud, the horizon was not visible. Taen saw no trace of the returning fleet. Resigned to wait, she sighed and settled herself in the lee of the loading winch.

A heavy packing crate had been left in the sling. Cords creaked as the wind tossed it to and fro. Irked by the sound and soaked to the skin, Taen huddled under her cloak, attention glued to the horizon where at long last the dark reddish triangle of the first sail sliced the gloom. The rest of the fleet followed behind. Anxious to catch the first glimpse of *Dacsen*, Taen did not notice the blond tassel of frayed rope overhead, where the line securing the crate crossed the pulley.

The first ply snapped with a whipcrack report. Taen started, looked up, and saw the box swing ominously in the sling. But the chill had cramped her muscles and her body responded sluggishly as she started to rise. The crate shifted before she moved clear. Added strain snapped the rope. Ironbound wood ripped free of its constraints and fell, crushing Taen's slender ankle.

The Sathid matrix watched dispassionately as the returning fishermen found her, barely conscious in the soaked folds of her cloak. They lifted the crate with careful hands, and said little to the brother who carried his sister home. One of the younger cousins was sent to fetch the Storm-warden.

But when Anskiere arrived, he had no magic to mend Taen's shattered leg. He explained as much in a tone subdued by regret, while the gale whipped across Imrill Kand and the wind tore at the shingles with a shriek like Kor's Accursed. Emien watched the Stormwarden gather his gray cloak about his shoulders. Without taking time to speak to the boy, the sorcerer stepped out into the night, letting a gust of rain across the threshold. Within the hour he had calmed the storm enough to send a boat to the mainland for a healer. But Emien had never forgotten the fact that his presence had been ignored.

Taen's convalescence progressed slowly. The Sathid learned patience and endurance through the days she lay abed suffering the pain of her healing leg. The Stormwarden spent hours visiting her and his walks into the hills with Emien were curtailed. At first the boy moped sullenly in the kitchen until his mother scolded him for idleness. Deprived at one stroke of the sister and the sorcerer who were his only friends, he spent his afternoons alone in the meadows and refused to seek other companions. Aware of his resentment but unable to console him, Taen bore her own misery in silence; as a cripple, she could never fully earn her keep in the hard life of Imrill Kand. The fleet would forever sail without her.

While she dreamed through the weary months of recovery, the Sathid deepened its grip on her mind. Slowly, experimentally, it sorted what it had learned and in the first poisoned seed of conflict sown between Taen and her brother, it found the weakness it sought in her character. The girl perceived Emien's shortcomings well enough, but cursed by the clarity of her gift she also understood him. Bereft of the security of her father's love, she would forgive the boy, though his flawed personality caused her pain and destroyed her emotional equilibrium. There the Sathid read potential for conquest.

The matrix probed for more detail. With utmost delicacy it examined every aspect of Taen's relationship with her brother and through that dis-covered the estrangement created by her loyalty to Anskiere. The Sathid weighed alternatives. While Taen relived the anguish brought on by her brother's rejection of Imrill Kand, it gained maturity. Soon the matrix and the girl's mind became inseparably interlinked. The Sathid's psychic strength combined with Taen's gift of empathy and expanded her abilities to paranormal proportions.

A day came when the Sathid launched the girl's awareness beyond the bounds of her own subconscious. Above the capsule which encased her body, a needle quivered in a meter embedded in the control console set to monitor her life functions. The Vaere noted the deflection and began actively to monitor. The Sathid sought a deeper hold to secure its bid for power. Taen would face her brother in Kisburn's court again; but with the Sathid's psychic strength now linked through her gift, she would learn more of his character than she ever wished to know. . . .

Emien ran full tilt down the corridor leading from the King's apartments, unaware his movements were observed by his sister and an alien matrix. "Wait!" he called after the small blond footpage who raced ahead of him. "You promised."

But the child, who was barely twelve and a recent addition to Kisburn's household, hesitated only an instant, then ducked through the portal which led to the King's private orchard.

Emien swore in exasperation. Though exertion went poorly with his best velvet tunic and fine silk shirt, he put on speed and hurried after. He caught the heavy door panel before it swung closed and sprinted down the steps. Cold struck through his thin sleeves. Dead grass crackled under his boots, stiff with winter frost, as he dodged between the statuary of an ornamental fountain; the basin stood clogged with ice and dead leaves. Emien cursed again, annoyed by the fact he had left his cloak behind. But the boy he chased must be equally chilled, clad as he was in the royal livery.

"Stop!" Emien called. "Do you always keep your word this loosely?"

But the page never slackened pace. Emien caught a glimpse of maroon brocade through the bare boughs of the fruit orchard, and with a scowl of black anger he leapt the stone wall and pursued. Twigs scraped his face as he fended the branches away from his clothes and his breath clouded on the frigid air, but gradually he closed with the child, who ducked like a frightened rabbit into the densest part of the orchard. A scant step behind, Emien reached out and closed his fist in light blond hair.

The page yowled and tripped over a root. Yanked off balance, Emien missed stride. Both boys rammed into the unforgiving trunk of a pear tree.

Scuffed by bark and the sharp ends of numerous twigs, Emien scowled down at the footpage who had nearly caused him to tear his best shirt. "You're a nuisance," he said sharply.

The page lifted his chin, frightened of the older boy but determined not to cower. He leaned against the tree, panting heavily from his run, and refused to answer.

"When does Tathagres go for audience with the King?" demanded Emien. "The lists were written this morning. Surely you've seen them by now. Did you think I gave you that silver for amusement alone?" He caught the page's collar and twisted the cloth cruelly around the child's throat. "We had an agreement. Dare you break it?"

White-faced, the page shook his head.

Emien released his hold, dusted his hands on his tunic. "I thought not." His tone turned peevish. "Fires! It's not as though you were giving away state secrets, or anything. Now give. When does Tathagres have audience?"

The smaller boy swallowed and wiped his nose. "Tomorrow," he said miserably. "Did you have to mess up my tabard?"

"Did you have to run me around the King's gardens?" Emien mimicked. He rummaged in his pocket and tossed a double copper to the ground by the child's feet. "Give this to the maid. If she complains, tell her you were lucky to get off so lightly."

The page regarded the coin with visible reluctance. Although his skin was blue with chill, he waited, shivering under the trees, until Emien had gone. Then in a fit of helpless rage he stamped the coin again and again into the weeds before he returned to the palace.

In her capsule beneath the ground on the Isle of the Vaere, Taen experienced the footpage's humiliation as though it were her own. For the first time since her dream began, she recognized the increase in her ability as a dream-reader. As yet oblivious to her peril, she tested her new powers and found she could skip from Emien's consciousness into the minds of others in his presence. The experience excited her, went to her head like wine. And like the nestling discovering the first use of its wings, she decided to accompany her brother when he went to spy on the audience between King Kisburn and the witch Tathagres. The Sathid did not object. Her response to Emien's cruelty precisely followed the pattern it sought to establish.

The Sathid and Taen waited with Emien as he crouched in the dusty darkness of the hidden passage behind the audience chamber. Exhilarated by his own daring, he pressed his eye to the small spy hole concealed by the room's ornate decor. On a bet, he had bested the chamber guard three times with practice foils, with access to the passage his claimed forfeit. The guard was an unimaginative fellow; linked with the Sathid's powers, Taen picked up the man's feelings without effort.

Though relieved not to be losing his beer money, the guard had agreed reluctantly to Emien's plan. He could be tried for treason if the boy were discovered. But gambling of any sort was forbidden to the guard, and the boy could cost him a month's docked pay if the captain was informed of their wager. Like many another in Kisburn's court, the guard placed little trust in Emien's scruples; Tathagres' young squire had a look of dangerous ambition about him, and his dicey temper was certainly no secret. He was fast becoming the sort of person nobody wanted to cross.

While the guard sweated at his post, Emien studied the officials present in the council chamber. Only three of the King's advisors were present. As usual, Lord Sholl sat to the right of the throne, bald head tilted behind his hand while he whispered in the royal ear. To the left of the arras stood the court's grand Conjurer, a position held by any of three sorcerers who currently held the King's favor. Tathagres had not yet arrived. As a boy raised to a fisherman's poverty, Emien stared, still enthralled by the presence of the King.

His Grace of Kisburn was slender, stooped, and barely thirty-three. He had a face like a mouse, quick, shifty eyes which missed very little, and a mind whetted to a fine nervous edge. His aspirations knew no bounds. Though he looked like a sickly scholar, engulfed in his heavy robes of state, the idea of conquest obsessed him. He ruled with a quick sharp hand, and if dissidents at court claimed he listened a bit too readily to Lord Sholl, his Grace the Ninth Sovereign of Kisburn never made foolish decisions. Emien watched with envious fascination as the King shook his head in denial. Lord Sholl straightened in his chair, lips puckered with displeasure. For a moment he looked as if he might speak again. But the King waved his hand impatiently, dismissing the issue, and that moment the doors opened to admit Tathagres. The King glanced up expectantly.

Emien leaned closer to the spy hole, rapt with anticipation. Today his mistress intended to end the long months of waiting. If the King approved her proposal, they would return to assault Cliffhaven with an army, and at long last Anskiere would fall. Taen, as observer, suppressed her dismay. Unless she remained passive, her brother would discover her presence and raise defenses against her.

Tathagres strode boldly into the audience chamber, unencumbered by her usual court finery. Emien was startled to find her clad in a man's heavy riding leathers, boots, tunic, and breeches impeccably brushed and a cloak of dyed wool falling in luxurious scarlet folds from her shoulders. Except for Lord Sholl, the advisors regarded her with stiff disapproval as she bowed neatly before the royal dais.

Tathagres unpinned the brooch at her throat and flicked her cloak over her arm with an air of confidence difficult to disregard. Emien was forced to admire her tactics. In a court entangled with corruption and intrigue, Tathagres abandoned any feminine wiles; with an air of uncompromising directness, she brought nothing to the audience chamber but the sure recognition of her own power. And though custom demanded that the King speak first, her stance gave the impression that she waited for him to petition her for information.

The King leaned eagerly forward, wiry fingers laced together in his lap. "Have you come to tell me your plan concerning Cliffhaven? If not, be brief. My patience is growing short where you are concerned."

Behind the King's shoulder, two of the advisors exchanged surreptitious whispers. With the major war fleet lately smashed to splinters by

Anskiere's storm, most of the court opposed further dealings with Tathagres; shipwrights labored day and night to replace the broken ships, but at least a year had been lost to damages. Only Lord Sholl supported Tathagres, and to the annoyance of many he still held the King's favor.

The witch behaved as if the setback never occurred. "If I bring about the defeat of Cliffhaven, our bargain still stands. With the Kielmark fallen, your passage through Mainstrait would stand unopposed and the Free Isles would lie open for invasion. You will deliver me Keys to Elrinfaer tower then, is that understood?"

One of the advisors stiffened at her affront. "With permission, your Grace." The King nodded irritably, granting him leave to speak. "Lady, may I point out that the loss of the war fleet seriously hampers any invasion campaign at this time?"

Tathagres smiled, her fingers still on the folds of her cloak. "When Cliffhaven falls you may replace your ships." She dismissed the advisor with a slight toss of her head, and addressed her next line to the King. "Why not invade the Free Isles with the Kielmark's fleet? His ships are known to be the finest vessels on Keithland. After his defeat, they will be yours to command as spoils."

The King settled back. Jewels flashed on his doublet as he drew a fast breath. But he tempered his impatience before he spoke. "Defeat Cliffhaven? You jest. Without an inside accomplice, it cannot be achieved."

"It can, your Grace. If you give me leave, I can deliver the fortress intact."

"How?" the King demanded, at last unable to restrain his eagerness. To his left the advisors shifted apprehensively in their chairs. Lord Sholl's expression remained impassive, but he toyed with his rings, his hands betraying his anticipation. To Emien, watching, it seemed as if the first advisor to the King held a stake in Tathagres' plan. But Taen, through the expanded resources of the Sathid matrix, caught the peripheral discomfort of the man's two colleagues; they were very much aware Lord Sholl was party to the witch's schemes, and the idea displeased them hugely.

Having won the edge in her exchange with the King, Tathagres lifted her cloak from her arm and draped it carelessly over the back of a carved chair. "Have I leave to sit, your Grace?"

The King assented with a gesture of annoyance. "How do you propose to take Cliffhaven? Many have tried." He did not belabor the fact that the wreckage of seven royal assault fleets littered the sea bottom beyond the Kielmark's harbor; the former sovereigns of Kisburn had many times emptied their treasuries in attempt to eradicate that den of renegades.

Tathagres arranged herself in the chair with maddening grace, and spoke only after she had settled herself in comfort. "I had other tactics in mind," she opened, as if answering the King's thought. She glanced up at the dais, her violet eyes gone chilly as arctic sunset. "There are those, among Kor's Accursed, who are willing to become your allies. How invincible would Cliffhaven be against a force which included demons?"

CHAPTER XIV

Bid for Mastery

The advisors shot bolt upright and the taller one banged his fist on the table top with a crash that shook the candlesticks. "That's madness!"

"You'll bring about our ruin!" shouted the other. "Kordane's Blessed Fires, witch, no man bargains with demons with impunity. Never in Keithland history has there been a precedent. And may I remind that Kor's Brotherhood will never sanction your alliance. That would enrage the populace, surely as tide, quite possibly provoke a revolt against the crown." The advisor paused for a near-hysterical breath.

But the King spoke before he could continue. "I would hear what motivates the demons, Lady. Why should they wish to support us?"

The advisors subsided with a rustle of brocades, their worry evident, even to Emien who observed still from the peephole. But linked with the Sathid matrix, Taen could perceive their minds directly; both men regarded Lord Sholl with a mixture of panic and admiration. His opinion very likely might spring the King's decision beyond prudent limits.

Taen considered Lord Sholl through Emien's eyes, and encountered the same disquiet she remembered from the first time she followed Emien to his apartments, as if the chief advisor's form were somehow draped in shadow. Although she had not attempted direct contact with the man's thoughts, he glanced up and stared at the peephole, perhaps aware someone observed him. Taen felt Emien repress a shiver of discomfort; the secret passage hid him from view, and probably none other than the King knew a peephole existed in the wall. Presently Lord Sholl looked away and Emien found everyone in the chamber had stilled to hear Tathagres' reply.

"The demons have a grievance with Anskiere." She paused a moment, her eyes distracted, as if she collected her thoughts. But a glance at Lord Sholl betrayed otherwise. Judging by his rapt, predatory expression, Emien would have bet silver upon the possibility the chief advisor was privy to her plans.

Tathagres resumed. "They wish the Stormwarden's death and access to the sanctuary shrine at Landfast. The Council of the Alliance will certainly defend the Brotherhood's interests; they'll not accept surrender, and for that they must fall. Demons have no scruples, every man knows. They'll direct their own campaign if they must. But since your interests lie along similar lines, why not make an alliance and so preserve the isles under a Kingdom overlord? I can negotiate for his Grace. The consequences shall be mine alone, this I promise."

Lord Sholl touched the King's sleeve, leaned close, and spoke into the royal ear. None in the room heard his counsel. But Taen, quickly becoming more adept with her added powers, quite easily tapped the royal mind with no one the wiser for her prying. She overheard the chief advisor's whisper as clearly as if the man had directed his advice to her.

"My King, you must be aware of the ramifications of this. The woman is in league with demon powers and has been for quite some time. Better Kisburn controlled her than leave the option for an enemy to exploit."

Taen detected the fact the King's intereest was engaged. As a spoiled product of a decadent court, Kisburn held a suppressed fascination for the forbidden, interlaced like thread through a tangle of morbid curiosity. Beneath the state concerns which framed his desire for expansion, he ached to level Cliffhaven, at last eliminate the Kielmark's humiliating demands for tribute on shipping through the straits. Kisburn also coveted the Free Isles, saw their addition to the Kingdom as vindication for an early and shameful defeat at the council table. Taen picked up enough echoes of passion underlying the royal ambitions to convince her; with very little encouragement, the King could be persuaded to accept Tathagres' proposal, dangerously immoral though it was.

Taen withdrew, distressed by her discovery. With Emien involved, her worst fears would be realized should demons be called into alliance by Tathagres. She could not allow such heresy to proceed unimpeded. Her loyalty to her brother lay too deep. Somehow she would reach him, set him free of Tathagres' influence. Yet even as she resolved to act, the Sathid within her gathered itself expectantly; the trap it had set to bring about her defeat was nearly ready to be sprung.

Beyond the peephole the advisors groped, desperately trying to raise an argument to counter Tathagres' proposal. "You suggest heresy," said the stouter of the two. He clutched his chain of office as if it were a fragment of the Blessed Relic, proof against the works of Kor's Accursed. "How dare you encourage your King to transgress Kordane's Law? The arch priests should have you burned."

Slowly, maddeningly, Tathagres smiled. "Let them try." She paused, and for a single fleeting instant her expression sobered. Only her eyes brightened with the same joyous challenge Emien recalled from the time she had commanded him to land the pinnace on Skane's Edge. In link with him, Taen felt the chills which prickled the length of her brother's spine. But she had no time to trace the cause of his uneasiness before Tathagres resumed.

Her tone was deceptively soft. "The truth is, they dare not lay hands on me."

The grand Conjurer caught his breath, his sallow complexion gone pale. He froze like a painted icon in his seat by the King's left hand and beyond him the advisors fidgeted, suddenly sweating above the stiff cloth of their collars. Taen needed no empathic skills to understand how greatly they feared Tathagres' powers. No man on the dais could touch her with impunity. Only Lord Sholl and the King seemed unconcerned by the woman's implied threat. The rubies in the chief advisor's rings flashed as he laced his fingers together on the table top; his colleagues' discomfort served only to amuse him. And a rushed glimpse of Kisburn's thoughts showed him weighing possible ways of evading the justice of Kor's Brotherhood, should the alliance prove viable. If anything, the added edge of danger in the plan attracted him the more. Now frantic to avert a decision all but complete, Taen turned her Sathid-born talents upon the disingenuous person of the King's chief advisor.

Her probe went amiss. Accustomed to the layered configuration of the human mind, its fixed preoccupation of past memories and learned passions, Taen was immediately baffled by hazy fields of patterns, a snarled confusion of sensation human reason could not sort. The alienness of the images overwhelmed her and she faltered. That instant, something slammed closed around her mind.

Dizzied, isolated, Taen strove to recover her balance. For a second she sensed the shape of the forces which sought to hold her trapped. Their strangeness defied comprehension. Alarmed, Taen tapped her reserves, and with a sharp stroke severed the link. There followed a flurried moment of confusion. When at last her inner vision cleared, Taen found herself restored to Emien's perception.

He crouched in the dust-dry darkness behind the peephole, doubled over by an excruciating pain in his head. Hammered by the effects of a backlash he did not understand, the boy moaned. He pressed a hand to his aching brow. And through the discomfort her own interference had brought upon him, Taen heard Lord Sholl's voice ring out across the council chamber.

"There is a spy present, your Grace. Did you place an observer behind the wall?"

Both advisors exclaimed in surprise, cut short by curt orders from the King. The doors to the audience chamber banged open. And through the jabbing waves of discomfort in his head, Emien realized the feet which thundered down the aisle outside belonged to royal men-at-arms sent to apprehend him. The wave of panic which shot through him disrupted Taen's equilibrium. She had no time to consider her peculiar encounter with the chief advisor's mind before Emien rose, slamming his elbow clumsily against the wall.

"Kor!" exclaimed the Conjurer. "There *is* someone back there."

That moment, the access door to the passage crashed open. Dust eddied against sudden light as guardsmen shouldered through. Emien whirled to run. Almost immediately a mailed fist closed over his wrist. The guard yanked him around, shoved his face toward the door.

"Fires!" The soldier's voice carried an unmistakable note of disgust. "You're nothing but a squire." He hauled Emien out of the passage, but his grip on the boy's arm became slightly less punishing. Frightened but defiant, Emien permitted the guardsman to escort him down the corridor and on through the portals of the audience chamber.

Over the chatter of the advisors Emien heard Tathagres speaking in a tone entirely free of inflection. ". . . My personal squire, your Grace. No, I did not send him to spy. He did so upon his own initiative."

Held pinioned in the grip of the guardsmen, Emien glared sullenly up at the men on the dais. The advisors' agitation had mellowed into speculative curiosity and the Conjurer simply looked bored. Only Lord Sholl regarded Tathagres' black-haired squire with the tireless intensity of a carrion bird, until Emien flinched and turned away.

His Grace of Kisburn tapped agitated fingers against the pearl buttons on his cuff, his expression sour with displeasure. "Take him away," he said to the guards. "I would have him questioned later, to determine whether his behavior warrants a trial."

"No!" Tathagres rose sharply from her chair. Her cloak slithered unheeded to the floor and the clink as the brooch struck the tiles sounded like a cry of distress against the silence. "The boy is mine. None will lay hands on him. I demand that he be released at once."

"You're impertinent," snapped the King. "How badly do you want the Keys to Elrinfaer?"

"How badly do you want Cliffhaven?" Tathagres tilted her head, and with an imperious grace no court woman could equal, touched her fingers lightly to the neck band at her throat.

Between the guardsmen, Emien started. The movement attracted Lord Sholl's attention. His gaze intensified upon the boy, and with an unexpected thrust of force, Taen felt him seek contact with her brother's mind. How the chief advisor had acquired a dream-reader's talent remained a mystery, but his touch was crude. Emien noticed the presence which sought to exploit his thoughts. Hair prickled at the back of his neck. In attempt to disrupt the intrusion, he gasped and flung back against the guardsmen's hold.

The King sat sharply forward, antagonized by the disturbance. But the royal displeasure had no effect upon Lord Sholl. He brushed past Emien's discomfort, rummaged ruthlessly to discover whether the boy still harbored the source of the touch which had molested him earlier at the council table. Rather than reveal her presence, Taen withdrew, darting like a fish into shallows out of reach. Presently Lord Sholl abandoned his search. But his expression of annoyance bespoke the fact that he would forget nothing until his suspicions concerning Emien were fully satisfied.

"You will release my squire," said Tathagres to the King. "I tell you he is mine. Would you contest me?" She phrased her words politely, but Taen saw into her heart and read murder there. And during the moment the girl tested the witch's intentions, a portion of Tathagres' mind engaged with a presence within the golden band at her throat. Although her body remained standing before the King of Kisburn in the palace audience chamber, her thoughts traversed a vista of darkness.

Swept along by the dream link, Taen accompanied the witch into a dimension of nightmare. Wind arose, buffeting her like the rustle of bats flying from their roosts at twilight. She recoiled, repelled. But the tenacity born of her island upbringing lent the girl strength to overcome shaken nerves. She clung to the contact. Presently the suffocating blanket of shadow dissolved into light, as red as sunrise viewed through thunderheads.

The illumination brightened, flared suddenly to blinding intensity. Sensing the advent of evil, Taen battled an urge to withdraw. Suddenly a wave of savage spite overpowered her. Through the window of Tathagres' consciousness, the girl perceived the demon faces of Emien's dream. Only this time the vision was direct and imminently threatening. Taen held on for her brother's sake. Though blistered by the ferocity of the demons' hatred, Taen reached beyond, to partial understanding of their intentions. Not only did Kor's Accursed grant Tathagres her power, they sought control of Emien as well.

"No!" Taen's horrified protest reverberated through the fabric of her contact, and snapped the dream link a bare second before Tathagres engaged with the demons. Yanked back to Emien's perspective, Taen felt an unseen force strike the hands which restrained her brother's wrists. The guardsmen shouted and staggered back, releasing their grip. Weapons held no edge against sorcery; deaf to the King's shouted command, the soldiers fled the chamber, unwilling to risk further contact with the boy.

"Don't try my tolerance, your Grace," said Tathagres, unmoved by the commotion set off by her action. The advisors watched, white with alarm, as she bent and retrieved her cloak. "I will await your reply, but not long. My patience, like my time, is limited." And with a nonchalance which bordered on insolence, she motioned Emien to her side and departed.

The boy followed on his mistress's heels, barely able to refrain from gloating. He discovered a bitter, vindictive pride in Tathagres' manipulation of the King, and, inspired by a wish to emulate her skills, he quickly regained his shaken confidence. Taen pulled back, sickened. Peripheral emotions still leaked from the audience chamber, pervading her dreamsense; through the advisor's dismayed affront, she felt the King's appetite for risk bite into her awareness with the cruelty of a spring frost. There could be no doubt; he would choose the demons' alliance, if only to intimidate his rivals.

Taen tempered her distress with a stout resolve. She would stop the corruption of her brother. Trained by the Vaere to dream-read and heartened by confidence in her increased powers, she decided to attempt contact with Anskiere once again. Perhaps now she could call him back to her brother's aid. Except that the instant her young determined heart became dedicated to that quest, the Sathid rose up to prevent her.

The alien matrix pinned her thoughts without warning, then struck a psychic blow which sent her reeling back, stunned and surprised and in agony. At first unaware the entity which opposed her used the same powers she controlled scant seconds before, Taen felt herself plunged back into the mind of her brother, but deeper than she had ever ventured previously. She fell, as if into darkness. And poignant as a minor arpeggio of harp strings, emotions pierced her until her whole mind rang in concert with the boy's unbearable pain.

"Your brother Emien is a cruel man, his deeds unfit for forgiveness," said the Sathid within her mind, its voice framed as her own, or perhaps that of her mother. Laced in the depths of nightmare like a fish in a gill net, Taen tried to raise her voice in denial. But her throat pinched closed and no words passed her lips.

"See for yourself," continued the voice of the accuser, and Taen found herself unable to close her eyes against the vision which battered her awareness.

She saw her brother Emien stride the length of *Crow's* pinnace, a length of knotted cord in his fist. The boat tossed, her bowsprit flung skyward by wave crests which thundered and crashed over the razor fangs of a reef. Emien threatened the rowers in a voice gone ugly with rage. And with the same hand he had used to dry Taen's tears as a child, he lifted his lash and brought it down with all his strength on the helpless backs of his oarsmen.

Taen shouted denial, but her protest went unheard. Blood flowed down the naked backs of the men, spilled in thick drops to mingle with the bilge, while Emien shouted like a madman, sounding more and more like his Uncle Evertt.

"No!" Taen shouted. "It's not true!" But vividly etched by her gift the details said otherwise. The pinnace slammed into rock with a boom that deafened thought. And Taen fell, through a dying man's cry of agony, into darkness once more.

The Sathid pursued, hounding her with remorseless certainty. "Your brother is a murderer, a breaker of the codes of life. Let him be condemned."

Taen whimpered in protest. But through the firelit boughs of a forest glen, she watched Emien select a rounded stone, and with a clean, vindictive throw, end the life of an elderly man. The victim crumpled, lay still in the wilted folds of his black cloak. And stung into action by fierce disbelief, Taen searched the mind of her brother. His memory confirmed the scene she had witnessed, the emotions etched by the remorse of an act best forgotten.

Taen retreated, stunned. Emien was no longer the tormented but guiltless brother she had loved on Imrill Kand. Somewhere, somehow, he had become hardened and insensitive in a manner not even his mother would accept. Wounded by the change and unable to adjust, Taen abandoned herself to pain. And anticipating victory, the Sathid moved to imprison her.

While the girl's will lay passive, it fashioned barriers, using the shattered remnants of her faith. The instant her love for Emien shifted to hatred, her confinement would be complete. The Sathid paused for a moment to gloat. How very smoothly its takeover had proceeded; the girl hardly resisted at all.

Absorbed by her grief, Taen felt an echo of the Sathid's triumph. The emotion rang false. Whether Emien had murdered or not, she could not abandon him to Tathagres' demons. Rededicated to her earlier resolve, her emotions polarized, and at once she recognized the image and the voice to be that of an enemy. Not Lord Sholl; this one knew her, used her mind and her memories against her in an attempt to break her spirit.

Taen struck back. With the anger of the betrayed she smashed through the Sathid's grip, recalled the image of the victim Emien had struck down with his stone. But this time she viewed the completed action and recognized the man in the black cloak as Hearvin, one of Anskiere's oppressors and evil in his own right.

"Liar!" she acccused the Sathid. "Who gave you the right to meddle?"

"I need no right," the Sathid replied. "I am a part of you." And as Taen paused to question the statement, the matrix added, "See for yourself."

Taen focused her scrutiny inward. With every available discipline Tamlin had taught her, she examined the source of the Sathid's intervention and discovered it to be inextricably linked with her powers as dream-weaver, its character a mirror image of her own. The Sathid had spoken the truth; the opponent she faced was herself. Yet because that self had encouraged her to abandon her brother, break the integrity of her upbringing upon Imrill Kand, Taen perceived the matrix to be the dark side to her character, that flawed facet of selfishness which sought to overturn gentleness and love with discontent.

"You see," said the Sathid. "We are one. To oppose me is to deny your own resources."

But words did little to ease Taen's suspicion. To follow the Sathid's logic was to invite the same mistake Emien had made to the detriment of his own self-worth. And as the survivor of misfortune which had left her a cripple in a society where bodily health was a necessity, Taen had already accepted the fact she could never be whole. She would reject the Sathid's proposal though she had to suffer lifelong deprivation. And because she believed its interference to be an extension of her own small-mindedness, she condemned it ruthlessly, left not the smallest quarter for argument.

"I will help my brother no matter what he has done," said Taen firmly.

The Sathid returned with a laugh which bounced demonic echoes across the fields of her awareness. "You're an idealistic fool. Do you truly know the brother you intend to save? I think not. For Emien is becoming someone far different than the brother you grew up with. If you try to help him now, it is apparent by his character he would kill you."

"No!" Taen pulled back, tried to thrust the irritating presence from her mind. But it was part of herself, and inseparable. She found no release from her nightmare.

"If you look, you will see," invited the Sathid.

And challenged by her own self-honesty, Taen sought the measure of its statement. "Show me. But I'll not be convinced by half truths. If Emien is evil, let me see for myself."

Goaded by the Sathid's cold reasoning, Taen sought her brother, sank downward into the limitless wells of Emien's subconscious, through territory within his mind unknown even to himself. She visited a landscape of insecurity. Sensitive to a fault, Emien saw his early years as a siege against the relentless and wounding concerns of his elders; the pressures of survival on Imrill Kand allotted no space for his fears. With only Evertt to share the workload, necessity often forced Marl to ask his young son to shoulder a man's load. Isolated by his perception, Emien hid his suffering, strove to meet expectations too great for a child to master. Life became a ruthless experience, a joyless siege of endurance. He despised the hardship, for it exposed his weaknesses without mercy.

Taen unraveled his personality with utmost patience. Tangled at the core of his being, she found Emien longed secretly to inflict cruelty, as if causing hurt to others might somehow ease his starved feeling of inadequacy. Yet twisted desires alone did not make a criminal. Desperate in her care, Taen searched further.

She traced the emotions underlying her brother's admiration for Anskiere. The Stormwarden alone had breached the boy's melancholy following the death of his father. Taen explored the trust which had grown between the sorcerer and her brother firsthand. The contact initially had been a fragile thing, tenuous as the miracle of birth or a light in the darkness of midwinter. Through the sorcerer's guidance, Emien discovered happiness and laughter and the bright new joy of self-acceptance for the first time. The news of Tierl Enneth and Anskiere's guilt had fallen with the devastation of a cataclysm. The fact that he had given his innermost love to a condemned man whose crimes were beyond human pardon threw Emien into towering, ungovernable fury. All his frail new stability collapsed like sand castles bashed flat by the tide.

The blow of that discovery sheared through Taen's defenses. She experienced the panic Emien had known as he raged, blinded by the brutal solitude of betrayal. Through the dream link, the sister experienced the fear, the horror, and finally the first sour seeds of resentment. For Emien never accepted responsibility for his own unhappiness. If Anskiere had brought down ruin and death with the same powers he had sworn to the protection of Tierl Enneth, all that he lived was a lie. His teaching left

Emien vulnerable, and another victim for the spoiling unkindness of fate. Driven by a venomous tide of bitterness, the boy wished he had never tasted the illusion Anskiere had brought: that life could reward a man who aspired to develop his strengths, and that security and happiness were things of faith within reach of any who strove. Feeling his contentment slip forever beyond reach, Emien abandoned belief.

Scourged by the sharing of her brother's loss, Taen beheld the birth of his ultimate desire. Emien sought a way to crush the fear which lurked within the darkest center of his being; he wished a weapon, power great enough to ensure that no man nor sorcerer nor any agency of fate's design should ever judge and find him wanting. Never again would he suffer manipulation at the hands of one he loved. For now he trusted no one.

Imprisoned behind the brickwork of an untenable position, his spirit ached for release. Taen perceived that her brother's misery knew no limits and understood none. He could not achieve peace without first acknowledging failure; and goaded by Tathagres' contempt, Emien found it simpler to kill.

He believed his sister had died, drowned without mercy by Anskiere's hand during the foundering of the galleass *Crow.* To accept her as alive, safeguarded by that same sorcerer's hand, was to negate what had come to be the foundation of his existence. And though he did not yet know the extent of the wretchedness his suffering had created, Taen beheld the truth the Sathid had foretold. Emien would murder before he would forgive himself the error of condemning Anskiere, even if the life he took was that of his own sister.

The Sathid poised itself; the moment it awaited had come to pass. The girl's loyalty surely would crumble under the knowledge, and in that instant, when the impact of rejection weakened her, the matrix would achieve permanent dominance over her will.

Taen felt the first stir of the Sathid's expectancy. She pushed it back, sharply and as unreasonably as a spoiled child. All but undone by the loss of her brother's trust, she did not welcome its intrusive sharing of her grief. No logic could console her loss. The Sathid waited with the cold patience of a serpent. It had measured Taen's vulnerability and extrapolated from there, centering its attack upon the one event which would create her greatest distress; the outcome was as inevitable as frost at the end of summer. After years spent judging Taen's character, the matrix anticipated that pain would shortly break her spirit.

But the moment never came. To Taen, daughter of generations of fishermen who had braved the caprice of ocean storms, Emien was not lost until he was dead. If the Stormwarden could not spare her brother, at least he would know a way to alleviate the boy's misery. The girl roused herself. She would seek Anskiere. And pressured by the dogged edge of her determination, the Sathid discovered it had underestimated her capacity to hope.

The conflict now was joined, with no advantage left but surprise. As Taen reached for the power to bridge the distance to the ice cliffs, the Sathid lashed out. It struck with the physical agony she had known when the crate crushed her ankle, its intent to throw her off balance.

Stabbed by a white-hot wave of pain, Taen perceived the Sathid for an enemy. Although it had merged with her mind, its will was a separate entity, and now it stood as a barrier between her and Anskiere, who offered Emien's sole chance of deliverance. Dizzied by the savagery of the matrix's attack, she clung to consciousness with the desperate grip of a sailor cast adrift on a spar. To yield was to invite oblivion. And having mastered the torment of injury once before, Taen endured. She would not give in to torture. She had seen into Emien's wounded spirit, and death itself could not make her choose the same self-betrayal.

"I will reach Anskiere." Her words emerged mangled by suffering, but her intent was fixed. "Set me free."

The Sathid shifted focus, assaulted her mind with a score of hurtful images compiled from her memory. Taen watched the houses of Imrill Kand smashed to a snarl of weathered gray boards by the fury of an ocean storm. The matrix showed her the same desolation the inhabitants of Tierl Enneth had known when Anskiere's powers destroyed their homes and families. Icy gusts flattened her skirts against her knees, hampering her steps as she trod the choked remains of the village streets. Beneath the slivered beams of her cousins' home, she discovered the bones of the Stormwarden she sought, knotted like tide wrack in the tattered wool of his cloak. The skull regarded her acccusingly, eye sockets clogged with sand.

"No!" Taen wrenched against the Sathid's hold, forcing the scene to dissolve. She tried to counter its ugliness with her own memories of beauty, but the images twisted in her mind, corrupted by the matrix; as she reached for spring wildflowers on the tors of Imrill Kand, her hands grasped withered thorns. The warmth of the solstice fires blew away as dust transformed to stinging sleet, and the small violet shells she had once collected on the beaches at low tide rotted as she touched them. The Sathid's malice knew no limits. Unwilling to watch everything she loved desecrated by its spite, the girl sought the coarse mind of the fish trapper Tamlin had often borrowed for her training.

And as nothing about the fish trapper's existence had ever been dear to her, the Sathid found no hold to exploit. It hesitated, thrown off balance, and in that instant, Taen's will predominated. Her dream-sense cleared. She saw herself once again through Emien's eyes. He sat, limp and trembling on a bench in the palace courtyard. Tathagres supported his elbow, her expression sharply concerned.

"What happened?" she demanded. "Did you faint?"

Taen guessed at once that her conflict with the Sathid had not proceeded without effect on her brother's mind. Even as the matrix gathered itself for a second assault, she felt the boy's painful confusion, and saw also that Tathagres' sympathy masked deeper feelings, strung like beads on a wire of mistrust. Yet the Sathid allowed no scope to explore further. Like a swimmer rising for a gasp of air, Taen gripped her brother's mind with inarguable firmness and forced speech past his lips.

"I'm a little dizzy," the boy replied. "The guardsmen weren't very gentle when they caught me." And before she released him, Taen cast a veil of confusion over her brother's thoughts, that the disorientation he had experienced following his departure from the King's audience chamber could not be too clearly examined. Then as the Sathid sprang to engage her once more, she dove down through a twisting spiral of space and time to the dockside inn of an island village, where a familiar and boring acquaintance clad yet in reeking oilskins stood beneath a shuttered window, begging the favors of a buxom tavern wench.

The Sathid sensed the fact that its control was slipping. Unprepared for the defensive, it scrambled for strategy, but found nothing in Taen's recollection to suggest her reason for seeking the personality of the fish trapper. Denied any direction, the matrix chose the familiar. In the same manner as it had transformed Taen's memories of the shells and the wildflowers and the solstice fires, the Sathid fixed on her object of concentration and created the illusion of its opposite.

Taen's opinion of the fish trapper's method of courtship was precisely defined, no trial for the Sathid to encompass. And the simplistic mind of the fish trapper provided an easy opening. With full command of a dreamreader's skills, the matrix shaped its resistance and altered the fellow's perception.

Standing chilled but hopeful amid the frost-browned stems of last season's herb garden, the fish trapper experienced brief disorientation. The instant his muddled senses cleared, he discovered a spray of seven red roses clutched in his callused hand. Shocked speechless by the sight of flowers in the dead of winter, he noticed the remainder of the Sathid's illusions more reluctantly. For nothing about him was the same.

The mildewed oilskins stood replaced by a cloak of brushed gray felt. His hip-high, fishy-smelling boots disappeared, transformed into soft calf leggings with silver buttons and embroidered cuffs. And the wild red snarl of hair and whiskers which habitually buried the man's neck and most of his features appeared clean and neatly trimmed, revealing an expression of bug-eyed astonishment.

He swallowed twice and raised a trembling finger to touch one of the roses. A thorn scraped his knuckle. Convinced the illusion was madness, he shouted aloud in disbelief.

The noise displeased the object of his passion. Above his head the shutters banged open and the tavern wench thrust her head out, her mouth opened for carping complaint. With its ruse nearly ruined, the Sathid was forced to intervene. It included the woman in its dream spell and extravagantly added a velvet waistcoat to the fisherman's attire.

And finding the suitor beneath her window was not the tiresome pest who brought the reek of cod into her taproom each evening, the woman yelled with predatory delight. Here stood a clean, strapping fellow who obviously had wealth by the look of his clothing; and roses in winter were a luxury no island doxie could expect unless she were courted by royalty. This one never hesitated. She smiled, hiding her broken tooth with her tongue, and swooped over the sill to be kissed. The fish trapper's eyes went wide at the sight of what bounced within inches of his nose. And unable to contain her humor over the fish trapper's ridiculous predicament, Taen burst into peals of laughter.

The Sathid recoiled in dismay. In the spectrum of human emotions, ridicule lay furthest from the cowering dejection of defeat. And having only Taen's upbringing within the harsh environment of Imrill Kand on which to draw conclusions, it understood very little of humor, except that its attempt to intimidate had failed. Flustered, it abandoned the structure of its attack.

Caught with her face half-smothered in the greasy beard of the fish trapper, the tavern wench emitted a muffled yell. She tried to yank back, but the fellow by now had thrust a fist inside her blouse. Bleached linen tore with hardly a pretext of modesty. The woman yelled again, while her suitor stared crestfallen at a bodice stuffed with woolen rags.

The sight reduced Taen to a quivering paroxysm of mirth. In vain the Sathid tried to reestablish its hold; but the comical expression on the fish trapper's face overwhelmed the girl, and her hysterical laughter could not be controlled. Baffled by frustration the matrix withdrew, and above the capsule which sheltered Taen's body, meter after meter quivered and dropped within the green sectors of the dials. The Vaere, standing by, recorded the fact. The girl had triumphed in her struggle for supremacy. Her laughter gradually dwindled to manageable proportions. She had defeated the Sathid and claimed the full command of a dream-reader's powers for her own.

Taen barely paused to acknowledge the victory. The instant she discovered her will was no longer contested, she collected her scattered thoughts. Though every nerve cried out for rest, she called her dream-reader's skills into focus. For Emien's sake she drove outward once more, and sought the sorcerer Anskiere.

CHAPTER XV

Anskiere's Geas

The ice cliffs reared above Cliffhaven's northern headland, white against the dirtier gray of storm clouds. Beneath, voracious winter seas chiseled the spellbound ice into caverns. Spray struck with stinging fury more bitter than any seasonal cold, and the air bit with the brittle edge of an Arctic night. Here, Taen returned to seek the sorcerer Anskiere.

This time she saw the wards, made visible through the expanded awareness of the Sathid link. Shifting curtains of blue-violet light radiated like a corona from the cliff face. Taen traced their energies deep into the earth, layer upon interlocking layer, in search of the Stormwarden's presence. Frost pervaded her senses, enfolded her innermost mind with the white desolation of a snowfall. But the energies which had disoriented her before now parted cleanly. Although the powers Taen had won from the matrix granted no influence over weather, Anskiere's works were Sathid-borne; seen through the lens of her newfound mastery, their structure was comprehensible. And following a pattern intricate as the laces woven by the elderly women on Imrill Kand, Taen unraveled the spell toward its source. The whistles of the frostwargs echoed distantly, with overtones as dreadful as she remembered. But Taen passed them by, untroubled by the crippling fear of her former experience. Soon, at the vortex of the wards, she confronted the cone of silence and darkness which had formerly defeated all her skills.

She paused there to renew her concentration. No cause which held Anskiere confined would be slight. Already weary from her battle with the Sathid, she dared not tap the final ward with less than total caution. Here misjudgment might prove fatal; and a single slip could easily cause damage beyond any power in Keithland to mend. Taen cast forth her dream-sense with a touch of utmost delicacy, and spun awareness like a cocoon around the barrier to sound the most central of Anskiere's defenses.

The configuration she encountered proved to be strangely familiar. Through the expanded perception of her dream-sense, Taen recognized the triple ring of force which once shot blazing bands of light around the wings of the stormfalcon she had released from the galleass *Crow*. But now Tamlin's schooling granted her more complete understanding. The interlace of power shaped the defense wards of a sorcerer's staff; a single touch would kill any being not attuned to their resonance. But Taen sensed a flaw in the structure.

Something about the ward's continuity seemed amiss. Its symmetry stood less than perfect, as if something sometime had struck its harmony slightly out of balance. Taen explored the anomaly with her dream-sense. The wards had certainly been disrupted, if only slightly. Resonance of tampering lingered still, and its nature made Taen spring taut with alarm. Someone with unfriendly intentions had entered here before her. Their passage had left a gap in the defenses. Although Taen held insufficient knowledge to assess the full extent of the damage, she recognized the touch behind the sorcery. Whoever had intruded upon the Stormwarden had been the instrument of Kor's Accursed; the culprit was certain to be Tathagres herself.

Discovery and revelation roused Taen to rage. When the witch had magically transported herself and Emien to Kisburn's court, the powers she manipulated had surely been Anskiere's; she had once tapped his staff to raise the sea at Tierl Enneth. Suddenly frightened for the Stormwarden's safety, Taen thrust her dream-sense recklessly past the wards and sounded what lay beyond.

She encountered Anskiere's awareness, sharp and immediate and demanding as the living presence she recalled when the sorcerer controlled the weather on Imrill Kand, but with one difference. Anskiere slept, his will quiescent, as if he hoarded his resources for a day of awakening yet to come. He seemed undisturbed. Apparently even Tathagres dared not disrupt a sorcerer trained by the Vaere. Softly Taen folded her awareness into the Stormwarden's. So light was her touch that he did not rouse from stasis as she joined with him in his dreaming.

Anskiere's sleep shaped a landscape of broken hopes, sharp with the memory of strife; for seven decades Stormwarden and Firelord had labored, their talents joined to form a single force. Together they had subdued eleven species of Kor's Accursed, and finally undertaken the imprisonment of Keithland's most terrible oppressors, the Mharg-demons from Tor Elshend. Although the two sorcerers had worked, mind within mind, for more years than the life span of most men, Taen found no love between them.

Half buried in the shadows of emotion which cleft the Stormwarden's dream, the girl experienced the venomous, spiteful twists of Ivain Firelord's character. This malice had wounded Anskiere, for he alone remembered Ivain before the Cycle of Fire forever upended his sanity. Anskiere returned such cruelty with sympathy, and once with a trust which nearly proved his ruin. For Ivain had betrayed him at the height of their contest against the Mharg-spawn. The Stormwarden survived and continued alone until he achieved the demons' confinement, but the scarring left by Ivain's malice never healed.

Now Taen beheld the implications of the frostwargs' release; shackled by shared understanding, she saw that Anskiere's life was fully dependent on a Firelord's skills. Tuned to the Stormwarden's aspirations, her dream-sense replicated the decision to release the geas to call the heir of Ivain into service. The choice rebounded with echoes of tragedy. Anskiere fully understood that the boy who answered his summons must someday suffer the fate of the father. No man who attempted the Cycle of Fire escaped its mark of madness. For that reason, Ivain's name was remembered with hatred, though the young man who first accepted his training from the Vaere had been loved for his generosity of spirit.

Burdened by Anskiere's past and by his agonized surrender to the only choice left available to him, Taen tuned her awareness to the spell which shaped his final hope. And since that hope also encompassed the fate of her only brother, she plotted the path of the geas the Stormwarden had shaped to summon the son of Ivain Firelord. The line of force struck out to the northwest, spanning the open sea with the directional clarity of a light beacon. Suspended by the dream link, the girl followed the geas.

Her search began without effort. Guided by the precision of Anskiere's handiwork, Taen sped over the wave crests with the ease of a skipper bird's flight. She traveled unaccountable distance within a matter of seconds, tracking without landmark beneath the flat overcast of the winter sky. Suddenly the spell wavered. Taen faltered. Wrenched by the resonance of violence, she tried to brake her speed. But the geas suddenly exploded around her, its linear progression jagged like crumpled wire into eddies of spent strength.

Overturned by confusion, Taen lost its track. Through a horrid, stunned moment, she tumbled on the edge of the void, struggling to sustain her contact with the place where the geas disrupted into chaos. Her control gradually prevailed. The dream link stabilized. Oriented once more, Taen drifted exhausted. Below her, the snow-covered roofs of a fishing village nestled closely against the slopes of a mountain coastline. Smoke curled from the chimneys, and through perceptions strangely altered by her dream-sense, she smelled the fragrance of birch logs. A crude road led out of the settlement, its switched-back curves rising tier upon tier up the slope until it lost itself into ranks of stunted evergreens.

Taen scanned the village inhabitants with a dream-reader's awareness. But she found nothing more than the simple thoughts of fisher folk, concerned with the mending of nets and baking bread and fretting over the thickness of the ice which choked the harbor; Taen felt it improbable that the subject of Anskiere's hopes would be concealed among such work-aday folk. More likely the heir of Ivain lived farther distant, well beyond the break in the geas created by Tathagres' transfer. Confident of her hunch, Taen abandoned the village, turned her focus northwestward in a direct line from Cliffhaven. Her search carried her across the high drift-bound passes of the Furlains and on through the hill country on the far side, where the trees of Seitforest thrust matted boughs against the winter sky.

There above the bare crowns of the beeches, Taen encountered traces of Anskiere's geas. The pattern was hesitant, visible to her dream-sense as snarled trails of light. It steadied as she progressed, gradually becoming structurally intact. No power coursed across the spell. Like a conduit shattered in midspan, the break beyond the Furlains had disrupted the continuity of the geas Anskiere had designed to summon Ivain's heir to Cliffhaven. But Taen easily read the spell's orientation from the segment which remained. Its path resumed, straight as a draftsman's line across the rolling dells of Seitforest, to end at last in the dooryard of a forester's hut.

There Taen discovered a fair-haired boy about Emien's age, bundled to the neck in furs. His breath frosted on the clear winter air as he grunted, hefting a heavy pack onto the slim frame of a drag-sleigh. By the restless, self-questioning intensity of his thoughts, Taen knew at once she had found the subject of the geas' creation; this slim, unremarkable boy was the Fire-lord's heir and Anskiere's hope of deliverance.

Bare-headed and with cheeks flushed from the cold, the boy never noticed the presence which observed his movements. He fussed irritably with a knot in the cord he had brought to secure the pack to the sleigh, hampered by gloved fingers and the whipping tug of the wind. Never once did he swear. In silence, he worked the tangle free, his brows drawn into a frown over dark brown eyes. Taken by his single-minded preoccupation with the task, Taen paused, her concern momentarily eclipsed by curiosity. She watched the boy lash the pack with painstaking care. He finished with knots as neatly done as any tied by a fisherman's son.

The door to the cabin banged open. The boy looked up. A tall, lean forester clad in a cape of marten emerged, black hair streaked heavily with white tumbled across his shoulders. He crossed to the boy's side and knelt beside the drag-sleigh.

With the caution of a man bred to the wilds, he tested the tension of the cords. Then he straightened, satisfied, and clapped the boy on the shoulder. "Fine job," he said softly. "Did you remember the striker and flint?"

The boy tapped the pouch at his waist, and although he spoke no word, the shy smile which touched his features revealed feelings of fierce pride. The forester's praise was desperately important to him. Sensitive to the fact that the fate of Anskiere, Emien, and perhaps the well-being of Keithland itself depended upon this boy's uncertain shoulders, Taen reached out to sound his thoughts.

Her entry was silent as an owl's flight and her quarry unsuspecting. Called Kerainson Jaric, the boy carried the mark of a recent and painful injury. He worked as apprentice to the forester, Telemark. A silent, earnest lad, Jaric took desperate care in his craft; he pushed himself ceaselessly, as if to overcome some greater deficiency than the weakness of convalescence. But when Taen sought the patterns of his immediate past, she encountered only emptiness and an anguished sense of shame. To her dismay, Kerainson Jaric possessed no conscious memory of his past or his parentage.

His plight moved Taen to pity. With full command of her dream-reader's skills, she reached to find out why, and experienced a disquieting discovery. Jaric's affliction resulted from the combined damage of a head wound dealt by outlaws and the backlash of Tathagres' interference at the time she had disrupted the geas. The boy could be made to remember. But through one stolen glimpse of the past he had forgotten, Taen understood enough to know that restoration of his memory would be doing him no kindness. Yet lacking Jaric's inborn talent on the opposing side, the demons would surely triumph, Anskiere's imprisonment would become permanent, and the Keys to Elrinfaer would fall into Tathagres' hands. Taen withdrew from the boy in the clearing, troubled by the realization that his peaceful life with the forester was destined not to last.

The instant the psychic net of Taen's awareness resumed normal proportions, the Vaere collapsed the time-differential which governed her, restoring the capsule which enclosed her to Keithland's main continuum. The girl within slept peacefully, her hair grown long and as glossy as the plumage of a raven through the lengthy years of her confinement; her body by now had fully matured. But the cycle of Sathid mastery had exacted a heavy toll upon the girl's physical health. The Vaere found her weight dangerously slight and much of her vitality depleted by exhaustion. Should Taen be removed from the capsule's protected environment in her current weakened state, there would be risk of disease; but her sleep patterns were normal. Rest would eventually restore her resilience.

Yet the months to come would develop the prime factors which determined humanity's survival. The Vaere tinkered probability figures as if fretting. Taen had uncovered new information during her passage into mastery. Merged, the facts shaped a picture distinctly threatening. The Vaere computed a second set of extrapolations and deduced potential disaster from the figures; for it appeared that the demons had dared to meddle directly with human politics for the first time since the crash of the *Corinne Dane.* If Taen's perceptions were accurate, the chief advisor to King Kisburn was almost certainly an alien shape-shifter. That posed immeasurable threat as Lord Sholl's influence could be seen behind the King's heated ambition and his decision to trust Tathagres. The Vaere perceived the entire campaign against the Free Isles as a plot to set the Landfast libraries into demon hands. If the Alliance fell, the heritage of humanity would be irreparably lost.

Lights glittered like stars on the consoles as the Vaere sequenced equations. Now more than ever before, Taen's talents as dream-reader were needed; she alone could challenge an alien shape-shifter and disrupt its influence over the affairs of the men it had selected as puppets. But her mastery of the Sathid also left her vulnerable. The Vaere knew that the frail girl its capsule sheltered would be ruthlessly destroyed should the demons discover her existence. Only two held power enough to protect her; the Stormwarden, still helplessly enmeshed in a defense spell to contain the frostwargs, and the untrained heir of Ivain Firelord.

The Vaere drew conclusions from its calculation with something akin to emotion. Taen would need to spend most of the winter inside the capsule recovering her physical strength. During that interval, she must engage her dream-reader's powers, restore Jaric's memory and drive him over the Furlains to the village of Mearren Ard. Once the boy made contact with the sea, Anskiere's geas should begin to resume its effect. The Vaere balanced the odds and found the margin for error nonexistent. Even pressed by the geas' cruel directive, Jaric could not possibly sail for Cliffhaven before spring; by then the armies of Kisburn would already have left for the Straits, with the Kielmark's defeat all but inevitable.

The issue at stake was no longer limited to Taen, or even to the uncertainty of Anskiere's rescue. By the Vaere's analysis mankind's very survival depended upon Kerainson Jaric's potential mastery of the Cycle of Fire. And should Lord Sholl learn from Tathagres that Ivain had left an heir, the demons would hunt the boy down and kill him.

Had the Vaere been human, it might have despaired. The balance of the boy's future rested within Taen's influence as dream-reader and a race against the exigencies of time. For the facts converged with ruthless persistence. Should Jaric fail his inheritance, the demons would achieve their final vengeance against mankind. And the stakes which the Vaere surveyed reflected all the uncertainty of a horse race. Since humanity's preservation lay in Jaric's hands, plainly Taen must send him to the ice cliffs and to Anskiere before Kisburn's armies arrived.

The straps of the drag-sleigh cut deeply into Jaric's shoulders as he yanked it clear of a thicket. Snowfall dusted his hair and melted flakes dripped unpleasantly through his fur collar. Yet Jaric never thought to complain. By midwinter, drifts would lie thick and soft beneath the trees, burying obstacles which now hampered the drag-sleigh's runners. Jaric looked forward to the time when Telemark would lift the oiled frames of the snowshoes down from their peg in the loft. The gap in his memory distressed him less when he had a new task to master.

The forester moved through the snowbound forest with practiced silence. Jaric followed, towing the drag-sleigh gracelessly over a fallen log. The straps bit into his hands and runners grated over bark with a dry metallic ring. Once again the packs snagged on a branch. Snow showered down wetly over Jaric's neck. He paused to shake the ice from his shoulders.

Telemark stopped and glanced back. "Here," he said as the boy labored to catch up. "Let me pull the sleigh for awhile."

Ashamed, Jaric shook his head.

The forester regarded the boy, a stern set to his weathered features. "Jaric," he said at last, "there are rules a man does not break if he lives in the wilds during winter. The first is never to deplete any resource unnecessarily."

Telemark reached out with startling speed and clapped Jaric on the shoulder. The blow was not rough. But it caught the boy squarely and painfully on muscles already worn out by the weight of the sleigh, and he flinched reflexively.

"You're tired." With gentle sympathy, the forester pulled the straps of the drag-sleigh free of Jaric's grip. "If you push yourself to exhaustion, who will help me set camp and build the fire?"

The boy sighed and nodded. He stepped aside while Telemark tugged the sleigh clear of the log. Although the man's face was averted, Jaric understood the forester was still concerned over the fact that he seldom spoke since his recovery from the accident. Occasionally disappointment showed in the forester's manner, though he never troubled to mention the subject.

Jaric bit his lip, watched Telemark haul the drag-sleigh with what seemed careless strength. Yet his rhythmic stride and the unbroken swish of the runners reflected more than years of accumulated skill; the man's haste described frustration. Jaric hated to distress the forester who had granted him shelter and healing; still, he avoided speech. Words disturbed him, created interference patterns whose echoes would not be stilled, as if they represented more than the simple sound of their pronunciation. To speak was to become disoriented, lost in the blackness of the void where memory ended and where the unknown tantalized him endlessly with unanswerable questions. Like a mariner cast adrift in fog-bound waters, Jaric clung to the particulars of the moment. In silence he listened for the marker which would guide him back to the past he had lost.

The weather worsened as afternoon progressed. Blinded by the thickening fall of flakes, Jaric stumbled often into branches and his boot cuffs became packed with ice as he waded through freshly drifted thickets. The terrain grew rougher, sliced by steep-sided gullies and the black unfrozen sheen of running water. Yet the boy pressed on without asking for rest. Telemark halted well ahead of sundown beneath a high shelf of rock. The wind drove the snow in smoking clouds off the exposed crest of the ridge and flakes tumbled, hissing, through the bare poles of a lean-to beneath.

With his back to the rocks, the forester set his boot on the drag-sleigh and leaned crossed arms on his knee. "Do you think you can set up the shelter?"

Jaric smiled, at home with the silent snowbound forest and the prospect of making camp as he never could have been before leaving Morbrith. But no memory of his former helplessness returned to trouble him as he knelt and set his hands to the cords on the sleigh.

Telemark laughed and bent to assist him, "Let me have my bow and two beaver traps. Do you suppose I can lay the traps and bag dinner before you can make camp and start a fire?"

Jaric grinned, yanked off one mitten with his teeth, and tore industriously into the knots.

"Right, then, it's a race," said Telemark. "If you win, I'll begin to teach you the quarterstaff. The wind keeps the snow thin on the bluff. The footing there should be adequate."

The forester unlaced a bundle and pulled forth two steel traps, each with a length of chain ending in a forged ring. Then he strapped on his quiver of arrows, took up his bow and his axe, and disappeared silently into the wood. Jaric barely noted his departure. He unloaded the drag-sleigh with exuberant haste and tugged the patched sailcloth shelter free of its ties. Snow cascaded down his cuffs as he tossed it over the poles of the lean-to, and an icy wind billowed the canvas while he fought to lash the lines to secure it in place. But Jaric was exhilarated by the contest and barely noticed the discomfort. He spread the dropcloth and stacked the supplies safely inside. Then, running and sliding in the fresh-fallen snow, he pulled his mittens on again, seized the straps of the drag-sleigh, and went off in search of firewood.

He returned with a full load, breathless and laughing. Warmed by his exertion, he stripped off his mittens and went to work with flint and striker. Falling snow dampened the shavings. Jaric cupped his hands, huddled against the wind, but the spark fizzled again and again into frustrating curls of smoke. The boy glanced over his shoulder, certain Telemark would arrive at any moment. But when at last he coaxed a small flame from the chips, the forester had not yet returned.

Jaric stacked logs over the blaze with miserly care. Then, elated by his accomplishment, he settled on the empty frame of the drag-sleigh and stretched his boots toward the fire. As the glow of the flames deepened to ruddy gold, the boy listened with every muscle strained taut for the sound of Telemark's step. Snow fell, hissing into the flames like the whispered secrets of ghosts; the birch logs crackled and popped, blackening into ash, while beyond the circle of firelight live branches creaked under winter's burden of ice. The wet patches on his leggings steamed and slowly dried. Jaric pulled his cloak hood over his head and tried not to worry. Often Telemark moved with such quiet that wild animals themselves did not hear him. If he was delayed, chances were the storm had made the game scarce.

But the first logs crumbled into coals without his return. Daylight slowly failed and twilight shrouded the wood beyond the ring of firelight. Jaric rubbed his mittens restlessly across his knees, felt the sting of heated cloth as his leggings pulled taut across his shins. Nightfall was imminent. Telemark should have come back by now. With the excitement of the contest forgotten, Jaric stared off into the gloom and considered the ugly possibility that something might have gone amiss.

The thought caused him great distress, that the only living person he had known since his accident might be threatened. With the wind getting stronger, he dared not sit waiting any longer. Jaric rose and entered the lean-to. He pulled a twist of oiled linen from the supply pack. His hands shook as he wound the cloth around the end of a stick and secured it with wire. Yet he completed the task with the exacting care the forester had taught him, now acutely aware the winter weather would not forgive ineptness. Then he thrust the stick with its linen wrappings into the fire.

The oiled cloth caught and flared, shedding a brilliant wash of light across the campsite. Jaric buckled on Telemark's spare knife, shoved a dry cloak under his arm, retrieved his lighted torch, and stepped beyond the safe warmth of the firelight into the icy blackness of the night.

Snowfall had all but obscured Telemark's trail; only slight, rounded depressions remained of his footprints, and where the brush grew sparsely, drifts had already covered all trace of his passing. Jaric suppressed the temptation to hurry. If he made a wrong turn in the dark, he might never regain the forester's path. And the wind was rising. The torch flame guttered, streaming oily smoke into the boy's face. He blinked stinging eyes, thrusting the stick at arm's length. If Telemark had been injured, there was a very real chance he might freeze to death before Jaric found him.

The boy pushed through a stand of young pines, guided by the fact that the branches had recently been swept clean of snow. On the far side the ground dropped off into a steep-sided ravine. A stand of saplings cast long, weaving shadows by the light of the torch; sheltered by the bank, snowflakes whirled, glittering with diamond-chip reflections. Jaric ducked under the fallen branch. Withered clusters of oak leaves raked his cheek and his boots slid in the uncertain footing. But as he progressed down the slope the wind dwindled; here where the snow accumulated more slowly, Telemark's tracks were more distinct.

Jaric squinted through the storm. Open water glinted at the bottom of the embankment, black against the reflective white of the shore. The brook was wide and deep enough for beaver trapping; the boy proceeded with caution. The ground was treacherously obscured by snow and a misstep could end in disaster. Despite his care, Jaric slithered down the final slope, whipped by the trailing tendrils of a willow tree. The torch threw off sparks like midsummer fireflies as he flailed his arm for balance. His boot splashed into the shallows. The water showed treacherous furrows of current between its bed of snowcapped rocks. Jaric caught a branch and barely prevented a fall. He paused, breathing hard, and waited for the flame to steady. Upstream he heard the faint rush of falls. Telemark's footprints led in that direction.

The boy turned along the stream. He made slow progress. The terrain was icy, crisscrossed with fallen trees jammed in haphazard array against the sides of the ravine. Jaric stumbled clumsily over dead branches. Worse, the torch showed the first flickering signs of failure. The boy cursed himself for neglecting to bring along an unlit spare. Telemark's footprints proceeded through the darkness ahead in a seemingly endless row; if he returned for a fresh light, all of his search might be in vain.

The splash of the falls grew louder. The flame sputtered against the wind, reduced to a sullen red glow. Through the shimmer of falling snow, Jaric made out the densely piled twigs of a beaver dam. The sight encouraged him. Telemark would have selected such a location to set beaver traps. Sheltering the light with his body, the boy hurried anxiously forward. The tracks ended by the edge of an eddy pool. There the ground lay strangely disturbed, as if a pine branch had been used to sweep the snow smooth. Jaric drew closer and saw a freshly cut sapling angled downward into the water's icy depths. He recognized the configuration of a freshly set beaver trap, and gave the area wide berth. The trap itself would be set on the stream bottom, its steel ring affixed to the pole well beneath the surface of the water. But any scent of man's presence would warn off the intended prey.

Stumbling over the uneven ground, the boy worked his way past the dam. The bank on the far side lay smooth and white, unmarred by traces of man's presence. But an exposed band of wet mud showed darkly at the water's edge; the level of the pond had recently been lowered. Jaric frowned and retraced his steps. Probably Telemark had pried a break in the dam, then left the second trap set in wait for an animal to come and mend the damage.

The boy drew abreast of the dam. In the uncertain glimmer of flame which remained of his cresset, he studied the glistening cross-weave of mud and twigs which spanned the throat of the gully. The hole, if any existed, was lost in darkness, and the tangled interlace of branches visible near at hand offered perilous footing for a man with unreliable light. Jaric assessed the situation and saw he had no choice but to return to camp for a fresh torch, then seek a safer crossing downstream.

The realization filled him with despair. He clamped his fingers around the torch shaft and shivered, cold and forlorn in the darkness of Seitforest. The mournful spill of the falls overlaid the higher-pitched sigh of wind through the treetops on the ridge. Jaric hesitated and stood listening, as if by sheer desire he could fathom Telemark's location before the torch died. For an instant his longing was desperate enough that it seemed the forest itself paused to share his pain. Suddenly dizziness claimed him. Jaric swayed, grabbed hold of a tree branch for balance. But the moment of disorientation lingered, and in the dying glare of the torch he beheld the vision of a woman's face.

She was young, perhaps his own age. Hair as black as fine velvet curved softly over her shoulders and her blue eyes regarded him levelly from features set with earnest concern.

Jaric gasped and started back. His hand jerked reflexively, and the torch guttered, nearly extinguished. But the girl's face remained in his mind as if her presence locked his very thoughts in place.

"Do not fear me, Jaric," she pleaded, and the tone of her voice pulled at the depths of his heart. "I appear to you as a dream, but I can help you find the one you seek."

"Telemark?" Jaric spoke loudly, startled by the sound of his own voice. The darkness and wind swallowed his words without echo, and for a second he thought he heard someone calling from the far side of the stream.

"The man you search for lies beyond the beaver dam," said the girl. "His foot is wedged, and he is injured. You must go to him at once."

Jaric released his grip on the tree, took a hasty step in the direction of the dam.

But the girl shook her head impatiently. "No." Her dark hair swirled and her face abruptly vanished into mist, but her voice lingered in his mind. "You must cross farther down. Beyond the first trap you will find stones where the footing is safe."

Jaric roused and discovered himself staring, half dazed, at the surface of the water. "Who are you?" he demanded aloud.

No answer came to him but the sigh of the wind in the branches. Yet above the ceaseless spill of the falls, he was now certain he heard Telemark calling his name. The voice was faint but unmistakable. And if not for the strange enchantress's sending he might have missed it.

Jaric whirled, sliding in the fresh snow. He plunged down the bank. The distance to the eddy pool and the first trap seemed longer than he remembered. Shadows spun and danced under his feet as he moved, and the torch hissed, fanned to temporary brilliance by the passage of air. The crossing lay as the enchantress had promised, a row of flat boulders spanning the dark rush of current like footings of an incomplete bridge. Jaric felt his palms break into sweat, shaken by certain evidence; the woman's sending had been something more than a fancy born of fear and distress. But concern for Telemark drove him onward without time to spare for thought.

Dense brush lined the far bank of the stream. Jaric crashed through, careless of ripping his cloak. His feet slipped often on the steep rocky ground. Jaric slowed, counting his steps to maintain patience. A fall would snuff out the cinder which remained of his torch.

"Jaric, over here." The forester's voice sounded hoarsely above the wind, yet quite close, from a point just down the slope.

Jaric followed the sound, ducking impatiently through a stand of briars. Thorns hitched his sleeve. He yanked clear, thrusting the torch high overhead. And in the faint orange light of the coals, he saw a rumpled form sprawled in the snow.

"Telemark!" Consumed by sudden sharp fear, Jaric slid down the embankment. The forester lay with his foot wedged between two fallen trees and his shoulders propped against a rock further down the bank. The knife left stabbed upright in the ice by his hand, and a white slash in the bark of the near trunk which pinned him revealed a desperate struggle to free himself. But the tree was too thick for the blade to be any help, and bending uphill against the pain of a twisted ankle in the end had exhausted his strength.

"Jaric." The forester smiled, though his lips were blue with cold. "The axe is down by the stream. I dropped it when I fell."

Jaric knelt, tugging the spare cloak free of his belt.

But Telemark frowned impatiently. "Go now," he said quickly. "Find the axe while you still have light."

The boy bit his lip. Tossing the cloak over the forester's still form, he rose and scrambled down the bank. The axe lay dusted with snow, its haft partly submerged in the stream. Jaric retrieved the tool from the water. Its weight dragged unpleasantly against muscles already aching with weariness. Jaric hefted the axe to his shoulder and took a stumbling step back up the slope.

That moment the torch went out. Jaric clenched his fingers around the wet axe handle and wondered whether he had endurance enough to free Telemark and see him safely back to the campsite.

CHAPTER XVI

Dream Weaver

Jaric knelt at Telemark's side, sheltering his friend from the worst bite of the wind with his body. Snowflakes whirled madly past and settled in white patches over the spare cloak which covered the injured man's shoulders. Telemark needed care and warmth and every comfort which could be gleaned from the supplies left in the packs back at camp. Jaric estimated the lean-to lay close to half a league distant, too far to travel without light, and with the storm becoming steadily worse, time was of the essence. The boy wished he could curse the inconveniences of fate. But words stuck in his throat and the raging despair he felt at Telemark's misfortune found no expression but stillness.

Moved by the boy's bleak silence, Telemark spoke from the darkness. "Jaric, many a problem will seem impossible at first sight. You must remember that no man can handle more than one step at a time. The most troublesome difficulty must be broken down into small tasks, each one easily mastered. Any predicament which cannot be dealt with this way will prove your undoing. This is not such a one. Trust yourself. All will be well, and sooner than you presently think."

The advice brought little comfort when measured against the fact that Telemark suffered the continuous discomfort of his twisted ankle. Yet with the same blunt courage Jaric had shown the day he regained consciousness in the care of a stranger, with no past and no memory of self, he placed total trust in the forester. He had nothing else. Either Telemark spoke truth, or both of them risked death by exposure in the stormy winter night.

The forester reached out and clasped Jaric's wrist with fingers already numb with chill. Through the contact the boy felt the deep tremors of shivering which racked his friend's body. He guessed Telemark's calmness was probably a brave facade, for the forester understood the gravity of his situation and Jaric was too perceptive to be fooled.

Whether Telemark sensed the boy's distress could not be told from his manner. "Did you find the axe?"

"Yes." Jaric swallowed. Determined to remain steady, he continued, though words came with difficulty. "I'll make a fire."

"Good lad." Telemark released his grip and settled wearily back on the snowy ground. "The branches on this fallen log appear to be seasoned.

Work slowly. Better I wait for warmth than you slip with the axe in the dark."

Yet Jaric knew the fire must not be delayed for very long. The wind was rising. It rattled through the treetops in heavy, whipping gusts, driving snow before it with stinging force. Unless the boy could shelter Telemark from the cold, and quickly, the forester would slip into delirium and thence to unconsciousness. Jaric selected a dead bough. He hefted the axe, swung it downward with a steadfast stroke, well aware that life depended upon his performance. Steel bit into wood with a ringing thump. The branch shivered and cracked, and snow showered down, sifting wetly over the tops of Jaric's boots. He jerked the blade free, snapped the limb off with his foot, and chopped into another, knowing if he stopped for a moment, weariness and fear would freeze him in place.

He worked with no thought of rest. After a time his movements settled into a rhythm entirely independent of thought. The axe handle raised blisters upon his palms through his mittens, but he felt no discomfort. Exhaustion robbed the sensation of meaning, and his muscles responded mechanically to the needs of the moment. Only after he had accumulated a sizable pile of branches did Jaric lay the axe aside. He scooped a hollow in the drift at Telemark's side, using a stick to scrape the ground clean of snow. Then he hastened down the embankment and returned with an armload of stones, still dripping from the stream. With shaking hands he lined the depression with rocks, stacked the wood in the sheltered place at the center, and at long last set to work with striker and flint.

The storm hampered his efforts. Gusts whirled the sparks away into the dark and scattered the last dry shavings he had brought in his pouch. Grimly Jaric drew his knife and carved fresh ones. Snow settled on his wrists as he whittled, chilling his skin until his bones ached with cold. Telemark had not stirred for some time. Afraid to find the forester's condition grown worse, the boy hunched resolutely against the elements. He struck another spark. This time the chips steamed and caught. Jaric hoarded the flame between his hands like gold. One twig at a time, he coaxed the fire to grow, all but singeing his fingers in the process. Then he draped his cloak over an overhanging branch as a wind break, weighted the hem with two rocks, and bent anxiously over Telemark. The forester lay with closed eyes, unresponsive to the boy's touch.

Jaric spoke, though the necessity stung his throat. "Can you feel your feet?"

The forester stirred sluggishly, his answer unintelligibly slurred. Jaric could only guess at the meaning of the gesture which followed. Cold had begun to slow Telemark's reflexes, and presently he would no longer be capable of rational action.

Cognizant of the fact that the forester's situation was critical, Jaric lifted a brand from the fire. He searched until he located a long sturdy stick, dragged it back, and wedged one end between the logs which trapped

Telemark's foot. Then he leaned every ounce of his weight on the farther end. The branch creaked under his hands. Dead bark split, baring wood like old bone in the firelight. Jaric closed his eyes and pulled until his tendons burned from exertion. The upper log shifted slightly, then remained fixed as a boulder. Jaric coiled his body, heaved the stick in desperation. But the makeshift pole only snapped with a crack that stung his palms, with nothing gained but frustration.

Shivering from stress and exertion, Jaric abandoned the stick. He fell to his knees in the snow and feverishly explored Telemark's trapped leg with his hands. His work had not been entirely in vain; the logs no longer pinched the limb so tightly. But the ankle had swollen badly. To drag it free would cause the forester great pain, and could cause unaccountable damage if any bone had been broken.

"The bone's intact," Telemark murmured, aware enough to realize what was happening. "You must tug until the leg comes clear."

But Jaric preferred not to take such a chance. He trimmed the edge of Telemark's boot sole with his knife, and slowly, carefully began to ease the foot free. Gently as he worked, Telemark gasped at the first slight movement. He bit his sleeve to keep from crying aloud as the boy lifted his twisted ankle clear of the logs.

Jaric supported his friend's shoulders, helped him to sit up. The fallen trees offered a reasonable backrest, and while Telemark settled shivering into the damp folds of the cloaks, the boy chafed his limbs to restore circulation. Then he turned to assess the extent of the forester's injury. The leg was not broken. But the flesh was bruised, swollen, and painful to the touch and certainly unfit to bear weight. And the storm was growing more violent by the hour.

"We cannot stay here." Telemark's teeth chattered with cold, and even the slightest speech seemed to tax his remaining strength.

Jaric touched his friend's arm, bidding him to be still. His brows drew into a troubled frown as he considered what should be done next. If he cut a stick for a crutch, the forester could move. But first he must have time to become thoroughly warm. The gusts struck with such fury no brand could long stay alight, and progress through the forest with an injured man would be tortuously slow. Jaric knew he faced a trip back to camp to fetch oiled rags for torches. But he dared not leave Telemark alone until he had cut enough logs to keep the fire going in his absence.

Jaric lifted the axe once more. Although his shoulders and arms trembled from exhaustion, he crossed to the foot of the nearest fallen tree and brought the blade down through the air in a clean, hard arc. Steel struck wood with a punishing jar. The impact left Jaric numbed to the elbow, yet he raised the axe for another stroke, and another. Chips flew, flickering into the shadows. Log by single log, he built a pile of fuel to ensure Telemark's survival, even should misfortune strike a second time and delay his return.

Drifts had piled waist-high between the thickets by the time Jaric departed alone to fetch fresh torches from the campsite. The boy plowed stubbornly through the heavy snow, too tired to feel any sense of his own achievement. He labored all that cruel and stormy winter's night to bring Telemark back safely, unaware he had surpassed, in strength and skill and perseverance, every limitation he once despised in himself as a sickly apprentice at Morbrith.

Dawn cast a pall of gray through the blizzard by the time Jaric lowered Telemark into the lean-to's shelter. He saw the forester securely wrapped in furs, then braved the torment of the wind once more to dig the accumulated snow and sodden ashes of last night's fire from the pit. The boy dared not rest until he had laid down fresh wood and covered his handiwork with canvas, ready for lighting should warmth be needed at short notice. Then, with his ears ringing with weariness and his body bruised and shivering with exhaustion, he stripped off his boots, wet leggings, and tunic. He rolled into his own blankets and almost instantly fell asleep.

The storm lifted toward afternoon. The sky blew clear of clouds and the temperature fell, leaving the forest brittle with cold. Jaric woke to the blinding glare of sunlit snow. Telemark had risen before him. A pot boiled above the fire and the boy smelled the enticing odor of brushpheasant and herbs cooking within. He began to rise, grunting as the pain of stiffened muscles protested his first movement. Brought fully awake by the sting of his blistered palms, Jaric recalled Telemark's accident, and the agony of endurance he had suffered the night before. Alarmed by his friend's empty blankets, the boy pulled a fresh tunic from his pack and tugged it clumsily over his shirt. He shoved his feet into icy boots and grabbing the frozen folds of his cloak he left the shelter.

Telemark sat with his sprained ankle propped comfortably on a log before the fire. His bow and skinning knife leaned alongside a bucket of hot water, and a soggy pile of feathers lay strewn around his feet.

Jaric gestured at the forester's injured leg, a confounded expression on his face. Then he directed a questioning glance at the cooking pot. "How?"

Telemark laughed. "I threw out grain. Brushpheasant are lazy creatures, particularly after a snowfall. They'll often risk a handout from a human rather than scratch for themselves. Are you hungry?"

Jaric nodded. He settled himself on the woodpile, spreading the icy cloak across his knees to dry. Telemark watched his companion's stiff, careful movements with every bit of his former acuity.

"Boy," he said softly. "Wherever you come from, and whoever you were does not count here. Last night you managed a man's work, and did it well. You have every right to be proud."

Jaric stared awkwardly at his hands, afraid to smile, fearful that if he acknowledged the forester's praise something inexplicable might intrude and ruin the moment. He longed to share the strange vision he had experienced by the beaver dam; to tell the forester of the black-haired girl who appeared in a dream to guide him. But the necessity of framing thoughts into words daunted the boy. Before he could manage a beginning, Telemark spoke again.

"You will have to set the traps alone until my leg heals. If I instruct you, do you think you can manage?"

Jaric looked up, brown eyes widened in surprise. Never had he considered the possibility that the forester might trust him to handle traplines by himself. Yet even as he sat, aching and tired, with his features stamped with the marks of last night's stress, he knew he could cope with the responsibility. Whatever his lost past, his work the last night had fully proven his capability.

"I can do my best," he said levelly. For the first time since he had recovered consciousness, confused and nameless in the forester's hut, speech came easily to his tongue.

Though pale from weariness himself, Telemark's stern countenance broke into a smile. "Good man," he said softly. "Fetch me the pack with the traps and I'll show you how we bag marten, silver fox, and ice otters."

Through the sunlit afternoon, Jaric worked in the clearing under Telemark's direction, learning the particulars of the trapper's trade. At dusk he loaded his pack and strapped a parcel of equipment to the frame of the drag-sleigh.

He rose at daybreak. Leaving Telemark to manage the campsite, he set off alone to lay the first of the winter traplines.

Early on he covered only as much ground as he could manage in a single day's hike. But he learned quickly. His confidence grew to match his skill. A week passed. The catch lashed to the drag-sleigh at the end of his rounds increased steadily; by the time Telemark's ankle recovered enough to manage the inner circuit of traps, the boy had progressed to the point where he could choose his own route. The day soon dawned when, with hard-earned pride, he loaded the sleigh with provisions and the spare cloth shelter and set off to manage the outlying territory on his own.

Jaric came to know the winter woods as home, whether under the trackless blanket of new snowfall, or the crisp cold of a diamond-clear sun. During the weeks which followed, he struggled over heavy drifts with the drag-sleigh in tow, day after long day; he chopped his own wood for each evening's fire, and gradually grew stronger. His face tanned from constant exposure to the weather. And the results of his labors filled the drying shed back at Telemark's cabin with the rich smell of curing pelts.

Midwinter's eve came, marked by austere celebration at the cabin. For hours Jaric stared into the fine, smokeless flames of candles made from beeswax, brought out specially for the occasion. If ever he had known such beauty in the past, his mind could not recall it. Silent with reflection, the boy sipped mulled wine fresh from the heat of the fire, unaware the forester studied him intently in return.

The shirts which had clothed an unsteady convalescent last autumn now fell without slack from shoulders grown broad with new muscle. Telemark noted the change but offered no comment. Sturdy and self-reliant as Jaric had become, and resilient as his outlook seemed, the fact he could recall no memory of his past lay like a shadow upon his young heart. Deprived of any knowledge of his origins, the boy lived like a man haunted by ghosts. Every commitment became a risk; each achievement, a footing built on sand.

But midwinter was a poor time to dwell upon somber thoughts. "Come to the shed," said the forester, a glint in his blue eyes. "I have something to show you." He rose and tossed Jaric a cloak from the peg by the back door and the boy followed him out into the night.

Telemark unbolted the shed door, kicked the snow clear of the sill, and tugged the heavy panel open. Jaric waited while the forester pulled a striker from his pocket and lit the candle in the near wall bracket. The flame grew, hesitant in the draft. By its first unsteady light, the boy saw a gleam of new metal on the worktable. He exclaimed and moved closer. There, still shiny from the forge, stood a full set of traps, laid out in Telemark's habitually neat array. Speechless, he turned and faced the forester.

Telemark picked a stray thread from his sleeve, embarrassed by the intensity of the boy's gaze. "I made spares during the time I was laid up. And I was right to do so, it would seem. You know enough now that we can keep two lines of remote traps going. Are you willing?"

Jaric reached out, traced the sharpened jaws of an ice otter snare with tentative fingers. He disliked killing animals; like him, they ran unknowing to their fate. But Telemark was never callous with his craft. He took only what he needed, cleanly and well, and never demanded more for the sake of greed. The forest was his livelihood, also his only love. Even with no past experience from which to draw conclusions, Jaric understood he might never know a better friend. The compassion and the trust represented by the forester's gesture touched him deeply. For a moment he could not answer. Yet the expression on his young face told the forester far more than any word.

The boy would accept the responsibility he had earned. By springtime, he perhaps would have bagged enough pelts to purchase a decent sword and knife. And certain Jaric's destiny did not lie with him in Seitforest, Telemark prayed silently that the boy would have time and the chance to finish the learning he had begun.

A month passed, the forest peaceful under winter's mantle of snow. A fortnight's distance on foot from Telemark's cabin, Jaric settled with his

feet to the embers of his campfire. Tired from an arduous day tending
traplines and satiated by a meal of stewed rabbit, he leaned back against
the trunk of a gnarled old beech while the sky changed from pale violet to
the heavy indigo of dusk. The expedition had gone well. The drag-sleigh
lay piled high with pelts, including several from the rare six-legged ice
otter, whose highly prized fur was beautifully mottled in silver and black.
Telemark would be pleased. But morning was soon enough to contemplate
the trip back to main camp; for now, Jaric delighted in his evening alone.

Here as nowhere else he felt at peace with himself. Seitforest took on
an austere beauty all its own in the dead of winter. Its law was harsh but
fair and its silence made no demands upon a troubled spirit. For competently as Jaric managed the responsibilities of his traplines, the gap in his
memory tormented him, leaving a hollow of emptiness at the core of his
being no achievement could erase. He felt as malleable as soft clay, fitting
the mold of Telemark's life, but owning no shape of his own. Jaric had
hammered that mental barrier with questions until his head ached with no
success. His past remained obscured until even Telemark ceased promising
that time would restore the loss.

The boy picked a stick off his woodpile, jabbing at the embers of the
fire. Sparks flurried skyward, bright and brief as the blossoms of the night-
flower vine, which opened but one hour at eventide and wilted immediately
thereafter. The image stopped the breath in Jaric's throat. His fingers
tightened until bark bit roughly into his palms. *Where had he seen such flowers,
and when? By the time he had regained awareness after his accident, frost had already
withered the greenery in Seitforest.*

Jaric shivered. Suddenly inexplicably dizzy, he filled his lungs with icy
pine-scented air, but the moment of disorientation lingered. Gooseflesh
prickled his arms though he was not cold and his ears rang with a strange
singing note like nothing he had ever experienced.

A log settled, scattered embers into the snow with a sharp hiss of
steam. Jaric started. He rubbed his sleeves, driving away the chills with
self-deprecating logic, until a glance at the fire set them off once more. In
the bright heart of the flames he again beheld the face of the woman who
had guided his search the night of Telemark's injury. Her black hair was
bound by a circlet of woven myrtle; the delicately colored blossoms
matched her blue eyes. Since no such vines could possibly be in bloom at
midwinter, Jaric knew she must be an enchantress. Her beauty left him
utterly confused.

She spoke, and her voice rang oddly inside his head, as if her message
originated many leagues distant. "Kerainson Jaric, look upon me and know
my face, for I shall return to you this night in a dream. I offer you full
memory of the past you have lost; but in exchange I must also demand a
price."

Her image wavered and began to fade.

Frantic to know more, Jaric shouted, "What price?"

But his words echoed across the empty forest unanswered and the fire burned as before. Jaric clenched his fists until his knuckles pressed as bloodless as old ivory against his stained leather leggings. The girl's mysterious promise made him blaze with impatience and her unearthly beauty inflamed his mind. Wracked by frustration too intense for expression, the boy wrapped his arms around his knees and stared restlessly at the sky. Stars glittered like chipped ice through silhouetted branches and somewhere above the thickets to the north an owl hooted mournfully. Seitforest remained unchanged in the winter darkness, except that the peace which Jaric found in evening solitude was now irreparably destroyed. Miserable and alone, he threw another log on the fire then bundled his cloak tightly around his body. He diverted the anger he could not express into the motion. Yet no human effort could lift the chill the enchantress had seated in his heart.

Wind arose in the night, pouring icy drafts through the patched canvas of the lean-to's meager shelter. Jaric curled like a cat in his furs, sleepless and tense. With bitter irony he wondered whether the enchantress' sending had been nothing better than an illusion born of his own unanswered needs. His disappointment was so intense that the enchantress' second sending came upon him unnoticed. One moment he lay with his head pillowed in the rigid crook of his arm. The next, his eyes closed and he fell into relaxed sleep.

Jaric dreamed he stood in the center of a twilit clearing. The air was clean and mild, and grasses flowered under his boots. The wintry gloom of Seitforest stood replaced by a towering ring of cedars whose age and majesty held no comparison to any woodland known to mortals. At once the boy knew he beheld a place beyond the boundaries of time, and there the enchantress chose to meet him.

It never occurred to him to feel afraid. "You were long in coming to me," he accused as she stepped into view between the trees.

Her shift glimmered white in the gloom, falling in graceful curves over her slender body. Although the glade remained eerily still, her presence reminded Jaric of music and torchlight and the rustle of fine silk on a midsummer's night. The associations arose unbidden, left him uncertain and confused, for the memories seemed those of a stranger.

"No." The enchantress touched his hand with small warm fingers. Jaric found her nearness disorienting. She gazed deeply into his eyes and spoke as though she shared his most private thoughts. "The memory is your own, Jaric. You grew up at Morbrith Keep. The Earl who rules there often guested great ladies in his hall."

Jaric felt his chest constrict. He forced himself to speak. "Earlier you mentioned there would be a price for my past."

Although the enchantress was a woman grown, a look of uncertainty crossed her features, as if a child suddenly gazed out at him through wide blue eyes. She glanced down, but not quickly enough to hide a fleeting expression of sorrow. Jaric guessed, after the open longing in his tone, that she already knew what his answer would be. Whatever her terms, he would accept; if he did not, the desperation, the loss, and the question of his own identity would eventually drive him mad. It was no fair choice she offered; that she well understood, and the fact pained her. She looked down as if fascinated by the flowers at her feet.

But her discomfort was not great enough to make her lift the restraint she had placed upon him. "The price is this: you will cross the Furlains at the earliest possible opportunity. When you reach the coast and the town of Mearren Ard, your fate will pass into the hands of another more powerful than I."

The enchantress looked up, her expression honestly distressed. "Jaric, I swear by my life. The destiny which awaits you is of crucial concern to those who safeguard the people of Keithland. Anskiere of Elrinfaer is wiser than any but the Vaere. He would not ask your service lightly."

But neither names nor the girl's entreaty held meaning to one who had no past loyalties to bind him. Jaric's lips thinned, a look entirely alien to the frightened boy who had once fled Morbrith keep on a stolen horse. "I accept," he said flatly.

Although the enchantress had won the concession desired by the Vaere, the victory was bitter. Jaric's decision arose from no feeling of compassion for Anskiere, nor for humanity's endangered existence. He consented only to gain knowledge of his birthright; and better than any, Taen knew the consequences were heavier than he could possibly imagine.

Telemark tossed down his polishing rag, hung the last kettle on its hook in the pantry, and succumbed at last to restlessness. Jaric was a week overdue. Unwilling to admit the depth of his concern, the forester paced the cabin's confines, searching for any lingering trace of untidiness; but he had cleaned, polished, and mended every belonging he owned twice over since his own return several days ago. No more loose ends remained to distract him.

He sighed and crossed to the window. Twilight settled over Seitforest, the gloom beneath the beeches all stillness and indigo shadows between the high crests of the drifts. With mid-winter past, the snowfall lay deepest, before the first thaw swelled the stream beds. There had been no severe storms of late; already the sun shone warmer in the afternoons, offering easy weather for travel, even with a loaded drag-sleigh. The trapline Jaric covered had been set over mild terrain, far from any traveled route where outlaws might lurk. The boy should not have been delayed.

Telemark left the window to pace once again, irritated by his own vulnerability. In all other matters he had learned to be fatalistic. The solitary life of the forest suited him; he had no need of companionship. Yet somehow Jaric's earnest desire to excel and the soul-searching depths of his silences had captured more than the forester's sympathy. Telemark roamed past the hearth for the fiftieth time that day; perhaps it was the fact that the boy carried the terrible mark of destiny that had caused him to bestow every protection in his power, even for the brief space of a winter. Few men were unlucky enough to be the focus of a sorcerers' dispute, far less stand noticed by Llondian prophecy. And Jaric was so very human. It was impossible for any man with sensitivity not to be moved by his plight.

Telemark paused again by the window. Night deepened over the forest and the trees bulked black and twisted beneath a thin sliver of moon. To the untrained eye nothing seemed amiss. But something in the shadows along the path beyond the shed caught Telemark's attention. His fingers tensed on the window frame. He looked more carefully and saw the faintest suggestion of movement. Impatience drove him to act before logic could restrain him.

Telemark ran to the door. He snatched the lantern from its peg, cursing the tremble in his hand as he fumbled for the striker. The first spark missed the wick entirely. The second caught. Without bothering to pull on a cloak, Telemark let himself out into the icy cold of the night.

The lantern cast arrows of light between trees limned by the flash and sparkle of hoar frost. Dazzled after the dimness of the cabin, Telemark squinted, unable to tell whether anything moved on the path. Worry made him stubborn. He refused to consider the idea he might have been mistaken.

"Jaric?" The word died on the air without, echo, leaving silence.

Telemark lowered the lantern, overwhelmed by disappointment. He reached for the latch on the cabin door. But before he could let himself in, he picked up the sound he had strained to hear through five uneventful days; a sharp ring as the drag-sleigh's runners scraped across the rock by the bend in the path.

"Jaric!" Telemark whirled and crossed the clearing at a run.

The lantern swung, jounced by his stride, and by its flickering light he saw the boy stumble out of the woods, towing a full load of pelts. Nothing appeared to be wrong. Yet as Telemark drew nearer he saw that Jaric, who was usually fanatically neat, looked raffish and unkempt. His cheeks were unshaven. Dark circles ringed eyes which contained a poignant and painful awareness.

"Jaric, what happened?" The forester set the lantern on a stump. He caught the boy in a fierce embrace, as if the solid feel of him might reassure the feeling of foreboding which had plagued him week long.

Jaric clung with a desperate grip, but after a moment straightened up. "I know who I am," he said. The dull edge of resentment in his tone raised the hairs on Telemark's neck. Memory of the Llondel's vision and of the boy's inexplicable destiny gave the man a powerful urge to weep. Instead he grabbed the lantern and gestured back toward the cabin. "Let's go home. You can talk later."

Jaric drew a heavy breath. He leaned into the straps of the drag-sleigh as if the sweat-stained leather was all that held him bound to the earth. "I have a debt, also," he announced.

And Telemark suddenly understood why the boy's step was so heavy. It appeared the fate foretold by the Llondel demon had at last overtaken him.

The forester walked at the boy's side, forcing himself to remain calm. "The tale can wait," he said, sensing reluctance behind Jaric's need to talk.

They stopped together by the cabin's door stoop. Telemark hooked the lantern on a bracket overhead and bent briskly over the drag-sleigh. The lashings had been tied with painful perfection, as if Jaric had tried to negate the inevitability of his future through single-minded devotion to his present craft. The pelts were expertly dressed, not a hair pressed against the grain during packing, and the axe blade gleamed, newly sharpened and oiled to prevent rust.

The boy and I are much alike, Telemark thought, and suddenly bit his lip as he realized how deeply his influence had rooted. Jaric had possessed no past and no self-image except what example his healer had provided him. Now, such a meager measure of stability was all the boy had to stave off the devastation of utter upheaval; the reckoning meted out when Jaric first entered Seitforest had been cruel but just. Before his accident, the boy had been singularly unfit to survive.

With the gentleness he would use to soothe a wounded animal, Telemark spoke. "I knew all along you would not be staying here. But how and when you leave is your choice alone. Until then this cabin is your home." He forced himself to concentrate on the untying of knots as Jaric drew a shaking breath that came very close to a sob.

At that Telemark could not help but look up. Tears streaked Jaric's face in the yellow glare of the lantern. Behind the boy's flooded eyes, Telemark saw agonized self-awareness and the just pride of accomplishment earned through the hardships of the winter woods. But undermining such knowledge lay a hunted, desperate self-doubt, as if some blight from early childhood had arisen to haunt the grown man. For suddenly there seemed very little of the boy left in the person who stood silent and determined at the forester's shoulder.

Torn by unbearable sympathy, Telemark could restrain his inquiry no longer. "How much did you learn?"

Jaric bent and began to loosen the lines with mechanical practicality. "Nearly everything. I know where I grew up and the names of the parents who bore me. I know I am not Kerain's true son, but the get of a sorcerer." He paused, unwilling to mention any name, and seemingly also unwilling to accept it. "That is the reason I left Morbrith Keep, where I was raised. But I know nothing of how or why I came to leave. Nor do I know why I am going; only that I must go."

His fingers froze on the knots. He looked up, meeting Telemark's gaze squarely for the first time since his return. And the forester saw he lived in horror of discovering what other surprises might lurk behind those memories still denied him.

But even Telemark's keen intuition could not guess the full truth; that Jaric's own mother had almost certainly tried to kill him in the very hour of his birth. The other children of the Smith's Guild had never allowed the boy to forget the fact. Kerain's account of his betrothed's crime lay inscribed in the records of Morbrith. As a scribe's apprentice, Jaric had checked the registry for himself and found in the cold words of the Earl's justice the transcription of testimony alongside the entry which sentenced an innocent man to hang.

The child Kerainson Jaric had grown to manhood without ever coming to terms with the horror born of his mother's rejection. Now posed tenuously at the edge of his first recognition of self-worth, the dream-weaver who guarded the last lost threads of his past demanded that he renounce the only happiness he had ever known in exchange for service to a second sorcerer whose name was linked with four thousand deaths. Pinned between the self-discovery learned under Telemark's guidance and a life-long feeling of inadequacy Jaric struggled, inwardly deafened by overpowering conflict.

"I must cross the Furlains to the town of Mearren Ard on the coast," he said in a tone stripped of emotion.

The boy's words struck Telemark like the last statement of a man condemned. He caught Jaric's wrist in a forceful grip. "That may very well be. But you'll go nowhere before I have gone to Corlin market for supplies." Jaric's stricken expression caused him to gentle his manner at once. "Come in and get warm. The passes over the Furlains are closed at this season anyway, and a fortnight's rest will serve you well before beginning such a journey."

Jaric nodded. He resumed unloading the drag-sleigh as if all were restored to normal. But by the look of naked relief which settled over his features, Telemark knew the day of parting would be difficult. All he could do was prepare the boy as well as possible. For a start that meant the commission of a good well-balanced sword from the armorer in Corlin. But the forester mentioned nothing of his intention to Jaric.

CHAPTER XVII

Mearren Ard

Jaric perched on a stool of carved maple, one elbow braced in the sunlight which spilled through the south window of Telemark's cabin. With a freshly sharpened pen in hand, he listed the supplies the forester would purchase during his monthly trip to Corlin market. But the return of his former skill brought him little joy. The familiar flow of ink and the neat incisive script which emerged beneath his nib provided final proof the dream-weaver had not lied about his past; once he had been a copyist in the archives of Morbrith Keep. The certainty left him feeling trapped.

"Add potatoes," said Telemark, pacing between window and hearth in a manner grown routine to Jaric through his months of convalescence. "And lamp oil. That should cover everything."

Jaric dated the list out of habit and laid aside his pen. He stared at his fingers, now heavily callused, and sliced across the right thumb by a scar where an ice otter maimed by a trap had bitten him as he bent to deal a mercy stroke. The hands he studied no longer looked like those of a scribe. Evenings, when the fire burned in the forester's hearth, the past the dream-weaver had unlocked within his mind seemed remote, belonging to a frail sickly stranger whose sleep had been riddled with nightmares of his own inadequacy. Jaric clenched his fists in the sunlight, chilled despite the promise of spring's warmth. At night the dreams and the terrors of that former self flooded his mind, battering away the self-assurance he had discovered at Telemark's side. The boy lived fearful he would waken one morning and discover his earlier image to be the true measure of his worth. All of daylight's logic could not unravel his uncertainty.

"Jaric?" Telemark crossed his arms and leaned against the chimney. "I'll be gone for a fortnight. Be sure the temperature in the drying shed doesn't fall below freezing. I've started seeds in the planting box in the back corner."

Caught with his mind wandering for the fourth time that morning, Jaric nodded.

"Good." Telemark straightened up. He collected the list from the table-top. "Are you certain you don't wish to come? We could move the sprouts to the root cellar."

"I don't mind staying." Jaric rose as the forester moved about the cabin, gathering together last-minute items in preparation for his trip into town. The boy felt no regret from his decision to remain behind. Although

Telemark made no issue of the subject, newly planted herbs would do poorly in the root cellar; with Jaric home to tend the fire, the bottled stores would not need to be moved to prevent freezing and the near circuit of traps could be kept in operation.

Telemark laced up his knapsack and directed a keen glance at Jaric. "You'll be all right alone?"

The boy nodded. He jabbed the stopper into the ink flask and rose to help the forester carry the remaining supplies to the door. Outside the drag-sleigh waited, already piled with pelts. Jaric stood awkwardly aside while Telemark buckled on his sword belt and shouldered his bow. Thieves preyed on the fringes of Seitforest even in the depths of winter and the ice otter fur by itself was worth a prince's ransom. The forester never went to the ferry unarmed.

Jaric watched his friend prepare to depart with strangely mixed feelings. He would miss Telemark sorely. But since his return to the cabin, the enchantress who unlocked the memories of his past had sent no more dreams. If she only appeared when he was alone, the boy wished one last chance to question her before the passes opened; for his recollection of events was complete except for the circumstances surrounding his departure from Morbrith. More and more, Jaric sensed the missing facts were pertinent, that Taen had a reason for withholding them. Since her abilities as a dream-weaver permitted her to cross the mental barriers left by an injury, surely she could also create them at will. And Jaric had reason to suspect he was being manipulated.

Disinclined to linger once the drag-sleigh's load was secured, Telemark left for Corlin. He had barely disappeared beyond the bend in the path before Jaric applied himself to mending the gear he had worn out on the trail. By sundown the boy was determined to demand the reason why his life was of such interest to the sorcerer who had once drowned half the souls of Tierl Enneth.

But the dream-weaver did not appear to him that night nor any time following Telemark's departure. Jaric attended his chores with increasing frustration, convinced some fact of vital importance had been denied him. But his attitude in no way affected his work. He checked and baited the traplines conscientiously while the afternoons lengthened toward spring. The icicles dropped from the eaves of the cabin with a sound like shattering crystal and the stream lost its crust of ice. On the fifteenth day, Jaric returned from his rounds to find the drag-sleigh leaning against the weathered boards of the shed. Smoke curled from the cabin's stone chimney, delicate as embroidery against the reddened sky of sunset. Telemark had returned.

Jaric shouted. He burst into a run, knapsack banging clumsily against his shoulders. The cabin door opened as he reached the clearing's edge and Telemark stepped out.

He caught the boy in a smothering embrace. "Stow your gear quickly and come inside. I have a surprise for you."

Jaric did as the forester bid him. But when he returned to the cabin doorway, he hesitated. The closer he came to the inevitable moment of departure, the more jarring he found each variation from habit; never before had the forester brought anything unusual from Corlin. For one wild instant Jaric longed to rush back into the cold familiar darkness of the shed. But Telemark caught his arm firmly and hustled him across the threshold.

Wax candles burned festively on the table beside the window, but Jaric's eyes were drawn at once by the polished metal which gleamed in the light beneath. A sword, dagger, and pen-knife lay in a row, the bluish patina of new steel in sharp contrast to the rough boards of the tabletop.

Jaric gasped, his hand motionless on the door latch.

"Go on." Telemark prodded him gently forward. "I had them made for you in Corlin."

The boy crossed the floor as if the planking beneath his feet was thin and treacherous as old ice. Candles struck a haze of bronze highlights through his fair hair as he bent to examine Telemark's gift. The weapons were plain but beautifully made. Every detail bespoke painstaking craftsmanship and the result combined grace and beauty with a chilly sense of effectiveness. Jaric regarded the sheen on the cutting edge of the sword blade and knew at once that Telemark had spared no expense. From blades to crossguards, the set glittered with the watery polish of first-quality steel, and the pommels bore his name chased in silver.

Telemark crossed to the boy's side. "Try the balance," he urged softly.

Jaric glanced up, a stunned expression on his face. He made no move to touch the weapons.

Interpreting his silence, Telemark caught the boy's shoulders in a firm grip. "You earned them, down to the last copper," he said emphatically. "Did you think I had you lay an extra trapline so I could deck my windows out in brocade?"

He released his hold suddenly, lifted the sword from the tabletop, and thrust the grip into Jaric's reluctant hands. The boy stared incredulously, then managed to execute an experimental feint. Candlelight danced across the polished curve of the quillon. The size and weight of the weapon suited him too perfectly for coincidence; Telemark had evidently ordered the blades designed exclusively for him.

Jaric raised his eyes to the forester and spoke directly from the heart. "I thank you. Never in life have I received so fine a gift."

"Well then," said Telemark gruffly. "Don't be losing this one as you did the last."

He turned abruptly from the light, but not before Jaric caught sight of the tears which gleamed on his weathered cheeks. The boy laid the sword aside. Without speaking he threw his arms around Telemark's shoulders. And from that moment both understood he was closer to the father Jaric had never known than any person from his childhood at Morbrith.

* * *

Two weeks passed with deceptive swiftness. Comfortably settled into the routine of the trapper's trade, Jaric wished he could forget the price he had promised the dream-weaver in return for his past. But the nights grew inexorably shorter. All too soon Jaric wakened from sleep to the sound of rain hammering against the eaves of the cabin; come morning, he would have to leave Seitforest. Although the weather in the mountains had yet to break, a man traveling alone was best advised to cross the high passes early, before the first caravans of spring attracted bandits to lie in ambush.

Telemark rose at daybreak. He helped load the spare knapsack with journey cake, smoked meat, and cheese, as if preparing Jaric's supplies for a trip to check on a remote trapline. He spoke very little. His face looked drawn and tired. This time the blanket roll and the spare snowshoes would not be returning to their pegs in the loft.

He strapped the knapsack closed with brisk efficiency, then folded his arms and leaned on it, regarding the boy with a look of uncharacteristic gravity. "Jaric, listen carefully. I have something to tell you that I don't fully understand. But I believe it to be important and you may someday find the information useful."

The boy rested the snowshoes against the settle and devoted his full attention to the forester. Slowly, with many a pause for reflection, Telemark related his encounter with the Llondel demon the day he had tried to deliver Jaric to Kordane's Brotherhood in Corlin. He spared no detail, though the memory of his attempt to renounce responsibility for the boy he had rescued from the woods now pained him deeply.

But Jaric accepted the forester's judgment without criticism. "I don't know what the dreams meant either," he admitted after Telemark had finished. He tried to lighten the forester's mood. "When I find out, I'll be sure to let you know."

The boy and the man regarded each other for a long moment, each one aware the moment of departure could not be delayed any further. At last Jaric shouldered the snowshoes. He moved decisively toward the peg by the door where his cloak hung.

"Wait," said Telemark suddenly. He crossed the room, flung open a cedar chest which rested at his bedside, and delved deeply inside. "I want you to have this."

He rose with a cloak of ice otter fur draped over his arm. The garment was strikingly marked, luxuriously thick, and lined with the snowy fur of the forest hare. Through a whole season of trapping, Jaric had never seen such pelts.

"It's much too fine," he protested. The worth of such a gift was something a king might envy.

But Telemark tossed the cloak over Jaric's shoulders, in no mood for listening to argument. "This was to be a gift for my son on his eighteenth birthday."

Jaric's breath stopped in his throat. He had never guessed Telemark had any family. .

"Yes, I had a boy and a wife." The forester caressed the silky fur with fingers scarred from years of tending traplines. "They both died of fever while I was on campaign with the Duke's army. That was what made me quit the mercenary's profession."

He dropped his hand, saw Jaric's stricken face, and smiled. "I have long since finished grieving, boy. And it's lucky for both of us the moths haven't made a feast of those furs, for Eleith needs no bride price now. Take the cloak with all my blessing. It will keep you warm when you cross the mountains, but wear it inside out lest some bandit take your life to claim it for himself."

He did not add, as Jaric understood he intended, that the cloak could be sold at need, in exchange for immeasurable wealth. And finding no words for the occasion, Jaric embraced the forester one last time, gathered up his belongings, and stepped out into the slush of the dooryard.

Telemark lingered in the doorway long after the boy had vanished down the path to the southeast. The forester would miss Jaric and wonder often through the coming months how the boy fared; yet he also experienced the immeasurable satisfaction of seeing a task complete. Jaric had come to him helpless, frightened, and injured; he had left with the promise of growth and a future, however difficult his lot. If he never returned, Telemark would remember the boy at the moment he vanished into Seitforest. For although the fate which awaited him terrified Jaric to his soul, still he had discovered the courage to go forward and meet his destiny.

Jaric crossed the Furlains while the icy grip of winter still choked the passes with the cruelty of a giant's mailed fists. He struggled through blizzards which drove the snow in smoking clouds off the peaks. Other times, when the sky shone clear azure above his head, he felt the thunderous boom of the spring avalanches shake the mountain beneath his feet. But Telemark had schooled him well to the art of survival in the frozen heart of the wilds. Jaric reached the far slopes two weeks before the equinox, and from a notch cut between the forested foothills gazed down upon the fishing village of Mearren Ard.

The houses looked like toys after the square battlements and watchtowers of Corlin. Built of logs, with steeply pitched roofs shingled with cedar, the buildings nestled against the side of a hill which overlooked two points of land. A well protected harbor lay between, scattered with the specks of fishing boats lying at anchor.

Jaric propped his snowshoes against the shoulder of a snowdrift and carefully folded his rich cloak inside his knapsack. Then he set off down the muddy trail, a wry expression on his face. The silver in his pocket would not last long at a tavern, even in a settlement as tiny as Mearren Ard. If the only inhabitants were fishermen, his talents as scribe and his

knowledge of trapping were unlikely to be considered worthwhile com-
modities for barter. Either the sorcerer Anskiere made a prompt appearance to claim the service Taen had promised in the dreams or Jaric would
take up sailing; he had no intention of selling an ice otter cloak simply to
pay for his bed and board.

The sole tavern in Mearren Ard was all but deserted during the daytime. Jaric stepped in from the dirt track which passed for a street and
discovered a cramped taproom smoky from a fireplace in need of a chimney
sweep. An ancient man in oilskins hunched over a table in the warmest
corner of the room, hands cupped possessively around a chipped tankard.
His fingers were hooked into useless claws by arthritis, but the sharp clear
eyes of a sailor still gazed from his creased sockets. He looked on with
crotchety displeasure while Jaric presented his inquiries to the landlord;
but no stranger awaited the boy's arrival. Jaric himself was the first outsider to visit Mearren Ard, by land or sea, since winter had closed the
passes. The boy sighed and settled in silver for a room. He had no choice
but to seek employment and wait until Anskiere chose to present himself.

The taproom grew boisterous by evening, when the fishermen
returned. Having bathed away the dirt left from the trail, Jaric went downstairs, found an unoccupied table, and ordered a meal of spiced chicken.
He ate while the smoky air of afternoon became musty with the sea-smell
of oilskins drying by the back door. An assortment of men with weather-
beaten faces gathered at the bar, their boots strongly reeking of fish. They
called the barmaid by name, yet offered no pleasantries; all seemed to have
wives waiting in snug cottages, except for the wizened, arthritic fellow
who sat still in his corner as if he never moved from his chair.

Jaric finished his meal, conscious of fleeting glances from the taproom's occupants. No one attempted to approach his table. In the gruff,
tight-knit society of Mearren Ard, he was an outsider; the men would wait
for him to speak, and probably be relieved when he finished his business
and went elsewhere. But Jaric had given the enchantress his word he would
remain until Anskiere chose to contact him. Although he longed with all
his heart of pack his knapsack and return over the Furlains to Seitforest,
instead, he pushed the bones of his dinner aside and rose.

The man at the end of the bar looked up. He studied the blond
stranger who paused by his shoulder, his narrowed stare that of a man
who had spent a lifetime squinting over water, overseeing fish nets and
weather and stars for navigation. His manner was not friendly; Jaric's presence was an intrusion, but the fisherman withheld any judgment until after
the boy drew breath and spoke.

"I need work," Jaric opened. "Is there any man among you who could
use an extra hand?"

The fisherman grunted and set down his ale mug. All conversation
silenced around him as he eyed Jaric from head to foot, and the thick

drawl of his reply fell against stillness grown dense as an ocean calm. "D'ye sail, then?"

The boy answered with a confidence he did not feel. "No. I'm willing to learn."

Boots scraped on the taproom floor as the men shifted their feet and the spokesman grunted a second time. "What for? Have ye no trade, then?"

Jaric refused to yield to the mistrust implied by the words. "I spent the winter trapping in Seitforest."

"Crossed the passes, then?" The fisherman considered the cut of Jaric's leather tunic, then the well-kept steel of the knife at his belt. "Well, then," he said at last. "Tavish lost a son, onto last summer. He'll be in, soon as he sets his anchor in the harbor."

The fisherman gestured to an empty stool at the end of the bar and turned back to his beer. Any lad who crossed the Furlains alone before solstice was hardy enough company, even by Mearren Ard's rough standards; and Tavish sorely needed a crewman.

Jaric seated himself and waited, uncomfortably sure what the outcome of his request would have been had he lacked the experience of Telemark's teaching. But none of his uncertainty showed in his manner and presently the main door banged open. A burly man with a fox-colored beard stepped in, accompanied by another who was unmistakably his brother.

The fisherman who had spoken to Jaric immediately raised his voice over the surrounding conversation. "Tavish! Got a boy here who wants work. Never salted his boots, but he claims he's come in over the passes."

Tavish stamped the mud from his feet, shaking the planks in the floor. Followed closely by his brother, he crossed the taproom with the rolling gait of a man better accustomed to a sloop's deck than solid land; and Jaric found himself scrutinized once more by two sets of keen blue eyes.

Tavish scratched his beard with thickened, rope-burned fingers. "Crossed the passes, did you then?"

Jaric nodded.

"Let's see yer hands." Tavish caught the boy's wrists and examined the calluses on his palms. "Won't look so pretty after a season with the nets," he observed.

Jaric said nothing.

"Ye'll do, then." Tavish leaned across the bar and called for the landlord to fill three tankards. When they arrived, he hooded one for himself, passed one to his brother, and slammed the other down in front of Jaric. "Drink up, then. We sail an hour before daybreak. Boat's named *Gull*, and sure's tide, ye'll get seasick. Get over it quick and ye'll share the catch. Fair?"

"Fair," said Jaric. He tasted the beer and found it bitter.

Tavish grinned, amused by the boy's grimace. "Drink on't, then." And he emptied his tankard.

*   *   *

Jaric appeared by the dockside at the appointed hour. Cocooned in an early fog, he boarded the dory with Tavish and his brother, and on the way out to *Gull*'s anchorage, set hands to a pair of oars for the first time in his life. His initial effort was clumsy. With his back to the bow of the boat and the darkness obscuring the landmarks, he had difficulty maintaining a straight heading. But the same perseverance which had endeared him to Telemark and an uncompromising desire to learn soon stilled the dry remarks the fishermen of Mearren Ard customarily inflicted upon a greenhorn. If Tavish resented the loan of his dead son's oilskins to a stranger, he made no comment. For the next three days he applied himself to teaching Jaric the difference between sheet lines and halyards. Even to his impatient eye the boy learned quickly. Come evening the fishermen laid bets on his progress in the tavern. Yet sooner than any of them guessed, *Gull* raised full canvas and left the coastline behind to ply her nets in the ocean far from Mearren Ard.

For a day and a half, *Gull* plowed close-hauled through the swells of the northern Corine Sea, driven by the brisk winds of earliest spring. Foam jetted off the bow, white as combed fleece, and gulls dove in the sloop's wake. Jaric suffered a brief bout of seasickness. Yet he eased sheet lines and changed sail with white-faced determination, never once complaining. Shortly his body adjusted to the toss of a sloop's deck at sea. He stood his first full watch at the helm with a vivid sense of exhilaration, and presently even Tavish's dour brother accepted him as crew.

The nets were drawn in heavy with fish. Jaric pulled twine until his shoulders ached and slept dreamlessly in his berth during off-watch hours. The cold air and the wild expanse of open sea agreed with him, yet the boy took care not to love his new life too much. He knew his time aboard *Gull* could not last. Inexorable as the turn of the tide, his promise to the enchantress must be completed; the sorcerer Anskiere would someday claim his service. Yet the fate Taen had promised came upon him suddenly, in a manner not even she could have anticipated.

Two weeks out of Mearren Ard, Tavish steered *Gull* on a southeast tack. Off watch at the time, Jaric dreamed of restless winds and towering waves with thundering crests of spume. He woke, chilled and sweating, and not even scalding hot tea and a cloak of oiled wool could calm his shaken composure. He clenched icy fingers around his mug, feeling as if some alien presence tugged at his mind. The sensation left him edgy, unable to contain his straying thoughts.

Tavish shouted impatiently down the companionway. Jaric roused himself with an effort. He yanked on his boots and went topside to tend the nets. But the odd sensation which plagued his mind would not relent even in the fresh air above decks. Instead it increased through the morning, until he worked with the muscles of his jaw clamped tight to keep from crying aloud.

Noon came, sunlit and pleasantly warm. Jaric bent over the rail, hauling in the first flopping burden of codfish. Drenched twine dug into his fingers and his shoulders quivered as he strained to raise the laden weight of the net. Suddenly a sharp tingle swept across his skin. Dizziness coursed through his body. Jaric flinched. Stunned by horrified recognition, he recalled a horse and a dusty summer road and a punishing vortex of wind which had once driven him forward against his will. His disorientation deepened, drowning the memory under a singing storm of force. He fought it, even as the net dragged at his wrists; echoing down a tunnel of darkness, he heard Tavish curse in exasperation. Jaric struggled to clear his head. But his vision slipped relentlessly out of focus, and his breath went shallow in his throat.

That moment the air above his head split with a crack like lightning. Jaric staggered, eyes blinded. Power pierced his mind, cruel as the harpoons the fishermen used to gaff sharks. The net slipped out of Jaric's fingers. Cod tumbled back into the sea. Their bellies carved silvery crescents into the green of the waves.

Tavish shouted in anger from the helm. He flung the tiller down, bringing *Gull* into the wind. Patched canvas banged aloft, punched by a freshening breeze, and spray flew in sheets over the bow. But the curses died on the fisherman's lips as he looked up and saw Jaric. For an instant the boy's slim form seemed almost incandescent, haloed by a triple ring of blue-violet light; the image of a bird of prey hovered over his head, tawny gold with feathers barred in black.

"Stormfalcon!" shouted the brother in a tone gone treble with panic.

Tavish clamped the tiller in the brake and bolted forward. He reached Jaric's side just as the boy crumpled unconscious onto the deck, salt-crusted hair fanned like frayed silk over the collar of his oilskins. The fisherman met his brother's eyes above Jaric's still form, his mouth set with rare and desperate anger.

"Knew he was too good to be true, then," he said after a moment. A wave thudded against the sloop's side, tossing spray in the sunlight, and gulls swooped on stretched wings above the main yard. No trace remained of the sorcery which had manifested above the decks barely a moment before; except Jaric lay motionless as death against the aft stay, and no mortal remedy would rouse him.

"Should toss him overboard, then," said the brother.

"No." Tavish was adamant. "We daren't."

But neither of them cared to try more fishing that afternoon. Reluctant to touch Jaric even to move him, the brothers tossed an old blanket over his oilskins. Then they hauled in the nets and headed *Gull* about, setting course for Mearren Ard. Their family had seen a streak of bad luck since the death of Tavish's son last season; they wished no further curse to fall upon them for keeping a lad touched by a sorcerer's powers.

Late in the afternoon, *Gull*'s anchor settled and bit into the sea bot-

tom, once more within the safety of the harbor. The boy still breathed.
Tavish and his brother slung Jaric between them on the blanket and loaded
him into the dory along with the rest of *Gull*'s catch. After tense debate,
they returned to his room at the inn, where they dumped him in a limp
heap on the bed. Tavish raised crossed fists in the sign to avert evil sorcery
while his brother counted out the coppers Jaric had earned aboard the
fishing vessel. They left the coins in a neat pile on the boy's knapsack and
left the room, hurrying back to their boat without speaking. But word of
the incident spread swiftly throughout the village.

Traders from the south arrived that afternoon, the first to reach Mearren Ard since the roads thawed. The bustle of unloading wagons and preparing stalls for their oxen lent the tavernkeeper an excuse to avoid the
boy who lay in his back garret. By the time sunset traced the rooftrees in
gilt and copper, the taproom stood packed with the bodies of fishermen
come to hear the news brought by the traders. The room grew noisy with
talk. But no one mentioned the boy who had fallen ill of a sorcerer's curse
on the decks of Tavish's boat. Curious, the traders inquired about the
mysteriously occupied back room, but received no reply. For not one villager present dared risk the ill fortune which might result if Jaric's name
were spoken aloud.

"Jaric!" Taen's call plunged deep into his mind, reached him where he
struggled, overwhelmed by a vision of storm-tossed seas and darkness.
"Jaric, let me help you."

But he ignored the dream-weaver's call, no longer dependent upon
her knowledge. During the moment Anskiere's summons overthrew his
awareness, he had remembered his past in entirety, even to his desperate
flight from the Sanctuary tower at Morbrith. Old memories slashed like
torturer's knives, tore his last precarious peace to ribbons. The months
the geas had lain fallow served only to redouble its power; now reconnec-
ted with its intended subject, its forces struck with a resonance far
stronger than Anskiere intended. Raging tides of power coursed through
Jaric's body. Each second he deferred the call which pulled him southeast,
he suffered agony.

Yet this time he endured. With the strength he had learned from Telemark he fought to regain his will. Slowly, carefully, the boy constructed a
framework within his mind to bring the punishing directive of the sorcerer's summons under control.

"Jaric, let me help." Taen's image appeared before him in the darkness.
The flowers were gone from her hair, and her face was drawn, brows gath-
ered in poignant concern. "Anskiere was to summon you, but not even the
Vaere guessed the power would strike so hard. *I beg you, let me help.*"

But wounded by her betrayal, Jaric shut her out. She had known. She
had let him sail, aware the geas waited to snare him at sea beyond Mearren
Ard. All along she had watched, Jaric realized, but never once had she
trusted him with the truth.

"How did I dare?" The enchantress's voice lanced into his mind, sharpened by pain. "I could do nothing but follow the orders of the Vaere. No one intended to hurt you. Believe me."

But Jaric would accept none of her help. Lashed by an unwanted memory of Kencie's pity, he unleashed his frustration against the dream-weaver whose promise had brought him to such torment. Rage burst like flame across his mind. Taen's presence dissolved with a pang of regret, leaving him alone in his struggle. Slowly Jaric knotted the shreds of his self-control back into balance. Power flared and sparked, resistant as cold iron against his will. Yet the boy persisted with the same rugged determination he had shown the night Telemark had been injured by the beaver dam. Gradually he dominated the effects of the geas sufficiently to regain consciousness.

Dull light filtered through a single tiny window. Sunset had passed well into the gloom of evening. Jaric saw that he lay on his bed above the taproom, clad yet in his damp wool tunic. Someone had removed his oilskins, most likely Tavish. But he still wore his boots, and a coarse, fishy-smelling blanket had been left twisted in awkward folds around his body; it bound at his shoulders, making movement difficult.

Jaric sat up. He drew a ragged breath and shrugged the blanket aside, then pressed his hands to his aching head. The geas drove remorselessly against his mind; it required a supreme effort to stay the urge to leave the inn and run blindly down to the harbor. He could not swim the ocean; and the road which led along the coast turned southwest, out of line with the geas' summons. Bereft of alternatives, Jaric dragged his knapsack across his knees. Something metallic fell, ringing across the floor. Jaric swore, and in the half light caught the faint gleam of coins scattered at his feet. The boy interpreted their significance with a heavy sense of sorrow. Here, as in Gaire's Main, the sorcerer's geas marked him; not even Tavish would welcome his presence now.

Heartbroken, Jaric pulled the ice otter cloak from his knapsack. He buried his face in the silky fur, hoping he could maintain control of the geas long enough to buy passage out of Mearren Ard. Then he braced up his courage and rose to his feet. One last coin tumbled from his lap struck the bedstead with a bright, pure clang. Jaric winced. Smoldering with resentment, he slammed the door open. Telemark would forgive the sale of the furs intended for his son's bridegift. But Jaric swore by the air he breathed he would make Anskiere pay for the sacrifice. With his fingers clenched around the hilt of his knife, he descended to the taproom.

CHAPTER XVIII

Callinde

Jaric paused at the foot of the stair. Every sconce had been lit in the taproom, but the increased illumination added little; trestles and roof beams loomed through a blue haze of smoke. The close press of people hampered what ventilation the chimneys provided, and more than one fisherman smoked a pipe as he sat over his beer. The talk was loud, dominated by a black-clad trader Jaric had not seen previously. Daunted by the stranger's presence, the stale air, and a falsely boisterous atmosphere, the boy hung back in the doorway, listening.

"Oh, aye," said the man in black. He leaned back in his chair, stretched like a bear, then bellowed for the barmaid to refill his tankard. His listeners shifted restlessly while he wet his throat. "There's rumor enough from ports beyond the straits. Heard it from a sailor who'd been there, Kielmark's crazy, he said. Tribute won't satisfy him, not since some white-haired witch twisted Anskiere's power about. They say Cliffhaven got smacked by a storm so mean she damned near cracked the light tower in twain. Now every ship bound through the straits gets boarded, assessed, taxed, and sailed fully fifteen leagues on her way, manned by the Kielmark's own. Then she's turned loose and no apologies for it. No sorcerer, says the pirate, damn his arrogance to the Fires, no sorcerer will get close enough to Cliffhaven to meddle with his fortress of thieving renegades, sure's tide."

The trader paused to quaff his ale. He wiped his mustache on his sleeve and resumed. "Can't blame him, though, not entirely. Who'd trust a sorcerer? Not me. I recall my father telling how Ivain Firelord burned a hostel to cinders, all because the roof leaked and woke him from sleep."

The trader belched and rubbed his belly. Beside him a drover with sly eyes added a second tale of Ivain's cruel exploits, and in words framed by the consonants of an eastern accent another man recounted the drowning of Tierl Enneth by Anskiere. Hidden from view beyond the stair, Jaric overheard. He felt suddenly as if darkness itself had reached out and marked him where he stood. Morbrith's archives held testimony enough of the Firelord's mad viciousness. Jaric had read the accounts of those wronged who had appealed to the Duke's mercy for shelter; but the stories repeated in the dimness of Mearren Ard's taproom were colored with human emotion no written record could express. In the rough words of strangers, the boy received his first understanding of the stigma in the fate Firelord and Stormwarden had mapped for him.

"Fires, now, *we* understand." The bearded trader gestured to his audience of fishermen with conspiratorial brotherhood. "Nobody with a jot of sense would wish a sorcerer making spells on folks who lived on his own green turf. That boy will bring no good should you continue to shelter him, there's a promise. But talk can't hurt."

But the trader's expansive suggestion left the villagers close-mouthed as clams. The tension in the taproom suddenly became too much for Jaric to endure. Sobered by the knowledge that he could lose his life should his parentage be discovered, he left the shadow of the stair and entered the taproom, the ice otter cloak clutched like a dead animal between clenched fingers. Quietly as he moved, the nearest man looked up from his tankard and pointed. Heads turned. Conversation stilled abruptly, as though something intangibly evil entered through the door behind the boy's back.

Jaric continued his advance, though the silence unnerved him. Oblivious to the spilled beer which splashed under the soles of his boots, he took another step. The barmaid started and dropped a tin jug. It struck the trestle beneath with a crash that jangled every nerve in the room. The man beside her swore and raised crossed fists in the traditional sign to avert malign sorcery.

Hurt to the quick by the gesture, Jaric stopped. A half circle of wind-burned faces confronted him. Across the length and breadth of the room, not one expression held the slightest trace of welcome. Poised and alone, the boy caught impressions like acid imprints; here a chin jutted aggressively forward and there a veined fist gripped a chair back, spaced between pair after pair of hostile eyes. But the geas granted no quarter. Doomed as a hare before mastiffs, Jaric at last set his request into words. "I need a boat to cross the Corine Sea. I can pay handsomely for my passage. Is there a man among you willing?"

Movement rustled like a sigh through the room, as every fisherman present turned his back. The last bit of color drained from Jaric's face. He seemed a figure made of paper, slight and brittle and pathetically vulnerable. "This cloak would buy an army for a king!" he shouted. "Have you no pity?"

But his pleas stirred the villagers at Mearren Ard not at all. They stayed rooted, stony and stubborn as a fortress wall, even when Jaric flung the magnificent fur down on the nearest table, his cry of disbelief stifled with his knuckles. The geas pressured him with the persistence of a tidal current, near to drowning all reason.

The boy felt his control slip. Anger flared through him. Touched by a trace of his father's madness, he longed to blast the rooftrees of Mearren Ard with flame, until charred beams smoked like blackened ribs against the sky. But the passion ebbed as swiftly. Bitter and trembling and sickened by the vindictive turn of his thoughts, Jaric tossed sun-bleached hair from his face and glared at the backs of the villagers.

"Is there no man present who dares to remember the meaning of mercy?" He spoke no louder than a whisper, but his outraged accusation carried to the farthest corner of the room. "Give me nothing but a boat. I'll find a way to sail her."

"Hey, boy!" The black-haired trader rose from his seat near the bar. Respectably clad in wool embroidered with scarlet, he wore a dandyish beard. Sharp features and slitted eyes lent him an expression crafty as a rat's. "I'd give you gold for that cloak, boy." But the price he named was an insult.

Jaric closed his eyes, anguished by the memory of Telemark's face on the morning he had opened the old cedar trunk and pulled forth his only treasure. The boy's straits were desperate; every man in Mearren Ard knew it. Anyone marked by Anskiere of Elrinfaer had no fate to bargain.

"Boy!"

Slowly Jaric turned his head and located the drover who had addressed him.

The man leaned on the bar, pudgy knuckles crimped around a wine flask. His lips parted with amusement. "Mathieson Keldric has a boat he can't sail any more. Why not ask the old relic if he'd swap his craft for your fancy cloak?"

By the fellow's derisive tone, Jaric guessed the advice was ill spent, a crass effort to poke fun at his predicament. But the geas blazed like magma through his flesh, making each separate moment an agony more terrible to endure than the last. He had no choice but attempt the trader's suggestion.

Jaric's reply fell without echo in the packed stillness of the taproom. "Who is Mathieson Keldric?"

The trader grinned, displaying a jumble of stained teeth.

"There, son." And he pointed to the arthritic elder who inhabited the corner table by the hearth, as if he intended to die there. Half crippled by age and disease, the old man was the only villager who had not turned his back on the boy from Morbrith Keep.

Jaric gathered the ice otter cloak from the tabletop and reluctantly moved toward the fireplace. A chair scraped at his back. Someone whispered an obscenity. Evidently Keldric's boat was the butt of a well-worn joke, repeated out of pity for the old man's plight. But Anskiere's summons left no space for inquiry. With cautious steps Jaric approached the corner nearest the hearth. And Mathieson Keldric watched him with eyes the light clear gray of rain pools, his lips pursed in alarm.

Suddenly the old man straightened in his chair. He stared in open-mouthed amazement at a point just past Jaric's shoulder and his twisted fingers flew to his face. *"Callinde!"* He spoke the name barely above a whisper, but to Jaric the sound felt louder than a shout against the blighted stillness of the taproom. Yet none of the bystanders appeared to overhear.

"The trader mentioned you have a boat you might sell." Jaric ran his fingers anxiously through the silver-tipped fur of the cloak. "I have no coin to offer, but perhaps you would consider a trade?"

But Keldric acted as if the boy had never spoken. He gazed unresponsively into the air. His lips moved, but no word emerged. For a moment it seemed he would ignore Jaric's need as the others had, leaving him powerless to answer the geas' terrible summons. The boy swallowed, feeling desperation well up inside him. Pressure beat against his ears, savage as the whistle of air off a stormfalcon's wings, and the threat of unending pain raised sweat on his temples.

"I beg you," he said hoarsely, distressed that his anguish was turned to a public spectacle. "I must have a boat."

Mathieson Keldric stirred. He looked up at Jaric as though fully aware of his presence for the first time. "Trade? Fer that?" He inclined his head toward the cloak, and tangled white hair fell, obscuring his face. But Jaric thought for a second that the clear old eyes showed a glaze of tears. He started to move away.

"Well, then," said Mathieson Keldric gruffly. "Ye'll have to come to the docks. My *Callinde*'s a lady, straight down to her keel, an' I'd not let her go to a man who never set eyes on her. Fair?"

Jaric struggled to suppress the tremor which arose in his knees and traveled the length of his spine. "Fair," he said softly.

An ugly murmur arose at his back, threaded through by the louder voice of the trader and sibilant whispers of sorcery. Jaric heard; he realized old Keldric's attachment to his boat was legend in Mearren Ard. The fact the man had considered parting with her earned the boy nothing but suspicion from the villagers.

Forced to move before their muttering metamorphosed into threats, Jaric extended his hand toward the old man. He spoke without urgency, his phrases shaped with the courtesy learned at Morbrith's great hall. "Come, then, and perhaps the lady will approve."

The voices grew louder. As the old man pushed himself to his feet, Jaric felt the villagers' resentment rise against him, menacing as the rush of breakers over rock. But Mathieson Keldric's lame old body could not be hurried. He walked with painful, halting steps, steadied by Jaric's arm. Bystanders moved grudgingly aside, leaving a wide berth as the pair made their way through the door.

Jaric drew a deep breath of relief. The night was damp and chill after the close heat of the tavern, braced by the tang of salt. But the cold calmed the boy's nerves. He shortened stride to match old Keldric's limp, grateful for the fog which smothered the lane leading down to the harbor; murky weather at least spared him the accusing observation of the villagers. Soon the last cottage passed behind, lighted windows eclipsed by the black hulk of a warehouse.

Surf boomed distantly off the barrier point and the air smelled sourly of tide wrack and fish. Mathieson Keldric lifted a lantern from a hook on a piling driven deep into the sand of the strand. He fumbled with crooked fingers to manage the striker, but something about the resistant set of his back warned Jaric not to offer help. Although Keldric was ruinously crippled, he was not incapable; Jaric sensed that the boat he needed so desperately to buy was inextricably interconnected with the old man's pride. To interfere even in kindness would offend.

The spark spat against the dampened wick and hesitantly caught. Flame quivered behind panes patterned with crystalline whorls of salt as Keldric raised the lantern. The boy stepped behind the old man onto the wet planks of the east dock. Mist rolled past, breaking like ghostly surf over his feet; it seethed through the black teeth of the pilings, stringing droplets on Jaric's hair and clothing. Keldric moved forward, silhouetted against the fuzzy globe of lanternlight. Through the formless darkness ahead, Jaric saw the gleam of a braided painter, then a high curving prow and the angled line of a headstay. But the rank smell of decayed wood warned him, long before the antique shear of the thwart stood exposed in the lanternlight; *Callinde* was ancient and rotten, and nothing close to seaworthy.

Painfully aware the derelict hull was Keldric's sole treasure, a shrine preserved in memory of the brighter days of youth, Jaric's first thought was not for himself. For one stunned moment he ignored the inhuman wrench of the geas' directive and stared at the elder who waited at his side, gnarled fingers gripping the ring of the lantern with an air of desperate self-sacrifice.

"Why?" The boy searched for an answer in the clear pale eyes. "Why would you give her up, after all these years?"

Mathieson Keldric shrugged. "You've the need in you." He glanced at his hands and spat. "I can't so much as plane a timber any more, and *Callinde* looks sloppy as a whore."

But Jaric knew there was more. Silently smothering an anger he could ill afford to express, he waited to hear the rest.

Old Mathieson shrugged again, then glared defiantly at the young man's face. "Well, then. My wife, I saw her standing at your shoulder, back there in the tap. Black-haired she was, full of her youth, and prettier than ever I remembered when she was alive. Seems the old lady would have it so." Suddenly his expression changed to worry. "Ye won't want to be changing her name, then?"

Jaric turned abruptly away, poisoned by sudden revelation. Taen had intervened, plied her dream-weaver's talents upon a defenseless old man to help buy him passage. But bitterest of all was the recognition that he had no choice but accept; the battered old hull represented his only alternative if he was to escape the insufferable pain of the geas.

Misinterpreting Jaric's stricken silence, Mathieson caught the young man's sleeve in a clumsy attempt at consolation. "She'll bear ye safely, son, my word on't. A grand old lady *Callinde* might be, but there's no leak to her can't be fixed with tools and a sound bit of planking. Ye'll see, then."

Jaric straightened, regarding the old man with clear-eyed honesty. "Thank you. And no, I'll never be changing her name." He pulled the ice otter cloak from his arm, draped it across Keldric's stooped shoulders. "If you'll guide me with the carpentry, I'll make her new again, sound as the day she was launched. That's a promise."

Mathieson Keldric thrust his lantern into the boy's hand and spat on his palm. "Your oath?"

Jaric nodded.

The old man pressed his damp hand to his forehead and stared at his feet, abruptly embarrassed to have insisted on ritual. "Well, then," he said briskly. "Tools are ashore, and I sure's tide can't lug them like I did when I was your age. Or did ye not want to start now?"

"At once," said Jaric. "She ought to be hauled, though."

Keldric grinned. "Aye. That's work for two stout men." He threw Jaric a look of bright-eyed challenge. "How well can ye row?"

Jaric smiled back, his frustration partially alleviated. "As well as I must. Is your grand old lady rigged with oars?"

Keldric answered with a dry cackle of laughter. Aged and lame and heartbroken as he was, Mathieson was villager enough to find humor in Jaric's ignorance. "I've a dory, son," he drawled, and in the foggy darkness the night before spring solstice, proceeded to instruct the boy how *Callinde* should be towed from her slip.

Enfolded still within the capsule of the Vaere, Taen dreamed she sat in the timeless twilight of the grove. The pale folds of a silk robe clothed a maturity she had only recently come to accept as her own, and a basin of carved crystal lay balanced across her knees, much as it had for the better part of a fortnight while Tamlin taught her the art of casting dream images onto the surface of water. At present three companies of Kisburn's royal troops performed toy-sized maneuvers, bounded by the confines of the chased silver rim.

To Taen the exercise seemed a frivolous waste of time. Through her mastery of the Sathid, she could tap any mind on Keithland at will, then impart her findings through a dream link with the flawless purity of thought. Causing her recipient to *believe* he viewed an image within water was bothersome, an added layer of illusion for which she discerned no useful purpose. Taen sighed, while in the bowl the Grand Warlord-General delivered a command to his aide. Trumpets flourished, signaling inspection of troops was complete. Neat squares of pikemen lifted miniature weapons in salute and the lowering sunlight of late afternoon flashed against polished blades. Even to Taen's unpracticed eye the movement described lethal perfection. After rigorous hours of drill the troops were ready for action; Kisburn intended to sail his force to Cliffhaven within the fortnight, and Emien would go with them. Still Tamlin insisted she refine a showy set of illusions designed to add mystery to her dream-weaver's talents.

Touched by sharp anger, Taen tilted the basin. Water sloshed, scattering droplets over the rim. Kisburn's soldiers streamed into a muddle of scarlet and gold, then vanished as her contact dissipated. "Why?" she demanded, though the clearing at present seemed deserted.

Tamlin appeared instantly. His bells jangled in dissonant displeasure as he gestured toward the basin. "It's a necessary defense. The demons would kill you should they ever suspect your true capabilities. Not only are they telepathic, they also recall every memory of their forebears, back to the dawn of their history; fortunately for mankind they evolved no cultural need for ceremony or legend or ritualized religion."

Tamlin folded his arms across his chest, bushy brows knitted into a frown. "Twenty-seven generations have passed since the Great Fall. Through that time, I have cloaked mankind's most precious secrets in the forms of myth and legend. The demons attach no value to such things; they perceive no logic in faith and no reality outside of racial memory. They observe and fail to discover my intent."

Taen remained unimpressed. Tamlin shifted his weight from one foot to the other and irritably jabbed a finger at the bowl. "If your client believes he sees a vision in water, but that image does not exist for other eyes, then the demon who observes will dismiss the incident as mummery, the time-worn, traditional sort of fortune-telling many a common man will spend copper to hear. The demon does not comprehend man's craving to control his future. In this manner your true talent will pass unnoticed."

Taen traced her hand over the carved crystal, mollified by the tirade. "I'm sorry. I never guessed."

Bells clashed softly as Tamlin seated himself in the grass opposite her. He rested his chin on steepled fingers and spoke in gentler tones. "Understand me, child. More of mankind's heritage than is safe for you to know lies similarly concealed. Landfast itself has no other defense. To save its records from the demons, you must trust my judgment. Now engage your craft once again and show me how Jaric fares."

Taen leveled the basin between her knees, then waited for the water to settle. She needed the interval to steady her own nerves more than any other reason. As often as she looked in on Jaric since Anskiere's geas resumed effect, she had been unable to make peace with herself for his unhappiness; neither Tamlin's insistence nor Keithland's peril could negate her sense of responsibility.

Taen closed her eyes and carefully cleared her mind. Despite her trepidations, Jaric's presence flowed easily through the channel of her talents; through the process of restoring his memory, she had come to know his mind better than any person living. Her call arose like a bird, sped on the silent wings of thought to the north coast and the village of Mearren Ard.

With barely a pause for transition, Taen felt the salty tang of the breeze blow against her cheek, sea-scoured and overlaid by the pungent smell of spruce. Within the crystal basin an image bloomed on the water.

In a yard beside a weathered shed, new grass lay sprinkled like snow with the delicate curls of shavings; there Jaric bent over a trestle, busily planing a length of wood which would shortly replace a cracked thwart on *Callinde's* starboard side. Linen cloth clung to his sweating shoulders as he worked, and wood chips speckled his wrists, pale against sunburned skin. Impressed by the play of muscle in his arms, Taen reflected that the wenches of Morbrith Keep would probably treat him to a different sort of teasing were they to observe him now.

But the unremitting pull of the geas and days of constant toil left Jaric too worn to reflect upon himself; plank by plank he labored to restore *Callinde's* rotted timbers. The discomfort of Anskiere's summons permitted him no surcease, even at sundown when other men sought rest. Jaric worked through the nights by lanternlight, feverish and driven, until his fingers cramped on the tools and his body collapsed from weariness.

Watching the strong rhythmic strokes of the plane across the board, Taen ached to reach out, lend him the peace her dream-weaver's powers could provide. But Jaric would tolerate no trace of her contact since the day he had fallen on the decks of Tavish's boat. Convinced she had used him for her own selfish ends, the boy stayed isolated, though loneliness ate him hollow and his arm trembled with fatigue as he lifted the plane to clear the blade. Shavings fluttered to the ground, pale and delicate as moths. For all his inexperience, the boy handled the tool well; even old Mathieson found little cause for complaint. But the dream-weaver saw beyond competence to the measure of pain which inspired it; Jaric acted out of necessity. He derived no joy from his achievements.

Taen shifted the image, caused the basin's crystal rim to frame *Callinde's* hull. Whole sections of her starboard side stood stripped of planking, leaving the bared curve of several ribs exposed against the sky. To port, yellow boards contrasted harshly with the weathered timbers of her keel; Jaric had made remarkable progress. Still his craft was days away from launch; Kisburn's army would not wait. Swift as the clouds which hazed the horizon beyond Mearren Ard's docks, the King's ships would cross the sea; even the Kielmark's fortress could not stay demons.

Suddenly a blur of motion flicked across the edge of the image. Startled by its presence, Taen stiffened. She bent closer to the basin, a disturbed frown on her face.

Tamlin rose to his feet with a clash of bells. "Something's wrong," he said quickly. "What do you see?"

"I don't know." Taen focused her attention on Jaric, seeking the source of the shadow which had passed briefly across her contact. Yet the sunlight shone brightly in Mathieson's yard and Jaric worked on undisturbed. Concerned, Taen refined her scrutiny. The fine hands which once had penned copy for a Duke's library were now blistered and raw from handling adze and hammer. Stress had left the boy gaunt and exhausted. Beneath the sun-bleached hair which spilled over his brow, his eyes were deeply circled; but other than fatigue Taen found no mark upon him.

She looked up, defeated. At a loss to explain the intuitive prickle of warning which stirred the hair at the nape of her neck, she said, "I did see something."

"I know." The Vaere toyed with his pipe. "There's a reason."

But he would not say what it was. When Taen pressed for an answer, he simply vanished, and none of the usual cues would call him back.

Left to herself, Taen lifted the crystal bowl from her lap and laid it aside on the grass. Disregarding Tamlin's directive pertaining to the water, she gathered her powers as dream-weaver and with no more effort than daydreaming bent her thoughts back to Mathieson's yard and Jaric. She would watch, she decided, to see whether the shadow which had grazed the edge of her vision returned.

Westerly sunlight cast steepening shadows through the opened sections of *Callinde*'s hull. Sheltered from the sea breeze by the angled roof of the shack, Jaric set his plane aside and with a forester's precision laid a fire beneath the steam box. While the planks heated he took up the adze and began to dress an uncut length of timber. Taen watched the chips fly, pale and silver as flying fish in the failing light. The intensity of Jaric's determination awed her. Unlike Emien, this boy had survived the scarring left by the inadequacy which had poisoned his early years. Hurt and pressured and driven, so far he had managed to continue without striking out in hatred. Taen caught her breath. The comparison wounded. Beside Jaric, her brother's shortcomings stood exposed with devastating and bitter clarity. Taen twisted her fingers in the fine silk of her robe. She must not abandon hope. One day perhaps Jaric might guide Emien to regain his faith in human compassion.

Sunset faded over Mearren Ard. Jaric paused to wipe the sweat from his brow and light the lantern looped to a line on *Callinde*'s yard arm. Keldric's unmarried niece arrived with a basket of bread, smoked fish, and cheese. Oblivious to the invitation in her smile, Jaric thanked her, his manner restrained with the polish of Morbrith's high court. Beneath his courtesy Taen read the raw pain left by Kencie's thoughtlessness. For all his accomplishments, Jaric placed no faith in the change wrought within himself since his accident in Seitforest; although the prettiest girl in Mearren Ard lingered to watch him eat, he misread her admiration for pity. Misery kept him silent. And too shy to breach his solitude without encouragement, the girl twisted her chestnut hair back under her cloak hood and quietly left as she had for seven nights previously.

Jaric dusted breadcrumbs from his tunic and resumed work. Jostled by wind, the lantern turned the yard to a circle of wheeling shadows. Removed from the rest of humanity and merged with the rhythm of Jaric's mallet as he fastened heated planks to the hull with tree-nails of locust, Taen almost missed the transition even as it happened. The boy missed stroke. The heavy fastener's mallet banged squarely into his thumb, splitting the skin. He swore once without rancor, and twisted his shirt cuff over the cut to stop the bleeding. The wound itself was slight. But tired as he was, the pain opened an avenue of distraction; his control slipped. The force of the geas welled up inside him, a whirlwind battling to escape the slender check-rein of reason.

A gust blasted the yard, streaming the lantern flame like blood. Jaric cried out, bent to his knees with his arms cradled against his chest. Wind lashed the hair across his cheek. For one stark instant, Taen saw the black-barred wingtips of the stormfalcon beat in the darkness above his head. Then the vision left her. The disturbance died, leaving only the distant crash of the surf beyond the harbor. Jaric shook himself. He reached for his mallet with the dull mechanical motions of extreme exhaustion; unable to bear the enormity of his burden, Taen wrenched herself out of contact.

The grove surrounded her with maddening and changeless serenity. Taen clutched the silken robe about her shoulders though she was not cold and with all the urgency she possessed, summoned Tamlin.

The Vaere appeared at once. His hands were unoccupied by any pipe and his bells stayed utterly silent. "You saw the stormfalcon," he said softly.

Taen burst into tears. Irritated by the unwanted display of emotion, she nodded. "How did you guess?"

Tamlin seated himself in his accustomed place on the stone at the grove's center. "No guess, child, but a natural law of sorcery. Anskiere loosed an energy, the stormcall you perceive in the shape of the falcon. It built a gale, as he intended, and dissipated, carrying out the ruin of Kisburn's war fleet. Left to itself, the seed of that energy had no direction of its own. Under normal circumstances it would lie fallow until its creator unmade its pattern. But when Tathagres interrupted the geas which summoned Jaric, the break opened what once was a closed loop; a structure created by Anskiere stood out of balance, a circumstance he never intended. For such disharmony would attract and bind any loose ends he might have left lying about: in this case, the stormcall."

Taen twisted the thin silk of her cuff. "What will happen to Jaric?" And Emien, she thought, but did not broach that fear.

A bell chimed as Tamlin shifted position. "The geas and the stormfalcon stand linked. With each passing day the tempest will build. If we are lucky, Jaric will sail before it breaks."

But even without asking, Taen knew. *Callinde* could not possibly be ready in time. She swallowed, reluctant to confront the inevitable conclusion; Kisburn's entire war fleet had been crushed like chaff before the fury of that storm. Tortured by thoughts of Jaric's antique craft being smashed by a thundering avalanche of foam, she found her voice and spoke, hoping the Vaere could silence her fear. "Jaric might never make Cliffhaven."

Tamlin stood up, his pipe suddenly appearing in his hand. For a prolonged moment he puffed in silence, an expression which might have been
sorrow half veiled by rising smoke. "He might not. We can do nothing
more for him except pray that he will. He is Ivain's son. There is much
reason for faith in that."

But hope was not enough to sustain Taen through the days ahead,
while Jaric wore himself ragged repairing *Callinde*'s battered hull. The gaps
in her planking closed with what seemed agonizing slowness. By the time
he hammered the brass fittings on the raw new shaft of her steering oar,
the flat deadly calm Taen recalled from her time aboard *Crow* had already
settled over Mearren Ard. The fir trees stood still and silent on the slopes
above the village, unruffled by any trace of breeze; confined to the harbor,
fishermen varnished spars and swore at the glassy surface of the sea. And
though no man put words to the notion, all thought of the boy struck
down by a sorcerer's curse on the decks of Tavish's boat. Talk in the tavern
turned restless.

Jaric continued his labors, possessed and oblivious. He threaded new
halyards through the blocks of *Callinde*'s mast and stitched patches on her
torn sails. The calm broke in the hour she was launched. Keldric's niece
braved the icy, ripping gusts to make her way to the docks, a cloak of
green wool bundled in her arms.

"For you," she shouted, her voice barely audible above the shrill keening of the wind through the stays. Her comely features were scrubbed and
hopeful and her braids were tied with red ribbons.

Jaric scrambled out of the depths of a storage locker, his hair whipped
like spun gold against his neck. He accepted the gift with genuine appreciation, but his thanks were stilted with wariness.

"Try it on then, Jaric." Puzzled by his reluctance, the girl placed a
freckled hand on his arm.

Jaric flinched from the contact, startled. His dark eyes widened with
an emotion the girl could not understand. She stammered an apology and
retreated, bursting into a run past *Callinde*'s slip. The boy stared after her,
frozen in his tracks. He wanted to shout, to call her back and apologize.
But words stuck in his throat. He watched until the girl disappeared while
the wind screamed around his head, lashing the wool against his thighs.

"Old storm'll catch you in the harbor," warned Mathieson, shuffling
up beside him. "Better to wait her out."

Jaric shook his head. He tossed the cloak into the locker and latched
it closed, then untied *Callinde*'s docklines. Canvas cracked like a maddened
animal as he raised the main halyard. Clouds roiled above the masthead
and angry gusts puckered the water, sending wavelets curling off the steering oar. Old Mathieson spat and bit his knuckle. Only a madman, or the
most brave, would put to sea in such weather.

Frail against lowering skies, the boat drew away from the dock. Jaric hauled in the sheets, felt the lines slam against the blocks as wind filled the main. *Callinde* heaved, timber shivering as she gained way. Foam ruffled off her bow. Standing forlorn on the docks, old Mathieson Keldric saw her heel like a lady and run for the open sea.

"*Callinde* keep ye safe," he murmured. The gale parted the fur of the ice otter cloak which clothed his stooped shoulders; but pelts which would have pleased a prince meant less than nothing to him. With tear-brimmed eyes he watched the boat which had once been his father's grow small and finally vanish, another man's hand on her helm.

CHAPTER XIX

Stormfalcon

Mathieson Keldric was not the only observer to watch *Callinde* depart from Mearren Ard. On the Isle of the Vaere, Taen bent over the crystal basin, her vision centered with feverish intensity upon the dusky tanbark sail of the boat which tacked across the harbor. Past the headland, waves battered like rampaging cavalry against *Callinde*'s sides, sheeting spray from prow to keel. Jaric adjusted his course for the open sea and Cliffhaven. The steering oar dragged against his arms and the boat bucked and rolled, her wake a boil of froth. Yet Jaric held true to his heading, though *Callinde* seemed little more than a splinter tossed haplessly in the path of the elements.

The point fell swiftly astern. Taen's crystal bowl showed a froth of tumbling whitecaps, *Callinde* a murky shadow blurred by smoking sheets of spindrift. Reminded of the shipwreck and disaster which had traumatized her early childhood on Imrill Kand, Taen chased the contact from her mind.

The water obediently went blank. Although the basin's chased rim gleamed silver and ordinary beneath her sweating palms, Taen's conscience continued to haunt her. *Had she not interfered, Jaric would be in Seitforest still, safely tending traps with Telemark.* Taen raised the bowl with trembling hands. Her nerves refused to settle. Water dribbled like tears over her fingers as she placed the vessel on the grass by her side.

She had been a coward, she realized. The ordeal of Sathid mastery had carved a mark of horror deep within her mind; left the ugly certainty that Emien would betray those closest to his heart rather than confront the error of his ways. Taen ran her fingers through her long silky hair. She had used Tamlin's plans for Jaric as an excuse, permitted herself to believe the Firelord's heir could restore Emien through release of Anskiere from the ice cliffs. That way she need never confront her brother's twisted nature, might avoid entirely the truth the Sathid had revealed.

Taen stared at her hands. The fingers were longer, shapelier and more graceful than those of the little girl who had first landed on the Isle of the Vaere. She had grown up, but childishly permitted herself to shelter her fears behind the risks of others, even justified Jaric's discomfort for the sake of Emien's need. Now Jaric battled for his life against the force of Anskiere's sorceries. The dream-weaver who had influenced his fate felt shamed.

Taen dropped her hands into her lap. The calm of Vaerish enchantment left her restless. Its changeless security made Jaric's peril more vivid by contrast. Chastened by his stubborn display of courage, Taen saw she could never leave her brother's future reliant on the efforts of others. The possibility the Firelord's heir might fail had forced brutal recognition; she must try to recover her brother herself, even should she forfeit his love in the attempt.

Taen settled herself in the grass and glanced carefully around the grove. The clearing was deserted; Tamlin had not reappeared since his explanation of the stormfalcon's presence, nor did he respond to any call. Left entirely to herself, Taen ignored the crystal basin. For the first time since accomplishing her mastery, she closed her eyes and bent her dream-weaver's skills to Kisburn's court and her brother.

Subtle Vaerish twilight yielded before the hard-edged splendor of a palace ballroom. Candles blazed from tiers of silver sconces, casting brilliant and costly light across gaudily dressed nobles, tables laden with sweetmeats, and a quintet of royal musicians. The King had commanded a lavish celebration to honor the eve of the fleet's departure, and there Taen located her brother.

No trace of a fisherman's origins remained about the young man who perched on the silk cushions of a windowseat, twirling a filled goblet between his fingers. Emien had eliminated his accent; the hand which gripped the wine glass was elegantly uncallused. Clothed in a black velvet tunic with scarlet and gold trim, the boy radiated charm and dark good looks.

Several court maidens clustered about, vying for his attention. But Taen saw that his wit was barbed and his smile self-derisive. Emien found no joy in the ladies' company. That they should waste admiration on anyone who lacked influence and power made no sense to him. He received their flattery with secret contempt and the wine stayed untasted in his glass.

Taen gathered her dream-reader's skills. She had no desire to exert influence on her brother amid a chamber full of revelers, particularly where Lord Sholl was certain to be present. Somehow she must entice Emien to leave. Careful not to disrupt Emien's thoughts, Taen awaited her chance.

A ringletted blond exclaimed coyly. With a toss of her head, she flicked a trailing curl of hair across Emien's wrist. Her ribbons looped in his cuff. Taen seized her opportunity; while the girl's flirting distracted him, she slipped silently into her brother's mind. Emien laughed. He flipped the ribbon away without spilling his wine and returned a witty remark. But his thoughts were far removed from the gaiety of the ballroom, Taen discovered. In a private chamber, Tathagres and the King held conference, finalizing plans for the demon alliance against Cliffhaven. Later, Emien knew, Tathagres would sit alone before a burning candle, hands raised to the collar at her throat and her mind deep in trance. At that moment she would engage three different races of demons and bind them into service, her purpose to bring down Anskiere of Elrinfaer. Ablaze with desire to possess such power for himself, Emien wished he could be present while she spell-wove.

Taen recognized her opening. With a touch imperceptible as dewfall, she touched her brother's mind and sharpened his inner longing with restlessness.

The fair girl tossed her hair irritably over her shoulder. "Emien! You're not listening."

"I'm sorry." The boy rose and pressed his wine goblet into her hand. "Will you excuse me?"

"You're not leaving, Emien. Not so soon." The girl tilted her pretty head and trailed her fingers along his sleeve. "At midnight there are going to be fireworks."

Emien ignored the girl's touch. Oddly unmoved, he glanced quickly over the ballroom, but found no guest compelling enough to hold his interest. Oblivious to the dream-weaver whose meddling made him bored with the glitter, the festivities, and the young ladies, he pressed past his admirers without speaking. They stared after him in puzzled disappointment as he crossed the polished marble of the dance floor and disappeared through a side door.

The hallway beyond lay deserted, except for occasional uniformed guardsmen standing motionless at their posts. Taen shaped her touch into a compulsion, causing Emien to hasten his steps. His fine calf boots made no sound on the carpets as he turned down a darkened corridor and let himself outside, into the windy blackness of a colonnaded courtyard.

Moonlight shone through polished marble pillars and marked concise geometrics on the patterned tile beneath. Emien leaned against the door panel, felt the latch click gently shut. Unaware that a sister's compulsion had driven him to seek this deserted place, he shivered in the cold spring air and discovered he was not alone.

A woman waited amid the silvery landscape of last year's rose garden, her robe of light loose cloth rippling in the breeze. A moonstone gleamed on a chain at her throat, and fine black hair lay braided into coils about her head, laced with a wreath of myrtle blossoms. Stunned by her beauty, Emien gripped the doorlatch in astonishment. The night air stuck in his throat.

He raised his eyes to the oval of her face. As he studied the delicate arch of her brow and lips, a strange and haunting familiarity made his heart twist in his chest. *"Taen?"*

The woman smiled. The sweetness of her expression snapped the last thread of disbelief. Emien drew a ragged breath and dragged his fingers across his eyes. Her presence could not be real; only a dream born of wine and rich food. But when he looked again, she came closer, her step strangely wrong, and her body eerily ripened into maturity.

"No, I don't limp anymore, Emien," his sister said softly, as if responding to his unspoken thought.

She moved nearer. The thin silk of her robe swished softly through the grass, leaving darkened trails through the dew. Paralyzed by incredulity, Emien stood with his back rammed against the unyielding wood of the doorframe. Taen's shadow flowed ahead of her, an etched silhouette against the tiles. Two more steps would bring her to his side.

"No!" Emien raised his arm before his face, as if to ward off a nightmare. "Leave me!"

Taen closed the distance, stopped scant inches away. "Why should I go, brother? I bring no harm."

Even with his eyes hidden, Emien felt the warmth of her skin; he could still hear the rustle of silk across her breasts as she breathed. Stirred by the breeze, the skirt of her gown brushed gently against his leg. The boy flinched back, felt the iron rivets of the door bear painfully into his back.

"I never drowned." Firmly, deftly, Taen built the illusion of her presence into her brother's mind. Her voice echoed convincingly through the confines of the colonnade. "What you behold is the truth. When *Crow* foundered, Anskiere delivered me safely to the Isle of the Vaere. By the tales you can guess the rest. I have grown up, Emien. I am no longer lame. And I have discovered happiness beyond any I could have found on Imrill Kand."

Encouraged by her dream-weaver's skills, Emien reached out and touched a coil of her hair. But the warm reality of her served only to frighten him. He hardened his hand into a fist, bashed it with bruising force into the door at his back. His reply emerged half-strangled from his throat. "No."

Taen stared at him, heartbroken. "Why, Emien? Why must you forsake belief? What change has Tathagres wrought, that you find no joy in the news that your sister lives and is content?"

Emien twisted his face away, every tendon in his neck pulled taut with distress. His mouth quivered. Taen sensed the clamor in his mind, felt his thoughts wheel like a flock of startled birds as pride and fear and loyalty warred. She ached, sharing his pain, yet not for an instant did she relent.

"There is peace in honesty, Emien, and forgiveness in understanding. Look to your heart." Gently, Taen pressed against his mind, promising comfort and love. "Abandon Tathagres, my brother, for she holds you in contempt."

The words touched him. Emien spun to face her, his expression darkened with indecision. Taen had spoken the truth, dragged him naked into the light of judgment. Emien gasped. Blackened by the evil of his hatred, he buried his head in his arms and shrank against the door. But his sister's image pursued, engraved like a spell of remembrance against the inside of his eyelids. Her words beat against his ears, bright and innocent as his memory of the goat bells in the meadows of Imrill Kand.

"Mother misses you, Emien." Taen's voice softened, tormenting him with hope. "She mourns your absence more deeply than the death of our father."

The reminder suddenly became more than Emien could bear. He lashed out at Taen's presence in pain and rage and terror. "My sister is *dead!*" His shout rang deafeningly off the stone, sent ugly undertones echoing across the garden.

The defiant note of his rejection shocked Taen like a blow. "You shame your ancestors, brother. Would you betray them as well?"

But Emien had regained his footing, and her plea moved him not at all. "Yes." His voice throbbed with malice. "What are they but a miserable, stinking lot of fools? I will *never* waste myself remembering their useless lives, all drenched oilskins and cod nets. When I have done, their kind, and perhaps even the sea itself, will serve me."

His conviction rang vindictively across the dream link, poisonous as the venom of a snake. Taen perceived the evil in him and the depth of it sent her talent reeling out of focus. She wakened weeping within the clearing of the Vaere. The enchanted silence did little to restore her. The instant she parted contact, she had seen into Emien's heart, and known he chose against her out of greed. Since the first intoxicating taste of power, his hunger had increased to the point where he could not, and would never, give up his desire to rise in dominance over his fellow man. Taen drew her knees against her chest, her head bent with unconsolable grief. Tathagres had done her work well; not even Anskiere himself could recover her brother now.

Emien fled the colonnade, wrenched the door closed against the moonlit garden with a crash that shook the carved lintel. Trembling and sweating, he slammed the bar home, then stood panting, his weight braced against the cold steel. His sister was a small child, dead, *drowned beneath the waves. He had seen* Crow *founder.* The pain of his conscience gradually eased, exposed to logic and reason. His panic subsided. The grown woman who had appeared to him could only be a dream, a profanity shaped by Anskiere's guile and sent to undermine his purpose.

Emien smiled in the darkness. Suddenly exultant, he threw back his head and laughed. Obviously, his presence in Tathagres' plan *meant something.* He had been a fool not to see it. Why else would a sorcerer trained by the Vaere trouble with him at all? The idea consumed him, left him drunk with a reckless sense of importance. Perhaps Taen *had* survived, even told him the truth. If so, she was a creature of the Vaere, robbed of her childhood and used as a pawn against him.

Emien pushed away from the door and strode down the corridor. He was tired of waiting, sick to death of being manipulated. Intoxicated by a savage flood of arrogance, he hastened to his chambers. He would arrange Anskiere's destruction himself. The Kielmark would be too busy with the demons upon his shores to bother with a single man. Ice could be broken; mortal steel could pierce a sorcerer's flesh. Emien blotted sweaty palms on his black velvet tunic. If Anskiere died by his hand, that surely would earn even Tathagres' respect.

Emien stepped confidently into his chamber. The sconces were dark and the air chilly; the chambermaid had forgotten to close the windows at sundown. Leaving the door ajar at his back, the boy fumbled about on the mantel until he located striker and flint. He lit a single candle, then banged the mullioned casement closed, setting the flame streaming in the draft. Emien cursed the flickering light. He knelt beneath the slate slab of the mantel and began to lay a fire, no longer awed by the luxuriously patterned carpet beneath his knees. He had come a long way from the wooden planked cottage where he had been born. Nothing could ever convince him to return.

Emien struck a spark to the kindling and rose. He crossed to the wardrobe, flung the inlaid doors wide. Although the clothes within lay deep in shadow, his fingers moved quickly, sorting rich velvets and brocades by touch. He passed the soft weave of his favorite lawn shirt; this once, finery did not interest him. Instead, he chose heavy linen breeches, a leather tunic, and the sea boots he had purchased following the crossing from Skane's Edge. Preoccupied and impatient, Emien dumped the clothing across the bed and began to untie the laces of his cuffs.

He did not hear Tathagres enter the room at his back. Surprised by his presence, she paused in the doorway. The plain clothing on the bed, and the decisive set to Emien's back did not escape her notice. An expression of rapt calculation crossed her face.

Tathagres waited while the boy loosened his shirt. Then silently, she crossed the floor and trailed slender fingers against the bare skin of his neck. "Emien?"

He started violently, but did not whirl. Tathagres felt fine tremors of tension course through the flesh beneath her hand. But when the boy spoke, his words were controlled. "I thought you had business with the King?"

"It is finished." Tathagres shifted her wrist, caught the silk of his collar, and gently tugged.

Emien faced her reluctantly. Despite his determined restraint, the breath caught in his throat. Tathagres had dressed for the celebration. A gown of white lace clung provocatively to her slim waist; bracelets of gold wire circled her wrists. Threaded by a circlet set with amethysts, her hair spilled like spun glass over bare shoulders. A delicate scent hung on the air about her person. Unbalanced by her nearness, Emien ran an appreciative glance over the ripe cleft of her breasts.

Tathagres saw, and a thin smile of amusement touched her lips. She traced the line of Emien's collarbone with a teasing fingernail. "Why did you leave the festivities? It's very unlike you. Weren't there to be fireworks?"

The query seemed casual. But Emien felt the power behind her words; she could force the truth from him if she chose. Seizing what advantage he could, he feigned nonchalance, and told her of his experience in the deserted rose garden. "My sister Taen came to me in a vision. She may have survived the foundering of Crow. If so, Anskiere sent her to the Isle of the Vaere, for she appeared to me as a woman grown." He paused. Tathagres' touch against his skin made him ache. Although his body quivered with desire, he resisted fiercely, aware she used her beauty as a tool against him. "Taen's childhood was stolen from her. I would see the Stormwarden suffer for that."

Tathagres dropped her hand, frowning. Emien stepped back until his calves pressed against the solid wood of the bed frame. With barely concealed defiance, he resumed unfastening his shirt. Tathagres continued to regard him. She toyed with the bracelets on her wrists, elegant features preoccupied by an expression he could not interpret.

"Your sister urged you to forswear your oath of service," Tathagres said at last. She seemed almost wistful. "Is this why you choose to attempt Anskiere's death by yourself?"

Emien disguised a shiver by shrugging the shirt from his shoulders. He tossed the garment onto the bed. "Do you care?"

"Yes." Tathagres closed the distance between them. With her arms relaxed at her sides, she bent her head and laid it against the corded muscle of his chest. "It does matter." Her breath tickled his skin. "Did you not guess? We are fated to work together."

Her presence burned him, released emotions like the raging spring tides. Emien managed a harsh laugh. "In all things, lady?" He caught her slim wrists, lifted them with the powerful grip of a sailor. "Remember, I've seen you kill. Why did you come?"

Tathagres did not resist, though her soft skin reddened under his fingers. She tilted her head, her lips within inches of his mouth. "It is destined."

Her voice held a queer note of sorrow. Jarred by the inconsistency, Emien stared at her. For a second Tathagres' control wavered. In one unguarded instant, the boy perceived she was bound to some purpose whose origin could not be guessed; she offered herself against her inner will. The urge to take her became overpowering. Lust beat like storm surf through Emien's veins. Unlike the sentries murdered on Cliffhaven's shores, he saw he could claim her with impunity.

He loosed his hold, turned her slim hands palm upward in his own. She shifted her weight. A lace-clad hip brushed his thigh. Emien quivered in response, released her entirely. Tathagres slipped her hands around his waist. One thinly covered breast traced a line of fire across his chest as she leaned up and kissed him. For a moment, Emien resisted her pliant touch. Then, with vindictive resentment, he wrapped his arms around her shoulders and pinned her against him.

Passion unfolded like the rush of water over rapids. Plunged beyond restraint by physical need, Emien sank to the bed, bearing Tathagres with him; clothing rumpled beneath their combined weight. The boy tugged at the fastenings of her gown. White lace parted, baring her eager flesh beneath his fingers. He buried his face in her warmth, all reason forgotten. His body trembled as, with skilled and exquisite simplicity, she freed the points of his hose. Emien locked his fingers in her hair. Lost to all caution, he failed to note the bright edge of triumph in her smile as she parted her legs and accepted him.

Their union was consummated swiftly. Flung headlong over a stormy crest of emotion, Emien subsided spent. He lay back on the crumpled coverlet, his pulse beating languidly in his veins. For a very long interval he did not care to move. Tathagres lay still against him, one arm flung possessively across his chest. Emien regarded her, and saw that she slept. Candlelight softened her, lending her curves the grace of a masterpiece painted on velvet. The boy lifted a silvery lock of hair off her cheek, revealing the unearthly perfection of her features. For all his awe, a thread of calculation wove through the wonder left by his first experience with a woman.

She believed she had used him. Abandoned in sleep with her limbs relaxed against him, she seemed vulnerable as any normal woman; the parted line of her lips emphasized her girlish fragility in a manner Emien found disturbing. There was nothing extraordinary about her. Try as he might, he could not equate the lady at his side with the witch who had raised the whirlwind on Cliffhaven or argued with royalty in the council chamber. The thought occurred to him that the powers she employed might be borrowed intact from the demons.

Emien traced the gold band at her throat with light fingers. A thrill of excitement coursed through his body. The plan conceived on the heels of Taen's visit suddenly seemed ridiculous and inferior; his ambitions abruptly expanded. Now he would bide his time. When the opportunity was ripest, he promised himself he would gain Tathagres' powers for his own. Then would Anskiere of Elrinfaer have great cause to fear him.

Storm waves hammered *Callinde*'s stout timbers and the wind shrieked through her stays with relentless fury. The steering oar dragged at Jaric's shoulders with the strength of a maddened horse. His palms had blistered cruelly. After five days at sea, the ache of stiffened muscles made every hour at the helm a trial of torment. His clothing clung, drenched, to his frame, chafing his skin with each movement. Yet such discomforts paled beside the driving weight of the geas. Jaric sailed with every fiber of his being strained on the thin edge of delirium.

Callinde's compass plunged and rocked in its casing, scrolled needle wheeling as she yawed over the wave crests. Jaric ignored it. He needed no instrument to guide him. Anskiere's summons consumed his awareness and the direction of its call twisted every fiber of his being into alignment. *Callinde* tossed on her heading. The spanker was sheeted too snugly; that the boat handled at all was a tribute to the skill of her designer. Yet Jaric had no energy to marvel upon her virtues. He felt far too wretched to bother adjusting lines. Weariness sapped his vitality; each passing hour, his hold upon the geas deteriorated. With one foot braced against the starboard thwart, he battled to keep his sanity through an unending nightmare of cloudy darkness.

The gale howled steadily on a broad reach; sped by its violence, *Callinde* made swift passage. Barely six days out of Mearren Ard, the beacon of Cliffhaven arose through the gloom above the bow. Jaric scarcely noticed. He steered, blinded by hallucination; at times he saw the stormfalcon's tawny-and-black form hurtling above his head, talons outstretched for landing, and the bluish halo about its spread wings backed by a dazzling spike of light. The vision often lasted hours at a stretch. Disoriented and exhausted, Jaric hoped he could muster the presence of mind to bring the boat in safely. The shore toward which the geas directed him was fast drawing nigh.

The island loomed nearer, jagged and dark but for the orange spark of the beacon in the fortress's topmost tower. Sheetlines snapped and banged against the blocks as *Callinde*'s sails bellied, smacked by contrary gusts. Jaric felt the kick of current against the steering oar, and the earthy scent of wet foliage filled his nostrils. Floorboards rattled underfoot as the boat pitched over ever steepening crests. Breakers hissed off the high curve of the prow, tumbling shoreward in ravening ranks of foam.

Jaric braced his body against the toss of deck. His hands clenched on wet wood as he muscled *Callinde* straight. The roar of water grinding over sand deafened his ears and salt spray dripped like tears from his face. At any instant he might be dashed to splinters on the fangs of a reef, though Mathieson had assured him that a boat with shallow draft would beach safely on strange shores. Jaric fretted, nerves drawn taut as bowstrings. Keldric's faith lent no comfort; not even *Callinde*'s stout keel was proof against submerged rock.

The waves steepened, crested, showering spray over the bow. Jaric squinted ahead through stinging eyes. The boat bumped. Sand grated harshly over wood, and the steering oar jerked, aground. Jaric cried out as the shaft was torn from his grasp. He sprang forward to release the sheets. Loosed to the caprice of the wind, canvas snapped with whipcrack reports overhead. The following wave boomed and broke, lifting the ancient boat. Jaric bit his lip in near panic. But the old man's word proved reliable; *Callinde* rode the rampaging flood of surf like a seal. Her chines crunched into fine gravel and she came to rest at last on the northern strand of Cliffhaven.

Jaric uncleated the halyards and with shaking fingers dropped the canvas. Headsails and spanker slithered in wet heaps across the deck. Then he hauled the mainyard across the wind, secured the sheets, and leapt down into the ankle-deep chill of the sea. The geas clawed at his mind, battering him toward the edge of madness; somewhere on this dark shore, the ice cliffs he had only known in dreams held the fate promised by the Stormwarden of Elrinfaer. But Jaric denied the insufferable compulsion long enough to rig a double set of blocks to a stout boulder in the scrub. Though his hands were raw and his back ached, he warped *Callinde* beyond reach of the breakers and saw her secure from the tide. Not even for Anskiere's summons would he abandon Mathieson's boat to ruin.

The stormfalcon flickered at the edge of his vision as he fetched his sword and dagger from his sea chest. Grimly Jaric ignored it. Delirium was not far off, he knew, but this close to release, he was determined not to give in. Belting his buckler to his waist, he hastened shoreward. But progress was difficult. Dry sand mired his steps, and the first solid ground he had trodden in days seemed to buckle and twist under his feet. Dunes shortly gave way to thornbrakes. Jaric stumbled through the night, cruelly clawed by briars and tripped by roots and rocks.

Suddenly a man shouted, almost at his elbow. "You! Stranger! Halt there."

Jaric heard a harplike ring as steel cleared a scabbard. He froze. Then someone unshuttered a storm lantern, pinning him in a wash of orange light. Blinded, Jaric threw an arm across his face. By squinting against the glare, he picked out a gleaming hedge of spearpoints and the needle-thin line of a drawn sword; with the sea at his back he was cornered.

A man wearing a captain's collar and badges stepped to the fore. "State your business promptly, else you risk your life."

Raked by the tingling discomfort of the geas, Jaric clung to the frayed remnants of reason. Instinct cautioned him to preserve every possible advantage; he narrowed his eyes to slits, keeping his vision adjusted to the dark. Then, careful to screen his movement behind the brush, he gripped the hilt of his weapon and answered in phrases chosen with the nuance of a court emissary. "I come in peace, summoned here by the Stormwarden of Elrinfaer. I honor your laws, but will answer to him only. Permit me to pass."

"He's for the Kielmark," said the captain abruptly, and gestured the soldiers. Spear points flashed and lowered, arrayed like the spokes of a wheel with Jaric at the hub.

"Alive?" said a voice from behind.

The captain nodded curtly.

Through an incredulous rush of anger, Jaric saw his request would be ignored; the men-at-arms intended to detain him, by force if need be. And that, abruptly, became a setback his stripped patience could not endure. He shouted, launching himself at the light. Brush clawed his wrists. A spear hissed past his ear, clanged harmlessly into rock. Then his fist smashed into the lantern, tumbling it to the ground. The flame was extinguished, leaving eight of the Kielmark's crack sentries blundering in the dark with their night vision spoiled.

Jaric ducked, bruising his shoulder against a weapon shaft. The man who held it shouted, "Here!"

Behind him the captain snapped an order; someone leapt to restore the light. Jaric drew his sword and dagger, desperately repressing an impending recurrence of the stormfalcon's black-and-gold-barred form. He stumbled over a stick and blundered into a leather-clad arm.

The owner whipped to face him. Confronted by a darting glint of steel, Jaric parried. The blow glanced cleanly off his dagger. But the belling note of swordplay drew his attackers like wolves. Even over the wind Jaric heard the crackle of boots approaching through the brush. He riposted, savage and desperate. The geas sang like a chorus of sirens in his ears, wrapping his nerves in fire. He felt no other pain, even when his opponent's blade grazed his shoulder.

Jaric covered with his dagger, late, but not disastrously. His enemy dropped his sword, clutching a cut wrist. Another swordsman took his place. Jaric lunged. His weapon struck steel with a shock that stung his arm. The impact jarred his concentration for a fraction of a second. Light flashed like lightning above his head; the stormfalcon's image rippled and vanished against the sky. Instantly his position was known to every man-at-arms present. They converged at a run.

"Fires, it's sorcery all over again," someone yelled. "Kielmark'll chew bricks. Anyone want to wager?"

A screech of steel met his offer as Jaric caught his blade in a bind. He wrenched the weapon free. Behind him a spark stabbed the darkness. The lantern flickered, blazed, and shot the brush with sudden shadows.

"Merciful Grace!" Jaric whirled, overtaken. A half dozen sword points angled at his chest, red as blood by lanternlight, and the captain stood with a poised spear at his back. The ending was evident; still, for all their seasoned experience, no soldier present foresaw the final move.

"You'll be my death," the quarry whispered. "I never had a choice."

And with an expression of agonized despair, he rushed them. The captain reacted, barely in time. He lowered his spearshaft and cracked the intruder's head from behind. The blow buckled Jaric at the knees. Sword and dagger flew from his grasp. He tumbled gracelessly after them, into a sprawling heap among the thorn.

The captain stepped quickly to his side, blade drawn and ready to kill. When the trespasser did not move, he kicked him sharply in the ribs. "Get up."

Neither violence nor words raised any response. A gust rattled violently through the brush. But Jaric himself lay lax as a lump of dough beneath the folds of his cloak. At that, the captain yanked the helmet from his head and raked sweaty hair from his forehead. "Fetch the light, boys. He's unconscious."

He sheathed his steel. Shadows danced across the briars as a man brought the lantern. The captain seized the outflung wrist which extended beyond the edge of the cloak and yanked Jaric onto his back. The wind parted the light hair, tossed it back from a profile lean as carved teak. Blood threaded his collarbone above a coarse, handspun collar, and the hands showed glistening patches of raw flesh left from unrelieved hours at the helm.

"Kor." The captain grimaced in disgust. "Whoever he is, he needed landfall here rather badly. Look, will you? He's scarcely grown a beard." The man paused and wiped his palms, as if embarrassed by his duty. "Still, the Kielmark'll want him for questioning. Strap his wrists damned tight. Boy or man, he's caused us nuisance enough for one night."

A subordinate ran to the beach and presently returned with a length of line cut from *Callinde*'s main sheet; he bound Jaric's limbs with thorough caution. Another sentry retrieved the boy's weapons. Then, with characteristic efficiency, the company rolled the trespasser in the storm-sodden folds of his cloak and bundled him off to the Kielmark.

CHAPTER XX

Captive

After nearly a fortnight's absence, Tamlin materialized in the grove with a disorganized flurry of feathers and beads. "Don't bother with the basin," he said quickly. "What has happened to Jaric?"

"Cliffhaven's sentries have taken him prisoner." Taen needed no words to elaborate. Since the day Tathagres upset Anskiere's geas, all Keithland's shipping had felt reverberations of the Kielmark's displeasure. As a trespasser brought in by a sorcerer, Jaric's very life stood in peril. At Tamlin's request, Taen cast her dream-weaver's perception northward with the direct force of a bolt shot from a crossbow. Within seconds her talents resolved an image.

High arched ceilings splintered brisk footsteps into echoes; a guard captain and two subordinates strode the length of a hallway floored with checkered tiles. They hefted an awkward item slung in cloth between them. Taen refined the focus of her perception and the object became recognizable as Kerainson Jaric, wrapped in his own green cloak and tied wrist and ankle with a length of salt-crusted rope.

The captain turned a corner, stopped, and knocked loudly against a closed door. "Night watch reporting, Lord," he said clearly. "I bring a trespasser from the north strand."

A curse issued from the other side of the portal. Then the latch clicked sharply. Wrenched open from within, the panel swung with a chirp of hinges and the Kielmark himself beckoned the men-at-arms across the threshold. Clothed in a tunic of fawn velvet, he carried no visible weapon; but no man who served under him dared disregard his gesture of ruthless authority.

The guardsmen entered, bringing sand-caked boots and sodden accoutrements onto the carpets of Cliffhaven's formal library. Books lined the walls from floor to roofbeams and the mantel above the hearth was carved of rarest merl marble inlaid with silver knotwork; the air smelled of leather and parchment. A sly-faced trader in russet sat opposite a table half buried in charts. He looked on with curiosity as the men-at-arms carried the prisoner into the light.

"Excuse the interruption," said the Kielmark to his guest. He blotted ink-smeared knuckles on a sleeve already stained, and pointed to the middle of an exquisitely patterned rug. "Dump him there. And pull that cloak off him. I want a look."

The men lowered their burden to the floor. When they tugged the wool from beneath his body, the captive rolled limply onto his stomach; turned toward the firelight, his face seemed that of a starved child. For a moment even the Kielmark stared in surprise. Then with a surge like an electrical current, Taen felt his distrust resurface. The Lord of Cliffhaven bent briskly to examine the unfortunate who had dared trespass his domain.

Taen steadied the dream link, gently widened her touch to include Jaric, then transmitted her findings to Tamlin. "He's unconscious, not dead. A sword grazed his shoulder when they took him. The cut is shallow, nothing serious. The bruise on his head is worse, but not so severe as the injury he suffered in Seitforest."

The Kielmark caught Jaric's shoulder and turned him, astonished to discover the blood streaked across the pale skin of his neck. "He gave you trouble, then! How much?" As he spoke, he tore the boy's collar aside and probed the injury beneath with blunt fingers. "You had better report in full. How did he come here?"

"Alone." The captain's armor squeaked as he shifted his weight. "The boy sailed in, on a ratty antique fishing vessel rigged out with a steering oar, one headsail, a square main, and a right damned clunker of a spanker."

The Kielmark's hands paused on Jaric's shoulder. He looked up, light eyes gone dangerously direct. "He landed *that*, in this storm? Fires! He's a madman. No doubt he attacked you in the same vein of idiocy?"

The guardsmen shrank in the shadows, while their captain gripped his buckler with tense discomfort. Every soldier on Cliffhaven recalled the Kielmark's anger and the oath he swore on the morning the witch left his island besieged by the gale. Sprawled helplessly before the fire, Jaric's slim form aroused no other feeling but pity.

Taen felt the captain's dread through the dream link as he resumed his report. "Perhaps not. The boy came ashore armed but not expecting company. When we challenged him, he claimed to be under the summons of Anskiere of Elrinfaer."

At the Stormwarden's name, the Kielmark froze. Massive wrists flinched taut, straining the fabric of his embroidered cuffs. "Anskiere! By Kor, not again."

Bound by the dream link, Taen caught her breath in the clearing of the Vaere. Overturned by the fierce current of the Kielmark's rage, she dared not intercede, even to secure Jaric's safety. The man's distrust made him unstable to the verge of madness; should he discover his inner mind had been breached by a dream-weaver's powers, his reaction would bear little relation to reason. Careful to preserve his equilibrium, Taen braced herself to drive him unconscious, should he move upon Jaric; but his savage outburst ended swiftly. The Kielmark bridled his anger in cold reason, dark brows laced into a frown.

Taen shivered with released tension as his bunched fists eased, and he motioned curtly to the captain. "Continue!"

The man stared at the rug rather than meet his lord's gaze. "The boy kicked the lantern over, rushed us with a sword and dagger. There came a flash of light; one man claims he saw the stormfalcon's image appear. The rest of us were too busy to notice details. Lord, if the work was sorcery, it harmed no one."

The Kielmark rose with deadly grace. "Did you recover the weapons?"

The request was routine; one of the men-at-arms promptly produced Jaric's sword and dagger. The Kielmark accepted them. Without comment he removed himself to the candelabra which burned on the mantel. Flame-light shed bronze highlights over his dark hair as he bent his head, treating the steel to a lengthy inspection. Sensing him absorbed in concentration, Taen tentatively tried to ease the man's antipathy toward trespassers. With delicate precision, she extended her dream-sense, sent calm to blunt the edges of his urgency. But the Kielmark's mood proved resistant as tempered steel. Taen pitched her powers to the very edge of compulsion, but her efforts seemed futile as trying to stay an avalanche with thread.

Thoughtfully the Lord of Cliffhaven fingered the edge of the sword blade. Then he requested the conclusion of the captain's account, and once the tale was complete, deposited both weapons on the table alongside the green cloak.

"What sorcerer would carry Corlin steel?" he observed drily. "And at the end, when he was desperate, that boy should have cast weapons aside and used magic." Rubies sparkled at his collar as the Kielmark folded massive arms across his chest. "The boy's name seems to be Kerainson Jaric, unless he stole the sword, which I doubt. It suits him too well for size, and the steel is newly forged into the bargain."

Cliffhaven's sovereign paused, his expression drawn and tense with thought. No man present moved a muscle, and in the grove of the Vaere, Taen held her breath. At last the Kielmark stirred and studied the boy upon the carpet with eyes narrowed in speculative calculation. The captain noticed and relaxed visibly. Had reprimand been forthcoming, the Kielmark would already have delivered it. Unaware such forbearance might have been induced by a dream-weaver's presence, he watched the Lord of Cliffhaven rake his knuckles through his beard and at last deliver judgment.

"Lock the prisoner in the east keep dungeon. He's no sorcerer. But he could easily be connected with one, and a stormfalcon may be the reason for the current foul weather." The Kielmark stepped back to the chart table, preoccupied and irritable. He delivered his final instructions with his back turned. "Call a healer to dress that shoulder wound. When the boy rouses, see that he gets food and drink. Send word to me afterward. I want to question him, but I won't like the delay if he arrives in my presence hungry. Take no risks. Post two armed sentries by the cell and replace those ropes with iron."

The guardsmen saluted. They collected the prisoner from the floor.

Still wary of the Kielmark's frame of mind, they removed Jaric from the library with dispatch. The latch clicked under the captain's hand; he swung the door closed with preternatural caution.

But the Kielmark paid scant heed to the trespasser's departure. As he leaned over the topmost chart, Taen felt his thoughts turn jagged with concern. Presently he slammed his fist into the inked outline of Main-strait, and raised cold eyes to the trader in russet. "I don't like your news. It makes no sense. *Why would Kisburn send a force consisting of three ships against Cliffhaven?* There must be a missing factor." His tone turned grim. "I had better learn the answer before this gale lifts. If troops sailed at the time you suggest, the only thing holding those ships from running the straits is this hell-begotten west wind."

For long hours, the sovereign of Cliffhaven glared at the charts. He brooded as if his question waited to be read in the parchment under his hands, while on a table at his back the abandoned folds of Jaric's cloak dripped salt water onto his priceless carpet.

Taen dissolved the contact and directed a stricken appeal to Tamlin. She avoided speech, choosing to clarify Jaric's situation directly through her talents. Unaware that the boy sent to his dungeons was Anskiere's sole hope of release, the Kielmark permitted Jaric to live on the chance the gale was connected to his presence. As long as the motivation for Kisburn's aggression remained unknown, he needed the storm to aid Cliffhaven's defense.

"Jaric is in jeopardy." Taen searched the seamed brown features of the Vaere for some trace of emotion. Finding none, she elaborated. "I cannot control the Kielmark's actions from a distance. His will is much too defined."

She did not need to emphasize that Jaric's imprisonment could not have occurred at a worse time. His resilience had worn away through long days of passage; the moment he recovered awareness in the Kielmark's prison, the pressure of the geas would resume with intolerable force. Denied the freedom to appease its pull, Jaric might well lose his reason.

Tamlin puffed stolidly on his pipe, motionless. Smoke curled through his mustache and eyebrows and lazily circled his beaded cap. "You must go to Cliffhaven," he said simply. "There is no other alternative."

Taen sprang to her feet. She upset the crystal basin in her haste, and water soaked the grasses in a silvery flood. "How can I? The crossing would take days, and I have no boat."

The grove's enchanted silence swallowed her distress without echo. Tamlin blew a smoke ring; his feathers hung without a quiver in the still air. "I can send you in a matter of hours, never doubt." He lifted the pipe from his teeth and regarded his charge with unwavering black eyes. "Free Jaric if you can. But you must promise one thing in return: leave the island before Kisburn's ships breast the horizon, else risk your life as forfeit. Tathagres knows of your mastership; and Lord Sholl the shape-shifter has sworn to achieve your ruin."

Taen stared at her hands, pricked by apprehension. Often during training she had resented her confinement; now the grove which preserved the
heart of Vaerish mystery seemed a precious and peaceful haven, far
removed from the strife of mortal realms.

"Do you understand?" said Tamlin sternly.

Taen nodded, fighting an unreasonable urge to weep.

"Kneel, then." The Vaere gestured at the grass, his pipe oddly missing
from his hand.

Burdened by responsibility she could not refuse, Taen did his bidding.
The fate of Jaric and Anskiere and perhaps all of Keithland rested on her
shoulders. She trembled, feeling bereft of courage, while Tamlin raised his
arms above her head. Bells shivered in the air as he clapped his palms
together. The grove whirled and vanished; Taen's senses were riven from
her, and she plunged headlong into night.

The capsule which housed Taen was designed for mobility, though it
had not traveled from its cradle for close to a quarter century. Switches
tripped and closed in the Vaere's vast databanks. Mothballed machinery
responded. Systems powered up in preparation for launch to Cliffhaven;
electrical impulses flickered through circuitry as instruments checked
operational. Servo mechanisms unsealed the capsule and labored to ready
Taen's body for consciousness. Her limbs were clothed in a dream-weaver's
robes, made from cloth which had no visible seam. The colors ranged from
misty gray to blue-violet as light played across the folds and hem, cuffs
and collar were bordered in gold. As a final touch, a robot pressed a circlet
woven of myrtle over her dark hair.

Despite painstaking adherence to the details of a mythology the Vaere
itself had originated, its plan held a serious flaw. The capsule was a clearly
identifiable relic from the *Corinne Dane*'s support systems; derelict, it could
never have remained functional so many generations since the crash.
Demons possessed eidetic memory, passed on intact through each generation. Should the capsule be sighted during Taen's landing, the enemy
might discover evidence that the Vaere still survived. If that occurred,
the computer's presence would be hunted more fervently than Landfast's
records. But no other option remained if Taen was to reach Cliffhaven in
time to help Jaric. Mechanically dispassionate, the Vaere wired a detona-
tion cap into the guidance systems. With luck, Taen would debark unobserved and the capsule would not be noticed until the self-destruct signal
fired off the explosive. The Vaere entered Cliffhaven's coordinates with
unerring precision. Following one last check on the drive systems, it
sequenced the capsule for ignition.

Deep underground, on an islet mantled by a trackless wilderness of
cedar forest, a silvery object shot from a tube hidden beneath the surface
of the sea. It sliced through the water with a muffled whine of turbines
and blazed northward, scattering a trail of phosphorescent bubbles in its
wake.

*   *   *

In the still hour before dawn, an ear-splitting bang rattled every pane in the casements overlooking Cliffhaven's harbor. Roused from his sleep, the Kielmark leapt out of bed in a ferocious temper. Cloud-racked skies glowed dull orange beyond his window, silhouetting the roofs of the warehouses against the landing. Naked except for his ruby torque, the Kielmark bashed open his chamber door.

"Fetch the saddled horse and bring it to the west postern!" The sentry posted in the corridor vanished down the stair. Without further delay, the Kielmark grabbed breeches, boot, and swordbelt from his bedside. He bolted from the room without pausing to dress. Time enough to don clothes while he waited by the postern for his mount, which at best would be an interval of seconds; every hour of the dry or night, one horse in Cliffhaven's courtyard stood saddled and bridled, ready at an instant's notice.

The Kielmark sprinted across the outer bailey, sword sheath and belt buckle clanging between his knees. The glow above the harbor had already faded to dull crimson. Cursing, the Kielmark yanked his breeches over his thighs. A shout hailed him through the mist, punctuated by the staccato ring of hooves over cobbles. A groom appeared running; a hammerheaded gray trotted beside him on a leading rein, its stirrups already swinging free.

"To me!" The Kielmark grasped mane and vaulted astride before the animal came completely to a halt. Abandoning his boots in the courtyard, he clapped bare heels to his mount, sent it careening into the gale-torn darkness beyond the gates. He took the stair beyond at a canter.

Shod hooves rang like hammers striking sparks from the stone at each stride. The Kielmark yelled, flicked the reins on the horse's neck and recklessly made it gallop. At the first bend in the stair, he whirled the animal off the path and plunged downslope amid a bouncing rattle of rocks. Brush lashed his arms and thorn branches raked his bare toes; but the Kielmark made no allowance for discomfort. He reined his sweat-soaked mount down twisted streets to the dockside barely a minute after the blast.

Scattered clots of wreckage tossed in the bay; flames streamed like banners, lining the wavecrests a bloody red. A semicircle of guardsmen cordoned the shore, surrounding a solitary figure in wind-whipped robes. But the soldiers held their weapons pointed down at the sand, and their discipline in the presence of their commander seemed queerly lax. The Kielmark grimaced with displeasure. He drew his sword with a stupendous ripple of muscles, slammed the horse with his heels, and drove it, sidling, straight for the lines.

Angry enough not to swerve for the men who dove clear of his mount, he bellowed against the storm. "What passes here?"

But the answer became apparent the moment he broke through the cordon and pulled the horse to a halt. A woman stood on the strand, alone and weaponless. Her hair fell dark as starless night about her shoulders and a mystic's wreath of myrtle twined her head. By the flowers and the unearthly sheen of her blue-violet robes, the Kielmark recognized her for a dream-weaver. The guardsmen's behavior did not stem from carelessness; snared by the enchantress's influence, they struggled to lift weapons grown strangely unruly in their grasp. Sweat sprang along the Kielmark's brow. His great wrist trembled with the effort of keeping his own sword upright, for it suddenly seemed too heavy for his hand.

Anger tore through him. Two incidents of sorcery in the same night utterly stripped him of tolerance. In a tone of killing fury he addressed the woman who had dared turn her enchantments against his men. "What brings you here? Answer quickly. Your presence is most unwelcome."

The dream-weaver regarded him with an expression of clear-eyed appeal. "This night you took a prisoner, one Kerainson Jaric. I am here to ask his release for the safety of your realm and all Keithland. You must not detain him. He is Ivain Firelord's heir and his obligation is urgent."

Taken aback, the Kielmark lowered his sword. That the slight blond boy brought in by his guardsmen could be Ivain's son was a development he could never have anticipated. The fact explained much. The Lord of Cliffhaven lowered his weapon and braced his wrist upon the horse's neck; unsheathed steel clanged against his stirrup iron as he leaned forward.

"Who sent you?" he demanded bluntly.

The dream-weaver shouted to make herself heard above the crash of surf. "Tamlin of the Vaere, the same who guided Anskiere to mastery. If you wish the Stormwarden unbound from the ice and gone from your shores, Jaric alone can accomplish the feat."

The Kielmark swore. He straightened in the saddle, jabbed his sword into its sheath with undisguised irritation, and extended his hand to the dream-weaver. "Come here. I'll negotiate nothing without a roof to break the wind. Do you drink wine?"

Taen shook her head and tentatively stepped forward. Interpreting her approach as acquiescence, the Kielmark urged the horse ahead to meet her. He bent, caught her strongly in the crook of one elbow, and swung her up into the saddle ahead of him. Black hair whipped across his bare shoulders as he reined the horse about. With a gesture he dismissed the guards, then set off up the slope to the fortress.

Taen perched uncomfortably on the edge of a stuffed chair in the Kielmark's study, her robes arranged to hide the hands clenched whitely in her lap. The Lord of Cliffhaven paced like a wolf before the hearth, shirtless still, a cut agate goblet in his hand. He sipped his wine and treated the dream-weaver before him to a long unpleasant scrutiny.

He stopped without warning and spoke. "You are younger than you look."

Taen watched the flamelight flash and sparkle in the rubies at his throat. "The Vaere sent me only in dire need. Cliffhaven stands in greater peril than you know."

"Indeed?" The Kielmark's eyes narrowed. He waited a lengthy interval for a reply but Taen volunteered nothing. Day brightened slowly beyond the casement, dusting highlights like faery silver through the hair on his chest.

At last the Kielmark said, "You'll gain nothing through seeking to bargain with me."

Taen met his threat with brazen honesty. "My kind don't negotiate. Lord, if I wished to manipulate, I would do so, *without your consent if need be.*"

The statement struck a nerve. The Kielmark slammed his goblet down on the window ledge, splashing wine across his knuckles. The girl in the chair flinched, but did not retract her admonition. Poker straight in her gold-trimmed robes, she held her silence while the servant who had brought the wine rushed off for towels and an ewer of water. The Kielmark dripped on the tiles, oblivious. Though the girl seemed guileless and vulnerable, the myrtle wreath and the robe only came to those trained by the Vaere. At her own craft, this childwoman held as much power as Anskiere.

The manservant returned and after a glance at the Kielmark's face began mopping spilled wine without fuss.

Taen confronted the Lord of Cliffhaven with disquieting assurance. "I would rather deal directly with you." Her restraint seemed genuine; and inspiration for her following line was borrowed from his innermost heart. "The Stormwarden of Elrinfaer holds you in highest regard. In his stead, I bring you warning. Kisburn seeks conquest of the Free Isles. Cliffhaven controls the Straits and so thwarts an ambition now turned to advantage by Kor's Accursed. The demons desire Landfast. Through the machinations of Tathagres, they will support the King against you."

The Kielmark jerked as if he tasted poison. The flush which suffused his features sent the servant scuttling backward from the room. "Fires! He *dares,* does he?"

His fury struck Taen's awareness with the splintering force of a mallet. Taxed beyond previous limits, she strove to maintain control. "Lord, listen carefully. You must abandon Cliffhaven and evacuate your following."

The Kielmark's demeanor turned vicious with rage. Seeing his hand reach for his sword, Taen drove to her feet. Power radiated from her person and her voice became forcefully cold. "Lord, heed me. Time is precious and words are wasteful. Look, I will show you."

She spread her arms, loosed the full force of her mastery upon him. Tuned into sympathy with her will, the Kielmark had no choice but stare into the ewer. Images bloomed in the water. Through interlinked chains of circumstance, Taen led him on a journey which began in Kisburn's secret council chamber and proceeded through the debate-ridden governance of the Free Isles Alliance to a forester's secluded cabin beyond the

Furlains. In dreams the enchantress showed him Keithland's most poignant weaknesses; of Cliffhaven's strategic importance, she spared nothing.
Twisting the Kielmark's emotions into her pattern, she stung him first
with a King's thorny ambitions; ruled by her touch, the Kielmark tasted
the greed which had transformed a fisherman's guilt-ridden son into a
pitiless pawn, knew the cruelty of the woman who had instigated the
change. Battered in turn by a sorcerer's geas, he suffered the storm winds
of an ocean crossing and Jaric's lonely hours at *Callinde*'s helm. Taen
granted no respite. Shifting her image yet again, she drove him deep
beneath the ice which buttressed Cliffhaven's northern shore. There the
Kielmark heard the bloodlust-crazed screams of the frostwargs; he felt the
last desperate hope of a sorcerer treasured like a brother in a friendship.

"Free Jaric," said Taen. Her words reverberated relentlessly within the
Kielmark's mind. "If you do not, everything you value will come to ruin."

She released him with calculated abruptness. The water in the ewer
lost its sheen of visions, became ordinary and clear once more. The Kielmark started. Restored to his own awareness, he discovered tears on his
face. "You place me at extreme disadvantage," he said softly and reached
for the carafe to refill his goblet.

Suddenly a thunderous knock sounded upon the door. "Lord!" A captain with looped brass earrings stuck his head inside. "Come quickly.
There's trouble with the prisoner!"

The Kielmark dropped the carafe. It smashed shrilly on the tiles as he
ran full tilt for the door. He wrenched the panel open, jerking his head
for Taen to follow. The captain continued his account as they raced the
length of the corridor.

"The boy roused screaming. Tore the skin off his wrists trying to
break the fetters. The healer had dressed the swordcut and gone, and the
guard could find no reason for the prisoner's distress. Lord, he rose to
summon help. His second on duty opened the door and nearly went blind
from a discharge of sorcery." Panting for breath, the captain finished his
report. "The guard got thrown from his feet. He bade me inform you that
he saw the stormfalcon appear in the cell. Now a wind rips through the
keep like a hurricane let loose from its moorings, and not a man dares to
go near."

The Kielmark pounded the length of an arched hallway, shouting over
his shoulder to Taen, "Can you help?"

Breathlessly, she replied, "If Jaric still has his reason, yes."

The Kielmark whirled. Without breaking stride, he caught Taen in his
arms for the second time that morning. Bunched against his shoulders
with no more dignity than a bolt of cloth, the enchantress felt his powerful
stride lengthen until the guard fell tiredly behind. His fingers bruised. But
concerned for the Firelord's heir, Taen barely cared. She endured the sprint
to the keep without protest, her dream-sense ranging ahead to reach Jaric.

Contact loosed a flood of terror and pain; and a searing, untameable torrent of power whose intended course had been balked. The force built with each passing second, turning inward against Jaric's spirit with the wanton destructiveness of a cyclone. He had no will left to break, Taen saw. In a moment of shared horror, her control wavered. The geas surged across the dream link. For one agonized instant she knew the full scope of Jaric's suffering. The impact made her gasp. Untrained to handle such a terrible influx of energy, her connection dissolved, leaving her limp and disoriented in the Kielmark's arms.

Taen raised her voice above the noise. "My skills are useless until we reach Jaric."

The Kielmark nodded curtly. He leapt down a short flight of steps and crossed an open courtyard. Rain howled over the roofpeaks, slashing the hair across his brow. Taen's light robes became soaked within seconds. Gusts screamed across the yard, battering shutters and doors with insane violence. Yet the Kielmark would not be daunted. He ran on, until the keep loomed through the downpour, a fixed silhouette against skies churning with clouds. With his head bent against the elements, he ducked beneath the shelter of the arch and kicked open the keep's double doors.

Inside, the rain ceased, but the rush of air became deafening. Slammed by the drafts which eddied up from the dungeons, the Kielmark set Taen on her feet. He wrapped his arm about her shoulders; sheltering her with his own great bulk, they descended the stairwell. Step by labored step, he hauled Taen to the cell where Jaric lay.

The door had been battered open. Harsh white light blazed from within, spilling glare off the rough walls of the corridor. The damp air carried a whetted edge of ozone. Through dazzled vision, Taen caught a glimpse of giant wings, feathers barred in black and tawny gold. The blast of the gale drowned her shout. She clung to the Kielmark's wrist and pointed. But the man had seen the stormfalcon's presence already. He nodded, his profile lined in light above her head, then shouldered stubbornly forward. Wind hammered at his balance. Sweaty fingers bored into Taen's flesh as he reached with his other hand and hooked the grilled iron above the cell door.

Taen's face was buried in his shoulder as he strained to cross the threshold. She felt his muscles strain and quiver under her cheek. But the wind funneled through the narrow opening with the fury of a cataract, making headway impossible. The Kielmark leaned down and yelled into the dream-weaver's ear, "When you reach him, hang on."

Taen nodded, whipped by strands of her own loosened hair. She felt the Kielmark's arm bunch briefly against her back. Then he flung her bodily against the might of the storm, through the door and into the cell.

Blinded by the brilliance of the sorcery, Taen stumbled to her knees, then tripped headlong over a limp body. Lost to all sensation, Jaric failed to react. Unable to see, Taen groped. Her right hand bruised against chain. Links gouged her palm, cutting the skin. She twisted and caught hold.

Wind shrilled past her ears like the scream of a torturer's victim. Taen resisted its force. She slid her hand up past the fetter and seized Jaric's wrist. Her fingers dug into flesh gone dangerously cold and slippery wet with blood. Taen knew anguish at the discovery. While the stormfalcon's wings lashed the elements into primordial fury above her head, she steadied her talents to dream-send.

"Jaric!" Her call was desperate and her touch unerring; still her cry of compassion raised no response. Taen flattened herself against the stone at the boy's side and caught his face between warm hands. Then she sharpened her will like a weapon and thrust into his being, dream-weaving a shelter for the beleaguered mind under her touch. Quickly, surely, she cast a barrier across his thoughts which the geas could not penetrate. Isolated, the pinpoint concentration of its powers began to dissipate.

The painful brilliance of the enchantment flickered, then disappeared, taking the stormfalcon's image with it. In darkness, Taen wove her bastion tighter and stronger still. The wind dropped to a sigh, winnowing her robes about her ankles. Slowly she sat up and eased her cramped muscles. Jaric still breathed beneath her hands, but his mind held no glimmer of self-awareness.

Something metallic clinked in the doorway. A spark flared, revealing the Kielmark's square features in the glow of flame; a lantern stood braced between his knees, and he was frowning. As the illumination steadied, Taen returned her attention to the Firelord's heir who lay sprawled across her knees. Both wrists were abraded from thrashing against the chain; his eyes stared sightlessly from his pale face, and fine sun-bleached hair fell over Taen's wrists, matted into tangles by wind and salt. Confronted by his physical presence for the first time, Taen was startled to find he was smaller than her initial impression in Seitforest. She brushed his brow with careful fingers. Jaric did not stir; beneath the sodden linen shirt, his skin felt icy as death.

The light brightened and boots scraped stone at Taen's elbow. She glanced up, found the Kielmark standing over her with the lantern. His cold eyes were fixed intently upon Jaric.

Taen answered the Kielmark's thought before he spoke. "I don't know. Perhaps I can restore Jaric to consciousness, but the geas touched him brutally and your handling was just short of inhuman." She touched the chains with distaste. "These must be removed directly. Then I will do what I can. If you bear this boy any pity, provide horses and escort, that he can reach the ice cliffs as speedily as possible."

With uncharacteristic tolerance the Kielmark refrained from comment. Sovereign within his domain, he would take no orders, even from a dream-weaver trained by the Vaere. Too late Taen regretted the tactlessness of her demand. If he crossed her, she wondered whether she could influence him at all, volatile as he was, and savage to the point of unpredictability. With the breath stopped in her throat, she awaited his decision.

Still studying Jaric, the Kielmark knelt. He drew a key from his belt and caught the steel which bound the boy's wrists. The locks sprang with a sharp click. The Lord of Cliffhaven removed the fetters from his prisoner with strangely disturbing gentleness. Taen sighed in relief. Her fingers unclenched in Jaric's hair, and she bent as if weeping over the boy's slack form.

The Kielmark tossed the chain to the floor. He stood then, waiting with ill-concealed impatience for the jangle of echoes to fade. "Do you know? The boy is small, but exceedingly tough. He might just have what it takes to master the Cycle of Fire."

With that he thrust the keys back into his tunic and regarded the dream-weaver who had invaded his island. Wind had torn away her myrtle circlet; black hair rippled across her shoulders, twisted untidily into elflocks. "You have great courage," the Kielmark added thoughtfully. "I think you have earned yourself horses and escort. Beyond that I cannot help. I have an island to defend."

But far removed from mortal hearing, Taen did not absorb the meaning of his words; she had pitched all her concentration into her craft from the instant Jaric's fetters were released. Her touch ranged deep. Digging for one thin spark of awareness in the limp flesh under her hands, the dream-weaver did not see the Kielmark set the lantern at her side. He departed quietly, leaving her unaware he had discarded prudence entirely. Stubborn as sea-battered granite, the Kielmark intended to fight Kisburn and his compact of demons. While he lived, the fortress would not be surrendered.

CHAPTER XXI

Ice Cliffs

Lost in a shadowless void near the borderlands of death, Jaric felt a current intrude across his isolation. He recoiled sharply. Unwilling to face any more pain, he lay motionless as the flatfish, which settles on the sea bottom to escape the sharpened jaws of predators.

But the presence would not depart.

"Jaric!" The name pierced the core of his silence and shattered into echoes, each one a pledge of compassion. The call promised peace in a world he had been driven to forsake; it also offered healing. But memory of the geas' lacerating pain lingered like an open sore. Jaric dared not trust. Behind bars, locked in fetters, the voice would bring nothing but ruined hope, like the dream-weaver who had once betrayed him. Anskiere never forgot, never forgave; his geas could grant no reprieve.

"Son of Ivain!" The cry raised a flicker like light rays fractured by water. With weary desperation Jaric sought to drown the glimmer in darkness. His effort was battered aside. Images surged across his mind. They harried him in his solitude. Denied all rest, Jaric cried aloud. The presence broke through, flooded his mind with joy so pure he could have wept.

Sunlight broke into jewels on the surface of a river where a small boy sat with a fishing line. The child was himself and the moment a treasured memory from boyhood. The vision shifted without warning. Snow fell in Seitforest, each flake more intricate than patterned lace against the dark wool of his mittens; in a circle of lanternlight by the shed, Telemark regarded the pelts piled on the drag-sleigh. "You never give up, Jaric. I admire that in a man." The forester added praise for the fine woodsmanship of a boy who had never before trapped an ice otter.

Outside of dreams, Jaric winced in shame. He longed for the anonymity of Morbrith's archives, but sanctuary was denied.

"Firelord's heir!" The cry raised echoes of despair and the horror-ridden vision of Morbrith in ruins. But the Llondel who had originally framed the warning with images now was dust, bled to his death by an Earl's cold steel. Jaric knelt amid streets choked with bones. He shouted denial; but his anguish was ignored.

"Kerainson Jaric!" The call built to a crescendo of accusation, paired by a vivid view of Mathieson, who grieved alone on a wind-whipped landing, hands knotted in his collar of magnificent fur.

"No." Jaric shuddered. He rejected the vision's unbearable implication, that he was unfit to have demanded such sacrifice and all who had aided him acted in vain. Punished to respond in his own defense, Jaric stirred. His lashes quivered and he opened his eyes, to find that in truth the pain was gone.

His mind cleared of visions. The dream-weaver who once restored his past sat with his head cradled in her lap. But the shining black hair Jaric remembered lay snarled across her shoulders, no longer crowned with flowers. Her pale eyes were swollen from exhausted tears. The hands which gripped his shoulders trembled, warm in contrast with the damp stone floor where he lay.

"By the Vaere," Taen said softly. "I thought I had lost you." Her smile held such sweetness it stopped the breath in Jaric's throat.

A lantern burned by her knee. Beyond its yellow glow Jaric saw windowless walls and bars, and nearby a brighter gleam of steel chain. He touched his wrists and by the sting of torn skin discovered his fetters had been removed.

"The door is open also," the enchantress said.

Jaric sat up, eyes widened with sudden sharp mistrust. Once she had deceived him, and let him sail into suffering on the sea beyond Mearren Ard.

Taen caught his sleeve with firm fingers. "Ivainson, no."

The sound of the name made him quiver. Jaric's mouth flinched in remembrance of another older pain.

The enchantress released him and sighed with sorrowful regret. "There is a difference between pity and caring. Try to believe me. The last thing Kencie intended was to hurt you. I speak for myself also. The Vaere misjudged very badly concerning Anskiere's summons."

With evident discomfort, Jaric tugged his sleeves over the raw patches on his wrists. Taen had just interceded in his behalf; quite probably saved his life. "I'm sorry. You didn't have to come after me."

"I did." Taen rubbed at her own skinned elbow and ruefully smiled. "The rest doesn't matter. Can you ride? I can subdue the effects of the geas a limited time only, and the storm attached to your presence continues to build. We must go and ask for horses without delay."

She rose expectantly. For a long moment Jaric stared at the broken skin of his hands, his expression stiffly unreadable. Taen waited without probing his thoughts. Unlike Emien, Jaric did not turn vindictive or angry when fate twisted his life into knots.

At last he raised his eyes to her face. "I'll go," he said warily. "Do you suppose you could convince the guards to return my weapons and cloak? They were gifts, and the loss of them troubles me."

But the request became unnecessary. When Taen and Jaric emerged from the keep, both horses and Jaric's confiscated blades awaited, along with five of the Kielmark's guardsmen to escort them to the north shore.

Whipped into sheets by the gusts, rain slashed across the cobbled yard, abrasive as driven sand. The gale had worsened; it hammered horses and men with unremitting fury. Even inside the walls, the angry thud of surf against the breakwater slammed the air like the thunder of the Great Fall itself.

Jaric collected his sword and dagger and mounted a gray with an ugly head. The horse pawed restively as he gathered the reins, hauling against his hold with ears flattened against its soaked neck. Jaric took the pull in his fingers, trying to spare his lacerated palms. Unlike the morning he had fled Gaire's Main, he was no longer too weak to master the animal under his knees. Yet the discovery yielded little satisfaction. His body might have changed, but the sickly boy who once copied manuscripts could not be reconciled with the man who left Telemark's cottage in Seitforest. Neither the one nor entirely the other, Jaric wrestled endless uncertainty, for every aspect of his life had been shaped by the sorcerer's geas which had upended his will at Morbrith Keep. As Jaric rode out of the courtyard in the company of the Kielmark's guards, he wondered how he would feel when he arrived at the ice cliffs and confronted the Stormwarden at last.

Rain pelted in opaque sheets over the Kielmark's escort as they reined to a halt above the crest which overlooked Cliffhaven's northern shore. Gusts whined through the dune grass, and the crash of breakers against the beach head added deep throaty undertones to a storm still ominously building. Sopping and miserable, the riders sat with hunched shoulders and the horses stood with tails tucked against the wind, snorting the salt taint of spindrift from their nostrils.

One of the guardsmen touched Jaric's elbow and pointed toward the sea. "Over there," he shouted. "You'll come to a sandy beach. Just past where it breaks up into rock, you'll find the ice cliffs."

The surf broke too high on the strand for horses. Jaric dismounted and passed his soaked reins to the guardsman.

"We'll wait for you," called Taen. A small determined figure on the Kielmark's great chestnut, she shivered in robes dulled silver-gray by the damp.

Jaric nodded but did not linger. Uncomfortable with sympathy from strangers, he hastened down the bluff to the strand; the guardsmen who stood vigil on the ridge faded behind. Rain traced icy runnels down Jaric's collar, and eel grass hooked his ankles at each step. But, anxious to complete his journey, he felt no weariness. Presently the dunes gave way to packed sand; close at hand, the grinding boom of waves became deafening. Jaric ducked smoking drifts of spray, his cloak bunched over the hilts of his weapons to keep the salt from the steel. Fifty paces beyond the bluffs he reached a jagged stand of rocks. Glistening in the rain, stone rose like buttresses against the sheer face of a cliff; incoming breakers battered at the base, spouting geysers of foam.

Left no semblance of a path, Jaric splashed through shallows, hurried by the rush of the following breaker. He jammed his boot in a cleft and swung up onto the nearest formation. He dared not look down. The sea sucked and thudded bare yards under his boots, twisting ropy tendrils of weed through the fissures; a man in the water would quickly tangle and drown. Even if he fell clear, current would drag him under like a rag.

Jaric hauled himself onto a narrow ledge. Waves sheeted spray over his back. He crept forward, fingers gouged by barnacles. Yet he dared not move without handholds. Gusts slapped at his clothing, sharp with unseasonal frost. Ahead loomed the ice cliffs. But only when the ledge broadened beneath his feet did Jaric notice the view.

The seas rose beneath, green with lattice marks of current; then crested with a roar that punished thought and broke, hurling foam against steely bastions of ice. Awed by the breadth of the cliffs, Jaric glanced up. But the structure soared upward, obscured by coiling wraiths of mist. He inched across a crevice. The cliff shelved beyond, cut like a road across the face of a precipice. Beyond lay a steep drop to the sea. Breakers battered beneath with the force of primordial creation.

Jaric moved cautiously toward the brink. Pebbles rolled under his boots, bounced outward into air and vanished. He took another step and another. Sorcery flashed, sudden and blinding as lightning overhead. Wind gusted through the defile and built to a screaming rush of sound. Certain the geas had broken free of Taen's protective barrier, Jaric cried out. He flung both hands over his face, prepared to be ripped into agony .by Anskiere's implacable summoning.

But the storm died. Wind dropped, weak as a spent breath; the rain ceased. After the violence of rampaging elements, the land seemed deadened under an eerie and unnatural silence. Jaric lifted his head in wonder. Surf still broke over the reefs below, but the wave crests unraveled into foam and subsided, no longer flayed to tatters by the gale. Mist eddied over the defile. Trembling in the midst of calm, Jaric watched the storm dissolve around him.

Storm clouds tore asunder and sunlight cast a mantle of gold across Jaric's shoulders. Peace claimed him. Breezes whispered through his hair and a single black-barred feather drifted down. Jaric caught the quill as it passed. He turned its knife-edge length between his hands and wondered what should be done with the seed of the stormfalcon's power.

"Keep it safe, Ivainson Jaric," said the wind.

Jaric started. He stared wildly about, but the rocky escarpment remained empty as before and the ice beyond as majestically desolate. The voice could only be sent by the Stormwarden of Elrinfaer, who had wrought the stormfalcon's pattern and set the geas of summoning upon him. Before apprehension could defeat him, Jaric gathered courage and spoke. "I have come in accordance with your bidding. Dare I ask what purpose brought me here?"

"You are the Firelord's heir," the wind replied.

Exposed on his shelf of rock, Jaric could not know that deep within the fortress of ice Anskiere of Elrinfaer roused from the deep sleep of stasis. Guided by the stormfalcon's feather, his mind ranged to a ledge beyond his confinement, where a young man with earnest brown eyes awaited his fate.

Jaric shivered as the Stormwarden's presence encompassed him. Aware his person was being assessed, he knew a moment of cynical amusement; the Stormwarden of Elrinfaer would find nothing but a starved, sunburned youth with tangled hair, slight stature, and a talent for fine penmanship; small reward for such stupendous expenditure of effort. Bitterness deepened the lines of hardship around Jaric's mouth. No doubt Anskiere would conclude he had been mistaken to summon him at all.

But the wind swirled, sharply snapping his cloak hem. The break in the clouds widened. Slanting sunlight touched the ice across the fissure, firing the crystals like prisms. As a prison, the structure was awesomely beautiful; also more permanently secure than any dungeon created by man. Struck by sudden poignant sorrow, Jaric realized the Stormwarden of Elrinfaer was no longer master of his fate. He depended on outside help for his rescue.

The fact sparked a painful reminder of Jaric's earlier inadequacy. Trapped by despair, the boy struggled to define what surely was evident. "I am useless to you, sorcerer. I have no power to assist your deliverance. My father resented your hold upon him. He died swearing his debt would stand unpaid. I survived through another man's sacrifice, and I remain ignorant of any heritage of Ivain's. Let me go. I possess no means to help."

The wind whispered mournfully across the rocks. "Power is your rightful inheritance. The heir has potential enough to surpass his sire. But this you must discover for yourself. I did not call you here to force that choice."

"Then why?" Jaric's shout echoed in wild anguish off the face of the cliffs. "Why summon me at all? Why not leave me at Morbrith or Seitforest and let my days pass in peace?" He waited through dense and implacable stillness. For long minutes it seemed he would receive no reply at all.

"You were called through the debt incurred against me by Ivain," said Anskiere in the voice made of wind. "As his heir you are bound to undertake a task in my name. Complete my bidding and you are forever free of obligation. This I promise: should you succeed in the task, you shall gain everything you desire."

Jaric swallowed, His heart felt heavy as lead in his chest. Memory of the tales repeated in Mearren Ard arose unbidden in his mind. Anskiere was seldom mentioned without a curse and Ivain's name was forever linked with cruelty. Small, uncertain, and exhausted, Jaric feared the madness engendered by the Cycle of Fire more than death itself. Still, he summoned the dregs of his pride and phrased the question he most dreaded to ask. "What is the task?"

The wind subsided like a sigh. "You will recover the Keys of Elrinfaer and hold them safe until they can be returned."

No mention of the Cycle of Fire; Jaric took a deep breath, startled by the simplicity of the demand. The Keys to Elrinfaer lay in Kisburn's possession, within reach of mortal means; once returned to Anskiere, Jaric never need concern himself with the Vaerish mysteries which had ruined his father's mind. Ivain's debt charged him to complete but a single feat.

The sunlight shone more kindly over the black granite beneath his boots. Raising his eyes to the ice cliffs, Jaric knew a moment of puzzled regret. "What of yourself?" His question echoed across the chasm, rebounding off the rock. "Would you demand no rescue from me?"

But the winds did not answer. The sea boomed, changeless as time against the reefs below the cliffs. Slowly, disbelievingly, Jaric waited. But Anskiere offered no reply but silence. At last, with a shrug Jaric turned away from frost-locked cliffs and retraced his steps to the sea.

By the time Ivain's heir gained the beach, Anskiere drowsed within his prison of ice and rock. Troubled by the whistles of frostwargs, he dreamed of a prophecy told by a Llondel master seer. "It is given thus," the demon had said, repeating from flawless memory a piece of his heritage from a generation past. His alien tongue struggled to shape human words. "The fourth ancestor of my mother's sibling sighted a future. She saw there seven times seven Llondelei and a yellow-haired son of Ivain Firelord. Then her sight became colored with warning. Guard the boy's life, for should he recover the Keys of Elrinfaer intact, he will also master the Cycle of Fire. And then shall men and Llondel rise from Keithland on Koridan's blessed Flame, to live in peace in the heavens."

While Jaric climbed the bluffs above the dunes, the prophecy receded from dreams to memory. Anskiere of Elrinfaer settled once more into sleep, in hope the Llondel seer proved accurate. Just before he crossed the border of dreams into stasis, the Stormwarden caught the fading echo of a laugh; but whether the mirth was Ivain's or Tathagres' or a reflection from his own imagination, it was impossible to guess.

Jaric gained the summit of the bluff, startled to find the guardsmen dismissed. Taen remained, along with one other. Mounted on a huge black horse, the Kielmark himself gripped the reins of the gray Jaric had left with the guard captain. By bearing alone, no man could mistake the sovereign of Cliffhaven, though his cloak was cut from plain maroon wool and weapons and mail were ordinary. Perched in a saddle of leopard skin, his watchful eyes reflected chill like glacial water as the heir of Ivain stopped by his stirrup.

Jaric greeted the Kielmark with the courtesy due an Earl; unkempt as he was, he bowed with practiced grace. "Lord, I ask leave to sail. Is my boat still where I left her, or has she been impounded?"

The Kielmark ignored his request. Motionless on his tall horse, he studied the young man with all the imposing arrogance of his reputation. "What do you know of Anskiere?"

Jaric's chin lifted at the sharpness of the query. Brown eyes met blue with a shock of surprise; the boy had not expected to be balked. His resilient show of spirit sparked instant reappraisal by the Kielmark.

Jaric answered with cool impatience. "Perhaps instead I should ask the same question of you, Lord, for I desire nothing beyond recovery of the freedom I have lost. The Stormwarden summoned me through the curse set upon my father. The debt demands I complete one task in his service. Once again, I ask leave to sail from your shores."

The Kielmark's horse sidled irritably against the gray as his hand jerked the bit. "What was the task demanded of you?"

Jaric spoke in near defiance. "I must recover the Keys to Elrinfaer. Would you prevent me?"

"I don't need to." The Kielmark flung the gray's reins into the startled hands of the boy.

Taen gave a small cry of dismay. The Kielmark immediately wheeled his horse to face her. She had been weeping, Jaric noticed, or perhaps arguing. Her cheeks were pinched and white and the set of her jaw seemed far more determined than the situation warranted.

"Consider again, Lady." The Kielmark grinned with wolfish delight. "The Keys are in the possession of his royal Grace, the King of Kisburn, who moves against me with an army of demons. It takes no dream-weaver's talent to guess what would happen to any son of Ivain's, should he risk an encounter in that antique joke of a fishing boat."

Taen tugged the mare's bridle, her mouth compressed with affront. She chose not to reply. But maddened by the Kielmark's wounding words and the fact his own fate was at issue, Jaric stepped in front of her horse, prepared to intercede in her defense.

The Kielmark softened his tone. "I think you have no better alternative, daughter of the Vaere. I offer you fair bargain: allied with your talents, Cliffhaven has a chance against this threat of demons. Give me the number they send against me and dream-weave a cover for my men. In return I will deliver your shape-shifter to his gods and the Keys of Elrinfaer to Jaric."

Taen spoke without moving. "Lord, I have told you. My kind never bargain."

"Very well." The Kielmark shrugged, his expression bleakly forbidding. "Remember your choices." He jerked his reins from the mane beneath his hands and booted the horse around. Over the boom of surf against the shore he added, "Boy, you are free to sail. *Callinde* is warped to the south dock in my harbor. Take her and go with my blessing."

"No!" Taen twisted in her saddle, her face pale but composed. "I will stay. For Jaric's sake only, I do as you ask. But if you fail, may the Vaere curse your name to the very gates of hell. They promised my death if I disobeyed."

"Lady, no!" Jaric caught the mare's bridle, shocked by the sacrifice she proposed. "You must not risk yourself for me!"

The Kielmark ignored his protest, a wild light in his eyes. His stallion stamped the ground, punching great marks in the turf, but he kept his seat easily and his lips drew back in a great shout of laughter. "Kor's Fires, woman, I'll whip Kisburn into the harbor." He sobered with startling speed and glared over the taut line of the horizon. "My captains will think me sea-crazed when they hear what I propose. But my plan will work. *There will be no surrender here, not while I can prevent it. And so long as I live, you and Jaric will be safe, my oath as sovereign upon it.*"

The vicious pride in him brought tears to Taen's eyes. To the bitter edge of death the Kielmark's word would stand. But Tamlin's warning lay heavy on her mind as the man kicked his mount to a gallop. He vanished over the dunes to the south while Jaric stood like a man stunned by a blow. No power on Keithland could call the Kielmark back and change his mind.

Five days after Anskiere's second storm loosened its grip over Cliff-haven, King Kisburn's three warships entered the narrows of Mainstrait. The wind blew yet from the west, a misfortune which made the captains irritable; forced to beat every league of the way in ships overloaded with troops and supplies, passage had been grindingly slow. And with Kor's Accursed on board, the sailors muttered and started at every order, making signs against evil even while they worked aloft.

Except for Tathagres, only one man of *Morra*'s company remained at ease in the presence of demons. Disdainful of the stuffy cabin he shared with two lieutenants, Emien lounged on the foredeck with his back braced against the rail, a woolen cloak draped over the wood beneath his elbow. He felt peculiarly unclothed without the accustomed weight of sword and dagger at his belt. But since the Gierj-demons could raise no power in the presence of iron, not a man aboard the flagship bore arms. *Morra* had been stripped of anchors and chains, and fitters had replaced every scrap of steel gear with parts made of brass. She carried ballast of sand specially for the passage across the straits.

Denied the security of their weapons, the soldiers huddled below decks, nervously whispering. Their uneasiness moved Emien to scorn. After long delay, Cliffhaven lay just two leagues off the bow. The vindictive hatred Emien felt for Anskiere far outweighed any distrust of the demons brought along to achieve the Kielmark's downfall. Eager for the first stage of conquest to commence, the boy leaned over the rail beneath the rising angle of the headsails.

The breeze freshened, funneled between the gapped peninsulas of the straits. *Morra* sailed with every stitch of canvas pinched tight. Emien squinted at the wavelets and cursed; the tide had recently turned. Ebbing current would shortly reduce their headway nearly to naught.

The captain called for a leadsman to sound the depth, that the ship could be run to the limit of her draft on each tack. *Morra* ghosted close against a craggy head of land which loomed black and forbidding beneath a lowering moon. At least the light lay in their favor, Emien reflected sourly. Any ship set against them would be exposed like an inked silhouette against the silvered face of the sea. That the Kielmark would attack was certain; the Thienz demon had promised it.

The Thienz itself stood propped against the mizzenmast just aft of the helm. The stern running lamps were unlit; but in the reddish glow of the compass lantern, Emien picked out the dim outline of grinning toad-like lips, slitted eyes, and the crested headdress which adorned the creature's crown.

The leadsman's line splashed beneath Emien's perch. In a clear voice the man sounded the mark; five fathoms, then four, then three. The bottom was shoaling rapidly. The captain signaled and the boastwain shouted, "Ready about. All hands, man sheets and braces!"

The quartermaster spun the wheel. The boatswain called orders over the crack of canvas and tackle as *Morra* swung into the wind. Sails ruffled. Sailors heaved on the sheets. With a squeal of blocks, the lines banged taut and *Morra* laid onto her new tack. Downwind like an echo the following ship repeated the flag's maneuver. Excitedly, Emien searched the sea beyond the straits. The Kielmark's ambush lurked in the darkness ahead; alone among Kisburn's men, the boy was curious to see how the demons would send them to slaughter.

Suddenly the Thienz stiffened. Its massive head lifted, blunt face trained forward like a bloodhound tracking an elusive scent. But the Thienz did not pause to sniff the breeze. Half blind by daylight and utterly lacking a sense of smell, it possessed empathic sensitivity more developed than any Sathid-linked talent trained by the Vaere. From a position nine leagues distant, it sounded currents no human could perceive, and reliably listed the position, numbers, and attack plan of the Kielmark's defending fleet. Emien fidgeted in smug anticipation. The renowned Lord of Renegades had no chance against them at all.

The captain fretted behind the quartermaster's shoulder. "Do you sense anything?"

The Thienz whuffed through its gills, noncommittal. But its pose remained tautly attentive. Emien strained to overhear as the captain addressed the mate on watch. "Fetch Tathagres. The Gierj should come on deck. If perfect timing exists for attack, this must surely be the moment."

The Thienz stretched its gillflaps and croaked. Beaded ornaments gleamed upon knotted wrists as it lifted the appendage which passed for a hand and pointed. "Ships, twelve to port, seventeen to starboard. They are signaled by watchfire from the island yonder, and now captains hoist canvas. They will round the points on both sides and bear downwind in a line. They hope to engage us and board."

Metal jingled in the companionway. Clad in ornamental mail wrought of silver and a tunic of dyed leather, Tathagres stepped lightly onto the quarterdeck. She smiled to the captain, who plucked nervously at his beard. "They play straight into our hands, don't you see?" With provocative grace, she hooked her scarlet cloak on a belaying pin and regarded the six creatures which swarmed across the deck at her heels.

Ropy, lean, and blackened like clotted shadow in the darkness, the Gierj-demons scuttled round her boots. Their eyes glowed pale and lambent as sorcerer's candles. Emien shivered despite his interest. Of ten demon races left unbound, the Gierj were most dangerous. Spurred feet scraped against planking as they moved, furtive and quick as weasels, and formed into a circle. Their bodies appeared to melt into a single form as they lowered narrowed heads into a huddle.

"Distribute jackets to the crew," said the captain to the mate. The sweat on his brow was not entirely raised by heat; his thick hands trembled as he accepted his own cloak from the cabin steward.

The Thienz whuffed loudly and barked. Tiny as toys, the Kielmark's first ships rounded the massive shoulders of land up the straits. Emien snatched up his cloak. Wool prickled his skin as he pinned it snugly about his neck. But watching in starved anticipation as the ships rounded the point, the boy forgot to scratch.

The Kielmark's captains maintained position with seamanship unequaled the breadth of Keithland; precise as clockwork, each vessel swung before the wind for the run down the straits. Lacking a ship's glass, Emien could only guess their size and rig; visible only briefly, the enemy craft jibed neatly and steered just inside the shore, for a few brief minutes escaping the backlit cast of the moonlight. Once clear of the land's shadow, they came head on in formation. The outline of the first ship became hopelessly muddled by those following behind.

Emien smiled. Against human foes, the Kielmark's tactics would be powerfully effective. Yet with Gierj on board, the enviable skill of his crewmen served only to aid his defeat.

On the quarterdeck, Tathagres licked pale lips. Bracelets clinked on her wrist as she touched the captain's arm. "They make it easy for us," she said, amused by the man's discomfort. "Closely bunched, those boats will burn like Koridan's Fires, you will see."

But her complacence felt misplaced to a man who had twice battled the wiliest sea dog on Keithland and been defeated. The captain anxiously checked the heading over the quartermaster's broad shoulders time and again.

With the wind in their favor, the Kielmark's fleet bore down with startling speed. Tathagres plucked her cloak from the rail, cast it over her shoulders with languid grace. The Gierj began to chant. The leadsman called the three fathom mark over an unsettling quaver of sound. Men dashed to the sheets as *Morra* came about once again. Emien crossed the forecastle and settled against the starboard rail. Slowly the ship clawed away from the shoreline. The demons' incantation rose and blended into a single flowing note which set Emien's teeth on edge. No longer could he pretend to be comfortable with the creatures on *Morra*'s quarterdeck.

"Captain, shorten sail and heave to." Tathagres stepped into the circle of demons and carefully fastened her cloak.

Sailhands swarmed up the shrouds to reef canvas. The Gierj chant ascended in pitch, ringing across the sea like a discordant shrilling of flutes. Emien covered both ears with his hands and wondered how men in the shrouds could bear the sting of that inhuman sound.

Tathagres spoke in an alien tongue from the quarterdeck. The Thienz replied, gestured with scrawny arms, then lowered its bulk down the companionway. No longer were its powers of observation required; lined up like sheep for slaughter, the Kielmark's ships sailed to their doom.

The Gierj shifted pitch. Their song flung screeching discord across the waters. Inured to their presence, the grizzled quartermaster swung *Morra*'s bow into the wind and steadied the helm. The flagship drifted in the current, balanced like a moth in a draft, while enemies closed on both quarters. The wail of the Gierj warbled, abruptly descended and became a bare whisper of sound. Tathagres placed her fingers lightly against her neckband. She spoke a sibilant word and around her the temperature plunged into winter.

Air burned with startling cold in Emien's lungs. He gasped, knifed to the marrow by chill so intense his cloak stiffened like paper across his shoulders. Hoarfrost traced the ship like crystal in the moonlight, whitening rail and rigging and wheel; the quartermaster's mustache sprouted a rim of ice. Still the temperature fell. With fingers numbed and noses reddened, men blinked frost from their lashes.

The Gierj's song wavered and broke upon the air. Tathagres raised a stiffened arm to the advancing lines of ships. The temperature dropped yet again, bringing the terrible cold of Arctic night. Ropes cracked like old bones and timbers moaned as ice strained the wood. A sudden aura of sorcery blazed around the Gierj. The faces of captain and quartermaster shone blue and their breath plumed against the dark. Tathagres raised her arms. Energy shot like lightning from the Gierj-demons' midst and broke in a blaze of light over her palms. Emien squinted, but the spell grew too brilliant to bear.

He shielded his eyes with his hands. The Gierj's chant ceased, choked off in midbeat. A high, ululating cry burst from Tathagres' throat. Power exploded from her fingers and the night split with a peal like thunder. *Morra* drifted placidly, cloaked in ordinary shadow. But beyond her forestay Emien saw fire burst like the wrath of Kor across the Kielmark's advancing ships.

Flames speared skyward, pinwheeling sparks and debris across the surface of the sea. In the space of a single instant, every enemy vessel was transformed to a raging inferno. Above the crackle of blazing timbers, a barrage of agonized screams rebounded down the straits as Cliffhaven's defenders perished at their posts. Emien gripped the rail with sweating hands. The scope of the demons' destruction left him awed. Confused by elation and a sickened sense of horror, he watched, rapt, while twenty-nine ships burned to the waterline.

Unnoticed beneath the companionway, the Thienz pressed finlike fingers to its face, delicate psychic senses overpowered by the discharge of energy. Blinded to its own element, it rocked and moaned in discomfort, while the cold traced rims of frost about its gills. On the quarterdeck Tathagres stood poised like a cruel marble goddess while the Gierj stirred and scratched at her feet. They turned lean faces up the straits, dispassionate eyes reflecting the ruinous conflagration their powers had unleashed. The living stood motionless on *Morra*'s decks while the fires up the straits roared and snapped and at last subsided into smoke.

On the foredeck Emien shivered. His mouth curved with surly desire. No mortal on Keithland could withstand the forces summoned by the Gierj; the Kielmark would be brought to his knees like a child and even Anskiere's great bastions of ice would soften and dissolve into the sea. The screams of dying sailors no longer troubled Emien's ears. If he could defeat Tathagres, the powers of demons would be his to command.

CHAPTER XXII

Fallen Lord

Led by the flagship *Morra*, Kisburn's fleet of three cleared Mainstrait, contested by nothing but current and wind; if the vessels were forced to tack often to avoid the smoking snarls of wreckage which drifted across their course, none of the captains complained. The fact that the Lord of Pirates had been defeated on his own waters seemed impossible to believe; yet in the gray dawn, beneath a mottled cover of clouds, *Morra* and one companion vessel anchored in Cliffhaven's main harbor utterly unchallenged. The third was sent on patrol to watch for attack by sea.

Emien leaned on the quarterdeck rail, eyes trained intently on the dockside. The bronze penknife he had lately used to pare his nails lay forgotten between half-clenched fingers. He glanced up as Tathagres paused by his side. Still clad in the mail and tunic she had worn the previous night, she appeared fully refreshed. Her appeal quickened the breath in his throat. But this once Emien had no mind to indulge his desire.

"There are no ships at anchorage, Lady." Carefully noncommittal, the boy returned his knife to his wallet. "When we last put in with the Stormwarden there were upwards of thirty, and by sailors' accounts the Kielmark never slept with less than two score vessels on moorings."

But Tathagres awarded the comment even less concern than the possibility survivors might have swum ashore from the encounter in the strait the previous night. Posed with perfect grace against the rails, she studied the stone corners of the warehouses which usually housed tribute, as if expecting something.

"There," she said suddenly and pointed.

Emien looked. A shirtless figure raced through the alleys toward the harbor, a white banner streaming from a pole in his hand. "That's a trap," the boy said, surprised into rash words. "The Kielmark ran a man through with a sword once for objecting to the fact he had no white for surrender among the ensigns aboard his ships."

"He still doesn't." Tathagres smiled with pleased satisfaction. "What you see is a strip cut from a bedsheet. The Kielmark had no part in the matter, I assure you. My Thienz informed me an hour ago; it seems the Lord of Renegades has at last fallen victim to the lawless. His own men have betrayed him. We are about to be invited through the main gates and there the Kielmark himself will be delivered to us in chains."

Emien bit his lip in disbelief as the shirtless man leapt into a longboat, propped his makeshift banner in the bow, and cast off. Oars winked like matchstick against leaden swells, then drove in rhythmic strokes toward the flagship.

"Why?" he said. "Why now of all times?"

Tathagres shook her hair free of its jeweled comb and loosed a bright peal of laughter. "A spy brought word of the Gierj-demons. The sentries on duty in the tower watched their companions burn in Mainstrait last night." She pricked Emien's arm lightly with the prongs of the hair pin. "Don't fret over the remaining ships, my love. Cliffhaven is ours. With the Kielmark hostage, any captains who remain loyal will be easily managed."

But her attitude was too confident, Emien thought. Like the time Tathagres had murdered the guards by the ice cliffs, her air of reckless assurance grated against his sensibility. Yet he followed when she called the captain on deck to receive the longboat. Certain of her one true weakness, he wondered when he would have the opportunity to exploit it.

The chains which operated the front gates of Cliffhaven clanked across the winches. Heavy steel-bound portals swung wide and thumped against the walls, raising small puffs of dust. From his place to the rear of the King's advance guard, Emien heard a raucous scream of laughter backed by the incongruous notes of a flute. The Grand Warlord-General bellowed an order; the column began smartly to march. But the soldiers ahead had to clear the span of the arch before Emien gained a view of the courtyard.

A score of leather-clad men danced and cavorted in the open; others looked on clapping, all of them drunk except one. Chained by the wrists to the ring which normally tethered the saddled horse, a huge man knelt in their midst, his muscles knotted in wild anger. Blue eyes followed King Kisburn's entry with murderous intent. With a shock of disbelief, Emien recognized the Kielmark. The man's hair was filthy with dust. Flies buzzed about a gash above one eyebrow. The flagstone lay speckled with blood under his knees and the steel links dripped red from a swordcut across his forearm. But Emien observed that the men who had betrayed the legendary Lord of Renegades to defeat were careful to celebrate beyond reach.

The King commanded the Warlord-General to transfer the prisoner to the great hall. The flute player trailed off into silence and the dancers stilled to stare. Each recalled times when the Kielmark had killed for less. Five men moved cautiously from the lines, followed by the spokesman who carried the flag of surrender. Emien licked sweat from his lips. It seemed impossible that Cliffhaven could fall with no struggle after twenty years of dominance; countless bitter forays had ended in broken ships each time Keithland's rulers tried to break the Kielmark's stranglehold over Mainstrait. Yet nothing appeared extraordinary about the flag-bearer. With a snarl of hatred, he lowered his pole like a weapon and jabbed it savagely into the pit of the Kielmark's stomach. The man's body doubled, and he retched, gasping helplessly for air, while soldiers rushed in and unfastened the chains from the ring. They jerked the Kielmark to his feet.

Emien shivered in the morning heat, distressed that a ruler of such stature could suffer common vindictive abuse. Deeply shaken, Emien trailed the royal party down vaulted corridors.

Solid stone felt suddenly unsound beneath his boots and marching feet seemed to rattle the very keystones in the arches. The most defensible fortress on Keithland could not stand against human treachery. Sapped by growing insecurity, Emien passed between the gaudy trophies which littered Cliffhaven's great hall. His eyes saw none of the wealth. He chose a seat to the left of Tathagres, his thought trained with fanatical clarity upon the gold which circled her neck.

Guards sprang at the King's command. The chamber reverberated with the scrape of furniture as men cleared space for their prisoner. Seated in the Kielmark's own chair, Kisburn watched with fascinated satisfaction as his men hauled the Lord of Renegades onto the open floor in front of the dais.

The guardsmen tugged his chains, holding him spread-eagled and helpless before the royal presence. Prisoner regarded captor with a level glare of hostility. The Kielmark's chest heaved in great whistling gasps while blood dripped from his wrist, splashing scarlet stars on the marble. He waited in silence for the King to speak, but whether from stubborn pride or incapacity, no man present could guess.

"For a man who has terrorized shipping, your harbor seems strangely deserted." Kisburn stroked the leopard skin on the chair with lean ringed fingers, an expression of overweening satisfaction on his face. "Where did you send them?"

The former Lord of Cliffhaven grinned. "To the backside of hell, for all the good it will do you."

Guardsmen wrenched at the chains and his shoulders jerked. In a burst of fury the Kielmark yanked back. One of his tormentors slipped, crashing sideways into a basket of alabaster pears. The container overturned. Fruit shattered with a shrill ring of sound and a spray of sparkling chips scattered the tiles. The guardsman cursed and clawed to maintain his balance. For an instant his chain fell slack; the Kielmark insolently wiped the blood from his brow, smearing his sound wrist scarlet.

But his gesture of bravado was spoiled by a vicious rejoinder from the flag-bearer. "He lies, your Grace. The ships left last night, packed to the crosstrees with cowards. Most of us served Cliffhaven against our will, and others didn't fancy getting burned alive like pigs."

But the King seemed unconvinced. His jeweled arm lifted, gesturing to a halberdier. The man reversed his weapon like a quarterstaff. Six feet of studded beech rose and descended and the Kielmark's smile vanished with a gasp. The flag-bearer laughed, backed by sudden ugly silence. The halberd's steel-shod butt carved arcs in the air as the guardsman raised his weapon for a second blow, then a third.

Emien shrank in distaste from his place at Tathagres' side. He barely

heard the reply which emerged half-strangled from the Kielmark's throat.
The King responded with evident displeasure. Chain clanked. The halberdier closed once more, and fresh blood spangled the floor.

The play of petty emotion across the royal countenance raised hackles
on Emien's neck. In all probability the flag-bearer had told the truth; but
in vindication for past dishonor, the King was unwilling to quit. The boy
felt his stomach twist; linked with revulsion came cold fear that one day
the man in chains would be himself. Harrowed by vivid imagination, he
saw accusers lined up to condemn him, his drowned father closely followed
by mother, sister, and the sailors he had abused on *Crow*'s pinnace. Beyond
stood four deckhands sold to the galleys on Skane's Edge; these were
joined by the King's youngest page boy and a fat leering guardsman he
had cheated into subservience at cards. Each blow that fell upon the
Kielmark made Emien flinch and sweat.

The officers soon tired of the sport. Only the King remained unsatisfied. The abuse continued, ascending in violence until furnishings rocked
and scattered before the halberdier's obedient enthusiasm. Repelled to the
verge of nausea, Emien pressed his palms to his face. And spurred by her
squire's discomfort, Tathagres stood up.

Light from the windows sparkled over white mail as she picked her
way around the overturned rungs of a chair. "Your Grace, the prisoner is
no longer a threat to our position. The Thienz assures it. And with the
Kielmark hostage, any captains who remain loyal can be controlled. The
Gierj will gain you ships in time, but not if you waste the opportunity."

The halberdier straightened over the Kielmark's sagging form, uncertain. At last, with a wave of bored acquiescence, the King ordered the
sovereign of Cliffhaven removed to the east keep dungeon.

The victim staggered badly as the soldiers dragged him from the hall.
Shocked by his halting progress, Emien squeezed his eyes closed. A steward mounted the dais with a tray of wine and poured glasses in celebration
of the victory. The Warlord-General issued orders to complete occupation
of the fortress. The flag-bearer volunteered to close the boom across the
harbor; he left with a junior officer and two guardsmen. The remaining
troops were dispatched, some under orders to search the town and a few
to stand watch in the anteroom. Boots tramped across rumpled carpeting
and a blood-spattered expanse of marble with casual disregard; the Kielmark's legendary might was broken. His conquerers answered orders with
a cheerful swagger, certain of fame and spoils.

Once the light tower was manned and the town proved deserted, servants arrived and straightened the disarranged furnishings. Emien paid
little notice. Concerned with his own thoughts, he lingered when the
Thienz was summoned. While the Warlord-General, Lord Sholl, and
Tathagres seated themselves on the dais with the officers to conduct their
council of conquest, the fisherman's son from Imrill Kand watched on the
sidelines, plotting his mistress' downfall.

*   *   *

Motionless where he had fallen when the guards flung him through the door, the Kielmark sprawled face down in the same stone cell where he had lately imprisoned Jaric. Bruised, bloodied, beaten, he did not budge, even to ask for water. The King's guardsmen secured his chains and locked the door. Gloating over his defeat, they left him in darkness without bothering to post any sentry.

An hour passed, then two. Metal scraped faintly beneath the floor. A length of flagstone shifted, raised, and a stealthy whisper issued from a tunnel beneath. "Lord?"

Chain rattled as the Kielmark stirred. He turned his head and spoke through cracked lips. "No guard."

"Fires!" said the man in the hole. "They're fools, then."

The Kielmark offered no comment. Eager hands levered the stone aside and a man emerged, blindly drawing candle and striker from a pouch at his belt. Light bloomed beneath his fingers, revealing the intent features of the man who had played the flute in the courtyard. Still reeking of ale, one of the dancers climbed out after him, armed to the teeth and dangerously sober. He drew a key from his tunic, bent over the Kielmark, and swiftly unlocked the fetters.

Crusted cuffs fell open. In slow painful stages, the Kielmark rolled over. His expression hid very little. Cliffhaven's two wiliest captains looked on with concern and wisely offered no assistance as he sat up. Even by the weak flicker of candleflame, they could see things had gone badly. The Kielmark's ribs and shoulders were crisscrossed with mottled welts; his back was little better. To touch even in kindness would only increase his discomfort.

One of the captains swore.

The Kielmark looked up. His eyes shone baleful and pale beneath eyebrows matted with dried blood. "Did the signal arrive from the straits?"

The flute player raked dirt-streaked fingers through his hair. "Nine dead, a score and four with burns major and minor and the rest of the lot lying about in the brush, croaking like frogs, their throats left raw from screaming. But watching, they said, for your banner in the tower." He paused, suddenly contrite. "Are your ribs intact? You weren't exactly acting after the bit with the flagpole. Corley says he only followed orders, Lord, but there's a wager going round that you'll break both his legs."

The Kielmark grunted. Split lips parted across his teeth. "I'll settle for the Kingsmen's heads," he said bluntly. "On with it, then."

He pinched out the candle. Darkness dropped, hiding his suffering through a terrible interval while the captains lowered him into the tunnel.

Beneath the high vaulted arches of Cliffhaven's great hall, the Thienz coughed through its gills. It leapt to its feet with a shrill scream of warning and suddenly staggered, a crossbow quarrel bristling from its throat. Knocked backward by the impact it fell, smashing through the rungs of an ivory-inlaid globe stand. Keithland rolled across the rug and the chamber erupted into chaos.

"Treachery!" shouted Lord Sholl. He dove behind his stout oaken chair just as the tapestries slithered into heaps, revealing arrowslits cut through the stone walls behind. A storm of shafts flickered past the arched windows. The royal chief advisor rammed face-first into oak, pinned by an arrow through his back. The Grand Warlord-General slipped to the floor beside him, his mouth stretched wide in surprise. The advisor's flesh crumpled before his eyes, melting into a form not recognizable as human; but sorcery blazed above the dais, dazzling his vision before the change was complete. He died still wondering whether a demon had shared his salt.

Shielded by the crackling blaze of Tathagres' conjuring, Emien crouched in terror, while on the dais around him the royal council members slumped in their seats, struck down by enemy arrows. Since the Thienz's first cry, his mistress had leapt to her feet, her hands clenched over the band at her throat. She raised a crackling arch of light over the King. Any shaft which touched it exploded into sparks. But the rest of the arrows hissed to their marks with grisly accuracy; in seconds, Emien, Kisburn, and Tathagres became the sole survivors amid a slaughtered circle of officials. Yet she dared not relax her defenses. The archers continued to fire.

"All is not lost," said Tathagres urgently. "Help get the King to safety."

Unearthly reflections flickered across her face, spangling her jewels in light. Immersed in her wardspell, Emien felt currents of energy tingle across his skin. Ozone stung his nostrils. Suddenly exhilarated by his narrow escape from death, the boy caught the royal wrist and urged the stunned King of Kisburn to rise.

"You must walk, your Grace." Tathagres gestured toward the anteroom. "Outside I can summon the Gierj. Hurry."

The King rallied scattered wits. Shafts banged and clattered across the marble floor, deflected by Tathagres' sorcery. Seizing the chance for survival, Kisburn permitted Emien to hustle him down the dais steps. Tathagres followed on their heels, still conjuring. The attackers switched to spears. Energy crackled and whined overhead, devouring wood and steel with seemingly endless appetite. The party crossed the hall at a run.

Carnage met them before they reached the door, as guards posted in the anteroom belatedly acted in their King's defense. Men charged in disciplined formation, shields raised over their heads. But the tasteless opulence of the Kielmark's decor was designed to foil attack. The lines broke into muddled knots as men dodged between tables and chests. A lampstand toppled with a screeching crash and swords tangled in statuary. The archers slaughtered rescuers at leisure.

The King shouted and extended his arm toward an injured officer.

"Prevent him," Tathagres said quickly. "We can't stop here."

Her violet eyes raked the King with ruthless calculation; she meant the King no kindness, Emien observed. He gripped the royal tunic with bruising force. Thin shoulders jerked under the velvet. Emien knew a thrill of excitement. Never before had a man born to power suffered discomfort at his hands. He shoved the King toward the door. Kisburn stumbled gracelessly forward. Emien followed, stepping callously on the fingers of the officer who thrashed on the floor. With Tathagres a step behind, he plunged through the arch into the anteroom, beyond range of enemy weapons.

The heavy iron-bound panels beyond were closed, *barred from without*, cornering them like mice in a culvert. Emien whirled. He yelled warning, just as the archway leading to the hall exploded in a burst of red light.

Tathagres spoke through the glare. "Move aside. *Hurry!*"

She intended to break the doors with sorcery. Emien dove clear, dragging the King by the collar. The spell blazed at his heels. Shadows streaked the anteroom floor, spattered across with sparks, and the panels sagged on their hinges. Wood and steel unraveled into smoke, rendered ineffective as the weapons set against them in the main hall. But when Tathagres followed the King through the gap, she lacked her usual lithe grace. Use of sorcery taxed her, Emien realized; the discovery pleased him. If her powers were limited by ordinary human endurance, he wondered how long she could continue before exhaustion made her careless.

A guardsman sprawled dead before the doorway, the handle of a throwing knife sunk between his shoulder blades. Tathagres saw him and stopped. With enemies about the fortress and no time left for etiquette, she spun and faced the King.

"Where are your personal chambers? Take me there quickly. Your Grace cannot be properly defended in the open."

Reliant upon her protection, the King answered at once. But Emien noticed she kept one hand poised on her necklace as if she expected resistance. When the Warlord-General's aide ran into the corridor, a score of guardsmen at his heels, her expression showed open annoyance. *She regarded them as interference,* the boy deduced. With the conquest of Cliffhaven thrown into question, Kisburn's men were allies no longer. Tathagres intended to claim the Keys to Elrinfaer by force.

The aide saw the corpse. He skidded to a halt with a rattle of mail and gear and saluted smartly. "Your Grace, the enemy has closed and barred the main gates of the fortress. Archers fire on the courtyard. We've had to move the company inside."

He paused, breathless, and waited. But without the advice of Lord Sholl and his council, the King seemed strangely indecisive. He made no effort to assert himself as Tathagres intervened.

"Forget the gates. There's been an attempt on your sovereign's life.

The Warlord-General lies dead." She jerked her head at the charred ruin of the doors to the main hall. "You guards. Block this entrance." To the aide she added, "Fetch reinforcements. There must be passages behind the walls. Purge them if you can. You will receive further orders after I have seen your King secure."

The King accepted Tathagres' judgment without question. He dismissed the aide and fled in the direction of his chamber.

The Kielmark's fortress proved a maze of stairs and angled passages. Winded after his rush from the main hall, Emien halted with Tathagres and the King before a brass-studded portal. Two of Kisburn's personal honor guards flanked the entrance, vigilant and alert at their posts.

Tathagres' aggression softened like steel under velvet. She waited with poised patience while the guardsmen saluted their sovereign Lord, then stepped smartly aside to admit him. Tired, shaken, and wheezing, the King leaned heavily on the latch. The massive panels swung open, revealing a wide chamber richly carpeted in scarlet and gold. Kisburn hastened to a side table where a tray waited with a bottle of wine from the Kielmark's private cellars. Ignoring the gold-rimmed goblet, he raised the flask to his lips. Fine crystal rattled against his teeth as he swallowed and his fingers marked sweaty prints on the flask.

A choked-off cry made him start. The King whirled, dribbling wine down his chin. Beyond the opened doorway, Tathagres lowered one of the honor guards, dead, across the corpse of the first. She straightened with wicked intent, pulled the heavy panels closed, then placed her back against them.

From the side, Emien saw her grip the latch until her knuckles blanched against the brass. Fatigued at last by her sorceries, she used the doors more to support her weight than to forestall attempted escape.

But her eyes stayed cruelly alert as she regarded her prey across the airy expanse of the chamber. "Get me the Keys to Elrinfaer, *your Grace.*" She turned her shoulder to the wood, one hand raised to her necklace. "Or shall I force them from you?"

The King dropped the wine. The flask toppled across the tray and shattered, spattering glass over his gold-bordered tunic. A stain darkened the carpet under his boots as he gaped in astonished disbelief. Tathagres had betrayed him; Emien made no effort to contain the elated laughter which arose in his throat.

Jolted by the sound, Kisburn recovered a shadow of his royal propriety. He shook his head, wine-streaked fingers clamped over the table edge. "But the Chief Advisor assured me—"

"Lord Sholl is dead," Tathagres interrupted. Amethysts flashed as her fingers jumped against her neckband. *"Fetch the Keys."*

Why does she hesitate? Selfishly eager, Emien wondered. Usually his mistress flaunted power, taking pleasure in intimidation and superiority.

Emboldened by the thought that Tathagres might be tiring, Emien hoped the King would resist, compelling her to react until exhaustion lowered her guard.

But the murders in the council had shattered Kisburn's confidence. Deprived of the support of Lord Sholl and the Warlord-General, he lacked the backbone to fight. Emien looked on in disgust while his shoulders sagged, as if the gem-crusted chain of office which circled his shoulders suddenly grew too weighty for him to endure.

"I will yield you the Keys." Kisburn blotted his brow on his brocade cuff and glowered at the woman who blocked the chamber door. Robbed of dignity by defeat, his tone turned querulous. "I hope you have decency enough to leave after this. For your sorceries and your demons have brought my kingdom to the verge of ruin."

The King pulled a ring from a chain at his belt and crossed the room. Sullen and slow, he knelt before the heavy steelbound chest placed beside the hearth.

"Go with him," said Tathagres to Emien. Her voice held a brittle edge. "Be certain he tries no tricks. The Keys of Elrinfaer lie in a box of black basalt. You will know it by Anskiere's seal set in gold on the top."

Emien obeyed, feigning nonchalance. While Kisburn unlocked the chest and lifted the lid, the boy glanced furtively at Tathagres; her attention appeared absorbed by the King, who reached with jerky, uncertain motions and shuffled among the contents in the chest. Emien sidled closer. Careful to hide his movements, he raised his hand to his belt, closed his fingers over his knife, and pretended to peer over the King's shoulder. Slowly, nervously, he inched his blade from its sheath.

"Here." Kisburn straightened, a cube of dark stone balanced across his palm. The symbol of Anskiere's mastery was inlaid in shining gold on its polished surface, a stormfalcon centered within three concentric circles. To Emien, the seal promised power, permanent escape from the sovereign tyranny of sorcery. With a rising surge of triumph, he seized the royal shoulder and sank his dagger upward to the hilt in the soft flesh of the King's lower back.

Royal blood flooded warmly over his wrist. The King cried out, twisted, and sank in agony to one knee. Anskiere's box slipped from loosened fingers. Emien caught the object, felt its solid corners gouge his skin. Too late he noticed the cube possessed neither seam nor catch. If the stone contained an object of power, he had no time to search for the secret. With the hair rising at the nape of his neck, Emien straightened and faced his mistress.

Tathagres stepped clear of the doorway, both hands in contact with her neckband. Her murdered ally writhed in agony on the hearth, but she made no effort to help him. Slim, straight, and savagely beautiful in her silver mail, she met her squire's defiance with dangerous fury. "Fool," she said coldly. "Give the Keys of Elrinfaer to me."

Taen cried out from the depths of dream trance. Sweat dampened her brow and she twisted against Jaric's hands. He held her shoulders firmly, preventing her from thrashing against the gritty wall of the cavern. The tunnel which led from the east keep dungeon was narrow, hastily constructed, and shored up with scraps of timber and undressed rocks. Sloping gently, it opened into a muddy cave whose entrance lay hidden behind an outcrop above the harbor. There by the light of a single lantern a wizened healer cleaned and dressed the Kielmark's abrasions with old, careful hands. Throughout the disturbance, his touch on the wounds stayed neat and sure, and if his salves were astringent enough to make Jaric's eyes water, the King of Renegades ignored the sting. Like the Firelord's heir, he sat hunched and still, attention fixed with unwavering intensity upon the dream-weaver who sought news of the trap which closed over King Kisburn's attack force in the fortress above.

Taen shivered and abruptly opened her eyes. In a voice which trembled with shock, she said, "Emien has murdered the King. He wishes Tathagres' death also and has seized the Keys of Elrinfaer on the chance their powers might prove useful against her. As yet Anskiere's sorceries are beyond his ability to master."

"He's ignorant." The Kielmark fretted as the healer wrapped a fresh bandage on his forearm. "The Keys have no purpose except to preserve the wards over Elrinfaer Tower."

Taen offered no reply. Suspended once more in the dream link, she sagged against Jaric's shoulder. But the tension did not smooth from her young face as she merged her consciousness with Emien. Her hands remained clenched in her lap. The Firelord's heir stroked tangled hair from her brow, unhappily aware the Keys' recovery might now cost Taen's brother his life. More than ever before, Jaric wished he had insisted the dream-weaver leave before Kisburn's assault as the Vaere had directed.

But Taen remained unaware of the concern which troubled the Firelord's heir. Absorbed by the mysteries of her craft, she heard nothing as the Kielmark swore and excused the healer with an irritable flick of his wrist. Bound to her brother, she stood in a room paneled in gilt and cedar, the chilly weight of the Keys to Elrinfaer Tower poised between sweating fingers.

Tathagres confronted Emien by the doorway, both hands clenched to her neckband. "I warned you, boy." Though her tone was harsh with threat, she seemed strangely reluctant to engage sorcery and attack. Taen expanded her focus, seeking the reason; she caught the elusive flicker of something similar to fear in the woman's violet eyes.

But fatigue made Taen sloppy. Her dream search brushed Emien's frame of reference, tripped it slightly out of balance. The boy also sensed Tathagres' hesitation. Suddenly brazenly unafraid, he laughed and crossed the floor, treading fragments of glass into the carpet. Taen drew back, alarmed. But Tathagres watched her squire's approach without anxiety, cold calculation on her face. She did not shrink as he stopped, so close he hedged her against the brass-rimmed wood of the door frame. Neither did she flinch as, with a smile of insolent malice, he twisted bloody fingers in her hair and kissed the angry line of her lips.

Although her fingers never left the band at her neck, Tathagres softened slightly under his torch. Only when the boy stepped back and presented the Keys of Elrinfaer with exaggerated courtesy did she relax and lower her hands.

Tapped into dream link, Taen felt satisfaction flood like ice water through Tathagres' thoughts. *The boy could still be managed.* Relieved she would not need to contest him for possession of the Keys, she glanced toward the fireplace. The King lay dead by the andiron, his opened mouth pooled in blood. He could no longer be used as a hostage to threaten cooperation from the men-at-arms; to escape the Kielmark's trap she would need sorcery and help from her demon allies.

Taen dissolved her contact before the idea finished forming in Tathagres' mind. Once the witch engaged her sorceries, the link might reveal a dream-weaver's presence. Unwilling to risk notice by the demons, Taen wakened in the earthy darkness of the cave. She sat up, weary to the point where even her bones ached.

"Well?" The Kielmark knotted the ends of the bandage across his wrist, using one grimy fist and his teeth. He paid no heed to the healer's wince of annoyance. "What did you find?"

Taen met his impatience with words stripped bare by exhaustion. "Kisburn is dead. Tathagres has the Keys. She intends to depart for Elrinfaer at once, with Emien."

The Kielmark crowed loudly and grinned at Jaric. "We have her boxed. Every gate in the fortress is barred from the outside and covered by archers in concealment. The fleet arrives with reinforcements by afternoon."

"No." Taen shook her head, desolate in Jaric's arms. "Archers cannot stop her." She drew a quivering breath and qualified. "The witch calls upon the Gierj even as we speak. The instant the melding trance is complete, she will draw upon their power and transfer."

"She won't get away with it." Linen parted with a coarse scream of sound as the Kielmark tore away the excess bandage. With single-minded disregard for his stiffened, abused body, he surged to his knees and scrambled across the cave to the brush which screened the entrance. There he grabbed the bow which waited in a niche already strung, and nocked an arrow with a streamer affixed to one end. Scarlet flecks soaked the bandage as he flexed his wrist and drew.

The Kielmark aimed high and released; the arrow leapt outward in a long steep arc, streamer trailing like a comet's tail across the overcast sky. The shaft slowed, almost hesitated midflight, then plunged earthward with a rush. Behind the Kielmark's bulk, Taen and Jaric watched it fall, cognizant of the fact that the signal sentenced brave men to die. The arrow commanded the first stage of the attack to retake the harbor; but the fleet which should have supported the strategy had yet to breast the horizon.

CHAPTER XXIII

Elrinfaer

Tathagres engaged the powers of the Gierj-demons and Kisburn's private chamber dissolved in a shower of light. Red-orange sparks streaked across Emien's vision and vanished in a scorching blast of wind. Unlike the earlier transfer from the ice cliffs, the boy felt a bucking lurch. Sorcery whipped his hair into snarls as he tumbled through air and darkness. He landed gasping beside his mistress on a beach laced with stinking strands of kelp.

Emien looked up, disappointed. A glance showed them still on Cliff-haven; but outside the fortress walls just a stone's throw from the dockside. Bruised and winded, Emien struggled to his feet. Sand dribbled out of his cuffs as he straightened his swordbelt and extended his hand to Tathagres.

She accepted his help with none of the acid unpleasantness he remembered from Skane's Edge. The sorcery of the transfer had taxed her. Her delicate features were drawn and pale under a light sheen of sweat. Tremors of fatigue passed through her as she gripped Emien's arm. She stumbled to her feet as if the demons' powers had left her slightly dazed.

Emien watched like a starved cat, fingers inching toward his sword. Yet Tathagres rallied before he gathered the nerve to exploit her weakness. She swept a rapacious glance across strand, warehouses, and the line of the horizon beyond the boom which closed the harbor, and thought rapidly.

"Find a boat quickly and get us to sea." She flicked sand from her hair with an arrogant toss of her wrist. "To transfer to Elrinfaer I must merge again with the Gierj. This cannot be attempted within reach of men-at-arms."

Whether she referred to Kisburn's men or the Kielmark's pirates made no difference; both sides would carry steel. Emien complied without argument. Outgoing tide creamed over a breakwater fifty paces to the south. Beyond, the shore lifted into rugged bastions of rock too steep for safe anchorage. Northward past the untenanted jumble of dockside taverns and shops a wharf extended beyond the corner of a warehouse. Black against leaden clouds, an angular assembly of spars and rigging reared above the shingled roofs.

Emien pointed. "There."

Tathagres nodded. Together they ran over sand still packed from the tide. The beach ended, shored up by a breakwater of granite. Emien caught

Tathagres' elbow, steadying her as she climbed over rocks crusted with barnacles. A push would tumble her onto the jagged stones below. Since she intended a transfer to Elrinfaer, Emien chose patience. Pressed flat against weather-beaten boards, he hurried past the warehouse. The boat lay tied thirty feet out on the pier. She appeared unguarded. After a hasty glance at her lines Emien saw why, and swore under his breath. The boat was aged and ungainly. Yet her planking showed signs of recent repair and she still looked fit to sail.

Tathagres shared none of the boy's annoyance. Although she appeared peaked and tired, she spoke before he managed any complaint. "The boat must serve. The Kielmark has cleared his harbor of everything else."

"Let's hope he was thorough." Emien grimaced. "If that relic sails at all, she'll go clunky as a farmer's wooden bucket."

Suddenly a shout rang from the alley behind the warehouse. Steel clanged, announcing a rapid exchange of swordplay. Out of time to seek options, Emien caught his mistress's elbow and bolted for the dock. The foolish old fishing craft was surely preferable to getting trapped like rats on the shore.

Emien leapt across three feet of water onto the port gunwale; an engraved plaque beneath his boot named the craft *Callinde.* Leaving the docklines for Tathagres, Emien dove for the mess of rope at the base of the mast and uncleated the main halyard.

Callinde rocked sharply as Tathagres followed him on board. Without looking around, Emien hoisted. The heavy yard rattled up the mast, unfurling a patched square of sail. "Cast off," he said tersely, and whipped the line onto a cleat. "Let the stern off last."

Tathagres ducked forward, shadowed by canvas as Emien raised the jib. Wind caught the clew, snaking lines across the deck. The boy dug aft beneath bunched acres of spanker for the knots which lashed the tiller. His hand slammed into floor boards and he cursed. Antique to her last fitting, *Callinde* came equipped with a steering oar.

Line splashed into water and the high curved prow swung free. Tathagres raised the spanker as Emien slashed the stern line with his sword. *Callinde* drifted from the wharf, sails flogging aloft. Emien dove for the sheets, dragged them hissing through the blocks. Canvas fell taut with a whump; the old craft shouldered on starboard tack across the bay.

Emien hauled on the steering oar, eyes trained forward. Kisburn's two ships lay moored to leeward; water stretched ahead in an open line to the sea. Emien felt his hair prickle at the base of his neck.

"Mistress!" He bent to see past the spanker and discovered her kneeling by the mast. "The boom is gone from the entrance of the harbor."

Tathagres hurried to the gunwale and looked out. Her voice came back above the crash of spray beneath the keel. "Kielmark's work. The flag-bearer must have turned coat again."

A deep rumble sounded across the bay. Emien glanced aft, distressed.

The entire seaward side of a warehouse slid open to reveal stone crenelations inside. Two catapults reared behind and the barbed bolts of four loaded arbalests glittered through notches cut in the wall.

"Sail!" Tathagres' voice broke. "If they loose any bolts on us, I can manage."

Emien dragged *Callinde* straight—and shouted. One of Kisburn's ships had launched a longboat. Drawn by the frosty gleam of Tathagres' hair, six seamen bent over the looms, driving their craft straight across his path. Emien adjusted lines and tried frantically to coax more speed from his sails.

The first of the arbalests released. But *Callinde* was not the target; the bolt whined overhead and drove with a plume of spray into the waves off *Morra*'s stern.

"They aim to disable the Gierj!" Tathagres leaned over *Callinde*'s thwart and shouted to the officer in the approaching longboat. "Return to your ship and man your weapons. Defend the demons from steel!"

The officer saluted. His oarsmen reversed stroke, turning the longboat aside. Emien corrected *Callinde*'s course. Another quarrel tore through the air, followed by a third which grazed through *Morra*'s mooring ropes. The men at the arbalests would shortly perfect their aim, and over the splash of *Callinde*'s passage Emien heard the sour clank of the winch which cocked a catapult.

Tathagres crouched beneath the gunwale. "I'm going to summon the Gierj and pull us out before the enemy spoil their powers with steel. Make for the open sea. Whatever befalls, I must reach Elrinfaer with all speed."

Tathagres settled against the mast. She bowed her head on crossed arms, her hands in light contact with her neckband, and slipped gradually into rapport with the demons. Emien steered against rising gusts, irritated to discover how soft he had grown during his months at court. *Callinde* tossed like a wayward horse over the crests, wrenching his shoulders without mercy. Emien hauled her straight and bitterly cursed her designer. *Morra* fell slowly astern. Carried downwind, the keening chant of the Gierj-demons pierced through the rush of the wake. In a moment, his mistress would focus enough power for transfer. Frustrated by the speed of her magic, Emien hoped *Callinde* would end on a reef.

That instant the first catapult launched with a crack. Emien whirled, saw a dark line writhe in an arc across the sky. His joy abruptly disintegrated. The enemy fired chain shot. Steel links wailed through the air and splashed with a geyser of spray a scant yard shy of *Morra*'s bowsprit. Disturbed by the brief proximity of the steel, the Gierj chant dipped and leveled. Emien cursed in earnest. Iron in any form disrupted their powers; one strike to *Morra*'s rigging would cripple both flagship and demons.

Screened by the brush at the lip of the cave, the Kielmark sprawled on his belly, a brass-banded ship's glass focused on the harbor. Glad not to rely on Taen's talents for information, he watched soldiers delivered ashore by enemy longboats as they rushed in black lines for the warehouse. In a moment the men who manned the embrasure would be under attack. The whistle of the Gierj-demons shrilled across the harbor, eerily ascending in pitch. Unmoved as a boulder, the Kielmark counted attackers and calculated. The catapults had maybe three minutes to set their range.

An arbalest released. Steel rushed through the air, banged soundly into wood. The Gierj wavered and fell off pitch. The Kielmark lowered his glass and grinned boyishly at Jaric. "They'll have her," he said. "Quit sulking."

Jaric did not answer. Tense and still by the Kielmark's side, he fingered the blade of his unsheathed sword and tried not to think while Mathieson's boat drove steadily seaward, her sails curved taut to the wind. Taen had tried vainly to ease Jaric's discomfort since the moment Emien had slashed the docklines. The possibility the Keys to Elrinfaer might slip beyond reach troubled the boy less than his oath to Keldric that *Callinde* would be treasured and kept safe.

"Well, don't rust your fittings with tears," said the Kielmark. But his harsh face reflected sympathy and the Firelord's heir did not weep. "If we don't get flamed by Gierj in the next minute and a half I'll loan you *Troessa*. She's faster than *Callinde* and rigged for quick handling."

A catapult cracked from the warehouse. The Kielmark jerked the glass to his eye in time to see a sharpened length of chain snag *Morra*'s headstay. Steel whipped in an arc, slashing among tarred line, and the foretopmast jerked, angled brokenly forward. Chain slithered to the deck; and the Gierj chant unraveled into dissonance.

Tathagres cried out sharply from her trance. Sparks crackled across her knuckles and winked out. Flung back against the mast, she lay still, her throat bared to the sky and her hands slack by her sides. Emien could not tell whether she had died or was only unconscious. He dared not leave the helm to check.

Ragged shouting broke out astern. The roof of the warehouse which housed the weaponry burst into flame, smudging the sky with smoke. But the catapults launched still, their aim corrected and deadly. More chain shot scythed through rigging, leaving a trail of wreckage. Sailors died trying to clear the steel from *Morra*'s gear, while quarrels from the arbalests pocked her paint with scars. The Gierj were crippled; their chant rose into ragged wails of pain and tailed off into silence. By the time the men-at-arms overran the warehouse and fought the crew who manned the arbalests to a standstill, the entire forward section of the ship stood riddled with bolts. To remove the steel and deliver the demons from agony would require a crew and tools and hours of time.

Emien looked away from the harbor, his face a mask of disgust. The deckhands feared the Gierj; the confusion set loose by the Kielmark's ruse would grant them excuse enough to upset discipline. *Tide against a sand castle,* Emien thought, reminded of a bitter expression from boyhood. Kisburn's officers would never set *Morra* to rights. He had no choice but sail for Elrinfaer alone.

Callinde breasted the waves, steady despite her mulish lines. She reached the headlands of Cliffhaven's harbor faster than the boy expected. He glanced toward Tathagres. Sprawled like a porcelain doll on the floorboards, she showed no sign of consciousness. Emien licked salty lips. He might easily knife her as she lay helpless. Once he stole the necklace, he could at last bring vengeance on Anskiere.

Confident of his plan, Emien turned *Callinde* into the wind. The boat wallowed, jostling Tathagres' limp form. Emien ignored her, rummaging in a locker until he located a ship's glass. This time he would not be balked by carelessness. Bracing his foot on the thwart, he lifted the glass to his eye and swept it across the sea to check whether Kisburn's patrol ship lay in his path.

But the horizon was not empty as he expected. Etched like scrimshaw against a taut band of sky stood a line of masts, each flying the sea wolf blazon of the Kielmark. A wave lifted *Callinde*'s prow. Water broke with a hiss of foam beneath her keel as Emien crossed to the opposite thwart and trained his glass to the south. Ships approached from that quarter also, nearer still, and with the wind behind them. Carrying every stitch of canvas, the Kielmark's fleet returned to defend their island.

Emien collapsed the glass with a snap and sprang back to the helm. *Morra* and her sister ship were doomed. Caught in the path of two fleets, Emien's sole chance was to turn west on a reach and sail for the open sea.

The boy flung his weight against the oar. *Callinde* answered and headed off; wind filled the sails with a bang, jerked her into thirty degrees of heel. The cant of the deck tossed Tathagres limply into the bilge. Emien had no time to drag her clear. To port a brigantine peeled away from the pack and steered northwest to intercept him.

Unlike a tiller, a steering oar could not be lashed to hold a fixed course. Emien cursed the fact while the sky off the bow darkened under an angry rim of cloud. Squalls threatened. A prudent sailor would shorten sail. But to heave to, even to reef canvas, would cause him fatal delay. Gusts whistled through *Callinde*'s rigging. Spray rushed in sheets over the bow and the steering oar clunked and twisted under Emien's hands, difficult to control with so much sail aloft. He clenched his teeth, watching through slitted eyes as the brigantine closed on *Callinde*'s port quarter. Raindrops slashed his face. Emien hoped the storm would hide him. He raised his head and shouted crazily at the sky. Clouds opened and *Callinde* drove, reeling, into the opaque flood of a downpour.

Emien laughed and threw his shoulder into the oar. From where he stood at the helm the headsails where lost in murk. He headed off, saved from pursuit by gray curtains of rain. Rope burned through his fingers as he eased the lines, setting *Callinde* downwind to run with the squall. The Kielmark's fleet could never locate so small a quarry in such poor visibility; once the weather eased, he could put about to Elrinfaer where the power he ached to possess waited to be claimed.

The rain ended at midnight. Wind shifted to the north and clouds scudded across a burnished quarter moon. Needles of reflection gleamed over the wave crests as *Callinde* rolled on a broad reach, her wake a chuckle of foam astern. Cliffhaven had long since vanished behind the horizon. Secure enough to rest, Emien hauled the steering oar with chilled fingers. The headsails backed with a whispered flop. Hove to, *Callinde* drifted, silent and alone.

In the aft locker Emien found a rigging knife. He slipped it quietly from the sheath and tested the edge with his finger. The steel was well honed. With the blade poised in his hand, the boy crept forward. Tathagres lay sprawled on her back, white tunic stained from the bilge. Her face seemed girlish and innocent in the moonlight. Tumbled hair sparked like frost over wrists so slim that Emien could encircle them easily with the thumb and forefinger of one hand. The mail over her breast glittered faintly. Disappointed to find she still breathed. Emien stole closer, fixed with predatory intensity upon the thin gleam of gold at her neck.

He stepped into shadow under the sail. Suddenly his foot turned on the ship's glass, left against a stay. Brass clanged loudly into wood and Tathagres opened her eyes.

Emien froze. He buried the knife in his cloak with a whispered curse and bent with feigned concern.

Tathagres regarded him, chilly awareness in her violet eyes. She spoke with languid unconcern. "Oh yes, you're very clever." Her smile held stinging viciousness. "But I fear not clever enough. We are pursued."

Emien drew a frustrated breath. "I lost the brigantine in a squall line."

"No." Tathagres sat up, her expression haughty beneath tangled hair. "Not the Kielmark," she said. "Your own sister would stop you now. Taen follows in a boat built for speed. Are you going to sit here waiting for her?"

Emien jerked. Steel quivered in his poised fist.

Unsurprised by the knife, Tathagres laughed with wounding scorn. "Fool. We lost Cliffhaven because Taen gained a dream-weaver's mastery from the Vaere."

Emien's expression lay in shadow. But he listened; the hand which held the knife steadied until moonlight traced the blade silver against the darkness. Waves slapped *Callinde*'s sides, jostling her tackle aloft. Tathagres judged her moment and resumed.

"Your sister blinded the Thienz, tricked us all with illusion so the King would walk into a trap." The witch delivered her final line with calculated malice. "She intended you to die with them, Emien."

Breath hissed between his teeth. Coiled dangerously on the edge of action, the boy lifted his head and looked northward. Faint as a spark, a light gleamed on the horizon, too orange to be mistaken for starlight.

"The boat's name is *Troessa*," Tathagres added. "She was granted by the Kielmark as a reward for the ruin of Kisburn's men. Put up your knife. Else Taen will reach Elrinfaer before us and perhaps take your life."

The blade flashed and lowered. Emien drew an uneven breath. Wrung by unreasoning rage, he spun on his heel. Returned to the helm, he jabbed the rigging knife into *Callinde's* sternpost. Then he grabbed the steering oar with a wrench that slammed the fittings and turned the boat southeast. Sails cracked taut against the blocks. The starboard rail lifted as *Callinde* gathered way and headed toward Elrinfaer once more.

Highlighted like a cameo in the moonlight, Emien's profile was a mask of hatred as he steered to thwart the same sister he left Imrill Kand to save. Lost to his rage he paid little heed to the woman who watched from the shadows. Tathagres studied her squire, aware of his lethal edge. She smiled again, well satisfied. The boy would wait to murder until morning when he delivered her to the rock where Elrinfaer Tower rose from the sea.

Tathagres settled back and closed her eyes, hands curved protectively over the black cube of rock which preserved the wards of Elrinfaer. After dawn the purpose of her demon masters would be accomplished; yet strangely as she drifted into sleep her limbs twitched as if her dreams held a nightmare of horrors.

The night wore on. Even Kor's Accursed did not guess that Taen's talents sheltered another man from notice. Ivainson Jaric bent with dogged courage over *Troessa's* helm, his blond hair gritty with salt. Yet swiftly as the Kielmark's ketch could sail, Emien was the better seaman. Evenly matched, both boats plowed through the waves toward Elrinfaer.

The wind slackened to a mere whisper out of the north and by dawn fog smothered the coast, dense as oiled wool. Steering *Troessa* one-handed, Jaric reached across the cockpit and snuffed the lantern which had lit the compass dial through the night. Taen lay in the bow, collapsed in exhausted sleep, her hair spilled like a snarl of weed over her shoulders. Slim hands pillowed her cheek against the mild roll of the boat.

In the half light Jaric could almost forget how thin she was; mist obscured the marks of fatigue beneath her eyes, softening the angles where the bones pressed sharply against her skin. The defense of Cliffhaven had worn her, body and spirit. For three days straight she had spun interlocking veils of illusion over the island, concealing the Kielmark's intentions from the Thienz while men fashioned facsimiles of brigantines from derelict hulls and half-rotted fishing vessels. She had engaged her talents in the very presence of demons, brashly sending and receiving messages from the Kielmark to his captains. All that she achieved was out of loyalty to Anskiere. The thought made Jaric feel inadequate. At the dockside when

Troessa departed, the King of Renegades had sworn Taen an oath of debt, his surly features traced with tears.

Asleep, her dream-weaver's robes soiled with dirt and salt, she seemed a fragile child. Nothing about her appearance suggested a Vaere-trained enchantress; innocent features reflected no trace of the courage which enabled her to pursue a beloved brother as an enemy.

Sailing under a dank layer of fog, Jaric regarded the girl who had started out a lame fisherman's daughter from Imrill Kand. In her unremarkable beginning he found proof that strength could arise out of weakness. The realization lent hope that someday he might discover confidence and master his lot as Firelord's heir.

An hour passed, then two. Mist clung dense as eiderdown over the face of the sea. *Troessa* ghosted forward by compass heading alone, and over the creak of her gear Jaric heard the distant boom of breakers. Unless their course had been spoiled by current, the shores of Elrinfaer lay ahead.

Taen woke from sleep with a sudden cry of alarm. She threw herself at the bow. "No! Emien, no!"

Jaric leapt forward, caught her slight waist. His hands tangled in long dark hair as he dragged her back, shivering and weeping in his arms. "Taen, what's wrong?"

Sails ruffled overhead as *Troessa* swung pilotless into the wind. Jaric cradled the enchantress against his shoulder and ached for the power to shelter her. Surf crashed, nearer, and more distinct, over Elrinfaer's unseen shore. Taen looked up with anguished eyes. The dream link which woke her to nightmare ripped out of control and swept Jaric into rapport.

Possessed by ice-edged hatred, Jaric gripped *Callinde*'s thwart. She lay beached on the cream sand of a cove, her sails left carelessly sheeted. Yet the mishandling of the boat did not trouble him, since the emotions he experienced were another's; following the slender white-haired figure of his mistress, he leapt ashore in Emien's boots, fingers clenched round the haft of an unsheathed rigging knife.

Deadly, silent, he coiled his body and sprang. Steel gleamed in the fog. Consumed by poisoned triumph, he raised his arm and buried his blade to the crossguard in the woman's defenseless back.

Tathagres staggered and fell, pale hair scattered across unmarked sand. Her beautiful features twisted in agony as Emien tore her collar aside, reaching with bloodied fingers for the band of gold beneath. He caught the necklace, twisted fiercely. The metal proved hollow; it crumpled and split, spilling dark liquid over Emien's knuckles. Scalded by caustic reaction, his skin blistered and bled. Emien cried out. He jerked back, just as something *other* stabbed his mind like hot wire.

The contact broke. Wrenched back to *Troessa*'s gentle motion, Jaric stared in horror at the dream-weaver who lay against his shoulder.

Surf boomed loudly, dangerously close. Taen heard, pushing free of his hold. "Sail!" she said frantically. "Tathagres is dying, and Emien has the Keys."

Jaric stumbled over *Troessa*'s stern seat and threw his weight against the tiller. The ketch swung, maddeningly sluggish. Her canvas ruffled, flopped, and drew taut in the wind. Sudden thunder shook the air. Wind sprang up. A gust tore shrilly through the rigging and *Troessa* jerked sideways onto her thwart.

Taen clung gamely in the bow. With small desperate hands she clawed the jibsheet free. Canvas banged, frayed to tatters by the gusts. Spray dashed madly over the bow. Half-blinded by salt, Jaric fought for control of the helm. Ahead the mist streamed and parted. Hard alee lay a shoreline of terraced rock, and the windowless spire of Elrinfaer Tower raised like a spoke against the sky.

Troessa lifted, flung on the crest of a breaker. Jaric leaned forward, jerked her leaded swing-keel up into its casing. The wave broke with a rush, hurling the boat toward the shore. Jaric caught a hurried glimpse of *Callinde*, pressed flat on her side against a white crescent of beach; then Taen loosened the mainsheet also. The boom swung, blocking his vision. But Jaric needed no sight to confirm the small still form which sprawled beyond, under the edge of the rocks.

Troessa grounded with a scrape. Taen leapt the bowsprit and splashed calf-deep into the cold flood of the sea. Jaric followed. Foam swirled over his boot tops as he yanked a line from the bow. Emptied of weight, the light boat slewed sidewards as the following wave crashed around her rudder. Jaric leaned into the rope, grateful not to be wrestling the heftier bulk of *Callinde*. By the time he crossed shallows to the tide mark, Taen had gone on ahead.

Lightning laced the sky and thunder rumbled. Jaric thrust his hands into *Troessa*'s forward locker and pulled out dagger and sword. Wet leather sloshed against his feet, which became caked with dry sand as he ran up the beach. Ahead, lit by a savage flash of lightning, he saw the dreamweaver crouched over Tathagres' crumpled form.

"Stop Emien!" she shouted over the rising fury of the elements. "I'll stay with her."

Jaric hesitated. Dwarfed by forbidding rocks, he touched his sword hilt with uncertain hands, and wondered what Telemark had felt when he had killed as a mercenary in the Duke of Corlin's army. The thought raised every self-doubt which had poisoned his childhood at Morbrith.

"Go!" Taen's plea was a ragged peal of anguish. "Emien seeks to break the wards over the Tower."

Thunder slammed the air. Jaric shivered. With short sharp motions, he unsheathed sword and dagger. He discarded swordbelt and scabbards in the sand and sprang toward the rocks. Once in Seitforest he had surpassed his limits when Telemark's life lay threatened; now to spare Taen the horror of confronting her brother, he would face Emien with steel, and stop him if he could.

*   *   *

Taen watched through a blur of tears as Jaric vanished up the slope, torn by the insufferable fact that his success depended upon the loss of her only brother. But now was no time to indulge in useless emotions. Mastering herself with iron bravado, she mustered her powers as dream-weaver and centered her thoughts on the woman beneath her hands.

Tathagres lay on her side, hands outflung and still. Her bracelets had carved half moons in the sand under her wrists, and grit clung to her back and shoulders, darkened by spreading blood. Emien had withdrawn the knife and an ugly reddened tear showed through tunic and mail beneath. Taen brushed back a silky fall of hair, baring features whose pale delicacy remained beautiful, even approaching death. For all her Vaere training, Taen could do nothing to save her. But for the sake of her brother, she sent her dream call into the faltering mind beneath her hands.

"Merya?"

Tathagres' lids trembled and opened, baring violet eyes to the sky. Wax-pale lips trembled and almost smiled, for the name Taen used was that given by her mother. Blackness leached through her mind. With a sigh of painful weariness, Tathagres gave in to the ebbing tide; the memory lapsed.

Dream call wrenched her back. "Merya! What has Emien taken?" Desperate to know, Taen caught the fading image of a forest where once a father had forbidden a small girl to play. But the child disobeyed. Laughing, breathless, Merya skipped under the trees on the edge of summer twilight, enticed by the notes of a flute. But the musician ran merrily ahead, ducking through thickets and branches, perpetually out of reach. Suddenly darkness claimed her. Kor's Accursed fitted the collar to her neck, and thereafter she served as Tathagres, her human family forgotten.

Taen clamped her will around the threads of deteriorating life. She forced a desperate question. "The collar. Did it hold crystals from Sathid?"

Merya/Tathagres quivered. Thoughts flurried like sparks in shadow as she strove to answer the dream-weaver's call. *Emien, warn Emien.* The collar's legacy was misery; woe to the mortal who touched it, for his will would serve the powers of Kor's Accursed without hope to the end of life. *Warn Emien,* Merya sent, but her breath stopped before the message was complete.

Left no answer but the limitless night of the void, the dream-weaver shivered, wakened to grief and poignant revelation. Freed by death, the woman's peaceful pose suggested the humanity she might have had if her life had been her own. Taen saw that she and the child Merya were more alike than different. Each had been gifted since birth with sensitivity deeper than most human perception. Sheltered by Anskiere, Taen had been sent safely to the Vaere. But Merya, and now Emien, had not been as fortunate.

* * *

Lightning snaked across the rocks but no rain fell. Taen raced over sharpened outcrops of shale. Wind rattled the branches of scrub and thorn and thunder shook the ground under her feet. Certain the disturbance in the weather was caused by Emien's meddling with the wards, Taen climbed with desperate haste.

She paused, searched the barren heights, but saw no trace of Jaric or her brother. She engaged her talents to seek, but her dream search was overrun by churning fields of power. The wards over Elrinfaer were stronger than any sorcery in Keithland, Tamlin had said. The Mharg-demons confined there were dangerous enough to destroy all life. Now Emien tried to free them.

Taen plunged over a rise. Breath burned in her lungs. Forbidding against cloud-racked skies, Elrinfaer Tower dominated the ridge beyond a boulder-strewn ravine. Blue-violet light flared across the heights and light-ning lanced the ground, set off by discharged energy as the Keys set forces held stable for centuries into flux.

Taen ran, buffeted by a heated backlash of air. Over the rumble of thunder she heard a thin chime of steel. She swerved toward the sound, oblivious to the briars which ripped her shins. Sped by understanding of Merya's possession, she battered her way up the slope. If Emien had suc-cumbed to the powers which had claimed Tathagres, Jaric's fine scruples would prove no match for the black hatred of Kor's Accursed.

Taen dodged past a leaning boulder and crashed into brush on the far side. Steel flared through the branches, lit by a flash of lightning.

Thunder drowned the clang as a dagger glanced off a sword edge. Jaric staggered off balance and caught the riposte on his crossguard. Emien advanced. Faced in reality by the willful evil of the brother she had loved on Imrill Kand, Taen stopped, unable to react.

But Jaric recovered. Slighter, faster, he managed a feint and sprang clear. Gravel slithered under Emien's boots. He parried Jaric's dagger, then thrust. Steel screeched, stopped against the crossed fence of his oppo-nent's blades. Emien leaned, tried to break the bind with brute strength. Jaric threw him off. Through the savage exchange which followed, Taen saw the match was not even. Neither boy was experienced. But Emien had eight months training under Kisburn's royal swordmasters; Jaric had spent most of the winter tending traps in the snowbound wilds of Seitforest. Emien lunged. Jaric missed the parry, twisted, and crashed shoulder first into a thorny clump of brush.

Lightning flared at his back. Blinded, Emien slashed on angry impulse. Branches sheared beneath his sword. Jaric tripped and went down on one knee, close enough that Taen heard him gasp for breath. Emien smiled with inhuman triumph, sword angled for a killing thrust. Too late, Taen gathered her power to prevent him; emotion shattered her concentration. Her powers faltered, blocked.

Emien's sword leapt outward. Jaric jerked, desperate. Sticks clattered over steel as he wrenched his dagger up to guard. Metal belled on impact. Emien's blade snaked into air, deflected above Jaric's shoulder. Right arm extended, Jaric pulled but could not free his sword from the brush. Finding his opponent helpless, Emien crossed his dagger over his quillon and bore down with both hands.

Jaric resisted, tendons whitened in his left wrist. His muscles trembled with exhaustion, no match for his enemy's weight. The crossed tangle of steel lowered, creeping with inexorable finality toward his neck. Lightning fickered, illuminating the instant of Emien's victory. Knuckles blackened with burns pressed downward past Jaric's cheek. Taen saw the marks; with horror-ridden certainty she looked at her brother's face and there found savage, unreasoning cruelty. The demons had claimed him irrevocably.

Torn by grief, Taen cried out. The brother she had loved on Imrill Kand would have died rather than betray his own kind. Released by terrible mercy, she rallied her powers and struck.

Emien screamed and staggered back. Steel grated, sang, and separated. Jaric surged to his feet, his sword free at last. He sprang, prepared for resistance. But Emien crumpled to his knees. His weapons slipped from nerveless fingers and clattered, ringing, onto stone.

Jaric lifted his sword to his enemy's throat. Taen rushed in and grabbed the black stone which encased the Keys of Elrinfaer. With Anskiere's service accomplished, Jaric hesitated.

Taen sobbed in anguish. "For Keithland's sake, strike quickly."

But Jaric saw no threat in the frightened boy beneath his sword. Desolate in his despair, Emien wept uncontrollably. He appeared broken and pathetic in defeat. Jaric flinched in empathy. For a fraction of an instant, he wavered. Emien dove under his blade and fled. He crashed through the scrub and vanished into the darkness.

Taen gathered herself to follow.

But Jaric threw down his sword and caught her in his arms. "Leave him. What harm can he do?"

And drained beyond all endurance, Taen clung to the comfort of his embrace. Let the Vaere decide her brother's fate. She could no longer bear to pursue him.

Epilogue

Sand crumbled under the Kielmark's boots as he paced the edge of the tide mark on Cliffhaven's north shore. In late afternoon, while his captains celebrated at the fortress, he had gone walking alone on beaches at last free of enemies. His great bow hung at his shoulder. Lonely winds ruffled the hair across his brow as the Kielmark paused to breathe the ocean air, his indomitable pride tempered by sorrow. The victory had been bitterly won. Many fine men had died for no better purpose than the demons' desire to seed discord.

Slanting sunlight struck fiery reflections on the ice cliffs which reared above the sea. Defense against frostwargs and haven for a friend, Anskiere's sorceries still remained a magnet for trouble. Drawn by the inconsistency, the Kielmark squinted and saw a slender figure hooded in gray which crouched at the crest of the ice. A Llondel demon perched on the Stormwarden's stronghold, orange eyes lifted in challenge.

The Kielmark swore and unslung his bow. With no regard for danger, he nocked a broadhead and drew.

The Llondel hissed warning.

But reflexively intolerant of trespassers, the Kielmark aimed and released.

The arrow arched up, a splinter of gold in the sunlight. Following its flight, the Kielmark felt his thoughts explode into images; but the retaliation sent by the Llondel faltered, twisted awry by irrepressible joy. The vision of dismembered ships and a harbor overrun by strangers became muddled out of focus, overwhelmed by other, stronger tidings intended for the Stormwarden of Elrinfaer.

Doubled in discomfort on the sand, the Kielmark saw a wide vista of ocean. There *Callinde* sailed, the lighter, leaner *Troessa* in tow. Seated at the helm with Taen against his shoulder, Jaric steered for Cliffhaven, the Keys of Elrinfaer safely reclaimed.

When at length the Llondel released him, the Kielmark straightened. The demon had gone. But the wind sang a less minor pitch as it swept the rungs of the ice, and the sea broke sparkling like jewels over the rocks beneath.

Keeper of the Keys

Book Two of the
Cycle of Fire

For Virginia Kidd
in admiration, respect, and warmest friendship

ACKNOWLEDGMENTS

Special thanks to:
My youngest sister, for proofing, and two extraordinary friends, an author from the West Coast and a sailor from the East, for support and suggestions respectively. Lastly, to the friend no longer living, who reviewed the preliminary draft.

Prologue

Chilly wind slapped the swells into the whitecaps off the west shores of Elrinfaer, where, a lone fleck of color under frowning cliffs, a fishing sloop spread tanbark sails beneath the leaden gray of the overcast. She was an aged craft, patched and stained with the wear of her labors, but now her nets hung slack. Her occupants, two brothers, leaned idle on the landward rail. Grizzled and gray and dour, they squinted shoreward at a dark bundle of cloth sprawled on the sand above the tide mark.

The younger one spat into the sea. "It's a boy, that. Flotsam don't wear boots, not that I ever saw."

"You say?" The sibling grunted in disgust. "Only last week, you missed the buoy marking the headland. Near to run us aground for that, and now you claim you got eyesight!" Still, intrigued, he did not order the boat put about. "If that draggle o' cloth is human, I'll give a week's coppers, and buy you a beer a night."

"Ye'll lose, then." The younger brother laughed, and sprang to haul in the sheets. Dearly loving a wager, he braced himself against the shuddering heave of the boat as wind-tossed canvas thundered taut. "If he's drowned, I get his rings."

The elder brother caught the worn tiller. "We'll see." And he turned the sloop, which reeked of cod, and sent her dashing in a heel for the beach head.

Lashed ashore by a rampaging flood of surf, the craft's sturdy timbers grated and grounded against sand. The elder brother leaped the thwart, his callused, twine-scarred hands braced to steady the prow. The younger brother vaulted after and, kicking sand from his wet boots, stumped up the beach to determine the winner of the bet.

He bent over the dark lump by the tide line, sending gulls flapping seaward. Tentatively he touched, then drew back.

Impatient, the brother by the boat bellowed after him. "Well? Who's doing the buying this week?"

The answer came back, subdued against the boom and echo of breakers under the cliffs. "It is a boy." The younger fisherman paused, and slowly stood straight on the shore. "A sick one."

The elder brother cursed, the exhilaration of the wager abruptly gone sour. Now out of decency they must take on a passenger; sick, even dying, the wretch would need food and water, and the sloop's hold was not yet full enough to pay even the cost of reprovisioning. "Better bring him in," he shouted. "And the beer copper goes for his bread."

The younger of the two fishermen shrugged philosophically, then lifted the limp body from the sand. His find proved to be slight, black-haired, and dressed in the remains of fine clothing. The eyes opened in delirium were blue, and the hands ravaged by what looked like burns.

"He probably eats like a flea," the younger brother muttered as he arrived, breathless, and deposited his burden in the sloop's bow. "Weighs little enough."

But the elder brother remained unsympathetic. He jerked his head, anxious now to be away from shores that were deserted, ruins of the once fortunate kingdom of Elrinfaer.

"And anyway, you have the sporting instincts of a grandmother," groused the younger. He set his shoulder to the sloop and shoved her ungainly prow seaward. As she slipped, grating, into deeper waters, the boy in the bow groaned in the throes of fever.

"Would you have left him, then?" accused the younger, bothered at last by his brother's silence. When he received no answer, he shrugged; the castaway wore court clothes, badly torn, but the dirt on the tunic was fresh. Perhaps he would have wealthy relatives who would reward his rescuers for his safe return.

CHAPTER I

Betrayal

By evening, they gathered in the great hall on Cliffhaven, a rough-mannered crowd of sea captains, sailhands, and men at arms. All were exiles, lawfully condemned as thieves or murders by the Free Isles' Alliance or the outlying kingdoms; except one, a slight, black-haired girl, almost lost in the brocade chair where she sat with her feet tucked up. Her arms were sunburned and briar-scratched, her nose peeling; but the robes she wore had the pearly sheen of a dreamweaver trained by the Vaere. For that reason, the bearded captain who wended through the press of beer-drinking companions approached with guarded respect.

Jostled by celebrants, sailors with silver-hooped earlobes, and officers still wearing mail, he gained the relative peace of the corner. There the captain set his tankard aside. He had been assigned the task of ensuring the enchantress's comfort, and at present the girl wore a troubled frown. He had to yell over the noise; immediately he regretted that his shout sounded gruffer than he wished. "Taen Dreamweaver?"

At her name she looked around, pale eyes enormous under the shadow of her brows. Her age was eighteen, but seemed less. "Jaric isn't here."

"No? Are you certain?" Surprised the boy should be gone, the captain stroked the knife at his belt out of habit. He echoed the girl's concern as he scanned the crowd in search of the sole surviving heir of the sorcerer Ivain Firelord.

The victory celebration had been organized hard on the heels of war. The timbers of the main door still slanted, singed and blackened and half-torn from their hinges by a barrage of enemy sorcery. The crannies between revelers were stacked with broken furnishings, upholstery bristling with arrows. Men could not yet be spared from the labor of repairing defense works to clear the hall of wreckage, and the Kielmark, who ruled this den of renegades, was never a man to pause for niceties. Abetted by Taen Dreamweaver's talents, his garrison had just repulsed attack by an armada that included demons. By his orders, the survivors would have their chance to release their aftermath of tension, and to mourn the loss of dead comrades; but only tonight. Tomorrow captains, crews, and men at arms must be fit once more for duty.

The atmosphere was predictably boisterous, with arguments and slangs and bouts of arm-wrestling compounding into a crescendo of noise. Meticulously patient, the captain sorted through the motley press of renegades, all armed, some bandaged, and most laughing and expansive with drink. Yet from one end of the hall to the other, where the bodies of senseless sailors snored off their excesses in a heap, his efforts yielded no glimpse of the tousled blond head of Jaric.

Nearby, someone banged the pommel of his knife on a tabletop, denouncing the careless pitch of a cluster of singers. The captain winced, unsure whether dreamweavers cared for obscenities. He glanced back to the girl and found her worried gaze still upon him. "You searched?" he asked, referring to her Vaere-trained powers, which could trace the mind and memories of any man she chose with little more effort than thought.

"No." As if the question were painful to her, Taen knotted nervous fingers in her lap. "I don't have to. Jaric has gone to the ice cliffs."

The captain sucked in his breath. "Kielmark'll be stark tied. Better tell him now." Purposefully he recovered his tankard, his intent to steer toward the end of the room where the revelers pressed thickest, and the great booming laughter of the Sovereign Lord of Cliffhaven wafted over the lesser din of the crowd.

"Corley, no," said Taen, unexpectedly calling the captain by name. But if her powers of cognition were uncanny, the hand she laid on his arm to restrain was human, and sorrowfully thin. "I'll find Jaric, trust me. Don't risk what we both know will happen if the Kielmark discovers him gone."

"Kordane's Fires!" swore the captain. But she spoke sense, this enchantress with the eyes of a child. The Lord of Cliffhaven maintained sovereignty over the criminals who served him through wily cunning and a distrust that brooked no exceptions. Though only a boy, as Firelord's heir Jaric aroused the Kielmark's suspicion in dangerous measure, for even the finest fleets and fortifications in Keithland were useless against the potential of a sorcerer's power. Corley looked at the Dreamweaver, assessing, and saw by the set of her jaw that she would stop him reporting if he insisted; Vaerish sorceries made her capable. Defeated, he tipped his head heavenward, his words almost too soft to be heard above the noise. "Girl, on my life and manhood, I didn't hear you say that."

He glanced back to find the enchantress already going, her silver-gray robe an oddity amid leather leggings, studded baldrics, and the plainer linens of the sailhands. Corley watched, unsettled, as she crossed the crowded hall. The most hardbitten fighters in Keithland parted readily to let her by, some drunk and argumentative, but all saluting her passage with a sincerity rarely seen on their scarred and sea-tanned faces. The Kielmark had made no secret of the facts: without the Dreamweaver's help, Cliffhaven would have fallen to King Kisburn's army, and his demons sworn as allies would have spared no lives in their quest of vengeance against humanity.

Taen slipped between the bronzed bulk of a quartermaster and a sailor with missing teeth. Both raised their tankards in her honor, and as she vanished into the hallway, Corley silently longed to be elsewhere. The situation was a right mess; the Dreamweaver had defied her Vaerish masters to stay and defend Cliffhaven. No mortal understood the extent of her peril by doing so, but the Kielmark had sworn to remedy the lapse with all speed and set her on a southbound ship no later than dawn next day. Added to that, Jaric's hasty departure was the height of bad timing. Angry now that the boy could not at least have asked for escort, Corley's fist tightened upon his tankard. To leave the King of Pirates ignorant when two under his protection presently traipsed through the wilds of his domain in the dead of night bordered upon an act of insanity. Corley had served on Cliffhaven long enough to learn what his life was worth; he took a hefty swallow of beer, and decided precipitously not to honor the Dreamweaver's request.

But even as he strode forward to inform his master of the girl's departure, her dream-touch cut his mind. *'Don't!'*

Corley froze between steps and cursed. She watched, then, with the unknowable talents of her kind; her sending carried awareness that she would stop him by force if she must. Having no wish to test himself against sorcery, the captain sat carefully in the brocade chair left empty by her departure. He laughed, very quietly and not without humor. Then, much against his careful nature, he lifted his tankard and quaffed the contents to the dregs. If the Dreamweaver chose to follow the son of Ivain Firelord to the ice cliffs that imprisoned the Stormwarden of Elrinfaer, at least one captain in Cliffhaven's great hall decided he wanted no part of the matter. With luck and a little time, he could arrange to be drunk to the edge of prostration when the Sovereign Lord of Cliffhaven discovered both enchantress and sorcerer's heir gone from his party without leave.

Outside, a damp salt wind scoured the bailey. Clouds hazed the moon's setting crescent, and gusts off the harbor blew sharp with the scent of impending rain. Taen paused in the archway, blinking while her eyes adjusted from the candle-brilliance of indoors to the dimmer flicker of torchlight. Canny enough to be silent, she stifled the flapping hem of her robe with her hands, and looked carefully for the sentry; revelry on Cliffhaven could never be expected to slacken the diligence of the Kielmark's patrols. Yet no man waited, spear in hand, to challenge the girl in the bailey. Empty cobbles shone wet in the dew, and the ring which normally tethered the saddled horse lay flat, a steely disc of reflection.

At that, Taen caught her breath. She bent her Dreamweaver's awareness to the stables, and immediately encountered activity. Already guessing the reason, she narrowed focus, and found the sentry questioning the horse-boy. Between them they would not take long to sort out the fact that someone not under orders had removed the horse kept saddled and bridled in the bailey for the Kielmark's emergency use at any hour of the day or night.

Jaric, thought Taen; she muttered an epithet learned from the fishwives of Imrill Kand that would have reddened even the sophisticated ears of Corley, then stepped swiftly out into the wind. She must hurry before the sentry carried word to the Kielmark. Pounding, breathless, through the passage to the horse yard, Taen engaged the talents only recently mastered under the Vaere. The minds she sought to influence were less informed, and therefore harder to convince than that of Captain Corley. The bailey sentry was an old hand, well familiar with the Kielmark's temper; and the horse-boy was native to Cliffhaven. All through childhood he had seen men hung out of hand for disobeying orders. Beside that sure punishment, to him a dreamweaver's sorcery seemed the lesser risk.

Taen crossed abruptly from shadow into torchlight, making both sentry and horse-boy start. Neither truly saw her for what she was, a small, disheveled girl with trouble marking frown lines on her face. Their eyes took in the silver gray of her robes, and stopped, wary.

"Enchantress," murmured the horse-boy. "Kor's grace, don't bewitch us."

Taen paused, swallowed, and wondered if anyone would ever treat her normally again. "Ivainson Jaric is the key to Keithland's survival." She shifted her regard to the sentry, standing sweating in the light of the stable lanterns with his hands locked around his spear. "The Kielmark and the Firelord's heir must not meet at this time. The boy is distressed, enough to make him careless. He would cross your master, and certainly get himself killed. But if you loan me a mount, I can stop that, and ensure you won't suffer any consequences."

Neither the sentry nor the horse-boy was moved by the promise. The Kielmark's discipline was legend on land and sea, and no man who gainsaid him survived. A tense moment passed, the gusty dark laced through with the distant beat of the sea. Taen gripped her whipping robes, and strove to maintain patience. She would not use compulsion on these two, not unless she was desperate. But when the sentry whirled with a look of stark fear and bolted, she was unequivocally cornered. Her powers answered, reliably, and blanketed the running man's awareness. Between one stride and the next, he pitched forward, to land in a sprawl across the midden.

The horse-boy gasped.

"He's unharmed!" Taen said, and though her skills were still raw and new, she managed to translate awareness of just how unharmed directly into the boy's shocked mind. "Saddle me a mount," she added gently. "And please do believe me when I tell you I can manage the Kielmark's rages."

The horse-boy regarded her skeptically, as if he noticed for the first time that she was not so very much older than he; yet her powers had deceived demons. With a shrug and a shake of his head he turned to do her bidding. Only his attitude of nonchalance was spoiled by the fact that his knees shook.

Taen leaned back against the timbered half door of a stall. Relieved she had not needed to engage her dream-sense a third time, and taxed more than she cared to admit from swaying the sensibilities of Corley, she tried to stop worrying. Around her rose the black granite walls of the stoutest bulwarks in Keithland; surely for a short time more she would be safe. Tomorrow would see her on a ship bound for the Isle of the Vaere, only five days past the date imposed by the fey master who had trained her. Even if demons knew of her existence, they could hardly act so swiftly.

In the dark at her back, a horse snorted. Taen started forward, and barely managed not to cry out as a warm muzzle bumped amiably against her arm. She backed away, just as the horse-boy reappeared with not one but two mounts on a leading rein. The smaller he handed wordlessly to Taen; the other rolled eyes showing nasty rings of white. War-trained, it sidled as the boy tugged its headstall and expertly directed it through the passage, to the tether ringing the bailey. Taen sensed his preoccupied thought. Granting an enchantress a mount was perhaps excusable, but if the Kielmark chanced to ask for the saddled horse and found no animal ready, his great sword would answer the offense before he spent breath with questions.

Taen faced the blaze-faced mare she was to ride, and preoccupation with the horse-boy's problems faded before immediate troubles of her own. She was brought up among fisherfolk—the largest animals raised on her home isle were goats. Riding even the gentlest mounts invariably gave her the shakes.

She was still staring at the stirrup when the horse-boy returned. "Here," he offered gruffly. Before she could protest, he caught her around the waist and tossed her slight body into the saddle. "Go before the sentry wakens." And he punctuated the advice with a clap on the mare's hindquarters. The animal leaped into a trot, stirrups jarring painfully against Taen's ankles. Skewed sideways, she grabbed mane with both hands, and barely caught the boy's parting shout.

"If you're still here when that sentry recovers, he'll be honor-bound to put a spear through your back."

Jolted, gasping, through the gates into wind-tossed dark, Taen made a sound halfway between a sob and a laugh. Once she centered herself precariously within the saddle, spears became the least of her concerns; the Kielmark's rages and the ferocious loyalty of his men at least were predictably certain. The reactions of Invainson Jaric were not. Wistfully Taen wished the advice of her mentor on the Isle of the Vaere; for Jaric rode now to return the Keys to Elrinfaer to the Stormwarden, Anskiere, believing that once his errand was accomplished, his bond to the sorcerer would be ended. What he did not know, and what Taen had no gentle way of telling him, was that Anskiere now was sealed beyond reach within his wards beneath the ice cliffs. Without the presence of a firelord's skills, the Keys could not be returned to their rightful master. They could only be guarded, and perilously at that, for the demons would again seek control of the Keys they had narrowly been thwarted from gaining. Worse, if Kor's Accursed ever guessed the fact that Ivain Firelord had left a living heir, Jaric would become the prey in a ruthless hunt for survival, since his latent potential for sorcery might come to threaten their plots against humanity.

Taen gripped the reins. In an agony of fear and courage, she kicked her mount into a canter, and sent it clattering through the gates. Torchlight and the inner fortress fell behind. The mare slid, scrambling, down the broad stone stair which cut through a slope of thorn and olive trees. Below lay the town, a sprinkling of lights between the dark bulk of the warehouses. The harbor beyond was a scattered patchwork of silver and black shadows, the moored brigantines of the Kielmark's corsairs. Yet Taen did not head downward to the townside gate. Instead she tugged the mare to the right, through the northern portal that led to the ridge road.

The sentries let her pass with alacrity, since Jaric had passed that way earlier. The mare's gaits proved gentle on level ground, and since she showed no untrustworthy tendency to drag on the bit and run, Taen gradually relaxed. Her feet found the stirrups, and the rhythmic ring of hooves eased her mind enough to free her dream-sense. A nagging jab slapped her intuition in the night-dark lane before the outer gate.

She hauled the mare clumsily to a halt, at last giving way to irritation; a check on affairs back at the great hall revealed the Kielmark in a seething temper, bellowing orders to men at arms who scattered running to seek weapons, helms, and horses. Never doubting that Jaric and she were the cause, Taen narrowed her focus and sought the single white-hot thread of consciousness that mattered.

Thought answered her probe, sharp as a whipcrack. *'Enchantress! Meddler! What have you done this time? Where is Jaric?'* Dangerously unstable at the best of times, the Kielmark's mind now blazed with raw fury. Taen encompassed the essence, though it burned cruelly. Sweating with the effort of her talents, she bent impatience into calm, deflected violence into confusion, and madness into a hole wide enough to send coherent communication.

'Call off your men at arms. I will look after Jaric.' She sorted the spikes and angles of the Lord of Cliffhaven's thoughts, and observed that he already guessed the boy had gone to seek Anskiere. The ravening desire to deploy an armed patrol still overruled any attempt to instill temperance. Sad, now, Taen countered with the one fact that might restrain him. *'Let the boy be. He won't find what he most wishes to obtain.'*

Surprise answered, followed by calculation, followed by some keenly intuitive guesswork. *'The Stormwarden is helpless, then?'*

Taen sighed in the windy darkness. Mad, but wily as an old wolf, the Kielmark made few mistakes when it came to assessing Keithland's weaknesses. As his thoughts shifted rapidly futureward, to planning and intricate countermeasures, the Dreamweaver released the contact. She urged the mare on into the scrub pines on the heights, certain now that the men who ran to fetch swords would be called back to their beer. The

Kielmark would allow her to seek Ivainson Jaric without interference, and since the ways of enchantresses could be expected to foul even the most carefully laid network of patrols, probably the sentry would get by with a tongue-lashing.

Yet barely a mile farther on, with the trees tossing around her and the first raindrops spattering in the dust, Taen heard a drum roll of hoofbeats bearing down from behind. Not a patrol; the men who kept watch on the island's outposts never reported alone, and a relief watch would number five. Annoyed now, and chilled by the wet, the enchantress reined up and waited as the rider overtook her. Expertly slowed from a gallop, his horse clattered to a stop. Sparks shot from the concussion of steel shoes on stone, and Taen's mare sidled.

She controlled it, mostly by accident. Her reins tangled uselessly with her fingers, and her legs swung, clumsily inept. Still, she managed to keep her seat, even when the man she recognized as the sentry from the bailey jostled his mount against hers and tossed the heavy folds of a cloak into her hands.

"Kielmark's compliments," he shouted breathlessly. Then he grinned. "Said his patrols could see you weren't ambushed, but damned if he'd have you perish of cold."

Taen grinned back, recognizing Corley's deft manipulation behind the gesture. Then, as she flung the wool over her shoulders, her hand caught on the huge ruby which adorned the brooch at the collar. The most feared and powerful man in Keithland had sent her his personal cloak, and not as an afterthought. In sparing his fortress from Kor's Accursed, Taen Dreamweaver had earned something more complex than the Kielmark's gratitude. She strove to wring comfort from that fact. Ahead of her, the troubled heir of Ivain Firelord had a decision to make that would affect the continuance of humanity; and behind, painfully abandoned at Elrinfaer, was the brother she had lost to the demons.

For Marlson Emien, hope no longer existed. Collected from the sands of Elrinfaer by the unsuspecting charity of two fishermen, he lay limp beneath a shelter jury-rigged from tarpaulins as the first fall of rain pattered over the sloop. The brothers who took him in had treated his palms, unaware that his burns were a caustic reaction to bare-flesh contact with a solution of demon-controlled Sathid crystal. Neither did they guess that his fever was no illness but the effects of transition as the entities he harbored melded and established mastery over his mind. Irrevocably possessed by Kor's Accursed, Emien did not hear the foaming rush of the sea, nor the thump and rattle of planking as the sloop tossed, spume-drenched, on her heading. Cold did not touch him, even when run-off from the tarps leaked down his shoulders and back. His opened eyes stayed blind as marbles, his limbs still. Only his mind knew agony. As the Sathid coursed through his body, his awareness twisted in a pocket of nightmare, utterly powerless to win free.

The sister who sorrowed at Cliffhaven would never have recognized him now. Demon thought-forms overran his humanity and alien desires ravaged his spirit. Emien had known hatred; but never in life had he experienced the depth and intensity of spite which racked him as his new overlords raged over the loss of the Keys to Elrinfaer. A decade of intricate plotting had failed them, and once more their hope of exterminating humanity had been thwarted. Only one part of the grand design remained to be salvaged: a new pawn had been gained to replace Merya Tathagres. As the Sathid entity assimilated Emien's personality, the demons explored their find.

Voices rustled in the boy's mind, dry and numerous as dead leaves whirled by wind. The words were in no human tongue, and the speakers far distant, conferring in a place beyond the north borders of Keithland. Yet through the bridge of the Sathid-link they were a part of Emien, and Emien a part of them. Comprehension required no translation.

'Who, tell me, who is he?'

Another voice answered, gruffer, and curt with authority. 'Man-child, forsaken-one. Called Marlson Emien, but ours now, destined to become the bane-of-his-kind.'

'Knowledge, fast-tell-me, what memories does he possess?'

Demon thought-probes jabbed into Emien's mind. He moaned faintly under the tarp, powerless to hinder as demons rummaged ruthlessly through his being. Most of his past experience they discarded as meaningless, but not at all; where his new masters had interest, they poked and pricked and prodded, pitilessly sorting out what information they wished. They examined his childhood, the poverty and the shortcomings and the discontent he had known as a fisherman's son on Imrill Kand. No nuance escaped scrutiny. Demons knew the rough wooden loft where he had shivered in the misery of his nightmares, and the quiet, careworn widow who had raised him. They knew the peat smoke and tide wrack, and the sour smells of nets drying through twilights smothered in fog; and not least they knew Taen, the sister who had collected shells on the beaches, and run dancing through wildflowers with the goats on the tor until the day the accident had left her lamed. When at the last she had found her cure, her family lost her; for the Stormwarden, Anskiere, had stolen her loyalty and sent her for training to the Isle of the Vaere.

Here the demon probe paused, sharpened to cutting interest. Emien flinched. Unnoticed by his fisherman benefactors, he quivered and sweated in the sloop's damp bow, while the enemies of humankind pursued details of the sister's existence more thoroughly. The voices reached a fever pitch of excitement in the dark.

'Behold, this-proof, another Vaere-trained enchantress walks Keithland, to our sorrow.'

The probe twisted, gouged deeper, and exposed Taen's presence in the battle that had prevented Cliffhaven's conquest. 'Vaere-trained, yes, most cer-

tainly Dreamweaver gifted.' Now the grip in Emien's mind tightened and focused with cruel clarity upon the sister as he had seen her last, standing windblown upon the heights by Elrinfaer Tower. She clung, trembling, in the embrace of Ivainson Jaric, the Keys to Elrinfaer gripped in her whitened fingers. Her shift was torn, and her skin spangled with salt from an ocean crossing. The pallor of her face accentuated her exhaustion, and her black hair tumbled in tangles over shoulders grown gaunt with stress. Yet where human vision ended, the enhanced perception of demons gleaned more: a halo of greenish light shimmered around Taen's form, tangible effects of the Sathid-enhanced powers she had challenged and mastered. The voices whispered over this, and refined their scrutiny until patterns became visible in the aura, and abruptly their concern dissolved. The demons' murmured commentary transformed to ridicule that sang and echoed through Emien's being.

'She is undone, this Dreamweaver trained by the Vaere. Too soon sent to defend: see! The aura is distressed. Her crystals are yet immature, and imminently dangerous.' An interval followed, dense with murmurs of agreement. *'The compact need not fear Marlsdaughter Taen, Emien-sister. Doom stalks her, even-as-we-speak. The Sathid she mastered to gain her powers shall soon seek replication, and the changes effected upon her body will assuredly kill her.'*

Chilled, and now utterly still upon the rain-sleek planking of the sloop, the conscious spark that remained of Marlson Emien pleaded inwardly for explanation. The voices quieted, considered, and with a bitter flash of malice granted his request.

Their answer came shaped in dream-image. Emien observed a sorcerer who had served as Grand Conjurer to the Kings of Felwaithe seven generations in the past. Yet demon recall spanned centuries; the memory was replicated with a clarity faithfully sharp. During a time of war, a devastating assault by demons had brought this man to attempt an unsupervised bonding with a Sathid crystal. The sorcerer had survived to win mastery, only to perish afterward, as the entity he harbored cycled to reproduce itself. Granted vision by demons, Emien saw the man writhe in torment, his sickbed the flinty, lichen-crusted stone that comprised the fells beyond Keithland. He quivered and sweated, all control of his sorcerer's powers overturned by the nightmare throes of delirium. Even as Emien watched, the man's flesh became suffused and discolored, muscles tortured into knots of tension and agony. Then, in the hours before daylight faded, his shivering ceased. The congested purple of his bruises opened into ugly weeping sores. Sickened, gasping in the throes of his own horror, Emien saw shards of crystal erupt through the dying sorcerer's flesh. The man screamed. His piteous cries were swallowed without echo by the empty fells, as bit by bit his vitals were lacerated from within by knives of glittering mineral.

In the end, only crystal remained, a jagged-edged remainder of what once had been human. Agony seemed inscribed in the very form, here the suggestion of clenched hands, and there the contorted arch of the back. *Taen would die so.* She carried within her the seeds of a crystalline entity that should have been safely separated from her flesh before it acquired full maturity. Yet the Vaere had dismissed her prematurely, or so Emien believed, that she could counteract the plot of the demons who threatened Cliffhaven. Ultimately, the Stormwarden who lured her away had betrayed her. For that, the voices in the shadows agreed that Anskiere of Elrinfaer should be made to suffer payment.

The assurance had a calming effect. Emien no longer tossed in discomfort as his overlords resumed their analysis of his mind. Instead he subsided into feverish sleep, the whispers and the voices a litany against a background of dreams while the probe of Kor's Accursed turned from remembrance of Taen Dreamweaver to focus next on the boy who comforted her.

He was blond, salt-stained as she, and as confused. His shirt and tunic had torn on the briar; the limbs beneath were well muscled and tanned from long days at a sailboat's helm. Yet for all his wiry strength, this boy carried himself diffidently. He had thrown down the sword he had used to win the Keys to Elrinfaer, but his hands shook through the moment of his victory, and his sun-bleached hair blew back to reveal tear-streaked cheeks.

'Who?' demanded the voices. The touch of demons prodded and tore at Emien's memory until the slight, untrained heir of Ivain Firelord was identified.

Silence resulted then, stillness that hinted of rage and resentment. Vaere-trained sorcerers were ever a threat to demons, but, among them, Anskiere and Ivain Firelord had caused the fiercest damage. The former was prisoner, trapped by his own wards in the ice cliffs. But the revelation that Ivain had left an heir with talent and potential to match his skills caused consternation and anger and a raw desire to destroy.

'The boy must be hunted down,' fretted the first voice.

'Killed,' chimed in a second.

'Destroyed, most-utterly,' wailed a third, and the howl of multiple companions made Emien's mind ring with hate. He lay twitching in reaction, even as his demon overlords instructed the Sathid which directed his fate. '*Call in the captured pawn. Compel him, the moment the sickness of bonding relents enough to permit him to act. Let the man-child steal the boat from his fisherman benefactors and sail north to Shadowfane. Scait Demon-Lord must sample his mind and memories. Then shall the hatred of Marlson Emien be granted training and weapons; and Ivainson Jaric, Firelord's heir, shall be hunted down and slain.*'

CHAPTER II

Keeper of the Keys

Jagged, icy rocks tore Jaric's hands as he climbed. In darkness the escarpments beneath the ice cliffs were steeper and more perilous than he recalled, despite the storm which had harried him the first time he made the ascent. A wave thundered over the reef below. Spray sheeted his back and subsided with a hiss into the sea. The soaked wool of his tunic clung to muscles which quivered with fatigue, yet he groped for a fresh hold and clawed upward. One shin banged painfully into granite before his boot found purchase; pebbles skittered under his sole, the rattle of their fall swallowed by seething surf below.

The Firelord's heir winced and clung gasping to an outcrop. Neither danger nor discomfort could deter him. Until the stormfalcon's feather and the Keys to Elrinfaer were returned to the Stormwarden who was their rightful guardian, no portion of Ivainson Jaric's life could be called his own.

The boy shook sun-bleached hair from his eyes and reached for another hold. Scant yards above, he saw a rim etched faintly against the night sky: a ledge cut across the rock face. He jammed his foot in a cleft, thrust higher, and fumbled with scraped hands until he found a fingerhold overhead. A breath of cold washed over him. Jaric shivered in the darkness and transferred his weight. Inured to the pain of stressed tendons, he wrenched his body upward and hooked his forearm over the ledge. Above loomed the ice cliffs where abided the Stormwarden, Anskiere.

Although elsewhere spring thrust wildflowers through the thornbrakes of Cliffhaven, here ice glistened silver by starlight, towering cascades arrested in mid-fall by the relentless grip of winter. The view could dizzy the senses with its splendor, leave a man stupid and staring with awe until the cold stiffened his limbs. Jaric clenched his jaw and kept his eyes on the rock face. Although the cliffs had frozen barely a year past, sailors' tales already made a myth of them, fancifully describing galleries filled with riches, and jeweled chambers where Anskiere worked his spells in solitude. In fact, the glassy ramparts shaped a prison more secure than any dungeon fashioned by man. Here the granite was smooth, as if the escarpment itself was hostile to human presence. Jaric found neither crevice nor outcrop sufficient to bear his weight.

Aching with fatigue, he hitched his body closer to the stone. Defeat never entered his mind. Too many times the debt inherited from his father had ripped his life into loss and hardship; with the promised release from that bond waiting only yards above his head, Jaric ran his hands over rock and hooked a sloping edge. The hold was inadequate for the move he intended. Yet a fall onto the reefs below was less risk than guarding the Keys through the night. Demonkind had plotted and killed to acquire the powers Elrinfaer Tower safeguarded. Only a fool would believe they would not try again. Jaric set his weight on the toe left wedged in the crevice, tensed his fingers, and thrust.

He caught the ledge under both elbows as his feet kicked out into air. His body struck the lip of the outcrop, jouncing the breath from his lungs. For a moment Jaric teetered, muscles straining. Then his left hand began to slip. Gravel turned under his palm. Desperate, he hiked his shoulders and lost a torturous inch. A breaker hissed hungrily across the reefs; Jaric shut his eyes and tasted sweat. He twisted sideways and raised his knee, sensed rather than felt a bulge in the stone beneath his body. Trusting friction and luck, he hitched himself up and grabbed left-handed. His wrist slapped the ledge. Two fingers hooked in a fissure and thwarted gravity for one precarious minute.

Jaric caught his breath with a painful gasp. He knotted tortured muscles and dragged himself higher. Chest, waist, hips, he gained the ledge by slow inches. At last he heaved his torso over the edge of the rock. There he collapsed, exhausted, and for an interval hung with both feet dangling above the sea. Had the cold been less cruel he might have rested until his lungs stopped aching. But air currents off the ice cliffs bit through his sodden clothes and quickly set him shivering. Jaric rolled, brought his knee up, and flopped onto his side, panting like a beached fish.

Securely on the ledge at last, the boy fumbled with chilled hands for the leather bag strung on a thong around his neck. The hard corners of basalt inside dug into his palms, assurance the Keys to Elrinfaer Tower's great wards and Anskiere's stormfalcon feather remained with him still. Comforted by the belief that his responsibility to the Stormwarden would shortly be discharged, Jaric looked up, and only that moment discovered he was not alone.

Not a yard from his position, two points of orange glared like coals from the darkness; starlight traced a hooded figure with folded, six-fingered hands. Jaric hissed through his teeth. His shoulder banged painfully into rock as he sat up. Even as he grabbed for his dagger he knew that defense was futile. The creature confronting him was Llondian, demon and enemy of mankind.

'No.' The Llondel spoke no word, but its thought-image struck Jaric's awareness like a hammerblow. 'I am here for Anskiere.'

Cornered against empty sky, Jaric felt a mental tug, and images followed, of sea winds and salt wrack which threaded the demon's pattern for the Stormwarden's name. Speech was alien to Llondian kind; they communicated with thought impressed directly onto the mind, and when they chose, no mortal could inhibit their sending. Neither could man attack Llondel with impunity. Yet Jaric saw no choice. His freedom, and the survival of all Keithland, would be threatened should the Keys to Elrinfaer fall into demon hands.

That Anskiere might have Llondian allies was surely impossible; unwilling to challenge the demon's falsehood, Jaric phrased his reply like a peacemaker caught in a hostile court. "Then for the sake of the Storm-warden, let me pass."

The Llondel did not move. It regarded the human boy with no flicker of emotion, pupils slitted against irises of burning gold. *'Keeper of the Keys, you may not pass; nor will your bond to Anskiere be completed until you accept the heritage of the Firelord who fathered you.'*

Jaric flinched, haunted with dread, for the Cycle of Fire brought madness along with mastery of a sorcerer's powers. Not even demons could make him forsake his humanity and request such training from the Vaere.

"No," said Jaric. Guile would not avail him. Already the demon knew he possessed the Keys; certainly it would strike to kill. "I must pass. There is no other choice for me." Sweating with fear, the boy raised his blade.

The Llondel hissed warning. Its eyes darkened to sultry red, and seamed, six-fingered hands clicked against rock as it stiffened.

'No harm to you, Firelord's son,' the demon sent; but its image became that of a human body spared a fall on the reefs. The meaning was murder withheld.

Jaric struck with the full strength of his arm. The demon retaliated before the weapon cut. Images sheared like lightning through its victim's mind, upending all sense of existence. Jaric's blade clanged harmlessly into stone, scattering sparks across the outcrop as he fell limp at the demon's knees.

Imprisoned by Llondian imaging, the boy heard nothing, felt nothing beyond the sting of steel piercing his shoulder. Plunged through transition and darkness, he emerged, staggering to his feet, in another place, a closed chamber where torchlight glimmered off strangely carved walls. A slight, pale boy struggled in his arms. He held the human close, though it pained him, and with a horrid shock of surprise, Jaric realized that *the boy was himself.* In the dream he was *other*; his hands, the same hands which gripped the human child, were gray-skinned, six-fingered, and spurred. In one shattering instant, Jaric recognized the moment: through enemy eyes he shared the agony of the wound the Earl of Morbrith had dealt a Llondian in the sanctuary tower last summerfair. The knife thrust had been intended for the heir of Ivain, but a Llondel demon had died instead.

Jaric had no chance to unravel ironies. The dream-image rippled like windblown tapestry. Torch flame spat and flared in the wall sconce, then transformed to a Llondian's glowing eyes. *'One of us perished, Firelord's heir, that you might survive to develop your talents.'*

The implication was damning in its simplicity. Jaric resisted, desperate.

"Why?" His shout echoed in darkness. "Since when have demons concerned themselves with the affairs of men, except to bring discord and suffering?"

But exactly as before, the Llondelei smothered protest in dreams. Jaric felt himself hurled back to an earlier day when he had scaled the ledges of Cliffhaven to answer the geas set upon him by Anskiere. Soaked and shivering and trapped in the past, he saw rain clouds cleft by new sunlight. Amid sudden, miraculous calm, while storm-whipped seas tumbled raggedly over the rocks, he heard once again the command Anskiere had shaped on the wind.

"You will recover the Keys to Elrinfaer and hold them safe until they can be returned." But here Llondian influence twisted Jaric's memory, crushing his spirit with an overwhelming burden of guilt. The human boy had been negligent in his judgment; the Keys to Elrinfaer were endangered still, and Anskiere's request neglected.

The accusation shocked like a death wound. In hurt and pride and raging anger, Jaric protested innocence. He had discovered the Keys in good faith, left his home, renounced friends, even abandoned principles he held dear to complete his bond to the Stormwarden. The Llondel alone prevented his return to Anskiere. The injustice of his quandary whipped Jaric to blind and murderous frenzy. For an instant the demon could not counter the scope of his response. Its hold slipped, and dream-images fled like shadows before fire.

Jaric roused to cold and darkness and the sour smell of the sea. Sprawled on the ledge at the Llondel's feet, he stirred skinned knuckles. The knife was gone from his hand. He groped after it, brushed a fold of gray cloth, and instantly recalled the ice cliffs and his interrupted purpose. A lump pressed against his chest, proof that the pouch which held the Keys to Elrinfaer remained tucked inside his tunic; still he was defenseless. The demon could steal from him whenever it pleased, and its dispassionate stare made him feel like a mouse teased by a cat.

Jaric dragged himself to his knees. Before he reached his feet, the Llondel touched his mind again. It grasped the fact that he attributed its interference to cruelty, and the shallowness of his reasoning roused it to rage.

'Mortal fool,' it sent. *'Ignorant child. Do you not know what the wards over Elrinfaer Tower defend?'*

"No!" Pressured beyond caution, Jaric shouted his defiance. "How should I? All my life I was a scribe keeping records in a backlands keep. Did you think I asked to be involved in the affairs of sorcerers?"

'You are what you must become,' the Llondel returned equitably and, with pitiless force, overturned his senses.

Jaric staggered back, blinded by a cruel flash of light. Etched against the night he saw the falcon and triple circle that symbolized the Stormwarden's mastery. The vision had no sooner faded when a second image ripped into Jaric's mind, edged with a clarity that cut to the heart. The Llondel showed him the ice cliffs, but changed in a manner no mortal could perceive. Cascades rose in frozen rungs above the rocky reefs of Cliffhaven. Their majesty stung Jaric to tears, for here stood a monument to inexpressible sorrow. The expanded perception of the demon revealed a corona of light like lacework across the sky; here shone the wards themselves laid bare, patterns of force which bound the weather to eternal frost. Although understanding of the structure lay beyond the grasp of an untrained mind, Jaric perceived that the Sorcerer had borrowed energy from his own being to balance the existence of his creation. Sadness echoed like a song's edge. Before the boy could contemplate whose grief made him weep, the spell unraveled into night. But darkness offered no reprieve. Jaric plunged into silence and cold without end.

Frost shackled his limbs. His heart slowed until the bindings of his spirit loosened and his body lay a hairsbreadth from death; yet the existence Jaric shared was another's. Through the guidance of the Llondel, he experienced the fate of the Stormwarden of Elrinfaer whose powers had provoked such hatred among men. Anskiere lay suspended in stasis deep beneath the cliffs, his limbs enshrouded in ice. Though his flesh was imprisoned and helpless, his mind roved a landscape of dreams. Through the window of the sorcerer's memories, Jaric encountered strife and sacrifice, and a tragic understanding of the Firelord who had fathered him. . . .

Ivain had not always been mad. At one with a younger Stormwarden, Jaric knew the twilight dimness of an enchanted grove. For Anskiere, the place held memories within memories. Once a Prince of Elrinfaer, he had waited in the selfsame place and renounced his royal heritage for the powers of wave and weather. Now he sought the Vaere to answer a demand of his own, for a grievance weighed upon his heart. The Stormwarden called repeatedly, but the fey being who trained him to mastery did not appear.

In frustration, Anskiere shouted, his voice an echo among the cedars. "In the name of Kordane's mercy, what have your gifts brought Ivain? Of us both, he was the better man. Did you mean to break his mind? Answer!"

The Stormwarden held his breath and listened, but nothing moved in the grove. No shimmer of air disturbed the silvery gloom. The cedars brooded in breezeless stillness. Anskiere clenched his fists. "I spoke with the seeress at Cael's Falls. She said each time Ivain summons fire, the flame that he masters consumes his living flesh. He does not burn, she said, nor does he consciously suffer agony, not since the Cycle of Fire seared his soul to a cinder. He has no nerves left to feel. Did you know that the torment would steal his humanity from him? He once was the gentlest of men. Now he is spiteful and cruel, and cursed by his own kind."

But the Vaere did not answer. Heartbroken by that silence, Anskiere left the grove. Through the trials to come he never ceased mourning the ruin of the minstrel's son who had been his dearest friend. Although the

Vaere never accounted for Ivain's broken mind, years and experience tempered Anskiere's sorrow. As he wielded his powers to hold Keithland
secure, he found enemies more ruthless by far than any Vaere. The deadly
wiles of demonkind eventually made Anskiere understand that mankind's
chances of survival were slight without the defense of a firelord's skills.
Twisted as Ivain became, the Stormwarden never forgot compassion for
his friend, even on the day the two sorcerers battled the most terrible
demons ever to threaten mankind.

The Llondel's imaging replicated Anskiere's recollection of that
betrayal; the circumstances were not at all as common men believed. The
surviving Mharg-demon was ancient, broken in mind and body from Kordane's Fires; his wings were too scarred to fly, and his breath barely sufficient to wither the lichens he devoured for sustenance. Yet he had life and
hatred enough to fertilize one last, lost clutch of eggs, forgotten since the
Great Fall until demons recovered it from the sea bottom. The Mharg-
male buried his brood in the heart of Keithland before he died. In time,
they hatched and flew over the Tors of Elshend, to wreak final vengeance
upon mankind. In the towns, the priests prayed for Kordane's mercy. Had
their faith been the land's sole defense, all Keithland would have been laid
waste. But the Vaere sent Stormwarden and Firelord against the Mharg-
hatchlings. No archive at Landfast held record of the conflict; the priesthood dared not credit sorcerers, lest the faithful cease to supply the
temple coffers with their silver.

Slogging through reeds in the lowlands west of Telshire, Anskiere
wasted no thought on the priests' petty pride. But Ivain cursed long and
vehemently, his resentment sharpened by the suck and spatter of mud
beneath his boots.

"Prostrated themselves so zealously for Kordane's mercy they bruised
their kneecaps on the prayer carpets. And Great Fall, the hangovers from
the rites! You know they sucked the temple wine stores down to the lees?"
Ivain tossed back red hair and regarded Anskiere with dark, unreadable
eyes; eyes whose set and color were the same stamp as Jaric's, but old in a
manner no mortal could comprehend. "If a song of blessing for our efforts
strains their sotted throats overmuch, may they slip while pissing and
drown in their jakes."

Ivain kicked a clod of grass. A marsh thrush started up with a whir of
barred wings. Its cry rang over deserted fields, for the folk of Tor Elshend
had fled the peril of the Mharg-spawn. No one remained to tend the hearth
fires in the cottages. Ivain swore as if the emptied landscape could respond
to the vicious anger in his heart.

"It's you, I think, who overindulged in drink last night," Anskiere said
mildly.

Ivain laughed, a wild sound that frightened the marsh thrush's mate
from her nest in a nearby bush. She took wing after the male, a scrap of
brown and white against the overcast sky. Ivain flicked his fingers. The

bird burst into flame, transformed by his malice to a conflagration of feather and bone.

Anskiere flinched as the pitiful handful of cinders tumbled over and over in the air and crashed with a hiss in a reed bed. "That was ill done. Her fledglings will now die also."

Ivain shrugged without remorse. "All Keithland might perish as easily. Have you forgotten? The priests have, and how convenient it is for them! We who are their true defense against demons are feared, spit on, outcast, and unsung."

The cries of the marsh thrush's mate filled a comfortless interval of silence. Anskiere had no word to speak in behalf of Kordane's sacred brotherhood. Ivain's accusation was true, but much of the people's ill will toward sorcerers stemmed from his own spiteful nature. Anskiere could not share the Firelord's bitterness. What man could sow fields and raise children, knowing his family lay continually in peril? Kordane's priesthood offered faith, cloaked in illusions of tradition and security. Would a sorcerer be resented any less if men understood the truth, that they were helpless as ants before the threat of demons? Anskiere thought not. But Ivain continued to taunt his complacency as they hiked to the site where the Mharglings had broken nest.

"We could show them, smash one of their pompous little towns to wreckage." Ivain flicked a tick from the ragged edge of his cuff and laughed again. "You haven't the stomach for that, though, if you'd mourn the charred corpse of a thrush. Had the bird been a child, would you weep, or would you puke? Perhaps you'd discover a way to manage both at once."

Anskiere clenched his jaw. Unwilling to yield to anger, he regarded the fresh fronds of the willows, so like the palace grounds of his boyhood. Tor Elshend lay on the southern borders of Elrinfaer, and the stream-laced meadows and forested hills prompted remembrance of his royal sister and the times they had gathered wildflowers and herbs for the healer's cupboards. Now, in the boots of a Vaere-trained sorcerer, he did not leap the hummocks or pause to skip stones in the pools. Foxglove and faerylace crumpled under his step, and no memory could ease his longing for the Ivain who had first met the Vaere, a ready smile and a whistle on his lips.

But presently even nature offered no distraction from the Firelord's soured spirit; the wind brought a taint of rotted earth and the hills rose scabbed like old wounds between areas of new growth. Abruptly Ivain ceased carping. Shaken by the ruin of the tor's bright beauty, he walked at the Stormwarden's side and spoke no more of birds or vengeance. The grasses turned sere and brown underfoot. As the sorcerers neared their destination, the hillsides stank and oozed, and their feet slogged through a gelid slime of dead plants. No living thing remained of the forest or the wildlife which once had inhabited Tor Elshend. The Mharglings were not far distant.

Suddenly a hiss cut the morning stillness. Tension raised sweat on

Anskiere's neck. Though the air was mild with spring, he felt chill down to his bones. Ahead, where maples had once lifted full crowns to the sunlight, he saw branches stripped like the beams of a burned croft. A scaled head arose above them, patterned iridescently emerald, turquoise, and gold. The creature's snout was flat, slitted with four sets of nostrils; centered within a maze of scarlet stripes, its single eye glared, black as a bead, and intelligent.

"By the Vaere," said Anskiere. In size alone the demon was daunting. "We'll be lucky to finish this alive."

Ivain shrugged. Sarcasm sharpened his reply. "Does it matter? Never doubt, the Vaere has chosen our successors already."

The Mhargling spotted their approach. It opened toothless jaws and hissed warning, membranes glistening through the fumes which issued from its throat. If its bite was harmless to man, the vapors were not. Ribbed rows of ducts emitted caustic digestive gases, and the breath of the Mharg-spawn rotted forests, fish, and animals into slime with killing speed. The creatures lapped the remains to feed. In a season they could ravage every living acre of Keithland, and afterward neither soil nor ocean would support any life.

Anskiere licked dry lips. "Are you ready?"

Ivain replied with an obscenity. Without warning he ripped a fireball out of empty sky and dropped it in the Mharglings' midst.

Four heads snapped erect, warbling screams of fury over the crackle of flame. Membranous wings thundered on the air as the Mharg-spawn took flight, talons unsheathed for battle. Enraged and deadly and fully sixty spans long, they wheeled and dove at their attackers. Though nettled by Ivain's precipitous action, Anskiere was not caught off guard. He raised his hands with speed and wove a whirlwind in the demons' midst. Squalling surprise, the Mharglings tumbled, tangled, and pinwheeled earthward in a knot of threshing wings. They struck amid a blinding explosion of flame.

A gust of heated air stung Anskiere's face. He blinked away tears from the blast. Outlined in glare, the first wings arose, stretched upward, and beat strongly amid the fumes. The fact the Vaere had warned that victory would be difficult made the moment no easier to accept. Wings cracked as the Mharglings scuttled clear of the smoke. They took flight, utterly without scathe, except for scales which glinted a hot reddish yellow where the flames had touched them.

At once Anskiere knew he must merge minds with Ivain. Their skills must answer as one to counter the Mharglings' deadly speed. Fire daunted the creatures not at all; the air currents already cooled their heated scales. The Stormwarden buffeted them with gusts, yet they stayed separate from each other, knifing through turbulence like quarrels shot from a crossbow. *Tire them,* he decided, confident Ivain would catch his thought. *Wear them out and try to survive, and when they weaken, seal them living in a tomb of rock.*

But when Anskiere extended his awareness to mesh with the Firelord's mind, his linking thought touched emptiness. Mharg-wings flogged the air with the sound of storm surf battering sand. The creatures spiraled upward with a rattle of scales, and yellow fumes billowed from their mouths. Anskiere turned, fearful the silence in his mind meant he would find his companion injured.

Yet the Firelord stood unharmed, with his thumbs hooked negligently through his belt. His chin lifted as Anskiere faced him.

"We should teach those priests a lesson," Ivain said. A mocking smile spread over his lips. "The event would be sporting, don't you think? A Mhargling against a prayer?"

Flicked by a monstrous shadow, Anskiere whirled. His cloak snapped like a flag as he raised a gust to drive off the poisonous fumes. Still his eyes stung and watered, and the blown ends of his hair turned from silver to black. "That's madness!" he shouted, for a moment unwilling to face the Firelord behind him. "You'll kill us all, and for what? Simple jealousy?"

Ivain's eyes narrowed. "Not of the priests' popularity. Kordane's faithful are insects, to a man. Should we prevent demons from swatting them?"

Anskiere jerked and spun around. For an instant Stormwarden and Firelord regarded each other, one with outrage, the other with naked enmity. Then the Mharglings screamed and stooped for the kill; Anskiere experienced a tangible dissolution of resistance as Ivain relented. The sorcerers' powers merged.

Power coursed through Anskiere's body with the inexorable force of the tides; nerve, sinew, and bone sang with stresses never meant for mortal endurance. Yet the Stormwarden held firm. He joined with Ivain and fought the Mharg with the combined masteries of earth and fire, water and wind. The battle spanned hours, or maybe days, without surcease.

Anskiere called up tempests, and rain fell. Lightning slashed the sky, striking sword-metal highlights on scaled hides. Still the Mharg flew. The temperature plunged, and hail rattled into the ground. Battered by ice, the Mharg howled but did not land. Ivain split the earth. Lava spurted from the rift, red as an opened artery. The Mharglings yowled, enraged. They shot straight up. Anskiere belted them with a downdraft, without success. The Mharg-spawn hissed and wheeled northward, over the hills of Elrinfaer. Through a murky rain of ash, forests withered. Pine trees crumpled like sodden silk, and the wind reeked of death.

Racked by exhaustion and inflamed nerves, Anskiere pursued. His eyes became blinded by tears, that the land he was once to rule should suffer such ruin as this. Tired feet stumbled over blackened earth, and his robe clung to shoulders which steamed with sweat. Caustic slush blackened his boots where the Mharg had passed. The leather softened and dissolved and the slime burned his bare soles. Beaten by sleet and wind, the Stormwarden paused to wrap his blistered feet in his cloak. A Mhargling hissed down out of the dark. In an instant the ground became an inferno as Ivain chiseled an outcrop into lava and drove it off. Still the demons flew. The Vaere had warned that their strength arose from a world never inhabited by men. Tortured by fatigue, Anskiere wondered whether the creatures would settle at all.

"If they land just once, we have them." Ivain's face glistened with rain and sweat. Mharg-breath had long since singed his cloak to rags. "Did you notice? They don't care for molten rock."

Anskiere grunted assent, his throat too raw for speech. With a shiver of foreboding, he raised his eyes skyward once more. Repeatedly the Mharg-demons retreated to the north; if they were not brought to ground very soon, their rampaging would destroy the orchards which were the pride and the wealth of Elrinfaer. And close by lay villages and farmsteads he was bound by birthright to protect.

Aching, the Stormwarden rose to his feet. As he raised his powers to renew the fight, Ivain regarded him with curious malice. But the dream which unfolded through Llondian influence was nothing more than a memory. No warning could alter the past.

Sudden fire flared. The earth spewed forth dust to clog the Mharg-lings' lungs, and the Firelord's face became veiled by grit. Powers burned through Anskiere's hands, vast and wild as a cataclysm. He needed every scrap of concentration to manage them. No resource remained to examine Ivain's vagaries, and of necessity his peril went unnoticed. Storms shook the ground. A forest burned, branches seared to skeletons against a wall of glare. Still the Mharg flew; but at long last they showed signs of flagging. More often they glided, as if resting tired wings, and their attacks became sporadic, even sluggish compared to their earlier efforts.

Dawn broke. Dust drifted in the air. The sun glowed sullen orange above fields scorched to stubble. Anskiere pounded the air with gusts, and the Mharglings cut and wove in maddened circles to stay airborne.

"Open a shaft. They're slowing." The Stormwarden shaped his request to the Firelord in a croaking whisper, unable to manage more. His skin was patched with abrasions. Sparks had scored holes in his clothes, but his eyes were alight with the triumph of victory.

Ivain faced him over the gutted remains of an oak, hair streaked with grime. "Do that yourself." A smile brightened his smudged face. "It's not my kingdom at stake."

Anskiere stared, speechless with shock. At first he refused to believe Ivain's words were not simply another malicious taunt. But the face confronting him was that of a madman. Overhead the Mharglings screamed, banked, and shot off to the north. Torn between rebuke and compassion, the Stormwarden searched for means to restore Ivain's lost reason and stave off the destruction of Elrinfaer.

"Your countryfolk deserve the lesson." Ivain spat on the broken soil. "They should never have refused me hospitality last solstice."

"Vaere witness, you wrong them," Anskiere managed, his voice mangled with pain.

Ivain perched insouciantly on the fallen oak, his hands lax at his sides. With terrible finality, Anskiere felt the presence of the Firelord dissolve within his mind. Grief caught him like a blow. Separate and alone, Anskiere turned quickly lest the Firelord laugh at his sorrow. Elrinfaer still lay dearest to his heart; the Mharg-spawn would make a desert of the land, farms and cities and wilderness, and all his Stormwarden's powers could not prevent them. . . .

Bound into sympathy by the Llondel's link, Jaric screamed over and over in anguish. Never in life had he known such suffering as the Stormwarden experienced at Ivain's betrayal.

There seemed no end to such agony of spirit. From the depths of trance, the Firelord's son flung a desperate appeal to the entity which imprisoned his will. "Free me!" Jaric's cry battered like a moth against lantern glass, seeking light though it killed him. For an instant, he thought he glimpsed stars and the crashing of waves smoking over the reefs of Cliffhaven. His throat was lacerated from screaming, and his lips stung with the taste of tears. He rolled, gasping from the cold, and saw two eyes glaring down at him with baleful and inhuman indifference.

"Let me go." Jaric shivered. Lashed raw inside by the demands of forces he had no schooling to understand, and terrified of that legacy as never before, he was aware Anskiere's struggle to save Elrinfaer was doomed; whatever powers the Stormwarden summoned, their fury was surely more than a boy's untrained mind could support. "Do you wish my death?"

'No,' sent the Llondel.

It flicked gray fingers, and Jaric tumbled back into darkness. Through Anskiere's eyes, he watched Elrinfaer die, slowly, inexorably, like embers beaten to ash by rain.

CHAPTER III

Warning

No longer could Anskiere influence the direction of the demons' flight. Without Ivain's command of fire, the Mharg drove across inhabited lands unhindered. Their wake became a wasteland of towns filled with smeared corpses and rotting bones. The Stormwarden stumbled over broken ground where only minutes earlier a flock of sheep had grazed, guarded by a dog and a boy with a reed pipe. Livestock, grass, and child were now dead, reduced to unrecognizable masses of slime by the Mharg. Bereft of alternatives, the former Prince of Elrinfaer tried desperate measures to preserve his land from ruin.

Anskiere called down the cold. Power answered, streamed like water over a rockfall from his raised fists. The temperature fell, and fell again. Spring transformed to winter; in the space of a single breath, the heartland of Elrinfaer silvered under a spiked mantle of frost. Cattle stampeded in the pastures. Inside town walls, parents hustled children from the dooryards and slammed their shutters in fear. Anskiere shouted again, and the skies darkened. Rain fell in white torrents and froze to a glaze of ice. Apple blossoms wore hardened fists of glass; animals fled for shelter only to stiffen like statues in their tracks. Field hands died at the sowing, and women washing on the riverbanks cried in terror, their wrists trapped fast in black ice. Grim as death itself, Anskiere tightened the bindings of cold over Elrinfaer; crops might fail and people perish, but an armor of ice might possibly shield the land from the total devastation of the Mharg-breath. Seeds would survive the cataclysm, and some of the plants, and surely the majority of the people, enough to rebuild their losses after the crisis passed.

But the tactic failed. Mharglings swept from the sky and attacked an isolated homestead. Their poison reduced the ice to hissing steam and razed everything beneath to stinking slush. Anskiere wept. All his Stormwarden's powers could spare neither land nor people. Nearly broken by defeat, he splashed through a pool of filth. His foot snagged on metal, a gate hinge cast loose when the wooden post which supported it dissolved into soup. The sorcerer stumbled, caught himself short of a fall, and continued, trying not to think of the dead who had raised that fence for their cattle. Inflexibly schooled by the Vaere, a part of his mind still sorted options. His final resource, and Keithland's sole hope, rested in the sea. If the Mharg flew over ocean, one chance remained that Anskiere might trap them through water.

The western coastline lay over mountains, weatherstripped rocks with snowbound passes where roads stayed treacherous even through high summer; to the east, fifty leagues of farmland sprawled toward a shore settled by fisherfolk. Anskiere rubbed the blistered skin of his brow. The Mharg flew where they would; he could do little but follow and ply the winds, try to keep them airborne as much as possible.

The trials which followed melted one into another; Anskiere's days became a misery of existence between terrible events of loss. Storm force resonated through his body. The terrible ebb and flux of power heated nerve and sinew and spirit to pitiless agony, burning away his identity until he could no longer separate which pain was his, and which his kingdom's. Days melted endlessly into dark and time itself lost meaning. Still the Mharg flew. Events became jumbled; scenes lapped together like patchwork, each one a vignette of tragedy.

A city fell and a sister died, the same a young prince had promised to defend when he left seeking the mysteries of the Vaere. Her image haunted his memory, girlish fingers clenched around a scepter she had never wanted, and her fears checked by nothing but royal pride. She had been born with the sight. Now Anskiere wondered whether she had known she would die while he slept. The first night he succumbed to exhaustion, the Mharg had veered east and brought death to the fair court of Elrinfaer. Anskiere clenched his fists and the sky spat lightning. Flash after jagging flash split the dark as he stumbled through courtyards littered with bones. In grief the sorcerer summoned storms to cleanse the streets; his tears became the drum roll of rain.

Summer came, and dust blew over wasted acres. Anskiere climbed a rock face, barefoot, his fingers lacerated from gripping cruel stone. The Mharg circled lazily on an air current, jewel-bright against the zenith. But so long had Anskiere been immersed in storm-weaving, his eyes saw no sky but patterns of tangled light that mapped the force lines by which he read the winds. And his weather alone kept the enemies airborne, harried them westward over the peaks to the sea.

He knew hunger then; days of snow and sun glare and gale-driven ice. Some nights he was too tired to deflect the temperature enough to keep warm. Clothed in little but rags, he rested, shivering on bare rock. The Mharg roosted on the peaks and preened like painted gargoyles. The voracious demand of their appetites would drive them to the air before long. Anskiere forced himself to his feet. Solitary under glittering pinpoints of stars, he traversed a slope of moraine. Pebbles scattered dangerously under his feet, and the air rose cold off the snowfields. Under the cliffs where the demons slept, the Stormwarden raised a fist and summoned his powers. Wind arose, howling over the rocks, and slapped the demons from their perches. They launched with a screeling wail and turned downward toward the sea. Anskiere pursued. His memory of that night's run blended indistinguishably into the tormented days which followed. Storm-torn, savaged by the forces he shaped with his mind, he existed only as a tool for his craft. For a time he lost all awareness of self, his mind blistered beyond mortal recognition by too much power.

Later, bone-thin, the Stormwarden huddled on a beach, his head cradled on crossed wrists. Waves thundered over rock bare inches from his body. Matted hair clung to wet skin, and he breathed in sobs, too spent to move. Sixty yards offshore, a waterspout raged, battered by a screaming howl of elements. In its heart, the Mharglings lay trapped at last, but a week passed before Anskiere recovered enough presence to balance the forces which held them. The months of his labors had taxed him. He could not weave the energy strong enough to perpetuate itself. Daily he had to strengthen his handiwork, and he dared never leave the site.

Anskiere scavenged the beaches. Filthy as a shipwreck victim, he ate raw fish. Dragging the waterspout and the Mharg it confined up the coast, he at last reached a derelict light station on Elrinfaer's northwest shore. The keeper dwelling there was senile, a hermit who had neglected to tend his lamps for half a score of years. Clicking, muttering, and running his tongue over toothless gums, the man still had wits enough to listen when Anskiere asked him to brick every window in the tower with stones. The lightkeeper scratched his groin and spat. But he helped until the task was finished. The moment the last chink was sealed, Anskiere summoned his powers. He heated the air to a blinding inferno. Reft of Ivain's talents, he drove himself until, at the uttermost edge of life, the stones of the tower melted and fused, leaving no break in the walls. The new-made prison rose sheer and black from the cliff, and there Anskiere confined the Mharg. They would fly no more. In time, only eggs might survive, but the sorcerer cleansed the place with wind, leaving no moisture within to trigger a second hatching. The Stormwarden sealed the entrance, rested, then plied his mastery once again. When he finished, the Tower of Elrinfaer held secure under the strongest wards ever forged by a weathermage.

He wept at the end. Battered, ragged, and blistered from his labors, he sat on the cliff's edge while the waves creamed over the beaches and the gulls squabbled over flotsam in the tide wrack. In fingers that shook he turned a small basalt block which had once been a trinket of the lightkeeper's. The facets flashed over and over and over. Absorbed by the play of the light, Anskiere never heard the footsteps of the visitor who approached. Nor did he guess he was no longer alone until a familiar, sardonic voice called out to him.

"You did admirably." Ivain paused, thoughtfully tossing pebbles from hand to hand. His hair gleamed copper-bright in late sunlight. "Wrecked yourself, truly, and for what? The survivors will say you caused the devastation. Their priests will curse your name in song, and children learn to fear you."

Anskiere rose, clumsy with exhaustion. "There were no survivors. That's why the Mharg sought the sea. *Nothing else remained for them to spoil.*" He paused to control an anger he lacked the strength to express. "You're lucky the destruction didn't spread beyond Elrinfaer."

"Why?" Ivain's hands stopped in the air, and the stones fell rattling to the ground. "I'm tired of working for the Vaere."

Before Anskiere could respond, the ground parted. The sorcerer who was both Firelord and Earthmaster vanished beneath the soil, his laughter ringing like curses upon the air.

"I'll find you," whispered the Stormwarden. "When I do, I will bind you with a geas so potent you'll *never* forsake your kind again."

So began the hunt for Ivain which culminated at Northsea; forced at bay against the ocean, the Firelord crouched at the Stormwarden's feet. There, under duress, Ivain completed the bindings, stabilizing the enchantments which prisoned the Mharg-demons. The powers of his Earthmastery impressed the Keys to the wards into the cube of basalt that once had served as the lightkeeper's door stop. After, Anskiere had pronounced his sentence upon the Firelord who had deserted him at Elrinfaer, the bitter effects of which were to pass through the next generation, to Jaric.

That instant, the dream shattered. Flung precipitously out of the Stormwarden's memory, the son of Ivain tumbled through blackness. Sound, sight, all sensations were lost to him. The Llondel withheld any guidance. Abandoned to some nightmare pocket between his own existence and the sorcerer's past, Jaric cried aloud. He struggled to reorient, half-deranged by panic.

That moment a voice boomed out of the dark. *"Name yourself, trespasser! What brings you to intrude upon the Stormwarden of Elrinfaer?"*

No longer able to distinguish where dream-image ended and reality began, Jaric felt his awareness netted by a will like steel shackles. Power tore through him, ruthless and sure, stripping him to his innermost self. Threatened by total annihilation, he abandoned resistance. The touch softened and abruptly released. Light flared and dimmed. Thrown to his knees, Jaric opened his eyes to the sight of a carved stone fireplace, and a room that disoriented him utterly. No trace remained of ice cliffs, rain, or the chill of the windy night. His hands dug into the pile of a richly patterned carpet, and the clothing on his back was dry.

"Ivainson Jaric," said a voice at his back, gently, but terrible with command.

The boy rose. Bewildered and shaken, he faced the speaker, and for the first time beheld Anskiere of Elrinfaer. The Stormwarden waited before a faded square of tapestry. His robes fell from straight shoulders, the velvet creaseless and blue as the skies of summer. Firelight played over silver hair, jutting brows, and a face creased deeply by weather and hardship.

"You sought me," the Stormwarden said.

Jaric blinked. "Where am I? How did I get here?" He raised a hand to his tunic, groped, and found the Keys to Elrinfaer missing. Panic shook him. "The Llondian!"

"Sent you to me," Anskiere finished quickly. "This chamber is an illusion, no more and no less than a thought within my mind. And the Llondelei are not your enemy."

Jaric reddened. "They are demons."

"All races of Kor's Accursed are not alike. Some would consummate their hatred against man to the detriment of the rest. If the Mharg fly again, the Llondelei would perish." Anskiere watched with understanding as Jaric absorbed this revelation. "Where the Keys are concerned, the Llondel is your ally."

Jaric met the sorcerer's eyes, found them deep as the horizon at the sea's edge. He wanted to feel anger, but could not. Once he had believed that Anskiere had cursed the Firelord in vengeance for past wrongs. Now he knew differently. The geas delivered at Northsea had been created solely against need, that the betrayal which ruined Elrinfaer should never again be repeated.

Anskiere spoke into the silence. "When I sent my summons, I already knew Ivain was dead."

The statement held multiple meanings. Jaric felt his throat constrict. Ivain dead meant his heir must answer, perhaps repeat the tragedy engendered by the Cycle of Fire; this Anskiere had known. Even as he called, the grief of that decision had stamped irrevocable sorrow on his heart. The Stormwarden saw, down to the least ramification, exactly what consequences he had set upon the untrained shoulders of the boy from Morbrith Keep.

"If you have questions, ask them now. I will answer as best I can. This may be the last time we communicate." Anskiere clarified with unemotional calm. "In sending you to me, the Llondel has shortened the span of my endurance. She took a risk that won't be repeated."

"She?" Jaric looked up, astonished. He had never thought of demons as being female.

Anskiere returned a half smile. "They are not human, Jaric, but in some things the Llondelei are as mortal as you or I."

Mortal; Jaric flinched to hear such an admission from a sorcerer whose deeds had bent the very course of history. Yet the discovery should not have surprised him; the Stormwarden was not all-powerful. Prisoner himself, Anskiere dared not unbind the ice without a Firelord's skills; to loose those wards would release the frostwargs, demons themselves, and nearly as deadly as the Mharg. Jaric felt the blood go cold in his veins. How long could the Stormwarden survive in stasis beneath the ice, if no candidate mastered the Cycle of Fire?

Although Jaric lacked courage to voice his question, Anskiere answered directly. "My days will number less than the span of your own life."

The fire abruptly felt too warm at Jaric's back. He sweated, resisting an urge to step forward. "What of the frostwargs? If you die, will they escape?"

"Not immediately." As if sensing Jaric's discomfort, the Stormwarden turned and stared at the tapestry, which depicted a seascape in bleached blues and greens. The sorcerer qualified in a voice as worn as the thread. "The wards would deteriorate slowly. If electrical storms stay few and mild, the bindings might hold for a century and a half."

"The Vaere would send your successor," said Jaric.

"They might." Anskiere did not add that talent was rare; even the most gifted often failed to endure through the trials of a sorcerer's training. But his silence on the subject spoke volumes, and Jaric found none of the reassurance he sought. Every exchange with the sorcerer led him closer to the Cycle of Fire, until acceptance of the torment which had destroyed his father seemed inevitable as death.

"No," Anskiere whirled from the tapestry. He lifted eyes passionless as ice water and added. "The decision to undertake the Cycle of Fire can never be forced on a man. I charged you with one trial only: recover the Keys to Elrinfaer and hold them safe until they can be returned."

Jaric shrank from the sorcerer's gaze. Naked before perception which pierced through denial, and unraveled his dread of Ivain's mad fate to reveal the inner core of his shortcomings, for the first time he fully understood the burden set upon him. Memory replicated the conflict at Northsea and the doom Anskiere pronounced upon Ivain. *". . . And should you die, my will shall pass to your eldest son, and to his son's sons after him, until the debt is paid."*

As if cut by the lash of a whip, Jaric paled. His hands knotted beneath the cuffs of his tunic. "Can you not relieve me of the Keys?"

Anskiere replied with surprising gentleness. "Only if I am freed, son of Ivain. Until that day, you or your children after you, must protect the Keys from demons."

"I have no such powers of defense!" Too late Jaric wished the words unsaid.

Anskiere smiled, implacable. "You have the potential."

"No!" Jaric abandoned restraint. Cornered by the Stormwarden's presence, and inwardly seared by the shared recall inflicted by the Llondel's thought-image, he spilled the horrors which had festered in his mind since the moment he discovered his parentage. "Who am I to assume those powers? Kordane's Fires, sorcerer, how many people did my father harm before he ran a knife through his heart?" Once started, Jaric could not stop. His voice thickened. "You, *Stormwarden*, with all your wisdom and compassion, *how many died at Tierl Enneth?*"

The accusation died into silence. Jaric stood with his chin lifted; he could not regret his defiance. The reproach was surely just. All Keithland remembered the wave which had roared in from the sea and despoiled the shores of Tierl Enneth. Four thousand people had died, each one under the Stormwarden's sworn protection.

Anskiere bent his head, vitality and strength drained from him until suddenly he seemed an old man. "I'll explain, Firelord's heir, though I've told none before but the Vaere. I pray you have wisdom enough to understand." He lifted tired eyes. "The demons found a way to twist the human mind and seize control. A terrible thing, for those they choose to corrupt are the talented. One called Tathagres came to me asking for apprenticeship. She proved to be the demon's own, and she discharged the powers of my staff one day while my back was turned. Such a simple betrayal I never thought to guard against. The staff was protected; to this moment I don't know how she manipulated the defense wards and lived. But her meddling raised the seas and destroyed Tierl Enneth. The act was done to discredit me."

Jaric let his hand fall, shaken to discover sweat on his palms. "Tathagres is dead."

The sorcerer responded fast as a slap. "Did her secrets perish with her?"

"Perhaps." But Jaric did not finish the thought, that more likely the witch had bequeathed her corruption to another. Drawn as an overpitched harpstring, he closed his eyes, wishing darkness could obliterate the destiny his inheritance laid before him. The sorcerer held no answer but the Cycle of Fire to his quandary; and that fate Jaric was determined to avoid, lest power beget more wrongs for demons to exploit. Since the Llondel had emphasized the perils of mankind's survival, Jaric dreaded to be the one to upset the final balance and consign his own kind to extinction. With a curse of agonized denial, he wished himself elsewhere.

The carpet buckled without warning underfoot. Pitched off balance, Jaric fell but struck no floor. The room dissolved into air around him. Light melted into blackness, and the Stormwarden's final words scraped like the whisper of a ghost in a void.

"Demons will seek the Keys, Ivainson Jaric. Guard them well. Make what choices you must with boldness and courage. My hope and my blessing go with you, however you fare."

Jaric strove to respond, but words stuck in his throat. Over and over he tumbled, buffeted by powers beyond mortal control. When his voice broke free at last, he screamed with pain and fear. The sound stung him awake. Roused to cold and sharp rocks and the booming roar of breakers, Jaric opened his eyes on the northern shore of Cliffhaven. Clouds had blanketed the stars. The ice cliffs towered upward, shadowed white buttresses against the stygian dark of the sky. Shoreline, reefs, and rocks blended beneath, stark as a drawing in monochrome, except for two points of orange. The Llondel watched still from the ledge, her cloak tucked over crossed legs and her eyes emotionless sparks beneath her hood.

Jaric shifted and sat up. He set his back against granite and cautiously studied the Llondel, but found no visual clue to confirm her sex. Uncertainty followed; what if Anskiere's words had been a dream, or, worse yet, an illusion designed by the Llondel to blunt his sense of caution? Undermined by mistrust, Jaric groped inside his tunic. Only when his fingers located Anskiere's basalt block did suspicion leave him. If the Llondel had not stolen the Keys by now, chances were her intentions meant otherwise.

As if his thought cued movement, the demon blinked. Gray cloth sighed in the dark as she leaned intently forward. *'Firelord's heir and Keeper of the Keys, you have spoken with Anskiere. What now will you do?'*

The thought-image rang dissonant with threat. Jaric swallowed and found his throat dry. He was not out of danger yet. Carefully as he sifted answers, in the end only truth would suffice before the demon's empathic perception. Braced by bravado he never knew he possessed, Jaric attempted an answer. "I will safeguard the Keys as best I am able. But I will accept neither training nor power from the Vaere."

The Llondel hissed.

Jaric recoiled into rock. His next words came barbed with bitterness. "Did you know my father?" Desperate to be understood, he sent pictures flicking one after another through his mind; the Llondel would read them, he knew. Jaric showed the Firelord whose cruelty had so vividly marked the memories of man. Told in taprooms and singer's lament, and written in legal records, Ivain's capricious temper had inflicted destruction upon every corner of Keithland; burned hostels, slagged fields, and even the blistered hands of a stableboy too slow to bridle his horse.

Jaric finished, but the Llondel sat still as carved stone, eyes like candles under the shadow of her hood.

Uncertain what might move a demon to empathy, Jaric tried again. "Even when matched with noble intentions, the powers of the Vaere have brought grief to my kind." Once more the boy chose images, showed the grief which haunted Tierl Enneth after the discharge of Anskiere's staff let in the sea. "No matter how wise the sorcerer, power on that scale is too easily misused. I cannot." Jaric paused, swallowed, and doggedly resumed. "I won't be responsible for that kind of risk."

The Llondel hissed and surged into a crouch.

"No!" Jaric slammed both fists into his calf. "Wait and listen! There must be alternatives. *Won't you understand? Sorcery brings nothing but ruin.* If I must, I'll find another way to preserve my kind and return the Keys to Anskiere!"

A charged moment passed. Then the Llondel settled back with a ripple of robes. She extended an arm and with ritual deliberation scraped her spur along the stone between Jaric's knees. The sound raised hair on the boy's neck. Though the gesture was not customary among humankind, its meaning was unmistakable.

'I warn,' the Llondel sent. *'You are marked by the Vaere, and your path will be noted.'*

Chilled to the marrow, Jaric caught his breath, for the Llondian showed him an image of himself ringed by a triple band of fire. The pattern was all too similar to the seal on the Keys which symbolized Anskiere's mastery. The Llondel implied danger; she cautioned that the Firelord's heir would be not merely noticed, but *hunted*. The vision held warnings within warnings; Jaric's potential as a sorcerer posed threat to the demon compact at Shadowfane. His reluctance to develop those talents yielded no safety at all, for since he lacked the defenses of a Firelord's training, enemies might defeat him without risk.

But danger alone could not shake Jaric's resolve. Brutalized by memory of Anskiere of Elrinfaer's mastery, the undisciplined mind of the boy could not fathom the weather sorcery which had scoured the depths of his awareness. He knew only that resonance of such power caused pain; the pitiless and terrible self-command required to bend raw force into control daunted comprehension. No margin existed for doubts. Trapped by the realities of his own inadequacy, the heir of Ivain met the Llondel's silence with denial.

For an interval, man and demon sat locked in stubborn conflict. Then the Llondel whistled through the crescent slits of her nostrils.

'A true son of your father,' she sent. Sharpened with Llondian frustration, the comparison wounded.

Jaric recoiled. "No!" He spoke out in rising anger. "I'll have no part of Ivain's cruelty! By the Great Fall, even Anskiere said he couldn't force me to try the Cycle of Fire."

The Llondel trilled a mournful seventh. For a space her eyes burned with an almost human sadness. 'Firelord's heir, Keeper of the Keys.' She wrought image with the subtlety of a master musician, blending sight, sound, and ancestral memory into a wail of inflexible destiny. The illusion echoed through Jaric, choked his spirit with grief. 'Go as you will, son of Ivain. But take heed. O little brother of your race, take heed.' And his sight of the Llondel's face rippled deftly into dream.

Blanketed by a touch like fog, Jaric slipped into the pattern of her imaging. His awareness of ice cliffs and rock shifted, transformed to the wallowing toss of a boat on the open ocean. Barely larger than a dory, the craft carried patched sails, a gaff rig, and piled nets which reeked of fish. Through Llondian perception Jaric understood he viewed the present; this boat sailed *now* off the western shores of Elrinfaer. Two brothers in oilskins hauled twine over the gunwale. Unaware of observation, they worked in silence, lit by a storm lantern lashed to a ring in the sternpost. Salt-streaked glass threw starred patterns which swung with each roll of the boat, and in fitful intervals of shadow and light, Jaric noticed someone else sprawled on the floorboards in the bow.

Sweating in the throes of fever, the third man lay half-covered by a rough wool cloak. The arm flung over his face was streaked with dirt and sand, and clothed in ragged linen. Jaric saw glints of goldwork on the cuff. With a twist of dread he recognized the pattern of the weave. He examined the man more closely, saw fingers scabbed with blisters and seal-black hair caught in tangles beneath. Without looking further, Jaric knew. Here lay Taen Dreamweaver's brother, Emien, whom Jaric had forced to yield the Keys to Elrinfaer over the bared point of a sword scarcely three days past. The fishermen must have found him wandering the beaches and taken him on board. The sight of Emien's suffering should have inspired pity; instead, Jaric felt dread, as if something had gone irrevocably amiss.

From the depths of the Llondel's dream, he called out. "Why? What harm can Emien do? His mistress, Tathagres, is dead, murdered by his own hand on the shores of Elrinfaer. It was she, not Emien, who conjured through the powers of demons."

The Llondel responded with images. Jaric watched the fishing vessel blur, then shift in some subtle manner, as if a veil suddenly fell away. With eerie clarity, the scene that followed recorded what would happen in a time yet to come. Jaric saw Emien shed his wool covering, rise, and take an unsteady step. His eyes glistened with fever and his arm trembled as he grasped the gunwale to steady himself against the heel of the boat over the waves. The sullen set of the sick boy's features unsettled Jaric with foreboding; though Emien walked with the abandon of a sleepwalker, he acted for a purpose beyond the vague stirrings of delirium.

The boat wallowed over a crest and the lantern tossed. Shadows wheeled, pooling and receding over faded planking as the stern settled deeply into the trough. Twine chafed against the thwart, dragged seaward by the relentless pull of the water. The nearer fisherman swore irritably. His sea boots stamped against floorboards as he set his weight to his work; had he looked up, he would have seen Emien leave the bow. But, absorbed by their labor, neither brother noticed the fugitive they had rescued from Elrinfaer bend and search out the flensing knife stowed in the forward sail locker.

Only Jaric watched as quivering, blistered fingers tightened over the steel. Then the air surrounding Emien's body rippled, as if wind stirred curtains of light made visible. The boy's form shimmered with a glow similar to the aura which had surrounded the Stormwarden of Elrinfaer when Jaric had observed through the Llondel's perception. Yet, although related to power, this configuration was *other*, evil in itself. Plainly Taen's brother had inherited Tathagres' affinity for demon possession.

Jaric shouted, but in the half-world of the Llondel's dream, his voice made no sound. Reminded that he experienced nothing more than a prescient image, he watched helplessly as Emien wrenched the knife from the wood. The reddish aura flickered, strengthened, became a hard-edged veil of force. Infused by a rush of demon strength, Emien lunged and sank his blade in the back of the nearest fisherman. Hands slackened on the nets. Twine grated over wood, reclaimed by the sea, and the man slumped against the gunwale with a gurgling cry. Blood snaked across his oilskins, black in the lanternlight. With a yell of outrage and surprise, his brother spun around. He glimpsed a fevered face, tangled hair blown back from a demented smile. Then Emien's knife found his chest. The fisherman toppled backward into the silvery mass of his catch.

The boat rocked, unbalanced by the sharp shift of weight. Amid a hellish whirl of shadows, Emien cast the net free. Weights rattled and splashed into the sea. The man's dying struggles sank slowly beneath the waves as, heartlessly practical, Emien kicked the second corpse overboard. He moved aft and took the tiller. The fishing boat ducked, swung, and jibed. Canvas banged taut with a clattering crash of blocks, and the compass needle steadied on a northerly heading.

Guided by Llondian prescience, Jaric peered futureward through a stormy crossing that ended far north on the shores of Felwaithe. There the beloved black-haired brother of Taen Dreamweaver debarked, met at last by the masters who had chosen him for service. Haggard after his weeks upon the sea, Emien stumbled across the sand, to be caught by the waiting hands of demons.

Jaric whispered denial, in vain. Powerless to influence the course of events, he watched Kor's Accursed lift Emien onto a litter and bear him off to the northeast. The image rippled, changed. Jaric saw beyond the borders of Keithland to a vista of windswept rock. There the land lay barren, unchanged as the desolation before the Great Fall; nothing lived but the sparse growth of lichens. Outlined by empty sky, demon masters bore Emien up the slope of a jagged crag. A fortress reared from the summit, all gray angles and spindled tiers of towers. Overwhelmed by despair, Jaric beheld the keep and knew, though never in life had he gone there. Legend named that castle Shadowfane, prison of the damned and the stronghold of demon might. If Emien ever emerged, his purpose would be the ruin of his own kind.

CHAPTER IV

King of Pirates

Jaric awoke to a fine, soaking rain. Water dripped from his hair, spilled coldly through his fingers, and trickled across the rock beneath. The Llondian's dream left him desolate; trouble would come from Shadowfane, trouble such as Keithland had never known. His own responsibility could no longer be denied. Once he might have prevented the murder of the fishermen, even spared Emien the damnation of Shadowfane's dark halls. Huddled in the misty darkness of the ledge, Jaric wished he could forget the moment the Keys had been reclaimed on the shores of Elrinfaer; then he had held Emien at bay beneath the naked point of a sword, yet not struck home. Unmanned by the sister's grief and his own reluctance to kill, he had hesitated. Jaric bit his lip. No good would come from that moment of mercy. In letting Emien escape he had only left the demons another tool to work evil upon Keithland.

Slowly, stiffly, Jaric sat up. No orange eyes glared at him through the darkness. The ledge was deserted, empty rock silvered by a patina of water. The Llondel demon had gone. Free to leave, Jaric knew an instant of sharp distrust. Only when he ascertained that the Keys to Elrinfaer and the stormfalcon's feather remained safe beneath his tunic did he relax enough to assess his position. Drawn by a faint gleam, he discovered his knife on the stone, its handle neatly turned toward him. Nearby lay a second object.

Jaric leaned forward. Pebbles grated beneath his thigh as he transferred his weight and cautiously touched the dagger. No Llondian appeared to prevent him. Jaric closed his fingers over the hilt with a grateful sense of relief. He sheathed the weapon swiftly. The other item waited, forbidding and pale as bone in the dark. Jaric preferred to go without touching it; but his mistake with Emien at Elrinfaer had taught him never to leave an unknown peril at his back.

Jaric explored the object with tentative fingers. The surface felt strangely warm, as if it had recently lain close to living flesh. Carved of wood, and chased with fine whorls of inlaid shell, the thing was recognizable as a flute. Twelve holes pierced its shaft, spaced for alien fingers. Prompted by intuition not entirely his own, Jaric understood that the instrument had been left for him to use at need. If he sounded the highest note of the scale, he could summon Llondelei aid.

Alarmed by the perception, Jaric flinched. Only demon imaging could prompt an explanation of the gift. No doubt the creature lurked nearby, out of sight, yet watching still. Made cautious by fear, Jaric hesitated. No man dared trust a demon, and possession of any Llondian artifact could bring a charge of heresy within the civilized borders of Keithland. Harmless or not, the demon's gift must be refused.

Jaric returned the instrument to the niche and rose. Poisoned by mistrust, he suspected the dreams. His recent exchange with Anskiere's consciousness might all have been an illusion wrought by Llondian imaging. Possibly the creature had sought to relax his guard, undermine the tenets of his own kind, and, as with Emien, bring about his downfall. Though soaked to the skin and aching with stiffened muscles, Jaric flattened himself against the escarpment. He resumed his climb to the ice cliffs with driven determination.

Though the worst of the ascent lay behind, rain-slicked rocks made treacherous footing. Cold had slowed his reflexes, and a misstep could tumble him over the brink, send him crashing down jagged granite to drown, broken, amid the savage maelstrom of breakers and reefs. Jaric inched forward. The smell of seaweed soured his lungs as he breathed. The ledge sloped upward, to widen gradually into an outthrust shelf of rock. Anskiere's prison arose beyond, white ramparts dirtied by drifting fog.

Jaric felt dwarfed to insignificance in that place. Surf reared up, crested, smashed into foam against the ice; the cliffs amplified the hiss of falling spray until it sounded immediately underfoot. Wind sighed over the crags, driving rain that trickled coldly down Jaric's collar. When he had received Anskiere's summons before, the Stormwarden had called to him in words shaped of wind. Jaric had listened against a silence so complete even the sea seemed muted. But this time the elements reflected only the random patterns of storm and tide. No breeze, no word, and no welcome awaited the boy who carried the Keys to Elrinfaer.

Chilled and disheartened, Jaric braced his back against the rock face. "Anskiere!"

His shout reverberated across the chasm, lost amid drumming waves. Jaric lacked the heart to try a second time. No spoken word could reach the Stormwarden of Elrinfaer, and with a heavy sense of foreboding the boy suspected the Llondel's vision might be accurate. *Keeper of the Keys* the demon had named him; the title left him bitter. Nothing in life had prepared him for such responsibility. Since the day Anskiere's geas overtook him, he had acted without thought or strategy, forced to complete the sorcerer's bidding within a framework not of his shaping. Now, chilled by the discomforts of rain and fog, Jaric fought to choose for himself. He would seek his own course instead of answering power with like power; rather than attempt the Cycle of Fire with its ruinous train of consequences, he would search until he found some other solution. Surely somewhere in Keithland an alternative existed to answer the threat of the demons.

More alone than he had ever been before, Jaric laced icy fingers over his face. He knew the perils. Each hour that passed lent the demons of Shadowfane time to design against him; more than his own peace might shatter before he finished. One day Taen Dreamweaver would learn of her brother's alliance with the enemy; her Vaere-trained talents made discovery inevitable, for no mortal on Keithland could hide truth from her dream-sense. Despite her exceptional courage, the grief of Emien's defection might break her. Of all risks, that one galled Jaric most sorely. If he ever completed his search, he swore as Firelord's heir he would shelter her.

Dawn broke dingy and gray through the drizzle which fell over Cliff-haven. Half-buried in the oiled-wool cloak lent by the Kielmark, Taen Dreamweaver perched on a rock above the tide mark, waiting. Jaric would return shortly. She knew without extending her powers; since the Vaere had employed her talents to lure Jaric into the bindings of Anskiere's curse against Ivain, the Dreamweaver perhaps understood the Firelord's heir better than he knew himself. Yet the effects of that betrayal had scarred the boy, and bitterness and distrust still shadowed their friendship. With Jaric, Taen dared not delve deeply. He knew her touch, and far too much of Keithland's safety lay balanced in his hands for her to risk any chance of upset. She sat patiently through rain and the lingering shadow of night until Jaric chose to come down.

Daylight brightened the sky above the ice cliffs. Gulls banked and swooped on the air, scavenging morsels the tide had left amid rain-blurred profiles of rock. Taen peeled wet hair off her cheek and tugged her maroon hood forward to shield her face from the wind. The smell of soaked wool mingled with tide wrack and damp. She barely noticed her cold feet. Brushed inwardly by a change subtle as shifting current, she smiled for the first time in days; for, on a ledge above her vantage point, Jaric rose and finally began his descent. He weathered his disappointment well, thought Taen. She sighed with relief. A touch of color returned to her cheeks, and she lifted blue eyes to the cliffs where Jaric would soon reappear. Although the Vaere had rebuked Taen often for her impetuous nature, she could not help but hope. Both Anskiere's deliverance and Keithland's future depended on Ivainson's mastery of the Cycle of Fire.

The darkest hours of night had passed more easily than those last minutes while Jaric descended the ice cliffs. Taen rose as he leaped the last yard to the strand. He stumbled on landing, muscles stiffened from chill. Light hair tumbled down over his eyes in the rain. Even from a distance Taen could see that he shivered.

"Jaric!" Breaking waves drowned her call. Irritated, the Dreamweaver raised her voice again. "Jaric!"

He stopped and looked up, brown eyes wide with surprise. Pleased he had not detected her surveillance through the night, Taen muffled a grin behind one wool-draped wrist and ran to meet him.

She arrived breathless at his side and, tilting her face up to look at him, saw exhaustion stamped across his features. "You've got fish-brains between your ears." Her hands seemed childishly small as she worked loose the brooch which pinned her cloak. The moment the fastening freed, she flicked the wool open and bundled Jaric inside; the Kielmark's garment was generous enough to accommodate both of them.

"I'm soaked!" he protested.

"Fish-brains!" The word transformed to a gasp as the seal-wetness of him penetrated the dry layers of Taen's shift. "No, you don't," she added as Jaric tried to draw away. "You'll hate it more if I have to feed you broth in bed."

He did not smile, which was unlike him. Instead he glanced at the big, square-cut ruby which adorned the cloak pin. Taen felt him tense.

"That's the Kielmark's," Jaric said sharply. "He knows you're here?"

"Fish-brains is too generous," Taen replied. Warned by her dream-sense that contact with her body was adding to Jaric's uneasiness, she loosened the cloak slightly. "When his Lordship the King of Pirates noticed you'd left his banquet without permission, he shouted like a mad-man and told half his captains to arm themselves directly and look for you. I offered to come in their place. I told him I already knew where to find you." Jaric would know her words were understatement. The Sovereign Lord of Cliffhaven was about as easy to influence as a rabid wolf, particularly concerning strangers who trespassed on his island domain.

Yet Jaric did not probe beneath her light humor. In tight-lipped silence he lifted the brooch from her hand, then rammed the pin violently through the collar of the cloak. When he spoke, he answered the question she dared not voice; and the real reason behind the Kielmark's short-tempered concern: would he accept his heritage as Ivain Firelord's heir, or would he abandon the Stormwarden to the ice and leave Keithland in jeopardy?

"I'm going to the libraries at Landfast." Jaric paused, expecting rebut-tal. Taen held her breath, waited with patience like sword steel until he resumed. "If there is a way for me to avoid repeating the sorrows my father loosed upon men, I will find it without mastering the Cycle of Fire."

He took a sudden step forward. Taen stumbled against him as the cloak between them snapped taut. Reminded of her presence, Jaric flung an arm about her shoulders to steady her. "I'm sorry, little witch." He phrased the nickname with affection. "But I'm weary of the ways of sor-cerers."

Argument would not move him. Taen suspected he kept something from her, but the resistant set of his jaw warned against using her Dream-weaver's skill to probe deeper. If she attempted to tamper with his deci-sion, she would strike where he was guarded, so deeply did he resent the fact that he was puppet to a sorcerer's geas. Worn by more than her night-long vigil, Taen dragged her feet through the sand.

Jaric's fingers tightened against her sleeve. He freed his other hand and gently tucked an ink-black strand of her hair back under the hood. "Shall we return this cloak to the Kielmark before he sends one of his bloodthirsty captains to collect it?"

Taen nodded, resigned. She would have to trust him. The struggle to recover the Keys to Elrinfaer had opened new depths in Jaric; his decision to research at Landfast did not entirely disown responsibility. Still, the choice brought little reassurance. If Ivainson found no alternate answer, if Keithland's threat became imminent, with the Cycle of Fire the only choice left to ensure mankind's survival, Taen foresaw an unpleasant consequence: the Vaere might command her to betray him, just as she had done once before.

The weather grew worse as the day progressed. By the time Jaric caught and bridled his horse, rain battered the earth in white sheets. Leaving the cloak to Taen, he helped her into her saddle, then swung astride his own mount. Bent against a whipping north wind, he reined around toward the main fortress of Cliffhaven. Taen endured the ride, uncharacteristically silent as the horses carried them inland. The terrain sloped upward. Dune grass gave way to thornbrakes, and rocks thrust through mossy tufts of ground cover. The hills beyond lifted into serried ranks of mountains, and cedar-crowned summits reared above valleys choked with fog. The air warmed as the ice cliffs fell behind. The horses scattered droplets from sweetfern and wildflowers, and splashed through streams in the fells. One league from the beach, the two riders broke through to the cliff road where the horses made better speed. Hooves clattered over a beaten track shored up with stone, built to allow fast passage for the Kielmark's patrols. Well before midday, Jaric and the Dreamweaver pulled their steaming mounts to a walk beneath the flint-black walls of the harbor fort.

Jaric led toward the town side entrance, a cramped archway which pierced the fortifications between the matching black turrets of the gate towers. Rain glistened over rounded, weather-scarred stone. Beyond the crenellations loomed the angled roofs of artisans' alley, shops and forges jammed like blocks against the steep pitch of the slope.

Jaric drew rein before the wall. As Taen stopped her horse beside him, he shook the water from his hair and inclined his head toward the town. "You go in. I'm going on to the harbor."

A sudden clang of metal from the gatehouse obscured Taen's protest. Both riders started in surprise as a siege shutter crashed back.

A bearded guardsman leaned out. "You'll both come in," he shouted. "Kielmark's orders. He sent me along to escort you."

Jaric's mouth flinched into a line. He touched heels to his mount. Hooves banged on wet cobbles as his horse sidled around to face Taen. "You didn't," he accused.

Taen shook her head, at first unable to speak over the din as the guardsman wrestled the siege shutter closed. "I told the Kielmark I would find you, no more. He summons us through no act of mine."

The officer reappeared in the shadow beneath the archway. "Hurry along!" His shout sounded surly. "The watch already sent word of your return, and the Kielmark waits."

Jaric did not obey. His brown eyes remained intently fixed upon Taen, and his heels made no move in the stirrups. The Dreamweaver shifted uncomfortably in the saddle. Her fingers clamped on the reins until her horse shook its neck in protest. To defy the command would be madness; the Kielmark was ruthlessly swift to punish inefficiency, and the rogues who served him often killed rather than provoke his anger. The officer strode impatiently from the archway. Raindrops caught like jewels in his mail as he closed his hand over his sword hilt. Even then Taen dared engage no dreamweaver's power to search Jaric's reason for delay. If Ivainson were ever to trust her again, her word alone must suffice.

The officer hissed through his teeth. "Have you both gone *crazy*?" He spoke out in genuine dismay, and with a start of relief Taen recognized his voice.

"Corley?" She twisted in the saddle to be certain. Rain had darkened the man's beard to burnt chestnut; a mouth customarily crooked with laughter now bent into a grim scowl of annoyance. No ordinary officer of the watch, Deison Corley was the Kielmark's most trusted senior captain. His presence could not be ignored.

"Jaric," Taen pleaded. "Will you come?"

The boy accepted the fact that he was beaten with open reluctance. A shiver whipped his frame as he reined his horse toward the gatehouse. Taen's animal needed no incentive to follow. Corley saw his charges turn, and ran to escape the downpour before his last dry patch of clothing became sodden. He preceded them under the arch, his surcoat mottled with damp across broad shoulders.

"Kor!" The captain's clipped north-shore accent lifted over the confined echo of hooves. "I should have the both of you back to polish gear after this. Two things the Kielmark hates alike, and that's rust on his ships or his officers' swords."

Taen grinned beneath her dripping hood. The complaint was all bluff and banter; Corley, she knew, kept whetstone and rag in his pockets. During idle moments he maintained the disconcerting habit of sharpening his knives one after another in succession. Once, during a lengthy council of war, Taen had counted nine separate blades on his person; barracks rumor claimed there were more.

Hunched against the weather, Corley glanced over his shoulder at Jaric. "Well," he said to the stiff-faced boy. "Ride at my back, mad as all that, and I'd sure feel less nervous if you'd swear."

The quip raised no response. The storm met them with a white wall of water on the far side of the archway, and Jaric rode in bitter silence.

Battered by wind and discomfort, the party passed through narrow, switch-back streets to the Kielmark's inner stronghold. Jaric stumbled badly when he dismounted. Only then did Taen realize his behavior stemmed partly from chill. Exhausted after his nightlong vigil on the ice cliffs, the boy was numbed to the point where mind and muscle would barely respond. Taen called upon her powers as Dreamweaver and touched Corley's mind with concern.

The captain's eyebrows rose. He flashed Jaric a startled glance and bellowed irritably for the horse-boy.

But the child on duty ran from the stables already. He caught the reins Corley flung with deft efficiency, relieved Taen of her mare, and jerked his head at Jaric's gray. "Let that one go. He's battle-trained to stand."

"On, then." Corley caught Jaric's arm in a firm grip and steadied the boy's first steps. Bent against the downpour, Taen followed the two of them across the rain-sleek slate of the bailey.

"Kor *damn* the weather!" Corley stepped through the vaulted arches from the dooryard. "Made just to please the ducks."

Blotting his face on his surcoat, he marked puddled footsteps the length of the hallway beyond. Taen shed her cloak as she walked, and nearly repeated Corley's oath as a thick lock of hair snagged on the Kielmark's ruby pin. She worried at the tangle with her head tilted sideways, out of habit veering toward the entrance to the main hall.

"No, Lady," said Corley without turning around. Cued to the Dream-weaver's change in direction by the sound of her footsteps, he added more kindly, "The Kielmark waits in his private study."

Taen yanked her hair free of the brooch and irritably hurried to catch up while the captain steered Jaric up a short flight of steps. She followed the length of a corridor floored with gold-veined marble. The ironbound door at the end lay ajar, firelight shining through the crack.

Corley shouldered the panel open without knocking. "I have the both of them, Lord, sopped as fishes, but secure."

The door swung wide, revealing a patterned expanse of carpet, carved chairs, and tables untidily sprawled with charts. Flame-light glanced over gilt carving and curled parchment, and cast crawling shadows across walls lined with books. No method attended their shelving; Cliffhaven castle held priceless treasure, plundered and gathered as tribute from ships which hailed from the farthest corners of Keithland. But the owner cared nothing for neatness. A pearl and lacquer side table supported a box of rusty horseshoes, and a smiling marble cherub danced with the Kielmark's buck-ler and great sword slung across its wings.

A man muscled to match that weapon rose from behind the charts. Candles flickered in the draft from the door, spattering light over eyes pale and restless as a wolf's. Beneath wavy black hair, the Sovereign Ruler of Cliffhaven wore an expression ominous as thunderheads. "You're late," he opened sharply. "The watch reported twenty minutes ago." Rubies sparkled in the torque at his throat as he moved around the table.

Corley offered no excuse, but turned and gently latched the door. Long years in the Kielmark's service had taught him when to keep silent. Left facing Jaric, the Lord of Cliffhaven treated the boy to a glance of rapacious intensity. Then he crossed the chamber in three fluid strides.

"Young fool." The Kielmark caught Jaric's shoulder, spun him deftly into a chair, and bellowed for a servant to bring mulled wine. Then he gestured for Taen and Corley to be seated.

"Don't mind the wet clothes," he barked as Taen hesitated. "There are plenty more pretty chairs in the warehouses by the dockside."

Taen sat, wincing with the abused brocade. As the candle flames steadied and brightened, she noticed that the Kielmark's leather tunic was creased and soiled with ship's tar; his nails were rimmed with dirt, and his hair lay in soggy curls against his neck. No doubt he had come directly from the wharf, where his men shortened docklines against the rising wind.

Restless as live coals, the Kielmark paced before the hearth. Although his face lay in shadow, his displeasure could be felt the breadth of the room. He stopped without warning and spoke. "Kor's Fires, boy, the Dreamweaver told us you wouldn't raise Anskiere. Did you have to stay out sulking all night?"

Jaric stiffened, and Taen stifled a cry behind her knuckles.

Before she could speak, the Kielmark rounded on her, eyes slitted with keen speculation. "Ah, so you didn't tell him."

Taen shook her head, annoyed to see her efforts wasted. As Jaric turned resentful eyes toward her, she tried desperately to mend the damage caused by the Kielmark's thoughtlessness. "You wouldn't have listened, Jaric. No matter what anyone said, you would have gone to the ice cliffs to see for yourself."

Yet Jaric misinterpreted. His grip tightened on the arms of his chair until the fingers stood white against the wood. Fair, wind-tangled hair dripped water down the line of a jaw just starting to show a beard. Barely eighteen, he was ill prepared to contend with the fate Ivain Firelord had bequeathed him. Caught by a moment of pity, Taen reached out with her powers, and brushed lightly through the surface of his mind in an instinctive desire to reassure.

Jaric felt her touch and flinched. Cut by his mistrust, and unpleasantly aware of how closely the Kielmark followed the exchange, Taen tried again. Her tone turned sharper than she intended. "Jaric, I needed no Vaerish sorceries to see your desire to be released from Anskiere's geas."

That moment the latch clicked. The Kielmark spun on light feet as the door opened and a grizzled servant entered with a tray. Wary of his master's mood, the man moved with maximum speed and no noise. He rested his burden by the box of horseshoes. The scent of spices and hot spirits filled the room as he began to pour from a cut-crystal carafe.

The Kielmark caught up the first tankard the instant it was full and personally handed the steaming drink to Jaric. "You're numbed witless from the cold, boy. A girl-child could knock you down with a rag doll."

Jaric lifted the tankard to his lips. He managed a shaky swallow, and a thin flush of color suffused his cheeks. The Kielmark folded his arms; as if softened by a woman's touch, his stance relaxed, and Taen sensed the tension leave him. Corley released a pent-up breath, pulled a knife from his boot, and with soft, rhythmic strokes scraped the blade across the whetstone in his other hand. As if the habit signaled safety, the servant resumed his duties.

"Now," said the Kielmark. Parchment crackled as he braced his weight against the chart table and swept a glance around the chamber. "Here is what I propose."

But his tone of voice suggested outright command. As Taen accepted mulled wine from the servant, she understood no debate would be tolerated. Corley knew also. His steel sang crisply under the pressure of his hands, and his deep, cinnamon eyes stayed shadowed under his lashes.

"My brigantine *Moonless* is provisioned and a full crew stands anchor watch." The Kielmark hooked his thumbs in his belt. "When the tide turns, she'll sail and take you both to the Isle of the Vaere under my flag."

Jaric perched his tankard between his knees. His cheeks flushed red in the firelight as he looked up. "No."

Corley's whetstone bit into steel with a clear and savage ring, and the servant fled from the chamber. Taen felt a stab of dread. Fearfully she watched the Kielmark's sword arm bunch until the muscles strained the stitches of his cuff.

"Boy, I didn't hear you say that."

"You will." Jaric lifted his chin with unprecedented composure. "My boat *Callinde* was a loan. She must be returned to a fisherman in Mearren Ard."

Deliberate as a cat, the Kielmark straightened. Corley's fingers froze on his knife, and the whetstone's whispered stroke went silent. Taen's skin prickled with alarm. With the sensitivity of her dream-sense upset by an overpowering threat of violence, she saw Jaric must desist, or risk destruction. She acted without thought, and initiated the rapport shared through the dangerous recovery of the Keys to Elrinfaer. For she knew the single fact which could forestall his headlong course and protect him from the Kielmark's wrath. Given no time to soften fact, Taen balanced her gift, bent Jaric's mind to a place leagues distant, and forced him to see.

Under her influence, the chamber rippled, transformed, became a misty shore haunted by the dissonant cries of gulls. In the smoke-dimmed interior of a shack which reeked of fish, a girl wept over the body of an elderly man. Closed in death, his eyes no longer shone with the piercing clarity of a sailor; work-crippled hands lay slack against mottled, silver-tipped furs costly enough to clothe a prince.

Through the rapport of the dream-link, Taen felt the echo of Jaric's shock as he recognized the girl and her uncle. His grief cut like a cry through darkness, for the man, Mathieson Keldric, had once answered a boy's desperate need and traded his only treasure for a cloak of ice otter fur he had not wanted. Repaired and seaworthy, *Callinde* had sailed; Jaric had been spared, but the loss of a beloved boat had broken the old man's heart.

The link shattered, dissolved into firelight and book-smell as Jaric wrenched free. "Kordane's Blessed Fires!" He turned tortured eyes to Taen, and she read there a desperation beyond her ability to fathom. "You might have spared me that!"

She stared at the carpet, her toes jabbed angrily into patterned wool. Tears stung her lashes. She held them back, determined Jaric should not see. Spare him she could not; had he persisted in sailing for Mearren Ard, the Kielmark would have lost his temper, and in the unpredictable reaction which followed, the Firelord's sole heir might easily have been killed.

"So," the Kielmark concluded. Muscle rippled under his tunic as he braced one arm against the mantel. "You'll not be sailing to return your craft to a corpse."

Jaric sat spear-straight in his chair. Steam drifted from his tankard, wound lazy ribbons through the air before him. "Neither will I sail for the Isle of the Vaere. I'm going to Landfast to study the libraries instead."

Corley stopped breathing. The Kielmark released a great, rowdy laugh, but the sound held menace like barbs wrapped in velvet. "I'd kill you," he said simply.

"I'd let you." Jaric's hands remained motionless in his lap. He held the Kielmark's furious gaze and his voice continued, passionless as ice water through the charged atmosphere of the room. "Better I died, I think, than accept the madness, the recklessness, and the cruelty of my father's heritage."

The Kielmark's brows knotted. His eyes narrowed in surprise and he glanced swiftly at Taen.

The enchantress nodded, dream-sent a spurious message much as she had when in the heat of the battle she had helped defend Cliffhaven against the demons. *'He means it, Lord. Jaric has been pressured as much as a man can be, and still believe in himself. Remember and be cautious. He faced down the Stormwarden before you, and lost.'*

The Kielmark stretched like a dog kicked out of sleep. He ran thick fingers through his hair and suddenly grinned. "You're a bold one, I'll give you that," he said to Jaric. "And more like Ivain than you'd know, there's fact if ever you discover manhood enough to face it." His manner changed, abruptly turned to challenge. "Why Landfast?"

Jaric drew a shaky breath and spoke over the careful scrape of Corley's knife. "I intend to find an alternative answer to sorcery."

"Ah." The Kielmark pushed off from the mantel, began restlessly pacing the rug. "Then you'll sail there on *Moonless,* and Corley will captain."

Jaric made a slight sound. Before Taen could gather a shred of power in defense, the Kielmark plucked the sword from the cherub's back. Steel sang from his sheath with killing speed. In one spinning instant, the bare blade lay poised against Jaric's neck. Corley froze in place. Taen felt her hands break into sweat. With painstaking control she balanced her awareness, knowing all the while her powers were useless. Whether or not she stunned the Kielmark unconscious, the sword lay too close for safety. If the hand that held the weapon loosened, the weight of the blade alone would cut the flesh beneath.

The Kielmark spoke into sudden stillness, his voice barely audible over the snap of the fire in the grate. "You'll listen, Firelord's heir." His fist tightened; steel pressed against Jaric's skin, drawing a thin bead of blood. "One hundred and eighty-four of *my best men* lie dead because of the Keys to Elrinfaer. I'll not repeat the experience, not for pride or any man's protest. Where you go, the Keys go. Demons and trouble will follow like sharks on a gaffed fish. You know this."

The Kielmark's wrists flexed, and the sword lifted so abruptly the edge sang through the air. "You may have your time at Landfast. But only if you and that Dreamweaver board *Moonless* at once. There's a man waiting at the docks with a longboat. If you wish, your sloop *Callinde* may go along in tow, but you'll sail *nowhere* without my escort. Am I clear?"

Jaric swallowed, nodded, and touched a finger to the tiny drop of blood on his neck. Beside the Kielmark's great bulk, he seemed slight to the point of fragility. His brown eyes turned poignant with uncertainty, as if he doubted his choice. Yet at length he stirred and stood.

"So," said the Kielmark. He sounded strangely tired. "You're dismissed."

Like a warning, Corley's whetstone and knife stayed silent. Taen set her tankard down. Her hands shook and she dreaded the act of standing. Sapped by a sudden, fervent desire to be safely back on the Isle of the Vaere, she shut her eyes to regain her composure. A touch smoothed the hair against her shoulder. Taen looked, found Jaric before her with one hand extended. He half lifted her to her feet. Through his wiry strength, she felt the tremors which shook him; but whether he shivered from cold or the aftermath of fear she could not tell.

"Corley, I want a word with you." The Lord of Cliffhaven rested his sword point downward against the carpet. He stared through the rain-washed glass of the casement, and did not move until Dreamweaver and Firelord's heir had departed.

CHAPTER V

Crossing

The latch clicked shut, and the sound of footsteps dwindled down the passage beyond the Kielmark's study. The Lord of Cliffhaven sheathed the sword he had turned upon Jaric and carefully lowered his muscled bulk into the nearest chair. Light from the candelabra fell full across his face, illuminating abrasions and bruises left over from his ruse to defeat Kisburn's army. Four days with too little rest had not encouraged healing. Deison Corley studied the Kielmark's pose with perception well honed by familiarity, and at once understood what the effort with the sword had cost. The captain bent with all the tact he possessed and sheathed his dagger in his boot. Then, absorbed by the movement of his hands, he straightened, flicked his wrist, and caught the slender blade which slithered from his sleeve. With what seemed limitless patience, he set steel against whetstone and began rhythmically to hone the point.

"That boy is a brash one," the Kielmark said presently.

Corley scraped his blade across stone and grimaced. "Got a will like one of Tierk's new anchor chains. And the girl's no different. Ever wonder how old she was when the Vaere took her for training?"

"Taen?" The Kielmark rested his chin on his fist. "She told me once." His voice resumed quietly over the whispered ring of the dagger. "The last memory she had before her passage into mastery was that of a ten-year-old girl."

Corley's hands faltered, stopped. "Kor's Fires!" But blasphemy was inadequate; with an incredulity that prickled the hairs on his neck, the captain recalled Taen's part in the recent battle against Kisburn's army. She might wear the body of a grown woman, but in years and worldly experience, she was poignantly, vulnerably young. "Did you know her age before you asked her to dream-weave those defenses?"

"No," said the Kielmark abruptly. With Corley he made no effort to school his manner. "Count on this, though. The Vaere themselves are desperate. Jaric is their final hope for Anskiere."

Steel sheared ringingly across whetstone. Corley remained silent, aware as no stranger could be that orders were forthcoming.

The Kielmark straightened without warning. "You will sail *Moonless* to Landfast. Place Jaric in the hands of Kor's priests, for trouble will nest with him like swarming wasps and he mustn't be caught defenseless in the countryside. I want the Dreamweaver clear of danger. She broke her oath with the Vaere to remain here and save Cliffhaven. Guard her life as you would my own, and return her to the Isle of the Vaere."

Corley set his whetstone on his knee and laid the little knife aside. He knew the Lord of Cliffhaven well enough to expect more instructions.

The Kielmark rose. Propped by one arm against the edge of the table, he fished beneath horseshoes and with a clanking jangle of metal, retrieved a leather sack. This he tossed to his captain. Corley stretched and fielded the object without upsetting knife and whetstone. Coins chimed as he thrust the bag beneath his tunic.

Across the room the King of Pirates stared at sky through the casement. "Someone well versed in arms made sure that Jaric carries a very fine sword. Corley, you must see he finishes learning how to use it. Instruct him during the crossing to Landfast. When you make port, use the gold to hire the city's most skillful weapons master. He will pose as a tutor, but actually serve Jaric as bodyguard. The boy is not to know. Let him believe his teacher saw talent, and chose a gift to develop it."

Cued by a shift in his master's stance, Corley slipped his whetstone in his pocket. He sheathed the knife with an almost imperceptible movement and stood, awaiting the Kielmark's final instructions.

"Make a safe passage, old friend." The King of Pirates clapped Corley's shoulder in a rare gesture of concern. "I'd trust this task to no other."

"Fires." Corley rolled his eyes at the ceiling, a devilish grin on his lips. "You would've, and for a song, too, if Selk's old hag of a wife hadn't tripped on that hen and done herself in with a pothook. One yell from her, even demons'd flee. Any kid old enough to eat meat would've taken to weapons in self-defense."

The Kielmark rewarded him with a genuine shout of laughter. "Get out," he said, gasping. "Warp *Moonless* out of the harbor, or I swear I'll attach Selk's wife's maiden sister to your pay share!"

Corley laid his hand on the latch. "Don't. She's community property. We're saving her for the light tower in case the fog bells ever crack." And he spun through the door before the Kielmark's quick mind could find a rejoinder.

The rain abated, but wind arose to replace it, whining through the stays and rattling *Callinde*'s mast and yard with the abandon of a madman drumming sticks. Docklines creaked against the bollards as Jaric stepped aboard. Bundled in a cloak of green, hand-spun wool, he knelt on the floorboards and set both hands against the sternpost. The wood was checked and gray; the marks of the tools which shaped it had long since worn away, battered out by a generation of weather. The fingers which had done the carving now lay cold, forever stilled.

Jaric bent his head, vision marred by wet lashes. "I'm sorry," he said, as if the old boat could hear in place of the crippled fisherman Taen's dream-image had revealed in death. "I never intended to keep her."

A gust slammed the dock and *Callinde* rolled, lines groaning with strain. Jaric sank down beneath the lee of the thwart. He stared at palms scabbed over with blisters from the steering oar, record of his storm-ridden crossing from Mearren Ard. He drew breath into his lungs, and felt trapped, felt selfish to be alive after the sacrifices others had made to see him safely to this moment. Once he had excused himself on the grounds of the Stormwarden's cruelty; but since the Llondel's intervention, that defense no longer sheltered. Anskiere's decision to call the heir of Ivain into service had been founded on nothing but compassion and desperate need.

Jaric clenched fingers into fists. A solution must lie at Landfast; he had to search, and quickly, before the demons completed their work with Emien and struck again. If he refused the Cycle of Fire without finding an alternative to defend the Keys to Elrinfaer, then, in accepting *Callinde* to complete Anskiere's summons, Jaric saw that his actions had murdered the fisherman, Mathieson Keldric, as surely as if he had knifed the old man directly. Tears were useless. Grief would mend nothing. The niece who had woven the cloak on Jaric's back would mourn, and marry, and eventually forgive the ruin he had caused. But rocked by the lift of the swell under *Callinde*'s keel, the boy understood he could never make peace with Mathieson's memory until he had accomplished the legacy of Ivain.

A shout rang out from the shore. *Moonless*'s boatswain waited with a line and a longboat to warp *Callinde* from the wharf. Jaric rose and made his way forward, running a hand along the thwart for balance. Worn, net-scarred planking contrasted with the sharper edge of new timber; though built to an ancient design, the craft was sound and well tested by the sea. Still Jaric fretted, checking the tension on the rigging and fussing to be sure each halyard was cleated. Once she was under tow, no one would be aboard to ensure *Callinde*'s safety.

Boots clumped on the dock. "Tide's turnin' lad. Corley's crackin' his knuckles on the quarterdeck, an' it's the crew who'll suffer if he heats up."

Jaric nodded. Wind fanned pale hair across the collar of his cloak as he bent to secure a locker. But the gear inside had shifted somehow and pressed the cover askew. The latch would not quite close. "I'll be a minute."

"Going t'fasten lines, then," said the boatswain. *Callinde* rocked under his weight as he stepped aboard.

Jaric opened the locker, reached to reorganize the contents, and instantly froze. *The ash flute he remembered from the ledge on the ice cliffs lay crosswise on top of the spare headsail.* But in the main harbor under the vigilant eyes of the Kielmark's sentries, how had a Llondian demon managed to leave it and go unobserved? Jaric drew a quick breath. Forward, the boatswain leaned over the bow threading towline. While the seaman's back was turned, the boy grabbed the demon's offering and flung it over the rail.

Delicate wood struck the sea with a splash, and its silver and shell decoration sank swiftly out of sight.

Jaric banged the locker closed. Mathieson's death left his confidence shaken; more than ever, he wished no help from demons. Caught by a queer surge of anger, the boy rammed the latch home and hastened to assist the boatswain.

Moonless sailed from Cliffhaven under full canvas and a sky scattered across with shredded drifts of storm cloud. Fair weather would bring a drop in wind; driving his command on a beam reach, Corley ordered the staysails set. As the boatswain bellowed instructions to the crew, the captain left his place by the wheel and paused at the stern rail, absorbed by the bobbing prow of *Callinde*.

Cautious of his mood, the quartermaster steered as if mesmerized by the compass. Canvas cracked overhead. *Moonless* shivered, heeled, and gathered speed as the staysails bellied taut. She sailed without incident through sunset into night, but Corley remained on deck. The Kielmark's order was simplicity itself. Why, then, could he not shake the feeling that trouble brewed like a storm front just beyond view over the horizon?

Yet at first the captain's apprehension seemed entirely unfounded; *Moonless* made swift and easy passage across the Corine Sea, her crew in good spirits, and her two passengers apparently secure. If Taen worried over her disobedience of the Vaere's directive, she appeared not to fret. Mornings she could be found clinging to the netting under the bowsprit, hair blowing in the breeze, and her laughing face drenched in spray. Mealtimes she teased the cook in the galley, and the off-watch crew corrupted her sense of fair play by teaching her to cheat at cards. The first mate especially liked to bait her until she blushed. He did so without fear of retaliation, until one night all on shipboard were disturbed by his yells of angry outrage. Taen was found by the scuttlebutt, crumpled helplessly with laughter. Under the amazed stares of the deckhands she admitted to filling the mate's berth with live fish. Called in to mediate, Corley belatedly recalled that the Dreamweaver had been raised on Imrill Kand, where bait and hooks were the staples of survival. Thereafter, he assigned her the task of filling the dinner pot with her talents, though the card games continued, with stakes of dried beans used for winnings.

Jaric smiled over Taen's popularity with the deckhands, but he did not join her antics. Corley's promise to the Kielmark kept the boy busy with sword and dagger, through exhausting hours of practice. A week passed, then two days more. His hands blistered, grew new layers of callus, and Corley's exacting instruction turned briskly unforgiving. Jaric sweated, striving to master his footwork while the captain hammered blow after blow against his guard. The sun shone hot on the deck, striking blinding reflections from the swells. Squinting against glare, neither tutor nor student noticed that Taen did not sit by the stern scupper with her lines, as she usually did in the morning. The quartermaster and the mate were aware; but with *Moonless* lying twenty-eight leagues from port, neither one thought to interrupt their duties to inquire why.

Taen lay in the heat of the stern cabin, hands pressed tight to her face. Above decks, she could hear the clang of swordplay, and Corley's voice exhorting Jaric to mind his guard. The drill had begun at daybreak, and near noon showed no sign of ending, though *Moonless*'s master estimated landfall by sundown.

"Watch it!" Steel chimed and stilled. "Your feint was too wide." Feet thumped planking. "Go again, Jaric, *move*."

The din resumed. Taen flinched and buried her ears in blankets. No matter how inclement the weather, Jaric's practice kept schedule. Ofttimes Corley drove the boy to exhaustion, yet Taen never heard a complaint. Ivainson did his best to learn. White-faced and determined, he persisted, though the roll of *Moonless* marred his control time and again; Corley battered him dizzy with ripostes and cursed him often for clumsiness. This morning, with the voyage all but over, the captain insisted on exchanging practice weapons for rapiers.

Metal scraped and parted. "Better," gasped Corley. A dagger clanged a cross guard, and something bumped the deck. "*Damn* you, boy, I said watch that footwork!"

The Dreamweaver *felt* rather than heard Jaric rise and lift his sword arm. A rapid exchange followed, the ring of tempered blades repeated over and over until Taen felt battered by the continuous onslaught of sound. Buried beneath the sea-dampened weight of her blankets, she sought the calm taught by the Vaere, that inflexible inner stillness she perfected to bring her Dreamweaver's talents into focus. Yet, oddly, the discipline of her craft served only to increase her disorientation. Swept by a rush of heat, Taen felt her ears ring as if with fever. The clash of swordplay thinned, suddenly faint as the jangle of the wind charms which hung from the eaves of the house where she had spent her childhood. Sifted through a febrile mesh of memory, the present slipped away. Corley's curses whirled like leaves in darkness.

Taen struggled to orient her dream-sense, separate vision from presence, and restore awareness of her cabin on board the brigantine. Control eluded her. Too late Taen recognized something amiss. Images swirled through her mind, fragmented glimpses of other people's lives drawn from the island of Innishari to the south. The bell of steel deepened in Taen's ears, gradually acquired the slower rhythm of a blacksmith's hammer. Heat burned her face, traced ruddy lines through a beard, *not her own*; yet even as she wrestled to regain her own identity, she felt the ache of sweating fingers clenched on iron tongs and turning a glowing horseshoe upon an anvil. The Dreamweaver snapped the link with a touch sharpened by fear. Yet as the smith's awareness faded, her perception did not return to normal. Tools transformed in her grasp, became the worn wood of a broom handle. Coal-fire cooled into the packed earth of a door stoop where a farm wife shooed six bedraggled hens from a measure of dried corn. The chickens took flight, squawking, and the air turned sickeningly around them. Taen blinked, whirled into the dusty, cluttered confines of a shop where a weaver wound gray wool on his shuttlecock. Desperate now, she banished the dream, firmly bent her mind away from the town and back to the clean, open sea.

Salt air slapped her face like wet cloth. Gasping, Taen centered her awareness, and immediately saw she had failed. *Moonless* plied westward, amid the archipelagoes of the Free Isles' Alliance. There the sun shone fair at the zenith and the islets scattered near Landfast notched the horizon. In place of this, her dream-sense had spilled her into a place of storm-tossed whitecaps and stark, pewter-gray swells which matched no sea where the brigantine sailed. Terrified, Taen tapped her reserves. Power flared and sparked, but would not answer; the image escaped her control like water through a sieve. Sliding downward into panic, Taen beheld an object awash on the breast of the swell. She thought it was a snarled length of fishing net negligently abandoned to the tide; until she noticed the catch which dragged between the painted marking of the floats. Showing through the twine were fingers, a jacket of rent oilskin, and boots.

Certain the corpse was a vision from her own past, Taen shouted, "Father!"

Yet, tossed over a crest, the body turned; foam subsided to reveal hair that was not black but fair, and trailed like weed across the swollen features of a stranger. Taen shuddered. Too shaken to struggle, she abandoned her mind to the vision. Mist drifted like gauze over the water, shrouding the net's grisly burden. Even as the fog thickened, Taen caught the glint of a knife sunk in the breast of the dead man's jacket. Before she could ponder the significance of the murdered fisherman the sight melted into featureless white, then gray; light drained out of the day, and night fell unbroken by lantern or star. Sound arose through that unnatural dark like bubbles from the depths of a well. Taen heard a door slam faintly, and footsteps. Someone's hand touched her shoulder; the blackness around her crackled. A sheet of fire shot across Taen's mind, blinding orange-gold and white with a heat which did not burn. Strangely, she felt none of the terror which had infused her earlier dreams. A human presence lay behind this conflagration; someone restless, intense, whose touch was nearly as familiar to her as that of the brother she had lost.

Taen started violently and woke, jarring her cheek against the bulkhead. "Jaric!"

"Are you all right, little witch?" His voice was filled with concern, and very close by.

Taen blinked, realized how severely she trembled. Not trusting her voice, she did not speak as Jaric drew her gently into the light which filtered through the salt-stained panes of the stern window. Disoriented and inexplicably cold, Taen looked up, met eyes whose brown lay shadowed under brows hooked into a frown. The ties of Jaric's shirt swung unlaced at his throat; his skin glistened, finely sheened with sweat, and his nostrils flared slightly, as if he was winded from recent exertion; normal enough if he had just left practice with Corley. But Taen sensed a detail out of harmony in the instant she touched his mind.

"I was on the way to fetch the ship's healer when I heard you cry out," said Ivainson. "Are you ill?"

There *was* something; his voice confirmed the fact. "No," said Taen. Brought fully and sharply awake, she shoved a hand into the crumpled blankets of the berth and sat up. "I had a nightmare, no more." She studied Jaric intently, but found nothing. Afraid he would leave before she could trace her suspicion, she qualified quickly to delay him. "I dreamed I saw a murdered fisherman floating in the waves."

Jaric stepped back, his expression abruptly guarded. But Taen noticed nothing beyond the crimson-splashed knuckles of the hand held pressed against his side. Her breath caught in her throat. "You're hurt!"

Jaric shrugged in immediate reassurance. "Only a little. Corley cursed me well for carelessness, and rightly. The mistake was mine."

His voice held jarring relief. Startled, Taen looked back to Jaric's face. Diverted by concern for his cut hand, she took a moment to recall the words she had used at need, which, surprisingly, had distressed him. Then she wondered why mention of a dead fisherman should prove so alarming. Jaric's stance suggested reluctance; he would refuse answer if she asked. Taen considered using her dream-sense. But that instant the lookout called from the masthead. *Moonless* crossed the perimeters of the Landfast defenses, the net of energies woven by the initiates of Kordane's brotherhood to ward against entrance by demons. Taen sensed the barrier as a prickle of cold force. For an instant she shivered, gripped by a power that ruthlessly tested her humanity; then the moment passed. Sunlight through the stern windows rinsed away the discomfort.

Jaric seized the interruption, backing hastily toward the companionway. "Have you ever seen the towers of Landfast?"

"No." Infected by his excitement, Taen kicked bare feet free of her blankets. "I'll meet you on the deck, but only after you've shown the healer that cut."

"Shrew," said Jaric. He grinned amiably. "Would you throw something at me if I refused?"

Taen brandished a fist. Jaric ducked in mock fright through the companionway and left her. As the door banged closed the Dreamweaver sighed, her pretense at levity abandoned. A force beyond her understanding or control had inflicted visions upon her; the event was no slight matter. She had disobeyed the directive of the Vaere, and if this was the first sign of the consequences, no strategy of the Kielmark's could aid her. Against mishaps by sorcery, all of Corley's skill with weapons and seamanship could offer no safety at all. Taen slipped unsteadily from her berth. Much as she valued her freedom, now, her return to the Isle of the Vaere could not happen quickly enough.

To Jaric, standing wind-whipped by *Moonless*'s rail, the towers of Landfast thrust like fat spearmen ranked against serried banks of cloud. Although he had never beheld the Free Isles before, the city which governed the Alliance had fascinated him ever since his apprenticeship as copyist in a backlands keep. Here lay the heart of human endeavor. Scholars claimed that the Landfast archives preserved even the mysteries of Kordane's Blessed Fires. Maintained by Kor's Grand High Grace and a staff of priests and initiates, the libraries contained the histories of all mankind, preserved since the Great Fall.

Familiar with the landmarks through a painting which had hung in Morbrith's copy chamber, Jaric touched Taen's arm and pointed out several slender, silver-domed spires which soared skyward from the central cluster of builders. "There, do you see? Those are the sanctuary towers of Kordane's shrine, where seventeen masters guard forbidden texts. The archivist who taught me said no woven cloth, nor any item which will sustain flame, is permitted in that place, and that the inner-circle brotherhood undertake a vow of isolation. They enter, never to leave."

Jaric fell silent, his face animated with wistful excitement. To a boy whose childhood had been limited to books and writing, Landfast held wonder and the promise of dreams. In bright sunlight, amid the bustle of sailhands and shouted commands, he could for a time forget the terrible burden which compelled him to visit these shores.

The wind freshened, then shifted northeast. Driven on a broad reach, *Moonless* shuddered under tautly curved canvas. She rounded the headland with her bowsprit and star-crowned figurehead glistening through flying sheets of spray; then, ducking like a haughty maiden, she jibed and bore down upon the light beacons marking the jetties which flanked the harbor entrance. Landfast lifted ahead like a jeweled diadem set of a sea-beaten headland of sandstone. Black against tawny bluffs, wharves, shops, warehouses, and fish shacks cluttered the shoreline beneath; and shadowed by the painted towers, the docks at the bay side teemed with boats of scattered shape and description, some inhabited, others packed to the thwarts with vendors and wares.

Corley called orders from the quarterdeck. Jaric roused from his reverie. He shed his shirt and passed it to Taen. Then he set his bandaged hand on the ratlines and swung himself up to join the topmen who clambered aloft to shorten sail. The cut on the back of his wrist did little to blunt his dexterity, and work on the main royal yard granted him a splendid view of the city, with its narrow twisting lanes, bronze statuary, and tiled courtyards.

Corley left the quarterdeck, and the mate called commands in his place.

Flying the scarlet and silver wolf which blazoned the Kielmark's standard, *Moonless* backed sail. She dropped anchor inside the barrier islet of
Little Dagley with the enviable precision that earmarked every vessel in
Cliffhaven's fleet. A crowd of frowning men clustered on the harbormaster's dock to watch. But no lighter launched to claim anchorage fees.
Hated, respected, feared, and left strictly alone, the Kielmark's vessels
plied every port in Keithland exempt from tolls or tariffs. Though merchants and officials complained waspishly, they voiced their bitterness out
of earshot. To arouse Cliffhaven's ill will brought ruin to trade, since any
shipping bound for eastern kingdoms must run the narrows of Mainstrait;
there the King of Pirates imposed an inflexible demand of tribute in
exchange for amnesty from his fleet of corsairs.

Last to descend from the rigging, Jaric found that the boatswain and
second watch had already launched a longboat. Corley stood with knuckles
buried in his beard, briskly selecting his oarsmen. Clad unfamiliarly in
dress colors, he wore bracelets on both arms and a maroon doublet with
the Kielmark's badge of rank embroidered in gold on his right shoulder.
But genteel trappings could not blunt his dangerous air of command; fine
cloth and hose only emphasized weapons whose hilts bore no ornamenta-
tion but the oiled sheen of purpose. As Jaric swung from ratlines to deck,
the captain called out to him.

"Fetch your things, boy. Shore party's nearly ready, and I've no mind
to linger in this port."

Jaric pushed past the crewmen, heading for the companionway and his
cabin. As he rounded the mainmast, he caught sight of a figure huddled in
shadow beyond. Taen sat on a bight of rope, hair tumbled like ink over
slim shoulders, and her face hidden behind clenched and bloodless fingers.
That, and an impression of unbreathing stillness about her person, roused
Jaric to sharp anxiety.

He hurried to her side. "Taen?"

She started slightly and looked up. Blue eyes remained unfocused in
her elfin face and her skin was chalk-pale. Her hands trembled; the instant
she noticed, she hid them in the crumpled cloth of her shift. "I left your
shirt on your berth. Better go there and gather your things. Corley's irritable." When Jaric hesitated, she forced a smile. "I'm going to miss you,
that's all."

Something very different troubled her. Only once before had she
sounded this strained, and that the time her brother had done murder.
But having had his innermost will overturned and bound to a sorcerer's
service, Jaric was wary of involving himself in the particulars of Vaerish
mysteries. He shrugged away concern with a forced grin. "Miss me? Not
likely, but when you leave, certain sailors on this vessel are going to be left
at a loss. What do you suppose they'll make of the beans they've hoarded
as winnings?" He paused and touched her thin shoulder. "You'll be safe
on the Isle of the Vaere."

Taen looked up, too quickly. At once Jaric knew he had been careless, that his distress over Emien's fate lay too near the surface of his thoughts. He ducked behind the blocks of the main halyard, and left before Taen's intuitive powers could probe his distress. In haste, he caught his heel in the line left flaked on the deck.

"Clumsy!" Taen called as he stumbled. "Watch out! You'll break your silly nose."

Jaric hurried on without rejoinder; and because for the second time that day her Dreamweaver's powers would not answer will or reason, Taen never guessed his silence was involuntary. Wrenched by the innocence in her upturned face, and the trembling fingers she had stilled with the same courage she had used to engineer Cliffhaven's defense, Jaric watched ocean, pinrail, and shrouds shatter through a lens of unexpected tears. He feared for Taen. He never realized how much until now. Her fragility never seemed so poignant, for once her brother reached Shadowfane, her presence would be known to the enemy. Landfast's great libraries must contain an alternative to the Cycle of Fire; if not, there would be no haven. Kor's Accursed would not rest until they had destroyed the Dreamweaver who had wrested away their conquest at Cliffhaven.

Taen was gone from the deck by the time Jaric returned. He carried sword, dagger, penknife, and a spare shirt bundled in the green folds of his cloak; heavy on the thong at his neck hung the Keys to Elrinfaer and the stormfalcon's feather. Looking for the Dreamweaver's dark head among the crewmen, Jaric found the longboat already laden and waiting. He cursed Corley's efficiency as the boatswain caught his elbow and impatiently steered him to the rail. "Get aboard, boy."

Reluctant to leave without saying farewell, Jaric grabbed the beaded wood and resisted. "Have you see Taen?"

The boatswain shook his head, copper earrings swinging. "Cap'n's temper's up," he warned. "Don't try him when he's hurrying." And he pushed Jaric firmly toward the battens.

Callused hands tugged Jaric's bundle free, tossed it carelessly down to the oarsmen in the longboat. Hustled from *Moonless*'s decks, Jaric descended into shadow and stumbled awkwardly into the rocking longboat below. The instant his feet touched floorboards, Corley ordered the craft cast off. Oar shafts bit into the sea. The strong backs of six crack seamen bent to their stroke, and Jaric half tumbled into the last empty seat.

His bundled weapons landed in his lap, thrown without gentleness by Corley. "Put on your sword belt, boy. I didn't blister your hands at practice these days only to see you robbed in the streets because you kept your steel swaddled in wool. Hereafter you'll *never* walk strange shores without arms, understand?"

Jaric bit his lip against anger. He rose, braced his knee against the aft oar bench, and buckled on sword and dagger while frantically searching the faces at *Moonless*'s rails. The officers had already begun to disperse the crew; Taen was not among them. Wedged uncomfortably between the bony frame of the ship's purser and an empty water cask, Jaric watched *Moonless* shrink astern as the pull of the oarsmen drove the longboat toward the main wharf at Landfast. The creak of leathers in the rowlocks and the rhythmic splash of the looms replaced conversation for what seemed a very long time.

"Boy?" said a voice over the rumble as the rowers shipped oars.

Jaric lifted his eyes from *Moonless*'s tracery of masts and saw the purser regarding him, hooked features keen with interest. "I'll tell the lass you looked for her."

Jaric considered the man's hooded eyes, then the clever fingers laced in his lap, their precise, waiting stillness seldom found in honest trade; rumor held that the purser had courted women and stolen their jewels before he took sanctuary on Cliffhaven. "Thank you," Jaric said, and left the issue there. He did not trust the man enough to add that Taen acted oddly, and might need help. On that matter the boy resolved to speak directly to Corley.

The longboat drifted to the wharf, caught and steadied against the swell by her forward oarsmen. Jaric rose at once. But blocked by men lifting casks, and buffeted in the swirling commotion of the landing, the boy took several minutes to reach the piling and pull himself onto the damp boards of the dock. He looked, but could not locate Corley's maroon tunic in the bustle. Though he called, his shout became lost amid the clatter of hooves and iron-rimmed cartwheels as two wagons passed on the street; whips cracked, and drovers yelled for clearance with deafening persistence.

"Cap'n's gone, boy," said the nearest of *Moonless*'s seamen through the tumult. He paused to tie a red scarf above his creased eyes. "In a hurry he was, to finish his business ashore." Misinterpreting Jaric's concern, he added, "Not to worry, then, he left instruction fer yer *Callinde*. She's to be towed in an' given free dockage, same's if she were one o' the Kielmark's own. Harbormaster'll tell you where. If he cusses, spit on his rugs and ignore it."

Jaric turned away from the seaman's grin. Bitterly concerned, he realized he would have to catch Corley in the streets. Not an instant remained for talk. Leaving the seaman, the boy dodged *Moonless*'s rolling water casks and ran. The wharf was a maze of activity. Forced to twist and duck through stacks of baled cargo and drying fish nets, and jostled by brawny, half-naked longshoremen, Jaric raced headlong for the town.

CHAPTER VI

Landfast

Crooked, narrow, and jammed with carts and stalls, the streets of Land-fast were a difficult place to locate a man in haste to finish an unknown errand. After running down three dead ends and tripping twice over the same grape seller's basket, Jaric abandoned his search for Corley. Frustrated, sweating, he braced his arm against the sun-warm bricks of a hostel to catch his breath.

The press of commerce swirled around him, overlaid by the spiel of a woman selling cakes for coppers. Two straining mules and a wagon laden with beer casks rumbled by. The spinning hubs of the wheels narrowly missed Jaric's hip. When he made no effort to step clear, the drover cursed and brandished a whip; but Jaric's sword and dagger, and the scowl beneath his tangled hair, made the man continue without further argument. The boy himself remained unaware that his appearance had intimidated a stranger twice his age and weight. A flock of geese flapped around his boots, arched necks lifted away from a girl with a stick who prodded them to market. She smiled invitation at him, her small feet dancing beneath lifted skirts.

Yet Jaric shrank and turned his face away. Even now he could not forget the teasing he had received from the serving wenches at Morbrith. The teeming streets, and the racket with attendant strange smells and bustle, made Landfast a world removed from Seitforest, where he had wintered. The beginnings of self-reliance he had learned in the trapper's trade became displaced by uncertainty; even his feats of seamanship lost significance, until every recent accomplishment seemed delusion wrought of dreams. With the dust of the city in his nostrils, the resolve made in the open air of the ice cliffs now seemed vain folly. How inadequate were his hopes to safeguard the Keys to Elrinfaer, far less protect Taen Dream-weaver from the brother she had lost to Shadowfane.

Jaric straightened, and pushed off from the wall before the tremble in his gut became an outright urge to run. His last and most sensible option was to write a note addressing his concern for Taen's welfare and trust the crew of the longboat to deliver it to Corley. Ink and paper could be found with the archivists, where Jaric intended to apply for work to earn bread and board. Although his plan now seemed futile, to do nothing invited despair. Resigned, the heir of Ivain Firelord tucked his bandaged wrist under his sleeve, and hastened to overtake the cake seller.

She accepted his copper with a quizzical expression. Then, with her trays balanced against a packing crate, she raised a plump hand and tucked her hair in her cap while Jaric asked directions.

"You'll want the residence of the Grand First Archivist, then." Belatedly discovering her fingers were still sticky with sugar, the woman abandoned vanity and let her arm fall. "Go up the east stair, boy. Pass two courtyards, and you'll find the door between the checkered towers beyond Lionsgate."

Jaric phrased his thanks with court courtesy. He moved to depart but the passage of mounted couriers in plumed helmets forced him to leap back, or be trampled. Raised in an earl's household, he instinctively shielded the woman from the horses' streaming trappings.

"You have the manners, then." The cake seller studied him curiously. She looked beyond scuffed boots and uncut hair, and either his slenderness or his uncertainty aroused her sympathy. "Have a cake, boy. And I won't keep your copper."

Jaric shook his head with startling vehemence. Painfully he had discovered that motherly behavior was inspired only by the helpless. Ignoring the cake in the woman's outstretched hand, he shoved his way back into the press. Nothing in Landfast could bring him to turn back, even when a pony shied back in its traces, showering straw on the cobbles and earning blasphemies from an oat farmer's wife.

Inland from the harbor the crush of traffic became less frantic. Warehouses and seaport trade gave way to guildhalls and houses. The streets rose steeply, cleft by switchback turns and a chaotic crisscross of alleys. Jaric found his way with difficulty, for the thoroughfares here were jammed with people and beggars on foot. A few lanes were sparsely traveled, like the street of cloth weavers with its clatter of looms and the heated reek of dye pots. Jaric spotted Lionsgate long before he climbed the east stair. Supported by pillared arches, cats carved of amber marble reared above the tilted slates of the rooftops. Jaric squeezed past a trio of quarreling merchants and stopped, his purpose obscured by awe.

To one side, between the shaded facade of two buildings, he saw a circular plaza of sand-colored marble. Grilled gates closed off the access, and neither people nor carts passed through. Deserted in sunlight, patterned stone inlay described the four points of the compass, and the center bore the stars and fire-burst symbol of Kordane's Brotherhood. Jaric turned toward the place, impelled by curiosity. But at the end of the access lane, a voice called out in challenge.

"Halt, boy! None may pass this way."

Jaric started back, even as a sentry stepped smartly from the shadows by the gate and lowered an enameled ceremonial spear. His helm was plumed and decorated also, but the facings were steel; and his weapon was tempered and honed to a killing point. Aware of the boy's confusion, and the plain sailor's linen that clothed him, the guardsman eased his stance. "You'd be new to Landfast, then, boy?"

Jaric nodded. "I'm trying to get to Lionsgate."

The sentry gestured down a side street. "That way, boy." Then, seeing Jaric's eyes still fixed on the forbidden plaza, he lowered his weapon and leaned on the shaft. "No man goes there but priests initiated to the mysteries. Yonder's the entrance to the sanctuary towers of Landfast."

"There?" Skepticism colored Jaric's tone as he regarded the polished paving. No door was visible.

"The stair leads underground, and the locking mechanism that hides the entrance is a secret kept by the Inner Echelon." Suddenly out of patience, the sentry seated his spear butt with a clang against the cobbles. "Now get along, boy. Regulations forbid me to jabber with passersby, and the captain of Kordane's guard has a mean way with slackers."

Reminded that his own errand would fare poorly by delay, Jaric hurried on down the side street. Houses with jutting balconies shut out the light. The air beneath was sea-damp, and smelled faintly of garbage. Town sweepers did not pass here to clear the gutters, and apparently the resident tenants were too lazy to tidy their door walks themselves. Since their shutters were latched closed in full daylight, Jaric wondered whether this was an alley of brothels. Ahead lay an intersection, and beyond, a small square, the final ascent to Lionsgate. The staircase to the arch was all but empty, since commerce slowed in late afternoon. Anxious to speak with the Grand First Archivist before the libraries closed at eventide, Jaric tackled the steps at a run. Near the top, panting, he spotted the twin towers the cake seller had described, their bases faced with bands of checkered agate. The doorway framed between bore a device of scrolls and crossed swords, symbolic of knowledge's double-edged legacy.

Jaric leaped the last triplet of stairs and hurried headlong through the arch. The shadows slanted steeply toward sunset. The longboat must not leave the Quay without his message to Corley.

The entrance to the scribes' hall stood open in the heat. The tiled foyer within proved invitingly cool, and musty with the smells of ink and old parchment. A clerk in brown robes rose from an ambry as Jaric entered. He banged the doors closed with ill-concealed annoyance, and stared at the boy who confronted him, a hand-woven cloak of green wadded under an arm tanned as a sailor's.

The clerk sniffed, unimpressed. "Are you lost?"

Jaric shook his head once, sharply. "I've come to ask for work."

The clerk twitched his lips. "We don't hire swordsmen."

"I'm not a swordsman." Jaric stepped forward, desperate to save time.

"Fisherman, then," said the clerk. He gestured, openly vexed. "Get back to your nets. You're too old for apprenticeship."

Jaric stiffened. His eyes narrowed. "Are you deaf? I said work, not apprenticeship. I know my craft."

The clerk's brows lifted. He glanced again at the sword, noticed heavy calluses on the boy's hands, and took a step back. Muttering for his visitor to wait, he walked precipitously toward the stair. Jaric paced back and forth before the ambry through what seemed an unreasonable span of time.

At length the clerk reappeared. He leaned over the balustrade, an overweening sneer on his lips. "The master in residence will see you. Mercy on you if your claims were boasting. The man dislikes nuisance, and the Grand Magistrate's his drinking crony."

Too annoyed to react to threats, Jaric bounded up the stair, unbuckling his sword belt as he went. He followed the clerk down a carpeted hallway, past door after door which opened upon rooms of books. His escort showed him into a chamber, rich rugs slashed with sunlight which spilled through lancet windows. Jaric paused past the threshold, momentarily dazzled.

The clerk poked sharply at his elbow. "Are you an oaf? Bow before your betters, boy."

Jaric ignored the prompt. Squinting, he took a step toward the broad desk with its stooped, white-bearded occupant. Then, suddenly timid, he stopped. The towering shelves of books, the ink-smell, and the still air wakened unwanted memories of his childhood at Morbrith. Once the silence of the copy chamber had been his only refuge from the cruel jibes of his peers.

"You come from the Kielmark's brigantine?" rasped the elderly man at the desk. His spectacles glinted white, unfathomable as the eyes of dead insects.

"Yes, Eminence." Jaric lifted his burden, carefully laid weapons and cloak on the marquetry table near his elbow. "But I'm not in Cliffhaven's service."

"That I know." The master in residence raised a crabbed hand and beckoned the boy closer to his chair. "Pirates have small use for written words."

Jaric stifled an unwise urge to contradict. Plain in his thoughts lay the Kielmark's personal study, walls lined floor to ceiling with volumes any prince might treasure. The books had not been for show, he knew; once in curiosity he had pulled one down and found it clean of dust.

The elderly scribe leaned forward. "You're very quiet, boy."

"Oh, he talks, all right," offered the clerk from the doorway. "The question is, can he write?"

"That's quite enough!" The old man stood. A collar ornate with embroidery and pearls dragged at the cords of his neck. "You have work to do, yes? Well then, leave me to mine!"

After a venomous glance at Jaric, the clerk spun and departed. As his steps faded away down the hallway, the master in residence returned his scrutiny to the applicant standing by his chair. One hand was bandaged; the other bore marks from the sword and the sea. And gold hair fell untrimmed over the muscled leanness one saw in the shoulders of the young who trained for posts in the Governor's guard. Still, this boy had features too sensitive for a fighter; and his manner, a queer mix of diffidence and impatience, harbored no arrogance at all.

The master in residence sighed and sat. The faintest of smiles crinkled his cheeks as he pulled off his spectacles, rubbed eyes of clearest gray, and said, "Are you perchance in some difficulty?"

Jaric drew a troubled breath. "I need work, as a scribe or a copyist. I can also tally accounts. Only, if you'll have me, I would beg use of a pen and an hour's leave to deliver a note to a friend."

"Well, then." The master pulled open a drawer. Blue-veined fingers dipped within and emerged with a square of parchment. He thumped the sheet on the boards before Jaric and gestured impatiently at the quill which rested in the inkwell by his wrist. "Write your letter first, boy."

Jaric bowed his head. "Master, you are generous."

His voice had steadied. The accent at last was plain, of north-shore origin, but cultured. This boy had not learned his speech or his manners in the farmsteads. His scarred fingers gripped the pen with recognizable expertise, and as line after line of even, cleanly phrased script flowed beneath his hand, the master ceased to watch.

"What are you called, boy?"

Jaric's writing did not falter. He answered with the surname given him by the Smith's Guild of Morbrith, for everywhere Ivain's name was remembered with vicious hatred. "Kerainson Jaric, Eminence."

"Then, young Kerainson, have you quarters?"

Jaric signed his missive and reached instinctively for the sand tray. He dried the excess ink quickly and well, blurring no letters in the process. "I have a boat."

The master in residence grunted. "Open to the sky, no doubt. Well, it isn't raining. Tomorrow is soon enough to arrange your bed and board."

Jaric raised uncertain brown eyes. With his letter clutched to his chest, he waited, afraid to speak.

"Well, get along, boy." The master in residence restored his spectacles to the grooved skin of his nose. "Deliver your note, but get back here sober by sunrise. I've three keeps full of books to be copied, and never enough hands for the pens."

Jaric barely waited to voice his respects before bolting for the door. Running by the time he crossed the threshold, he forgot to pick up the sword and dagger left on the table by the entry. Hall, stairs, and landing passed by in a blur of haste, and as he crossed the foyer he answered the clerk's sour query with breathless words.

"I'm hired."

Afternoon had all but fled. Landfast's towers framed a sky blending toward the fallow gold of sunset. Surely *Moonless*'s longboat had departed by now; Jaric raced for the stair and cannoned squarely into a man coming in from the outside. Fingers clamped like trap jaws on the boy's wrist. A neatly delivered push spun him off balance, and he crashed, sprawling into the stone pillars of the railing.

"Why the haste?" said a voice, consonants clipped with annoyance. "Are you a thief?"

Jaric shook the hair from his eyes and looked up at a lanky man with a seal-brown mustache. His body was clothed in russet trimmed in black, and sinewy wrists lay crossed at his waist, hands lightly gripping the hilts of a jeweled sword and dagger.

"Your pardon, master." Belatedly remembering his abandoned weapons, Jaric's fingers tightened. The letter in his hand crumpled slightly. "I am much in haste." He pushed himself away from the pillar and attempted to walk past.

The man moved like a fox. Steel sang from his scabbards. Blades flashed blue in the sunlight and fenced the boy on the stair. "I *said*, are you a thief?"

White, angry, and desperate, Jaric stared at the weapons angled at his chest. "I haven't stolen anything! Ask the clerk, and then let me pass."

The points remained so steady they might have been nailed in place. "You aren't very convincing, ship-monkey. The clerk could be your accomplice."

Jaric gasped, shocked. He jerked a glance at his antagonist, and saw him smile, teeth glinting through his mustache; but the eyes above were cold blue, and the brows questioning, as if the exchange were deliberately meant to provoke.

"Why insult me?" said Jaric. "I've neither sword nor dagger, and wish no quarrel with you."

The stranger laughed. "No sword and no dagger? Then certainly I'll skewer you where you stand."

"Oh no," a voice broke in from behind. "You won't bloody this stairway with fighting."

Jaric whirled, just as a robed figure emerged from the hallway. Clutched awkwardly in his arms were two familiar weapons bundled in a salt-stained green cloak. With a grimace of distaste, the clerk unloaded his burden next to Jaric. The metal on the scabbard guards grated, dissonant as a knife on a whetstone, as the cloth settled against the stair.

"Take your dueling elsewhere." The clerk set his hand on the chased brass doorknob and gave a mighty pull. "That's an order from the master in residence." He ended with a smirk as the panel began to swing.

The door crashed closed. Jaric swallowed and spun to face his tormentor. "Be reasonable. There's no purpose in fighting over accidental clumsiness on my part."

"Except, dear boy, that I want to." Scarred from years of sparring, the man's hands stirred impatiently. "Carry on."

Jaric straightened, ash-pale. "I won't."

"Ah," said the man. "But I think you will." Again he moved, so fast his blades sparked like fire in the sun.

Jaric felt air whicker past his knuckles. The letter in his hand parted, sliced cleanly in two. The severed portion drifted, turning over and over, and settled across the cloak with Taen's name and his own signature slashed cruelly in half. For a stunned second, Jaric forgot to breathe. Then he bent and recovered his steel. In anger he drew and attacked.

Blade met blade with a furious clang of sound. From the first moment Jaric had no doubt he faced a master swordsman. The stranger's parry met him, lightly, easily, and the riposte followed in a smoky blaze of light. Jaric caught the stroke on his cross guard. The force rattled his teeth. Too furious to care, he beat, feinted, lunged, and gained two steps on the stair.

"Oh, very nice." The man smiled, foxlike, through a crossed barrier of blades. He disengaged and struck.

Jaric's foot slapped the edge of the step. Forced to parry high, he twisted. His opponent's dagger darted out of nowhere, cleanly eluding his guard. The boy felt a tug. A breath of cold kissed his sweating skin. He lifted his arm to cover and saw his sleeve was slit. But the touch might as easily have gone home to maim muscle and sinew.

Forced back a pace, Jaric riposted. "You're toying with me." His blade struck a guard implacable as stone.

"Perhaps." The man in russet caught his sword in a bind and twisted. "But it's a game you must win, yes?"

Tendons tightened in Jaric's wrist. Feeling his fingers shift on the sword grip, he responded as Corley had taught, and escaped getting disarmed. His heel bashed hard against a riser. Belatedly he discovered he had lost a step.

"Tell me," drawled the man. "Is the note for a lady?"

Busy defending himself, Jaric said nothing. Cut, parry, riposte, the steel whistled and clashed until his ears rang with sound. The continuous jar of impact stung his hands. At some point, unnoticed, he received a nick on his thumb. Blood laced his wrist, and sweat ran stinging under the bandage from his morning's mishap.

Then, with the rail pressed to his side, and the breath burning in his throat, Jaric saw an opening. His sword thrust shot under defending block, and opened a line of red on the stranger's collarbone.

The man collected himself instantly. He leaped backward. His feet landed lightly on the cobbles at the foot of the stair, yet he cast down his weapons. Steel chimed deafeningly on stone. Poised to follow through, Jaric checked his rush. Hair slicked damp to his forehead, he waited, panting, while the man pulled a cloth from his sleeve and delicately dabbed his cut.

"What, no shout of victory?" The man's hands stilled and he looked up.

Jaric did not voice the obvious, that anytime previously the stranger could have sliced him to ribbons. In a few breathless minutes, the boy had perceived how pitifully inadequate were his skills; a fortnight of Corley's training had barely sketched the rudiments of technique. But this time the man refused to break the silence. Jaric shivered, set his sword point against the stone, and asked the only question that mattered. "Why attack me?"

The man kicked his dagger aside and mounted the steps. "For devilment, I suppose." His breath betrayed no sign of exertion.

Jaric gritted his teeth. "Then devil and demons take you. *I couldn't spare the time!*"

He turned on his heel, retrieved his buckler and cloak. The slashed letter fluttered under his feet as he sheathed his weapons with short, angry jerks. A hand touched his elbow. Jaric recovered his torn note and whirled, his face a mask of fury.

But the stranger laughed no longer. His brow knitted with contrition and he said, "I'll make it up to you."

"I doubt it." Jaric pushed past. "You've no idea what you've done."

"No." The man shrugged and fell into step beside him. "But you're not without talent, you know. I could instruct you, as compensation. The next time someone sought to delay you, your lady need not be kept waiting."

Jaric stopped. A bitter laugh escaped his throat. He regarded the swordsman, who held his bloody handkerchief pressed beneath his collar, and whose light eyes remained shrewdly intent. The boy's features twisted, assumed a look wholly Ivain's. "That won't mend it," he said.

But by his tone, the swordsman understood that Corley's protégé saw the sense in accepting. Not without friendliness he offered, "My name is Brith. If you come to the practice yard by the city guard's quarters, we can start tomorrow."

"I'll consider it." Jaric was curt. *"Now let me go!"*

Sunset silhouetted the humped profile of Little Dagley Islet and the waters of Landfast harbor deepened slowly to indigo. Loud in the evening quiet, the last wagons rumbled away from the dockside. Brith crouched in the dooryard of a spice shop and watched the boy, Jaric, who lingered alone by the wharf. Sea wind tossed the hair from his face, revealing a glint of unshed tears; while, beyond the beacon towers of the inlet, a brigantine flying Cliffhaven's colors shook out her stunsails and scudded south for the Isle of the Vaere.

Brith swore softly. He tossed his stained handkerchief in the gutter, and wondered again why the Kielmark's foremost captain should concern himself with a boy who hated fighting. The swordmaster shrugged and, feeling the laces of his collar fret against his cut, cursed again. The pay was generous, but the idea he might spend the night skulking like a dog in an alley had never entered his mind when he accepted responsibility for Jaric. On the verge of rising to coax his charge to consider retiring to the comfort in an alehouse, Brith froze.

Jaric spun abruptly and threw something, his arm a blur of force. The watching swordsman ducked hastily as the object struck the boards above his head. It bounced once, and rolled to a stop against the instep of his boot. Brith retrieved what proved to be a letter, crushed and wadded into an unreadable pulp. Cautiously the swordsman looked up and found Jaric on the move once more. Stealthy as a cat, he followed.

His charge strode to the dockmaster's shed and pounded on the panels until the door opened. The official inside thrust forth an angry face and swore until his lungs emptied of air. Although no money changed hands, he finished with directions. Jaric left without thanks. He interrogated a beggar and a street urchin for knowledge of landmarks and, poorer by two coppers, eventually found his way to a slip where a fishing boat of ancient design creaked against her lines.

Brith tensed. If the boy tried to cast off and chase the brigantine, the swordsman did not fancy the prospect of stopping him; but Corley's orders had been explicitly clear: Jaric was to be trained for the sword, and under no circumstances should he leave the shores of Landfast. But the boy apparently realized his *Callinde* could never match *Moonless*'s speed under full canvas. He made no effort to sail, but tossed his weapons, unoiled, into a locker, and sprawled prone beneath his cloak. Brith guarded and listened, and at length settled resignedly against a damp pile of fish net. If the boy wept, no sound betrayed him. Perhaps in the end he slept, for nothing moved on board *Callinde* until dawn silvered the horizon to the east.

Wrapped in the fog by daybreak, *Moonless* shuddered over a swell. Canvas rippled aloft and fell taut with a coarse smack. Shirtless, and clad hastily in hose and boots, Corley arrived on the quarterdeck. He squinted at the compass without pausing to consult the officer on watch.

The quartermaster blinked moisture from his lashes. "Wind's changing."

"I know." Corley gazed over the rails. Beyond the curve of the swell, the air lay dense and dead, horizon buried in mist. "Stuns'ls will have to come down. We're in for a blow, I can feel it." Deftly he skirted the wheel and shouted orders to the boatswain.

Moonless came alive as men leaped for the rigging. Corley watched, unsettled and critical. When his cabin steward appeared at his elbow with a shirt, he accepted the garment with a preoccupied frown.

"Where's the Dreamweaver?" He dragged the laces tight at his throat and adjusted his cuffs, eyes fixed intently on the activities aloft.

Sensitive to the captain's mood, the steward replied concisely. "The girl's asleep, Captain. She's been very quiet."

Too quiet, Corley suspected, but did not voice his thought.

His stillness prompted the steward to qualify. "I'd guess she misses the boy. Any man with eyes might notice that she and Jaric were close."

"Enough," snapped Corley. He raked tangled chestnut hair with his fingers and finished with a gesture of dismissal. "I'll be down to look in on her shortly."

Taen might pine for Jaric; but the captain had not missed the fact that she had failed to come on deck to bid her companion farewell. Since leaving Landfast, she had made herself scarce, behavior markedly changed from her earlier habit of riding the bowsprit with her hair flying in the wind. The fighting spirit observed during the defense of Cliffhaven could not be reconciled with a girl who suddenly languished in emotional sentimentality. But with storms pending, and canvas being shortened aloft, no captain worth the Kielmark's pay would be caught below decks. Taen's vagaries would have to wait.

Corley checked the weather gauge and frowned again at the compass. Lines squealed in the blocks overhead as the crew shortened sail. Mist trailed through the yards, shredded to scarves by gusts. The waters heaved gray and leaden beneath, fretted by the faintest whisper of disturbed air. The wind had definitely shifted. Since speed had dictated a westerly course through the narrow channel that separated Landfast from Innishari, *Moonless* had only a scant margin of sea room. Should the weather deteriorate before midday, she would have to put about. The Kielmark's captain paced anxiously. Conditions would inevitably get worse. He had been too many years at sea to misread the signs. If, as he suspected, some difficulty beset Taen Dreamweaver, he had but one desire, and that to make landfall at the Isle of the Vaere as swiftly as ship and sinew could manage.

Watery sunlight struck through the fog as day progressed, striking highlights against the waves. Yet the brightness proved short-lived. Hounded by rising wind, storm clouds rolled in from the south, darkening the mist to sickly green. Stripped of flying jibs and topsails, *Moonless* reeled closehauled, thudded by swells which struck with the might of siege engines. Spray dashed the quarterdeck.

Sodden, Corley shook water from his hair and shouted commands to the boatswain. "Reef the main! And send the slowest man below to batten hatches."

While the crew swarmed aloft, the captain flung away from the rail and nearly belted into the steward, who brought him a cloak of oiled wool.

Corley accepted the garment with a bitten word of thanks. "How's the Dreamweaver?"

The steward seemed taken aback. "Sir, I don't know."

"Why not?" With his brooch poised to stab cloth, Corley phrased his next words with warning care. "I thought I told you to look in on her?"

"Your pardon, sir." A gust forced the servant to raise his voice. "You said you'd see Taen yourself."

Corley rammed the pin into place and twitched the cloak over his shoulders. "Damn the weather," he replied. "I did say that. Check her for me and report back, could you?"

"Aye, sir, at once." The steward left.

Corley hastened to the binnacle, glared at the compass, and swore afresh. "Kor's Fires, the wind's veering again. We're going to end with a west wind, but too late to matter." He met the quartermaster's glance with anxious eyes. "I don't like the drift of this. Seems like we're getting a fall tempest, three whole months out of season." Neither man belabored the obvious, that with the archipelago of Islamere lying east, a westerly gale might force *Moonless* north to gain leeway.

"Bad luck," murmured the quartermaster.

Fast as a whipcrack, Corley answered. "Do you think so?"

The officer paled above the spoke curve of the wheel. "What else? Demons cannot shift weather, and Anskiere's bound in ice."

A gust struck. Stressed canvas boomed in protest, and *Moonless* flung into a heel. Water pressed against her rudder, and the wheel creaked, slipping in the quartermaster's grasp. Corley reached and caught the spokes, adding his own weight to maintain the brigantine's heading. For a moment the two men strained, feet pressed to the wet planks of the deck. Then the wind eased, and the pressure abated.

"Boatswain, send a man to assist with the helm!" The instant the deckhand arrived to relieve him, Corley took a log reading and retired below.

Returned from Taen's cabin, the steward found his captain in the chart room. Light from a gimbaled oil lamp flickered over Corley's shoulders, flashing and sparking through salt crystals in his hair as he bent with dividers and pen, working out the running fix. Patient, the steward waited until his master looked up.

"Captain, you had best come. The Dreamweaver is ill. I cannot rouse her."

Corley's eyes steadied, dark with decision. After a moment he spoke softly. "By the Great Fall, that's bad news." If the Vaere had chosen this to penalize her for breaking her oath to return, the timing couldn't be worse.

He straightened and blew out the oil lamp. Crossing to the companionway ladder which led onto the quarterdeck, he cracked the hatch cover. The chilly smells of rain and seawater swirled into the cabin as he shouted against the storm. "Bring *Moonless* about. We're going to have to run northeast."

With the gale closing from the west, no other choice remained. Islamere's jagged shoals lay too close for safety, and no time remained to beat clear of the southernmost reefs; frustrated, concerned, Corley saw his hopes for a fast passage balked. The Isle of the Vaere lay due south.

The captain banged the hatch and hastily secured the fastening. "Fetch the healer," he snapped at the steward, and without pausing to shed his damp cloak, he headed for Taen's berth.

CHAPTER VII

Dream-storm

Gale winds whined through masts and rigging, and *Moonless* tossed, spray flying from her bow like foam from the jaws of a beast. Sprawled loose-limbed against the lee board of her berth, Taen Dreamweaver heard the thud and rush of seas whipped to fury by the storm. She struggled to determine whether the sensations were reality or another sequence of the nightmares which had beset her since the morning Jaric disembarked at Landfast. Yet as if her senses were locked in shackles, her mind remained in darkness.

A hinge creaked, stiff as the door to the cottage Taen had known as a child. Orange light suffused her awareness, centered by a pinpoint of flame. A male voice called her name. Powerless to respond, she did not answer. The light moved closer, fell blinding across her face, and she smelled the hot reek of oil.

"Taen Dreamweaver," repeated the man. Cloth rustled very close by. "You're right, she's not sleeping. What in Keithland could be ailing her?"

Taen had heard that voice before. She wrestled to identify where; for an instant an image like an acid etching formed in her mind, of the Kielmark flinging chart after chart across the table in his study at Cliffhaven castle. Then the veils of delirium closed over her once more, and words bounced like echoes across the dark.

". . . something decidedly amiss."

Someone's fingers closed over Taen's wrist. Shapes slashed her awareness, inspired by a presence edged and dangerous as sword steel. The Dreamweaver cried out from the depths of trance. Gasping, she at last perceived that the person who touched her was no nightmare born of a troubled mind but solid flesh and blood. His concern pierced the depths of her until her dream-sense rang with echoes. The grip shifted on her arm, transferring her limp weight into the care of another whose self was a warm muddle of worry. A cup brushed Taen's lips. Stinging liquid ran down her throat. She stirred and choked, but after a moment the elixir cleared her mind. Taen quivered and opened her eyes.

Awash in a flood of lanternlight, she saw faces crowded against the low beams of the cabin: the wrinkled visage of the healer, the cabin steward's bald head, and the Kielmark's bearded captain, salt-streaked and mettlesome, the violence of character which had prompted her vision of swords held flawlessly in check.

Corley spoke before the others could react. "Kor's grace, she's come to." His hands pressed deep into the blankets by the Dreamweaver's side as he leaned close, openly ignoring the healer's request to give her space and air. "Girl, what ails you?"

"No ordinary sickness, that's certain," snapped the healer from behind. "Let me through."

Corley waved him silent. "Taen?"

"I don't know." Dizzy and confused, the Dreamweaver wished she sounded less like a lost child. "My dream-sense seems overturned. I have visions . . ." Her voice trailed off, and she was terrified by her own words. *What had happened to her mastery?* Yet the fear cleared her mind a little. Her voice became stronger. "Corley, whatever happens, take me to the enchanted isle. Tamlin of the Vaere will know how to help."

"You'll get there." Corley straightened with an expression unexpectedly grim. He left the bedside abruptly and ducked through the companionway, but not before Taen sensed his thought: *how could he tell her that an out-of-season storm had diverted the brigantine's course due north?*

Relieved of the captain's bothersome presence, the healer jutted his bearded chin and took charge. "Out!" he snapped at the cabin steward. "The child needs no gawkers hanging about."

Taen stirred as he chivvied the steward past the bulkhead. "I don't mind," she said.

"Oh, sure." The healer thumped his satchel of remedies on the sea chest in the corner and testily shook his head. "You'll be that much better without yon gossip poking his nose into corners."

The elder arranged his brazier on a slate. The shuddering toss of the brigantine appeared to cause him no difficulty, for he spilled none of his phials as he concocted a bitter-smelling potion of herbs. Taen drank the mixture with heroic distaste, at which point the steward reappeared with a tray of hot soup. The healer admitted him grumbling, and lingered to make certain she ate. At last he packed up his satchel and left. Taen slept. For several days no dreams returned to trouble her.

But the storm grew worse. The wind reached gale force, screaming like a demon out of the west, and battering the wave crests into streaming tails of spindrift. Stripped to bare spars, *Moonless* reeled and tossed, seawater rolling green through her waist. The off-watch crew huddled wet as seals in the forecastle. Lashed beside the helmsmen, Corley oversaw his command night and day from the quarterdeck.

Taen learned to disregard the monotonous clang of the bilge pumps. She ate cold fare with the crew; seas were too rough to permit any fire in the galley, and, lacking that central place of warmth, the brigantine became dank and cheerless below decks. Still, Taen was a fisherman's daughter. Inured to the discomforts and the perils of the sea, she badgered the sailhands until they laughed, and put red pepper in the cook's jerky so he would stop carping about the fact that his food was never hot. Watching her bright spirits light the brigantine from stem to stern, not even the healer guessed her dizzy spells had returned. Taen fought to stay active. Burning resources and wit like festival candles, she knew if she returned to her berth to sleep, the dreams would overwhelm her once again.

But a morning arrived two days later when the dawn watch entered the galley dripping rainwater. They shouted coarse jokes about wet weather causing ringlets, and one by one fell silent as they noticed Taen sprawled against the woodbox, her skin dry and burning to the touch. Neither noise nor shaking could rouse her.

"Inform the captain," snapped the boatswain.

Dragged unceremoniously from his hammock, the healer rammed a path through the gawking crewmen to Taen's side and found Corley newly arrived from the quarterdeck.

Unkempt from ceaseless exposure to wind and water, the captain paced until he heard the healer's prognosis: this time the girl had drifted too far for mortal efforts to avail. Her cure, if any existed, lay with the Vaere.

"See her to a berth." Corley shut red-rimmed eyes, for a moment overcome by fatigue. Then he shivered like a dog and added, "Storm's lifting. By daylight we should be able to put about and resume a southern course."

But weather balked his plans again by midday. The heavy clouds broke, replaced by a sky the clean cobalt of enamel. Capricious winds shifted and winnowed and stilled. *Moonless* wallowed becalmed over a round-topped procession of storm swells. Her gear crashed and banged aloft, and the smoke from her galley fire rose straight as a spire overhead. Silent, Corley took sun sights and consulted his charts. Tempest and current had set *Moonless* far to the east and north, leagues from her desired course. The Isle of the Vaere presently lay twenty days' sail under perfect conditions; but without wind for her canvas, the brigantine rolled dead as a gaffed fish in the water. Suddenly sensitive to every ache in his tired body, the captain laid his dividers aside and bellowed for the officer of the watch.

The man arrived tardily. Curt to the point of rudeness, Corley demanded the reason, and received a second round of ill news. Inspection of the hold revealed casks worked loose by the storm; most of the water stores had been fouled with seawater.

As the officer delivered his report, Corley resisted a consuming urge to cover his face with his hands. *Moonless* would need to make landfall within eight days to take on water, else the crew would suffer shortage. Kor defend the innocent, thought Corley; the girl who had kept his sail-hands grinning through a bout of the most evil weather he had seen on the Corine Sea would now have to wait on more than the wind for help.

Taen never felt the hands which lifted her from the galley deck and carried her, wrapped in blankets, to the narrow berth in the aft cabin. Lost in a maze of dreams, she knew nothing of the healer's attempts to rouse her, nor did she react to the thumps and shouted commands from the hold where the sailhands labored to secure the ruined casks. Her mind assumed a course all its own. Personalities deflected her, temporarily flooding swirls of color and dimension across her inward eye; then they passed, and the images ran together into a world of twilight and shadows. Taen drifted, time and self forgotten.

Later the light faded entirely. Muffled in night like felt, Taen sailed through an eddyless void. Neither moon nor stars pricked the depths, and no lantern shone to mark any haven or dooryard where she might find peace and rest. How long she drifted could not be measured, but imperceptibly, the quality of the blackness changed. She perceived a spark of illumination. Distant, but warm as candle flame the light drew her like a moth.

Blindness lifted from Taen's dream-sense. She found her awareness centered in a dusty attic chamber stacked with books. There afternoon shadow streaked a copy table where Jaric bent over parchment and a scroll with handles of gold-stamped wood. A brief shiver gripped him. Though the room was neither cold nor dark, he paused, laid his pen aside, and reached with ink-stained fingers for the striker to ignite the oil lamp.

"Never mind, boy." A scribe with rumpled silver hair shuffled out from behind a row of shelves. "No sense burning lights, now. If your eyes are tired, you can finish translating that treatise in the morning."

Jaric rubbed a crick in his neck. "You don't mind, Brother Handred?"

The elder unhooked his cane from a chairback and limped across the chamber. Through dust-streaked cuffs and an assortment of ancient food stains, Taen saw that he wore the deep blue robe of Kor's Brotherhood. "The master in residence told me you stayed all night."

"I was reading," Jaric admitted. "I didn't start copying until dawn."

"Well, then you're plenty tired." Head cocked like a bird, the priest thumbed through the pages piled at Jaric's elbow. The script was clean and straight, and probably without errors; whatever the scarred state of his hands, this boy had been trained well. "You've done enough for one day."

Taen felt the ache of Jaric's weariness cut through the dream-link as he rose to his feet. "I can go?"

The priest nodded. "Eat. Get some sleep. You'll work the better for it come morning."

But rest never entered Jaric's mind as he pushed back his stool and picked a path through the stacks to the door. The boy *Moonless* had delivered to Landfast was changing, Taen perceived. The teaching of Corley and another swordsman called Brith had bent Jaric's mind toward a mold which accepted no excuse for weakness. More and more, necessity forced him to set aside the fears which had poisoned his childhood at Morbrith. He remembered to buckle on sword and dagger before he entered the streets. Now better acquainted with Landfast, Jaric chose back streets and alleys least traveled. Within minutes he reached the dockside.

"Alms, young master," called a one-handed beggar who leaned on a bollard. A mangy tomcat crouched by his feet, and clothes already patched shapeless needed another round of mending at elbows, knees, and cuffs.

Jaric tossed the fellow a silver with the unthinking reflex of habit.

"Thank'e." The beggar jammed the coin in his boot and straightened with a crooked grin. "Boat's bailed for ye, master. Best check the starboard bowline. She's chafed a bit, from the storm."

Jaric paused while a wagon rumbled past. "I came as soon as I could." He reached into his pocket, groped for another coin.

"Leave be, boy." The beggar shrugged. "I do well enough by you."

Jaric tossed a copper, spinning, into the air. "Take it for the cat, then. I've no family to feed."

"Right, aye, then." The beggar caught the coin with the speed of a striking snake. Taen saw him stare after as Jaric ran down the dock to the slip where *Callinde* lay tied.

Linked through the dream to the boy's concern, the girl stepped aboard the ancient boat. After a hasty glance to ascertain whether the floorboards were dry, Jaric ducked around the headstay and ran anxious hands over the dockline the beggar had mentioned. Frayed plies scraped under his fingers; the rope must certainly be replaced. Squinting against the low sun of afternoon, Jaric bent and unfastened the aft locker. He reached beneath the folded canvas of the headsail in search of his store of spare cordage, and froze suddenly in mid-motion. Taen felt a chill jolt through him. Startled, she shared the apprehension which tightened his chest as he dug under the sail and dragged forth an object that *could not* have been there, yet was. Jaric sank against the thwart, the cold, pale length of an ash flute clenched hard between his hands. Inlay flashed silver as he turned it. The breath came fast and dry in his throat.

Moved to concern, Taen probed him and encountered stark edges of fear. She never learned why. As if roused by her dream-touch, Jaric stiffened. He flexed his wrists in sharp denial, and the delicate shaft of the flute snapped. Splinters glanced in the sunlight, fell whispering to the deck; and Taen cried out, for as the ash wood broke asunder, a wail of purest sorrow echoed within her mind.

She protested without thought. *'Jaric, no!'* The makers of the flute offered their gift without malice. They wished only to aid him, defend him from harm.

But the words of the Dreamweaver in his mind only caused the boy to start up in alarm. With a guilty gesture, he tossed the broken instrument into the harbor. As it sank from sight, Taen saw that memory of its origin was linked to another event Jaric had determined to hide. Reflexively she pursued the reason; and the dockside where Jaric tended *Callinde* vanished, swept away by the whine of wind across desolate acres.

Taen looked down from the carved archway of a tower and saw a place of treeless rock. Bare except for scabrous splotches of lichen, hills fell away to a gray horizon. Trapped by dreams, the girl knew she gazed from a window far distant from Landfast, beyond the borders of Keithland itself. Even as she wondered how a thought from Jaric's mind would lead her here, she sensed movement in the chamber behind her.

'*He will be all you hoped for, and more,*' said a voice whose overtones grated like rusty metal.

The words formed no language spoken by man, but, gifted with a Dreamweaver's talents, Taen understood the meaning. Touched by nameless dread, she turned from the window to view the chamber behind her. Within a vaulted hall of stone, crimson carpets covered a raised, central dais. A mirror pool of black-veined marble reflected a table and carved chair whose yellow-eyed occupant possessed no human features.

'*Bring him hither,*' bade the demon on the dais. His tone whistled like flutes. He leaned forward, rippling skin all mottled and scaled like a lizard's. Orange spines tipped fingers, ears, and the armored plates visible beneath the hem of the garment which swathed his spindly torso. Gold chains winked above spurred ankles.

'*I enter, Lord Scait.*' The original speaker strode from the shadowed depths of an antechamber. It moved with the raddled gait of a hunchback, followed by others who supported another apparently ailing or injured. By the fleshy curves of their gill flaps, Taen recognized the toadlike Thienz, empaths whose kind had allied in the attack against Cliffhaven. All but blind in daylight, the demons advanced on rubbery, webbed feet. Crested headdresses clinked, beads and jewels keeping time to their ungainly stride. The party stopped by the pool-side, reflected upside down in the water as they offered obeisance to the figure seated on the dais. Taen took a careful look at the other, who bowed woodenly in the grip of wiry Thienz fingers. And her heart twisted terribly inside, for there stood no demon but a human male in ragged, salt-stained clothing.

Black hair lay tangled against the filthy cloth of his collar. His sea boots were torn with wear, and his face a dead mask of exhaustion. Granted a clear view of his features in the pool, Taen felt the vision tighten like a noose around her mind; for the man held between the hideous bodies of the Thienz was Marlson Emien, her natural brother, last seen when he had fled Jaric's sword beneath the Tower of Elrinfaer. But Emien's expression of lifeless uninterest was one his sister had never known before.

'*This is the dissident who succeeds the witch, Tathagres?*' said Scait from the dais. '*He came of his own will, you say. Is that so?*'

Emien gave no sign of recognition. His eyes remained fixed, a cold and passionless blue, while the demons discussed him in images which translated in no tongue spoken on Keithland's soil.

'*Lord, that is so.*' The spokesman for the Thienz stepped to the lip of the pool. Beads clinked on either side of its jowls as it bobbed its blunt head. '*This Emien-that-was desired the power of his mistress-now-dead. He did murder to claim it. See, Lord, mighty-and-greatest, there are burn scars on the man-flesh of his hands. By this be certain the crystals once-stolen-from-Llondelei ensure our permanent domination of his body. His fate is yours to command.'*

Scait's lips curled, revealing razor rows of sharklike teeth. *'Has he talents? Information? Bring him hither, that I might test his mettle.'* The lizard demon flicked spiny fingers and beckoned.

The Thienz-demons clustered tightly together. Though small and awkward of movement, they proved surprisingly strong. Webbed, toadlike fingers propelled Marlson Emien past the mirror pool, pressing him prone on the carpet before the dais.

The Demon Lord arose, and with the detailed horror of nightmare, Taen realized his throne was comprised of preserved human remains. Wishing to turn from the image, but unable to abandon knowledge of her brother's fate, she whimpered in the depths of trance, even as the demon ruler of Shadowfane set spurred hands against the sides of Emien's head.

The probe must have been cruel, for despite the restraint of the Thienz, the boy's body arched against the floor. His scream echoed piteously off the vaulted ceiling of the hall; but no mercy was shown him. Scait Demon Lord arose from his examination with the satisfaction of a scavenger sated upon carrion. Yellow eyes glittered with excitement as he transmitted his findings to the Thienz.

'He has abilities, this manling stolen from Keithland! A sorcerer's latent potential, did-you-not-see: had he not forsaken loyalty to his kind, he might-have-gone to the Vaere and caused-us-sorrow, even as Ivain and Anskiere before him.' Here the demon croaked in sour irony. *'Now he is ours. Let him be called Maelgrim, for when his talents are mature, he will both be deceived, and act the part of deceiver, our tool and the bane-of-his-kind.'*

The group spokesman cleared its throat with a croak. *'Lord-mightiest, there is more. Marlson-Emien-Maelgrim has a sister of equal talent. She has trained already with the Vaere, and walks Keithland as Dreamweaver.'*

The demon on the dais swore in slit-eyed fury. *'Corinne Dane, Accursed! How can this be?'* Spurs clashed against ankle ornaments as he sprang precipitously to his feet. *'Explain!'*

The spokesman for the Thienz bobbed in deference. *'High-mightiest, when the shape-shifter, Tathagres'-ally, perished during the assault on Cliffhaven, it sent a message most-strange through its death-link. The Karas claimed it was Dreamweaver-betrayed. This boy has memories of a sister who proves-this-was-truth.'*

Listening, Taen felt as if a sliver of ice pierced her heart. She struggled to influence her dream-sense, bend it away from the horrors of this place; but her effort dissipated, smothered by dark. Powerless to control her Sathid-enhanced talents, she had no choice but observe as Scait bent for the second time over the prone form of her brother. Emien flinched from the touch. He whimpered and writhed as the Demon Lord ransacked his mind for information. The Thienz before the mirror pool clustered together, trembling and hissing softly among themselves. Their discomfort translated across the link and oppressed Taen's dream-sense with foreboding.

Yet even this did not prepare her for the violence of Scait's reaction. His spurred grip tightened on Emien's flesh, almost drawing blood. Then, as the import of his findings registered, he recoiled as if burned. His whistle of alarm struck echoes off vaulted stone ceilings; beneath the dais the Thienz stilled utterly as their overlord's yellow eyes lifted and fixed upon them.

'Cowardly toads! Fools! The sister-Taen-Dreamweaver is no threat to Shadowfane, dying as she is of her Sathid. But the other, Ivainson-Firelord's-heir-Jaric! That one could inflict death and sorrow upon-us-all.' Scait bared his teeth and, agitated as never before, raised his long hackles before inferiors.

The Thienz wailed in alarm, almost tumbling over each other as they shrank from the wrath of their lord. Scait harried them with imprecations and curses, but Taen ignored their meaning. Terrified for Ivainson Jaric, and consumed with the need to warn him, she struck out with all her strength against her prison of dreams. Yet her struggle accomplished no more than the frenzied wingbeats of a moth. Taen felt her dream-sense ripple, darken, and refocus on the same stone chamber at Shadowfane.

On the dais, Scait flexed his spurs and crouched once again over Emien. *'The sister can show us where. Weakened as she is by changes in her Sathid, she might be vulnerable if we seek to manipulate through the affinity that remains between her and this, her brother.'*

The Thienz spokesman whuffed its gills. *'Your will, mightiest.'*

Stillness fell, broken by a rasping scrape as Scait honed the edges of his teeth by grinding his jaws together. As the Thienz pressed closely around him, he reached a last time for Emien.

Taen never felt the Demon Lord and his minions combine their powers. She knew only a moment of red-hazed perception, as the minds of Kor's Accursed encompassed her brother. Then their probe struck, a blazing arc of force that stabbed like sword metal into her awareness. She recoiled, unable even to cry out. The defenses that should have answered her Sathid mastery failed utterly, sundered as she was from control. Demons snapped her frail web of denial. With a thrust like pain, they seized upon the subject of their desire and plundered. Two words they tore from her, *Cliffhaven*, and *Landfast*; both would be searched for the purpose of destroying Ivainson Jaric.

Taen barely noted Scait's fierce crow of triumph. Dazed by the demon's whirlwind withdrawal, her battered human awareness grasped only fragments of the instructions he gave to his underlings; vaguely she understood that the demon compact at Shadowfane would meet to hear tidings. Emien would be trained as a weapon against Keithland, and assassins would sail to hunt Jaric. This was the will of Lord Scait.

The Thienz wailed mournfully in consternation, for saltwater immersion was a hazard to them. But their spokesman groveled before the dais without protest. *'Your will, Grand-mightiest.'* Its crested headdress rattled as it shuffled back among its colleagues. Then, croaking among themselves, the Thienz gathered Emien between them and marched him unprotesting from the hall.

The impact of implication became too much for Taen to endure. Grief for her lost brother and fear for Ivainson Jaric momentarily upset reason. She cried aloud, every fiber of her being reviled by the betrayal she had been entrapped to commit. Sundered by the violence of her rejection, the thread of the vision snapped. The demon's vaulted council hall vanished, swept away in the torrent of her Sathid change. Sound beat against Taen's ears, shrill as wind through winter branches. Orientation crumbled with it; the girl's awareness tumbled over and over, banished into darkness and primordial cold. Ice cracked like old bones around her, shackled her feet to bedrock stillness. Stars sprang into being, needle pricks against an endless field of night. Solitary, aching, Taen sought but found no landmark from any place she knew. No effort availed her. Again and again she spun thought, only to strike against impenetrable bounds of nightmare. The strange words spoken by demons whispered and sighed through her thoughts, uncipherable as the tracks of ghosts.

'. . . Dreamweaver . . . no threat . . . dying as she is of her Sathid. . . . Ivainson-Firelord's-heir-Jaric . . . could inflict death and sorrow upon-us-all. . . .' And always, with a tearing edge of pain, her concern circled round to Emien. '. . .came of his own will . . . did murder. Let him be called Maelgrim . . . our tool and the bane-of-his-kind.' Horror and memory blended, until one became inseparable from the other.

Taen struggled afresh to escape to her prison of dreams. But the images she wrestled muddled like ink only to blossom anew in her mind. Her endeavors earned no respite. Dream-sense returned nothing but the desolation of absolute emptiness, and in the end, frayed to a febrile sleep of exhaustion, she drifted forgetful of her purpose.

The presence stole upon her unawares. A soft chink of bells and the click of beaded feathers at first passed unnoticed, an insect rustle of sound teasing the limits of awareness. Nailed to immobility by the vacuum brilliance of the stars, Taen ignored the interruption. But the disturbance waxed insistent, and was joined after a time by a ruddy glimmer of light. The girl felt her consciousness caught and bridled by a touch so light she never thought to protest. Dream-sense aligned like mirrors in her mind. Light cut like a blade across blackness. Taen recovered self-awareness like a sleeper wakened, and found herself in the presence of Tamlin of the Vaere, the same who had trained her in the ways of power.

Fey, impertinent, the creature had changed not at all since her departure for Cliffhaven. Scarcely half the height of a man, he stood with his clay pipe tucked amid an unkempt nest of whiskers. Skin crinkled around eyes unfathomable and dark as jet. From folded arms to stitched calf boots, Tamlin radiated an impression of quickness and reprimand.

"Girl-child, you broke faith. That's trouble." The tiny man shrugged in irritation, and bells and beads danced on the thongs laced through his sleeves. "I warned you, made you swear. You should have left Cliffhaven long since."

Tired to the marrow of her bones, Taen had to gather energy simply to answer. "I had to stay."

"Did you so?" Tamlin snorted through his pipe, and smoke rings lifted, silvered by the light of his presence. "Now your life is endangered."

A spark of resentment rose in Taen. "Would you rather the demons won Landfast? Had I left, the Kielmark's defenses would have fallen. Who would have guarded Mainstrait against invasion then?"

"You're ignorant. Foolish as well." Tamlin twirled the end of his beard between his fingers, and a thoughtful crease appeared between his brows. "Listen now, or perish. Your dream-sense has become unbiddable because you left my guidance before your cycle of mastery was complete. The Sathid crystal you bonded to extend your talents now reaches maturity within your body. The process should have been overseen by the Vaere. Yet you left Cliffhaven too late for our helping."

Taen felt cold touch her heart. *"I can't awaken out of this?"*

"Be silent." Tamlin bit down on his pipe, hands stilled against the fawn cloth of his jacket. "Remember this, whatever befalls. If you cannot reach the enchanted isle, seek the makers of Jaric's flute. They alone can save you."

"Riddles?" said Taen, frightened now, for Tamlin's presence had suddenly begun to fade. The glow of his pipe reddened like a coal, and slowly diminished. Sharp in the ebbing twilight, the Dreamweaver recalled an image; again she saw the scarred fingers of Ivainson Jaric tense, twist, and the delicate shaft of a holed instrument snap into splinters and bent wire.

"Tamlin, the flute you mentioned is broken!" Taen's protest echoed across emptiness; the Vaere was gone. The darkness of his passing closed over Taen's head, even as the green waters of Landfast harbor had once swallowed the fragments of the flute which offered her sole hope of survival.

CHAPTER VIII

Search

The days lengthened toward summer, and in Landfast, oldest settled city in Keithland, the fruit sellers' stalls smelled fragrant with ripe strawberries. Unmarried girls wove ribbons in their hair for the dances to celebrate the planting, and though the season made them eager for courting, Jaric could only stare wistfully at their smiles. Days he spent copying manuscript in the towers where the archives were stored, and in the long hours before twilight, he met Brith in the training yard for arms practice. His sailor's tan faded, but his calluses did not. He cleaned and oiled his steel each night as the lampsmen made rounds to light the wicks along the Lionsgate stair. Then, as Brith and his cadre of off-duty guardsmen gathered, laughing, to visit their alehouses and taverns, Jaric slung his weapons across sweating shoulders. Bound by Anskiere's geas, he stepped into the gathering dark to begin his search for means to safeguard the Keys to Elrinfaer.

He went first to Kordane's shrine. An acolyte met him within the tiled arches of the forecourt. The man wore a robe of blue, the single gold star which adorned his collar showing he had sworn life service barely one year past. He could not have been much beyond Jaric's age, yet he carried himself with an arrogance that seemed common to all junior officials in Landfast. The acolyte regarded the baldric, sword, and dagger slung across the visitor's shoulders, and his lips pursed with disdain, even as he executed the bow of ritual welcome.

"Have you come to worship?" The acolyte straightened, chin lifted for the negative he expected would come.

Jaric stared at him, the disappointment inspired by such brusqueness politely kept hidden. "I wish to speak with the head priest."

"*Head priest?*" The acolyte sighed, loftily amused. "You're backlands-born, aren't you, soldier? We have no head priest here. Only his holiness the Master Grand High Star."

Jaric accepted this without the least sign of discomfort. His hands gently shifted the sword belt. "Does he have a shorter title?"

"'His Eminence' will do." Nettled by the chime of steel cross guards, the acolyte added, "You don't need those in here."

"But I didn't come to worship," Jaric reminded. "If his Eminence is too busy with devotions, please mention that the matter concerns Keithland's defenses."

The acolyte raised his brows at this, as if he doubted any connection a boy with a north-shore accent might have with the preservation of civilization. Still, the single star on his collar was no match for sharpened steel if argument arose; he spun with a flap of dark robes and jerked his head for Jaric to follow.

The anteroom of Kor's shrine was lamplit and chill, the walls being faced with black marble, and the floor polished stone with no carpets. Dark hangings with the gold-sewn sigil of the priesthood seemed to swallow what little light was available, and the raised dais with the reliquary and public altar were shadowed and dim with mystery. Footsteps and voices echoed under lofty vaulted ceilings; the few worshippers clustered by the offering chests spoke in whispers, and acted apologetic if their children made noise or their sandals scraped inadvertently. Jaric waited where his guide indicated. Still holding his weapons, he dropped no coins in the offering chest; nor did he ask the attendant on duty to light any lamps for loved ones. Taen deserved such a courtesy, he knew. But the thought of crossing the chamber was daunting, and a particularly demanding practice with Brith had left his muscles in knots. Weary, hungry, and anxious to be quit of the Keys, Jaric debated the propriety of sitting down on the floor where he stood. Then the acolyte returned and beckoned him through a door into the inner sanctuary.

Beyond lay a drafty expanse of stairwell. The stonework was pierced at intervals with lancet arches open to the outside, and by the lack of glass Jaric guessed the acolyte had led him through the oldest portion of Kor's sanctuary. Here at one time the openings would have been covered by siege shutters, for the walls were dressed and buttressed like a fortress, and the risers worn by the generations of tramping feet.

"Tell me your name," wheezed the acolyte. Since he was a man unaccustomed to exertion, his second ascent of a very steep climb exacted a punishing toll.

"Kerainson," Jaric replied, and winced inwardly as his tired legs protested the length of the stair. Yet he managed with better grace than the acolyte, and finally took pity as the man began to gasp. "If you tell me where, I can go on my own."

The acolyte rolled his eyes. "His Eminence would send me to fast. Don't tell him?"

Jaric shook his head, then memorized what seemed an unduly complex set of directions. Three flights and two corridors later, he knocked on the one door he found that had the Brotherhood's star and fireburst inlaid in gold into ebony.

"What!" barked an impatient-sounding voice from within. "If it's the accounts from the grain tax, leave them for tomorrow, will you?"

"I'm not the accountant," called Jaric. Gently he lifted the latch.

A gray-haired man in a rumpled smock jumped up and peered over the papers piled on his desk. The lamp which burned by his elbow lit apple cheeks, a harried frown, and hands better suited to a farmer. "Ah, the visitor, yes, do come in."

Jaric took a startled step into the room. "You're his Eminence the Grand High Star?"

"Eh? No." The man noticed the sword and dagger slung across his visitor's shoulder and blinked. "You don't need those in here." Then, belatedly remembering the question only partially answered, he said, "I'm his Eminence's secretary. Tell me why you came, and if the matter warrants, I'll refer you."

The boy made no move to lay aside his blades. Neither did he speak, but instead reached one-handed to his collar and lifted a sweat-stained thong over his head. A small leather pouch dangled from the ends. He loosened the drawstrings with his teeth, then dumped the contents onto the only square of desk not littered with paperwork.

A heavy object tumbled out. Black, cube-shaped, it clattered like a die and stopped with a device inlaid in one side uppermost. Lamplight flickered over the triple circle and falcon, sigil of Anskiere, once Stormwarden and sworn defender of Tierl Enneth. The secretary sucked in a surprised breath, then bit off an exclamation as a second item settled with a whisper of sound beside the first. Scratched wood framed the black-and-gold-barred length of a stormfalcon's feather; even here, fenced by papers and pens and the clutter of sheltered living, the spell-wrought thing radiated the chill of gales driven by sorcery.

"Kor have mercy," murmured the secretary. He directed a nervous glance at Jaric, as if seeing him for the first time. "Where did you come by those? Are you the Stormwarden's emissary? You knew his powers leveled Tierl Enneth? Four thousand people drowned, they say. Should Anskiere ever again set foot on any isle of the Alliance, he stands condemned to death by fire."

Jaric said nothing. For an extended interval, the flash and gleam of lantern flame over Anskiere's gold seal was the only movement in the room. Then the secretary jerked open a drawer, raked out a pair of spectacles, and jammed them over his ears. "Wait here, boy. Wait." And near to shaking with agitation, he burst through the door behind his chair.

A taller man stepped through a moment later, the secretary tagging anxiously behind. The newcomer wore no robes but trousers and shirt close-fitted to his body. The fabric was knit rather than woven, the emblem of office in sewn silver and indigo on his chest. More agile than the secretary, with a face barely wrinkled and hair dusted gray at the temples, he turned sharp, dark eyes upon Jaric, then glanced at the desk, to the items isolated between tiered stacks of accounts.

His voice proved as authoritative as his attitude. "Kerainson? Pick those up and bring them in."

Brisk but not unkindly, he held the door open while the boy filed past. The chamber beyond was sumptuously carpeted. White-painted walls contrasted with polished stone sills; but Jaric had no eyes for the view of Landfast which sparkled four stories down, alight with lanterns and life. He stared instead at row upon row of bookshelves laden with gold-stamped bindings and rare texts. The lettering was scribed in religious runes, which he lacked the schooling to decipher. Yet the promise of new knowledge offered fascination enough; surely Kordane's Brotherhood possessed means of holding the Keys to Elrinfaer secure from demons.

"You're standing on the sacred symbol," admonished a voice at his back.

Jaric started, and belatedly noticed he had strayed beyond the carpet. The floor beneath his boots was configured like a seal. A polished mosaic of lapis lazuli and agate depicted Kordane's Fires as they first arced across Keithland's sky, condemning mankind to exile until such time as the last demon was vanquished or killed.

"I'm sorry." The boy stepped back with an embarrassing chime of sword steel. Painfully diffident, he stilled his swinging blades and found the Grand High Star smiling at him.

"You don't need those in here," said his Eminence softly. "But keep them by you if you feel the better for it. Only sit, please. I've a stiff neck from looking over accounts, and watching you walk circles is a distraction I'd rather avoid." Strong, pale hands lifted a chair from the corner and thumped it on the carpet before the books. The Grand High Star seated himself on a nearby divan, his attention apparently fixed on the wrought-brass candlestand which supported the only light in the chamber.

Jaric slipped his baldric from his shoulder. He looped the leather over the chairback and settled stiffly on the seat, the Keys to Elrinfaer and the stormfalcon's feather clenched in white knuckles in his lap. Then, granted audience with the man in the highest echelon of Kor's priesthood not sworn to seclusion, the boy struggled for words to begin.

The Grand High Star rescued him from discomfort. "You are the heir of Ivain?"

Jaric flinched, wishing he had the courage to lie; but the eyes of the priest on the divan were unforgiving, behind their kindliness. "Eminence, how did you know?"

"You look like him," the Grand High Star said bluntly. "And Cliffhaven's news ofttimes travels in the gossip of sailors. The priesthood has heard that the curse pronounced by Anskiere at Northsea had been loosed within Keithland."

"I never knew either sorcerer," the Firelord's son admitted miserably. Wariness showed in his bearing as he opened his fists and bared the Keys to Elrinfaer and the feather.

"No, boy," said the Grand High Star. "The Brotherhood cannot shelter those things in your care."

Jaric returned a stricken look. "But—"

The Grand High Star waved him silent. Then he rose and crossed to the doorway. After a few quiet words to the secretary standing without, he nodded, shut the panel, and promptly returned to the divan.

"Ivainson, the works of Kordane's Brotherhood and the doings of sorcerers have never intermixed. By oath an initiate must maintain, nurture, and defend. But sorcerers, particularly ones trained by the Vaere, seem compelled to meddle, so far to the detriment of mankind. The destruction of Elrinfaer should have taught your Stormwarden the futility of challenging demons. It did not, and four thousand more innocents died at Tierl Enneth."

"But I have no wish for a sorcerer's powers!" Jaric burst in. "Instead I seek means to avoid them."

The Grand High Star tapped his signet with its carven seal of office. The boy seated hopefully before him never moved, even as he sighed and spoke. "Firelord's heir, the priesthood cannot help."

That moment a knock sounded at the door. Jaric started, hands tightened convulsively on the Keys to Elrinfaer. But the panel only opened to admit his eminence's secretary. The man carried a tray laden with sweet pastry, cheese, and ale. He set this on a side table and, with a bow to his superior, departed.

The Grand High Star smiled as the latch clicked shut. "You seemed hungry," he said to Jaric. "If my order can do nothing else, at least I could be certain you got supper."

The solicitude was impossible to refuse. Jaric returned Keys and stormfalcon's feather to the pouch on the string at his neck. He reached tentatively for the cheese knife; and the Grand High Star of Landfast waited without speaking while the boy shed his self-consciousness and ate. Only then did his strength become apparent, innate, but too often obscured by uncertainty. His hair needed a trim, and his clothing was simple, but the manner in which he broke his bread would not have been out of place in a king's hall.

Anxious not to tax his host's attentiveness, Jaric soon set his ale mug aside. "The sanctuary towers of Landfast are the most secure stronghold upon Keithland. Why not safeguard the Keys to Anskiere's wards there?"

"Because demons covet the breaking of those wards, Jaric." The Grand High Star settled back. Carefully, patiently, for he understood the disappointment his words would bring, he explained that the knowledge stored in the sanctuary towers was too vital to be risked. "The priests who enter there stay for a term of life, and not even I know what secrets they guard. Were they to add the wards of a Vaere-trained sorcerer, demons might attack to gain possession of them. Better the Keys fell to Shadowfane than that the legacy of mankind became jeopardized."

Jaric forgot the half-eaten pastry in his hand. "But I thought the outer defenses—"

The Grand High Star seemed suddenly burdened with sadness. "Jaric, what I'm about to tell you is unknown to men on the streets, and in peril of your soul you'll never repeat it. But the ward you encountered upon entering Landfast waters was no defense at all, only a screen maintained by the more talented initiates of the Brotherhood to detect the presence of demons. Should Kor's Accursed send spies, or even an attacking army, no disguise will shelter them. Our citizens will gain warning of invasion. After that, defense of this city must rely upon ordinary force of arms."

Crumbs jumped as the pastry dropped from Jaric's hand onto the tray. He stared, shocked, at the haunted countenance of the Grand High Star, and suddenly understood: this man's fatalistic serenity and Ivain Firelord's contempt of the priesthood both stemmed from the fact that mankind's survival hung balanced on the most fragile of threads. The impact of implications stunned the mind. For if this priest spoke honestly, the bulwark of Landfast's defenses was based on bluff. In all of Keithland only the Vaere-trained owned effective powers against demons. The enormities of Elrinfaer and Tierl Enneth gained a new significance, and, almost, the Cycle of Fire seemed less a mad recourse, and more a remedy of desperate necessity.

Jaric forgot courtesy. Miserable with fresh doubts in the one place he hoped to find solace, he rose and grasped his sword belt. But his move to depart was caught short by the steely voice of the Grand High Star.

"Ivainson Jaric, listen well. You came to Landfast to gather knowledge. Wise or not, your quest shall not go unsupported. There are treatises in the secular archives pertaining to Keithland's defenses. These will be made available to you for study."

Jaric spun just short of the doorway and bowed. "I am grateful, Eminence."

"Don't be." The priest seemed suddenly remote behind the badges and signet of his office. "I must also restrict your stay here, since your presence shall inevitably draw unwanted attention to this city. Felwaithe's royal seer already warns that the compact at Shadowfane seeks your whereabouts. You have leave to remain until the fall solstice. After that, I recommend you apply to the enclave of wizards at Mhored Kara, and beg them to offer you shelter."

Jaric accepted this banishment with startling poise. His dark eyes remained steady, and the hand on his sword no longer trembled. "Like you, the kingdom conjurers can warn. They have little ability to guard. If demons overtake me, and the Mharg fly free, how long do you think your sanctuary towers will stay standing?"

The question was impertinent; the highest-ranking priest in Landfast answered through white lips. "Until eternity or man's salvation, by the grace of Kordane's Fires."

"I hope so," whispered Jaric. And he spun with the reflective grace of a swordsman and departed.

All the way home, through streets bustling with Landfast's frenetic nightlife, Jaric thrashed through the facts revealed by the Grand High Star. Jostled by sailors on shore leave, and whistled at by more than one aging prostitute, he shut his eyes, sweating and cold and angry by turns. Who enacted the greater injustice against mankind, he wondered: the priests with their fabrication of illusions, or the Vaere-trained, whose perilous powers sometimes killed the innocent? The question nettled like a thorn, his own fear a litany beneath. The only surety in Keithland was the tireless hatred of the demons.

"Anskiere forgive me," murmured the boy, surrounded by strangers; for like the righteous, ignorant populace of Keithland, he had condemned what he had not understood. Tierl Enneth's deaths might perhaps be justifiable; but in terror Jaric knew he could not accept such responsibility for his own. The Cycle of Fire was a curse he would escape if he could. And he would, he must, though the demons crushed him to powder as he tried.

Ivainson Jaric never spoke with the Grand High Star of Kor's Brotherhood again, but the next day after sword practice, he called back at the shrine. Now the acolyte at the entry greeted him with solicitous respect, and conducted him to the librarian in the chamber of secular archives. There, by the command of the Grand High Star, an impressive collection of documents and books had been compiled. All were bound in black leather, and not a few had locks.

Though the chamber that housed them was vaulted with high, airy domes, large enough to diminish the tallest of men, Jaric felt confined. Here, for the first time he could remember, he found no security in a place of knowledge and learning. The evil and the doom threatened by Shadowfane's compact seemed to poison his heart against hope. Inexplicably he thought of Taen, even as he perused the first titles. Haunted by growing doubts that his search would prove futile, he barely noticed the librarian behind him raise crossed wrists in the traditional sign against evil. Need to escape the Cycle of Fire overshadowed any social stigma of Ivain's inheritance. Jaric lifted the first book from the shelf and retired to an alcove overlooking the merchants' wharf. There he wedged his sword in a notch between cushions and, with feet braced against a worn corner of wainscoting, began to read.

Sundown came quickly. Beyond the window the city towers streaked shadows across the hump of Little Dagley Islet. Carts rumbled away from the dockside, and as the harbor beacons glimmered orange through twilight, the whistles and shouted jokes of the longshoremen faded as they sought their wives, or refreshment in the taverns. Jaric squinted in the failing light, and barely glanced up as the librarian brought a stand and two spare candles. He managed a nod when the man retired for the evening, leaving instructions concerning the visitor for the night watch.

Jaric read as if the treatises and the essays were not long-winded, or repetitive, and tediously interrupted with religious overtones or outright misconceptions. He dared do no less. A paragraph carelessly skimmed might contain the one fact he needed. Some of the works on the hilltribes' rites were available nowhere else on Keithland; the wild clansmen who practiced them were easily provoked to killing, and their ways were little known to outsiders. Evangelists of Kor's Brotherhood were among the few to venture among their camps. Jaric studied until his eyes stung and the light wavered. He finished the first book in time to light a fresh candle from the failing wick of the last. He reached next for a collection of essays, absently kneading a cramp in his thigh. The words were archaic and stiff, difficult to follow. Jaric persisted, while the second candle burned down to a dribbled stub. In time, the third and last of his lights flickered out. The glow of a rising quarter moon lit his way as he returned the books to the librarian's desk.

Jaric pushed open the wide double door, and caught the watchman napping at his post.

"It's after midnight, boy," groused the man as he shuffled yawning to his feet. He fumbled at his belt ring and the rattle of his keys echoed down deserted corridors as he unlocked to let Jaric out.

The streets outside were equally empty, except for scavenging dogs and disreputable sorts who rummaged in trashbins for their livelihood. Ivainson walked between shuttered houses, past lamps with their wicks trimmed low. He kept one hand on his sword to deter footpads, but his thoughts were detached as he contemplated the rites of the clansmen, whose chosen high priestesses were ritually blinded as maidens. The barbarities described in the texts were disparaged by the priests; yet the visions experienced by the women after their cruel initiation were indisputably true seeing. They possessed power to unmask demons, even shelter their folk from the malign influence of dream-image that Kor's Accursed sometimes employed to lure isolated humans to their deaths. Whether the Presence behind the springs that were the center of the clan priestess's devotions truly held power to guide, advise, and protect was a claim no devout missionary dared endorse without risking trial for heresy. The point was moot, from Ivainson's standpoint. Valid as a religion or not, the clan tribes' beliefs were not adequate to safeguard the Keys to Elrinfaer, or stay frostwargs and win Anskiere's release.

Jaric's curse of frustration rang in the emptiness of weavers' alley. His quest was a vain one, surely. If the clansmen, or any conjurer, priest, kingdom, or alliance within Keithland held force or knowledge enough to suppress the demon compact, *they would have done so.* Unbidden, the thought followed, that Anskiere and the Vaere-trained who preceded him had courageously endeavored the same, despite the mistakes at Elrinfaer and Tierl Enneth.

"No," said Jaric aloud. An alternate to the Cycle of Fire *must exist.* Yet the suspicion his conviction was false drove him into a run.

His baldric and weapons chinked faintly in the dark, and his footsteps echoed like whispers against the locked doors of the buildings. Rats dashed from their scavenging, and the glassless lanterns of the poor quarter flickered to the disturbed air of his passage. The boy pushed harder. Sweat stung his eyes, and the breath rasped his throat. The pouch on its knotted thong swung to his stride, the Keys to Elrinfaer banging painfully into his breastbone. Jaric closed his hand over sharp corners of basalt with a half sob of panic. Why should he be chosen to shoulder such a burden? As a child, he had been weak, ridiculed by his peers, and inept at anything resembling conflict. What talent had his mad but gifted father owned, that the pain of a sorcerer's legacy should fall to a son he had never known?

The empty streets held no answer, only the reminder of humanity's fragile and inadequate defenses. Still running, Jaric could not escape facts. Centuries had passed since Kor's Fire had fallen from heaven. Demons whose numbers had once been small had multiplied, even as men had; Shadowfane's strength increased with each passing year, while mankind's defenses had evolved very little. One day the balance would swing. The compact would strike, and under attack by powers of mind and sorcery, men would strive and perish. Was he, Ivainson Jaric, by himself responsible for light and darkness, good and evil, survival or death? The question ripped him with anguish and doubt, and he ran faster, his feet a blur over the cobbles. The poor quarter fell behind; smells of sea-rotted timbers and waste faded, replaced by hearth smoke and new paint. The houses of rich merchants arose on both sides of the street, each with stoutly shuttered windows and inset dooryards planted with shrubs. Sometimes a light shone through, where a man or his wife tallied accounts in the lateness of the night. Oblivious as insects before the killing advent of frost, they went about their industries unaware of the doom which threatened. Jaric gasped. His chest burned with exertion, yet he raced onward, past a crossroad with a shrine to the Sacred Fires. Beyond, scrolled columns rose amid pools of lamplight; a wrought-iron gate spanned the roadway between, blocking the path of his flight.

"Halt!" cried a voice from the shadows.

Jaric stumbled, caught short of a fall by unyielding bars of iron. He hooked his fingers to stay upright. Dizzy from exhaustion, he recognized the perimeter defenses of the sanctuary towers guarded by the highest of Kordane's priests.

"What passes? Are you in trouble?" demanded the sentry on duty. Pressed against cold metal, and numb to most else, Jaric lifted his head. Thinking the boy fled from footpads, the soldier had stepped from his post to survey the street for thieves, or maybe a murderer.

"I'm alone," said the boy between gasps.

The soldier returned a puzzled look.

Jaric chose not to explain. He leaned his cheek against the gate to recover his breath, his eyes fixed on the tiled court beyond. Torches blazed over the entry to the towers where priests guarded knowledge too precious to risk to demons. The brightness seemed to sear his eyes. He closed them, even as the grief of a sorcerer's inheritance ached in his heart. Willing or not, Ivain's heir must answer to his father's legacy; accounting would be exacted for Keithland's need.

"You can't linger here, boy," snapped the sentry. He lifted his halberd to prod, and Jaric nodded.

Certain of nothing but his own weaknesses, and the inescapable probability that his search of the libraries was wasted endeavor, he loosed his grip on the grillwork. Anskiere's curse would never leave him. By burden of blood relation, he must act; but only when hope was exhausted. Responding at last to the impatient shove of the sentry, Ivainson Firelord's heir straightened. He began the long walk to the boardinghouse, where a bed waited, and the transient oblivion of sleep.

Yet now even that peace was denied him. The leathery smell of aged books followed Ivainson into rest, and that night, for the first time, he dreamed of demons. They sailed in black boats, toadlike forms with webbed fingers hunched in silhouette against the lacy foam of the swells. Pale eyes glinted in the dark of the open sea, and the hissing croaks uttered in place of language threaded menace through Jaric's sleep. He tossed in his blankets, threatened by a purpose remote and pitiless as the constellations which shone unchanging overhead. Elusive, evil, dangerous in the extreme, Thienz demons lifted blunt snouts to the south. The thrust of their intent stabbed outward, searching, circling, frustrated to bitter and repeated fury by the wards which protected the isle of Landfast. *'He is there,'* Shadowfane's chosen whispered among themselves, mind-to-mind, as one being. *'Ivainson Firelord's heir hides there.'*

And from the boats on the open sea, cold reached out and touched Jaric, sending chills over his sweating skin.

The vividness of the nightmare wrenched him awake. Soaked and shaking, he threw off his sheets and paced the floor. But the worn pine boards beneath his feet did not reassure. The solidity of the boardinghouse walls seemed somehow less substantial than the lift and hiss of waves beneath the keels of Shadowfane's black ships.

Jaric perched in the window seat. He wrapped his arms around his knees and regarded the towers of Landfast, while sunrise burned the gray east to red, and finally to gold as bright as Ivain's command of flame. On this day, as any other, farm wagons and drays laden with fishmongers' barrels rumbled through the streets, bringing produce to market. The whistles of the milk sellers called buyers to their doors to haggle, and the bell towers sounded carillons at daybreak. Yet the familiar wakening of Landfast reflected precarious tranquility. Warned by the Llondel on the ice cliffs, and the visions of Felwaithe's seer, Ivain's heir no longer dared presume the black ships and their searchers were anything other than real. More weary than ever he could remember, Jaric reached for boots and tunic. He needed all the courage he possessed simply to face another day in the libraries. As he tied his laces, his hands clenched in terror. Where, for love of all he knew in life, would a backlands scribe like him find strength to combat such as the Thienz, with their ability to steal thought and override the living will of a man?

Five days after the storm the Kielmark's brigantine, *Moonless* drifted still in the northwest reaches of the Corine Sea. Far from any land, she lay like a speck upon water flat as sheet metal. The sky glared cloudless indigo overhead. Shirtless, his shoulders bronzed by pitiless sunlight, Corley paced the quarterdeck, the tap of his booted feet measured against the nerve-wearing creak of cord and timber. He strode from wheel to compass to railing, and back, repeatedly, until his officers adopted tact and fell in step with their captain as they reported. The slow-witted who did not received sharp words and a glare biting as frost.

The ship's healer paused at the head of the companionway ladder; absorbed in his own troubles, he called out without first gauging the prevailing mood. "Captain? I think you should accompany me below."

Corley spun on his toes, hands poised as if he expected attack. "Best tell me why." When the healer hesitated, he snapped, "Quick, man! Is the Dreamweaver dead?"

The healer shook his head, fed up with eddyless air and the captain's dicey temperament. "Not yet. But without help she soon will be."

"Kor's *Fires!*" Corley's tone blistered. "Do you think I can raise the wind? We're no slave-bearing galleass, to row our way out of a calm."

The healer gripped the rail and stood in steadfast silence. Presently Corley raised his brows, and his hands dropped loose to his sides. "I'll come. But nothing under Keithland's sky that I do will be any use."

Shadow pooled under his feet as he stepped to the companionway and followed the healer into the airless confines below decks. Taen lay on a pallet in the healer's quarters, her hair spilled like ebony silk across the sheets. Her eyes were open, but misty and unfocused above the curve of her cheeks; worse, her perfectly motionless limbs made her seem a sculpture in wax. Never had Corley seen a girl look so vulnerable. With her indomitable spirit absent, the fact that Taen was a child inhabiting a woman's body became arrestingly plain.

"Kor's grace, is she breathing at all?" Corley knelt by the pallet in alarm.

The healer coughed uncomfortably by the companionway, his head bent beneath the beams. "Her life signs are very weak."

Corley lifted the girl's wrist from the sheets. Her bones felt frail as a bird's, and the pulse raced shallow and quick under his finger. But where the consuming restlessness of his character had once driven her awake through a touch, now not an eyelash flickered. Close up, Taen's skin was feverish and dry, the hollows of her face a shadowed, translucent blue.

Corley raised helpless eyes. The healer, who could not face him, sighed and shook his head. "I don't *know* what's ailing her. Only the Vaere could say."

At that the Kielmark's sternest captain settled Taen's wrist back upon the coverlet with unabashed regret. "*Damn* the wind! After all Taen did for Cliffhaven, she deserves better." He paused, his lips thinned with conflict. Then he met the healer's glance, and all trace of profanity vanished from his speech. "You know it's too late, now, for the Isle of the Vaere. If the wind came up this minute, I have no choice. *Moonless* must run straight to the nearest shore for water."

The healer remained mute. The captain's decision was not made callously; with empty casks, not a man of *Moonless*'s company would survive to reach the Isle of the Vaere.

Corley's boots scraped against wood as he rose. "This will haunt me the rest of my days." He smacked his fist to his palm in frustration. "The Vaere warned her, yet she chose to stay and defend. The Kielmark will be bitter when he hears."

Aware that his voice was painfully altered, he stopped, pushed past the pallet and departed. The healer stared mutely at Taen's face, death-pale, but still possessed of an innocent and unearthly beauty. The girl was doomed, surely; for the closest landfall was the deserted shore of Tierl Enneth.

CHAPTER IX

Ash Flute

In a fourth-floor garret of Landfast's main library, a single candle guttered, and wax dribbled and froze like old ice against the base of the stand. The flame flickered out as Jaric closed the book he had finished reading. He made no move to strike a fresh light, but lifted another volume from the table and hitched his stool closer to the window. Far beneath the sill, blots of shadow underhung the people and wagons which jammed the square; diminished by distance, the noise of the traffic through Lionsgate sounded thin as the clatter of toy figurines. Jaric paid no heed. Propped on one elbow with his fingers jammed into tangled hair, he leafed through the pages of yet another history of the Great Fall. This book was far older than the others. The covers were cracked and worn, and the text archaic. Jaric touched the lettering, felt a texture that differed from inked parchment or reed paper. He knew a moment of excitement. Perhaps this account contained information the others lacked. Driven by the conviction that time was growing scarce, the boy perused the older writing eagerly. Hope died as he read. The most ancient record in Landfast's stacks only repeated the same events, beginning with Kordane's Blessed Fires which had seared down from the divine province of Starhope and set men and demons upon Keithland to contend for survival. There followed the usual lists of First Elders and their offspring, who had dispersed and settled, establishing the civilized bounds of Keithland.

Defeated, Jaric bit his lip. His eyes ached, and his stomach cramped with hunger; in the weeks since his audience with the Grand High Star, he had neglected meals and sleep while he poured every spare minute into studying the records of Landfast. As he had guessed, his efforts brought him no nearer to safety than the moment he had encountered the Llondel demon upon the rocks of Cliffhaven. Tired and disheartened, the boy flopped the book closed and buried his face in his hands. The spiel of a fish seller drifted through the opened casement, underscored by the clatter of hooves and wagon wheels. In daylight, amid the bustle of Keithland's most populous city, his beginnings at Morbrith felt very far away; Emien and the perils of Shadowfane seemed unreal as the tales told by firesides to frighten children. But at night, dreams of black boats and demons continued to break his sleep. Then the leather bag which held the Keys to Elrinfaer weighed all too heavily. Ivainson stirred and dropped his hands.

As he reached dispiritedly to replace the book on the stack, his fingers snagged an edge where the glue had loosened on the binding.

The damage made him pause out of instinct. His earliest training had been by an archivist concerned with the preservation of ancient records, and repairs had been part and parcel of the daily chores. Jaric examined the worn place, and discovered a protruding corner of parchment that logically should not have been there.

The leaf was yellowed and flecked with age. Jaric bent closer and perceived traces of lettering, faded nearly illegible. Certain the fragment was not an integral part of the book, he tugged it gently free. The parchment fell into pieces as he uncreased its tight folds. He lined up the edges in the sunlight, and saw lettering. Written in an informal hand rather than the script of a trained scribe, the message itself proved cryptic.

> What I write here is forbidden, since the charter established by the Landfast Council. But how else can a man protest what he knows to be futile? With the Veriset-Nav unit lost in the crash, no ship can find the way back to Starhope; the heritage so carefully sealed in the sanctuary towers will inevitably prove useless. If the Council's policy endures, will our children's children ever know their forefathers ruled the stars?

Jaric frowned, fingers tapping anxiously on the tabletop. Nowhere within the records had he encountered anything to match the context of this strange note. No archives mentioned an artifact called Veriset-Nav unit; Anskiere might command wave and weather, but how could a man hold influence over stars? Even the sorcerers knew them as lights in the sky, changing with the seasons, and useful only for navigation. Perplexed, Jaric considered the city beyond the window. The Landfast Council still ruled the Free Isles' Alliance, but the sanctuary towers were the perpetual domain of the priests. Now, as never before, he distrusted the platitudes of the Grand High Star of Kor's Brotherhood. Their secrets were perhaps deeper than anyone guessed. The knowledge he sought might indeed lie locked within the great, cream-colored spires which notched the sky above Lionsgate.

The door latch clicked sharply. Jaric started from contemplation and glanced around as a blue-robed priest entered the chamber. He strode toward the table by the window with an air of querulous admonition, his mouth pursed and his brows drawn into a frown.

"Young man, why are you idle? Does our guild pay you copyist's wages to sit staring at sky?"

Jaric leaned on his forearm, covering the scrap of writing he had found; the note's contents were certainly heretical, and if he wished continued access to temple records, the Brotherhood must never find reason to question his faith. Jaric met the priest's suspicion with a show of boyish innocence. "I thought Brother Handred was making the rounds today."

The priest sniffed. "You're impertinent. Brother Handred is busy. Now answer me. Where are your pens?"

Jaric sighed. "This is my day off." Slowly, surreptitiously, he closed his fingers over the parchment.

The priest coughed. "Well, then. Who gave you permission to disarrange the stacks and leave books piled all over the library?"

"Brother Handred," Jaric said sweetly. With the paper safely crumpled in his palm, he rose. "I'm finished anyway." In a move designed to provoke, he reached across the table and lifted a book by its pasteboard cover.

The priest flinched. "Stupid boy!" He snatched the volume from Jaric's hand and smoothed the pages closed. "Brother Handred will hear about this! How ever did you get hired without knowing the proper way to handle a book?"

Jaric shrugged, then flexed his wrists, that he might appear more like a sailhand caught out of his element than a trained copyist.

"Well," huffed the priest. "Get along, boy. I'll tidy your mess." He clutched the piled books protectively against his chest, and glared until Jaric passed the doorsill.

In the cool shadow of the stairwell, Ivainson paused and slipped the parchment with its strange writing into the bag along with the stormfalcon's feather and the Keys to Elrinfaer. He tugged the drawstring taut and replaced the thong beneath his collar with a curse of sharp frustration. Lacking an intimate's training and vows, he had no way to gain entry to the sanctuary towers of Landfast. The guards and fortifications that surrounded them were enough to daunt a small army, far less a determined thief.

Light slanted steeply through the doubled arches at the base of the stairwell, showing noon was now past. Jaric hastened across the tiled foyer, wary of being late for sword practice. Brith's lessons were always tougher when his students forgot to be punctual. Midday glare whitewashed the marble paving beyond the main floors. Jaric stepped out into heat and the busy press of traffic. Sweat slicked his back beneath the thick linen of his tunic. Startled to remember that solstice lay barely a fortnight off, he realized a full year had passed since Anskiere's geas had driven him from Morbrith Keep.

"Boy! Watch yourself!" A carter's whip cracked, and his team of draft horses curvetted sideways with a deafening rattle of hooves. Jaric dodged the spinning rims of the cartwheels. No longer intimidated by the press in Landfast's streets, he passed the snapping row of pennants which marked the council hall of Landfast, then turned into the street of the potters' guild. The guest house where he had lodgings lay in the alley beyond. Hoping to avoid the landlady's chatter, the boy ducked through the pantry entrance; usually the kitchen was deserted at this hour of the day.

Jaric grabbed a fresh roll from the bin. He chewed with wolfish appetite as he climbed the back stairway to his garret room. From the chamber opposite, he heard the carping voice of the downstairs tenant complaining of moths in the blankets. The landlady returned an epithet and tartly suggested he admit his paid woman through the door instead of the casements; then perhaps the insects wouldn't fly at the candles and end up nesting in the bedclothes.

"But I put the flame out *before* I let her in!" whined the tenant; a silence developed as he realized what he had been tricked into admitting.

Jaric grinned and gently closed his door. He threw off sword belt and tunic and piled them on his bed. Then, with one hand busy loosening laces at his throat, he opened the lid of his clothes chest and rummaged inside in search of summer-weight garments. The shirt he wanted lay folded beneath his trapper's woolens. Jaric tugger impatiently. The cloth pulled free of the chest, and a light, slim object tumbled out, clattering hollowly across the floorboards.

Breath stopped in the boy's throat. Chills pricked his neck as the Llondian flute he had smashed and sunk in the harbor rolled to a stop beside his knee. Shell inlay gleamed in the light from the dormer. The delicate wooden shaft lay unmarked, as if no breakage had occurred. Jaric shuddered. With the shirt balled up in his fist, he settled back on his heels. The forester, Telemark, had once told of a Llondian demon which had waylaid him after a storm of sorcery had destroyed the contents of his cabin. When the forester recovered from the encounter, he had found his shattered flasks miraculously mended and restored to the shelves, and every displaced item in his cabin set to rights. Now, confronted by the flawless surface of the ash flute, Jaric wondered whether Telemark had trembled with fear as he did now. The powers of the Llondelei were beyond human comprehension.

The shirt slipped from the boy's hand as he reached to retrieve the instrument from the floor. The instant his trembling fingers touched the wood, Llondian images snared his mind. His perception of walls, floor, and room buckled, replaced by a lonely, wave-washed shoreline. The hills beyond stood crowned with jaggedly gapped walls, and houses that were roofless and forsaken to the elements. Gulls dove and swooped against empty sky. Pilings thrust blackened stumps through the seethe of the swell, the wharves and shops they once had supported torn cleanly away. Jaric understood he viewed the ruins of Tierl Enneth, the city blasted to wreckage by the powers the witch Tathagres had stolen from Anskiere's staff.

Yet, through Llondian perception, the boy observed that the landing of what had been the richest city in the Alliance was not deserted. A ship's boat drove through the booming froth of the breakers, her oarsmen trained and steady, and their stroke expertly timed. The man in the stern was *Moonless*'s boatswain; and as if Jaric's recognition were a cue, the Llondian image tightened and focused solely upon the boat.

The craft held other familiar faces. Hatless, his shoulders glistening with spray, Corley sat in the bow with a cloak-wrapped form in his arms. By the strands of black hair which looped his wrists, Jaric realized whom the Kielmark's captain sheltered. In anguish he cried out Taen's name; the empty beach and dismembered dwellings beyond echoed his despair over and over to infinity.

'Not dead,' soothed the Llondel presence in his mind. 'Yet your Weaver of Dreams is very ill. The landing you view will not occur for another fortnight, but unless you sail to the shores of Tierl Enneth, and there summon help with the ash flute, Taen will perish. Heed well, little brother of your race. Should the Dreamweaver die, the hopes and the efforts of your forebears will have been in vain.'

The image of the longboat wrenched out of existence, replaced by the screams of frostwargs etched against the silence of ice-bound caverns. For an instant, Jaric shared the icy vigil of the Stormwarden of Elrinfaer. Then his perception turned, vanished, and coalesced into the peat-smoke dimness of a fisherman's shack where the niece of Mathieson Keldric grieved for an uncle buried in the tide. Cut by a keen edge of sorrow, the boy cried out and abruptly wakened to the touch of a hand on his shoulder.

"Are you ailing, boy?" Solicitous with concern, the landlady smoothed the hair from his brow.

Jaric drew back from her touch. "I'm all right. Just tired." Worried lest she notice a demon artifact beneath her roof, he glanced at the floor. But the ash flute no longer lay on the boards beside his knee.

Skirts swished softly as the landlady straightened. "You work far too much, you know. Boys your age should be carefree. Haven't you the time for a girl?" She clasped her hands at her waist and ran an appreciative glance over Jaric's muscled shoulders and the finely drawn line of his brows. "That's a pity, don't you see?"

"No." Embarrassed by the elderly woman's regard, the boy spoke curtly. "I've troubles enough without adding girls to the tally." He reached to recover his fallen shirt and froze as he discovered the flute beneath the cotton.

The landlady retreated to the door. "Well, boy, I'll allow you the wisdom in that. Some men spend their whole lives, and never learn." With a snort of annoyance which had more to do with the downstairs tenant than any vagary of Jaric's, the woman ducked into the hallway and departed.

Her step faded on the stair. Jaric rose swiftly. He unwrapped the flute and tugged the thin shirt over his head. Leaving the lacings at cuff and collar untied, he pulled cloak and sea boots from the closet. Concern for Taen left no room to question the Llondel's intentions. Jaric emptied the clothes chest and tossed his few belongings into the folds of his cloak. As he knotted the wool into a bundle, his thoughts leaped ahead to the difficulties of passage between islands. Tierl Enneth lay eighty leagues to the north across a shoal-ridden strait. Safer waters lay eastward, around the tip of the archipelago, but that route might take too long, particularly if the wind blew from the north. Callinde's shallow draft was better suited to avoiding reefs than making time on a windward heading. Grimly Jaric buckled on his sword and dagger. He left a neat pile of coins on the clothes chest to pay for his bed and board, then slipped out by way of the pantry stair.

Determined to avoid the bustle in the streets, Jaric hurried into the torturous maze of byways and alleys which riddled the districts between thoroughfares. Because his route lay shadowed by gables and the clustered spires of the town, he never noticed the man who emerged from the arched gate of a nobleman's entry and followed his steps. Preoccupied with concern for Taen and intent upon reaching the harbor before the turn of the tide, the boy raced over puddled brick and ducked under the dank stone of cross-bridges. As he crossed a slash of sunlight between houses, the man who pursued caught sight of the cloak bundled under Jaric's arm; he swore and redoubled his chase.

Jaric rounded a corner. Confronted by a five-way intersection where several alleys converged around mossy foundations of stone, he hesitated and, unsure of his bearings, chose blindly. The man who dogged his tracks saw his quarry run down a known dead end. He chuckled and slowed to a jog, confident he could reach the harbor ahead of the boy.

Minutes later, Jaric leapt over the rotting boards of a tavern's rear stair and found himself blocked by the mortared bricks of a courtyard wall. Too winded to curse, he whirled and retraced his steps. One turn-off led to the locked gates of a root cellar; another sent him sliding and panting over a refuse heap. Broken glass skittered under this boots, startling a starved dog which foraged among the garbage. Jaric gave the snarling animal wide berth, nostrils revolted by the smell of rotten meat. Ahead, sunlight stabbed down through the grate of a culvert; beyond rose the lampposts which flanked the entry of the Lanterns Inn. Restored to familiar territory, Jaric continued at a run. He sprinted down the street of the spice grinders and, still sneezing from a cloying miasma of cinnamon and pepper, arrived breathless at the quayside.

Sea air slapped his face, damp and fitful, and straight out of the south. The boy squinted to windward and frowned to find a low band of clouds beyond the crosshatch of ships' rigging. The breeze might favor a crossing to Tierl Enneth, since *Callinde* sailed best on a downwind heading; but weather from that quarter invariably brought rain. Passage might be miserably wet. Jaric waited while a beer cart rattled past, then bolted for the wharf where his boat lay tied.

The tide had just turned. In the harbor, a cargo bark raised sail; sailors' gruff voices blended in a chantey, accompanied by the rattle of anchor chain through the hawse. Anxious to catch the current to his advantage, Jaric threaded his way through the jam of commerce on the docks. Half running, he rounded a mass of piled fish nets and all but impaled himself on the point of an unsheathed sword.

"Kor!" Jaric bounded back. Cloth spilled from his arms as he dropped his bundled belongings and drew his own blades from their scabbards.

"Why the haste?" said Brith, in precisely the tone he had used the first time they met. Unlike the sessions in the practice yard, his mouth showed no smile beneath the brown tips of his mustache. The eyes he fixed on his pupil remained cold and steady.

But Jaric was no longer the timid boy who had cowered from a fight on the steps before the scribes' towers. Desperate with worry for Taen, he lifted his sword and attacked.

Brith's block met him, effortlessly executed and seemingly solid as stone. "Where were you off to, boy? Didn't we have a practice scheduled this afternoon?"

Harried backward by a fast attack, Jaric managed a breathless reply. "I haven't time. Why concern yourself? Fires! Sometimes I think you have nothing better to do than follow me around!"

Steel clanged vengefully against Jaric's guarding blade. Stung by the force of the blow, the boy guessed at once that this encounter was no spar for sport. Brith's eyes were narrowed slits of annoyance, and his attitude that of a man who fought in earnest. Pricked by intuition, Jaric feinted and kicked clear of the nets at his heels. "You've been following me. Why?"

Brith drove into a lunge and recovered with his habitual neat footwork. "Where were you *going*, boy?"

"Sailing!" Jaric twisted to avoid a rolling cask. A longshoreman cursed and ordered him out of the way, then sprang back as Brith's sword whined through the air and clashed against the boy's cross guard.

"No, boy." Brith beat at Jaric's guard, driving him toward a stacked pile of lumber. Steel clanged and shivered under the force of his offensive. "I'm paid the Kielmark's gold to keep you safe at Landfast. Won't see my hide roasted by his first captain because I broke my trust. Put up now." Jaric wrenched clear of a bind; Brith cut at his fingers and scored a glancing touch. "Drop your sword, do you hear?"

Stung, bleeding, and angered beyond reason, Jaric executed a whistling riposte. After Anskiere's demands, the Kielmark's high-handed attempt to meddle became an intrusion not to be borne. Only the innocent would suffer; distressed by the threat to Taen's life, and incensed by Brith's superiority, Jaric felt something snap within his mind. He focused every ounce of his being on the fight. As his sword battered against Brith's guard, his lips curled with a grim understanding. Unlike the weapons-master, he was under no constraint of the Kielmark's; if he must, he would strike to kill.

The shift in the intensity of Jaric's style caught Brith by surprise. The swordmaster deflected a fast cut to his chest and escaped with a tear in his tunic. In the exchange which followed, he lost two steps. When the boy beat and lunged and nearly maimed his face, he was forced to recognition; somehow, Jaric had lost his inhibition against fighting. "Kor, boy! Had you applied yourself like this earlier, I might have taught you something worthwhile."

Icily silent, Jaric continued to attack. Brith abandoned speech. Although the boy was still too inexperienced to best him, for the first time the guardsman required total concentration to defend himself.

Swordsman and pupil circled like dancers across the dock, the flash of parry and riposte licking between obstacles. The belling clang of swordplay carried stridently over the bustle. Longshoremen loading a nearby lighter rolled their casks upright and perched on the rims to observe the fight. Brith and Jaric wove back and forth. Unaware of their audience, they skirted pyramids of stacked barrels, baled cloth, and the heaped mounds of fish nets. Other workers joined the longshoremen, and presently a crowd formed. Coins clinked in callused palms as the sporting ones among them exchanged wagers, then energetically joined the spirit of the dispute by shouting encouragement to whichever duelist they favored to win, the seal-dark man with the fast sword, or the blond boy who met superior skill with determined defiance.

Idlers gathered and the crowd swelled larger. At any moment their commotion would draw the attention of the town guard. Brith redoubled his efforts, aware he must subdue the boy at once or risk getting fined for brawling in public. Steel rang dissonantly. Brith hammered at Jaric's guard, then, in a twist, caught the boy's sword in a bind. Through the sliding ring of blade on blade, he sensed the tremor of flagging muscles. The boy could not last much longer. Though competently executed, his technique was now wholly defensive. As the weapons wrenched apart, a fast feint and a lunge might corner him against the lumber pile. Confident of victory, Brith drove in with the agility of a fox.

Jaric parried the attack, twisting to avoid a step back. His elbow snagged on a plank. The wood fell with a boom onto the dock. A moth-eaten cat shot from a cranny just as Brith lunged. His boot struck the animal a glancing blow in the ribs. The cat yowled and fled. Distracted, Jaric glanced sideways for a fraction of an instant. Brith's blade hooked his cross guard and, with a single stroke, disarmed him. The sword pin-wheeled from the boy's hand and fell ringing onto wood. Deafened by a chorus of cheers and groans from the onlookers, and pressed hard against the lumber by the points of his opponent's steel, Jaric panted and shifted his dagger to his right hand.

"Desist," snapped Brith. He also breathed heavily from exertion. "You're beaten now. If you don't quit, I'll have to hurt you." His sword flicked like a snake.

Flattened against stacked planks, Jaric missed his parry and, trapped in another bind, caught a warning scratch on the wrist from his opponent's dagger.

"Drop your knife," commanded Brith. His sword arm flexed, bearing painful pressure against the boy's stressed wrist.

Still Jaric refused to relinquish his weapon. "How many times did you warn that chance can ruin a victory?" And his brown eyes showed a hint of laughter as a board thrown from the sidelines struck the weaponsmaster squarely in the back of the neck.

Brith buckled at the knees and crashed at Jaric's feet. The swords-master's head had barely struck planking when a familiar, one-handed figure darted from the crowd and piled squarely onto his shoulders. Breathless, the beggar lifted his face to the boy. "Kicked my cat, this lout sure did."

"I saw." Jaric grinned. He bent wearily and recovered his sword, then gathered up Brith's weapons as well. "Can you hold him long enough for me to cast the lines off my boat?"

The beggar raised both eyebrows and answered with a gap-toothed smile. "Surely, boy, surely."

"Thanks." Jaric flexed bleeding fingers, and hurled the swordsmaster's weapons over the lumber pile. They plunged with a splash into the shallows by the breakwater. Brith could find them easily enough, but only at ebb tide. By then *Callinde* should be well beyond the harbor. Jaric could buy provisions in one of the fishing villages north of Landfast; after that the rain would hide him from further pursuit. Ivainson tossed a silver to the beggar, collected his bundle of belongings from the dock, and shoved through the bystanders who now argued loudly over the validity of winning bets, since the beggar had clearly foiled Brith's victory. By the time the boy boarded *Callinde*, the shouts had transformed to a brawl. As a uniformed guard on a war-horse thundered over the docks to intervene, none but the beggar noticed the fishing boat slip her docklines and hoist sail for the open sea.

In keeping with the advent of summer, weather from the south brought low clouds, and then mist which lowered clinging and gray and turned finally to drizzle. Light winds held *Callinde* to an easy, northerly course, but she was not the only craft to ply the Corine Sea. North and east, on a close-hauled course for the heart of the Free Isles' Alliance, a scarred old fishing boat with no flag of registry sailed under orders from Shadowfane. Her sails were gray with mildew and her hull dark; the face of her helmsman was the toadlike countenance of a Thienz. Alone of seven companions, it hunched over the compass, rain dribbling runnels over the ornamental crest of its headdress. Yet the others huddled in the lee of the mainmast were not sleeping. Joined mind to mind, they bent their thoughts toward Landfast, whose barrier ward shone to their perception as an icy halo of light. This no demon could cross without rousing the wrath of men. Though their quarry lay on the other side, this difficulty did not distress the Thienz, who turned their every resource to the hunt. Humans by nature had short memories for trouble; sooner or later they grew complacent and misjudged, and for the day such folly overtook Ivainson Jaric, the Thienz waited with a patience no human could match.

Night fell. Rain blew cold in the face of the helmsman, and he rose with a whuff of his gill flaps and shook droplets from his headdress. At his movement the tranced Thienz stirred from their huddle. They shambled to ungainly feet and sought a meal of fish, snatched live from a barrel by the masthead. Then, with backs hunched against the gunwales, they gnawed through scales and fins and cartilage. The youngest of them whistled soulfully, deploring the salt in the flesh. Its elders rolled tiny, half-blind eyes in shared sympathy. Though water was the natural abode of their kind, the deep pools of fresh streams and lakes were their proper element. Boats were a curse to limbs designed for swimming, and the surrounding sea an evil best not mentioned. Its rich solution of minerals could leach the gills of an immersed Thienz, bring death by poisoning and suffocation. For sea-going brothers, awareness of mortality permeated every lift of the swell. Yet Lord Scait commanded. The company sent to hunt Jaric licked fish from webbed hands, oppressed and silent with a distress they dared not express.

At length the Thienz who had served as helmsman groped its way to a nook by the mast. One of the others took its place in the stern, knuckles gripped to the tiller and its snout lifted to the wind, since it maintained course by senses unknown to humans. The rest of the Thienz finished their meal and, picking scales from pointy teeth, drew together to resume communion with their purpose. Collective consciousness pooled, focused as always upon the ring of defenses surrounding Landfast. The hard lines of the wards lay unchanged, and, surrounding the fringes, the clustered flickers of illumination that were men and the crews of wooden ships scattered like beads on dark velvet. Thienz-memory recalled a time when ships had been metal, ablaze with the brightness of energy fields. The mighty star fleets of ancestors once had tracked such sparks of light through the vast deeps of space, and all but obliterated humanity. But the remembered glory ended in captivity and cruelest exile, and survival became a thing steeped in hatred. For that, Thienz braved oceans and sour fish and at last found reward for their patience.

A light-mote brighter than the others emerged from the glow defined by Landfast's wards. As it cleared the energy barrier, its pattern grew more distinct, and, with a hiss of triumph and malice, the Thienz narrowed the focus of their search. They knew, without mistake. The aura of this man brightened and blazed, a hard-edged beacon that seared sensitive perception almost to pain. So did humans with a sorcerer's potential appear to the minds of demons. The Thienz-eldest croaked, shivering with ecstatic anticipation. The perilous vigil had ended. For whatever reason, Ivainson Jaric sailed beyond the protection of Landfast.

The Thienz collective flicked thought to the helmsman, who flung the tiller hard over. Two youngest left the link to adjust sail, and the dark boat scudded into a heel, gunwales pressed into a reach. Her course was set now to race, for from Jaric's untrained, unshielded thoughts the demons had pried the required facts. He sailed in haste for Tierl Enneth, his hope to spare Taen the agonies of the Sathid death.

The night fell close as ink over the Corine Sea. Droplets rolled like sweat over the face of the Thienz helmsman, and its wiry limbs trembled. Tierl Enneth lay seventy leagues off, against a contrary wind. Yet the shores of that isle housed a ruin, empty of all but the bones of slaughtered men. With diligence, and determination born of hate, Thienz might win two prizes, Ivainson Jaric, Firelord's heir, and Marlsdaughter Taen, who might yet make a weapon to pair with the brother already in thrall to Shadowfane.

Though fitful and unsteady, the winds blew from the south through-out Jaric's passage from Landfast. Drenched by intermittent rain, and exhausted by the pull of the steering oar, he muscled *Callinde* through the narrow strait which separated the mass of Tierl Enneth from the splinter islet of Hal's Nog. Shaking drenched hair from his eyes, the boy clung grimly to the helm. He had been twelve days at sea. Now, in the final hours of crossing, the channel was treacherous with rocks. Current ran counter to his course, and a single miscalculation could sliver *Callinde's* stout tim-bers, leave him awash in the hammerblows of breaking swells.

Gulls looped and screamed above the yard as daylight failed. Overcast skies blackened into night like starless ink. Jaric blotted dripping fingers and groped in a locker for the flint to strike the compass lantern. He longed for the safety of anchorage. Every sinew ached with exhaustion. Waves crested and boomed to starboard, carving crescent swirls of foam which warned of submerged reefs. Yet Corley was due to make landfall with *Moonless* the following afternoon; Jaric had no choice but run the strait's perilous waters in darkness.

Sheltered by the damp folds of his cloak, the lantern wick flared and caught. The boy latched the glass closed, knuckles stained red by the glimmer of flame within. The air smelled heavy with rain. Dreading reduced visibility, Jaric bent strained eyes upon the waters off *Callinde's* bow. While the waves remained dark, he sailed safely in the deeps of the channel. But should a faint slash of spray suggest the presence of white-caps, he hauled on his steering oar and dragged in the sheets, setting his frail craft to weather to claw clear of the shoals. He lost count of the number of tacks he made long before midnight. Left only guesses and the glimmer of the compass lamp to guide him, Jaric fought to stay alert. More than once he caught the cloying scents of earth and wet grass, as his course strayed close to the shore of Hal's Nog.

The rain held off until dawn, then resumed with wretched persistence, turning waves and whitecaps a pocked, leaden gray. Jaric huddled in his cloak and blinked droplets from his lashes. With visibility reduced to scant yards, he dared not relax vigilance, even for a second. Beaten with exhaus-tion, he never knew the precise moment when he cleared the straits and entered the wide, safe harbor of Tierl Enneth.

Yet, in time, he noticed that tidal currents no longer kicked and curled around *Callinde's* steering oar. The swells under her keel silvered and flat-tened into wavelets, the first sure sign he had reached protected waters. Weeping with relief, Jaric abandoned the helm. He set his anchor, dropped canvas, and settled to rest under the partial shelter of the mainsail. Wind through the rigging lulled him. He slept finally, unaware that two addi-tional vessels bore down upon the harbor where *Callinde* took shelter. One was Corley's command, *Moonless*, bearing a battle-trained crew of eighty. In the other, a black vessel seen only in dreams, eight Thienz licked their teeth, driven onward by Scait Demon Lord's directive to kill.

CHAPTER X

Tierl Enneth

Mist rolled across the harbor of Tierl Enneth and cloaked the ruined city in gray. The drizzle which began at dawn still fell in the early afternoon when, like a phantom haunting waters where moored ships once swung with the tide, *Moonless* ghosted in under the whispered flap of her staysails. Her deckhands sang no chanteys. In somber silence, they dropped anchor, furled canvas, and swayed two longboats out. The first craft they loaded with empty casks which bore recent marks of repair. Corley commandeered the second. Scowling, his maroon tunic darkened with damp, he accepted the blanket-wrapped weight of the Dreamweaver from the healer's anxious arms. Leaving command of *Moonless* to the first mate, the captain descended the side battens one-handed and settled in the stern seat of the boat. He arranged Taen in his lap, and paused a moment to look at her. Rain beaded her lashes like tears; pale as a porcelain doll, the girl barely seemed to breathe.

The healer glared reproachfully down from the waist and tried one last time to object. "She ought not to be moved."

Corley ignored him. With a curt jerk of his head, he ordered his sailhands to proceed. The boat jostled under the added weight as four brawny men stepped within. They positioned themselves on the benches and threaded oars through rowlocks in subdued silence.

"Take her ashore, then," murmured Corley. His eyes never lifted from the girl in his lap. Looms lapped into water. As the Dreamweaver's head rolled with the pull of the first stroke, the Kielmark's most hardened captain bit his lip and wondered whether he was right to trust the dream which urged him to convey the failing girl to land. He had no fey skills; only a sure eye for weapons and a knack for managing men. But when his sleep had been torn into visions four nights in a row by an image of Taen dying in screaming agony unless he carried her with him into Tierl Enneth, Corley chose to act. He had nothing to lose. Barring a miracle, the Dreamweaver was already lost.

The oars dipped and lifted like clockwork; expertly handled, the longboat hissed through the waters of the harbor. Surrounded by the smell of sweating men and damp wool, Corley regarded the landing of Tierl Enneth, once Keithland's most opulent trading port. Flotsam-snarled sands and wrecked dwellings now sheltered no life but seabirds. Crabs picked at the pilings of the emissary's dock, where past generations of royalty had debarked to fanfares of trumpets. If Landfast was the seat of government and antiquity, Tierl Enneth had nourished the arts, until Anskiere's sorcery smashed city and inhabitants without warning.

The oarsmen threaded a careful course between the shorn bollards of the traders' wharf, and the boat grounded on the strand. Men leapt from the bow to steady the craft against the curl of the breakers as Corley rose from the stern. Bearing Taen, he stepped over the gunwale and, careless of the water which swirled over his boot tops, waded shoreward while the crew beached the longboat.

The ruins loomed ahead, gray stone tumbled like bones against the lighter gray of the mist. Corley stood dripping on the seaweed at the tide mark. Uncertain what to expect, he scanned the slivered ramparts which remained of the harbor gate. The sculptures of eagles had been torn from their niches, and the great arches rose gapped and broken against the sky, spoiled past memory of design. Weeds presently grew where gilded four-in-hand coaches had thundered over marble paving.

Despite the company of the men at his back, Corley shivered. He tightened his fingers in the blankets which sheltered Taen, and suddenly realized Tierl Enneth was not entirely deserted. A figure in a dark cloak walked amid the looming mist of the ruins.

Corley tensed. Taen's helpless weight prevented a fast reach for his sword. On the point of tossing her into the arms of the nearest oarsman, he saw the approaching stranger throw his hood back. Sun-bleached hair tumbled in the wind, and with a shock of surprise, the captain recognized the face.

"Jaric! Kor's Fires, boy, what are you doing here?" Corley strode briskly forward, his uneasiness transformed to annoyance. "Brith was under orders to keep you safe at Landfast!"

Jaric paused by the crumbled breakwater, brows knotted with an anger all his own. "I owe no loyalty to the Kielmark, nor any of his henchmen. I came here for Taen."

As the boy leaped down to the strand, Corley sensed changes; Jaric carried himself with an unthinking self-command. If he had sailed to Tierl Enneth for the sake of the Dreamweaver, how could he possibly have known *Moonless* would make landfall there of all other ports in Keithland?

Jaric drew nearer; Corley noticed the scabs of a recent fight on his knuckles. "Did you best Brith?" he demanded in surprise.

"No." The boy looked worn, exhausted utterly from his passage. His clothing and hair sparkled with salt crystals, and his hands were chapped from the sea. "He tried to stop me." Reluctant to elaborate, Jaric bent over the blankets and studied Taen. "How long has she been like this?"

"Too long." Corley hefted the girl and settled her more comfortably against his shoulder; her cheek rolled limply against his neck. "Do you know how to help her?"

Jaric looked up, eyes darkened with sudden and painful uncertainty.

"I've been instructed. But by Kor's divine grace don't ask anything more." He lifted his arms to take Taen.

Concerned by the boy's fatigue and by his studied lack of comment on his encounter with Brith, Corley shook his head. "Wherever you're going, I'll carry her."

Jaric stiffened, distrustful of the captain's motives. He might face another fight should Corley try to balk him; and delay would cost dearly. Taen's still limbs and cold flesh warned how near she lay to death.

Corley sensed the boy's suspicion and softened his tone. "I won't stop you, Jaric. Just show me where to go." With crisp decision, he addressed the crewmen who lingered nearby. "Return to *Moonless*. Tell the mate to post an anchor watch until I return. I'll signal for a longboat by lighting a fire between the pillars of the harbor gate."

Jaric watched with trepidation as the sailhands moved to depart. "Do you act for the Kielmark?"

"No." Corley qualified without pause. "I act for the Dreamweaver who once spared every soul on Cliffhaven from Gierj-demons."

"Then leave your sword and knives behind," said Jaric.

Deison Corley clenched his teeth with a visible jerk. His lips tightened to an expressionless line, and for a long, dangerous moment he regarded the boy on the strand before him. Yet Jaric stood his ground with staid resolution; and something about his stillness disarmed the captain's affront.

Without speech, Corley hefted Taen, and transferred her limp weight into the arms of the boy. Gravel crunched at his back as his men busied themselves launching the longboat; unwilling to leave his blades unattended on the strand, Corley reached swiftly to unbuckle his sword belt.

But Jaric impulsively changed his mind. "Never mind, I'll trust you."

Corley looked up. He searched the boy's troubled expression through windblown strands of Taen's hair, and suddenly understood. Probably Jaric's guidance came from a source as fathomless as the dreams which had entreated the captain to bear the Dreamweaver ashore in Tierl Enneth. Sympathy filled Corley for the upheaval caused by a destiny too weighty for even a sorcerer's heir to encompass. "You won't be sorry," he said gruffly.

With an emotion very near to gratitude, Jaric restored Taen to the captain's capable arms.

Thick fog muffled Tierl Enneth. Its whiteness erased the outline of the beach head, and the hiss of unseen breakers turned ghostly, a mirage of disembodied sound. The forms of captain, Firelord's heir, and Taen Dreamweaver became lost to the eyes of the crewmen aboard *Moonless,* yet the limits of visual perception were not shared by demonkind. Aboard the fishing vessel dispatched to destroy Ivainson Jaric, the Thienz assigned as watcher observed the exchange on the shore. Even as Corley accepted the limp weight of Taen Dreamweaver and turned with Jaric to bear her toward the ruins, the demon signaled its companions.

'Man-fools, we have them, with-certainty.' The Thienz ruffled its crest, amazed and elated by the hapless ways of humans. For the Dreamweaver lay unguarded, unconscious to danger; and though the presence of latent power wrapped a haze of confusing energies about the Firelord's heir, the Kielmark's captain had a mind decisive as a sword's edge. His intentions were plain: directed by Ivainson Jaric, Corley planned to bear Taen Dreamweaver to an unspecified place, and upon his given word, the Kielmark's men at arms were to stay behind.

The companion Thienz whuffed their gill flaps, pleased-for-Scait, while the watcher showed them Corley turning toward the ruins. The captain and the two-who-were-prey turned unsuspecting toward deserted dwellings where no-human-ally-now-lived.

'Ours,' hissed the Thienz at the helm, its reference to the Firelord's heir. It clicked sharp teeth and pulled the tiller with anticipation, even as the response of its companions swirled and buffeted its awareness. The harbor must not be risked, with the vigilant presence of eighty men at arms. But the landward side to Tierl Enneth's ruins was unguarded since the devastation unleashed by Anskiere's powers. Thought-forms flickered with rising excitement as the demons plotted. The sloop could be landed under cover of the mist, then concealed in a cove beyond view of the brigantine's sentries. Thienz would creep ashore. On dry land, well removed from the accursed dangers of salt water, the Kielmark's captain and his blades could most-easily be overwhelmed.

'Then shall Ivainson-Firelord's-heir perish, to the sorrow of mankind and the Vaere.'

Whetted for the kill, a Thienz crew member sprang to harden sheets. Fingers ill suited for handling rope slipped and gripped in eagerness to tease the sails into perfect trim. The sloop responded, rounding to the slight breeze and swinging shoreward. Yet as the sails snapped gently taut, the watcher hissed warning from the bows. Wide lips curled back from small, back-canted teeth, and its thought-lash of startled annoyance slapped through the minds of its companions.

'Men move beyond the walls of the city-now-fallen, many-men, stop-see, they might bring danger.'

Two Thienz abandoned the lines. They crowded around the spokesman and at once melded awareness to scout this new development. Chafing, almost reckless in their haste, they pressed to sample the human minds who presently converged upon the meadows beyond Tierl Enneth.

The demons' probe met the taste of dust, and beast-smell and the sweaty reek of oiled flesh. Wagon wheels creaked, and somewhere a singer intoned a chant in queer, quarter-tone intervals that jarred the eavesdropping Thienz with unpleasantness. Shadowfane's minions delved deeper to escape the irritation. Beneath the surface patterns of sensory perception, the enemy minds they touched were strangely unstructured by logic. Their thought-colors blazed like beacons, twisted to resonance by fierce counter-currents of emotion. The watcher-Thienz saw and sorted implications, even as a presence among the humans noticed the eddies generated by demon meddling. Warned off, the Thienz withdrew. Their probe dissolved without trace well before that guardian awareness coalesced and stabbed out in challenge.

The dark boat rocked gently in the mist, its occupants stilled to listen. 'Clan tribes,' hissed the watcher. 'They gather to celebrate the solstice, and with them rides she-who-sees-truly, a sightless-one trained to read memory.'

A wail arose from the helmsman, echoed in octaves by its companions. Thienz could not pass that way, for clan priestesses never failed to detect the presence of Kor's Accursed. Other Thienz paused in their tasks, turning wide, near-blind eyes toward the shadow the watcher's body imprinted upon the air. 'Trouble for us, but also hindrance for Corley-Jaric-Taen,' they intoned in return.

The shared song of the hill tribes' enthusiasm swelled yet again. Wild clans on the move might complicate the will of Lord Scait, but all was not lost. The humans hunted by Shadowfane would be forced to travel far afield, since clan tribes celebrating solstice would be dangerously inclined to violence. Strangers who trespassed upon the rites quite often got themselves murdered.

The dark boat rocked as the Thienz turned hands to their sailing. They bailed, and eased lines, and cheerfully bickered over who-next-should-share-helm-watch; while, as a descant to physical action, they braided words and mental musings into plans for night landing followed by ambush in the misty fells past Tierl Enneth.

Poised at Corley's side with one foot on the breakwater wall, Jaric felt as if he stood at the edge of the unknown. The Kielmark's captain would keep his word, though his life became the cost; yet the boy fretted, wondering how Corley would react when he discovered they acted under influence of the Llondelei demons. Distressed that Taen's life should depend on the whim of Kor's Accursed, Jaric slipped one hand beneath his cloak and touched the shaft of the ash flute. Contact roused a cold tingle of energy; a presence touched his mind, urging him quickly into the mist-choked ruins of Tierl Enneth. Aware no choice remained but to trust in such a guide, the boy drew breath and started forward.

Corley leaped the shattered stone of the breakwater. Trained to move in silence, he followed the boy's lead across cobbles slimy with moss. Except for the fact the captain carried Taen, Jaric might have forgotten the presence of his companion. Once within the city, cracked walls rose up on either side, the hiss of breakers echoing between like the mournful whisper of ghosts. Wind sighed over tenantless thresholds, and gull droppings streaked the fretwork of sills and chimneys. To Jaric, Tierl Enneth was a city haunted by the resonance of misused powers. Only bones remained, scattered by scavengers; once he tripped over a skull, and eye sockets clogged with fungi stared accusingly at his back as he passed.

Distressed by the emptiness and the mist, Jaric whispered unthinkingly aloud, "Why weren't they buried?"

"Too many dead," said Corley, and the boy flinched at the sound of a human voice. "Very few had relations left living to care."

Shocked speechless, at last Jaric understood the undertones of sorrow which had haunted the Stormwarden's manner; Tathagres' transgression had permanently cost Anskiere his peace of mind. Amid the smashed houses of Tierl Enneth, the boy's doubts resurfaced with vicious intensity. Evidence of tragedy wider than his worst imagining confronted him on all sides. The silence, and the empty, gaping doorways, infused fresh desperation in his need to escape the Cycle of Fire. What were Vaere-trained sorcerers if not evil, that demons could deflect their formidable powers against mankind? Shaken numb by the catastrophic scale of Anskiere's failure, Jaric stumbled through doorways and gardens overgrown with briar as he followed the ash flute's directive.

Late in the day, the sun broke through the fog. Purple shadows slanted across the western lanes of Tierl Enneth. Wreckage was less evident on the landward side of the city; yet even those dwellings left whole sheltered no inhabitants. Windows gaped fireless and black, and alleys lay deserted. Guided by the Llondian artifact, the Firelord's heir and the Kielmark's captain reached the far wall of the city in the wan light of the afterglow. Darkness obscured the arch of the trade gate which pierced the inland fortifications. Above, the battlements rose intact, notched like the spine of a dragon with scales of green ivy. Jaric stopped briefly to admire the pair of eagles which capped the portal, their outstretched wings tipped in gilt.

Corley paused and shifted Taen's weight to his opposite shoulder. "Are we going through?"

Jaric nodded. Though twilight was nearly spent, the tingling pull of the ash flute showed no sign of diminishing. Dogged by rising uneasiness, the boy pressed on toward the arch.

Shadow closed around him, dense as spilled ink. Corley followed on his heels. The air smelled of damp and moss, and the stone deflected the sound of their footsteps into echoes. Directed through darkness by no more than the mental pull of the ash flute, Jaric hastened his pace. Suddenly his shoulder crashed into rock. He gasped in near panic.

Corley spoke calmly over the boy's shoulder. "Turn left. Before the city was destroyed, an iron gate was kept barred during the night. The tunnel on either side was built with a crook to foil siege engines."

Jaric pushed away from the stone, his fear changed to regret. The finest of engineered defenses had not spared Tierl Enneth; the survivors of the cataclysm had chosen to relocate rather than rebuild their homes. A few paces ahead, Jaric brushed past the rusted remains of the grill. Then the corridor bent once more. The far arch loomed ahead, scattered across with clusters of orange light.

"Kor," swore Corley in disbelief. "Could those be campfires? I can't believe it." He lengthened stride, reached the far entrance of the tunnel, and, with Jaric at his side, looked out over the countryside beyond.

Blurred by streamers of mist, the valley that nestled between ruins and hills lay riddled with hundreds of torches. Music wafted faintly over summer's chorus of crickets, cut across by raucous shouts. Painted wagons, lighted stalls, and the packed earth where dancers circled all formed a familiar pattern. Jaric needed no words to qualify; identical seasonal gatherings had occurred beneath Morbrith's walls each solstice throughout his childhood. Tierl Enneth itself might lie deserted, but wild clansmen from the hills still gathered there for summerfair.

Corley shifted his weight, settling Taen in the crook of his elbow. Her face appeared as a pale oval against the mouth of the tunnel. When Jaric did not speak, the captain scuffed his boot irritably against the cobbles. "We have a problem." Clansmen were distrustful of strangers and quick to anger at any time; when they were drunken and euphoric from the rites of the solstice, their belligerence became unmanageable. "We could wait for full dark and perhaps slip past without being seen."

"No." Jaric released a quivering breath. The Llondian flute directed him straight toward the heart of the festivities. Aware as his companion of the dangers, and agonized by Taen's helplessness, the boy resisted an urge to fling the artifact to the ground.

"Carry the Dreamweaver, then," said Corley grimly. "Before long we'll both be glad my blades weren't sent back to *Moonless*."

The mention of weapons earned no response but an unreadable glance from Jaric; the boy made no effort to accept the burden of the unconscious girl. And frayed to a nervous edge by the prospect of crossing a summerfair on the very eve of the solstice, Corley's great hands knotted. Taen's blankets pulled taut, and a lock of her hair tumbled free and streamed in the wind.

"Wait." Jaric stepped back and, with abrupt decision, reached beneath his cloak. "Steel may not be necessary."

Had Corley been amenable to religion, the boy might have begged a blessing from Kordane for understanding. But from a captain trained on Cliffhaven, Jaric knew he could expect no better than a split second of reason before a sword stroke. Wary of the consequences, he pulled the ash flute from his belt.

Inlay glimmered with the iridescent gleam of shell; not even fading light could conceal the stops, which numbered twelve, too widely spaced to suit even the longest human fingers. Corley studied the artifact, then glanced at Jaric's face.

He spoke with controlled gentleness. "That's Llondian, am I right?"

Jaric nodded, openly distressed; mere possession of demon handiwork was heresy punishable by death should he ever stand trial under the priests.

But Corley made no outcry. "Well," he said quietly, "if you think that

thing will protect us from quick-tempered clansmen, by all means use it."
At Jaric's startled silence, he shrugged. "Boy, the ways of a sorcerer trained
by the Vaere are not those of a man. Anskiere consorted with Llondelei.
Even the Kielmark knows."

Jaric lifted a hand and carefully tucked Taen's fallen hair back under
the blankets. "You're not afraid?"

The captain drew a quick breath. "All right, yes, I'm afraid. Did you
think me a brainless fool? I've a half sister who's a hillman's get, and still
I can't fathom their ways. But this much I'd bet. Alone, without help, we'll
surely end up spitted on clansmen's daggers."

Relieved, Jaric summoned courage and struck out from the archway.
Corley followed, tense and beginning to sweat. Thornbrakes and meadow
grass had overgrown the trade road beyond, muffling their passage to a
sibilant swish of undergrowth; dew spangled their boots at each stride.
Corley lifted Taen to his shoulders to keep her blankets dry. Silent but
for an occasional grunt of exertion, the captain stayed close to Jaric's side
until the light of the clansmen's bonfires streaked their faces like ceremonial paint. Close up, the smells of roasting meat and incense mingled with
the odors of sweat and the manure of horses. A bowed instrument rasped
arpeggios to the stamp of dancing feet. Ragged, painted, and scantily clad
in the furred skins of animals, the clansmen and their women spun like
shadows between a circle of torches lashed onto poles. Both sexes carried
steel. Daggers, short swords, and quoit rings gleamed from belts and
shoulder scabbards, and bone-hilted knives protruded from the tasseled
fringes of boot tops.

A stone's throw from the perimeter, Jaric tripped on a branch. Sticks
snapped beneath his feet as he scrambled to maintain balance. Corley
grabbed his elbow and steadied him, too late. By the fireside, a man whirled
and broke away from the dance. He spotted the intruders, pointed, and
raise a yammering shout of alarm. The music died as the revelers laid aside
their instruments.

Corley froze between steps. "Use your whistle, boy." He pitched his
words with urgency, for the interlaced patterns of dancers unraveled like
torn knotwork. A fist-shaking mob coalesced around the first man. Shoulder to shoulder with their husbands, women tossed braided hair over their
lithely muscled backs. Steel flashed in the torchlight as one clansmember
after another drew knives.

Jaric raised the flute to his lips. He made no attempt to seek the stops,
for the Llondel demon by the ice cliffs had instructed him to sound the
highest note on the scale. The crowd charged from the fireside with an
eerie, quavering scream, just as the boy drew breath and blew into the
mouthpiece.

The flute sang out with a tone so pure it pierced the clamor like a
needle through cloth. The very air seemed to shatter. The note swelled,
deepened, raising resonant harmonics beyond the range of hearing. Vibra-

tions spread outward like wind, touching the living essence of plants and livestock, and fraying the thoughts of men into patterns never meant for mortal minds. The attacking hillfolk jumbled to a halt and fell silent, knives forgotten in their hands; and like ripples settling from a stone tossed into water, the seething hordes of the summerfair quivered and stilled and quieted.

Jaric lowered the flute, leaving the crisp snap of torch flames isolated in a pool of silence. His head rang and his limbs trembled. Somehow he retained the presence of mind to stumble forward. Trusting Corley to follow on his heels, he entered the summerfair; and the torches burnished his hair like gold struck by sunlight.

That moment an eldritch cry split the stillness. An ancient woman burst from the mass of clansmen. Clothed in garments of knotted leather, she raised fleshless arms and swayed toward Jaric. Corley hung back as, in the singsong syntax of trance, the crone raised her voice and spoke in the tongue of the clans. Her guttural syllables chilled Jaric like the touch of winter ice. His step faltered, and he stopped, alone within the ring of flame-light. He knew whom he faced. A year past he had met this woman's counterpart in a backlands settlement called Gaire's Main; the prophetic words spoken then still broke his sleep with nightmares. As priestess of the spring on the isle of Tierl Enneth, the woman was crazed through a lifetime dedicated to ritual dreams and oracular vision. Her word superseded all law among the clans, and should she speak against them, very likely he and Taen and Corley would perish at the hands of her maiden initiates.

The woman uttered one last word and snapped her jaw shut. Beaded locks of hair rattled around her shoulders as she stamped her foot, spun around, and ran to the tailboard of a wagon piled high with wreathes of ceremonial flowers. Nailed to the wagon's crosstree was the traditional offering to the blessed Flame, a circlet braided from the fire-lilies which bloomed only at solstice. Jaric held his breath as the priestess leaped, snatched, and landed bearing the sacred circlet. Before he could move a muscle, the woman whirled. For a single suspended instant, his frightened gaze locked with the blind pearl-white of her eyes.

Then the priestess stamped again. She whispered in the common tongue of Keithland, yet her words reached the boy as if she spoke in his ear. "Aye, so, ye are the one." And she threw the wreath.

Orange, gold, and butter-yellow, the flowers fluttered through the air and landed squarely on the crown of Jaric's head. The clansmen gasped. Though not a man among them spoke, they knelt as one on the packed earth. Only Jaric and Corley and the blind priestess remained on their feet in the torchlight.

Corley stepped swiftly to Jaric's side. "Best move on. The Lady has granted us safe-conduct."

The boy roused with a start. Fire-colored petals tangled with strands of his hair as he twisted to face the captain. "Do you know what she said?"

Corley answered with reluctance. "Yes." But to his surprise Jaric did not demand a translation.

In a voice half-choked with misery, the boy said, "Please, if you can, will you tell them to *get up?*"

Corley swore. Clutching Taen closely to his chest, he shouted in the coarse tongue of the clans. With a ragged rustle of movement, the people rose to their feet. Someone shouted at the far edge of the crowd, and a drum boomed through the night.

"Go now," said Corley in Jaric's ear.

The drumbeat quickened, then broke into wild rhythms of exultation. Though Jaric longed with all his heart to flee, he forced himself to step forward with dignity. Painted, braided, and reeking of sweet oil and the exertion of their revels, the clansfolk parted and deferentially permitted him to pass.

With Corley at his shoulder, the boy strode through a living corridor of flesh which extended the breadth of the summerfair. Hands plucked at his clothes; children peeped with unblinking eyes from the fringes of their parents' leggings, and grandmothers murmured over the blanket-wrapped Dreamweaver cradled in Corley's arms. Dazzled by the glare of the torches, Jaric kept on, though his knees trembled and his knuckles blanched against the shaft of the ash flute long before he crossed the final perimeter of wagons.

Darkness closed over him on the far side. The priestess shrieked again at his back, and flutes and fiddles joined the drums' rejoicing. The hillfolk resumed their solstice dances beneath torches which smoked and streamed in the wind. Jaric plunged gratefully through the dew-drenched grass of the meadowland. He did not speak, even as the summerfair shrank behind, and the campfires dwindled to orange glimmers down the valley. The land became rough, cut by ravines and small, rock-strewn streams. At length the moon rose, round and full in the east. The pine forest which bordered the fells loomed ahead, outlined in silvery light. Still Jaric showed no sign of slowing. Corley shifted aching shoulders and wondered whether he dared to pause for a rest. Suddenly, with a queer and desperate violence, Jaric stopped.

He yanked the wreath from his brow. The soft bells of the fire-lilies crushed between his fists as he drew breath and demanded to know the meaning of the priestess's prophecy.

Aware how close the boy was to breaking, Corley answered with patience. "She called you Firelord and Demonbane. She said danger would track you as winter follows spring." Slowly, with painstaking care, he eased the Dreamweaver to the grass and continued. "She told her people not to obstruct us, for the sake of the girl who would defend all men from the Dark-dreamer yet to come."

Something in the captain's manner cued Jaric to the fact that there was more. "Go on."

Stooped over Taen's still form, Corley sighed. "The Lady said one day you will go forth and steal power from the very heart of Shadowfane. If you survive that quest, mankind will endure to see Kor's Fires rekindled in the heavens."

Jaric hurled the wreath to the ground with a wrenching cry of anguish. "Shadowfane?" His voice held a raw edge of fear. "Do you know how misguided her faith is? Great Fall, I'm *no man's savior!*"

"You're Ivain Firelord's heir," Corley said matter-of-factly.

The scent of mangled flowers hung heavily on the air between them. Jaric twisted his face away, eyes shut hard against tears. "Ivain was a murderer. I've no intention of following in his footsteps."

Corley, who knew men, had wisdom enough to keep silent as Jaric whirled and ran. Aware the boy must come to terms with his fate by himself, the captain sighed and gathered the Dreamweaver from the ground. He followed at a walk toward the forest.

The Llondelei waited at the edge of the pines, their gray cloaks mottled like smoke in the moonlight which spilled through the boughs. Confronted by a hiss, and movement, and a glowing circle of eyes, Jaric started back and slammed into Corley.

Both humans froze as thought-image knifed into their minds. *'Danger stalks from behind.'* The Llondelei dealt a shadowy glimpse of creatures rustling through what looked like scrub grass. Before their meaning entirely resolved, they added a fleeting likeness of Taen's face, the glossy black of her hair crowned with myrtle. Silent, impatient, the tallest of the three demons lifted six-fingered hands toward the girl.

Pressed tight to the captain's side, Jaric felt Corley shrink in the dark. "Let them take her," the boy said quickly. The demons would use force if they resisted.

Yet already the Llondelei had sensed the captain's hesitation. They acted without warning. Jaric felt a jab in his head like hot wire. He tumbled, his eyes full of moonlight, and never felt his body strike the ground. Two Llondelei stepped across his prone form; they caught Taen as Corley's knees buckled. Thought-images passed briefly between Llondian minds. Then, with a mournful whistle, the female among them bent and stripped Jaric of his sword and dagger. She grasped the wrists of the Firelord's heir and hoisted him onto her back. More silent than the rustle of a leaf, she bore her burden after her fellows and vanished into the forest.

CHAPTER XI

Corinne Dane

Corley awoke to birdsong and the cold trickle of dew down his collar. Daybreak brightened the tops of the pines, and a six-legged three pecker rattled the branches overhead, stabbing for grubs beneath the bark. Alarmed to discover Taen and Jaric missing, the captain rolled to his feet and gasped at the pain of stiffened shoulders. Fully alert, and frantic with concern for his companions, he searched the ground for sign of the Llondelei. Yet the surrounding mat of pine needles showed no trace of a track. Only a sword and dagger of Corlin steel remained; surely, after his experience with Brith, the boy would not have abandoned his weapons, except under duress.

Corley swore and brushed twigs from his hair. Whatever beneficent connection Anskiere might have with the Londelei, Taen and Jaric lay in demon hands with no human weapon to safeguard them. The captain would not give them up without a search. Though his stomach was pinched with hunger, and his body ached from his night in the open, Corley never hesitated. He gathered Jaric's weapons from the ground and set out to seek his companions.

Mountains thrust like the armored spine of a lizard down the length of the island. The forests cloaking their slopes proved dense and seamed with gullies, too rough for a single man to cover effectively. Faster, more efficient than most, Corley quartered acres of remote dells, occasionally crossing the rutted tracks cut by the clan tribes' wagons. He startled satin deer from their grazing, and brushpheasant from their nests, but encountered no sign of the Llondelei.

Only as the day wore on, he felt increasingly unsettled, as if he sensed something following. Time and again he checked his back trail, yet nothing arose to justify his suspicion. Slowed at last by hunger, he paused by a stream to whittle snares in the late afternoon. The facts of his predicament were not reassuring. If the demons intended Taen and Jaric harm, by now no man could help them. Yet the Kielmark's orders had been explicit; Corley saw no alternative but to return to the harbor and wait. If his two charges survived, surely they would return to Tierl Enneth and *Callinde*.

In a place of purplish twilight, shadows danced in patterns on tree trunks. Wind rustled through alien foliage; no, Jaric decided, the sound he heard was *not wind*, but spring water singing over pebbles in an underground channel. Enveloped in the overlapping images generated by collective Llondian consciousness, the boy strove to separate dream from waking reality. He lay on a mat woven of rushes, surrounded by the earthy confines of a cavern that was surely the Llondian demons' burrow. Yet even as his mind framed the concept, an influx of images contradicted; *this here-now dwelling was a place of misery and exile.* Home raised memories of moist air and shadows, of endlessly whispering breezes and lacy tendrils of vegetation. That wood was *other*, a place inconceivably distant from Keithland's forests. The sun there shone red, little more than a dim star overhead.

Jaric puzzled to fathom how any sun might resemble a star. Disoriented by the waking dreams of the demons who sheltered him, and troubled with concern for Taen, he propped himself on one elbow. An oil lamp shaded by panes of violet glass dangled from a chain overhead. A weak flicker of flame illuminated a chamber bare of furnishings, except for the grass mat and a clay ewer of water cradled in a three-legged stand nearby. The earthen floors were beaten smooth. Walls shored with timber bore incomprehensible patterns of carving, and scarlet hangings curtained the archway to an alcove beyond. Uncertain whether he was prisoner or guest, Jaric wondered whether the structure concealed a door. According to Kordane's Law, prolonged exposure to Llondian imaging could drive the human mind to madness. Yet the boy would not consider leaving without searching for Taen.

Leave, Kordane's Law; Llondian consciousness plucked fragments of thought from his mind, and the unfathomable caprice of their kind melded the concepts. The illusions the demons employed in place of spoken language overwhelmed Jaric's senses, and the cave's board walls shattered into a starburst of light. Disoriented, the boy fell back on the mat. He threw his hands over his face, but the light endured. Indelibly impressed on his mind's eye, he saw the conflagration streak earthward across blackness spangled with stars. A roar like thunder filled Jaric's ears. Deafened, his vision blistered by forces too awesome for comprehension, he endured as Llondian memory unveiled the glory of Kordane's Fires at the time of the Great Fall.

'Corinne Dane, *probe-ship.*' Borrowed human words strained to encompass inconceivably strange concepts. '*Stole Llondelei from Homeworld,*' that place of soft shadows and rich soil and magnificent, towering trees. Jaric experienced a withering flash of hate. '*Your kind, stole us away, Homeworld,*' Star-sun, lost sun, red as a stab wound in the sky. Wrung by hostile emotions, Jaric cringed and cried out.

The image shifted like a jarred kaleidoscope. '*Peace; this human is Ivainson Firelord's heir, let him be.*' Restored to the unthreatening interior of the cave, the boy felt the demons' enmity subside.

Shaking, Jaric unclenched his hands. He pushed sweat-soaked hair from his eyes and sat up. Two coals of orange glowered from the alcove where the curtain hung; a Llondian demon watched him from the dark.

Jaric forgot his fear. "What have you done with Taen?"

'*She who spins dreams?*' The Llondel stepped into the chamber, a gray, six-fingered hand extended to steady the boy as he rose. '*Come.*'

Jaric shrank from the demon's touch. He reached his feet unaided and discovered with distress that his weapons were missing. "Where's Corley?"

The Llondel hissed. Its spurred fingers flinched into a fist, and, like a slap, Jaric received an impression of a sunny forest glade. There crouched the Kielmark's chestnut-haired captain, toasting fish on a stick over a campfire. Yet the image did not reassure. Disquiet troubled Jaric, as if something evil lurked in the shadows beyond Corley's campsite. But the Llondel allowed him no chance to explore the premonition.

The image dissolved abruptly into dark, lit by baleful eyes. '*Follow.*' The demon pushed the curtain aside and beckoned.

A narrow corridor extended beyond, minimally illuminated by lamps paned with the same violet glass. Left no choice but to obey, Jaric stepped forward. His heels clicked against tiles of glazed ceramic. Unable to see as well as the demon who guided him, and curious what might lie behind the doorways which opened at intervals off the hallway, the boy lagged slightly behind. His footsteps reverberated within the burrow, bewildering his ears with overlapping layers of sound; imperceptibly, his self-awareness frayed into dreams. Jaric stumbled. He pressed a hand against the wall for balance as, adrift in the flux of Llondelei consciousness, his mind crossed the far borders of Keithland. Inside stone towers at Shadowfane, he perceived a young man crouched with his arms locked over his ears. A strange, reddish aura shimmered over his form; unsure if the phenomenon was induced by imagination or Llondian prescience, Jaric looked closer. Through the shifting curtains of light he saw scarred fingers and a familiar tangle of black hair.

"Emien?" he called, though he had not intended to speak aloud.

Hard, spurred fingers clamped Jaric's wrist. The connection broke before the man in the tower could answer, and Ivainson felt himself jerked backward, into the violet-tinged shadows of a corridor beneath the earth. '*Stay close,*' admonished his Llondian guide. '*Heed, or risk your mind. If you stray, I cannot shield you from the dream-melding of the burrow.*'

Jaric shared the jumbled reactions of many in the instant before the demon released him. '*Ivainson, Firelord's heir; strong-willed, yes? Look, he seeks the Dark-dreamer before time.*'

"Dark-dreamer?" the boy said aloud. "Do they mean Emien?"

The Llondel hurried forward without answer. Presently it paused, pointed through a side door, and jabbed Jaric's mind with a fleeting impression of Taen Dreamweaver's face. The boy needed no further incentive. He entered the chamber hard on the demon's heels and stopped, blinking in the glare of unshielded candles.

Forced to squint as his vision adjusted, Jaric made out the hooded forms of three Llondelei clustered around what appeared to be a wooden tub filled with hot water. Through the steam which drifted and coiled above the rim, he saw a dark, wet head, and the flushed features of the girl whose memory had haunted him since the moment they parted at Landfast.

"Jaric?" Taen's voice was weak, but tinged with unmistakable reproach. "Corley said if you followed *Moonless* from the Free Isles, he'd skin you with the dullest of his knives."

"Well, he didn't. After four weeks of worry over you, every blade on *Moonless* had an edge that would split a cat's whisker." Astonished by the tightness in his throat, Jaric rushed to embrace her. Quickly as he moved, the demons reacted first. One behind caught him by the shoulder and yanked him back, while two in front sprang to their feet and caught his hands. Spread-eagled and helpless, Jaric struggled to reach Taen; but Llondelei thought-forms hammered his protest to silence.

'Never you touch, not now.' The command was qualified with an impression of his inner self perpetually locked into sympathy with Taen's powers as Dreamweaver. Jaric saw his potential as Firelord's heir rendered impotent at a stroke, *all because he had ignorantly embraced the Dreamweaver before her illness left her.* Llondian images detailed a ruinous sequence of catastrophes which mankind could suffer as a result: cities burned, refugees starved, and civilized Keithland crushed before an onslaught of demon foes.

Released with a suddenness that jarred thought, Jaric stumbled to his knees. Shaken, afraid to rise, he searched the demons' inscrutable eyes. Then, rubbing a cut where a spur had accidentally scored his wrist, he appealed at last to Taen. "I don't understand."

"How could you?" A trace of an impish grin touched her lips. "I don't guess the mysteries of the Vaere are part of the Landfast archives."

"No." Jaric responded to a prod from the demon at his back, and seated himself on a mat at Taen's side. Though the glistening skin of her shoulder was close enough to touch, he clenched his hands tightly in his lap.

"The Vaere were desperate when Cliffhaven was endangered by demons. I was sent to intervene," Taen said. "At the time, my Dreamweaver's mastery was incomplete."

But Jaric knew she left out details to spare him. Taen had been dispatched to Cliffhaven to preserve his own life from the combined effects of Anskiere's geas and the Kielmark's unpredictable temperament. Against the will of the Vaere, she had stayed on and engaged her talents in Cliffhaven's defense so that he could recover the Keys to Elrinfaer in safety. Anguished that Taen's suffering had begun with disobedience in his behalf, Jaric covered his face with callused palms.

"Ivainson, no, you can't blame yourself!" Taen rested her cheek against the rim of the basin. Wearied by the inadequacy of speech, she engaged her craft as Dreamweaver.

Her thoughts touched Jaric's mind as softly as a falling leaf. Gently she made him share an understanding she had only recently acquired through the Llondel who cured her illness. The powers of the Vaere-trained were created through a bond with a living matrix called Sathid. Upon maturity, the crystals caused an incompatibility with the body, which developed into a coma. At that time, the crystals would procreate by transforming the living tissues of the body into seed-matrix. Death was the usual result. Yet since Llondelei also derived their imaging abilities from Sathid bonding, they knew ways to separate the mature crystal from the body without harm. The process was easily disturbed; physical contact at the wrong moment could cause the matrix to cross-link, augment the imprint of a second mind alongside that of the first master.

Demon thought-forms defined the matter further. Swept into an explanation of dreams, Jaric observed that the Stormwarden of Elrinfaer's formidable control of wind and wave derived from two Sathid matrixes. The crystals formed the foundation of his powers, and to protect them from enemy meddling, he sank them in a capsule beneath the polar ocean. Driven beyond the icy deeps, the boy traversed a series of interlinking associations called forth by Llondian consciousness. In a whirl of past events, he saw enemies march from Shadowfane. They murdered Llondelei guardians and stole the last of their native stock of Sathid matrix. The crystals were pure, never having bonded previously; no others could replace them, except on Homeworld under the scarlet star. Once returned to Shadowfane, hostile hands experimented with the matrix and discovered what Llondelei always knew. At the time of separation, Sathid crystals could bond again; any who attempted to share the influence of an impressed matrix risked total subjugation to the will of the original part-ner. And since the matrix itself inherited the experience of each successive master, the crystal itself grew stronger, wiser; it, too, might contend for mastery. Thus had Jaric nearly destroyed a balance when he tried to touch Taen, and thus did the compact at Shadowfane create pawns to commit atrocities against mankind.

Freed from the imaging, Jaric recalled the caustic burns which had disfigured Emien's hands since the hour he had murdered his mistress, Tathagres. Abruptly he remembered Taen's presence. He stopped his spec-ulation, but not before the Dreamweaver caught the direction of his thoughts.

"My brother stands in grave danger. The Llondelei know Tathagres served Shadowfane. She carried Sathid already impressed by demons in a collar of wrought gold. Though the witch herself was not matrix-linked, the enemy controlled her by the crystal's influence. Through her they channeled their designs against Anskiere and Cliffhaven. But when Emien broke the band from her neck, the matrix contacted his skin. Very likely he will succumb to direct possession. Any talent he has could be developed to the detriment of our kind."

Jaric felt the breath constrict in his throat. For a suspended interval he studied Taen's face through the steam which clouded the tub. The girl's eyes showed fatigue, their color shadowed under lashes like ink; but her expression reflected concern rather than grief. As yet she seemed unaware that Emien was held captive at Shadowfane. Dry fingers brushed Jaric's arm. He started and found a Llondel crouched at his shoulder.

'*Once, she saw,*' sent the demon. Its touch intensified in his mind. '*The girl received the image in delirium, and for the sake of health, we let her believe she experienced a nightmare. But she cannot be kept ignorant much longer.*' Slitted nostrils flared; and drawing the boy into sympathy, the creature inclined its head toward the Dreamweaver.

Jaric beheld the chamber and its inhabitants through the altered perception of Llondian eyes. Candlelight threw off a hurtful, greenish cast; and Taen's person shimmered with the blue-violet aura which accompanied the maturing presence of a Sathid bond. Its pattern radiated changeless and clean as light refracted through dewdrops at dawn, then vanished, blotted into darkness by a second view of the black-haired captive huddled within Shadowfane's walls. In contrast, the patterns emanating from Emien's form gleamed an angry scarlet, contorted as a hillwoman's knotwork.

The image faded away. Subjected to the expectant regard of the Llondelei, Jaric realized the demons expected him to intervene. Logic demanded that he develop his sorcerer's potential to combat the anguish Emien would unleash against Keithland. But the revelation that all Vaerish powers, even the Cycle of Fire itself, were derived from mastery of a Sathid matrix changed nothing. Tierl Enneth's plight had affirmed his aversion to sorcery more deeply than ever before.

Frustrated to despair, Jaric challenged. "Why should you care what becomes of Keithland? Kordane's Law holds all demons alike. What separates your kind from the builders of Shadowfane?"

The Llondelei hissed with affront. Taen cried aloud, but her warning went unregarded. The demon at Jaric's side caught his wrist in a crushing grip. Its spurred palm drove deep into his flesh, and he tumbled headlong into an inferno of heat and violence.

The night-dark forests of Homeworld exploded into fire, slashed by energy weapons carried by invaders. Jaric watched a stand of torched trees buckle and fall. Droves of batlike fliers took wing, shrilling piteously as the flesh seared from their bones. A small band of Llondelei fled the conflagration. Driven from their burrow in confusion, blinded by smoke, and disoriented by the cruel brilliance of the flames, they ran only to be captured. Darts tipped with drugs whined through cascades of airborne sparks and struck the running forms. One after another, Llondelei tumbled to earth and lay still.

White-suited creatures advanced across the swath of smoldering vegetation. Their bodies resembled a man's, but instead of faces, their heads were glassy, featureless windows with blackness inside. Jaric screamed in terror. Yet the dream did not relent. Bound to memory of Llondian disaster, he watched helplessly as the enemy piled their stunned captives in a fearsome metal wagon. The vehicle jolted into motion with a roar, and the dream-image went dark. Jaric endured a period of jostling movement and noise. Then, like a beacon in a sea of confusion, he heard a human voice.

The woman's accent was foreign, her tone openly distressed. "Commander Keith, I must protest! The inhabitants of Llond's world aren't dangerous. My God, they don't even have space travel yet!"

A gruff voice replied. "They register psi strong enough to ruin us. That's enough to list them among the enemy. Complaints don't count a damn since Starhope was besieged. And God? If *Corinne Dane*'s mission fails, if mankind doesn't find a defense against powers such as your Llondelei possess, the only human survivors will be those colonies enslaved by the Gierj. Since the Book of Revelation didn't mention that ending, you can assume the rest of old Earth dogma was fiction also. Now get back to your post!"

Jaric strove to make sense of the words. Denied sight, and confused by religious references whose meanings seemed strangely skewed, he puzzled over the term *Corrine Dane*. Llondelei consciousness caught the name in his mind, and the dream upended, flung him with sickening vertigo into a vista of blackness and stars. Adrift in the vastness of space, Jaric beheld a vast, metal engine. Its surface was cluttered with incomprehensible symbols, and a shiny, bewildering array of struts and vanes and lights. 'Corrine Dane, *star-probe-ship*,' sent the Llondelei who imaged the dream. An explosion of blue-white light followed; the engine shot forward like a meteor, scribing a line of fire across the dark.

Tumbled through sequence after sequence of images, Jaric at last understood; the Blessed Fires praised by Kordane's priests were nothing more than a corrupted reference to this same ship, *Corinne Dane*, which once had sailed the vast deeps of the heavens. The Llondelei granted no time to examine the impact of this discovery. Images patched Jaric's thoughts like mosaic work. He saw scores of Llondelei caged in metal while *Corinne Dane*'s mighty fires transported them across inconceivable distance. Twelve races gathered from other worlds shared the confinement of the Llondelei. Gierj, Karas, Mharg, Thienz, and frostwarg, and other demons whose shapes Jaric did not recognize: all huddled imprisoned in the ship's dungeon. With restless thoughts and endless hatred they plotted against the humans who had captured them; humans whose lonely, isolated minds made them such easy prey that now their last outpost among the stars battled desperately to stave off extinction.

Joined with Llondian consciousness, Jaric shared the suffering of captives who pined for the forests of Homeworld. He cringed from the tortured scream of machinery as other demons' vengeance wrenched *Corinne Dane*'s guidance systems out of sequence. Rudderless as a ship in a storm, the great craft hurtled through the atmosphere of a far, uncharted planet. Smoldering wreckage smashed and scarred a barren landscape with the marks of the Great Fall.

Jaric screamed as his sight again went dark. Beset by the pain of Llondelei survivors, he breathed air that was dry and thin, hurtful after the moist damp of Homeworld. One with demon memory, he crawled from the wrecked framework of *Corinne Dane,* a castaway on an unknown world. Forced to forage for fish and lichens, Jaric endured cruel cold and blizzards. He knew the discomfort of seasons set out of harmony with his anatomy. Sorrow and despair beset him as companions weakened and died. Weeping for release, he suffered the hardship of the Llondelei who survived and reproduced. Even after the humans at Landfast seeded the first forests upon the barren hills of Keithland, the exiles never ceased to mourn for the lost land of their ancestors.

Jaric screamed. Battered by generation upon generation of Llondian grief, he recalled the thoughtless words he had uttered before the images trapped him. *"Why should you care what becomes of Keithland?"* As if his guilt keyed release, the dreams fled from him like shadows before light.

He recovered awareness, shivering on his knees in yet another underground cavern, but this chamber was smaller than the one which had sheltered Taen. Jaric raised himself shakily from the floor. Wetness slicked his thumb, blood from the stinging puncture left by a Llondian spur. The demon who had inflicted the wound waited at his shoulder, motionless in the violet light of the lamps. It offered no image as the human boy recovered his composure; and shamed to the core, Jaric was too embarrassed to speak. He stared at the far wall, and there saw a board laid generously with bread and fruit.

The Llondel bade him sit down. The boy complied, startled to awareness of his own hunger. But the influx of alien thought-images had left him feeling vaguely queasy. His awareness seemed oddly separate from his physical body. Perception of solid reality frayed at the edges, unintegrated as oil on water. Aware that time spent among the Llondelei could only intensify such disorientation, and that madness lay at the end, Jaric buried his face in his hands.

He did not hear the demon rise at his back. Its feet made no sound as it stole from the chamber, leaving the curtain open for another who entered in its stead. Unsteady on her feet, one hand braced to the wall for support, Taen Dreamweaver tugged at the wool robe the demons had loaned her. She regarded the bent head of the Firelord's heir and managed a wan smile. "Why don't you eat? Illusions don't smell like peaches, and if I tried, I could count the knobs on your backbone from here."

Jaric spun around. "Taen?" He scrambled awkwardly to his feet and hesitated, arrested by uncertainty. "Are you . . ."

"On the mend," Taen finished for him. "Except this darned wool itches like the thistle cloth we used to rub down goats." She stepped to his side, bringing freshness and a calm that dispelled the nausea brought on by demon thought-image.

Abruptly suspicious, Jaric helped her to sit on the mat. "You aren't using your powers to steady me, are you?" Through the contact he felt her trembling. The weakness of her appalled him.

"No." Taen picked up a peach and bit into it. "A Dreamweaver's aura can heal. Had you forgotten?"

"Yes." Recalled to manners, Jaric reached for a loaf and broke a piece off for the girl. "We have to get out of here."

Taen looked at him with her mouth full. A tinge of color had returned to her cheeks, and her blue eyes were laughing. "You make a terrible sailor," she observed. "Always wanting to change the wind. Will you eat that chunk of bread, or are you just going to sit there bleeding on it?"

Jaric dropped the crust with self-conscious embarrassment. He looked for a napkin to blot his thumb, but found none and had to settle for a strip from his cuff, which was torn anyway.

Taen continued as he bound his cut. "The Llondelei will free us in their own time, I think, but not before the Sathid matrix expelled from my body fully crystallizes."

Jaric regarded the board as if the bread were an enemy that had betrayed him. "We might have been here days already."

Taen punched him, ineffectively, but with the fire of her usual spirit. "It's only nightfall outside. That makes one full day, and the last without supper. Eat, or I will use my powers. You'll need your strength. If my legs don't stop wobbling by tomorrow, who else do I have to carry me back to *Moonless?*"

The Llondelei returned when the last of the peaches were consumed. Two of them escorted Taen to a place where she could rest; illness that preceded the maturation of her Sathid matrix had left her exhausted, and even through his preoccupation, Jaric noticed she had difficulty keeping her eyes open. Though he would rather have sat with her while she slept, the Llondel who remained forbade him.

'Follow.' The image that touched the boy's mind was tinged with urgency and an indefinable weight of regret.

Taen's presence had eased the immediacy of his despair. Jaric dusted bread crumbs from his shirt and went where the demon directed.

It led him deep into earth, yet the timber-shored walls of the burrow held none of the dank chill he might have expected. The tiled corridor they traversed was dry and warm, if eerily lit by the violet-paned lamps. With no image offered in explanation, the Llondel guide stopped and flung open a door. Jaric entered the chamber beyond at its command, his feet rustling through a mat of sweet rushes. The room was large, even more sparsely furnished than the others he had seen. Here the air had a close smell, as if animals were kenneled nearby. Suddenly, in the gloom of the far corner, Ivainson saw movement, Llondelei; but these differed from any he had observed so far. Four gray-skinned youngsters tussled like puppies on the rushes, and something about the savagery of their play set his hair aprickle.

The human boy held still, awaiting a cue from the demon at his side. None came. Except the Llondel young noticed Jaric and broke apart with whistles of surprise. Lankier than human children, their silvery skin ridged with sinew, they approached with trusting curiosity. The grown Llondel made no effort to exchange images with them, but stood motionless. At last, confused by the adult's poised stance, and driven to uneasiness by the wild, animal innocence reflected in the eyes of the young, Jaric spoke. He hoped he would not offend. "Why have you brought me here?"

Gray cloth rustled. The Llondel's furrowed face turned toward him. Beneath the embroidered cloak hood, Jaric saw the creature's slitted nostrils widen; the light in its eyes shone subdued and sad. *'No Sathid.'*

The image rang with tragic overtones; cut to the heart by forced empathy, Jaric felt helpless tears blur his eyes. At his feet the cublings squealed and scattered playfully. With breathless, gleeful whistles, two smaller ones pounced upon the largest, and presently the entire group tumbled into a knot of fists and knees. Puzzled by the incongruity of the youngsters' behavior in the presence of opposing emotions in the adult, Jaric found his answer; since Llondelei communicated entirely through shared mental images, spoken language did not exist among them. Any Llondian young born since Shadowfane's theft of the Sathid were deaf and blind to their own culture. Even if words could be made to compensate for the loss, the ancestral memories of Homeworld would be forgotten within a generation. Priceless heritage, and the cherished identities of forebears who lived before the Great Fall, would become irretrievably lost.

Jaric pressed his bandaged thumb to his side. Reduced to silence by the weight of tragic consequences, and saddened by the Llondelei cublings who cheerfully hammered each other with six-fingered fists, the Firelord's heir strove to lighten the plight of the Llondelei. "What of the Vaere? If the sorcerers they train are Sathid-linked, another source of the crystals must exist."

The Llondel lifted spurred hands and pushed back its hood. It turned a rounded, earless head and regarded Jaric with anguished eyes, then answered. Like Kordane's Law, the Vaere held all demons alike. The Llondelei far-seekers had searched in vain for their isle. Though Taen could reach Tamlin with a thought, the far-seekers received only silence.

Jaric tried again. "But Anskiere was Vaere-trained. Would he break his loyalty to consort with Llondelei?"

'Yes.' The demon's images turned forcefully emphatic. *'Anskiere was born a prince among men. Where he perceived injustice, he had strength to follow the dictates of his heart.'* In a condensed rush of pictures, the creature showed Jaric the far-seeker who had befriended the sorcerer, and the pact sworn between

Stormwarden and Llondel in the twilight seclusion of a forest glade. He heard words spoken as Anskiere of Elrinfaer promised to intercede with the Vaere in behalf of a wronged species. But hope was brief. Wrung by disappointment and a sweeping change of scene, Jaric perceived the tragedy of Tierl Enneth, then the towering prison of ice which prevented the keeping of that oath.

'*Keeper of the Keys, Firelord's heir, are you blind to destiny? The survival of your people, and also Llondelei, lies with your mastery of the Cycle of Fire.*'

"No," whispered Jaric. But his denial proved futile. Out of patience, the demon overturned his senses with brutal abruptness.

He saw himself ringed with the Sathid aura of a sorcerer's craft, but blindingly brilliant, stronger than even that of Anskiere of Elrinfaer. *Centered within a nexus of power, his flesh charged to near incandescence, he would make war upon Shadowfane's demons.*

"No. Ivain my father went mad!" Jaric's shout echoed through the cavern, scattering the Llondelei cublings. But the images battered into him without surcease.

By the Firelord's grace, Corinne Dane's fires will rise once more, bearing Llondel and human to the stars in peace.

Jaric exploded into white-hot anger. He broke the demon's hold upon his mind and flung back a step. "No! There must be an alternative!"

The Llondel answered in words, underscored by finality irrevocable as death. "*Ivainson Firelord, for that you are already too late.*" Eyes flared like coals beneath the cloak hood. The adult demon trilled a mournful seventh, and Jaric felt his will milled under like sand in the teeth of a storm tide.

CHAPTER XII

Destiny

Caught in a moment of wrenching disorientation, Jaric blinked to clear eyes that were stung by change. He looked upon night and the orange glow of a fire. The Llondel allowed him an instant to recognize the campsite where earlier the Kielmark's senior captain had toasted a fish for supper. Then demon thought-image swept away self-awareness, and Ivainson Jaric *was* Deison Corley, waking from sleep with the hair on his neck prickling with the sense of impending danger.

Even as Corley closed hands over his daggers, shadows moved, studded with the glint of eyes touched by firelight. Thienz-demons come hunting from Shadowfane closed in to take their prey, not the Firelord's heir they sought, but another: the chestnut-haired captain who had set up the Kielmark's counterattack during Kisburn's assault on Cliffhaven. Because of Corley, a Thienz, six Gierj, and a Karas shape-changed to human form had been slain. The demons reached for the captain's mind to initiate their attack. As they melded awareness with his thoughts, their eagerness seeped through the contact; and chilled by an influx of malice not his own, the captain jerked his first dagger from the scabbard. He had no chance to throw. His human will suddenly reeled under a demon-inspired compulsion to turn his blade against himself.

In the nursery chamber of the Llondelei burrow, Jaric cried out, the sound of his own voice unheard in his ears. He never saw the cubs who scattered away, eyes flaring in alarm, from the dimness of the far corner. Trapped wholly in Corley's awareness, the boy knew only desperation as the Thienz drove the captain toward suicide.

But the trained instincts of the fighter were not easily overpowered. In the moment Corley raised his knife, Thienz-bound against himself, the unconquered portion of his mind rebelled. He seized the only available recourse, and shoved his left hand to the wrist in live coals.

Pain came white-hot and immediate. Entwined in rapport with their victim, eight Thienz suffered equally. They screamed as one. Their hold upon Corley sundered, and even as reflex jerked the man's scorched flesh from the flame, he whipped back his knife hand and threw. The blade caught the nearest Thienz in the throat. Its death-dream diverted its fellows a split second, enough for Corley to close his fingers over the cold hilt of his broadsword. He yelled, shattering forest silence, and drew. His first stroke sliced two of his antagonists in half.

The survivors scuttled frantically into the night-black thickets. Corley could not see them. But Thienz-demons would sense each other; their counterattack would be sudden and coordinated, and against five he would be lost. The captain struck blind. Twigs and small saplings sheared under his blade. Slashed greenery whipped straight to jab him as he pressed forward, each step taking him farther from the fire that had been his salvation. Yet he did not hesitate in false hope. He had read the histories. Repeat tactics never worked on a Thienz. His only chance was to cut them down before they managed to regroup.

Yet his enemies had melted like ink into the night. Corley shook back sweat-soaked hair. His seared hand throbbed, and his breath rushed raggedly through his throat. Necessity forced him onward. His sword stroke stayed even, a scathing lethal arc he had practiced to mechanical perfection. With wry fury, he wondered whether his corpse would continue the motion after the Thienz had crushed his spirit to whimpering defeat.

Then, without warning, the captain's inner musing became wrenched away and replaced by another reality.

Jaric smelled sweetrushes. Yanked back to separate awareness, he dimly recalled falling to the floor in the nursery of a Llondelei burrow; but a dream-image bound him deeper into night. He could neither tear free nor influence the demons who manipulated his mind.

'Firelord's heir, you were cautioned long ago on the ice cliffs; now Shadowfane's minions come hunting, and Keithland holds no haven.' Revelation followed, cruel as death: Jaric and his companions had nearly been overtaken on Tierl Enneth. Only because Llondelei influence had directed them across the midst of the clansmen's summerfair had they been spared from attack. Since the tracking Thienz had presumed civilized humans would never attempt such a course, the ambush they prepared had been foiled. Cursing, yowling among themselves, Shadowfane's hunters lost precious time and their prey by going around, beyond range of the blind priestess's sensitivity to demon presence. Now, with Firelord's heir and Dreamweaver out of reach, the Thienz vented their frustration upon the luckless person of Deison Corley . . .

Their next strike battered the captain to the edge of unconsciousness. The sword flew spinning from his hand. He crashed after it, landed heavily on his shoulder. Briars tore his face. His teeth gouged up a mouthful of dirt, and his vision went utterly black. Still he fought. But now his enemies were guarded; pain could no longer free him. All he had left were the knives concealed on his person, though he might only get the chance to use one. Trapped like a rabbit in a warren, Deison Corley reached for the blade snugged in the sheath against his thigh. Around him, the Thienz closed in.

Jaric twisted, savaged doubly by Llondelei accusers. "You'd let Corley die!" he charged in return. "Your kind saw his peril, and yet did nothing to save him."

The Llondel returned no mercy. Unlike the heir of Ivain and the Dreamweaver, the life of Deison Corley held no consequence to the far-seers of their burrow. The man's continued well-being concerned the Llondelei not at all: *Jaric had disregarded all warnings; that the Kielmark's captain should die was just consequence.* The guilt cut like a whip.

"No!" Jaric's anguished denial rung without echo within the burrow's earthen walls.

'*Then who else among mankind shall end contention?*' The Llondel showed him Corley, struggling in the night with his dagger in the guts of a Thienz who had strayed within reach. Human and demon thrashed over and over in leaf mold, entangled and sticky with blood. Jaric tasted salt. Dream-image and self muddled together, his own tears indistinguishable from Corley's sweat as the captain fell limp, mind-bound victim of the four Thienz left living after the ambush.

Jaric felt his face ground on the rushes. He whimpered, flayed raw by remorse as the demons closed, vindictive in their desire to maim. Still he could not snap the fear which rejected Ivain's inheritance. Though he shared the suffering and the death of a friend, the bones of four thousand unburied corpses bound him to horrors far worse. The multitudes slain by sorcerers' mistakes shackled the heir of Ivain against action, and for this the Llondelei named him coward.

"More than one captain died at Elrinfaer and Tierl Enneth!" Jaric flung back. "Must human endeavor be limited to Vaerish mysteries and the Cycle of Fire?"

As if in vindication, an arrow slashed the dark. The shaft struck and buried to the feathers in the neck of the Thienz who crowded to kill. It tumbled thrashing to the ground. The demon beside it spun with a snarl toward the brush. This one was mature enough to carry venom, and Jaric saw the glint of poison sacs distended to bite.

Then, beyond the thicket, a shadow moved. The creature staggered and fell, the beaded leather haft of a hillman's dagger stuck in its chest. As one, the Thienz survivors abandoned Corley. Flight availed them nothing. As Corley threw off the effects of their hold, ten leather-clad tribesmen dashed silently from the thickets. A hail of javelins transfixed the last two Thienz from behind.

Relief lent Jaric the boldness to repudiate the judgment against him. "There, humans *can* kill demons without sorcery!"

Llondelei consciousness denied nothing as Corley rose from the ground. Half-dazed, cut in a dozen places where branches and Thienz claws had mauled him, the captain still retained presence of mind to thank his rescuers in clan dialect.

The leader of the foray hid surprise at the fact that an outland captain spoke his language. He jerked his dagger from the nearest corpse, feathered ornaments trembling at his wrists as he raised the bloody blade. "No thanks are due, seafarer, and none accepted. Our Lady sent us hunting for Thienz, not to win tribe-debt for sparing the carving of city-man skin."

Corley bent with a grunt, retrieved his longsword from the leaves, then leaned heavily on the cross guard. Tired, battered, and stinging, he regarded the clan chief entirely without rancor. "Health to your horses, then," he said.

The hillman raised painted eyebrows; here stood a town-born wise enough to tribe ways that he returned insult with blessing; this from a warrior great enough to slay four of the enemy before he succumbed to their mind-tricks. Guardedly acknowledging respect, the clan chief turned his fist outward in salute. Then he and his fellows spun soundlessly and the image of their leaving vanished utterly into dark . . .

Jaric's reprieve ended, his awareness of Corley ripped away by a tide of contempt. *'Foolish boy, did you think peril ends here?'* Without waiting for answer, Llondelei consciousness tore away his defense, stripped him vulnerable before self-evident truth: young Thienz were the compact's lowliest and most expendable resource. Their auras were least detectable to humans, which made them suitable as errand runners to Keithland; but before the mighty of Shadowfane, the powers of these were insignificant. Angered now, the Llondelei tightened their net. Cruel as the death of hope, they toppled Ivainson Firelord's heir headlong into nightmare. . . .

Images hammered into him with the force of physical blows. The Dark-dreamer emerged from Shadowfane. Commanding the same powers Taen employed for good, the brother spun ringing webs of nightmare. Misfortune harrowed the people. Farmsteaders on the northern borders of Hallowild died screaming in their cottages; others woke crazed from sleep and butchered their families. Cattle and crops died of neglect in the fields, and weeds wove shrouds through the bones which lay whitening in the dooryards.

"Spare them," whispered Jaric, but his words became the sated croak of scavenger birds. He heard laughter as demons praised their chosen, one called Maelgrim who had once been born a fisherman's son on the isle of Imrill Kand.

A demon hissed, and stone walls crumbled. Jaric saw dead men at arms in Morbrith livery stare open-eyed at the sky. Within the bailey, amid a litter of shredded parchment, the master scribe who had taught a lonely boy to write pleaded on his knees for mercy. Yet the Dark-dreamer saw into the victim's mind and there encountered memories of Ivainson Jaric. Maelgrim spat in the dust, and the ascending whistle of Gierj-demons rang across the valley where corpses rotted in the sun. Parchments ignited into flame, and Jaric's scream blended with that of the archivist at Morbrith, who burned alive on a pyre fed by his own life's works.

"No!" But the images spun faster, slivering the soul of the Firelord's son to agony: Taen dead, spitted on the knife of her brother, *all because a recalcitrant boy refused the fate of his father!* Black hair clotted in a pool of scarlet where she fell. Her death brought an end to the powers of the Vaere-trained, and the demons advanced unhindered.

The eastern kingdoms of Felwaithe and Kisburn did battle and failed, proud cities razed one by one to rubble while the countryside smoked with the burned-out shells of farmsteads. The wizards of Mhored Kara came singing to the field and perished, slaughtered beside their familiars without any bard to commemorate their passing. The images continued, relentless. Gierj-demons sang in another place, and fire swept across the thornbrakes of Cliffhaven. Bleeding, riddled with burns, the Kielmark howled curses as he and his men roasted like slaughtered animals. On the north-shore cliffs, dirtied tons of ice softened and slithered seaward with a roar like a spring avalanche. Bloodthirsty whistles echoed over the roar of flames. When the heat subsided, the frostwargs scuttled to freedom, and their segmented legs scattered the bones of the Stormwarden of Elrinfaer who had once confined them. Roused, murderous, crazed to insatiable frenzy, the creatures rampaged across the straits. No Firelord stood forth to curb them.

Broken at last by grief, Jaric wept. Yet the images knifed through his tears with terrible clarity. Landfast became desecrated by demons. Priests died, disemboweled, and the knowledge preserved by Keithland's first, starfaring generations was torn from broken towers. Forever ignorant of their heritage, the townsmen trapped in the streets suffered diabolical torment as the Dark-dreamer culled the weak from the strong. Demons bred the survivors for slavery.

Jaric's tears became the salt-wet tumble of storm waves. Crouched in despair over *Callinde*'s rail, he cast the Keys to Elrinfaer into the sea, that Kor's Accursed might never recover them. Yet atrocity did not end. Maelgrim Dark-dreamer and his pack of Thienz chased down their final quarry, the heir of Ivain Firelord whose latent masteries held Keithland's last chance of recovery. Winded and beaten after a long, hopeless flight through the wilds, Jaric stumbled to his knees against the granite cliffs of Northsea. His captors closed in, Emien among them, his eyes bereft of all trace of humanity. Jaric gasped air into burning lungs. At bay and cornered, he stared at the sword blade which quivered in triumph at his throat.

"You showed mercy and granted me life, once," said the brother whose hand had murdered Taen. "I survived to know my true masters. Shall I offer you the same courtesy? The Keys to Elrinfaer are lost, but your talents might yet unbind the Mharg."

Jaric tensed, his final, desperate act an attempt to throw himself on his enemy's blade. But the Dark-dreamer engaged his mastery and slapped him aside unharmed. Captured alive, and bound by the Thienz, *Ivainson saw himself delivered to Shadowfane.*

"No!" His protest echoed off walls of windowless stone. Demons came. They slashed Jaric's flesh with a knife, and poured the dissolved crystals of the living Sathid into his wound. Shackled by demon malice, Jaric experienced the first unbearable torment of the Cycle of Fire; *if he survived, Kor's Accursed intended to command his powers. Their will would become his own, and he himself would betray Anskiere's trust, break the wards over Elrinfaer Tower, and release the horrors within.*

"*No!*" Jaric howled in the throes of insufferable anguish. Flame consumed his limbs. The blackened flesh of his hands peeled from splayed bones. "*No!*" Tendons popped and sizzled and sparks shot through the eye sockets of his skull. "*No!*" Riven by madness, the son of Ivain would raise fire and sear the last human life from Keithland. "*No, no, no!*"

"Jaric!" Taen's voice echoed through a roar of flame. *Taen Dreamweaver, who died bleeding on the dagger of her brother.*

"No, Jaric, will you listen?" A girl's cold fingers reached through curtains of fire and grasped his shoulder. Charred muscles burst under her touch. Jaric screamed in mortal agony.

"Ivainson Jaric, *wake up!*" The fingers tightened, shook his body with desperate violence.

Jaric moaned and opened his eyes to the gray folds of a Llondian cloak. He flinched and started back, but small hands caught him close. Taen's face loomed over him, backed by sky and the sun-dappled leaves of a forest.

"Jaric?" With a tenderness that tore him to the heart, the Dreamweaver smoothed the damp hair from his brow.

Tatters of nightmare fled, but waking thought could not disperse their memory. Jaric drew breath into a throat stung raw from screaming. Shattered, shivering, he clung to her, afraid to close his eyes; afraid if he lost sight of her for an instant, he might drown in the morass of despair inflicted by Llondelei far-seers.

"Kor's grace," said Taen unsteadily. "That was bad." She endured the grip of his hands, though his fingers gouged into her back. Patient, and near to crying herself, she numbed the worst of his anguish until equilibrium could return.

Jaric steadied under her touch. His quivering gradually subsided, and he loosened his locked muscles with an effort that was visible. Pressed against Taen's side, he twisted at last and examined his fingers. The skin was tanned and healthy, unmarked by any trace of burns. With a final shiver, he said, "You know what they tried to tell me."

Taen met his eyes. Now she could not prevent the tears which coursed down her cheeks. She said nothing. But Jaric knew that through his dream, the Llondelei had permitted her to discover the fate which awaited her brother.

Tortured by her steadiness, Jaric lowered his gaze. "Kor! I *can't* try the Cycle of Fire, do you understand?" He rammed his fist into the chilly dampness of last season's leaves, and watched a spider scurry in panic across his knuckles.

"I understand what will happen if you won't," said Taen in a voice kept painfully calm.

Jaric rolled away from her and wrapped his arms around his knees. He would not ask if she knew of the attack upon Corley; not immediately. "Where are the Llondelei?"

"Gone." The cloak borrowed from the demons rustled as Taen shifted position. She did not touch him. "Once the Sathid finished crystallizing, I was free to leave. They released you in the forest a short time later. I used my dream-sense to find where."

But her words became background to echoes of the nightmares wrought by Llondelei. Their meddling in Jaric's mind had offered warning. Dared he proceed without heeding? Eight hunters from Shadowfane lay dead, but their kindred at Shadowfane would already have sensed their fate. More attacks would follow; if demons overtook *Moonless* in force, Corley's crewmen would be no match for them. Aware through deep disquiet that the Dreamweaver had stopped speaking, Jaric hid his face in his hands. His words emerged muffled. "You're well, then?"

Taen reached out and tugged his wrist until he surrendered. With a smile so genuine it caught the breath in his throat, she placed a small amber stone in his palm and closed his fingers over it. "There. You hold the foundation of my power as Dreamweaver. Tamlin has urged that I hide it, lest demons use it against me. Why must you believe the legacy of the Vaere-trained is an intolerable burden?"

Jaric sighed. His emotions felt threshed over and over until only the husk of feeling remained. Yet his expression softened slightly as he gathered the girl close. "If anyone on Keithland could convince me, little witch, you would be the one." He paused then, too lacerated to hide the fear which tangled his inner self. The Llondelei had shown him horrors. Terrorized by another possibility, that Keithland might also fall to ruin because he embraced the Cycle of Fire only to repeat the madness that had made Ivain devastate Elrinfaer, Jaric fixed on the last place his quest had left unsearched. "I have one more plan left to try."

He returned the crystal to Taen's hand. Then, looking down into her trusting blue eyes, he found himself caught by an irrational rush of desire. Flushed to the roots of his hair, Jaric resisted an urge to kiss her. "Will you help?"

The words came queerly strangled from his throat. Aware of his discomfort, but not the turmoil which prompted it, Taen replied with a brave attempt at humor. "Help do what, you fish-brained scribe?"

"I need to subvert the priests and break into the sanctuary towers of Landfast," said Jaric. Driven in his need to escape destiny, the idea firmed, a shelter against a future too terrible to contemplate. If a defense against demons existed, it surely must lie within the heritage of the first men of Keithland; records might still survive from the ship, *Corinne Dane*. But to break the security of the priests was treason of the first order, a direct violation of the Landfast Charter. Smudged with dirt, with his shirt torn and small sticks hooked in his hair, Jaric braced his shoulders in anticipation of rebuke.

Taen grinned. Then the incongruity between his request and his appearance broke her control; she burst into peals of laughter. Jaric's brown eyes widened with hurt. Before he could retreat, she sobered and caught his callused hand. "I can do better than that. If you want, I can pick secrets from the mind of the Supreme High Star himself. But first I think we should get back to *Moonless*. If we delay much longer, a certain captain I know will be whetting his knives down to needles."

Sensitive to the signs that weakness lingered yet from the Dream-weaver's harrowing illness, Jaric controlled his impatience to be far from the burrows of the Llondelei; he matched his pace to Taen's as they hiked through the breezeless summer morning. Noon came and went. By after-noon, the pair reached the forest's edge, where they rested. Withdrawn and broodingly silent, Jaric stared across open meadows. The broken towers of Tierl Enneth lay etched against the skyline beyond, blue with haze, but eloquent with still-remembered tragedy.

Braced against a tree trunk, Taen Dreamweaver plucked a tassel of pine needles from her collar. The intensity of Jaric's stillness disturbed her. "You're very quiet."

The boy shrugged. Distressed by his reluctance to answer, Taen sounded his mood with her talents. Jaric felt her touch. He jerked back, tensed as if to move on; and balked by his restlessness, the Dreamweaver could discern nothing of the reason for his worry.

She spoke of ordinary things to disarm him. "The Llondelei didn't keep your weapons." Attuned even to particulars, she shrugged her cloak from her shoulders and qualified. "Corley carried your sword and dagger safely back to *Moonless*. I contacted him to be sure."

Yet mention of the captain seemed only to intensify Jaric's silence. "He knows you're safe? Then he'll want you back on board as soon as possible."

Taen frowned, now certain that the stresses implanted by Llondelei dreams absorbed Ivain's heir still. A glint of pure mischief lit her eyes. "You can't fret all the time. I won't let you." Without warning she launched herself at him, piling shoulder first into the hardened muscles of his middle.

Caught unprepared, Jaric gasped. He overbalanced, fell rolling into soft grass with Taen clutched in his arms. Her hair tangled in his shirt laces, then scattered across his face, fragrant with the herbs used to sweeten her bath. Wakened to the fact that the touch of her was pleasing, Jaric ceased struggling and lay back with her warm weight sprawled across his chest.

Taen spoke, her words muffled by the cloth of his sleeve. "Do you mind if we take a nap first?"

At a loss to answer, Jaric swallowed. Her nearness disoriented him. He could feel the pound of his heart against her cheek, and the pressure of her hip against his groin stirred his blood with desire. Abruptly he tried to pull away.

"Don't, Jaric." Taen shifted and caught his ears between her fingers. "You're not a scrawny apprentice anymore. And if I were a serving wench from Morbrith, I'd treat you differently than you remember." With an impish grin, she released him and began to tickle his ribs.

Jaric broke into laughter. Yet his mirth caught in his throat, transformed to a wrenching sob of despair. Llondelei warnings had cornered him, unveiled a painful sequence of destiny no sane man could tolerate. Aware how sorely he needed release, but not that he feared for her safety, Taen applied her mastery and deftly overturned his control. Immediate tears flooded his face. With the last of his pride, Jaric twisted his face into the grass and wept.

Taen curled next to him, her arm across his shaking shoulders. She said nothing, offering only the comfort of her presence. But when he finally steadied, his expression no longer seemed a mask of agonized endurance. Though the grief instilled by the Llondelei visions had not left him, now he observed the summer meadow with calm; the strength and the life in his limbs could be appreciated without shrinking in horror of tomorrow.

"You cheat like the daughter of a Landfast merchant," Jaric accused the Dreamweaver at last. Yet he spoke without rancor.

"Daughters of Landfast merchants don't roll in the hay with vagabonds." Taen climbed to her feet and shook grass seeds from her fallen cloak. "Are you going to spend the rest of the day on the ground with the ants?"

"I should." Jaric grinned and rose also. "The worst they ever do is pinch."

He caught Taen and pulled her into his embrace. Then, too embarrassed to express himself, he opened his hands and whirled abruptly eastward toward Tierl Enneth. Taen fell into step at his heels. Reassured that the quality of Jaric's mood had changed, she did not badger him from silence.

Except for occasional gullies, the terrain offered easy walking. Still, sundown spilled shadow across the hills by the time Dreamweaver and Firelord's heir reached the site where the clans had celebrated summerfair. The painted wagons had departed, leaving torn earth and the dried mounds of horse droppings. Jaric and Taen trod a flattened expanse of grass where dancers had celebrated solstice. But the desolation of the place now was total, with the tenantless dwellings of Tierl Enneth brooding black against amber in the afterglow.

The pair hastened their pace. They entered the wall through the damp mouth of the arch, Taen wrapped in the Llondian cloak, and Jaric shivering in his torn tunic. Dusk deepened over streets and towers; in time their legacy of bones became veiled kindly in darkness. Taen grew weary. Jaric caught her stumbling; he supported her lagging steps, then carried her outright. This once her physical nearness did not move him. Now more than ever before he had no wish to linger amid ruins whose sole testimony was a sorcerer's failure to protect.

At last Jaric heard the rhythmic wash of breakers ahead. The lane he traversed widened and joined the avenue which led to the sea gate. The harbor glistened silver in starlight beyond the gapped span of the arch. Blackly outlined against sandy shore, a boat waited with four oarsmen lounging by the thwarts.

A man's voice called from the breakwater. "Jaric? The Dreamweaver warned me of your arrival." Corley leaped the wall and extended brawny arms toward Taen. His left hand was poulticed, and on his wrists the scars of old battles were scribed across with fresh scabs. Overset by remembrance of what might have resulted had the clansmen not interceded, Jaric lost all inclination to speak.

As he surrendered the Dreamweaver to the captain's care, Corley added, "I saved your sword and dagger, boy, but, Kor! I'll flay you with the dullest knife on *Moonless* if you ever again give up weapons without a fight."

The tapers burned low in Shadowfane's great hall in the early hours before dawn. Shadows crawled grotesquely over the skulls used as end caps on the posts of Scait's tall throne, but the Demon Lord did not sit. He paced, the click of his spurs upon stone an uninterrupted rhythm since the news which had drawn him from council. Back and forth he passed across the dais; no underling dared to approach. Finally he flicked a thought-query at the Thienz who knelt with snout pressed to forelimbs at the foot of the stair by the mirror pool.

'*What passes in Keithland, one-who-cowers-beneath-my-feet? The report from your underlings at Tierl Enneth is carelessly overdue.*'

The Thienz raised features gone yellow and creased with age. Too experienced to be cowed by its overlord's irritable insult, it whuffed air through its gill flaps and chose words. "Lord-mightiest, I offer news of a mishap."

Scait stopped poised between steps. The long hackles at his neck ruffled aggressively, a warning noticed at once by those favored advisors gathered across the hall. They stopped murmuring and lifted their eyes from the wax model of Landfast which had preoccupied them through the night.

"Speak," commanded the Sovereign Lord of Shadowfane. A neat movement spun him round, and he sat very stiffly on his cushions.

The Thienz repeated its bow, then rose on ridiculous feet. It offered image to explain. Scait received with narrowed eyes, sharing the view of a woodland dell in the highlands of Tierl Enneth. Between innocuous thickets of greenery lay the dismembered remains of eight Thienz sent to apprehend Jaric. Insects had hollowed the bodies; bones showed white through shriveled flesh, but decay did not affect the feathered tokens staked through the victims' torsos.

"Clansmen," hissed Lord Scait. His hackles bristled in displeasure, and his spurs scraped reflexively over the skulls. "How did this happen?"

The Thienz sang a mournful note. "Treacherous are the tribes of Tierl Enneth, Great-Lord. Their seeress sees much we wish would stay hidden. They dissipated the death-dreams of the fallen; most-unforgivably, little memory survives."

Scait's body stilled. At his silence, the boldest of the favorites abandoned her fellows and joined the Thienz by the dais. "Lord," she intoned. "If Taen and Jaric sought the burrow of the Llondelei on Tierl Enneth, what-chance the Dreamweaver survived?"

Scait's eyes flicked up. He bared teeth to silence the nattering of his underling, for her noise added nothing. Why the Llondelei should support humans was not fathomable; but that they might have chosen to spare Taen Dreamweaver from Sathid death must not be lightly dismissed. In the deep, chill hour before dawn, Scait weighed options. His next move must be planned with boldness, or mankind might gain another Vaere-trained sorcerer as ally. The boy Ivainson Jaric must be apprehended without thought for losses.

"Here is my command," said Scait. The favorites straightened to hear, and the Thienz swiveled small, half-sightless eyes toward the throne. "Send forth underlings to steal boats from human fishermen. The victims must be carefully chosen, isolated from their families and far from any harbor, for the rulers of Keithland must not be made to suspect." Here Scait paused and narrowed his focus upon the Thienz. "These boats you will load with a venomed elder, and those of your kind who have least seniority. They shall sail south into Keithland at the earliest opportunity."

The Thienz rocked in keenest anticipation. Though the young who were appointed would receive such orders with trepidation, that Taen-Dreamweaver-who-killed-brothers-at-Cliffhaven might be found and ripped apart was cause for joyful sacrifice.

Yet even as the Thienz rocked in anticipation, Scait sensed the cause of its jubilation. He sprang from his throne, crossed the dais in two steps, and descended the stair beyond at a bound. "You will *not* set the hunt after Taen Dreamweaver."

"Lord!" objected the Thienz, then abruptly smothered its protest as the spurred thumb of its overlord flicked out and pricked its neck.

"The boats will seek the Isle of the Vaere." Gently, cruelly, the Lord of Shadowfane bore down. Blood beaded around his spur, and the Thienz twitched, even as it received its instructions. "At all costs your siblings must find and kill Ivainson Jaric before he finds his way there."

Pinned and helpless, the Thienz repressed an ingrained reflex to cower. "Mightiest-high-one, your will shall speedily be done. But if the Dream-weaver has recovered her powers, she will cloak the prey from our sight. What means shall locate the one-you-desire-killed?"

Scait withdrew his spur and delicately licked the point.

Since the slightest taste of blood could stimulate the insatiable appetite of his kind, the Thienz scuttled in terror from underfoot. But the Great Lord's feeding instinct remained quiescent as he turned lambent eyes to his favorites. One or two waited with short hackles raised, as if they questioned his judgment concerning Taen; perhaps their hidden thoughts contemplated something more grave than disapproval. In the annals of the compact, combat had been called against rulers with less provocation than this.

But Scait dismissed such threat and turned his back, challenging belligerence with contempt. "The girl is nothing at this time but distraction. Dally for her now, and we risk facing a trained Firelord."

One among the favorites dared a small sound of dissent.

Scait whirled, deadly and graceful and utterly sure of his dominance. "Against Taen Dreamweaver, we have her brother. Had you forgotten? His powers will begin to stabilize within the next few days. Then shall a ruse be framed to snare the sister." The Sovereign Lord of the demons slashed the air with his spurs, and the long hackles at his neck bristled fully erect. "This is my plan. Who among you dares disapprove?"

Dawn spilled gray through the high windows of Shadowfane's great hall. In its light, the tapers smoked and guttered, while with manes smoothed in agreement, the sycophantic circle of demons all bowed to the will of their overlord.

CHAPTER XIII

Maelgrim

After rest and food and an accounting of events in the Llondelei burrow, Corley put away his whetstone and sheathed the impeccable steel of his knives. To the relief of his crew, he ceased to pace the quarterdeck through the night and the day while Taen recovered from the exhaustion of her ordeal. Still, watches were kept with strict regularity, and a scout network continued to quarter the shoreline for Thienz-sign. Since they discovered nothing more threatening than a fishing boat abandoned in a thorn thicket, *Moonless* remained at anchor off Tierl Enneth.

But Jaric's restlessness would not abate. More silent than usual, he avoided company, and even Taen had difficulty drawing him out.

"Sulk in peace, then," she retorted in exasperation when for the second time in an hour the boy retreated into the chart room. After that the Dreamweaver resorted to card games to fill her time. The sailhands resurrected their stakes from knotted stockings and sea chests. More than a few groused that dampness had transformed their former winnings to sprouts. For a time, the cook found it necessary to forestall looters by barricading the bean stores in the galley. Loud-voiced, boastful, and vociferously protective of the Dreamweaver who teased them to laughter, the off-watch crew aboard *Moonless* settled comfortably back to routine. Corley reviewed reports from his scouts between stints of cursing the healer. When the persistent, meddling fool finally stopped worrying at his scabs, the captain channeled his own excess energy into resuming Jaric's education at arms.

Corley then drove his charge relentlessly to assess the effects of Brith's teaching. He found Jaric's attitude changed in more than technique. Where once the boy had handled his blades with a tentative, even fussy finesse, he now struck out boldly. Gratified by the belling clang of solid blocks and parries, Corley grinned, then pushed the boy harder. But now the captain added occasional words of praise between epithets. That teacher and pupil both used the practice to vent their internal frustrations did not matter; in a short time, the Firelord's heir would be capable of defending himself with a fair degree of skill.

By the seventh day, Taen had recovered equilibrium enough to resume command of her Sathid-born powers. Jaric endured his morning sword drill with evident impatience; the instant Corley excused him, he hastened below decks and tossed his sword on his berth without pausing to oil the blade. At last, Taen could turn her talents to dream-search the secret knowledge of the priests who lived in seclusion at Landfast. Pitched to feverish anxiety, Jaric hurried to the Dreamweaver's cabin, only to find her absent.

The captain's steward reassured him. "Taen said you'd ask for her. You'll find her waiting in the chart room."

Jaric voiced a breathless thanks. His steps slowed as he made his way aft and stepped through the chart room door. The lantern swung gently over a table cleared of maps. Taen sat with closed eyes, her breathing gentled in the peaceful rhythm of sleep. Jaric saw with trepidation that she had already focused her dream-sense and begun the tedious search; for amid Landfast's populace, few minds held knowledge of the mysteries guarded by Kor's Brotherhood.

Jaric eased the door closed. Too restless to sit, he paced, his head bent to accommodate the low ceiling. Nerves and the stifling heat thrown off by the lamp made him sweat. The sanctuary towers had been sealed by the founders of the Landfast Council; to break their edict constituted treason. Yet should demons conquer the Alliance, that same knowledge would be threatened. The heritage and purpose of Keithland's forebears might surely be lost. Burdened by the horrors of Llondian prophecy, Jaric crossed and recrossed the space between table and chart locker. Only one fact mattered: if the sanctuary towers failed to yield answers, all that lay between Keithland's continuance and mankind's survival was himself, and the Cycle of Fire.

Hours passed. The lamp burned low and finally flickered out. Smoke spindled up from its spent wick. Jaric struck a spark to a candle he found in a locker, then sat and busied himself with oil flask and wicking string. With the meticulous care learned under a forester's guidance, he cleaned the lantern and set the flame burning once more. A golden circle of light illuminated the cabin. Across the breadth of the chart table, Taen lay motionless in trance. Her hair spilled over her wrists, ink-black against pale skin. The curve of her cheek lay tilted toward Jaric; if her lashes and brows seemed delicate as a master artist's brushstroke, any image of perfection was marred by the broken thumbnail which peeped beneath her chin. Devoid of jewel or artifice, clad in a shift of plainest linen, the girl owned all the spare beauty of a wild creature of the wood. Jaric felt his breath catch.

He set aside the knife he had used to pare wicks. As if the smallest disruption might break the spell and rouse her, he clamped his oil-streaked fingers in his cuffs. Earlier he had been unable to keep still; now, if an enemy burst in and challenged him with a naked blade, he would have found it impossible to move. Blood rushed through his veins. His skin went hot, then cold, and he swallowed painfully. This girl had been all things to him: betrayer, confidante, a friend who had badgered him until he laughed, and a kindred spirit who had eased him through times of anguish; but suddenly, in the undefined space between one breath and the next, this same girl became the one treasure in all Keithland that he could not bear to lose.

Jaric regarded Taen with a hunger he never knew he possessed. The lamp burned lower by his elbow. Memories of the matronly ridicule he had suffered at Morbrith faded until, almost, Jaric imagined he could touch this woman and receive her welcome. *Moonless* swung against her anchor line, disturbed by a breath of wind. Draft from the hatchway tumbled a strand of hair across the pink curve of Taen's lips. She stirred, her brows pinched into a frown. The same breeze eddied across Jaric's sweating skin. He shivered and abruptly recalled his fate. Between himself and the girl across the table lay futures too terrible to contemplate: the bloodied knife of the brother who would kill her, or the madness of the Cycle of Fire. And if he hesitated in his choice, if he delayed one day or one hour too long, Thienz might destroy them both.

Jaric shoved violently to his feet. He stifled a raw cry and braced his fists against the bulkhead. No alternative offered relief. Of the countless cruelties Ivain had inflicted upon Keithland in his madness, his mistreatment of women was least forgivable. Jaric understood that to complete his father's heritage, he must first sacrifice his feelings for Taen. On this, his self-control wavered dangerously. If the search of the sanctuary towers failed him, he wondered whether he would have strength enough to leave her, as he must, since the presence of the Firelord's heir would inevitably draw enemies. Jaric stared down at his hands. He dared not look toward the chart table. If he did, even once, the sight of the girl would break him.

No hand moved to trim the lantern wick. At length the flame trembled, thinned to red, and sparked out. Taen sighed in the darkness. Warned by a rustle of cloth, Jaric knew she awakened. He waited with taunt muscles, yet failed to hear her step. The first he knew of her presence was a feather-light touch on his shoulder.

"Jaric?"

He whirled, backed against the unyielding frame of the bulkhead.

She could not read his face in the darkness. "Jaric? What's wrong?"

Ivain's heir fought his voice level. "You surprised me."

Blind himself in the shadow, he heard her sandal scrape the deck. Then the striker snapped. Haloed in the light of new flame, Taen closed the glass shutter and stretched on tiptoe and hung the lamp from the hook above the chart table.

She faced him then, and he saw her eyes were full of tears. "I didn't find what you need."

Pained by her anguish, Jaric took a moment to understand the import of her statement.

"The minds of the priests in seclusion are beyond my reach," Taen resumed. "I cannot tell why. Perhaps the stone of sanctuary itself forms a defensive barrier." She hesitated, and the disappointment she felt on his behalf cut Jaric to the quick. "I turned from the towers, and tried the mind of the Supreme High Star, whose sacred title is Guardian of the Gates. He alone knows what secrets the tower protects. Jaric, you'll find no help against demons at Landfast."

Safe beyond range of her touch, the boy lifted brown eyes to her face. "Tell me why."

Taen answered reluctantly. "The sanctuary towers contain keys to Kor's Sacred Fires, also answers to the riddles of eternal space and time. But by divine decree, that knowledge must be withheld from man until all demons are vanquished from Keithland."

Jaric closed his eyes. Sweat on his skin caught the lamplight like gilt, and his chest heaved as if he had been running. Taen had phrased her findings in religious terms, but through Llondian memory, Jaric perceived more. Almost certainly Landfast preserved plans to the engine *Corinne Dane,* heritage of mankind's origin among the stars. How many would be slaughtered if demons knew such knowledge still existed? Even now the anguished words of the starprobe's long-dead captain echoed in Ivainson's thoughts. *"If* Corinne Dane's *mission fails, if mankind doesn't discover a defense against powers such as your Llondelei possess, the only human survivors left in creation will be those colonies enslaved by the Gierj."*

Corinne Dane had flown, and crashed like a stricken bird on hostile soil. Jaric swallowed, dangerously near to weeping. His last hope had failed, left him lightless in the shadows of his weakness. In a moment of gritty honesty he admitted he had built dreams only to delay, for since his interview with the Grand High Star at Landfast the truth had been apparent. Had a weapon against demons existed, *Corinne Dane's* band of castaways would never have formed the Landfast Council, nor drawn up their charter of secrecy; they would have rebuilt their broken ship and brought rescue to their beleaguered civilization among the stars. Instead, for a span of centuries, Keithland's people had struggled for survival, precariously defended by the talents of Vaere-trained sorcerers. Jaric drew a shuddering breath. Safe haven no longer existed. If he asked passage to the Isle of the Vaere, or fled from *Moonless* to spare Taen from the Thienz who tracked him, already he might be too late. Racked by indecision, Ivainson Jaric opened his eyes.

The lantern flame wavered, recently brushed by a draft. The chart room stood empty. Attuned to the depth of his distress, Taen had possessed the wisdom and the tact to leave him in solitude.

Corley ordered *Moonless* under way at the turn of the tide. The clank of the capstan and the rattle of chain through the hawse reverberated the length and beam of the brigantine, yet Taen barely noticed the din. Weary from her dream-search of Landfast, she sat on her berth in the darkness, her heels tapping restlessly against the wooden locker beneath. She needed no Dreamweaver's talents to sense Jaric's apprehension of the Cycle of

Fire. Distressed that she could not console him, and afraid if she sought counsel from the Vaere that Tamlin would command her to intervene and force Jaric to accept his father's heritage, she longed for the wise comfort of Anskiere of Elrinfaer.

Moonless shuddered as her anchor ripped free of the seabed. The rhythm of the capstan's pawls quickened, and feet thumped on the decking overhead as sailhands rushed to man sheets and braces. "Steady as she goes!" yelled Corley from the quarterdeck. The brigantine lifted into a heel as yards of unbrailed canvas caught the wind. Taen settled with her back against the bulkhead. She did not weep. Though emotions knotted the core of her being, she was the daughter of an Imrill Kand fisherman, born to hardship and loss. She had learned early to temper misery with practicality. If Jaric refused the Cycle of Fire, not even the Vaere could change his mind. To wish for the guidance of an absent sorcerer would not cure the problem; and the effort of the morning left her drained. Aching, and unsettled by problems too great for her powers to encompass, she rested her head against the bulkhead.

Light sleep claimed her unawares. The security set about the sanctuary towers at Landfast had been complex, taxing in the extreme to unravel; concern for Jaric had driven her to an imprudent outlay of energy. Now, drifting directionless in dreams, Taen failed to safeguard all her channels. A compulsion crept in, not her own, but threaded through her thoughts with a tact that could only come from one who had known and loved her. Slowly, subtly, the intrusive presence blended with the essence of her will; and presently subtle prompts became conviction.

Since the demons' strike against Keithland involved the brother they held captive, Taen saw clearly where duty lay. In the past, she had failed to save her brother from the guilt-ridden misery which had pressured him to forsake his own kind. Now the only option left was to prevent him from becoming a weapon against humanity. She must engage her mastery, contact Emien in the heart of Shadowfane, and attempt to break him free of the demons' influence.

Spray sheeted across *Moonless*'s stern as she rounded the headlands of Tierl Enneth and jibed for the open sea. Jounced against the bulkhead as the spanker boom slammed onto starboard tack, Taen centered her awareness. She did not feel the draft which spilled through the grate, nor did she smell the sea breeze, spiked with the scent of impending rain. Never did she imagine that her intent had been molded by enemies who shaped a snare. Unwary, and drawn by love, her dream-sense carried her awareness across the wild barrens beyond the borders of Keithland.

Gusts whined across the stone spires of Shadowfane; echoes like the keening of grief-stricken women penetrated even the depths of the dungeon where Taen found Emien. The man she recognized as her brother crouched in darkness within the barred confines of a cell. His face was hidden behind scarred fingers while a Sathid matrix cross-linked to demon masters deepened its grip upon his mind. Careful not to disrupt his equilibrium, Taen extended her dream-sense and tentatively encompassed his thoughts.

At once, she knew nightmares. Prompted by the crystal's guidance, Emien relived events from his past as vividly as the day they occurred. Taen merged with his consciousness as fluidly as water flowing into a pool. Through her brother's dreams she observed a storm-lashed vista of ocean. Wind screamed, blasting the wave crests into spray, while the sibling she remembered clung with wet hands to the gunwale of a pinnace. Numbly he watched the galleass he had abandoned founder among the swells. Though the vessel was half-veiled in spindrift, Taen recognized King Kisburn's flagship, *Crow*, which had borne the Stormwarden in chains from Imrill Kand. She, a girl of ten, had stowed away to free him. Emien had boarded later, with a vow to bring his sister safely home; instead he had lost her.

Now the demon-controlled Sathid he had inherited from his mistress compelled remembrance. Battered by storm winds of Anskiere's making, Emien watched the galleass settled beneath the waves. The Dreamweaver who shared his memory felt the grief and sick anger which thwarted him from tears; for the boy believed his younger sister was still trapped in the galleass' hold. The blame for her death was entirely his. Wretched with loss, he knew guilt; *the familiar, terrible guilt he had suffered when his father drowned in the net his own carelessness had entangled.* Mourning could not absolve him; crushed beneath an overwhelming weight of responsibility, Emien sought release in vicious anger against the Stormwarden who had lured his sister into danger.

Taen saw her chance, but lost any opening to act.

The demon-controlled Sathid which supplanted her brother's will arose like a cyclone of force. It splintered Emien's spirit like a hammer-blow. The self-inflicted anguish of a sister's death became multiplied tenfold, twentyfold, twenty hundredfold, until agony become the sum of his existence. Taen lost her grip. The torment which harrowed her brother sucked her deep into the recesses of his mind, and through his mouth she screamed and screamed again. Emien's cell rang with echoes while slowly, painstakingly, Taen recovered a semblance of control.

But for the brother entrapped at Shadowfane, the agony continued. Tortured beyond reason by despair, he sought oblivion. Power blocked his desire. Demon voices addressed him through the Sathid link which bound his conscious will.

'As Emien, you suffer needless loyalty for a sister who later betrayed you. As Maelgrim-demon-honored, you can spare yourself. Would you choose to renounce this memory?'

Thrashing in unbearable anguish, Emien whispered hoarsely. "Yes. Set me free."

'So be it. Become Maelgrim.' A sigh like wind passed across the link. Bound to the consciousness of her brother, Taen perceived a series of sparkling flashes. Storm-tossed ocean frothed beneath the pinnace's keel; exactly as before, Emien regarded the foundering pinnace. Only the remorse he once had felt for his lost sister was gone. Now the anger and hatred for Anskiere remained, resonating through Maelgrim's awareness like the tireless toll of fog bells.

Prompted by the Sathid, the boy dreamed on, of the white-haired witch whose incomparable beauty had captured his loyalty. He noticed no eddy as the sister who shared his vision drew back from his mind. Horrified by the demon's meddling, and utterly careless of risk, Taen delved into her brother's memories with every shred of her skill. There she found that the sibling she had known and loved during childhood had changed beyond recognition. Where Emien should have recalled his mother and his home on Imrill Kand, his sister found gaps braced by bitterness, resentment, and malice; his inborn humanity was shattered nearly past hope of mending. In time, Taen saw that all compassion would perish, leaving a demon abomination named Maelgrim.

That transformation must not happen undisputed. Roused to outrage and fury, the Dreamweaver focused her will. As her brother cried out under a fresh onslaught of torment, she raised a veil of resistance across his mind to block the demon's designs.

For an instant Emien's screams ceased. Sharing his moment of reprieve, Taen knew the drafty damp of a cell where a lost, beloved voice cried out. "Sister?"

Then with the subtlety of a chess gambit, Shadowfane's minions narrowed their trap. Power arose, a storm song of force terrible as the wail of the damned. Slammed by a barrier of limitless dark, Taen mustered resistance; the vigor of her own Sathid link answered the demons' challenge. Her offense struck their barricade with a tortured flash of sparks. Forces thundered and spun like a cataclysm unleashed. The restraints set upon her by demons shivered, thinned, and finally tore asunder. Taen blazed through the gap, prepared to defend Emien's mind.

But the ravaged entity which remained of the brother she had loved did not stand in her support on the other side. *The entire sequence had been a ruse, designed and intended to imprison her.* Whirled haplessly into the destructive malice of Maelgrim, Taen felt herself seized and mangled by rage which understood no limit. Frantically she tried to withdraw. Her defense came too late. Demons controlled Maelgrim; and since their servant had been born her brother, his talent potentially matched her own. Even as Taen sensed the roused awareness of his matrix, demons assumed control. They urged the cross-linked Sathid to attack. Energies surged across the link and attempted to manipulate her own powers against her.

Taen bolted in terror. Should the enemy succeed in awakening her own Sathid's awareness, she would be crushed, her will extinguished as swiftly as a candle in a gale. The consequences of defeat stopped thought. Blind with panic, and still depleted from her session that morning with Jaric, Taen mustered her remaining resources into a flare of raw power. She strove, yet failed to snap the dream-link. Harried across distance by the malevolent entities of Shadowfane, Taen tried to quench her powers within the circle of her own awareness; surely no evil could challenge her within the security of her cabin on *Moonless*.

But the assumption proved false. The demons retained their hold. As Taen dissolved ties with her brother, enemies reversed the polarity of the link with a stinging lash of force; and for the space of a heartbeat, the Dreamweaver became Shadowfane's puppet. Through her consciousness, the enemy assimilated all, brigantine, crew, and captain. Taen experienced a savage flash of annoyance as the demons recognized Corley; his machinations had cost them a victory at Cliffhaven, as well as the lives of eight Thienz on Tierl Enneth. Yet Shadowfane's minions did not pause to strike. Instead, voraciously hating, they discovered one they despised more, one they hunted because in time his talents might mature to threaten their designs: Ivain Firelord's heir sailed on board a brigantine whose destination was the Isle of the Vaere.

Taen screamed aloud. Unable to endure any threat to Jaric, she convulsed and ripped into the depths of her being. Life-force itself became tinder for her rage, and the conflagration raised a white flash of power. The result tore through the demons' hold, and she woke disoriented in darkness.

Panting in the dampness of her own sweat, blinded and choking on tears, Taen took several seconds to recognize her surroundings. *Moonless* reeled in the throes of a squall. Waves thudded against the brigantine's sides, shivering timbers and keel, and wind shrilled through tackle and rigging with the savagery of a witch shrieking curses. Ragged with exhaustion, and tormented with self-reproach for the dangers brought on by her lapse of discipline, Taen pushed herself upright. That moment the companionway door banged open.

Deison Corley burst across the threshold. A lantern swung from his fist and his bronzed hair dripped rain. "Kor's grace, what's happened?"

"Demons." Taen fought to steady herself. "The compact at Shadowfane has taken over my brother. His powers are theirs, and through him I was lured into contact. Kor's Accursed attacked me across the link."

Corley swore; shadows spun crazily across the cabin as he raised the lantern to a hook set in the deck beams overhead. "List the damage. Quickly."

Taen drew a shaking breath. "The enemy knows *Moonless* is bound for the Isle of the Vaere."

"Destinations can be changed," snapped the captain. "What else?"

"Jaric," Taen began. As Corley surged forward in alarm, she backed her voice with a Dreamweaver's compulsion. "No! Things aren't that desperate! The demons have no knowledge of Jaric, except what they could sort

from my brother's memories." Taen qualified with an image drawn from
the past, and Corley shared the immediate impression of a frightened,
diffident boy, flattened at swordpoint against a thorny tangle of brush; so
had Jaric appeared to Emien upon the shores of Elrinfaer at the moment
the Keys were won. Taen's meaning was poignantly clear; without the support of a Dreamweaver's mastery on that day, Ivain Firelord's heir could
never have completed the Stormwarden's bidding.

"Jaric's changed a great deal since then," Corley conceded. "But you
know that's stinking little protection. Won't count a dog's damn against
the might of Shadowfane. The boy must be warned."

He snatched down his lantern and moved to go; and Taen's perception
caught the concern which filled the captain's mind. When Corley had
entered the chart room to plot his course, Jaric had learned *Moonless* would
sail for the Isle of the Vaere. A brief but stormy confrontation had
resulted; reflexively, Taen reached out for Jaric's thoughts, her intent to
measure the impact of the captain's insensitive rejoinders. The quality of
the silence which met her all but stopped her heart.

"Wait!" Frantic with worry, Taen Dreamweaver leapt from her bunk.
"Corley, wait, I'm coming with you."

She bolted through the companionway. Rain slashed her face, backed
by a howling wind. Hard on Corley's heels, the girl struggled to climb the
wet and heaving ladder. Even as she gained the quarterdeck, a shout from
the officer on watch hailed the captain.

"Boy's gone overboard."

"Quartermaster, hard alee!" Corley bellowed. He thrust the lantern
into the startled grasp of a sailor, then bolted for the rail. His brawny
hands snatched up the line which secured *Callinde*. "Boatswain! Stand by
to man the tackles!"

With a stupendous heave of muscles, Corley dragged the towrope in
hand over hand. Coils flaked across the deck, and presently *Callinde*'s dark
shape loomed through the squall. Gold against the white of the waves, a
head broke the surface of the sea. Jaric shook the hair from his face and
clung like a limpet to *Callinde*'s prow. Even as the Kielmark's captain
sought to drag him back, Taen arrived, slight and soaked like an otter
beside Corley's great bulk. She saw steel flash in Jaric's hand. The line
sang, short and sharp, and splashed slack into the sea.

Corley dropped the severed rope and swore. With barely a break in
motion, he threw off his sword belt and began to strip his person of
weapons. He intended to swim for the boy, Taen saw.

She caught his elbow as the first of his knives clattered to the deck.
"No! You must not follow him!"

Corley jerked free, a dagger in each hand and a murderous frown on
his face. "Why not?"

The Dreamweaver raised her voice over the flapping din of canvas as
the brigantine rounded to weather. "Jaric's pushed to the edge already, can't
you see? And aboard *Callinde* he'll be safe if demons strike at *Moonless*."

Corley cursed, on the brink of diving overboard.

Taen shouted. "Not even the Stormwarden dared force Jaric to the Cycle of Fire! Would you break his mind trying?" And she braced herself to protect with her Vaere-trained powers as enchantress.

Rain slashed across wood and oilskin and the flogging yards of canvas overhead. Finally Corley jammed one knife, then the other, into the sheaths at his wrists. "Kor's eternal Fires, girl. If I could lay hands on that boy's hide, I'd flay him quick. Will he *ever* learn not to jump ship without his weapons?"

Shivering, her hair fallen wet around the delicate lines of her collarbone, Taen stared after the vanishing shape of *Callinde*. And shocked back to reason by the stricken expression on her face, Corley caught her close.

"Jaric's tough, you know that, girl. However hard he's pushed, I never yet saw him run." A gust caught the spanker even as he spoke, recalling Corley to his neglected command. Belatedly he remembered he must chart a new course for *Moonless*, away from the southerly heading Shadowfane's compact would expect him to hold for the Isle of the Vaere.

Taen sensed his thought. Suddenly she longed for the village of her birth, a harbor so remote that Anskiere himself had chosen the site as a refuge after the disaster which destroyed Tierl Enneth. Imrill Kand as a haven made sound sense. Warned and alert to her peril, she would never again let her defenses slip; and if demons did trace *Moonless*, a northwesterly course might provide a foil for Jaric and *Callinde*.

"Put me down," she demanded of Corley. "Then sail me home. Please. Put about and go east to Imrill Kand."

The captain regarded her with the level attention he usually granted to equals. "You're sure? Luck won't forgive if your judgment's sour, and to sail that course will be in defiance of the Kielmark's orders."

Taen tilted her head with a shaky ghost of a smile. "The same tired argument? I thought we wore that one out on the night of your master's victory party."

Corley sucked air through his teeth; irritation and laughter warred on his rain-drenched face as he released the Dreamweaver abruptly. "Don't ever count on that one, girl." After an interval trading glares, his humor finally won out. "The day I give over my command to a cheeky, wet snip of a girl, those dogs in the forecastle will be sewing my carcass into sailcloth. Now that fact's understood, will you go get dry? You've given *Moonless*'s healer and my steward enough gray hair without adding pneumonia to their troubles."

CHAPTER XIV

Hunted

Dawn broke between squalls. Sunrise peeped through the last, low-flying clouds and scattered an arching magnificence of rainbows, but Jaric regarded their loveliness with little joy. *Moonless* and Tierl Enneth had long since vanished over the horizon. Alone upon the sea, the boy huddled in *Callinde*'s stern with both hands clenched to the steering oar. West winds drove his boat on a broad reach. Once he cleared the archipelago beyond the point of Tierl Enneth, he would turn south to Landfast and every indulgence a port city could provide. Until then, during a fortnight-and-a-half passage through mild summer weather, Jaric had solitude and too much time to reflect. He sailed *Callinde* and tried desperately to keep thoughts of Taen from his mind.

The night fell calm and star-studded. Jaric hove his boat to and ate a meager meal from his stores. Rocked upon the face of the sea, he slept only to waken screaming in horror of the Cycle of Fire. Later he tried tending the steering oar from sunset to dawn; but fatigue inevitably betrayed him. Against his will his eyes closed, and nightmares caught him at the helm. *Callinde* bore off her course; time and again the rattling crash of jibed sails battered Jaric back to wakefulness. In despair he buried his face in his hands and wished for stormy weather. The present, changeless blue of water and sky reminded him endlessly of Taen's eyes.

Conditions remained fair, though the wind rounded to a southwest heading. Forced to tack, Jaric revised his course and beached on a wild spit of land west of Islamere. There he trapped game, foraged tubers for the food locker, and refilled his water casks. Since *Callinde* sailed poorly to weather, he camped four days until the winds blew easterly, then crossed the final leagues to Landfast under gathering sheets of cloud.

Lightning laced the sky and thunder crashed when at length he rounded the islet of Little Dagley. Torrents of rain dimmed the light beacons on the jetties to weak haloes. Worn to exhaustion, and harassed by the pound of the squall against the sails, Jaric threaded a cautious course between the anchored ships and mooring buoys which cluttered the inner bay. He rounded *Callinde* to windward and at last dropped sail by the harbormaster's shed.

A dock lackey in fresh-looking oilskins caught *Callinde*'s lines. Jaric jumped ashore. He failed to note that the servant eyed him with wariness. Drenched, bearded, and ungroomed after a three-and-a-half-week passage, the boy warped his boat to the bollards. Muscles bunched under his wet skin, and the scars left from recent sword cuts shone livid and red across the knuckles of his dagger hand. Preoccupied and weary, Jaric ducked past the lackey and barged through the doorway of the harbormaster's shed to negotiate dockage for *Callinde*.

The master on duty leaped to his feet so quickly the beribboned beret which displayed his badge of office slipped down across his eyes. "You again! Fires, and what could you want *this* time?" He straightened the hat, revealing a droopy mustache and an anxious frown.

Jaric stopped in his tracks. Water dripped from his tunic, spattering the swept boards of the floor. "I want dock space for a fishing boat ten spans in length."

He raised a hand to his belt. The official flinched, but the boy drew no weapon. Instead Jaric pulled forth a leather bag and spilled a flood of coins on the counting table. Silvers bounced, rolled, and clanged into stillness, while the man behind the table slowly turned pale.

"Well?" Jaric gestured impatiently. "Are you deaf and blind? I said I want—"

The official lifted a trembling hand. "I *heard*. And I remember. You're master of *Callinde*?"

Jaric nodded.

"Kor!" The man dropped into his chair as if his legs had failed him. "Would you ruin me? That boat's marked in the Kielmark's registry. *No fee*. Do you hear?"

Jaric made no move to retrieve his coins. "I swore no fealty to Cliffhaven." But the anger in his tone made the ribbons in the man's hat quiver all the more.

The official swept the silvers into a heap and shoved them across the table with a rasping jangle. "Corley himself named you for the Kielmark's exemption. I won't be jeopardizing the trade of every guild in Landfast, knowing that. D'you think I want to hang because I brought Cliffhaven's retribution, and only a wharf fee to show for it? No. Get out. *Callinde* docks free until I'm personally informed otherwise."

Jaric shifted his weight to depart. But the harbormaster bolted from his chair and plucked at the young captain's sleeve in sharp distress. "Boy, please. Don't be leaving any coin."

Jaric swore. "If honest silver bothers you, then give it to the one-handed beggar with the tabby cat."

The official released him in dismay. "Which, the one who got arrested for striking the guards' master of arms?"

Jaric jerked and stopped, hands knotted into fists; and the harbormaster recoiled into the table, inciting a tinkle of coins.

"*Arrested?*" The boy sounded strangely heartbroken. *Must everyone who befriended him come to harm?* The beggar who had downed Brith had probably saved Taen's life. Grief caught Jaric off guard, twisted, and became anger.

"Send the silver to pay the beggar's fine, then!" he shouted at the dock-master. "Tell him to spend what's left, along with my apology for the prison charge."

The official drew breath to protest. But the boy stormed through the door, leaving water puddled on the floorboards, and a troublesome pile of silver on the table. The harbormaster swore. He called the man on dock watch in from the rain and, with utmost distaste, dispatched the fellow to the town prison with Jaric's coin and orders to free a one-handed beggar and a cat.

Rain glazed the slate roofs of Landfast, and cold, whipping wind chased the run-off into currents across the cobbles. Jaric slogged through the storm with his head down. He had no particular destination, only a driving need to forget the leather bag full of sorcerer's wards which swung at his neck, token of the destiny set on him by a father and a weathermage he had never known. That he could not compromise his fate without losing the black-haired enchantress who had captured his heart caused him pain beyond bearing. Jaric splashed through puddles until he found himself by the Docksider's Alehouse. Drenched and morose, he pushed the door open and entered.

The taproom was crowded with patrons from every walk of the water-front. Tracking footprints across brick that was already wet, Jaric pressed between a knot of dice-throwing sailhands and two merchants who argued with a captain over bills of lading. A pot boy stoked the fire on the hearth beyond, his face flushed red as nearby longshoremen shouted unflattering comments about his skinny frame. Once Jaric had been the butt of such jokes. Unaware how greatly he had changed since his initial passage from Cliffhaven, he hurried to the bar, where he tallied what remained of his coin. He spent all but two coppers on a wineskin. Then he retired to an uncrowded corner and sought the oblivion of drink.

When he was a scrawny apprentice at Morbrith Keep, unwatered wine invariably caused Jaric to fall asleep. Now, in the smoky air of a Landfast alehouse, the remedy chosen to drown his sorrows did not take immediate effect. Ivainson hunched in his dripping clothes, while the talk of a dozen groups of men swirled around him. He listened to debates over prices of silk and wool, a discussion of shipping hazards, and several rounds of sailhands' tales relating mishaps at sea. All the while, rain drummed on the roof shingles, relentless as Keithland's doom. The afternoon wore on. Gradually the wineskin grew flatter. Jaric regarded the ebb and flow of patrons with owlish eyes. He sat unresponsive when the one-handed beggar his money had freed burst in, jubilantly flipping coins while the tabby on his shoulder batted playful paws at the flash of the silver. The vagabond ordered beer for himself and his pet, and half the men in the taproom burst into laughter.

Jaric settled his chin on his fists. Too moody to respond when the redheaded barmaid paused by his elbow to flirt, he closed his eyes. The girl's smooth skin reminded him unbearably of Taen. Presently the barmaid plied her charms elsewhere. The wineskin lay empty beneath the boy's hand, and at last the drink overwhelmed him. Jaric settled into sleep that felt like death.

The boy woke to coarse words and a hand shaking his shoulder. He blinked, stirred, and found a burly man in a leather jerkin standing over him, shouting.

"Get up, tar-knuckles. Time to lock the doors. This isn't an inn, and nobody stays the night."

"I'm no sailor," Jaric muttered. He tried to straighten, groaned, and pressed both hands to his aching head.

"Don't matter what," said the man. He caught the boy's tunic and yanked. "Out with you."

Thrust to his feet, Jaric stumbled. His clothing reeked of wine, and movement made his stomach heave. He started on unsteady legs toward the privy behind the bar.

The man in the leather jerkin wasted no breath on warnings. He seized Jaric by the collar, propelled him forcibly across the tap to the door, and pushed him into the night. The boy tripped over the steps and sprawled face first into a mud puddle. He raised himself, shuddering, while the door boomed closed, then promptly fell, sick to his stomach. When the nausea subsided, Jaric settled his back against the tavern stoop and took stock of his position.

The rain had ceased. Stars glittered like frost overhead, gapped by the black silhouettes of the Landfast towers. Wretchedly alone, and chilled with the aftermath of sickness, Jaric wiped mud from his face. He rose clumsily to his feet and turned down the alley toward the dockside and *Callinde*.

The lane between the tavern and the shoreside warehouses loomed black as a pit. Dizzy from the wine, Jaric walked slowly, one hand braced against the alehouse wall. Refuse and run-off from the storm squelched beneath his boots. Between a cranny in the foundations, he heard the furtive crunch of a rat gnawing a bone; the sound ceased as he passed, then resumed. Jaric stopped. Overtaken by nausea, he crouched in the street once again. Yet instead of wet paving, his hands brushed the icy flesh of a man stretched prone in the alleyway.

Jaric recoiled with a cry of surprise, all sickness shocked from him. He explored further, felt a length of torn cloth and a sinewed arm. Suddenly a furred creature threaded between his knees. Jaric started back. He lost his balance and sat sharply on the cobbles, just as the beast leaped into his lap. It rubbed against his chest and meowed.

Recognizing the beggar's cat, Jaric shivered in relief that swiftly changed to worry. He pushed the animal away and bent over the man who lay prone in the street. Lanternlight flickered at the mouth of the alley. Dimly Jaric made out the form of the beggar, his one empty cuff pressed wet to the cobbles. Bruises mottled his face.

"No," whispered Jaric. He required no imagination to deduce what had happened: the beggar had carried silver into the alehouse, then boasted of the wealth and the freedom bestowed upon him by a young swordsman who had returned to pay his fine. Probably footpads had attacked him as he left, beat him senseless for his money, and dragged him into the alley to die.

Jaric touched the old man's face, felt cold skin and a flaccid mouth. No roguish, world-weary smile animated those lips now. Wrenched to the heart, Jaric bowed his head.

"No," he repeated. Grief overwhelmed him. Another friend lay dead. Unbidden, the boy remembered Taen and the fate mapped out for her by Llondian dream. Jaric felt a smothering sense of panic. Dreams had shown him death. But never until now had he experienced the reality. These cold hands, *her cold hands, Maelgrim would knife her*; the cat huddled forlorn in the alleyway; *himself, bereft.*

"No!" Jaric's shout rang, echoing, through night-dark streets. The fears twisted inside him changed, transformed to cruel regret; the chance he might cause a catastrophe like Tierl Enneth paled to insignificance by comparison. Ivainson did not hear the jingle of mail, or the footsteps which approached. Slammed hard against the end of dreams and hope, he wept to realize that nothing in life could wound him so deeply as the eventuality of Taen's murder.

That moment the cat streaked away. A dazzle of lanternlight fell full across his face, and an authoritative voice demanded, "What's happened here?"

Jaric opened his eyes, squinted, and felt the steel of a guardsman's sword prick his throat.

The blade jerked. "Quick, thief. Answer sharp. Did you murder for money?"

"No." Jaric lifted empty hands, spoke around the pressure against his larynx. "Search me. You'll find no coin."

The guardsman spat. He did not lower his weapon, but seized the boy with a gauntleted fist and hauled him to his feet. "Perhaps I caught you too soon to find coin, yes?"

Sickened to the core, Jaric stiffened. "Search us both, then! This man was my friend."

The guardsman bashed him back against the building and raised the lantern. Flame-light flickered over the sprawled form of the beggar, opened eyes and bloodied jaw glistening like macabre paint. Jaric turned away.

The guardsman grunted. "Some friend. That's old Nedge. Thief himself, did you know? The executioner chopped his hand as lawful punishment." He released his hold on Jaric and sheathed his sword in disgust.

"Kor curse his flea-ridden corpse. I'll have to clear him out before he starts to stink."

Distastefully, the man at arms prodded the beggar with his toe. "How long's he been dead, d'you know?"

"No." Jaric rubbed his wrists, outraged by the guard's callousness. No matter what his crimes, no man deserved to die without the pity of his fellows. As that thought turned in Jaric's mind, logic drove him one step further; unless he mastered the Cycle of Fire, Anskiere would perish similarly, deep under the ice cliffs with no friend to care.

That moment the beggar stirred. A snore escaped his lips. Steel flashed as the guardsman started back with a curse. "Kor, the stupid sot! Got himself drunk, didn't he? And probably bashed his silly head passing out in the street."

Jaric almost shouted with relief. *He had not caused the beggar's death.* The sudden, lifting rush of departing blame snapped a barrier within him. Self-doubt imprisoned him no longer. Offered the reprieve of a second chance, he seized the freedom to choose. He would go to the Vaere. No failure, no loss, and no fate carried worse penalty than the guilt of a loved one's death. If he could act to spare Taen, the risk of his father's madness must be accepted.

"Get on your way," said the guardsman curtly.

Jaric lifted his chin, his hair glinting gold in the lanternlight. "One moment," he said. With deliberate defiance, he loosened the laces at his throat, drew off his linen shirt, and spread it over the beggar who lay in the street. "This man is my friend, thief or not. Let him sleep in peace." And with a level glance at the guardsman, the heir of Ivain Firelord rose and strode off, to seek *Callinde* and the open sea.

Summer haze hung a moon like a yellowed game piece over Cliffhaven when *Moonless* returned to her home port. Despite the late hour, her crewmen furled sail with matchless efficiency. Yet the anchor had barely bitten into the seabed when signals flashed from the light tower caused Corley to yell for a longboat. No man dared delay direct summons from the Kielmark, far less a message coded urgent.

Blocks squealed in a night of oppressive stillness. The instant the boat splashed into the harbor, Corley departed for shore with all the speed his oarsmen could summon. Too impatient to wait until the craft drifted to the dockside, he leaped a span of open water to the wharf.

An officer with a lantern met him. His skin sparkled with sweat above his unlaced collar, and his chest heaved, as if he had been running. "Best hurry, man. Kielmark's in his study, pacing."

"Kor," said Corley sourly. "He wouldn't by chance be in a dicey temper, now would he?" Without pause for answer, he stripped off his own tunic and shirt and sprinted through close, late-season heat.

Except for an occasional sentry, the streets by the wharf lay empty.

Corley raced past closed shops and darkened houses with only the echo of his footfalls for company. The stair which led to the fortress left him winded after long weeks confined to a ship's deck. Yet when the guards waved him through the gatehouse, he did not slow down to walk. If the Kielmark sent for audience demanding all speed, he would be counting every second with resentment until his captain arrived.

Corley passed the repaired portals of the great hall, then hastened down the corridor which led to the study. The door burst open as he rounded the last corner, and the Kielmark thrust his head out.

"Kor's Fires, another minute, and I'd have ordered you spitted, captain." The Lord of Cliffhaven spun and paced savagely from the threshold.

Corley followed into the candlelit clutter of the study. Breathless after his run, he bent a keen gaze upon his master. The Kielmark was stripped to leggings and boots in the heat. He paused before the opened square of the casement, the muscles of his back and shoulders quivering with suppressed tension. Throwing knives gleamed in a row upon his belt, and both hands were knuckled into fists. Suddenly he whirled from the window. The eyes he trained upon Corley shone ice-pale with anger. "Demons take judgment, man, *what were you doing in the north?*"

Corley ignored the question. With an expression of mild inquiry, he lifted his wrist and blotted sweat from his brow. "What happened here?"

The Kielmark surged forward with a frenetic burst of energy. He drew one of his knives. A flick of his wrist spun the blade the breadth of the room, to strike quivering in the stacked logs by the hearth. As if the violence steadied him, the King of Pirates leaned back against the sill. "Thienz-demons came hunting. Now tell me where Taen Dreamweaver is, and quickly."

"She's safe." Corley qualified promptly. "Though not on the Isle of the Vaere, as you ordered."

The Kielmark straightened with warning speed. "I said, where?"

"Imrill Kand." Corley smoothed the crumpled cloth of his shirt and tunic, and draped the garments across the back of a nearby chair. Then he sat. "Between a run of contrary weather, an illness related to the maturity of her mastery, and a vagary of Jaric's, the original plan had to be abandoned. Taen asked to go home. I saw no reason to prevent her."

"Kordane's Blessed Fires!" exclaimed the Kielmark, his consonants bitten and sharp; then without warning he burst into laughter. "Made the damned demons chase themselves, snouts to tailbone, you did."

Corley slipped a dagger from his boot and the inevitable whetstone from his pocket. "You say? How?"

The Kielmark pushed off from the window. He bent, wrenched his throwing knife from the log, and thoughtfully tested the edge of the blade with his thumb. "Shore patrol here captured a fishing boat off North Point. They found it crammed to the gunwales with Thienz-demons who thought they could drift off Cliffhaven's shores with impunity, even spy and pick the thoughts of *my* following. The stinking toads!"

Corley's steel sheared across stone. "Thienz lurking inside the bounds of Keithland? That's bold. I trust you taught them a lesson."

The Kielmark raised murderous eyes, the knife haft poised in his fist. "I lost a man bringing those Accursed in. Two demons I killed outright, for that. The third died very slowly. It talked before the end."

Cautioned by his master's tautness, Corley stilled his hands. "Was that wise?" With a single thought, a Thienz could relay its suffering clear back to Shadowfane.

"Then their masters will think twice before they send another such envoy, won't they?" said the Kielmark. When Corley offered no comment, the King of Pirates turned on restless feet to the window. Moonlight silvered the curled hair on his crown as he continued. "At first I thought that demons came seeking the Dreamweaver. But the Thienz I tortured said differently. Shadowfane seeks to locate the Isle of the Vaere. They tried tracing *Moonless*. Only my most reliable captain sailed them all over the Free Isles' Alliance, every place but the southwest reaches where she belonged. Man, I sweated and I counted hours until you made port. Thank Kor the weather went contrary. If my original orders hadn't been balked, who knows what might have resulted?"

The Kielmark considered his captain, and frowned as he noted that whetstone and knife lay motionless. "So?" he said softly. "The Dreamweaver is on Imrill Kand, alone, but she can cloak herself with her craft. I trust Jaric remains under a guardsman's protection, securely inside the Alliance's defenses at Landfast?"

Corley placed his weapon on the bare wood of the table, then faced his master with steady eyes. "Five weeks past, Jaric went to sea with *Callinde*. Not even Taen would say where he went."

The Kielmark exploded from the window. The candles in the sconces guttered furiously as he crossed the carpet. "Great Fall, were you daft?"

"No." Corley smiled. Another man might hang for such a transgression; but he had stopped enemy knives at the Kielmark's back so many times, they might have been the same flesh, so tightly did their loyalties interweave. "That boy is marked by fate. I saw a hill priestess name him Demonbane at the summerfair rites on Tierl Enneth. Her clans paid him homage like a holy one. He went, Lord. I doubt a man could have stopped him without causing him injury."

The Kielmark hefted his knife, impaled it in the trestle next to his captain's, then shrugged his massive shoulders in resignation. "Either Jaric will return one day with a Firelord's powers, or else he'll wind up dead. I cannot shepherd every sorcerer's brat who rebels against fate. But Taen is another matter. Cliffhaven's debt to her is too great. You will dispatch five ships to safeguard Imrill Kand."

"The fishermen there won't like interference," Corley pointed out.

The Kielmark slammed the table with his fast. "Bedamned to the fishermen! Choose the finest crews in the harbor. Then return here and deliver your report."

Corley rose to depart with troubled thoughts. Unless the demons' true quarry was the Firelord's heir, why should Thienz risk themselves within the borders of Keithland seeking the Isle of the Vaere? No chart listed its position; even to find the place required the talents of a trained sorcerer. Now, too late, the captain regretted the fact that he had yielded to Taen's request. Jaric should never have been permitted to sail without escort.

Night fell swiftly in Keithland's lower latitudes. Braced against *Callinde*'s sternpost, Jaric chewed a strip of dried meat and watched the afterglow of sunset dapple the western waters gold. Around him the sea stretched to the horizon, empty. A fortnight had passed since the peaked profile of Skane's Edge had disappeared astern. Still the boy found no trace of the fabled Isle of the Vaere. Jaric swallowed the last of his savorless meal and rubbed his hands on his breeches. The water flasks were nearly empty. If he encountered no land in the next three days, he would be obliged to head about and return to Westisle to restock his supplies.

A glance at the compass showed the wind steady from the south. Jaric ran a calculating glance over the mild swell and the clear arch of the sky, then sheeted headsails and spanker on opposite sides. With the mainsail furled on the yard, *Callinde* would ride out the night hove to. After a quick check to be sure all gear was stowed, the boy settled in his accustomed nook in the stern.

Twilight deepened over the face of the ocean. Rocked upon the waves, Jaric lay still and listened to the slap of *Callinde*'s halyards. Stars pricked the cobalt of the zenith overhead. The boy watched them brighten, and wondered whether Taen watched the same sky many leagues to the north. Presently weariness overcame him. His eyes fell closed. Of necessity, Jaric slept lightly at sea; even a slight change in weather could endanger him if he failed to rouse in time to adjust *Callinde*'s sails.

Alone in a world of wind and waves, Jaric rested dreamlessly. When the late-rising summer moon lifted above the horizon, a presence brushed his mind. Gently, furtively, it probed his sleeping thoughts for information. Jaric stirred against the stern seat, vaguely aware the disturbance originated elsewhere.

"Taen?" he murmured, wondering whether she might have tried contact. But the presence subsided at the mention of her name. Jaric sighed. He nestled his head in the sun-browned crook of his elbow and settled back into slumber. The moon rose high over *Callinde*'s starboard quarter, tracing silver highlights over the wave crests. But Jaric no longer drifted alone. A whisper of foam sheared the water. A tiller creaked, and a dense black triangle of sail eclipsed the sky. As *Callinde* plunged into shadow, a wiry figure leaned from the newcomer's rigging and snagged the smaller craft's stay. Froglike hands caught her thwarts. In silence, two other figures leaped across the water between the rails.

Callinde rocked under the stealthy weight of boarders. Jaric roused in the stern, eyes opened and alert. Dark as ink against the stars, he saw two crested, lizardlike heads. Blunt, smooth-skinned faces trained toward him, revealing a glint of gimlet eyes and no nostrils at all. With a jolt of fear, Jaric recognized the Thienz. The creatures had been hunting since Taen's encounter with Shadowfane; but Jaric's stop at Landfast had muddled their search. Thienz had overtaken *Callinde* much farther south than they planned. Though the demons' eyesight was all but useless, they would stalk prey by sensing the thoughts in their victims' minds.

Desperate and frightened, Jaric fixed his attention upon the innocuous memory of a book he had copied as an apprentice scribe. The text had expounded at boring length upon the particulars of planting; in hopes that farming might mask his intent from the Thienz, the boy eased back his sleeve, where he kept a knife to slash rigging in emergencies. The haft slipped coldly into his palm. One Thienz stiffened in the bow. Jaric jerked his blade from the scabbard and threw.

Steel flashed and struck. Air whuffed through the demon's gill flaps. It staggered backward, the knife buried to the hilt in the folds of its broad neck.

Expecting the swift, crippling attack upon the mind which had brought down Deison Corley, Jaric kicked off from the stern seat. He could not know that, even untrained, the intensity of his inborn potential made his awareness difficult to grapple. His hands shook as he tripped the latch on the locker beneath the steering oar and snatched the spare rigging knife from its bracket. Bitterly he regretted the sword left on *Moonless* as he confronted the demon who remained.

It carried a short, curved saber, unsuitable for throwing, but deadly enough against a man armed with nothing but a knife. Jaric moved forward with caution. Frantically he reviewed the strategies taught by Corley and Brith. The Thienz did not wait. Disadvantaged by poor eyesight, and sensing murder in the boy's mind, it raised its blade to cut the head stay and bring down mast and rigging in a tangle to trap its adversary.

Jaric launched himself with a shout. Unable to clear the mast before the demon's blade fell, he sawed frantically at the headsail halyard just above at the cleat. Plies popped and parted, and the line snapped. Loosened canvas slithered in a heap over the bow. Knocked off balance, the Thienz tumbled across the thwart with a croak of surprise. Its sword flailed clumsily through the air as *Callinde* swung into the wind. Jaric lunged and stabbed it in the back. Flesh shuddered under his hand as he jerked his steel free for a second strike, then a third. The slick heat of the creature's blood on his hands caused the breath to gag in his throat. Half-sick with shock, Jaric stumbled back from his dying enemy. He shrank against the thwart and only that moment noticed the boat which trailed *Callinde*, a second party of demons poised by her rail to board. Moonlight glanced off blowguns and darts pinched in demon fists. Jaric freed his feet from the miring folds of the headsail. Even with his enemy half-blind, numbers threw the odds against him. Very likely the darts carried poison.

Wind ruffled the spanker. Slack canvas slammed taut, and, lacking the balancing force of the jib to hold her hove to, *Callinde* sheared ahead. Only one refuge remained where Thienz could not follow; undersized forelimbs hampered them from swimming without their heads immersed, and their gills did not function in salt water. With a short gasp of fear, Jaric caught the jib sheet on *Callinde*'s lee side. He flipped it overboard. Then, in full view of the demons, he leaped the other rail and dove.

As he struck the water he heard a wail from the Thienz. Their dismay touched his mind like dream-sense; they had expected the weak, indecisive boy Emien recalled from Elrinfaer, not a strapping young man who threw knives. Their mistake would not be repeated. Even as sea water closed over the boy's head, the demons relayed their discovery to colleagues at Shadowfane.

Callinde gathered way. Jaric swam under the keel and surfaced to lee-ward. His hands scrabbled frantically over planks. If he missed the sheet line he had thrown, his boat would sail past, and demons would have him at their mercy. Jaric thrashed, felt rope snake past his shoulder. He grabbed and clung. The jerk as the plies whipped taut stripped the callus from his palm, but he dared not cry out. Aware that *Callinde* would swing and jibe against the drag of his weight on the line, Jaric thrust his dagger between his teeth.

He hauled himself in hand over hand. Foam swirled to his chin, slapped his face, and set him choking. Jaric struggled for breath, and felt a mental stab as Thienz sought his mind. He ducked fast, sucked salt water around his blade on the chance that demons might think him drowning. All the while his hands stayed busy on the line. Fighting the drag of the water, Jaric hauled himself alongside *Callinde*, then kicked and hoisted himself up to the jib sheet block.

Over the rail he glimpsed Thienz beginning to board. *Callinde* swung, delaying them; her spanker flapped sullenly as her sternpost crossed the wind. Jaric dangled with his feet in the sea. Hanging from his hands, he worked aft along the thwart while the yard carved an arc across the stars. *Callinde* balanced between port tack and starboard, then jerked as the enemy entered her cockpit. Jaric caught the knife from his teeth. Waiting with his mind locked on images of darkness and sea water, he felt the boat turn further. Wind blew cold on his cheek. Then air filled the spanker with a thunderous flap of canvas. The boy yanked himself up, reached over the thwart with a desperate heave, and slashed the spanker sheet at the block.

The boom swung across the cockpit with killing speed, smashing the Thienz where they stood. Darts showered in the moonlight, to fall rattling amid floorboards and a flailing mass of demon-flesh. Jaric jammed his knife between the thwarts. He hauled himself bodily on board and, with the breath burning in stressed lungs, plunged across the cockpit. Barring his heart against mercy, he stabbed and cut throats until the last toad-fingered hand fell limp.

At the end, he leaned gasping against the stern seat. Blood streaked his arms to the shoulder, and his tunic dripped seawater dyed red. Pilot-less, *Callinde* jibed again; the shadow of her sail scythed across the deck, then passed, exposing carnage drenched in moonlight. Overtaken by hor-ror at the killing his hand had engineered, Jaric cried out. He doubled up over the rail and retched until his stomach emptied. His nausea took a long time to subside. When at last he raised his head, he saw that the demon ship drifted aimlessly. No helmsman took her tiller to resume chase.

Yet Jaric dared not assume all the Thienz lay dead. *Callinde* wallowed over the swells, littered with corpses and the silvery needles of spilled darts; she could not sail until cut lines were spliced and set right. Jaric pushed himself to his feet. With shaking hands he set about the task of lashing the spanker boom and clearing his decks of the dead.

CHAPTER XV

Stalkers

Morning came in a wash of copper and gold, with *Callinde* sailing briskly on a southwest heading. Jaric crouched over the helm, both eyes gritty from sleeplessness, and his fingertips raw from splicing lines. The attack and its aftermath had left him spent, and though at dawn he had grappled to the Thienz vessel and boarded to make certain none of his enemies remained, empty decks failed to reassure him. The demons would be back. Jaric dared not rest until *Callinde* was well away from her present position.

The breeze slackened as the day warmed. Jaric set about the repeated task of lashing the helm, then shook the last reef from the main and changed to the larger headsail. Then he fetched a biscuit from his dwindling stock of supplies and munched while he made a restless survey of the horizon.

The sea stretched empty, except for the saffron-dyed sails of a fishing boat out of Innishari. Yesterday the presence of other craft would have been a welcome reassurance that *Callinde* did not fare alone upon the ocean, but now any boat might carry enemies. Jaric lost his appetite. To sail the empty south reaches with no more weapon than a rigging knife suddenly seemed a fool's errand. If he were killed or taken, the Keys to Elrinfaer and Anskiere's wards over the Mharg would become a fearful liability to Keithland. The boy tossed his crust overboard for the fish to finish, then freed the steering oar and brought his boat about. His search for the Isle of the Vaere must wait. The level in *Callinde*'s water casks was getting low anyway. Since Westisle lay four days' sail due north, Jaric decided to visit the markets there. Perhaps by trading every belonging he could spare, he might arm himself well enough to repel boarders.

But his plan lasted no longer than the span of a still afternoon. The wind died to a breath, and the waves rolled, varnished by calm. Stopped dead in the water by the caprice of the weather, Jaric cursed, and longed for Taen, and finally exhausted himself with worry. He shipped the steering oar in frustration. Curled in the slanting shadow of the headsail, he slept with his head on crossed wrists.

He woke in the silver chill of twilight. Early stars pricked the zenith, the sea an expanse of darkened indigo beneath. Jaric rose and stretched the stiffness from his limbs. He splashed seawater on his neck and face to relieve the sting of sunburn, then stepped to the bow and leaned on the headstay to reconnoiter. South, the boundary of water and sky met in a line unbroken by any sign of life; but to the north, between *Callinde* and the direction of Westisle, spread the pen-stroke silhouettes of nine masts.

Jaric's skin prickled warning. No fishermen he ever saw would drop canvas in a calm and risk missing the first change in the wind. Occasionally the Kielmark's vessels used such a ploy to conceal themselves in the dazzle of sunlight reflected on water. But only the most inept of pirates would sail in fishing smacks and sloops, far from the wealth of the trade routes. What bore down from the north could only be Thienz drawn by the death-dreams of last night's slain.

Jaric shut his eyes to forestall panic. He resisted the first, overwhelming impulse to spring headlong for the steering oar. The compulsions of Thienz traveled poorly over water and at present *Callinde* lay distant enough to keep him beyond reach of demon manipulation. Jaric forced himself to think rationally. He must wait until dark to put about. Then the stalkers from Shadowfane might not see his boat change heading, and if luck blessed him with wind, *Callinde* might flee beyond the horizon before morning.

But the waiting proved painfully difficult. Jaric paced and sweated as the sun lowered, the last rays staining *Callinde*'s sails bloody red. The afterglow faded slowly from the sky, and with it went sight of the masts which loomed to the north. Jaric assumed the stern seat in cover of darkness. Sweating in icy fear, he took up the steering oar and sculled *Callinde* around. No breath of air steadied her keel on the new course, an easterly heading he hoped would enable him to tack and make port in Harborside on Skane's Edge. The presence of the Thienz made landfall there all the more necessary; his mug now scuffed bottom when he had dipped into his cask for a drink. If the enemy kept him at sea after his stores ran out, thirst and starvation might kill him without the inconvenience of a fight.

Left no task in the calm but to battle his own apprehension, Jaric stared north until his eyes stung. His vigil was lonely, a solitude more relentless than any but a sailor could know. Nothing met his search but night-dark waves, broken by the occasional sparkle of phosphorescence where schools of fish disturbed the surface. The dark had swallowed his enemies. No means remained to determine whether the drift carried their boats near or farther off. Every noise made Jaric start, even the slat of *Callinde*'s gear as she wallowed windless in the swell. By the time the constellations turned to show the harvester overhead at midnight, the boy's nerves were sawed raw. Light would have helped. But the glow of the masthead lantern would mark his position like a beacon, and very likely draw the demons to try a mind-probe to bind him. Recalling Corley's evasive action with flame when Thienz had meddled with his thoughts, Jaric fetched the lamp from a locker. He cleaned and trimmed the wick by touch, then made certain the reservoir was filled with oil. As a final precaution, he dug deep in the aft locker and removed a cask of oakum, a mix of pitch and fiber used by shipwrights to caulk the seams between planking. At need, the stuff would burn mightily; to set such a fire on shipboard would be an act of extreme desperation, but better *Callinde* were destroyed than to let demons kill him for the Keys. Jaric wedged the cask beneath the stern seat with a muttered apology to the shade of Mathieson Keldric. Then he sat with striker and rigging knife near to hand, and thought of Taen between fervent prayers for breeze.

Wind answered in the dark before dawn, but weather came with it, blotting the summer sky with sheets of low-flying cloud. For once not cursing the threat of moisture in the air, Jaric hardened his lines. *Callinde's* sails banged taut. She gathered way, driving forward into the swell. Spray shot from her bow, and sternward her wake trailed a comet tail of phosphorescence. Her young helmsman leaned into his oar and smiled with fierce exhilaration. Rain would hide him; if he rigged the spare sail with a catch basin, run-off could replenish his cask. Stormy weather might lend him resource to thwart both thirst and the Thienz.

Yet fortune granted only small favors. The clouds lowered and spilled thick, misty drizzle, and the wind slacked to the barest hint of breeze. Jaric hunched over the steering oar. More wet seemed to trickle down his neck than ran off the spare canvas to fill his catch basin. By dawn barely enough air moved to fill *Callinde's* sails, and beyond ten yards, the waves lay swallowed in drifts of featureless gray. The possibility that Thienz might lurk unseen at any quarter of the compass preyed upon Jaric's thoughts, wore at his spirit until he was angered enough to want to shout and cry by turns. Instead, he lashed *Callinde* on course, fetched out whetstone and rigging knife, and returned to his post at the helm. With the oar clamped in one elbow, he resorted to Corley's habit of sharpening steel to pass the hours.

Day brightened over *Callinde's* yard. Still the mist did not lift. It mantled waters the gray on gray of dull metal, and damped the shear of steel across stone as Jaric whetted his blade. He continued long after the edge was keen, just to keep his fingers busy; but as the morning progressed, that remedy was not enough. The fog swirled ghost-shapes around his boat and strung jeweled droplets on his lashes. He blinked them away, yet in time this seemed too much effort. His eyes grew heavy. His hands stopped the motion of whetstone and blade, while his mind strayed unnoticed across the boarders of waking, into dream. . . .

Waves and the dull red of *Callinde's* sails lost color, became the whiteness of snowfall in Seitforest. Jaric failed to arouse at the transition, wrought as it was by the touch of the enemy upon his mind. Cold and stillness lulled him. His senses knew nothing but the slow spin of flakes whispering through bare branches, the soundless settling of snow into hollows. In time the leaf-patterned forest floor became featureless as spread linen. Even the creeks froze and drifted over, the trickle of water

over rock silenced until the season's distant changing. Winter bound the
land, and Jaric, into tranced peace. His body assumed the numbness of
extreme cold, and his mind became lost in ice-white landscape. Enspelled
by dreams, he did not feel his fingers loosen, or hear the clatter as his
knife fell to *Callinde*'s floorboards. Nor did he notice when his arm slipped
from the steering oar. *Callinde* lost way, her sails slatting fretfully aloft.
Beaded with droplets from the mist, the compass needle wandered in circles as his boat drifted rudderless over the waves.

And the dream-cold deepened. Knife-keen, it pierced the very mantle
of the soil and touched the trees to the roots, freezing the dormant life
within. Boughs bent, burdened under cruel shackles of snow. Wood gone
brittle with chill snapped, eerily soundless in the wintry air; frost chewed
through the bark like acid, and ice crystals pried and pressured, and burst
the fastness of stone. Soon the whiteness ruled supreme. Sprawled like a
corpse against *Callinde*'s thwart, Jaric felt no pain. He knew no alarm, no
sorrow, no feeling at all, even as the cold penetrated his body and reached
to stop his heart.

Near the end another sound intruded. Faint with distance, and sweetly
brittle in the still air, the chime of goat bells penetrated the Thienz-
wrought tomb of cold. Sluggish with trance, Jaric fumbled after the
source. The white which blanketed his vision thinned slightly, and insubstantial as ghost-image overtop he saw a hillside patched with wildflowers
and heather. The land was rough, torn in places by weathered spurs of
granite. There a black-haired girl sat amid a milling herd of brown goats.
The vision of her was indistinct, as if viewed through the shallows of a
running stream. But her warning rang clear as the bells through the winter
chill which gripped him.

'Jaric, the Thienz have set a dream-spell on you! Jaric!'

But the whiteness rendered the words as sound without meaning, a
disturbance that floundered and died into silence. The girl's image dissipated, and the hillside with its cloak of heather and fern dimmed to wispy
shadows. Before long the void devoured them entirely. Thienz-bound, Jaric
drifted reasonless as a stone.

Yet the presence of the Dreamweaver did not entirely fade. With all
her skills, Taen gathered herself and struck out against the cocoon that
demons had woven around the awareness of Ivainson Jaric. Her urgency
pried like a knife, and this time broke through.

Jaric roused. The workings of his mind and body felt swathed in a tide
of whiteness and he could not orient. Uncertain whether the presence he
remembered was a temptation of demons designed to weaken him, or illusion born of longing and his own imagination, he murmured Taen's name.

Her answer brought raw-edged fear. *'Jaric, you must break free!'* At last
allowed foothold in his conscious mind, she spun dream-sense and
attacked. The demons' prison shivered before the impact of her powers.
Taen struck again, utterly exhausting her strength. Unable to maintain

contact, her touch faded, even as the barrier of numbness which threatened the life of Ivain's heir weakened and suddenly collapsed.

Cold needled wakened senses with an onslaught of terrible pain. Jaric recoiled. Ripped by agony into full remembrance of *Callinde*, the ocean, and the fishing boats laden with enemies determined to take his life, he doubled over in the stern seat. His brow cracked unwittingly into the steering oar. His howl of shock and surprise was torn away by wind, and he roused fully at last, brought around by the maddened thrash of canvas. The weather had changed, totally. Mist had given way to clouds and driving rain. Water streamed in streaks off sails and spars, while *Callinde* pitched over white-capped waves, her lines lashing untended through her blocks. Panting like a distance runner to regain the air his slowed lungs had neglected, Jaric made no move to remedy his lapse of seamanship. He reached instinctively to rub his bruised forehead, then stopped to stare at his hands. The flesh was barely cool to the touch. Yet to the eye the skin was mottled purple-white, as if exposed to extreme cold. The inner ache and the agony of returning circulation were quite real, and the effects wrung Jaric to dizziness. The illusion of winter that Thienz had used to ensnare his mind had apparently afflicted his body with all the effects of frostbite.

The implications terrified, that Thienz he could not see might bind the human mind with visions potent enough to kill. Jaric stuffed his aching fingers under the tail of his tunic, but more than cold touched his heart. His search for the Isle of the Vaere had nearly ended here, adrift on the lonely ocean. Ivain's inheritance and Taen's hope of life might have been wasted before his potential could be challenged by the Cycle of Fire. Frightened to action, Jaric rose upon shaky legs. Since the machinations of the Thienz did not carry efficiently across water, the demons who had tried murder would not be far off.

Shivering and alone, the heir of Ivain Firelord sprang forward and hardened *Callinde's* slackened lines. As his boat rounded, her sails punched taut by the wind, he bounded back to the steering oar and strained every muscle in his arms resetting his interrupted course. He shied from thinking of Taen, whose need had inspired him to seek the Vaere, and whose intervention had certainly spared his life. He dared not consider the headache which tormented him, nor the lingering ache of frost that gnawed at his fingers and toes. He bound all his resources to sailing, and the north-northwesterly heading that would see him safe to Skane's Edge.

The squall came on suddenly. Between one gust and the next a downpour lashed the waters, flattening the wave crests and kicking up spray in opaque white sheets. Jaric sailed by his compass, his hands clenched fast to the steering oar, for the storm left him blind. No visibility remained to show whether he sailed toward freedom or the heart of the demon fleet; and as the wind shifted round to the north, he fought the buck of the swell. Clinging to the helm, he drove *Callinde's* bow windward to the limit of her sturdy design. Then the squall passed. The skies hung moiled and black, and the sea foamed angry spray beneath. Jaric squinted through the spray which sheeted off the bowsprit, but no trace of mast, sail, or spar marred the waters ahead. Storm still curtained the sternward horizon, hiding any presence of Thienz pursuit. Since Jaric saw no sign of the demon fleet, he concluded he must have drifted past their location in the calm, and only Taen's intervention and the cover of the fog had spared him. Afraid to leave the helm even for a drink of water, he sailed, while nightfall darkened around him.

Clouds smothered the stars, and the ocean heaved black as a pit. Jaric huddled in damp clothing, the play of wind over *Callinde*'s sails his sole means to hold course. On a clear night with the polestar visible, such crude measures might have worked, but not now. Squalls and mists meant changeable weather, and under such conditions the wind would not blow consistently from one direction. Sooner or later, Jaric knew he must take a compass bearing to check his course. The lamp he had trimmed and tended earlier waited, hooked still to *Callinde*'s thwart. The tin shutters were latched closed, and the wick dry and ready; still his hand shrank from the striker. Loath to make a light lest he give his position away to the Thienz, he made no move from the helm.

Callinde sailed on through the dark. Slave to the demands of his boat, Jaric rested his head on crossed wrists while the thrum of water over the steering oar translated through bone and flesh. Despair ate at his heart, though no Thienz appeared to attack. Staring, morose, at the tail of phosphorescence kicked up by the keel, Jaric saw a brief flicker of lightning astern. A squall moved in from the east, sure sign the wind had shifted radically. The compass check could no longer be delayed, unless he wished to risk doubling back and sailing head on into the demon fleet. Bending with the taste of fear in his mouth, Jaric reached for striker and lamp.

He slid aside the shutter on the lantern, the grate of metal on metal a scream against the natural sounds of water and wood and canvas. Jaric's fingers shook as he snapped a spark. He gave the flame barely an instant to catch and steady before he snapped the shutter down to a slit. Light yellow as a pen stroke parted the blackness of the night. Jaric wrestled the steering oar into the crook of one elbow, then raised the lantern over the binnacle. The compass revealed a disappointment. *Callinde* currently sailed due west, and had done so for an unknown span of time. Until the stars or sun could be seen for navigation, Jaric could not fix his position. Worse, to reach Skane's Edge, the old boat's poor performance to weather would force him to tack.

Jaric hardly bothered to curse the cruelties of the sea. With the breath gone ragged in his throat, he hauled the steering oar round, then burned his forearm as a chance wave jostled the heated frame of the lantern into his flesh. Reflex made him flinch, and another jerk as *Callinde* wallowed broadside over a swell caused the north-facing shutter to slide open. Light slashed across the water; it caught like sparks on a shear of foam, and the wet-black glisten of timber. Jaric stifled his scream of terror. Not a stone's throw off his thwart sailed one—no, two—no, *three* Thienz vessels. How long they had stalked him in darkness he could not guess, but that they were within range to attack was beyond all remedy. As if the weather mocked him in his weakness, the wind lay in favor of the demons.

Jaric slammed the shutter back over the lantern. He looped the carry ring over a hook, even as Thienz yammered their cry of attack. Their collective psychic assault ripped his mind as he slammed his full strength against the steering oar. The effort came too late. Jaric's defenses sheared away like slivers under a joiner's chisel. The demons knew his inadequacies; through the frenzy of their bloodlust leaked the satisfied memory of the night they had stalked and studied him. No cranny of his mind was unknown to them, no weakness, no strength, and no resource. The force of their compulsion was beyond any power in Keithland to deny, for the Thienz had shielded against outside intervention. This time no Vaere-trained Dreamweaver could break through to wrest their quarry away. Ivainson-Firelord's-heir-Jaric-Thienz-quarry would perish now, for the compact and the glory of Scait.

The boy wept tears of fury and frustration, even as his hands disobeyed his inner will and did the bidding of enemies. The steering oar turned on its pins, and *Callinde*'s bow swung obediently through the eye of the wind. Jaric thrashed, in vain. He owned no Firelord's defenses to counter the grip that shackled his will. *Callinde*'s prow turned inexorably south. Her sails whipped taut and she shouldered ahead, directly toward Thienz who lusted to rend the son of Ivain Firelord limb from limb. Their excitement charged the contact, bruising their victim with images of blood and torn flesh; once he was aboard their black boats, his dying would be horrible and slow. Spurred to inspiration by extremity, Jaric attempted the unthinkable. He stopped struggling against his captors, without warning pitched his efforts into concordance with theirs. His own added strength drove *Callinde*'s helm hard over in the direction their compulsion demanded. The abruptness of her swing caught the demons by surprise. With a yammering yell of dismay, they slackened their designs upon Jaric, but already the heavy, curved prow of Mathieson's fishing boat sheared wide of the course they intended.

The great, patched main caught wind with a bang. *Callinde* lurched and Jaric slammed forward. His shins barked into the sail locker, yet he clung to the oar, dragging his boat another two points to port. The grand old vessel responded, gathered way, and lumbered into a heel that parted the swell, straight for the Thienz vessel that centered the enemy fleet.

Wails arose from Thienz crewmen. Demons unraveled like crochet-work from their perches on the rails, while the helmsman of the center-most boat jerked the tiller hard starboard to avert collision. The sloop jibed, but not handily enough. The iron-banded edge of *Callinde*'s keel

post hammered crunching into her side, while Jaric slammed head-first
into the steering oar. The force of the collision stunned the Thienz hold
upon his mind.

Bleeding from a cut lip, and confused by the hellish toss of shadows
thrown by the lamp, Jaric retained barely enough presence of mind to keep
his grip on the helm. He reacted on nerves and instinct. With his boat
locked still to the enemy's, he kicked the heavier *Callinde* into a jibe.

Timber grated and shrieked. The bolted iron fittings which reinforced
Callinde's bow savaged the lighter sloop. Splinters gouged up; pale and
pointed as knives in the lamplight, they showered into the foam. Jaric
glimpsed the riven boat. Its attendant pack of Thienz were very close, the
eyes of each gone wise and liquid with fear. The malice of their curses
slapped stingingly into his mind. Then a swell shouldered the locked craft.
The high curve of *Callinde*'s prow grated another point to port and hooked
a stay on the enemy boat. The Thienz who manned the sheets shrieked
alarm.

Strain snapped water like smoke from the cable. Jaric had only an
instant to brace his body before the floorboards shuddered and the following wave heaved up and under *Callinde*'s bow. The stay on the demon boat
snapped with a whipcrack report. Thienz crew scrambled over themselves
in attempt to slacken lines, but none could act swifter than wind. A gust
thundered into the sloop's mainsail; canvas bellied and her unsupported
mast screamed and cracked. Thienz wails rent the air. The backstay
knocked the helmsman flying as the shorn timber scythed sideways. Canvas
braked its descent, lent a stately, deceptive grace to impending disaster;
then spars and tangled rigging bore downward, plowing a furrow of death
among the Thienz. They scattered across the deck, tripped by ropes and
battered down by trailing blocks. Jaric watched the carnage with numb
horror, while the sloop's tackle and sails settled toward the waves.

The impact kicked water sixteen spans into the air. Billowing yards of
canvas followed and scooped sea with a jerk that ripped the sloop's chain
plates from her bow. The Thienz vessel heeled, glistening like a fish. The
following swell drove her hard against the butt end of her fallen mast,
impaled her timbers with a boom like a battering ram. Dark toad-shapes
spilled screaming into the waves. Salt water burned the tender flesh of
their gills, smothered their cries to silence. The ranks of demon survivors
abandoned the energy patterns of coercive attack. They moaned in communal anguish as the boy who had been their quarry clung to *Callinde*'s
backstay. He shouted in savage elation, while drowning Thienz spun
death-dreams before the waves extinguished their memories forever.

Callinde drifted free, her timbers gouged with scars. Old Mathieson's
craft mark had been sturdiness, not style, not speed, and not grace. Jaric
could have wept for love of the quirks of north-shore fishermen, but two
other boats filled with Thienz gave no surcease. Even as one vessel hove
to in an effort to rescue the demons still clinging to the wreck, the second

jibed and bore down on *Callinde*; now the heaviness of her hull worked against Jaric. The sloop the enemy had stolen from the more affluent fisherfolk of Felwaithe was lighter, leaner, and faster. To race her with *Callinde* would be the errand of a fool.

Jaric did not try. As the Thienz drove their craft to take him, he bent and wrestled his cask of oakum from beneath the stern seat. The lid proved stuck fast. He pried and split his fingers on the seal, to no avail. The gabble of Thienz voices drew inexorably closer. Spray carved up by the sloop's bow damped the boy's cheeks, even as he swore and reached for his rigging knife. He hammered the cask top with the blade. Splinters gouged his skin as he ripped through and seized a tarry mass of caulking compound. By now the Thienz vessel shadowed *Callinde*'s quarter. Only seconds remained before the death-dreams of the less fortunate ceased to preoccupy those enemies who pursued.

Jaric straightened just as the demons grappled his mind. His hand jerked toward the sheet line, urged by Thienz compulsion to let the sails run free and allow them to overtake and board. The boy resisted. Crying out for the pain, instead he closed his fingers over the lantern ring. Nerve, bone, and sinew, his will was resisted by the Thienz. Determined, whipped onward by fear and love for Taen, Jaric heaped oakum through the shutter and onto the flaming wick.

Pitch-soaked fibers flared like lint. Seared by a wash of flame, Jaric felt the Thienz within his mind shift beyond reach of his pain. He seized the small instant of reprieve, spun, and flung the lantern.

It arced hissing over water. The moment of flight seemed to span eternity, or the dark end of time. Then the brand crashed tumbling against the headsail of the oncoming Thienz vessel. Flaming clots of oakum spattered forth, to cling and burn and ignite.

The Thienz squalled in fury. Backlash through their mind-probe stung Jaric like a whip, and energies savaged the channels of his nerves. The torment unraveled his control. He crashed backward against the stern seat, gasping. The shaft of *Callinde*'s steering oar jerked abandoned circles above his head. But the wood stood in stark silhouette against leaping veils of flame. Powerless to move, Jaric wept in triumph. His enemies were defeated. The Thienz sloop burned, sails and rigging, and presently the hatred that gouged the boy's inner awareness receded as the attacking demons were forced to abandon their prey and contend instead for survival.

Battered, bruised, and sticky with pitch from the oakum, Jaric crawled to his feet. No Thienz engaged to prevent him. He set blistered hands to the steering oar, and tenderly swung *Callinde*'s bow downwind. Her main filled with a bang that stung his ears, and the lines whumped taut. Spray shot from the bow, jeweled carnelian and ruby in the light of the conflagration astern. Then old Mathieson's boat did what she was best suited for: she gathered herself and raced before the wind.

The oar steered to a feather touch downwind. Jaric sank wearily against the sternpost, his feet stuck to the decks by spilled gobs of oakum. His only knife lay buried somewhere beneath the tarry mess, which would have angered Corley. Jaric closed his eyes. His imagination showed him Taen, teasing like a harridan over the black pitch that would rim his finger and toenails throughout the coming fortnight. But the humor and the exultation suddenly soured. Thought of the Dreamweaver's reaction to the fate he had narrowly avoided caused Jaric to shudder, then explode into racking sobs. Almost he had lost everything, the Keys to Elrinfaer and Keithland's future. Aftershock overturned equilibrium, left him feeling reamed and empty and lost. But throughout the tempest of reaction, the boy clung to his purpose. *Callinde* held to her course like a bird migrating before the killing storms of winter.

The glare of fire receded astern. Jaric shook tangled hair from his face, surprised to find that hunger pinched his middle. He had forgotten meals for what seemed like days. Determined to concentrate on the ordinary, he pried sticky fingers from the helm and sought out the biscuit cask. But once the food was in hand, he found himself too frayed with exhaustion to eat.

Spray waterlogged the hardtack in his fist. He licked at salty crumbs and adjusted lines, and stubbornly refused to look back in the direction of the carnage his hand had wrought among the Thienz. The boat which remained would come for him. Of that he had no doubt. Somehow, against hope, he must be ready when demon attack carved his inner will into a weapon. Jaric forced himself to take sustenance. He sailed, wary with nerves and determination, and never guessed so inconclusive a victory might alter the stakes against him.

Callinde had vanished over the horizon by the time the Thienz had rescued their last survivor from its perch on a floating spar. They hauled it on deck, where it crouched dripping and mewled of its misery, for waves had splashed it, and its gills burned unmercifully. Fluid clotted its lungs from even so brief an exposure, and perhaps-near-to-certainly its companions would be sharing its death-dream by dawn. At last, irritated, the seniormost Thienz cuffed it to silence. The chastened one scrabbled sideways into a corner and licked its webbed fingers, while companions undamaged by salt water laid out the crushed bodies of their dead, communed with their wounded to ease the pain, and crooned laments for the lost. The night was all but spent before the survivors who were Jaric-defeated gathered beneath the mainmast to pool resources and send word of their plight to Shadowfane.

The content of their news roused much consternation. Scait's favorites and the senior members of the compact convened hastily in the main hall. Though the Lord of Shadowfane was feeding, none dared assume the risk of leaving him uninformed. A wailing junior Thienz was dispatched through the door of the dining pit to summon him. It lost an arm, before the meaning of its message penetrated the instincts that drove Scait's frenzy. Reason returned to the Lord's savage eyes. He bridled his appetite before he succumbed to the urge to slash the errand-Thienz's throat; but the anger roused by its message spiked the Lord's hackles with malice. He granted the underling's heroics no reward, but left it moaning and bleeding amid the hacked remains of his meal.

The Sovereign Lord of Shadowfane stalked from his dining pit and joined the meeting in the great hall with his lips and his foreclaws unwashed. His jaws still crunched the fingerbones of the underling who had informed him of Jaric's escape, and only the most ambitious of his favorites were not cowed. Those bold ones watched with predatory patience as he strode across the floor.

'So, Ivainson-Firelord's-heir-Jaric is a human with courage to be reckoned with.' Scait paused, licked his teeth, and glared at the rows of cringing favorites. 'A curse on the seed of his father, he must be dealt with.'

No demon stirred around the mirror pool as their overlord ascended the dais and sat. Claws scraped softly on cured human flesh as he settled on his throne and glared down at the wizened Thienz who hastened forward to crouch at his feet. 'Show me Jaric's aura, Thienz,' commanded Scait. 'As he lives now, not the inadequately translated memory of Taen-brother-Maelgrim.'

Beads clashed as the Thienz elder rose. It blinked wrinkled lids at the Lord on the throne and insolently flapped its gills. Then, having established the fact that it had not been intimidated into compliance, it squatted and offered an image.

Scait shared with his eyes narrowed to slits. Thienz-memory gave him Jaric, poised by lanternlight on *Callinde*'s decks; to the eye he was still a human boy, muscled from his hours at the helm, and tanned and tangle-haired from exposure. But demon senses perceived more than flesh. Surrounding Jaric's form spread intricate patterns of energy startling for their complexity.

The Lord of Shadowfane bared his teeth. Seven decades he had studied the enemy. In that time, he had arrogantly presumed to claim knowledge of humanity's native endowment for psychic development. In depth he had dissected the inborn talents of Merya Tathagres and, most recently, Marlson Emien. He had once even gazed upon a Thienz-wrought image of Taen Dreamweaver. But never before had the aura of a man birth-gifted with a Vaerish sorcerer's potential been unveiled to demon sight prior to training and mastery. For the first time, Scait realized how rare, and how precious, and how *fearfully strong* was the ability latent in the individuals chosen for dual Sathid bonding. Yet, paired with the staggering capacity for power, this boy who sailed to claim his right to the Cycle of Fire owned a naïveté, a defenselessness born of the fact that he had yet to access the well of resource within him.

This observation bent Scait's thinking into change. His eyes stayed hooded, but his favorites did not mistake the expression for sleepiness. Their Lord's very stillness bespoke warning, and the experienced among the council waited in poised anticipation for their master to stir and straighten.

Scait chose speech to communicate, which confirmed that he plotted deep, yet would not confide indiscriminately in his underlings. The risk he intended to take was perhaps a greedy one, but Jaric's talents offered possibilities whose dangers were two-edged. More than the Keys to Elrinfaer might be won for humanity's downfall. If Ivain's heir were captured alive, the compact might develop and enslave his vast potential through bonding to a previously mastered Sathid. Then all his Firelord's powers might be used to rip Keithland into chaos. The vengeance planned for centuries against humans might be completed at a stroke.

Scait's lips widened into a leer as he spoke his will to the ancient Thienz. "You will assemble a third fleet to sail in support of the dozen vessels still quartering the south reaches." A murmur arose in the chamber, stilled by a gesture of Scait's forelimb. "No more inexperienced young will be entrusted. By my command, only the strongest and eldest Thienz will embark upon this voyage, for I wish the pawn Maelgrim to go along. He will use his training to secure my desire. Let him not fail. Ivainson-Firelord's-heir-Jaric is to be captured and delivered living to me."

CHAPTER XVI

Storm of Crossing

Gusts off the sea jangled the wind charms the Imrill Kand fishermen hung from their eaves for protection against ocean storms. By that sound, and by the shouts of the children who chased the goats through the streets to pasture on the tors each dawn, Taen woke aware that she was home. Although she opened her eyes to the loft that she had known as a girl, with the same faded counterpane tucked beneath her chin, the present allowed little chance for reminiscence. Too much had changed during the year of her absence. The brother who had slept in the cot across the loft was now forever lost to demons.

Taen rose. She dressed hastily in trousers and tunic that had once been Emien's, with a cast-off shirt of Corley's thrown overtop for warmth. This she gathered close with a belt of knotted string, tied as a gift by *Moonless*'s sailhands. Her Dreamweaver's robes of silver-gray stayed folded away in the cedar closet, as they had since her arrival. To the Imrill Kand villagers, the garments were uneasy reminders that she had returned to them an enchantress, transformed by the mysteries of the Vaere from a crippled child of ten to a grown woman in little more than one year's time. Accustomed as Taen was to isolation, this new alienation was a misery she tried not to dwell upon. Briskly she combed and braided her hair, then descended the ladder to the kitchen.

Her mother heard her despite the fact that Taen no longer had a stiff ankle to drag and clatter over the rungs. Marl's widow never looked up from kneading dough, but called out to her daughter with her back turned. "Here's you going barefoot again. Step on something sharp, or catch chill, and don't come crying to me for pity."

"Now who's acting the witch?" Taen jumped to the floor, grinning. "My boots are by the stove, drying, since last night. You didn't see them when you made fire for the bread?"

The old woman made a sound through her nose. " 'Twas before daybreak, then, girl. And you shouldn't stay out on the tors after nightfall. Could come to grief on the rocks."

By the smell, the first loaves were baked through. Taen twisted the tail of Corley's shirt around her fingers and retrieved the pans from the oven. "I know," she forestalled, even as her mother drew breath to warn that her sloppiness was bound to cause burns. No matter that a moment later she banged the bread pans down with a clatter and ended licking a blistered thumb.

"Stubborn." Marl's widow set her dough in a bowl to rise, then turned around, wiping her hands on her apron. Careworn, and aged by sorrow from the loss of husband and son, she regarded the daughter the Vaere had changed into a stranger she barely knew. "You'll be going to the tors again?"

Taen nodded. She preferred to work alone, where she did not have to watch folk she had known since girlhood making the sign against evil behind her back.

"Might be rain later," said Marl's widow. She brandished a damp fist at Taen, who had twisted a corner off the fresh loaf and crammed it into her mouth. "You're old enough not to do that."

"That's what the cook on *Moonless* said." And Taen sighed as the cooling bread was removed beyond reach; the barley and smoked fish her mother offered instead made a dull substitute. The Dreamweaver picked at her plate without enthusiasm. Jaric's danger, and the threat of the demons who tracked him, fretted at her thoughts always; but this burden must not be shared here, for the sake of the brother whose betrayal shadowed this house like cobwebs. Of necessity, Taen kept to the ordinary. "What was Uncle Evertt bellowing about?"

Marl's widow raised offended eyes to the window which overlooked Rat's Alley. "Wants the Kielmark's brigantines gone from these waters. No matter that they're here to defend. I told him to save his grousing for the tavern."

"And he didn't," said Taen, but without bitterness. Times had been hard for her uncle, even before Emien had lost the sloop. Even plain barley was a commodity on Imrill Kand. Taen scraped her bowl carefully, and wrapped the fish in linen for her lunch. "I can bring back herbs for the pot," she offered as she rose.

"Won't be back in time for supper, and ye know it." Marl's widow vanished into the pantry and reappeared with her sewing basket, just as Taen stamped her feet into damp boots.

"Take this, child. The cold's coming, and you'll need something against the wind."

Taen looked up, saw the cloak in her mother's outstretched hand. The fabric was woven of fine-spun goat's hair, russet, with borders of blue to match her eyes. The gift left her speechless, for she knew better than any that coppers were scarce under her uncle's roof. Taen searched her mother's face, and her delight withered before the certainty that the fabric could not be spared.

Her mother noticed the hesitation and frowned. "Not fine enough for ye, then?"

Taen recognized the look, and forced a lighthearted grin. "Only if you stole it." Then, lest she cry on the spot, she threw her arms around her mother's floury middle and squeezed.

"Settled with the weaver with the money I earned darning sweaters,"

Marl's widow confessed. "Evertt can't throw his weight around over that, and I'll sleep maybe, knowing my girl is warm without taking handouts from pirate captains' mates."

Taen exploded backward. "Corley?" she said incredulously, and ended sneezing the flour she had inhaled in her outrage. "He's Cliffhaven's top-ranking officer, and nobody's lowly mate."

"Go," said her mother. "Now, before I slap your backside for tearing the end off the new bread." And she bundled Taen and the cloak through the door, into the puddled brick of Rat's Alley.

Bemused, the Dreamweaver ran her fingers over the cloth. Then she smiled with the sweetness that had won the hearts of the roughest of the Kielmark's captains. "Thank you, Mother," she called, and started to pin the collar with a brooch of plain copper.

That moment the door flung open again, and a linen-wrapped packet of herring sailed out and struck her in the chest.

"Forgot your lunch," said Marl's widow. She banged the latch closed, but not before her daughter glimpsed her tears.

That, more than any other thing, impressed upon Taen the change her life had taken since Anskiere had sent her to the Vaere. She had come home, yet Imrill Kand retained little claim upon her loyalty; the villagers and their bitter struggle for sustenance seemed sadly diminished in significance. As a girl, she had longed for healing so she could work on the decks of a fishing sloop; how little she had bargained upon the fact that such simple dreams would lead her to join the Vaere-trained as guardian of Keithland.

The wind blew cold, ruffling the puddles in Rat's Alley; overhead, the luck chimes jingled in warning of autumn. Taen clutched the edges of her whipping cloak and left her uncle's door stoop. She passed the weather-board stalls of the fish-market, and the docks, and the Fisherman's Barrel Inn, and, remarked by a weaving, squalling flock of gulls, wended a tortuous path through a fish-stinking expanse of drying nets. Beyond lay the goat track which led to the upper meadows, and the rock-crowned heights of the tors. The gulls sped away on the breeze. Taen climbed quickly, where once she had limped. The shingled roofs of the houses diminished beneath, and clouds raced tattered and damp across the crags. Wind and the bells of the goats were the only sounds she could hear when at last she chose a sheltered cranny and settled herself within.

The sea spread like hammered silver from the shore, unbroken but for flyspecks of fishing craft, and the distant masts of a patrol ship from Cliffhaven. Secure in the knowledge she was guarded by vigilant men and weapons, Taen closed her eyes. Her dream-sense answered her readily now that she had gained experience. Within seconds her vision of harbor and village melted away, replaced by wider vistas engendered through her Sathid-born talents. The boats were specks no longer, but craft with crews who labored with sails and nets. Each man reflected his own pattern of fears and dreams; of emotions and desires and hopes that blended to fashion the spirit of an individual. Although Taen could sift the contents of men's minds with the same fascination that an archivist might show while studying books, she passed by. Her attention extended outward, across the wide waters between Hallowild and Felwaithe. She encountered no demon-sign; only one ship flying the Kielmark's blazon, and a ragged patch of mist. Except for that the seas appeared empty.

A prickle of intuition caused Taen to linger. She had been raised by the sea; all through childhood she had known weather to descend unexpectedly from the northwest, bringing peril to the fishing fleets, and silence in the houses where wives and mothers awaited their menfolk's return. The moods of storm and sea were studied and known and feared; yet something about this isolated fogbank roused the Dreamweaver to uneasiness. She sought the reason, and felt her hair prickle in alarm. This mist was not natural, but drifted purposefully south across wave crests buffeted by winds blowing due east.

Alerted to danger, Taen probed further. Fog hampered her dream-sense, clinging white and impenetrable. The swells crested and foamed, strangely muted, and the air felt oddly dense. Suspecting the handiwork of demons, the Dreamweaver quartered the area with care, yet nothing came of her search. No shadow of a boat moved within the murky mass. She drew back, cold, and prepared to try another pass; then she reconsidered. If demons sailed in strength, with resources forceful enough to blind her dream-sense with illusion, she would be foolish to expose herself further. The most she could accomplish from Imrill Kand was to warn the enemy of the fact that their presence had been discovered. Far better such trespassers were caught unsuspecting, and dealt with before they could cloak themselves and escape. Grimly Taen gathered her dream-sense. She sought across the waters for the irascible presence of the Kielmark's acting officer in command, master of the brigantine *Shearfish*.

She found the man on his quarterdeck, arguing with the cook over an infestation of weevils in the porridge. Taen repressed a smile, for the beleaguered cook cursed his captain under his breath in wildly original oaths before he raised his voice in defense.

"Man, you ask too much, when it was yourself came blundering into the bread room looking for crewman's contraband and sliced the sacks what held the oats." The captain of *Shearfish* glowered, but by now those deckhands within earshot were watching. As if his manhood were at stake, the cook pressed hotly on. "O' course the dignity weevils moved right in, could you ask them to forgo a bite with such plenty sprinkled about for the taking? Lucky I found the bag, I say, or we'd be eating bugs and their leavings the rest o' the way back to port."

"Enough!" snapped the captain, so abruptly the nearer deckhands jumped. The cook went suddenly pale. Taen chose that moment to intervene. She sent a warning and a plea to *Shearfish*'s master, to investigate the unnatural fog to the north; and out of respect for the services she had already rendered to Cliffhaven, her request carried weight. The subject of weevils died with alacrity. Even as Taen relayed details, the captain transferred his shout to the quartermaster; the great wheel spun at his command and *Shearfish* put about with a thunderous flap of sails.

Taen and the cook sighed with relief. While crewmen ran to polish weapons, the Dreamweaver withdrew. She sped her awareness southward as she had each day previously, to resume her watch for *Callinde* and Ivainson Jaric. Now the sick worry hidden within her burst free of constraint. Her last sight of the Firelord's heir had been the night she had discovered him under attack by demons. She had exhausted her powers to break the Thienz's hold upon his mind. By the time she had rested enough to resume her watch, she had encountered no trace of Ivainson or Mathieson Keldric's old fishing boat, though she had tried ever since, repeatedly.

First Taen swept the seas southeast of the Free Isles' Alliance. She had found a strayed trade vessel blown off course from Skane's Edge, and two small fishing fleets. No sign did she encounter of Firelord's heir on *Callinde*. That in itself should not have been discouraging. The Isle of the Vaere was a fey place, elusive to mortal perception and not always visible to the eye; no charts would show its position. Though any trained sorcerer could sense its location, Jaric would be sailing blind; and by now Taen was forced to assume he plied waters far off his intended course. The past day she had expanded the limits of her search. Still she found nothing. Her dream-sense encountered lifeless vistas the breadth of the southeast reaches, and now she fought against loss of hope. Logic insisted that continued effort was futile; stubbornly she held out. If Jaric had abjured his inheritance, or if storm or demon possession had interrupted his quest, the consequences and Keithland's peril were too final for thought.

Now Taen quartered the seas lying west and north of the fabled isle. She dream-read sailors in the ports on Westisle and Skane's Edge, but their minds held no memory of a fair-haired young man with an antique fishing boat. South she found nothing, not even traces of wreckage. Now only the wide waters to the east remained, the least likely place for a man sailing alone with a small craft and limited provisions.

Northerly gusts blew cold across the tors of Imrill Kand, moaning around crannies in the rocks where Taen sheltered. Her new cloak protected her body, but she barely cared that her fingers and toes were numb. With her awareness centered across the breadth of the Corine, she knew only seas that were patched gray and cobalt beneath the breaking cover of rain clouds. There the wind blew warm and damp from the west, its smell scoured clean with salt.

Presently another scent intruded. The taint was so faint she might have imagined it, the barest suggestion of something acrid. Taen paused, tightening her focus. A moment later, her heart quickened in alarm. The smell traveled clearly on the east breeze, now identifiable as smoke from charred cordage and timber. The source, when she traced, proved swathed in heavy mist, identical to the patch she had diverted *Shearfish* to investigate in the waters to the north off Felwaithe. Taen's dream-sense shrank in reflexive warning. The evidence overwhelmingly indicated demon-sign and battle; and what reason for both in this desolate stretch of ocean, if not Ivainson Jaric?

Pressured now by fear, Taen added caution to her search. Worse than discovery, she dared not let demons detect her probe, tap into it, and gain further knowledge of Jaric. Her mistake with Emien aboard *Moonless* must never be repeated.

The Dreamweaver entered the mist with the subtlety of snow drifting through air, and the net she wove to trace was fine-meshed enough to draw minnows. The fact that she might be helpless to intervene should she find Jaric in demon captivity made her palms sweat and her breathing shallow. But the tenacity of her Imrill Kand upbringing shored her spirit against heartbreak. To find him alive would bring hope, however dire his circumstances.

She pressed deeper, found a drift of burnt timbers but nothing else, only an icy, unnatural emptiness which made her flesh crawl. The mist pressed close about her dream-sense. It cloaked the wave crests and coiled like smoke through the troughs. Taen detected no life but schools of scavenger fish come to investigate the flotsam, yet her foreboding only intensified. Something lurked just past the borders of her perception, like movements glimpsed in a mirror. Her skin prickled as if she were watched by hostile eyes; despite the fact that she sat in the distant north, surrounded by rock and soil and thin grass grazed by goats. The entity which lurked in the mist seemed somehow *knowing,* as though her presence had been expected.

Taen paused. Even as she sought to refine her probe, a force brushed light as feathers down her spine. Suddenly she felt an overpowering urge to pull back, leave this stretch of ocean, and forget the traces of wreckage she had found here. Yet Imrill Kand offered no haven if the Keys to Elrinfaer fell to enemy hands. Certain her compulsion was demon-inspired, Taen braced to fight; if the Thienz who came hunting from Shadowfane saw fit to hide their machinations, she refused to be cowed. Power smoldered within her, clearing the mist for a target to strike. Yet her dream-probe encountered no Thienz; only the sudden, unexpected awareness of Ivainson Jaric.

The shock wrenched a cry from Taen's throat. Ablaze with unshed power, and poised for battle, she yanked back. Cold rock bruised her spine, yet discomfort to her body became insignificant before the whetted edge of weariness within her mind. Quite certainly the Firelord's heir had been unveiled because it suited the purpose of demons for him to be found. Yet Jaric was not taken captive. He sat alone at *Callinde*'s helm. His hair was sodden and wind-tangled, and his eyes stinging from lack of sleep.

The energies Taen had woven in search of him were still intact. Power flared in answer to his presence; she dampened the force instantly, but not before a spark of contact leaped through.

Jaric raised his head. "Taen?" he said, and the hope and the confusion in his tone almost broke the Dreamweaver who huddled in the cold in

Imrill Kand. That narrowest instant of pity proved fatal. The enchantress hesitated, and the trap she feared, the threat that instinctively cautioned her against maintaining any thread of rapport, overtook her. Thienz grappled a foothold through the contact.

Taen screamed in fear and pain. She slammed up defensive barriers, too late. Her compassion for Jaric ran deep, and the grip of the demons had penetrated through to its source. They had breached that innermost psyche where she was unguarded and their attack was engineered with devastating precision. Jaric had been used as bait, left free and in solitude expressly that demons might snare her. Once Taen Dreamweaver was rendered impotent to defend, her powers would not foil the demon's final possession of their quarry. The last living heir of Ivain Firelord would be taken as surely as a wheat stalk razed by a scythe. The pain of that ripped Taen open to more cruel revelation still: the guiding mind behind this most deadly plot had been not that of a demon *but that of the brother she had lost to Shadowfane.*

"No!" Taen's cry echoed over the tors of Imrill Kand. She struggled to repel the hold upon her mind, even as power flared and burned her resistance away to nothing. The being who now was Maelgrim had no mercy; all that remained of his humanity had been carved into a weapon for killing. He traded upon ties his sister would harbor, the same loyalty and stubborn love that had made her hesitate to strike him down once before on the heights of Elrinfaer. Maelgrim thrust through the Thienz net to cripple her.

Yet Taen did not crumple. Weeping bitterest tears, she mustered and deflected the killing blow. Her dream-sense flashed white under the paralyzing agonies of conflict. Her mind reeled under the backlash, and the suffocating hold of the Thienz released. Taen reached immediately to retaliate, to strike at the source of Keithland's peril before Jaric could be captured or slain. But no force answered. She had dangerously overextended herself, and her powers were utterly spent. Sapped of energy, Taen opened her eyes to gray mist, and a wind that scoured across the rocks of Imrill Kand. Pain and cold wracked her body, and her eyes ached from tears.

She tried to stir, and could not. Her limbs felt locked in lead. Afraid now, for the chill might certainly kill her, she struggled to lift her head. Her vision became patched with darkness. Dizziness wrung her senses like grass stalks swept up in a whirlpool, and a fierce attack of nausea left her gasping. Jaric, she thought weakly, but could not rouse enough to focus her warning into dream-call. As the void swirled and engulfed her, Taen heard laughter from the man she had once called a brother. Then the sound shattered to echoes. Her awareness slipped sickeningly into night, even as the last terrible fact crackled across the link: the Demon Lord of Shadowfane wanted more than the Keys to Elrinfaer. He had commanded that Jaric be taken alive. Ivain Firelord might have been hated, even cursed for his cruelties and his malice. But the son bequeathed to Keithland might do worse; enslaved by demons, the boy and his prodigious potential for a sorcerer's mastery might be turned like a cataclysm against his own kind. A Firelord dedicated to destruction would surely end hope and extinguish humanity's chance of survival.

Had Taen retained even a glimmer of consciousness, she would have wept for sorrow, that the greatest fear of Jaric's heart should now so terribly become real. But her awareness extinguished like candle flame slapped by a downpour.

Night fell over the tors of Imrill Kand. The broken clouds of afternoon fused into darkness and whipping rain that slashed the rocks, and beat in icy sheets over mats of flattened grass. Bracken bent to the storm, and run-off drummed over a mud-spattered goat-fleece cloak that only that morning had been new. The Dreamweaver of Imrill Kand lay beneath, unmoving. Her hands glistened with rainwater when the lanternlight fell across them; the hair plastered sodden to her cheek swallowed reflections, seemed a shroud cut from the very cloth of death.

"Fires, she's here, then," said a soul-weary voice edged with bitterness.

A shout followed, and a rustle of oilskins, as the small band of searchers clustered together around the site.

More light flooded the cranny in the rocks where Taen lay. Evertt stamped mud from his boot soles to be sure of his footing on the rocks. Grim as the granite he trod, he set his storm lantern in a cranny. Then he bent and gathered his niece in his arms exactly as he would have hefted a net of fresh-caught cod, except that his movements were awkward with a grief only his dead brother might have recognized.

Her skin was very cold.

"We're too late," someone murmured. Already the dour men with their flickering lanterns dispersed to descend the tor.

"Perhaps." Evertt lowered his head against the driving rain, the girl cradled limply against his chest. "She breathes, but her spirit rides the winds." He said no more until he reached the doorstoop in Rat's Alley where Marl's widow waited in an agony of silence, even as she had for the husband and the son fate had torn from her before this.

Now, the same as then, Evertt could not meet her eyes. He stepped full into the light which spilled from the kitchen, Taen bundled loosely in his arms. The mud and the wet spoiling the cloak which had not protected made the mother gasp, but she did not ask. Still, beaten and worn with years, she did not ask.

Her aching, terrible courage made Evertt feel inadequate. Rage at his helplessness made him gruff, for he knew no other way to treat the humiliation, and the endless, grinding tragedy of life as he understood it. "Found her on the tors," he snapped. Then, sorry for his harshness, he tried to ease what he could not change. "Taen is too small for her task. But like her father, she won't believe it."

Which was Evertt's timeworn bitterness finding expression, as it always did, that his brother had been born knowing how to find joy in the face of adversity.

Marl's widow stiffened. "The sorcery could not kill her, any more than the storm did Marl." Bravery had, though, and now might do so again. Abruptly Marl's widow discovered she was not too hardened for tears. "Bring her in, then."

Evertt stepped into the dim warmth of the kitchen, and for once he was not nagged about the mud he tracked in with his boots.

Taen wakened to dry blankets and the dull red glow of the hearth fire. She lay on a cot by the settle. Her cloak hung on a chair, filling the air with the reek of damp wool, while wind and rain slashed the windowpanes, jangling the luck charms intended to ward storm violence from those within. Taen stirred under the coverlet. Her eyes stung. Her body ached, as if savaged by fever, and her heart bore a burden of pain greater than any she might have imagined when she accepted her training from the Vaere.

"Don't speak," said Marl's widow.

Taen turned eyes that were too old for the years she actually carried. Restless on her pillows, she framed a tortured question. "How long?"

Marl's widow found herself crying again, not in relief, but for the mysteries which burdened her daughter she would never again understand. "Your spirit has ridden the winds through a day and another night."

Taen grew very still. Her blue eyes acquired depths that wounded, before she closed them. *Too late, too late for Jaric.* Thienz had taken him as she slept, and the Keys to Elrinfaer with him. Even as the Dreamweaver's mind encompassed the knowledge, she sensed the demon boats which dragged *Callinde* in tow. Defeat had sharpened her dream-sense to knife-like clarity, and an image formed, of Jaric battered helpless by the vindictive triumph of the Thienz. His body lay wrapped in sailcloth, trussed in spare cordage purloined from *Callinde's* lockers. But far worse, his mind was left aware. The fate he would embrace at Shadowfane was known to him, and the horror of his knowing was reflected inward over and over by the mirrorlike spell of his prison. The demons could not kill him, by Scait's express command; but in bloodless malice they tortured the mind of their victim past bearing.

Taen could not penetrate Thienz's defenses with her dream-sense; that she saw at all was a cruelty arranged by the one Shadowfane named Maelgrim. Powerless to intervene, ravaged by the failure of her talents as never, ever before, the enchantress knew Ivainson Jaric well enough to guess the depths of suffering he could not express. Behind the glassy blankness of his eyes, his heart was screaming.

"When the net grows too heavy, the wise fisherman seeks help," said Marl's widow from the shadows by the cot in Evertt's cottage.

Taen swallowed, willing the images to leave her. She opened eyes flooded now with tears and forced her hands to unclench. "Who is left to help?" She stared at the roofbeams, hating the whipped sound of her words even as she spoke them.

Marl's widow leaned forward and rested work-weary arms upon the shelf of her knees. "The sea itself, if the powers beneath so choose." Then she abandoned the solace of proverbs with a sigh of exasperation. "Daughter, must you always seek to bend the wind?"

The words were very near the ones a Dreamweaver had offered Jaric in the burrow of the Llondelei. Now that time felt far distant, a child's dream of happiness. Taen kicked the memory to quiescence, before sorrow could choke her heart. The Keys might be taken, but the Mharg had yet to fly; leagues of ocean remained to be crossed before Jaric reached the dungeons of Shadowfane.

"So like your father you are," Marl's widow began, and stopped, for a glance toward the pillows made her breath catch. Taen's tears had stopped. Her face was no longer that of a girl, or even a woman, but that of an enchantress trained by the Vaere. Power rang from her, even as sound reverberating from steel under the hammer falls of a smith's shaping. Yet even now the familiar was not entirely lost; the Sathid-born force of the enchantress held that fierce, indomitable hope with which Marl had tempered the hardship of his days upon Imrill Kand.

"The sea will help, if the powers beneath so choose," Taen repeated. She turned a shining look to her mother. *"Callinde*'s provisions were low, her casks nearly empty. *If the demons bear the Firelord's heir to Shadowfane, they must make landfall, somewhere, for water."*

Her mother made the sign against evil, for the mention of perils beyond her understanding. She turned diffident eyes to her daughter, who was no longer of Imrill Kand, but inextricably bound to the turning of the world beyond. Only Taen did not see her mother's uncertainty. Her Dreamweaver's mind was already far removed by the powers that marked her craft.

Taen's awareness sped outward from Imrill Kand, straight as an arrow's flight. She wasted no time with openings, but roused the captain of the Kielmark's brigantine *Shearfish* with an urgency that shot him bolt upright in his berth. He narrowly missed slamming his head into the deck beams overtop, but purpose overrode his annoyance.

'Weaver of Dreams, I have patrolled the northeast reaches in the area you named,' he thought in answer to her query. *'My men saw no mists. If there were demons, they are gone.'*

But the negative report was a thing Taen had expected, since learning that Maelgrim's talents directed the powers of the Thienz. He would surely be sailing where her dream-sense had seen the fogs of cloaking illusion, and through mind-trance with the second fleet of Thienz to the south, his powers had augmented the trap that had sprung on Jaric. The eyes of men would see no trace to mark the boats which sailed from Shadowfane; but a Dreamweaver might. Taen bent her focus to Cliffhaven. If *Shearfish* bore her south, and the Kielmark mustered his men at arms, the chance existed that she might track the demon fleets. Though the sea was too wide, too open, to launch an attack upon enemies men could not see, on land, with the aid of her dream-sight, an army might manage an ambush when dwindling provisions drove the Thienz ashore.

The Kielmark sat at dinner. Before his table, an uncomfortable merchant captain stood with the bare steel of two captains pricking the back of his fine brocade doublet. He had thought to run the straits with impunity after sending ingots lined with lead in his tribute chests, and now was regretting his scam. Though the meats and the wines were very fine, the Sovereign Lord of Cliffhaven was not eating. For the merchant, that sign boded ill, but the judgment awaiting him was summarily put off. The King of Pirates sprang to his feet even before Taen had completed her message. Wine sloshed in the goblets as he shoved away from the table, yelling for his captains to leave the merchant in irons, and follow him afterward to the bailey. The Dreamweaver's rapport faded as he called for the saddled horse. Shouting commands to his captains even as he gained the saddle, the Kielmark wheeled his mount with a crack of hooves and galloped for the harborside gates.

Taen relayed another of his orders; and far north, the brigantine *Shearfish* came about with a crack of canvas and steadied on a new course for Irmill Kand.

But in the end all the flurry of preparation proved useless. When the Dreamweaver turned her perception south, the demon fleet which guarded Jaric did not ply a northerly course for Shadowfane, as anticipated. Natural wariness perhaps made them shun the lands of men; their stores might be too depleted to reach the mainlands which lay between the south reaches and Felwaithe's distant shores. But far and away more likely, with the Keys to Elrinfaer taken at last, the demons intended to ply north to free the Mharg. Taen saw with bitterness that the black ships with *Callinde* in tow sailed due east, for the southwest shores of Elrinfaer. No army could be gathered there to do battle for the rescue of the Firelord's heir; those lands had been stripped of habitation since Ivain's betrayal, and Anskiere's contention with the Mharg.

Skilled as the Kielmark's captains were, they could not outsail the winds. No fleet and no fighting men, no matter how well trained, could possibly cross the Corine Sea in time to matter. Even the wizards at Mhored Kara could not help, with trackless leagues of wilderness lying between their stronghold of towers and the western sea. Beaten, cut by cruelest despair, Taen rebalanced her powers. Nothing remained but to recall the Kielmark's brave ships. Afterward, defeat like ashes in her mouth, she gathered weary resources to frame one final message. This one sapped her in more than content, twisted as it must be across barriers of space and time. Tamlin on the Isle of the Vaere was last to learn of her failure. Once the demon fleet sailed from Elrinfaer, no force in Keithland could prevent Maelgrim and his Thienz from delivering Ivainson Jaric to the Lord of Demons at Shadowfane.

CHAPTER XVII

Lady of the Spring

Taen's sending reached the Isle of the Vaere in the still hours before dawn, yet no shadow of night darkened the grove on the fabled isle. As always, the oak trees stood without a rustle in silvery, changeless twilight, where nary a grass blade stirred. No little man with clothing fringed with feathers and bells manifested in response to the Dreamweaver's tidings; yet the being known as Tamlin of the Vaere received word of Jaric's peril and the Keys' loss nonetheless. The extent of the damage was no sooner understood when the entity which inhabited the grove sent a second call forth into Keithland. Directed to a certain spring in the forests southeast of Elrinfaer, this was a summons of desperation; for even the Vaere could not be certain the initiate of the mysteries there would accede to the demands of necessity.

The storms in the south reaches of the Corine eventually broke, but the swell took far longer to subside. The black fleet from Shadowfane tossed on a beam reach, and the jerk as *Callinde* rolled and snapped short on her towline became torment without surcease for Jaric. Each surge of the sea fetched his limp weight against the comfortless angles of wooden ribs and floorboards. His cheek and shoulder quickly chafed raw from the pounding. He could not move to east his misery, even to turn his head. Demons had trussed him in sailcloth and cord. They had lashed his wrists to the mast, then imprisoned his mind with ties more ruthless still. Fully aware of his battered and aching body, Ivainson Jaric was deprived of any control of his limbs. His thoughts were left free to agonize over his helplessness.

Defeat and humiliation became suffering from which no surcease existed. The Thienz sailed for Shadowfane, to deliver him alive to Lord Scait, along with the cloth sack which contained the stolen Keys to Elrinfaer. The seals over the wards which imprisoned the Mharg now hung at the neck of a demon; more terrible still, the critical potential for his Firelord's mastery would be enslaved, even as the Llondelei far-seers had forewarned. Jaric cursed the wind that bellied the black boats' sails. As *Callinde* was dragged inexorably northward, he ached for Taen, whose death at the hand of her brother would proceed undisputed. He thought often of the Stormwarden, whose geas of desperation had failed to bring rescue, and whose doom in the ice now was sealed. All the while Jaric's Thienz captors gabbled among themselves. They praised each other for the defeat of Ivainson Firelord's heir and they jabbed energies at his mind to taunt him. A day and a night passed before they gave him anything to drink, and then he suffered the indignity of rough handling as they poured water down his throat. The demons did the same with the food, an ill-smelling paste of raw fish that they chewed first to soften, their poison sacs sphinctered shut to prevent contamination that might inadvertently kill him. Had Jaric been left any physical response, he would have gagged rather than swallow, but even that reflex was denied him.

The winds held fair from the west. Spray fell full in Jaric's face, and his hair trailed in the bilge, which unavoidably came to reek of urine. The Thienz seemed unfazed by the stink. They gloated, and they trimmed sails, and they checked often to see that the towrope dragging *Callinde* and the lines binding their prisoner did not chafe.

Day followed day in a misery of animal suffering. Nights became a terror-ridden procession of nightmares as, over and over, Jaric relived the destruction of Keithland as foretold by the Llondelei dreamers. He saw Taen bleed under the knife of her brother, Anskiere's bones became trampled by frostwargs; and the jewel-bright scales of the Mharg flashed in sunlight over withered acres. Other times, his captors crafted images to torment him, of Scait Demon Lord on his throne of human remains, and of the dank dungeons carved beneath the foundations of Shadowfane. There, most horribly, the heir of Ivain would come into his inheritance; in mind-rending agony he would suffer the Cycle of Fire for the vengeance of demons against humanity. Powerless to move, unable to weep, and denied any means of dying, Jaric endured. He burned in the sun's harsh glare and shivered, drenched, through the squalls. There seemed no relief, except at rare intervals when exhaustion overcame discomfort, and he slept. Then his wretchedness receded before a dark like the void beyond eternity.

During such a time the Thienz reached the westernmost coast of Elrinfaer, their purpose to refill depleted water casks. Jaric did not rouse when the lookout croaked from its perch in the rigging. He did not feel the short, sharp tugs as *Callinde*'s towline was snubbed short, nor the bang of sails as the black ships jibed to run before the wind. The first he knew of the landfall was the jar and the grinding scrape as *Callinde* grounded on the shoaling sands of the barrier bar. The Thienz at her steering oar responded clumsily; the heavy craft slewed sideways, and all but broached as breaking surf boomed and exploded into spray against her portside thwart. Jaric was thrown hard on his back. Impact knocked the wind from him, and his bonds jerked his arms at excruciating angles beneath his body. He could not curl to protect himself. *Callinde* rolled queasily through the trough, while the Thienz at the helm whuffed alarm and tugged to straighten the helm. Before it succeeded, a second wave hammered down. Bruised against the mast, Jaric choked helplessly on the flood of water through the bilge. Soaked and limp as flotsam, he felt Mathieson's forgiving old fishing boat swing and plow like a dolphin for the shore.

She grounded with a jolt in the shallows. Jaric lay gasping as his captors seized the towline and dragged the ungainly craft ashore. Dazzled by the glare of noon sunlight, he heard the thumps and bumps as others boarded. Soon busy, toad-fingered hands untied the lashing which secured *Callinde*'s casks. More Thienz scrabbled over the gunwales, these to stand guard while the others searched for a clean spring ashore. Jaric endured their cuffs and their kicks, his opened eyes filled with sky, and the sour, reedy smell of marshland strong in his nostrils. Flies crawled on his scabs, and mosquitoes stung his face. Swarms clouded the air around the Thienz also, but the insects seldom fed, for the demons snapped their jaws and ate them. Queasy from thirst and days of unsuitable food, Jaric wished desperately for the freedom to close his eyes voluntarily.

That moment, a shriek rent the air. The nearest of the Thienz toppled over, its limbs thrashing in agony. It crashed heavily against Jaric's leg, even as the demon standing watch in the stern snapped straight, a feathered arrow pinned through its gills. It fell without outcry, while its companions shrilled the alarm.

Jaric noticed clan markings on the arrow before cries and screams rent the air and a spear stabbed, quivering, into *Callinde*'s sternpost. Another ripped through a Thienz trying to board. More demons swarmed to replace it, jostling and shoving to launch the craft bearing their prisoner back into the sea. Arrows fell in a hail to prevent them. Thienz crashed thrashing into the salt sting of the foam, while others dove to raise the sails. More shafts sleeted among them. *Callinde* lurched. A javelin struck the deck not inches from Jaric's ear, and a stricken demon clawed him in his death throes. *Still he could not move.* That he had need to was certainty, for hill tribes on a raid against Kor's Accursed were known to slaughter with berserk fury.

Callinde slewed in the lift of an incoming wave. Jaric fetched up against the pinrail. Then the mast tipped; the boat dragged seaward, spinning, the Thienz at her helm toppled with an axe in its back. The one at the bow who fought to shear the towline died next, of a dagger thrust to the groin. Then an eldritch scream rent the air, bone-chilling for its anger. The sound cut through the minds of the demons like a knife, and those closest wailed aloud in consternation. Jaric felt the bindings upon his mind give slightly. His heart flared with hope as a feather-and-fur-clad clansman leaped *Callinde*'s thwart. Then the boy's view was eclipsed by the head of the Thienz elder who commanded the fleet of black boats. An arrow transfixed its forearm; blood twined channels through its creased flesh, and its eyes were dark with pain, but its hands were vengefully strong as it tugged Ivainson upright by the hair.

'*Die in torment, Firelord's heir.*' Gills gaped red as wounds beneath its jowls as it opened its mouth. The venom sacs behind its foretongue discharged as it bit, sinking needle fangs into his victim's shoulder.

Jaric did not see the axe blow that severed the attacking Thienz's neck. His mind exploded in a haze of anguish. The poison racked him, each tear in his flesh a heated rivet of agony; and whether the fetters of demons still bound him became immaterial. He lacked recourse to recoil or even to scream. Riven through with suffering, he received the impression of a hillman bending over him with a scarlet axe. He tried to warn, to beg that the Keys to Elrinfaer be sought out and recovered from the hands of the demons who had stolen, all for the ruinous release of the Mharg. But words would not come. The sky and *Callinde* overturned, pitched him head-long into pain.

Sounds receded, overlaid by a roar like surf. Jaric knew vertigo, then the bitter tang of salt on his tongue. Somewhere an ancient, wrinkled crone lay dying. The vision of her body lying crumpled in white sand was imprinted sharp as sorrow through his torment. Almost he could count the knots in the interlaced leather of her garment; but why he saw the death of a hilltribe's seeress remained a mystery. His skin went from fire to ice to fire again, and his breathing seemed to rock the earth. Then came a jolt, and he saw clearly, a flat gray vista of swamp reeds and scum-caked pools. The feathered heads of the bullrushes seemed to advance upon him, twisted and tossed by wind that made no sound. Seed tips brushed his bitten shoulder and agony flamed from the contact. Darkness flooded his vision. His mouth went bitter and dry as ash, and his feet seemed to float. Taen, he thought, but her image ran like wax in his mind. For a very long time he knew nothing but the jumbled dreams of delirium, boats that sailed over blood-dark seas, and the grinding crash of masonry as the towers of Landfast were falling, falling, blasted to rubble in flames raised by sorcery.

In time the dream changed texture. Dry heat gave way to darkness and moisture, and a grinding, tumbling roar filled Jaric's ears. Behind that endless, rolling crescendo of sound he heard the treble clang of hand cymbals and chanting. The words were not intelligible, but by the inflec-tion, Ivain's heir knew. The speakers mourned the devastation of Keith-land. Where the cities had stood, curtains of red light were falling, falling into absolute dark where Mharg-wings knifed like razors . . . and though his guilt could never be absolved, in time he realized that the sound, and the ritual, and the plummeting curtain of illumination at least were real.

He lay on his side in a place that smelled of moss and cured fur. His limbs were unresponsive as dead meat, and his shoulder throbbed beneath the weight of an herb compress. Though his head swam with dizziness, Jaric determined that he lay in a cavern recessed behind a waterfall. The cascade roared and shattered into fine rainbows of spray not three yards from him, and on his other side a coal brazier spattered highlights like jeweled fire over walls of natural stone.

The chanting swelled and receded, changeless as breaking surf; somewhere in the background a woman keened in grief. Jaric fought to control his muddled thoughts. Powerless to stop the flight of the Mharg and reverse Keithland's doom, powerless even to prevent the tears which traced his cheeks, he watched the falls and wondered why, if life elsewhere were ending, his own wretched existence continued.

A sonorous voice interrupted from the shadows at his back. "The sorrows of the grievers are not yours, Keeper of the Keys."

Had paralysis not shackled his reflexes, Jaric would have flinched at the name given him by Llondelei. Yet not even his eyelashes flicked. Helplessness forced him to think, and analyze, and finally determine that the speech was heavily accented, not stilted with images as a demon's would have been.

The Firelord's heir labored through pain to understand more, when the speaker gently qualified. "The lament is for the ones who fell to Thienz-*cien* on the shores of the great sea, and under blessing of the Presence you lie in the Sanctuary at Cael's Falls."

Jaric knew a spinning moment of vertigo. Disoriented and hurting from the aftereffects of Thienz venom, he tried vainly to move, to turn and face the unseen speaker. His experience at Tierl Enneth and the treatises in the archives of the Landfast priesthood offered scant understanding of hilltribes' culture, but this much he knew: the Lady who kept the Sanctuary at Cael's Falls was word and law among the clans. Her will was supreme over all other seeresses and chieftains throughout Keithland. On a whim she could order him killed.

But struggle did nothing to alleviate the Firelord's heir's distress. At his back, the speaker uttered a phrase in clan dialect, and a person left the cavern with a soft rustle of leather. Jaric felt shadow chill his body as someone else passed between his pallet and the brazier. Then light and warmth returned and only the crash of the falls remained.

A hand touched his shoulder. He could not recoil or protest, even as the fingers gripped and pulled him inexorably onto his back. Then he did break into a cold sweat, for he had expected the wrinkled crone from the Llondelei dreaming of Anskiere's past. Instead, the Lady of the Spring at Cael's Falls was a girl with russet hair braided and coiled back from a waiflike face. Her age might have been twelve. The ceremony of her initiation had to have been recent, for her eyes were swathed in cloths that smelled strongly of healer's unguents. Her touch upon his flesh was unsteady. No doubt she still felt the ache of the knife which had taken her sight.

"The Lady of the Spring died on the strands with the others," she murmured, as if her mind tracked his thoughts. Once again he recalled the crone he had dreamed, her bone-thin face outlined in a wreath of dry seaweed.

The child bending over him qualified with a reproach that stung. "I am her appointed successor."

Her words seemed to shimmer with reflections: of knowledge with-held, and sorrows laid bare. Called to account for his delays at Landfast, Jaric thought of Taen, and then, sharply, of peril and his own helplessness. Again he tried to move, only to lose himself impotently in vertigo left by the Thienz venom. The falls hurtled around him, the churning maelstrom of their waters a sound like the grind of the wheels of fate. Turning, they would crush him, and Keithland would burn. . . .

The seeress stiffened. She snatched her hand from his shoulder and uttered a phrase in dialect, her tone all ice and hostility. Young she might be, but the power at her command was shatteringly evident. Jaric's delirium cleared before a surge of raw fear.

Energies he did not understand tingled across his skin. The seeress arose. She whirled, and the knot-worked leather of her garments fanned a chill over him even as the embers in the brazier flared white-orange. Hallucinations touched off by the poisons made her shadow seem to caper as she strode to the back of the cavern. Drapes hung there, fashioned of woven cloth, and sewn with pearl chipped from the shells of river mussels. The clan seeress whipped these back and cried out in a pure, singing tone that shivered the air like a bell. An ache suffused Jaric's bones; uncertain whether this was an effect of his sickness, or the resonance of unknown powers, he fought for breath. Black patches danced before his eyes. Through them he saw a slab as black as a pool under starless night. Intri-cate patterns were worked in gold upon its surface, concentric circles with interconnecting whorls that dazzled and confused the eye. Silhouetted like a spider on a web, the seeress sank to her knees. Like one tranced she raised her hands and touched the disc at the very center. No visible phenomenon resulted, yet Jaric felt a force vibrate upon the air. Unseen energies whined along his nerves, and the hair pricked at the base of his neck.

The sensation ceased when the seeress lowered her arms. As she broke contact with the slab she staggered slightly. Small and suddenly very frail, she dragged the curtains closed and then sank down until her cheek rested against the stone of the cavern floor. "You shall have help," she murmured to Jaric. "By the life of my people, I swear you shall be cured."

The bandages over her eyes seemed to run red, accusing him of crimes and suffering beyond hope of redemption. Whether this, too, was an illu-sion born of delirium, the heir of Ivain could not say. The thunder of the falls swelled around him until he screamed and toppled backward into night.

He roused choking, the bitter taste of herbs on his tongue. Someone supported his head; horny calluses dug into his cheek, and guttural voices spoke above a white, never-ending hiss of sound. Jaric felt the cold rim of a cup pressed to his lips. Stinging liquid filled his mouth, and he coughed and turned feebly aside.

"*Ciengarde!*" The exclamation had an acid inflection; and though the language was strange, Jaric understood. They called him by his name, the same name spoken by another seeress at midsummer, under the shadow of the ruins at Tierl Enneth.

"*Demonbane!*" called the voice again, compelling. "Drink of the elixir and live."

Again his mouth was poured full of liquid. The taste was acrid. Jaric swallowed and drew a gasping breath. His chest ached. He wanted, terribly, to run, but his legs were beyond feeling. The hands shook him, pinching him cruelly.

"*Ciengarde,* answer! Resume the burden of your fate."

Weakness washed through him. Aware Taen's life depended upon his reply, Jaric struggled, snatched air into lungs that were racked like a drowning man's. But his tongue would shape no sound.

His eyes filled, and he wept. As if his tears were a catalyst, he saw the ancient predecessor of the seeress. Robed in knotted black, her crabbed hand raised and pointing, she spoke no word. Yet her accusation struck Jaric like a blow. Each hour he had dallied at Landfast had engendered tragedy; the life of the boy recovered from demons on the southwest shores of Elfrinfaer had been measured and bought in blood.

No. But even in recoil, Jaric could not escape the will which summoned him.

The fingers that gripped his body tightened their hold without pity, and the living seeress's command rang out like a whiplash. "*Ciengarde!*" his hard-won core of conviction transformed to a stinging agony of guilt. "Answer!"

Jaric flinched. The seeress's hand moved as if to slap him, even as a mother might reprimand a stubborn son. Such presumption of authority moved the Firelord's heir to rage. Air dragged like sand across his lacerated throat. "I am here."

His words seemed to fall into a pool of blackness. The restraint loosened from his limbs. He sank, utterly spent, into drowsy warmth.

"He will live," someone pronounced in a girlish treble, while the roar of the falls hammered into echoes that swallowed light.

He woke next to daylight and the faintly rancid scent of the white bear pelt that covered him. Even the softness of the fur seemed harsh against his flesh, and the hand and wrist lying crossed over his chest flared an angry, congested red. There were scabs left from the ropes. Jaric closed his eyes, listening to the tumble of Cael's Falls. He smelled the moisture upon the air, a sweetness not unlike rain-washed moss, and he thought of Taen's laughter. Then memory returned, of a tavern, and too much wine, and a shame that cut to contemplate. He tried to close the fingers of the hand that lay upon the coverlet, his left, which he had lain upon through the long days of his captivity. A blaze of pain answered. But the fingers quivered, and slowly, ever so torturously, closed into a fist.

Jaric felt sweat drip down his temples. He gasped in shallow breaths and tried to move the other hand, the one he could not see, the one attached to the shoulder the demon had bitten.

"Ach! No!" And without warning, the female who had chastised him reached out and pulled his hair.

Jaric opened his eyes. The seeress of Cael's Falls bent over him, the bandages over her face replaced by a veil of woven straw. Through the chinks he glimpsed blind, scarred tissue, and a girlishly vexed frown; then the seeress turned and called to someone else beyond his view. An attendant wearing deerhides arrived and fussed with the dressings on his shoulder. By the ungentle twists and tugs of the older woman's hands, the heir of Ivain Firelord understood that his efforts to move had knocked his poultices awry, and that his healers were mightily displeased.

Jaric struggled to turn his head. "How long?" he whispered, unable to manage more.

But as always, the seeress anticipated him. "The days number ten and six that the Presence has guarded your spirit."

The news struck hard, now that hope had been reborn. Jaric forced air into his lungs and attempted to inquire of the Keys to Elrinfaer. Words grated painfully in his throat. "Tell me—"

Yet before he managed more the seeress turned away. She knew what he would ask, and more plainly than words the line of her back indicated an unwillingness to answer. Jaric persisted. With a wrenching effort of will he raised his left hand and hooked her garment. "Please."

The touch was a breach of etiquette. The attendant sucked air through her teeth with a hiss; in shocked reaction she grasped his wrist and snatched back his offending hand. Incensed, the seeress spun like a cat and faced him. Only the trembling lip that showed beneath her veil reminded that she was but a girl, alone and frightened as he. "When you are stronger, she that the Presence names Dreamweaver to Keithland will reveal those things you must know."

Jaric subsided against the furs, white-faced. Taen apparently was safe; but for how long? And what in Keithland had become of his trust to Anskiere, that he must wait to hear? But no further questions were possible, for the seeress turned stiffly and left his presence.

The attendant remained, fussing over his dressings. She accompanied her ministrations with scolding clicks of her tongue, until, provoked to rebellion, Jaric sought clumsily to muffle his ear with the furs.

The attendant prevented him, allowing his dignity less regard than the bother of a swarming gnat. "Lie still." And she finished with an epithet in clan dialect.

Jaric ripped out a protest. "I never asked for help."

His obliqueness required no definition. The hillwoman stopped, lightless black eyes fixed on his face. Her back was stiff, and her muscled shoulders scarred from what looked like an injury inflicted by antlers. She answered finally, in a stilted, broken accent. "The Lady is never asked. She acts only by the will of the Presence."

"And never questions," Jaric whispered, for even so small an outburst had left him limp.

The clanswoman bent brusquely to her bandaging. "To question is to die, *Ciengarde.*"

Angry, debilitated, and faint with pain and worry, Ivainson Jaric turned his face to the falls. When at last the seeress's attendant finished dressing his shoulder, he hardened his will with determination, then struggled to flex his legs.

The attempt served only to tire him. Hot with fever, he tumbled into dreams that rang with the powers of the Presence. He saw torches, a circle of leather-clad clansfolk who chanted laments for the dead. The deceased presented in state at their feet lay covered with dark cloth, sewn and knotted with abalone into the sigil of the seeress. Except this Lady's hair was not aged and white, but auburn; neither were her bared features those of a girl. The tribes of Cael's Falls mourned a grown woman. In flickering flame-light, Jaric observed that the leather ceremonial mask which covered her blindness was stained dark with new blood, the ritual of initiation itself the cause of untimely death.

Beside the bier stood a girl-child who might once have been sister, or daughter, or niece, but who now bore the mark of successor. She was robed without ornament in white fleece. Her feet were bare, and hair of matching auburn blew unbound in the wind. She lowered a torch with trembling hands. As she touched the ceremonial shroud of her predecessor into flame, her eyes remained vivid and steady. Through the closing rites of the ceremony, while the flesh of her kinswoman burned, she neither shrank nor wept.

Fire obliterated the scene, then smoke smothered flame into shadows.

"*To question is to die, Ciengarde,*" cried the voice of recent memory.

Jaric sweated on his bed of furs. The dark closed over his mind like a pool, and somewhere a very young girl screamed once in terrible agony.

Soon after, the vision lost coherence. Jaric tossed, adrift in a half trance between waking and sleep. Dimly he was aware of hands that raised him up, forced broth between his locked teeth. Once, when the falls danced white-etched in the lightning of a late-season storm, he sensed the seeress at his side, the Sight she had gained in place of vision trained intently on his face.

His lips shaped speech with great difficulty. "Was that your sister, or mother, who failed the old one's legacy?"

The Lady gave no answer.

Jaric drew a ragged breath. Though uncertain whether the storm-lit figure was a dream, an apparition, or a delusion born of strong drugs and poison, he persisted. "Someone close to you died. If you suffered the old one's inheritance in her stead, and my actions are to blame, I am sorry."

The hill priestess stirred, the sigh of her knot-worked robes all but lost in the rush of the falls. "Power cannot bend to sorrow, *Ciengarde*."

Jaric wrestled for strength to sit, but fingers reached out and bore him down. His helplessness that moment became a torment worse than pain. "Is threat to Landfast, to Keithland, to every living tribe under your protection not cause enough? Lady, I must know. What became of the Keys to Elrinfaer?"

His plea met implacable silence. Whether out of pique, or the inborn distrust of her kind, the seeress departed without reply. Dreams closed once more over the mind of Ivainson Jaric.

When next he awakened, he remembered, and did not ask again. Hill-folk came and went, tending his daily needs and changing his fouled dressings. The wounds in his shoulder gradually ceased to fester, and his intervals of delirium receded before increasing hours of lucidity. Yet the crippling weakness lingered. Jaric lay all but motionless, his senses filled with the crash and tumble of falling water. Two thoughts turned in his mind: had he claimed his inheritance sooner, his present suffering might have been avoided; since he had not, in his frailty only one argument remained that could force the seeress to break silence.

For all his determination, a week passed before he was able to try. Even then, he had to wait for the brief interval when the eldest of several healers assigned to watch over him fell asleep. At the first of her wispy snores, Jaric rolled on his good side. He tossed off the suffocating furs. The Thienz venom had left him devastatingly weak; the slightest movement left him breathless, his forehead slick with sweat. Still he drove himself, quivering, to his knees. There he paused, while dizziness sucked at his balance. He waited, eyes closed, for the vertigo to subside, which took a fearfully long time.

Perspiration cooled on his body and made him shake. Jaric bit his lip, forced his unwilling limbs to bear weight. The grotto wall lay barely two paces away, yet he reached it gasping as if he had run an endurance race. The curtains of the falls tumbled not an arm span distant. Backlit by moonlight, the water shimmered like faery silver, elusive and cold and forbidden. Jaric dragged himself upright against the stone and inched his way to the ledge.

Spray showered over him like needles of ice. Jaric licked his lips for the clean, wild taste of it. His knees were trembling. Beyond his feet the water poured in thunderous, downsweeping torrents into darkness. Defying vertigo, Jaric watched droplets bounce off his toes and whirl unseen over the brink. A mapping text read long ago in the Kielmark's library claimed Cael's Falls dropped three hundred feet into a cauldron carved into rock. A second, newer work claimed the drop to be triple that. With a scholar's curiosity, Jaric wondered which was true.

A sharp intake of breath cut short his reverie. Rough hands caught him back from the ledge, and he toppled in a heap at the feet of the Lady of the Spring. She wore no veil. Half-healed blind eyes seemed to sear him with reproach.

"*Ciengarde*": the word pure anger at his recklessness; had he fallen, the future of humanity would have found oblivion with him.

"Tell me what I need to know," demanded Jaric, though he had spent all his strength, and that moment could barely manage speech.

The seeress stamped her foot. Attendants rushed into the grotto, and at her command, they half carried, half dragged Jaric back to his furs.

When he woke the next morning, a pair of clan warriors armed with axes stood guard at his feet. Humiliated, and wretchedly infuriated by his failure, Jaric shouted out loud to the seeress, who was not present, but who most assuredly was listening. "Am I a prisoner, then?"

Yet when she answered his challenge, he started, for the roar of the falls had masked her approach. "No prisoner, *Ciengarde*, except to the fate which binds you." She stepped into view from the shadows behind his head, black-clad, and looking nothing like the child she actually was. Rooted in total acceptance of the powers which had torn her from youth, her poise was an embarrassment. Solemnly she extended his sword; knotted around the cross guard were the thongs of a familiar leather bag, darkened now with bloodstains. With a gesture of newfound respect, the seeress added, "No prisoner, son of Ivain Firelord. Never that."

Driven by a wild surge of relief, Jaric reached for the weapon. He had been sixteen when he learned of his inheritance; seventeen when he assumed Anskiere's geas. Now, at eighteen, he had seen the greatest of his responsibilities ceded to the judgment of a twelve-year-old child whose courage left him disgraced. Jaric forced himself not to buckle. The weight of the steel bore down upon him and emphasized how thoroughly the Thienz venom had devastated his vitality. He let the cold length of the blade settle across his chest, then, with fingers that trembled, fumbled and felt the hard edges of Anskiere's basalt block. The Keys to Elrinfaer had been recovered. Drained with release, Jaric gripped the sword and its burden of wards until his hands went white. "Thank you, Lady," he managed at last in a whisper.

The seeress watched with impassive, stony silence, as if a weight of sorrow measured her gift. Unmanned and desperate under the intensity of her gaze, and humbled by a debt he could not express, Jaric turned his face into the furs. She left finally without speaking, but the guards at his feet remained.

Another week passed. The days all dawned gray behind the tumbling cataract of Cael's Falls. Jaric labored at lifting his sword. Then as his hand began to steady, he tentatively attempted forms, while his guards commented in grunts upon his progress. Between times they played at knucklebones, and for Jaric the rattle of the game pieces seemed to keep time to his pain. In time his persistence must have earned the clansmen's approval, for when the healers came to change the dressings on his shoulder, or feed him, or perform other less agreeable tasks, his guards offered him privacy by turning their backs. Night and day Jaric fought to recover the health the Thienz venom had sapped. Gradually his tissues began to heal; his pallor left him first, and then the debilitating tremble. Dexterity returned, and slowly, grudgingly, balance and the beginnings of strength. In time, steadied between the shoulders of the warriors, he was permitted to stand, and then with difficulty to walk.

The moment he could cross the chamber unassisted, he demanded access to *Callinde*. The seeress denied him, until, by words and vehement gestures sketched upon the air, he made her understand that two fortnights' neglect should not be stretched out into three. His boat had fared poorly as a Thienz prize; ripped sails and rotted cordage might delay his sailing as surely as a relapse, and the demon hunters from Shadowfane would not wait to allow repairs.

Yet five more days passed before the priestess granted grudging consent. Jaric arose on the following morning and neatly rolled up his furs. He donned his cleaned and mended clothes, and buckled on his sword. The two warriors assigned to attend him were barely old enough for beards. They flanked his steps as he left the seeress's grotto and made his way down a passage whose left-hand partition was a perpetual curtain of water. The stone underfoot was glazed with damp, polished smooth by centuries of erosion. The wall on the right bore paintings of Kor's fall, and scenes of beast hunts and rituals whose meanings Jaric could only wonder upon. At last the corridor gave onto a ledge, and he stepped out into sunshine for the first time in thirty-seven days.

The dazzle of reflection off the falls seared his vision. Blinking until his eyes could adjust, his shoulder pressed to the cliff face for support, Jaric made out a series of wooden rungs slotted into notches in the stone. The breeze smelled of balsam and leaf mold, woodsy scents familiar from Seitforest. Below, the falls roared and spattered off jutting shoulders of granite, to dash into lace-fine drifts of spume in a cauldron far, far beneath. To a sailor's eye, the second of the texts had listed the distance more accurately. Jaric swallowed, sweating to recall the time he had stood swaying on that brink, and the seeress's just anger in the moment she pulled him back.

Behind him a warrior spoke in dialect, asking whether he was afraid of heights. Jaric shook his head. Below, like a model made of matchsticks, lay a scattering of huts and gardens, and the inevitable beaten circle of earth where wagons and teams of horses were picketed. Cael's Falls was a shrine rather than a settlement. Tribes came to consult their seer, or to leave offerings of food and fur for the staff who remained in her service. Beyond lay forests broken by pale marshlands and the russet basins of reed pools baked dry by late summer heat.

"How far is the sea?" Jaric inquired, in what stilted bits of dialect he had managed to master during convalescence.

The warrior in front of him grinned, his teeth very white against his weather-tanned face. "Follow."

Never certain whether the oblique answers of hillmen were the result of his poor pronunciation, or the perverse reticence of their kind, Jaric made his way down the ledge toward the rungs. The drop beneath was sheer. Not at all sure his strength would last the descent, he swung his weight out, over air, and laboriously started down.

There were alcoves with railings where climbers could pause and rest. Curled panting and sweating into the topmost of these, Jaric cursed his Thienz-weakened body while the warriors who accompanied him lounged upon the rungs above and below, laughing at a joke between themselves. Long before the ache in his muscles subsided, the Firelord's heir forced himself to his feet. He finished the climb this time without stopping, though the effort half killed him. He collapsed in a heap by the pool at the bottom, whooping air into taxed lungs. The fingers of both hands spasmed uncontrollably, and his vision spun.

"A fool for courage, you are," said one of the warriors, but whether he spoke out in mockery or disgust, Jaric never knew. The next instant he was scooped up in sinewed arms. Struggling not to inhale the ornamental feathers which trailed from his bearer's wristbands, he felt himself deposited on the withies of a skin boat. The floor tilted crazily as the second clansman stepped aboard and shoved off. Then the current snatched the frail craft from the bank.

Whirled dizzy, and further disoriented by a spinning view of sky and wind-tossed treetops, Jaric fought an unseamanlike urge to be sick. In time he recovered enough to notice the warriors paddling furiously, spray and sweat lending a patina to their bronze skins. The roar of the falls receded, replaced in time by another thunder as the coracle jounced and skated over the cross-currents of a rapid. Jaric managed, between dousings, to sit up. "How far is the sea?"

"Not far, *Ciengarde*," assured the warrior in the stern. He nodded forward.

Jaric turned to look as the coracle ducked and shot like a pinched melon seed into shallows. He raised himself to the gunwale in time to see a wall of dry reeds coming straight for his face. He yelped, ducked, and managed not to fall out as the coracle rammed and braked to a stop in an explosion of cattail down.

The warriors slapped their knees and laughed. Then, amid a confusion of gestures, they thrust broken reed stems into Jaric's hands and drew lots to determine who should drag the mired craft free.

The loser claimed his reed was a liar. Half in frustration, and half carried away by the exhilaration of the first freedom he had known in weeks, Jaric leaped the thwart to do the job himself. He no sooner touched bottom when he sank to his waist in brown muck.

The warriors stared at him, suddenly silent. Then the nearer one spoke. "*Ciengarde,* we usually use the pole wedged under the seat for this labor."

"Oh, Kor's Fires," exclaimed Jaric. "Did your seeress tell you I'd perish at the touch of a little water?" And he shoved the coracle so hard that both of his escorts overbalanced and fell with a smack into the brackish water of the reed bed.

They came up spitting mud, reeds pinched in the soaked draggle of their skin garments.

"How far is the sea?" Jaric demanded.

"Oh, very close," said the nearest, and with a wicked gleam in his eyes, flipped the coracle back and keeled him over full length in the swamp.

CHAPTER XVIII

Fabled Isle

The three occupants of the coracle reached the coast at noon, slapping at insects and scratching chafed patches where damp leathers had irritated their skin. By now Jaric wore one of the warrior's wristbands. The young man who had offered the gift had received in exchange the cuff torn off Ivainson's second-best shirt. Yet whatever ebullience had developed between clansmen and Firelord's heir during the coracle ride down the creek dissolved upon arrival at the estuary. The two warriors became broodingly silent from the instant they stepped ashore. While the gulls screamed and dove overhead, they sauntered onto the beach head, stripped, and without a word or a glance at Jaric, began to scour their muddy leathers clean with sand.

Left at a loss, and worn more than he cared to admit by the journey, Jaric finally searched out *Callinde*. She rested a short distance up the shore-line, beached dry above the tide mark. At first glance, little aboard her appeared amiss, but a stone's throw off her bow, between water and the ribbed detritus of weed left by the sea, lay a blackened patch in the sand. A great fire had burned there not long in the past. Abruptly Jaric felt a chill roughen his flesh.

Sand rustled beside him. He looked up to find one of the warriors at his side. "Tell me what happened," Ivainson said softly.

The clansman regarded him with expressionless eyes. "This is not a thing for telling under the daylight, *Ciengarde*."

Wind blew, stirring Jaric's hair; the plumage stitched to his tribal waistband twisted right and left against his palm. The sun overhead suddenly seemed too hot, and the air, inexpressibly icy. "Tell me," he repeated. "In the dark or the light, as *Ciengarde* I have the right to know."

The clansman bowed his head. As if signaled by the gesture, his companion down the beach shook sand from his leathers and arose. He walked still naked to his tribe fellow's side, and incongruously, Jaric realized they were brothers.

"We wait, then, for the twilight," said the elder.

Jaric nodded, and without speaking strode off to tend *Callinde*. He spent the afternoon sanding away splinters where arrows and spears had scarred her planking, and scouring the odorous stains left by half-devoured fish heads. Then he set lines and sails to rights, and mended the worn shank of a stay. In time the sky reddened. As the sun sank beneath the western rim of the sea, a high, keening wail called him from his labors. The hillmen stood upon the beach, their shadows trailing across the black-ened area where fires had burned not forty days before. They sank to their knees and squatted as the last sunlight died, and Jaric joined them. The cries of the gulls faded in the air. Twilight silvered the shoreline as, in words and stilted pictures scrawled in chilly sand, the heir of Ivain Firelord learned what the tribes of Cael's Falls had sacrificed to save him.

The clansmen ended their account with a ritual song of lament. Then, unwilling to bed down in a place where blood had been shed, they arose and silently disappeared into the woods. Full dark had fallen. Jaric knelt motionless in the starlight beside the dead circle of ash. For a long time he listened to the rush and boom of incoming tide. Throughout he ago-nized for each and every life his reluctance had destroyed; the months he had tarried at Landfast searching for an alternative to his inheritance had been paid for by the deaths of thirty-eight men and women, and twelve children, without counting the old seeress's first successor, who had per-ished during her ritual of initiation.

Jaric regarded the ashes, black as a pit in the darkness. Once he would not have understood the loyalty of the clans of southwest Elrinfaer, who had answered a summons that forced days and nights of travel with little food and no sleep, all for the sake of a stranger. That children had fallen ill under the hardships, and a wife had been left by the wayside in the throes of childbirth, could not be permitted to matter. The seeress had called the clans for a cause that brooked no delay. Jaric closed his hands into fists; the time was too late for regret. So said the young clansman who had recounted the struggle on the strand, where every tribe answerable to the shrine of Cael's Falls had stood forth to challenge the Thienz. The demons had guarded the Firelord's heir in force, and the powers they exerted upon the mind were by far too dangerous for a small band of raiders. Even children were needed to preoccupy the enemy. Unless Jaric was recovered alive, Shadowfane's triumph over humanity would inevitably follow, and even a single Thienz survivor might escape with the Keys to free the Mharg.

Victory had come to the clans, but at cost. The old seeress had died breaking the hold upon Jaric's mind. Her second, surviving successor was gifted with great talent, but woefully undertrained. Much knowledge had been lost. Admitting this, the young clansman had shrugged. "The sea will wear away the strongest shoreline, but *Ciengarde* must sail if the land is to remain fertile. Can a man abjure the will of the Presence, and live?"

Jaric traced a finger through the ash that remained of the thirty-eight who had died, among them the father and the sister of the brothers who had escorted him to *Callinde*. He drew a shuddering breath, but did not weep for the young boy who later had run himself to exhaustion and death, to bring the herbs and minerals the Presence had named to the priestess, that an antidote for Thienz venom could be mixed to keep hope alive.

Once the burden of such relentless sacrifice would have broken Ivainson Jaric. But not now; he had changed profoundly in the months between Landfast and his striving for the Isle of the Vaere. Now Jaric laid his palms upon gritty earth and quietly swore his oath to the dead. *Callinde* would sail at dawn.

That night, wrapped in the damp shelter of the mainsail, he dreamed of black ships, a fleet so vast that the ocean was sheared into foam by the streaming lines of wake. Wind moaned through a cabled forest of rigging, and through its dissonance, Taen's voice cried warning: Maelgrim Dark-dreamer sailed with these Thienz. If Jaric was overtaken by the brother enslaved to Shadowfane, Keithland's future would be irrevocably lost. Then the voice of Taen was joined by the wails of the hilltribes' dead. And always, relentlessly, the demon ships converged upon the southwest reaches.

In the dream, Jaric hardened lines until his hands bled. He guided *Callinde*'s steering oar with hairsbreadth precision, and coaxed maximum advantage from each gust. Yet old Mathieson's boat was too clumsy. The demon fleet gained effortlessly. Enemy sails swelled and eclipsed the sky, blanketing Jaric in shadow. Somewhere he heard Taen shouting frantic instructions; but the dark smothered her words beyond all understanding.

That moment, someone kicked his ankle. Jaric started, roused, and shot upright amid a clatter of sail hanks. He blinked sweat from his eyes, breathing hard, and by the canvas that slid loose around his shoulders recalled that *Callinde* lay beached on the shore of south Elrinfaer. The seeress of Cael's Falls stood over him. Her scarred eyes were tied with a veil that streamed in the breeze like smoke; stars shimmered faintly through gauzy folds, jewels for the unseen face beneath.

"*Ciengarde,* you are leaving at sunrise."

Startled afresh by her prescience, and wrung with the horrors left by dreams, Jaric nodded. He dragged himself warily upright and braced his weight against the back-canted shaft of the steering oar. "I must, Lady."

But the seeress had not come to deter him. "You seek the Vaere, *Ciengarde.*" Away from the echoing grotto, her voice seemed unfamiliarly thin. Yet with none of the uncertainty of the young, she raised her blowing veils and regarded him with eyes that saw no living boy but a spirit-world of mysteries.

Jaric shivered.

The seeress ignored his discomfort. As if speaking to air, she repeated a directive given her by the Presence within the shrine of Cael's Falls. Then her dispassionate recitation ceased. With the faintest rustle of gauze she lowered her veils and departed.

Jaric watched her go, a shadow against the scrolled curl of waves breaking upon the sands. In time her form merged with the black circle of ash, and she seemed to vanish from the face of the earth.

Her presence might have been a vision; Jaric regarded the lift and surge of the breakers, and the sliding, silvery rush as the backwash slid seaward to mesh with the foam of incoming waves. He wept then, not for the dead, but for the aching rebirth of hope. Without doubt the black ships and Taen's warning had been true dreaming; the Lord of the Demons had sent Maelgrim Dark-dreamer forth from Shadowfane to hunt him. But the most powerful priestess to serve the Presence had spoken from her shrine for the second time in the long memory of the clans, to grant a city-born the most significant guidance so far received from any source. It might, perhaps, be enough to thwart the Dark-dreamer and the designs of his demon masters. In terms a sailor could understand, the Lady of Cael's Falls had given Ivainson Jaric the location of the Isle of the Vaere. She had not done so for the sake of dead clansmen, nor even for the continued security of humankind. She had gifted the Firelord's heir because he had learned to embrace his destiny, fully and finally, for his own sake.

Jaric surged to his feet. He banged open the chart locker and rummaged within for a map of the seas south and to the west of the Free Isles. There and then in the starlight he made a calculation, and estimated a crossing of three weeks, provided the winds held fair. Too restless to sleep, he arose and checked *Callinde*'s stores; then, grateful for the water and provisions already laid in by the generous hands of the clansmen, he stamped on his boots. West winds tumbled the feathers on his warrior's wristband as he rigged blocks to drag *Callinde* toward the sea. Jaric set his teeth against the lingering weakness of the Thienz venom. Determined, pressured by hope and the bitterest of goals, he labored through the effort of launching.

At last, sweat-drenched and panting and ready to board, he stood in the shallows and looked back. The beach spread pale by starlight, blighted by the fire scar that had honored the bravery of thirty-eight dead. Jaric repeated their names one by one, then hauled his tired frame over *Callinde*'s high thwart. His hands trembled as he shook out canvas, and his head swam with dizziness. Slowly, painstakingly, *Callinde*'s bow swung. Her sails slapped taut to the wind. With apparent reluctance, Mathieson's ungainly craft responded to the shove of the breeze and gathered way, her wake a faint lisp over the deeper boom of surf.

Jaric turned his face to the sea. No longer did he sail for Taen alone, nor for the civilization so precariously preserved within the painted towers at Landfast. The wild tribes of Keithland had sacrificed loved ones for a future. To them he owed a blood debt that only the Cycle of Fire could absolve; lastly, for himself, nothing less could bring peace.

In the morning, when the two brothers assigned watch over Jaric returned to their post, they found the beach deserted. The dark, seared circle left by the fire for the slain was slashed across by the white drag mark left by *Callinde*'s keel.

The early part of the crossing passed smoothly. Mild weather lingered, and the winds blew steadily from the east. Days, Jaric basked in the sunlight, warily watching the horizon for sails that never appeared. Nights, he thought of Taen, while the stars wheeled above *Callinde*'s masthead, and the sails flapped gently to the dance of breeze and swell. Slowly the strength sapped by the Thienz venom returned. As league after league passed under the old boat's keel, Jaric's bouts of dizziness subsided; the morning came when navigational sights no longer blurred his vision. His shoulders and back deepened with new tan, except for reddened, angry weals left by Thienz teeth in his flesh. But now the scars itched more than they ached.

When the weather finally broke and rain rolled in from the south, the Firelord's heir had regained most of his health. Though his hands blistered upon the steering oar, he did not complain, but meticulously minded his heading, and checked and rechecked the horizon. No black fleet appeared. The sea heaved gray and foam-flecked, league upon empty league. Shearwaters wove like weavers' shuttles through the warp and weft of the swell, and once a pair of dolphins came to sport in the bow wave. Jaric watched their antics with poignant longing, aware as never before how circumscribed his own freedom had become.

Callinde crossed the latitude of Islamere. Jaric celebrated by eating the last of his dried apples, for the crossing to the Isle of the Vaere was now over halfway complete. No black fleet breasted the horizon to waylay him. Sunset spattered the waters bloody bronze, while a full moon rose like a pearl on gray velvet in the east. Jaric washed his shirts and tied them to the backstay to dry. Then, soothed by the familiar flap of laundry, the slap of loose reef points, and the creak and work of the hull, he settled barechested in his accustomed niche at the helm and waited for dark.

At midnight he awakened with the chill uncertainty that all was not well. The moon shone bright as new coin-silver overhead. *Callinde*'s decking gleamed in planes of shadow and light; no weather threatened. Each sail carried its burden of wind in perfect trim. The boat breasted the crest of a swell. The ropes bracing the steering oar creaked taut and slackened, and the yard bumped as *Callinde* dipped toward the trough, all sounds repeated a thousand times, but now their rhythm did not reassure. Jaric swept his eyes across a horizon etched white by moonlight. He saw no silhouettes of dark boats bearing down from the west. Only the sliding cross-hatch of ocean waves met his search, yet for some reason that set his teeth on edge.

He rose, and started violently as a damp shirt sleeve slapped his throat. *Callinde* splashed over the crest of another swell. Jaric yanked the offending laundry down and screwed it into a ball, which he wedged beneath the aft thwart. Jumpy as a cat, he paced port and starboard, checking sheet lines as he went. Nothing required adjustment. Finally, in sharpest unease, Jaric hooked the thong at his collar and closed his fingers around the hard basalt edges of the Keys to Elrinfaer. The stone felt cold beneath the leather; and the horizon showed no change.

Demons were there nevertheless, awaiting him. Jaric sensed their presence as surely as he breathed, and that certainty threatened to suffocate him. For this encounter, his peril was tenfold greater, since the weeks he had lain ill of Thienz venom had granted Shadowfane's second fleet time to ply south. Maelgrim Dark-dreamer sailed this time to intercept him. Jaric returned to the steering oar and gripped its solid wood with hands gone slippery with sweat. He owned no sorcerer's training to defend himself. Doomed by his human frailty, he bent his head and apologized for the hilltribes' dead, and old Mathieson, and Anskiere of Elrinfaer trapped in the ice. Then, as if memory were a catalyst, the thought of the Stormwarden gave rise to a desperate expedient. Jaric reached again for the pouch at his neck. With shaking hands, he jerked the thong open and drew forth the black-and-gold-barred length of the stormfalcon's feather. It gleamed silver-black by moonlight, seed of the most ruinous gale ever bound to a weathermage's bidding. Once that same storm had smashed a war fleet; another time Jaric had battled the edge of its violence on a hell-ridden passage from Mearren Ard to Cliffhaven. *Callinde* yet bore the scars from the batter of rampaging seas. In his hands Jaric cradled all of nature's most killing fury, conjured with the powers of the Vaere-trained he had most sworn to abhor; yet no other option remained. Here, alone, as prey of demons and the target of Maelgrim Dark-dreamer's hate, the feather and its potential for destruction offered the only weapon to hand.

Jaric dared not pause for second thoughts. If he did, cowardice would surely unman him. With a harsh, unsuppressible quiver of apprehension, he lifted the knife-keen stormfalcon's quill between his fingers, waited for a gust, and released it.

The feather skimmed away across the wave crests. Jaric watched its flight with his heart pounding, but no blue-tinged aura of force snapped into being. The weathermage's powers did not manifest to whip wind and wave to violence and storm. Agonized and uncertain, the heir of Ivain stood with his fists glued to the steering oar. Powerless to change the inevitable, he steadied to meet his fate. For Taen, for the dead clansmen of south Elrinfaer, for the sorcerer doomed to the ice, for his own integrity's sake, he must not quit until he had met his measure. *Callinde* would sail until the killing dreams of Maelgrim and his pack of Thienz manifested for the victory. Then Jaric resolved to hurl the Keys to Elrinfaer into the sea; afterward, if luck favored him, he might act swiftly enough to run his rigging knife through his heart, even as his father had before him, to spare the men of Keithland from the Firelord's powers which would assuredly ravage and destroy.

Far downwind from *Callinde*'s course, the stormfalcon's feather fluttered and spun, and settled finally upon the breast of the sea. It did not sink, but drifted there, a line silvered like a pen stroke in moonlight. But to a Dreamweaver's perception, the quill appeared as a bar of etched blue,

haloed with the fainter lattice of wards that held its violence in check.
Only one sorcerer in Keithland could unleash the great tempest from its
bonds.

Far off on Imrill Kand, Taen drew a shaking breath. Wind teased her
hair from her hood and set it streaming over her cheek. She brushed the
strands aside and her hand came away wet with tears. Days she had
watched, agonized, while Jaric closed the distance between Elrinfaer and
the demon fleet. Though he sailed to certain defeat she had dared not
intervene, even to offer the boy the comfort of her awareness. If she tried
any contact at all, her brother's twisted talents might sense her probe.
With his pack of Thienz to augment his powers, Maelgrim could obliterate her control and, through her, strike Jaric down. But now the stormfalcon's feather and Ivainson's brazen courage offered dangerous and
desperate hope.

Taen clenched her hands to still their shaking. Alone on the moon-
blanched tors above the harbor, she gathered her powers as Dreamweaver
and disturbed the sleep of Anskiere of Elrinfaer. For the continued survival of Keithland, she begged that he unbind the wards which curbed his
most terrible gale.

Dawn failed to brighten the southeast reaches of the Corine Sea. Mantled in clouds and sooty darkness, wind howled and slapped down out of
the north. *Callinde*'s spanker banged over into a jibe with such force that
her hull keeled and pitched Jaric off his feet. He fetched up against the
sail locker, knocked breathless, while the steering oar wrenched loose, and
two tons of antique fishing boat wallowed and careened through the spray.
The next gust nearly swamped her.

Jaric received a dollop of seawater in the face. Spitting and coughing,
he clawed through falling spray to the mast. He dared not think of bailing
before he reduced sail. Already the halyards hummed, plucked by the
unseen hands of the gusts. Dirty fingers of cloud streaked the sky to the
northeast and waves from that quarter raised ragged crests that exploded
into spindrift off the stern. Squinting against the burn of blown salt, Jaric
hauled the main down in flapping disarray. The forces of Anskiere's storm
had assuredly found release, for since dawn the weather had deteriorated
with unnatural speed. If *Callinde* were not quickly stripped to bare poles,
she would be battered to slivers.

Skinning his fingers in his haste, Jaric bundled the spanker beneath
the stern seat. Forward, the jib banged and jerked in rising gusts, slamming
fearful vibrations through the hull. The main yard thrashed against the
mast, and the waves seethed and hissed, bearded angrily with whitecaps.
Jaric wrestled the buck of the deck, and managed to furl the square main.
But the jenny fouled with the head stay, and the whipping loops of her
sheets had to be cut before they snapped themselves to tassels. Bruised
from crashing against stray bits of tackle, Jaric stumbled aft. Water sloshed

and sucked at his ankles. The curved sternpost kicked and dipped against sky as *Callinde* careened down a trough. Fighting for balance, Jaric slashed the lashing on the helm and struggled to wrestle his boat on a downwind course. Within an hour his hands were bleeding; still the waves steepened, until the bow dipped low and the surfing slide of *Callinde* threatened to punch her prow headlong into the sheer rise of the sea.

She would have to be slowed lest she pitchpole. After struggling to lash the steering oar, Jaric tore a length off the headsail and rigged a sea anchor. Though the safest course was to hang bow to and ride out the storm, he cleated his line to the sternpost. Then, shaking wet from his eyes, he braced his feet between the binnacle and the chart locker and grimly took the helm once again. If Anskiere's tempest were to founder him, he intended to go down on course for the Isle of the Vaere.

But the hours that followed became an agony of endurance more terrible than anything he could have imagined; the demands of his boat increased to a succession of critical disasters, each one of which threatened survival. The wind increased and buffeted his ears near to deafness. Seas heaped up in green, towering mountains whose heights wore spray like snow blizzards. To leave the helm under such conditions invited disaster. Yet as fittings tore loose, and lines frayed, Jaric had no choice. He lashed the oar, and relied on luck to keep his craft from broaching. Through a maelstrom of boiling foam, *Callinde* corkscrewed and thrashed, trounced like a chip in a millrace. Her mast whipped violently against her stays, stretching stout cable like taffy. Jaric looped belaying pins through and twisted up the slack in a terrified, stop-gap attempt to keep his spars aloft where they belonged. And he bailed, miserably, until his back muscles quivered with the weakness of exhaustion. If he paused, even for a minute, the weight of shipped water might founder his tiny craft.

Still the storm came on. Rain lashed down and lightning ripped the sky. Mathieson's stout planks flexed and sprung, and *Callinde*'s caulking loosened like wisps of dirty hair. Submerged to his elbows in bilge, Jaric labored on his knees to slow the leaks with oakum, then patched with old canvas when his earlier remedies failed. Above him, the compass spun like a drunk. The steering oar banged until the fittings threatened to crack, and to preserve those parts he could not replace, Jaric was forced to draw the pin and lash his rudder inboard. Tillerless now before the might of Anskiere's tempest, *Callinde* reeled her hapless way west.

Once Jaric saw a length of dark timber adrift in a snarl of cord. Through bruises and misery, and weariness that ached him to the bone, he managed a ragged laugh. At least one demon boat fared worse than he; yet if Mathieson's handiwork escaped ruin, the Dark-dreamer also might survive. Taen's brother was a sailor born; on board the pinnace from *Crow*, he had weathered this tempest once before. If Jaric were to reach the Isle of the Vaere to gain his mastery, he would still have to win past Maelgrim.

The eye of the storm passed over on the second morning, bringing a sickly, yellow-tinged sky, and a lull that left the seas sloshing and confused as the tilted contents of a witch's cauldron. Jaric seized the interval to whip *Callinde*'s sloppy stays; then he bailed, endlessly, his torn hands bound with wisps of frayed sail. He ached for sleep as the dying might plead for light. Instead he worked like a madman; by the nature of great gales, he could expect to be hammered with redoubled violence on the west side of the storm. Then the winds would reverse direction, against his desired course. Now, if the watery disc of the sun glimpsed through the clouds at noon could be trusted, the storm had driven him all but aground on the Isle of the Vaere.

A chill roughened Jaric's skin. He looked up, perturbed, and through tangles of his own hair peered at the horizon. There, after days of brute suffering and struggle against the elements, lay a sight to strike him to the heart: a black sloop sailed against a dirty drift of storm cloud. Her course bore directly for *Callinde*. Stripped by the storm of his mists and illusions, Maelgrim Dark-dreamer closed in for his conquest.

Jaric cast down his bailing scoop. Screaming denial, he lunged to unfurl the main. Yet even as his fingers pried the halyards from the cleat, he understood that such effort was hopeless. The winds had already shifted west. With her headsail in shreds, *Callinde* could make no headway to weather. Cornered now without alternative, Jaric abandoned the sail. Left no time for recriminations, he reached with stinging fingers and jerked off the thong which hung Anskiere's wards from his neck.

The pouch was sodden, the knotted ties swollen impossibly with damp. Jaric cursed. The little air pocketed within might prevent the Keys from sinking if he cast them into the sea still wrapped. Dreading the attack which might rip his mind at any moment, Jaric reached for his rigging knife. Too frantic to agonize over failure, he slashed; and the cube of dark basalt tumbled out into his palm.

The surface of the stone was unnaturally warm to the touch. Jaric turned the Keys over, and light rinsed his face, sudden, blue-white, and blinding. The falcon device set into the face of the cube glowed with a fierce energy that waxed brighter by the second. Terrified such change might be provoked by the meddling of demons, Jaric smothered the brilliance with his hands. Contact blistered his flesh. He fell back with a cry, but the resonance in the ward stone died away, keyed to response by a force entirely separate. A flash like lightning split the air. Mast and yard and rigging jumped out, inked lines against light. The ocean gleamed bright as molten metal, and *Callinde* became consumed by a scintillating explosion of rainbows that spiraled Jaric downward into dark.

Blackness suffused the boy's senses for an unknown interval, then tore asunder as a crackling burst of energy rent the air. Sparks pocked his vision, cold-white as starfields called up by Llondian imaging. Light followed. Jaric opened his eyes to sunshine, bewildered, shaken, and now certain that the sorcery which had transformed storm-torn night into day-light was no invention of Anskiere's. The Keys to Elrinfaer were now cool in his hand. Ivainson tucked them in his shirt and gripped *Callinde's* thwart. Tackle creaked as he straightened to view his surroundings. No sign remained of the demon fleet. His boat drifted alone upon a sea gone calm as burnished metal. No land relieved the distant edge of the sky; only an odd, silvery haze hung over the horizon. For no reason Jaric could name, the air smelled *wrong,* as if the untimely advent of day had also altered the season. The wind carried a tang of frost.

A glance at the compass showed the needle spinning in lost circles across the cardinal points of direction. Jaric checked in alarm. Denied sure means of navigation, he sought the position of the sun, and that moment discovered he was not alone.

A tiny man sat on *Callinde's* bow. He perched on the wet wood like a toy, stiffly formal in a fawn tunic and dark brown hose. The laces of his sleeves and boot cuffs were fringed with feathers and bells. Black eyes regarded Jaric from a face nestled amid windblown tangles of hair and beard.

Jaric reached reflexively for the knife at his wrist. His hand slapped an empty sheath. Too late he recalled the dagger dropped in the moment when sorcery had ripped him from reality.

"Violence will not avail you." Bells jingled as the strange man sprang from the rail. *Callinde* failed to rock beneath his weight as he landed, and his shoulder barely topped the rim of the portside locker.

Jaric backed until the hard edge of the sternpost jabbed his spine. "Who are you?"

"Keeper of the Keys, do you not know?" The little man tilted his head, fetched a briar pipe from his pocket, and thrust the stem between his teeth. With no pause to strike a light, he blew a smoke ring in the air and vanished.

Jaric shouted in astonishment. He dashed to the mast, but found no trace of his strange visitor. Only the smoke ring remained, drifting into a smeared oval above the ripped fabric of the headsail.

"I am Tamlin, and you trespass upon the domain of the Vaere," said a sudden voice from behind.

Jaric spun. The creature stood poised on the chart locker, his wrinkled face insouciant. A fresh triplet of smoke rings drifted around his head.

Ivainson steadied shaken nerves, strove to act as if such vanishings and reappearings held no strangeness at all; but his voice betrayed uncertainty. The forces which had plucked him headlong from Maelgrim's path had been Vaerish, and the mystery of them overwhelmed. "Surely you know why I seek the fabled isle."

Tamlin gestured, his movement an indignant flurry of feathers and bells. "Fabled? You presently observe otherwise. And demons tracked you, even over water. That's trouble more grave than you know."

Aware the being he confronted would abide by no human code, Jaric answered with care. "A seeress named me the bane of demonkind."

"And well she may," said the Vaere. "But Kor's Accursed grow bold in their plot to defeat Keithland. Now, after centuries of striving, they have what they sought longest, a man with a sorcerer's potential whose loyalty they command. Maelgrim is their supreme weapon. Dare you oppose the designs of beings many times more powerful than yourself? You could die, and still save nothing."

Poised with his hands against the mast, Jaric felt his palms break into sweat. Had he traveled so far and overcome such odds, had hillfolk died to aid him in reaching this place, only to see him refused through Vaerish caprice? Shaken badly, Jaric fought through diffidence to respond. "I am the Firelord's son," he said grimly. "Gladly would I leave responsibility to another, but Ivain left no better heir than me."

Tamlin tilted his head as though waiting for the boy to qualify. But Jaric added nothing. At length the fey man raised his brows. "Very well. If you prove worthy of your father's heritage, you shall undertake the Cycle of Fire."

That moment, though the sun shone warm on his back, Jaric felt chilled to the heart.

Tamlin raised his chin. "Listen closely and follow my instructions. The weather will change. When it does, you must sail before the wind. Take no heed of your compass. If you delay, even for a fraction of an instant, your life could be forfeit." Beads, bells, and feathers jangled as the Vaere raised his arms. Without warning, he clapped his hands and vanished.

"Wait!" Not at all certain he had understood such instructions, Jaric shouted Tamlin's name.

The little man did not reappear. Almost immediately icy breezes puckered the sea. Caught with his spanker snarled and his jib in ribbons from the storm, Jaric leaped and freed his last functional sail. *Callinde*'s square main unfurled from the yardarm; fortunately the boat required no other canvas for a downwind course. Yet as the boy moved to set the sheets, he frowned in puzzlement, for what weather he received came from no fixed direction; the breeze ruffles on the water seemed contrary and unstable. Even as Jaric sought to decipher their patterns, lightning jagged the sky. The air went dark as ink. Wind howled astern like the roar of an angry giant. Jaric bounded aft and seized the steering oar, just as canvas cracked taut aloft. Deafened by a stupendous peal of thunder, he felt *Callinde* reel forward under the blind fury of the elements.

Jaric wrestled the helm by touch. Waves broke into whitecaps under the stern. Spray splashed his face, and wind stung his back, sharp as a midwinter gale with the scent of snow. But the boy had no chance to contemplate the inexplicable shift of seasons; whirled like a leaf in a maelstrom, he fought to steady his course. Sudden energy slashed the sky. For an instant, the air seemed to scintillate, smashed to a prismatic orchestra of color.

Then the wind died to a breath. *Callinde* rocked upright. Blocks squeaked as her canvas billowed and settled into a gentle curve from the yardarm. Jaric blinked, restored once more to sunlight. Spray-soaked and shaking, he found himself sailing under the mild warmth of spring. The ocean ahead lay empty no longer. An islet rose like an emerald amid the waves. Beaches glittered, trackless and fine as powdered marble beyond the surf, and dunes crowned with grasses lifted against darker strands of cedar. The trees themselves towered spear-shaft straight, unscathed by ocean storm or woodcutter's axe. Confronted by a shoreline so peaceful it seemed bewitched, Jaric forgot to breathe.

Surf nudged the steering oar. *Callinde* surged shoreward on the sparkling crest of a swell. Recalled to his seamanship, Jaric recovered his breath with a jerk. He cast the sheet lines free and swung the yard across the wind just as *Callinde*'s keel grated on sand. The son of Ivain caught a line and leaped the thwart. Barefoot, salt-stained, and weary, he splashed through the shallows and set foot on the Isle of the Vaere.

By its very stillness, the place intimidated; the presence of the boat seemed a blasphemous intrusion. Harried by uneasiness, Jaric immersed himself in the ordinary. With careful hands he landed *Callinde,* lowered the yard, and lashed the torn sails. While he delved among the spare lines for a block and tackle to beach his craft above the surf, Tamlin reappeared.

The little man gestured with an agitated flurry of bells. "No need for that, boy. Can't you see? The weather here never changes."

Jaric set his shoulder against the side of his boat, rope trailing from his fingers. "What about tide?"

The Vaere set his hands on his hips. "Mortal, you jest. Water and weather abide here unchanged, until the day the first riddle is answered, or unless Kor's Accursed learn the heart of Vaerish mystery."

Jaric restored the rope to the locker and reluctantly fastened the latch. *Callinde* had been the proudest possession of an aged fisherman; the boy hesitated to entrust her cherished hull to the vagaries of an enchanted isle.

Bells clashed as Tamlin stamped his foot. "Mortal fool. I am the master of space and time. Are you doubting my ability to safeguard simple timber and cloth?"

"No." Jaric ran his eye over the boat, distressed that wood and rigging should suddenly seem so frail. By the time he recovered the courage to inquire what the first riddle might be, Tamlin vanished. Not even footprints remained to mark the place where the Vaere had stood on the sand.

A mocking tinkle of bells sounded beyond the dunes. "Keeper of the Keys, no man since the founders of Keithland remembers the first riddle. But if you seek a sorcerer's mastery, you must go to the grove at the forest's center."

Jaric loosed an exasperated sigh. When Tamlin did not reappear, he rummaged through *Callinde*'s gear until he located his boots. Then, with a shrug of resignation, he donned his footgear and hiked inland toward the dark stand of cedars.

The forest was rich with shadows after the reflective brilliance of the beach. In a single step, Jaric plunged from light into trackless tangles of undergrowth. His feet sank soundlessly into moss. The wood sheltered no wildlife; at a glance he saw that deer had never browsed the lower branches of the trees. The ground showed no trace of game trails, and since the moment he landed, the only birdsong Jaric noticed had been the sour call of sand swallows. The sole sound to disturb the stillness was the snap of sticks beneath his boots.

The gloom deepened. At first Jaric attributed the dimness to denser foliage, but as he pressed forward through the matted growth of thicket and gully, sunbeams no longer dappled the moss underfoot. Farther on, the light which filtered through the trees shone eerily silver, as if in this forest time itself stood suspended in the interval between sunset and darkness.

"I am the master of time and space," Tamlin had declared at the seaside. Unable to locate the disc of the sun, denied even the crudest means of guidance, Jaric battled uneasiness. With no visible effort, the Vaere had caused day, night, and seasons to change upon the face of the open sea. Here the boy sensed that he trod soil beyond the borders of any land known by men.

The wood grew darker. Twigs and trunks lay limned against shadow like an etching rendered in moonlight; yet no moon gleamed overhead. Jaric's step faltered. Sweating with apprehension, he thought of Taen, remembered how her eyes looked when she laughed, or badgered Corley about his quick temper. Fear of the brother left free to murder in Keithland drove Jaric forward. He crashed recklessly through the next stand of overgrowth. Light glimmered ahead, soft as summer twilight. Jaric stopped in awe, all terror forgotten. Through the black fringes of the cedars he beheld the grove of the Vaere.

Grasses spread green beneath a towering circle of oaks. Gray trunks rose like pillars in the gloom, supporting leafy crowns which arched into a vaulted ceiling overhead. Jaric stepped to the edge of the clearing. He felt springy turf give under his boots. Constellations of tiny flowers studded the ground, and the strange, silvery light seemed to blur all concept of time. Here lay the magic and the mystery of the Vaere. No man could turn back from this place; to enter the grove was to yield mortal flesh to forces which could alter the progression of nature with impunity.

Jaric crossed the boundary of the oaks with barely a pause to reflect. A stressful, tempestuous year had passed since he had fled Morbrith Keep, clinging helplessly to the mane of a stolen horse. Here for the first time he found peace, and a silence more abiding than the central shrine in Kor's cathedral at Landfast. Jaric settled himself to wait. The perfume of the flowers hung heavy upon the air. Weary from Anskiere's storm, and lulled by the changeless twilight, he sat on the grass and rested.

At first nothing happened. Jaric had time to order his thoughts, to realize at last that his safety from demons was secured. Granted reprieve from the demands of survival, he examined the guilt so recently and painfully inflicted by the seeress, whose clansmen had died for his uncertainty at Landfast. This the grove's stillness touched also. Inside the achievement of Vaerish protection, life and death became framed by a greater truth. Jaric understood that for all her far-seer's wisdom, the Lady of Cael's Falls had accused him wrongly.

Had he chosen his Firelord's inheritance without first finding himself, even had he acted in earnest duty for loved ones he longed to protect, he would have failed Tamlin's initial assessment. The Stormwarden had stated as much from his icy prison on Cliffhaven. No man could be forced to a sorcerer's mastery. A challenge as stringent as the Cycle of Five required a whole heart and a settled mind.

Drowsy now, Jaric recalled another scene, and a half-forgotten promise of Anskiere's that he would receive his heart's desire if he succeeded in safeguarding the Keys to Elrinfaer. But the memory of the boy he had once been, and what outgrown longings might have shaped his hopes, became obscured by the vision of Taen. The last time he had seen her had been in *Moonless*'s chart room, the lantern tinting her skin with the delicacy of fine porcelain. Hair had cloaked her shoulders like starless night. Aching for the sight of her, but free now to appreciate love as a miracle separate from his happiness, Jaric pondered the words she had spoken then. *"The sanctuary towers contain keys to Kor's Sacred Fires, also answers to the riddles of eternal space and time."*

Now the boy wondered whether Vaerish mystery might be linked to the same knowledge. But weariness overwhelmed him before he could reflect. Ivainson Jaric closed his eyes. Surrendered to the enchantment of the fabled isle, he fell dreamlessly asleep, even as his father had before him.

Epilogue

Anskiere's great storm blew and raged across the southwest reaches, to spend its fury in the empty seas far south of the Free Isles. The sorcery of its binding dissipated finally, leaving swells that churned and rolled green, bearded with flotsam and frothy mats of weed. There, across leagues of empty ocean, Taen threaded her awareness in dream-search. She found no boats, only smashed spars and ripped lengths of planking, rafted together sometimes with shreds of sails and snarled tackle. The Storm-warden's tempest had ravaged the dark fleet from Shadowfane. Scavenger fish now fed on the remains of the Thienz; if Maelgrim Dark-dreamer escaped the same fate, the Dreamweaver's probe detected no trace of his presence.

At last, content, Taen withdrew. As she collapsed the net of her awareness, she sensed isolated points of energy across Keithland's isles and mainlands. Here the seeress of Cael's Falls laid flowers of thanks and offering before the spring which gave rise to her powers. North and east, the King of Pirates penned orders on Cliffhaven, recalling his captains from patrol off Felwaithe and directing them instead to attend the merchant shipping which plied the straits. And in burrows in the wilds well hidden from the eyes of men, Llondelei demons reared dumb, unenlightened cubs with one less of their far-seers' prophecies waiting for fulfillment. The heir of Ivain Firelord had safely reached haven on the Isle of the Vaere, to challenge the Cycle of Fire for his mastery.

Taen roused fully to sunlight and the inquisitive tug of a goat who sampled a taste of her hair. She shouted, laughing, and, with the mercurial energy she had always shown as a child, sprang to her feet and chased the creature back to the flock. Then she turned her face to the wind, which smelled of autumn, and started home. Shadowfane still held demons who hated and plotted, while Jaric must brave the perils of a sorcerer's passage to power. But when the winds blew fair and favorably, the daughter of an Imrill Kand fisherman would not fret upon storms that might bring ruin. Tomorrow could only come after today.

Shadowfane

Book Three of the
Cycle of Fire

For Raymond E. Feist
true friend, talented author,
and
(my influence to the contrary)
an incurable enthusiast of jazz and the Chargers

ACKNOWLEDGMENTS

The finish of a series requires a great deal of thanks to the many individuals who helped the author along the way. In particular my appreciation goes to the following individuals, for efforts that made all the difference:

Terri Windling, for seeing three books between the lines of two, and asking gently to make it happen; Virginia Kidd, for her tireless efforts of negotiation; and Jonathan Matson and Abner Stein, for the same, but overseas; Soni Gross and Fern Edison, whose contributions above and beyond the normal call helped make the start a success; Peter Schneider, for off-the-cuff assistance with promotion; my parents, who put up with a lot of unreasonable dreams; my friend and former landlord, Daniel P. Mannix, who for eleven years gave me guidance and a roof under which to create; Beth Fleisher, my editor, for sharing my passion for sailing and twisted plots; Gene Mydlowski, art director, for belief in an author who happens also to paint; Elaine Chubb, copy editor, whose unfailing devotion to detail is a mystery and a miracle all by itself.

Prologue

The seeress of the well in Gaire's Main woke gasping in the straw of the stables where she sheltered. She shivered, blind eyes milky in the moonlight that spilled from the loft. The visions that had broken her sleep racked her still, bringing terror beyond anything mortal. The seeress stirred ancient joints and rose. Clothed in scraps of knotted leather, she groped down the dusty ladder and made her way past stall and grain stores, then out into the waning autumn night.

Beyond the barn lay a crossroad and a trough awash with muddy puddles. The folk of Gaire's Main presently used the sacred spring as a watering place for beast and household; to them the seeress was a senile beggar woman given to strange outbursts and mumbling. But tonight no confusion blurred her movements. She knelt on the chill ground and scrabbled through pig droppings until she located the stone that founded the mystery of her craft.

The slab was black, laced with metallic streaks of gold, and rinsed clean by overflow from the spring. Tears brimmed from the seeress's lashless eyes as she laid her palms against the talisman. Energy welled from the contact. With a cry of agonized relief, she surrendered her burden of dreams to its current. . . .

In the wind-whipped darkness of an ocean roiled by the aftermath of a gale, a boat with tattered sails rolled hove to in the swell. There a blackhaired man dressed in the cottons of a fisherman reached out to an injured Thienz-demon who clung to a drift of timber in the waves. Neither kindness nor compassion prompted the man's action; his spirit was not human, an evil sensed palpably across the fabric of the seeress's dream.

The rescued demon was not to survive its deliverance from the waves. As its toadlike fingers closed upon the man's wrist, the seeress sensed its agony, the burning sting of salt splashed into its gills. Poisoned beyond healing, the demon endured only long enough to deliver its death-dream, which held intact the death-dreams of others who had perished earlier, in a backlash of forces brought about by no natural means.

These memories the Thienz impressed directly into the mind of the human in the boat, for their significance to mankind's enemies offered proof that an artifact of paramount significance still existed. Untempered and entire, the death-dream of the Thienz seared like magna through the young man's awareness. When he screamed, the seeress screamed with him, and the well-stone beneath her hands relayed the dying demon's legacy to mankind's most ancient defender. . . .

On an islet far distant from Gaire's Main, the old woman's sending cut like the cry of a dying doe across a grove of enchanted twilight; there an entity known as the Vaere received her images with an understanding not given to mortal men. The news promised grimmest consequences. The dying Thienz had stumbled upon a secret centuries old. When that knowledge reached the demon compact at Shadowfane, its full import would be recognized. Then would the wardenship of the Vaere itself become threatened. Now the untried talents of the sorcerer's heir but recently come to sanctuary offered the only expedient. If Ivainson Jaric failed to master his father's talents, if he failed in the Cycle of Fire while the compact unriddled the mystery of the Vaere, mankind would suffer extinction at the hands of demon foes. . . .

The seeress broke contact with a quivering sigh; and silence ominous as the calm before cataclysm settled over the grove of the Vaere.

CHAPTER I

Riddle

Cold came early to the wastes beyond Felwaithe; frosts rimed the lichens and traced a madman's patterns on the bare rock of the hills. Here, far north of Keithland's border and the lands inhabited by men, a single lantern burned in a hall of bleak stone. Within its circle of light, Scait, Demon Lord of Shadowfane, sat upon a chair fashioned from the bones and the hides of human victims. He pared his thumb spurs to needlepoints with a penknife, while an immature Thienz ornamented with beads crouched at his feet, froglike limbs folded against its loins.

Scait flexed scaled wrists and paused in his sharpening. His upper lip curled over rows of sharklike teeth as he addressed his groveling underling. "What has occurred that Thienz elders send a hatchling to trouble my thoughts? Speak, tadpole! What tidings do you bring?"

The Thienz cowered against the icy stone floor. The sovereign of Shadowfane quite often killed out of temper, and this youngster brought ill news of the worst import. It flapped its gills in distress. "Most-mighty, I bring word of the boats sent into Keithland to capture Ivainson-Firelord's-heir-Jaric. Your servants have failed. Jaric has reached sanctuary on the Isle of the Vaere."

Scait hissed explosively. "*Seed-of-his-father, accursed!* How did one wretched boy slip past five dozen Thienz elders?"

Beads chinked against stillness; the Thienz battled an overwhelming instinct to flee, yet the flash of displeasure in its master's sultry eyes did not metamorphose into blows. Its crest flattened in reluctance against its blunt head, the youngster prepared to offer images of storm and death, and the wreckage of the fleet that had failed in its directive to take the gold-haired son of Ivain Firelord.

But the sovereign Lord of Shadowfane refused direct sharing. Instead he twisted the blade of his knife and pricked at the stuffed human thigh that comprised the throne arm. "I would know the particulars of Jaric's escape from one who is senior, and experienced. Fetch me Thienz-eldest, for no other will suffice."

The young demon bobbed hasty obeisance, then scuttled from the dais, its discharge of fear and relief a palpable stink in the air. Once clear of the steps, it spun and fled around the mirror pool set into the floor beyond. Scait watched with slitted eyes as it vanished into the gloom of the doorway; rage born of frustration bristled the long hackles at his neck. He had hoped to capture Jaric, enslave and manipulate his Firelord's potential for the ruin and sorrow of humanity. Now this recent failure by the Thienz invited terrible risk. Ivainson Jaric might survive the Cycle of Fire; then would humans gain another Vaere-trained sorcerer, one powerful enough to free Anskiere of Elrinfaer from his prison of ward-spelled ice. The paired threat of Stormwarden and Firelord would pose a serious inconvenience, if not a direct impediment, to the conquest planned by the demon compact at Shadowfane.

Scait paced, knife clenched between spurred fingers. He ground his teeth in agitation until the Thienz elder he had summoned presented itself before the dais.

Lest an underling of no consequence sense his distress, the Lord of Shadowfane smoothed his long hackles and sat. As the elder completed its obeisance, he scraped one spur across the bared edge of his knife and demanded, "How did Ivainson-Firelord's-heir-Jaric come to reach the Isle of the Vaere?"

The Thienz replied in words, the barest ruffle of its crest hinting defiance. "Ivain's-get-Jaric arranged the release of a weather ward of Anskiere's." Offered the clear, precise image of a stormfalcon's feather, and the blue-violet shimmer of sorcery that had released a ruinous gale across the southwest reaches, Scait bared his teeth.

The Thienz hastily continued. "Storm-death did not bring the bane of all Thienz-cousins sent hunting. Another hazard entirely prevented their closing with the prey." The Thienz closed tiny eyes and sent the death-dream salvaged from a failing survivor by Maelgrim Dark-dreamer. In precise, empathic images, the Lord of Shadowfane shared the last memories of three Thienz who had huddled in drenched misery aboard a boat many leagues to the south.

Only moments before death, they whimpered among themselves, their shared thoughts riddled with terror. The storm that Ivain Firelord's heir had caused to be unleashed had bashed and capsized and drowned the crews of seven companion vessels. The Thienz who sailed aboard the last boat trembled, fearful their own doom would follow.

Scait hissed. The dagger dangled forgotten in his grip as the doomed creatures' vision filled his sensors. At one with the memories of the Thienz who had crouched afraid in that-boat-sent-to-apprehend-Jaric, he, too, beheld the roiling and spume-frothed crests of gale-whipped ocean.

Suddenly the air seemed to shimmer. Sky and swells rippled, blurred, and shifted into pearly mist; then fog in turn dissolved, transformed to a prismatic chaos of energy, all shattered bands of color and light. The display lasted only a moment before cruel fields of energy blistered the Thienz's bodies. They fell, crying curses, the agony of their dying accompanied by wood that popped and steamed, and canvas that burst sullenly into flame.

The dream ended. Scait's lids snapped open, unveiling irises hard as topaz. Needle rows of teeth gleamed as he framed words in speculation. "Tell me, lowly toad. What memory does that death-dream call to mind?"

Possessed of the eidetic recall common to all demons, the Thienz squirmed uneasily upon the carpet. "This death was the same as that dreamed by ancestor-among-the-stars who died, trapped by the expanding field of a time anomaly when a ship drive malfunctioned. But such interpretation is questionable. Keithland's humans have lost all memory of technology."

"Not entirely." Scait snapped his jaws closed. Delicately he stroked his dagger across the arm of his throne. "Veriset-Nav," he mused triumphantly. "This dream gives proof beyond doubt. The navigational guidance module must have survived the crash of starprobe-*Corinne-Dane*-accursed. We have only to find it, and recover the unit intact, and our exile from home-star will be ended."

The Thienz wailed, its crest flattened against its earless skull. "Lord-highest, you suggest the impossible. Where can we seek? *Corinne Dane*'s emergency systems capsule plunged into ocean, destroyed." The Thienz paused to whistle soulfully, its tune an expression of knowledge lost.

But Scait ignored its protests. Preoccupied, he arose from his chair. Wire ornaments jangled against scaled knuckles as he paced the dais.

Like an ill-sewn frog puppet, the Thienz twisted its blunt head to follow its master's steps. "Mightiest, Set-Nav is lost, still."

"Perhaps not." Scait jerked to a stop. He leered down at the Thienz. "I say all along that Set-Nav may have hidden behind a persona called the Vaere."

At this the Thienz rocked back on webbed feet, snorted, then burst into croaking peals of laughter. "Mightiest, O mightiest, you surely jest! We know the Vaere! Human superstition, brought forward from earliest, most barbaric remnants of old Earth culture." All in the compact knew that Tamlin originated in a tale conceived by primitive ballad singers; funny indeed, if mankind might be witless enough to mistake the most sophisticated technology its people ever created with a make-believe creature of faerie!

"Silence!" Scait's short hackles lifted in warning. "Be still, one-who-forgets."

The demon beneath the dais quivered at the insult. It rolled whiteless eyes as Scait leaned over and thrust the knife toward its chin. "Myth or not, facts are these: Tamlin of the Vaere reputedly trained our greatest foe, Anskiere, and also Ivain Firelord. And, one-who-forgets, remember that humans possess no senses to differentiate between the dream-state and reality experienced! Recall that *Corinne Dane*'s Set-Nav guidance unit came equipped with mind-link modules."

Such machines could induce a man to dream for years, and still preserve his body. The Thienz blinked, jolted to sober reflection. The time-differential field of the star drive neatly accounted for the unnatural aging that afflicted those mortals who received their sorcerer's training from the Vaere.

Scait shot to his feet, eyes ablaze with excitement. "Now, one-who-forgets, let scornful laughter pucker your tongue with the taste and the texture of excrement. For I think humankind does not know its sorcerers are guided to mastery by technology its people once possessed."

The Thienz whuffed its gills, silent, while Scait subsided back into his chair. Strangely, terribly, the Demon Lord's reasoning suggested truth. Man might have forgotten his vanquished empire among the stars; yet an electronic guidance system endowed with intelligence, self-repair, and the logic to master the bewildering mathematics of interstellar navigation would never lose its loyalty, or its mission. As killers and imprisoners of creatures with paranormal endowment, Stormwarden and Firelord might indeed continue the starprobe *Corinne Dane*'s original directive: to discover means of defending mankind against the psionic warfare of aliens.

Curled in idle malice upon his chair of human remains, Scait qualified the Thienz's thought. "Toad, you misjudge. Deliberately Set-Nav may have cloaked its identity as Tamlin, that the compact might overlook its existence."

The Thienz twisted the tiny fingers of its forelimbs and moaned, while in abrupt agitation the Demon Lord stabbed the dagger to the hilt into stuffed human upholstery. "O toad, the death-dream of your companion brings promise of triumph-and-trouble. We must unravel the riddle of Tamlin, for time is precious. Ivainson-cursed-sorcerer's-heir-Jaric escaped us. Now, surely as stars turn, a firelord could emerge to balk us. If so, we might face the hatching of the Morrigierj unprepared."

The Thienz stiffened. It raised, then lowered its webbed crest, and a tremble invaded its limbs. The memories-of-ancestors knew Morrigierj, that grand-master entity spawned each three thousand years to bind the collective powers of the Gierj into a single force; of all sentients sworn to the compact of Shadowfane, the mindless Gierjlings owned a latent capacity for destruction that intimidated even the strongest demon. With a squeak of apprehension, the Thienz fled the chamber; it slid with a scrape of claws around the doorjamb and scuttled like a dog down the stairwell.

Scait laughed at its flight. His threat had been a lie designed to intimidate; when the silly Thienz paused to think, it would recall that no grand hatching could occur without maturity of a Morrigierj spore. Since his predecessor's death at Anskiere's hand, the Demon Lord held power against the machinations of ambitious subordinates; at best, his supremacy at Shadowfane was precariously secured. With his current plot to defeat mankind thrown into setback, underlings must be kept cowed to discourage rivals; for challengers there would be, unless Scait found means to counter the threat posed by the possibility of a new firelord. The discovery of Set-Nav, though of paramount significance, was of secondary importance to politics and power within the compact.

Scait thought bitterly upon Jaric. Once he had glimpsed the boy's aura; demon-perceived clarity had sensed the ringing patterns of energy that mapped a gifted human's aptitude for mastery of Sathid-bonded forces. Never until then had any demon imagined that humans, even rare ones, might hold so much latent affinity for power. Untrained, such individuals could easily be enslaved and turned to the detriment of their own kind; the loss of Jaric's talents stung doubly. Scait bristled his hackles in frustration. Humanity bred and proliferated like pest parasites. Except for the wizards inhabiting the towers at Mhored Kara, most were blind to the psychic energies of the mind. Perhaps among Keithland's teeming towns, other children born with such gifts were overlooked.

Scait blinked and shifted in his chair. If such children existed, they might be taken and exploited. Yet members of the compact could not cross into Keithland to explore without drawing notice. Subterfuge would be necessary.

The lantern suddenly flickered; in its failing light, Scait's teeth flashed in a leer of wild excitement. There existed one for whom such restrictions would not exist. Maelgrim Dark-dreamer's talents were already controlled by the compact; through him, a way could be found to conduct such a search undetected. Excited now, Scait reached in thought for the mind of the Thienz elder who had recently departed his presence.

'Where is Maelgrim now?'

The image sent in reply was prompt, but clouded with a resentment most probably effected by the ruse concerning the Morrigierj; Scait chose forbearance in his lust for information. All of Maelgrim's Thienz crew had perished of salt poisoning; alone in a boat severely battered by the aftermath of the storm set loose by Jaric, the Dark-dreamer currently struggled to patch tattered canvas, that he might sail for Shadowfane and the north. Scait clicked his spurs in irritation; his new plan must wait until the boy-slave-human returned, a delay that might extend through several months, since winter's inevitable gales would brew up weather unfavorable for passage. Forced to patience, the Demon Lord brooded upon the possibilities presented by rediscovery of the Veriset-Nav computer. Hours passed. The lamp flickered out and predawn gloom infused Shadowfane's empty hall. Spurred fingers stroked the dagger left embedded in cured human flesh, while, outside, wind wailed like a funeral dirge across the frost-blasted fells.

Twenty-seven generations after the fall of the probe ship *Corinne Dane*, the navigational computer that had calculated courses between stars analyzed its latest acquisition, a sorcerer's son who aspired to undertake the Cycle of Fire. Small, lean, and callused from the rigors of the storm that had delivered him to the fabled isle, Jaric was remarkably like his sire, Ivain; except here and there lay clues to differences that extended beyond mere flesh.

The boy's sun-bleached hair and seafarer's tan seemed oddly misplaced under the red-lit glimmer of the control panels. His clothing had been meticulously mended with a sail needle, before being torn again. His rope belt was not tasseled, but perfectly end-spliced; only his bootlaces revealed haste or impatience, one being tied with sailors' knots, the other whipped into tangles that the mechanical arms of the robots unsnarled with difficulty. The body beneath the clothing proved bruised and abraded, the legacy of hardship and stress.

The father had chosen his path to mastery in far less agony of spirit; unlike his son, he had arrived upon the isle with a companion at his side, his passage uncontested by hunting packs of Thienz. Much hope or much setback might arise from Jaric's experience. Unaffected by sentiment, the guardian of mankind's future reviewed his candidacy for the Cycle of Fire with precise and passionless logic.

The boy under scrutiny remained unaware that the creature he knew as Tamlin of the Vaere was an entity fabricated by a sophisticated array of machinery. Taken into custody from the woodland clearing where he had succumbed to drugged sleep, and bundled by robots into a metal-walled chamber hidden beneath the soil, Ivainson Jaric presently rested within a life-support capsule that once had equipped the starship's flight deck.

Servo-mechanisms labored over his body, completing hookups that in the past had enabled human navigators to interface with the Veriset-Nav's complex circuitry. Like every human visitor before him, Jaric would experience only dreams during his stay upon the fabled isle.

The Vaere had kept its true form secret since the crash of *Corinne Dane*. Ejected intact from its parent ship, the unit retained power generators and drive field; but with Starhope fallen to enemies, a distress flare would draw attack rather than rescue. Set-Nav found itself shepherd to refugees incapable of defending its data from aliens who could reprogram its functions for their own use. Even as the germ plasms of earth-type flora and fauna had survived and altered the face of Keithland, so had the guidance computer changed, adapted, and evolved, cloaked in a guise of myth. Despite time and attrition, its primary directive remained. Set-Nav even yet sought means to end the predations of psionically endowed aliens that mankind now called demons.

In its latest, most effective offensive, Veriset-Nav trained psi-talented humans to mastery of a double Sathid-link that gained them direct control over the elements. Jaric was the latest candidate for a procedure fraught with danger.

Of countless human subjects, only Anskiere and Ivain had survived to achieve dual mastery; but their success had justified the deaths of their predecessors. Paired crystals had granted them power enough to eradicate some species of demons and imprison others. The task of freeing Keithland from threat had begun. But talent capable of training for such feats was sparse, ever difficult to obtain; Ivainson, whose life was already sought by demons, possessed potential both precious and rare.

A switch closed. Lights flickered green over the access console, tinting

Jaric like a wax figure while programs designed for complex navigational mathematics exhaustively mapped his potential. The Vaere matched the crippling self-doubt of this boy's childhood against his determination to achieve a Firelord's inheritance. It tallied strength, weakness, and raw potential and completed its model with direct observations shared by the Dreamweaver, Taen. Information streamed into the data banks, then transmuted, meshed and interwoven to a sequence of intricate probability equations. Inflexibly logical, the Vaere calculated Jaric's potential to survive the dual mastery that comprised the Cycle of Fire.

The conclusion was disturbing. Never in Keithland history had the Vaere detected such raw potential for power in the mind of a man; yet the latent ability Jaric possessed proved coupled with a personality sensitive to the point of fragility, balanced upon a selfhood newly and precariously established. Considered alone, this analysis might have disqualified the boy from training; but now, with demons aware of the origins of the Vaere, the slimmest opportunity counted.

An access circuit closed. Alongside Jaric's statistics the Vaere added the composite analysis of Keithland, then an estimated projection of the Dark-dreamer's acquired power. The forecast proved bleak. Maelgrim's mastery derived from a Sathid already dominated by Thienz-demons; his talents would be like his sister's, but reversed. Where Taen wove dreams to heal and defend, her brother would spin visions to destroy. She could influence individuals; but with the combined might of Shadowfane's compact to back him, Maelgrim might instigate wholesale madness, corrupt governments, or incite soldiers to war against the very cities they were armed to protect. Before such an onslaught, even the defenses at Landfast might topple.

The Vaere sequenced scenarios of possible countermoves for days and nights without letup. At the end, only one held hope. Shadowfane's invasion might be deterred if the Stormwarden, Anskiere of Elrinfaer, were freed from the ice. That task required a firelord's skills. Time was too short to seek an alternate for the Cycle of Fire, even should a second candidate exist within Keithland's population.

Had the Vaere reacted as a mortal, such a quandary would have caused grief and trepidation; being a machine of passionless logic, it executed decisions within a millisecond. Jaric must be placed in jeopardy; after a brief training period, the boy must attempt Earthmastery. If he retained control after primary bonding, he must go on to attempt mastery of a second Sathid matrix, the most difficult challenge a sorcerer could attempt. He must endure and survive the Cycle of Fire. Should he fail, if the Sathid entities he must battle for dominance conquered his will, both he and Anskiere would perish. Then the defense of Keithland would rest upon a Dreamweaver's frail and inadequate resources.

Lights blinked and vanished, and the consoles went dark beside the amber glow of the life-support unit. Veriset-Nav initiated an entry command, and the circuitry that cross-linked the master navigator's capsule shifted status to active. Monitors winked to life, glowing blue over a boy framed in a nest of silvery wires. The heir of Ivain Firelord stirred in the depths of his sleep, even as the guidance systems from *Corinne Dane* induced the first of a series of dreams designed to prepare him for the trials of a sorcerer's mastery.

Unaware his senses were subject to illusion, Jaric believed that he roused to twilit silence in the grove of the Vaere. He opened his eyes to grass and flowers, and to the same enchanted clearing where he had earlier fallen asleep. A chill roughened his flesh. Nothing appeared to have changed, and that unsettled him. His hands still stung with abrasions from muscling *Callinde*'s helm against stormwinds. Both clothing and skin glittered with salt crystals, crusted by spray upon his person. Puzzled, for he had expected some sign of great magic, he blinked and pushed himself erect. The soil felt cool under his palms. Overhead, the trees arched in the silvery half-light like a congregation of leaf-bearded patriarchs. Irritated to discover that his body had stiffened during his rest on damp ground, the boy stretched, then froze with his arms half-raised. Tamlin of the Vaere sat perched on the low gray rock at the center of the grove.

An insouciant grin crinkled the tiny man's features. His beard tumbled in tangles over his fawn colored jacket. Beads and feathered bells sewn to the cuffs jingled merrily in rhythm with his booted feet, which swung idly above the tips of the flowers, and the pipe in his hand trailed smoke like braid through the air.

Jaric raked back mussed hair, wary of the lightless black eyes that watched his every move. "How long have you been here?"

"Always, and never." The Vaere made no effort to qualify his oblique statement, but bit down on his pipestem, drew, and puffed out a perfect smoke ring. "Are you going to ask why?"

Jaric tucked his knees within the circle of his arms and frowned. "Would you answer?"

Tamlin laughed. Feathers danced on his sleeves as he lowered his pipe, yet his mirth dispersed with the smoke ring. "I have no answers, only riddles. Do you still desire a firelord's mastery?"

Aware his integrity was under question, Jaric chose his reply with care. "I wish Keithland secure from demons." He rose, too nervous to keep still any longer.

"No difference, then, son of Ivain." The Vaere leaped from his perch and landed in grass that did not rustle; full height, he stood no higher than Jaric's hip. "To spare your people, you must conquer all weakness, then master the skills that were your father's. Are you prepared?"

"No." Jaric waited, tense down to his heels. Hemmed in by the eerie stillness of the grove, he shied from remembering the demons, and the fate that awaited the people and the woman he loved if he failed. "Is any man born prepared to suffer madness? I can do nothing more than try."

"You say!" Bells clinked briskly as Tamlin took a step forward. "You cannot survive the Cycle of Fire without first mastering the earth. For that, your resolve must be unassailable. *Is it?*"

Jaric swallowed. With a bitter heart, he pictured Taen Dreamweaver's smile, bright as the song of the woodlarks in Seitforest; he remembered the banners flying free over the towers of Landfast, and the Kielmark's wild anger when Cliffhaven stood threatened by armies with demon allies. These things he treasured, and longed to protect. But it had been the wild clans of Cael's Falls and their sacrifice of thirty-nine lives to preserve him from demon captivity that had irrevocably sealed his resolve to attempt the Cycle of Fire. Nothing short of death could deflect Jaric from his decision, though the passage to a firelord's mastery had worked upon Ivain a total annihilation of identity: a vicious, irreversible insanity that caused people across Keithland to fear him. Years after the morning he had ended his misery with a dagger thrust through his heart, Ivain Firelord was remembered with curses. The mention of his name caused folk of all stations to raised crossed wrists in the sign against evil brought on by sorcery.

Tamlin gestured and the pipe vanished instantly from his hand. He spoke as though he were privy to the boy's dark fears. "Son of Ivain, you will need more than determination. The Sathid crystal you must subjugate to gain Earthmastery will already be self-aware at the time it links with your consciousness. It will explore your innermost self, back to the time of birth, seeking weakness that can be turned to exploit you. How much of your past can you face without flinching?"

Though pressured where he was most vulnerable, Jaric refused to give ground. From the instant he reached the fabled isle, Tamlin seemed bent on intimidating him. The idea dawned that the Vaere's words might not be warnings but a ploy intended to provoke him.

"So!" Tamlin sprang aggressively onto the stone, his gaze turned terribly, piercingly direct. "Your mind is quick. But anger will not be enough to overcome what lies ahead. Shall I prove that?"

Without further warning the Vaere clapped his hands. A dissonant jangle of bells tangled with Jaric's shout as the ground dissolved from beneath his feet. His senses overturned, and he tumbled backward into a memory from his past.

CHAPTER II

Mastery of Earth

The fruit trees in Morbrith's walled orchard stood stripped of leaves, and branches rattled like bones in the grip of ice and wind. Yet the gardens Jaric recalled from childhood were not desolate, even in the harshest freeze of winter. The footprints of small boys rumpled the snow between the paths, and laughter rang through frosty air. Only Jaric, an assigned ward of the Smith's Guild, hung back from the rough play of his peers. On the morning of his fourth birthday, a big man who smelled of horses had taken him from the hearth of his latest foster-mother. From now on, he understood he would live in the loft over the forge with the rest of the guild apprentices. The other boys were older than Jaric by several years; in the cruel fashion of children, they resented the intruder in their midst.

"Why, he's nothing but a baby!" Garrey, the eldest, had mocked, and the rest followed his lead like a pack.

Cold air bit through Jaric's mittens. Longingly he watched the apprentices run and leap at tag-ball; earlier, Garrey had told him he was unwelcome to join their play. But the game fascinated a boy whose foster-mother had kept him separate from her own children, and whispered when she thought he would not hear that his presence brought ill luck to her house. Drawn by the laughter, the running, and the carefree scuffling of the young, Jaric edged closer. Unwittingly he crossed the boundary line of the game.

Garrey missed a difficult catch. A burly boy, but quick, he spun and dashed after the ball, only to encounter Jaric standing squarely in his path. He checked and slipped, and barreled heavily into the younger child. Knocked to one knee, Jaric struggled to regain his feet. Garrey whirled before he could run.

Scowling, his red face speckled with snowflakes, the larger boy curled his lip in contempt. "Hey! Milk-nose!"

He did not turn from Jaric as the tag-ball glanced off the wall beyond. The rebound became soundlessly absorbed by a snowdrift as Garrey's companions closed in a semicircle around the slight, blond boy who had clumsily spoiled their play. Jaric backed one step, two, then stopped, cornered against the thorny stems of a rosebush.

"You're not wanted," said Garrey. He stripped off his gloves and raised crossed fists in the traditional sign against ill fortune. "Your own mother tried to kill you, don't you know? And afterward, the father who spared your life got hung, condemned by the Earl's justice for her murder."

"No," whispered Jaric. "You lie, surely."

"Do I so? Then where's your mother, whore's get? And your father?" Garrey grinned, displaying gapped teeth where a horse had kicked him. His tone turned boastful. "I saw Kerain die. His face turned purple, and his eyes bled. Ask the Guildmaster." The older boy knocked Jaric to the ground with a savage shove. Other boys joined in, striking with fists and boots.

But Kerainson, whose upbringing had been charged to the Smith's Guild, hardly felt the blows that pummeled his body. A peer's thoughtless cruelty had revealed the truth behind the townsfolk's tendency to shun him. For the first time he had words to set to the dream that broke his sleep, week after restless week. The nightmare left him wailing in terror from a remembered flash of silver, followed by a man's bruising grip, and blood smell, and a terrible shout mingled with a woman's scream of anguish.

As Garrey's band of apprentices tumbled him over and over in the snow, Jaric felt the darkness of those nightmares return. He choked and bit his lip, but could not smother the scream that rose in his throat. Once that scream escaped, another followed, and another, until his senses reeled and drowned in reverberations of remembered fear.

That day in the past, the apprentices had pulled back. Alarmed, they fled the presence of the boy who screamed as if crazed in the snow. They ignored him when he recovered; and pursued by a horror no longer form-less, the boy had repeatedly fallen ill rather than watch their play from the sidelines. Now a man grown, Jaric felt both memory and snow melt away into air. His last cry rang without echo within the grove of the Vaere. Yet even as he separated past from present, the hands now callused from sword and sheet line remained clenched across his eyes.

Bells tinkled nearby. Jaric drew a shaking breath and forced his sweat-ing fingers to loosen. When he looked up, Tamlin stood over him, his bearded features vague in the twilight.

"Ivainson Jaric, to achieve a sorcerer's powers, you must first master yourself. The training will go hard for you. I say again, are you prepared?"

Jaric swallowed. He spoke in a voice still husky from tears. "Yes."

Tamlin did not relent. "Would you return to the memory you just left, and suffer the pain of that experience ten times tenfold?"

Blond hair gleamed in the half-light as Jaric lifted his head. Brown eyes met black, the former angrily determined, the latter fathomlessly dark. For a moment human and Vaere poised, motionless. Then Jaric rose. He glared down at the fey form of his tormentor, his stance the unwitting image of Ivain's.

"Yes," he said softly. "Send me back to suffer if you must. Only don't turn me away empty-handed. Should you do that, all that I value will perish. To watch and be helpless would be worse than any torment a Sathid could devise."

"Very well, then." Tamlin gestured with a shimmering jingle of bells. "You have earned the chance to train." He paused, and a gleam of admonition lit his eyes. "But remember, self-defense will not avail if on the day of trial no weapon is ready to your hand."

Tamlin winked and promptly vanished. Left alone in the glade, Jaric barely grasped that he had gained the chance to attempt a sorcerer's mastery. Instead, chagrined, he wondered how Tamlin had learned of the sword he inevitably forgot to carry, to the repeated dismay of his instructors.

Lights flickered, patternless as stars across the consoles, as the Vaere sorted the data acquired during Jaric's first trial of will. If the early figures showed promise, they also outlined need for major work to come. To survive the Cycle of Fire, Jaric must bring his present-day resilience to bear upon the inadequacies of his childhood. Motivated, not by hope, but by the relentless reality of numbers, the Vaere sorted options and prepared for the future.

Mechanical extensions trapped the small, squirming bodies of two earth-diggers from the soil beneath the forest floor. Barely a handspan across, the creatures lacked both eyesight and measurable intelligence; yet within their living bodies Set-Nav would create the seeds of a sorcerer's command of elements. Machinery hummed, and gears spun in frictionless silence. The earth-diggers squeaked protest as needles pierced their hides, inoculating each of them with a separate solution of Sathid matrix. Set-Nav placed the squalling animals in cages. The first would host its crystal until its flesh transformed to seed-matrix at the completion of the Sathid's cycle; when it was secondarily bonded to a human subject, memories stored from the matrix's previous existence would expand. From them Jaric must shape his Earthmaster's powers. If he succeeded, the remaining digger would be set aflame. Sathid matrix recovered from its ashes would initiate Jaric to the Cycle of Fire, if his courage did not fail him. For by the most conservative estimate, Set-Nav determined that Keithland had less than a year to offset the threat of Maelgrim. All too soon the dark dreams of demons would influence humanity toward destruction.

In Keithland the days shortened. Crops ripened to harvest, gathered in before the frosts that withered the stubble in the fields. Leaves cloaked the hillsides in colors until winter winds ripped them away; but while snowfall might silt the thickets elsewhere with drifts, time and season remained constant on the Isle of the Vaere. Grasses flowered soft as spring above the installation that housed Set-Nav. Securely dreaming inside his silver capsule, the boy who aspired to a firelord's mastery slowly completed his training. Through months of careful schooling, Tamlin taught him to reshape the nightmares of his childhood. The insecurities Jaric had known as an apprentice scribe were painstakingly unraveled, early uncertainty excised by the confidence of later achievements until recognition of his own self-worth underlay the boy's being like bedrock. For the first time in his life, Jaric could explore his past without feeling haunted by inadequacy.

Yet the freedom inspired by his accomplishment was not to last. The moment the odds of probability favored success, Set-Nav recovered the seed Sathid that had survived the first earth-digger's death and dissolved it in saline solution. Jaric felt no pain as the needle pierced his unconscious flesh. Even as an alien entity entered a vein in his wrist, he dreamed of a twilit grove; there a tiny man dressed in leather and bells delivered final instructions.

"Remember, your danger lies in the weakness within yourself." Bells tinkled as the Vaere wagged his finger at the young man who sat before him on the grass. He had been born slight, this son of Ivain; blighted early by rejection and misunderstanding, still he had grown to manhood. Now the hope of Keithland's survival rested upon his shoulders. Forcefully, Tamlin resumed.

"Fear must be controlled at all times, or you will be lost, forever subservient to the will of the Sathid. If you block the matrix's first attempt at dominance, it will revert and turn its previous memories of the soil against you. You are near then to victory, but do not be careless. At that moment, you must seize control and unriddle the mysteries of the earth. If you misstep then, you shall perish."

Kneeling, Jaric fingered the petals of a flower that rested against his knee. The softness of the bloom reminded him of Taen's skin; thought of her woke a tremble deep in his gut. He forced the memory away, only to recall the face of Mathieson Keldric, the elderly fisherman whose boat had borne him safely through seas and storms. Before Keldric and *Callinde* there had been the forester who had taught him independence, a master scribe who had given him literacy, and later, thirty-nine clansfolk who had lost their lives to secure his safety. Jaric reviewed the sacrifices made by the Kielmark, Brith, and sharp-tongued Corley; and lastly, he considered the Stormwarden, locked living in his tomb of ice. Except for his geas of summoning, Anskiere had forced no man's will, though his rescue depended upon sacrifice of another.

"Boy," said Tamlin softly.

Jaric flinched, and the flower stem snapped between his fingers. He glanced up, bleak with the realization that if he failed his father's inheritance, he would be more fortunate than his friends and fellows. Dead, he would not have to suffer through the demise of Keithland.

Tamlin folded his arms, his hair and beard shining silver in the gloom of the grove. "Boy, whatever your father's reputation, remember this: Ivain gave himself for the greater good. He preserved far more than he destroyed in the time he served Keithland as Firelord."

But where Ivain had begun his trial of Earthmastery with a shrug and a whistle on his lips, Jaric knelt in silence. He did not look as Tamlin's form faded away into air. Left vulnerable and alone, the boy felt a presence that was no part of himself stir within his mind; already the Sathid germinated inside his body. Since the matrix had previously mastered the flesh of the earth-digger, it did not grope, but quickly established contact with its new partner. Though every instinct rebelled, Jaric forced himself to remain passive, even as his awareness of the clearing slipped away, replaced by scenes from early childhood.

The memories unreeled more vividly than any dream; *then* became *now,* and Jaric regressed to the time he was a babe cradled in his mother's lap. Under the expanded awareness of the Sathid-link, he experienced his surroundings with a clarity no infant could have achieved. His mother's heart beat rapidly beneath his ear; she had carried him in haste to a woodland dell, a place of frost-killed leaves and tangled vines beyond view of any dwelling. The hand poised against her breast gripped the haft of a sharpened knife.

Jaric watched, fascinated by the gleam of the steel. Too young to understand peril, he saw his mother's knuckles whiten. She murmured an appeal for forgiveness, and a curse against Ivain Firelord; then she raised the dagger and angled the point to murder the son on her knee.

A frantic shout cut the stillness. "No!"

Leaves crunched under a man's running feet. Jaric felt his mother jerk as if slapped. She struck with desperate strength, caught short as the grip of Smithson Kerain imprisoned her fine-boned wrist. Jostled and pinched against the man's leather breeches, her child wailed in fear.

But the man's voice cut through his cries. "Kor's mercy! Woman, are you mad? *That's our son. Why should you kill him?* Your father agreed we could marry!"

The woman gasped with exertion as she tried and failed to free her arm. "This brat's none of yours, Kerain. Fires, why did you come here? Nothing I say will make you understand."

With a lunge that bumped Jaric onto his stomach, his mother snatched up the knife left-handed. She stabbed at the child a second time, single-mindedly determined.

Caught off guard as the steel arced down, Kerain shouted and snatched at Jaric's garments. He yanked the howling infant out of death's reach, while the woman cursed with astonishing viciousness.

Hard fingers bit into Jaric's ribs, jerking him upright. He continued to wail while the smith shouted angrily. "My love, are you sick? What could you expect? Should I turn my back while you murder our child?"

But the woman seemed not to hear. She doubled over, gasping. Blood ran between her fingers. Only at that instant did Kerain discover that his betrothed had continued her stroke and plunged the knife into her own heart. He screamed himself then, his grief blending with the shrill cries of the child. Crushed against the man's shirt of sweaty linen, Jaric knew terror and the mingled smell of blood and damp earth. Not until many years later did he understand that the woman had taken her life with her own hand.

Established now within the framework of Jaric's mind, the Sathid deepened its hold. Voracious, insistent, it assimilated more memories, passing through the time of upheaval while Kerain stood trial for the murder of his betrothed. Jaric lived in the care of a crabbed old midwife, guarded always by the Earl of Morbrith's men at arms. The woman was deaf. She did not always notice the baby when he cried; and the guards filled long days and nights with endless games of dice.

Kerain was convicted and hanged. Fed a potion by the midwife, Jaric slept through the execution. He was too small to understand the condemned man's final bequest, that the orphan be named his own get and raised as ward of the Smith's Guild. For Jaric the result was a loveless succession of foster homes, then a bed in the chilly garret over the forge. Driven by the influence of the Sathid, he relived the slights of his peers, the fights, the humiliation, and the lonely nights spent with his face muffled in bedclothes lest the other boys rouse when he woke crying out from his nightmares. Again he endured the degrading moment when, at ten years of age, he still lacked the strength to heft ingots of unwrought iron from the traders' wagons to the forge. In disgust, the smiths sent him back to work the bellows. But the fumes of the coal fire made him cough; work that other youngsters managed easily taxed Jaric's health. Age brought no improvement. As a slight, pale twelve-year-old, he proved too timid to restrain the mares brought in from pasture to be shod.

"Fires above, but you're useless!" shouted the master smith. Exasperated, he threw his hammer down with a clang and glared at the lad who shrank in the dimmest corner of the forge. "What can I do but apply to the High Earl for compensation? The guild can't waste silver to feed a ninny. Kor, we've got all the wives and daughters we need to cook and sew shirts!"

All the next day, Jaric huddled on his cot; the Sathid analyzed his misery like a starved predator while, in the yard beneath the dormer, loud-voiced men appointed a delegation to appeal to the Earl. They called Jaric from the loft with impatience, and joked over his girlish ways as they hurried him through the town to the council hall. In a solemn room filled with hard chairs and officials, Jaric listened while the smiths presented their case. The phrases *"cursed since birth"* and *"not Kerain's get"* occurred frequently. The boy they referred to twisted slender fingers in his lap. He tried desperately not to weep, while the Earl listened, frowning, his wrists and collar resplendent with emerald clasps.

The Sathid savored Jaric's discomfort as the petition grew heated. But before the Earl made judgment, the stooped old scribe who kept records interceded in the boy's behalf.

Master Iveg had a quiet voice. A moment passed before anyone noticed his offer. Then clamor abruptly stilled, and the elderly scholar's words echoed through the tapestried chamber. "If Jaric is a burden to the smiths, let him apprentice as a copyist. I need help with the archives anyway. If the boy applies himself, his earnings can pay for his upkeep at the forge."

"Done," snapped the Earl, impatient to be away to his hawks.

His decree changed the life of Kerainson Jaric. By day, the boy studied letters and books. The silence of the library became his haven; each night he dreaded his return to the loft, and the jibes of the smiths' apprentices. With years his roommates grew brown and boisterous and burly, while he stayed slight and pale. At fifteen, the older boys' boasts rang through the alehouse. They arm-wrestled for the chance to kiss the barmaid; and the wench, who was buxom and shameless, turned from them to chaff Jaric for his slenderness. She coddled him, bringing bowls of hot milk for his coughs. Once she caught him peeping down the laces of her blouse. She pinched his cheek like a child's; but the box on the ears he deserved would have hurt less.

Two years later, Jaric's delicate stature had not changed, except that he learned to excel at his scholarly trade. Then, without warning, Anskiere's geas sundered the life he knew at Morbrith. The Sathid was taken aback. It saw its subject outgrow the debilitating insecurities of childhood. Jaric acquired self-reliance under the guidance of the forester, Telemark, and strength through restoring the timbers of *Callinde*'s neglected hull. Through the experiences and the year that followed, the matrix realized with growing frustration that Jaric had faced and overcome every trace of his former softness. Only one chink remained in the boy's integrity when Tamlin's training was complete: Jaric still feared his father's madness, and the awesome potential for destruction inherent in a sorcerer's powers. This a Sathid parasite might exploit to secure its goal of permanent self-awareness. Accustomed to dominance from its interval with the earth-digger, it shaped its snare cunningly and well.

The bond between crystal and human consciousness evolved toward completion. Like a sleeper wakened from drugged rest, Jaric stirred within the stillness of the grove. At once he experienced the vastly expanded awareness that accompanied the Sathid-link. His thoughts rang strange and resonant with energy; intuitive perception and latent talent had now transformed to tangible force. Jaric experimented and discovered he could channel this power at whim. The crystalline entity encouraged curiosity, urging the fledgling mage to explore his newfound abilities.

Jaric stood, struck motionless by wonder. Preternaturally aware of the grass and soil under his feet, he blinked and realized he viewed the trees through altered vision. His eyes perceived the life force in the lofty gray trunks; each leaf was limned by a faint halo of light. If he listened, the boy could hear the plants around him, their growth and flowering a deep, subliminal buzz. The novelty overwhelmed him. At first he failed to realize that the living essence of the grove was also answerable to his will.

A moment later, a tree leaned to one side *simply because he wished to see beyond it.* Revelation struck with a rush that turned him dizzy. Stunned to find he could command the living forest, Jaric sat abruptly. *How could he marshal such power?* Touched by self-doubt, his imagination supplied visions of withered branches and trunks drained to sapless husks. The boy chafed his hands on his forearms in distress, until a presence within his mind jostled recognition that he could preserve with equal facility. Wards could reverse the effects of age and storm, even avert the depredations of the axe.

Soothed, Jaric failed to distinguish that the reassurance arose from an entity not part of himself. Unaware that the Sathid manipulated him, he found himself imagining ways to curb fate, perhaps defend the Dreamweaver he loved from the brother who threatened her life. Yet even as he planned, his fears betrayed him. Jaric recalled the ruins of Tierl Enneth with vivid and appalling clarity. Hemmed in by walls of crumbled stone, he stood exposed while unburied skulls accused him with empty, beseeching eye sockets. Fleshless mouths seemed to wail in anguish, reminding that Anskiere of Elrinfaer had taken oath to protect, then unleashed destruction when a witch enslaved by demons usurped his powers.

Jaric bowed his head. His hands whitened in his lap as he tried to shut the image out. But the Sathid tightened its net of terror over his mind. Every sorcerer trained by the Vaere represented a threat, a magnet for disaster and a target for demon conquest. The Sathid supplied grisly detail; Jaric saw his gifts raised against the sanctuaries at Landfast, his own hands drenched with the blood of the innocent slain. He cried out in purest despair, unaware of the enemy that sapped his defenses.

The Sathid felt him weaken; in a bid for swift and final victory, it seized the one thing Jaric prized above all else, and set that in jeopardy. Helplessly the boy watched as the wards he had raised to safeguard Taen twisted out of control. Power exploded with the fury of a cyclone and bashed her bones through rags of torn flesh.

"No!" Jaric clenched his fingers into fists. His mind seductively insisted that he could avoid such ruin if he chose to relinquish control; Taen could be kept safe if he yielded his mastery to wisdom. But the plurality of the concept rang false. Warned alert, Jaric corrected the Sathid's misapprehension. He realigned reason with a human fact he had nearly been lulled into forgetting: *no power on Keithland or beyond could induce him to betray the Dreamweaver of Imrill Kand,* for he loved Taen beyond life.

The Sathid drew back, uncertain; it knew little of love. Few clues existed to inform it of the nature of its error, for Jaric's past had been cruelly solitary. For a fractional instant, the matrix hesitated in its attack.

The reprieve gave the boy space to realize that the images of torment were none of his own. Now aware that the matrix challenged him for dominance, Jaric responded with anger.

The crystal counterattacked, cut him with reminders that Ivain's fine intentions had soured into unbridled wickedness. Like his father before him, so might the son ravage and betray. Jaric choked on denial. Driven to his knees by visions of Elrinfaer, of people and lands blasted by the depredations of the Mharg, he strove to hold firm. But the Sathid sensed uncertainty; it pressured him ever closer to despair. Battered into retreat, the boy backed his resistance with advice Telemark the forester had offered when he had confronted a seemingly impossible problem in the depths of a winter storm.

"Remember that no man can handle more than one step at a time. The most troublesome difficulty must be broken down into small tasks, each one easily mastered." On the night those words were spoken, Jaric had surpassed his former limits. He had saved the life of his friend. Later, perhaps, he might not manage power with total infallibility; but to the end of conscious will he could ensure he never harmed his own, even if his only means of defense was to yield up his life as prevention.

The Sathid queried the sincerity of its victim's resolve, and abruptly found itself cornered. Jaric's immediate past held record of an incident when the boy had risked his neck to the Kielmark's sword, all for the sake of a principle. A limit existed beyond which he could not be forced, and the crystalline entity had unwittingly transgressed that point when it had first suggested threat to Taen. Now only one resource remained; to subdue the will of its host entity, the Sathid must re-create fear drawn from the earth-digger it had dominated first, then pitch the result in assault against the human mind.

The shift in tactics caught Jaric unprepared. Without warning, he plunged into dampness and dark. Smells of roots and soil filled his nostrils. Suddenly a shower of pebbles and loose dirt rattled down around his shoulders; a falling slide of dirt mired feet, then legs, then hands. Jaric struggled to free himself, to no avail. Unlike the digger, he had no claws to tunnel. Earth compacted his chest, then avalanched in a smothering mass over his nose and face as, with demoralizing accuracy, the Sathid recreated the digger's memory of a tunnel collapse.

Jaric repressed the instinct to panic. Tamlin had warned of this last, desperate trick of the Sathid's. Only wits and the paranormal perception of the link would help him now. Survival depended upon Jaric's ability to unriddle the secrets of earth before suffocation overcame him.

Ivainson ignored the bodily clamor for air. He turned his new awareness toward the soil that imprisoned his body; humus, pebbles, clay, and moisture, he assessed the content of the earth. Even as he groped for means to shift its mass, the Sathid goaded his nerves. Fear shattered his calm. *He could not breathe! He would die here, entombed forever in an unmarked grave.* Sweat slicked Jaric's flesh. He expended precious moments restoring equilibrium, then drove his perception into the dirt once again. This time he sought energy, a life force similar to the aura the trees possessed, which he might tap to save himself.

Yet the earth proved stubbornly inert. Sand and stones had never lived; except for the stirring of occasional insects and worms, particles of soil were comprised largely of dead things, or organisms too tiny to matter. Jaric checked in dismay. Unsure where to search next, he resisted the raking pains in his chest. He must not give in, or his will would be lost forever. *Somehow, Ivain Firelord had untangled the secrets of earth and had won free before death overwhelmed him.*

Dizziness wrung Jaric's senses. Again he drew solace from Telemark's advice; strengthened, he resumed with dogged and desperate concentration, and studied each separate particle. Stone seemed least promising of all; yet Ivain Firelord had been known to step through solid granite on a whim. Harried by a wave of faintness, Jaric attacked the problem. He hammered at dark, unyielding matter until his head ached with effort.

'*You are losing,*' the Sathid interjected, '*Shortly, your flesh will succumb from lack of breath. Before you perish, my victory shall be complete.*'

'No.' Jaric resisted an impulse to curse. His head whirled unpleasantly, and his equilibrium was utterly disoriented. Only seconds remained for his bid to preserve free will.

'*You struggle for nothing,*' goaded the Sathid.

Jaric did not retort. Teetering on the edge of delirium, he strove to unravel the power within the earth. One instant he grappled with the particles that comprised the soil; the next, giddiness overbalanced his touch. The thrust of his thoughts slammed hard against the flinty surface of a pebble. Jaric had no reflexes left to brace and avoid impact. But the rock yielded. His astonished perception melted into stone with the ease of a fall into water. Here at last lay energy enough to move mountains, strung in symmetrical, glittering strands that awed the spirit with beauty. Inside each fleck of sand, each rock, each boulder, abided the strength of the earth. Like the Stormwarden's sources of weather and wave, an Earthmaster's dominion could never be exhausted. Jaric had only to apply his will to release the ties that defined the pebble's structure. The rush of freed forces would be more than ample for him to escape his prison of mud.

The process should have come fluid as thought. But smothered to the brink of unconsciousness, Jaric fought for clarity of mind. His lungs burned. Control eluded him; the energy strands within the stone slipped his grasp like broken chains of pearls. Even as he strove, and failed, pain lanced his body. His lungs felt wrapped in hot wire. And the waiting Sathid invaded, intending to secure control as he foundered.

Jaric recoiled. Stung into rage, he lashed back, forgetful of thoughts left joined within the structure of the stone. Lattices of matter splintered; energy roared forth with the coruscating fury of explosion. Stunned by a shimmering flash of light, Jaric cried out. He tumbled, twisting, onto green turf, then wept as a sweet rush of air filled his lungs.

Agonized and gasping, Keithland's newest sorcerer lay prone within the twilight of the grove. He waited, expecting the matrix to stir in his mind. Yet no whisper of dissent arose. He had battled the Sathid into submission. But its quiescence was only temporary; while Jaric rejoiced in his victory, a small digger screamed and died in an agony of flames. The Vaere recovered seed Sathid from the ashes. On the day the young master attempted the Cycle of Fire, the crystal he had subjugated would rouse to bond with the second. The paired Sathid would then seek domination with an exponential increase in power. Not even Set-Nav could prepare the heir of Ivain for such a trial. As they sought dual mastery, Tamlin had watched even the fittest aspirants die.

CHAPTER III

Return

Winter knifed across the barrens north of Felwaithe; wind sang mournfully over bare rock and winnowed the snowfall into ranges of sculptured drifts. This was a land of harshest desolation, but nowhere was the ice more bleak than on the crag where rose the demon fortress of Shadowfane. Snow did not settle there, but was packed by gales into hardened gray sheets, glazed shiny under the pale midseason sun. On just such a bitter day, a man clad in tattered sailcloth picked his way up the frozen slope. He moved cautiously, for the footing was treacherous, and the soles of his boots sorely worn.

Thienz sentries spotted him long before he reached the final ascent to the gates. Gabbling excitedly, they sent an underling to inform their senior. Yet this once, the presence of a human so far beyond the inhabited bounds of Keithland raised no consternation. The arrival of this particular man had been expected.

The Thienz senior instructed the messenger to return to its post with the sentries. Then, with a whuff of its gills, it scuttled quickly to inform Lord Scait that Maelgrim Dark-dreamer had returned from the south reaches of Keithland.

The sovereign of Shadowfane received the Thienz elder while still immersed in his bath cauldron. His eyes lit with keen anticipation, yellow as sparks through the steam that wreathed his scaled head. Since good news usually had a settling effect upon the Demon Lord, the Thienz elder stretched once and crouched, content to bask in the warmth and moisture; but this once it misjudged.

Scait waved away the spiny, six-legged attendants that scuttled busily about the chamber, stoking peat on the fires that kept his bath water boiling. To the bead-ornamented Thienz elder he said, "Send the Dark-dreamer to the main hall at once. Have him await me there."

The Thienz hesitated, reluctant to leave its comforts.

'Go now!' Scait snapped, his sending barbed with threat. As the Thienz started up and scrabbled off on its errand, the Lord of Shadowfane doused his narrow head one final time and stepped briskly from the cauldron. Droplets splashed from his scales, and struck with a hiss of instantaneous evaporation against the heated stone by the fire pit. Impervious to burns, the Demon Lord fluffed his hackles dry. As an afterthought, he sent

thought-image after the retreating Thienz. *'See the human's needs are met, toad.*
I will not love the delay if he faints in my presence from hunger or chill.'

The chambers comprising Shadowfane's interior were interlinked by a
mazelike warren of corridors. Stairwells bent and spiraled between levels
with the random twists of kinked thread. Human logic could decipher no
pattern to aid in the memory of its array, yet the eidetic recall of demons
mastered such complexity without effort. Scait hurried from his bath
chamber to the central hall on the upper level. He paused only to cuff at
the black forms of Gierjlings whose entwined, sleeping bodies blocked his
path. Lacking any overlord to animate them to purpose, the creatures were
mindless as vegetables. They blinked eyes the lightless gray of grave mist,
and moved chittering from underfoot. Scait kicked the tardy ones aside.
Unlike other demons, the Gierj were active and successful breeders; Keithland's climate gave their females and their fertility no difficulties. Lately
there seemed to be even more of them underfoot than usual. Scait made
mental note to inquire of the Watcher-of-Gierj whether their numbers
were on the increase. Then, excited by the prospect of beginning his grand
plan, and concerned lest one of his rivals should speak to the Dark-
dreamer ahead of him, the overlord of Shadowfane's compact hastened
with a faint scrape of spurs through the diamond-shaped lintels that
opened into the central hall.

The one who had once been Marlson Emien, brother to Taen Dreamweaver, sat on the stone by the mirror pool chewing on smoked fish. His
birth name no longer held meaning for him, if indeed he recalled his life
with a human family at all. Since the day he had been renamed by demons,
the mind of Maelgrim Dark-dreamer had become a warped snarl of hatred
and passions, controlled by a Thienz-dominated Sathid-bond. He might
retain the shape of a man, but his thoughts and his desires were Shadowfane's.

Since his return, his clothing of ill-sewn sailcloth had been discarded
for a tunic of woven wool. No other amenity had been granted by the
Thienz who had escorted him in. The fine cloth caught and clung against
his unwashed skin, mottled still with the ravages of frostbite and cold.
Maelgrim's black hair hung lank with tangles, and a three-month growth
of beard matted his chin. Still, though his body had been starved and
depleted by the abuses of weather, the awareness within was not dull.
Maelgrim looked up at Scait's entrance, his ice-blue eyes unblinking as a
fanatic's. In silence he prostrated himself before his overlord.

Scait noted the sincerity of the obeisance with keen satisfaction. Here
at least was one pawn who could never betray his loyalty. Snarling at
thoughts of other factions who might, the Demon Lord leaped onto the
dais. He seated himself with a predator's grace upon his throne, and since
in this case he need not intimidate to maintain supremacy, he allowed his
servant to rise.

Maelgrim straightened, half-squatting on his heels. He lifted a flesh-less hand and resumed gnawing his meal. The fish head he spat into the mirror pool, a transgression Scait forgave. The Dark-dreamer was more than a pet. He was a weapon exquisitely crafted for carving out vengeance upon the human inhabitants of Keithland.

Scait established his opening in words, that his finer concentration be available to sample Maelgrim's inner thoughts. "You have been long in returning."

The Dark-dreamer answered around a mouthful. "Winter in the north latitudes doesn't favor passage, far less with a boat whose sails are ripped to shreds."

Scait's mental probe sampled the truth of the words, and Maelgrim stiffened, very still with the awareness of his overlord's scrutiny. He waited, eyes fixed blankly on the morsel of fish in his grasp, while the master's presence explored; the weather had been terrible, storm after storm battering down upon an already sprung and leaking sloop. Only a fisherman's upbringing had permitted him to bring the boat safely in at all. Maelgrim had done well to achieve landfall at Northsea, but for resent-ful reasons of his own he had not hurried once he gained shore. As Scait rummaged through his memories to divine the reason, the Dark-dreamer flashed thought across the link. *'Thienz could have killed him at Elrinfaer, and didn't. Why not?'*

Awareness interlinked with the human's, Scait required no guesswork to answer. "The Firelord's heir possessed rare potential, and talents that might have been exploited for the benefit of Shadowfane's compact."

"But now he is free!" Maelgrim's hand clenched angrily, crushing the carcass of the fish. "Like my sister who was beguiled, and even as his father before him, he has gone to the Isle of the Vaere to be trained."

Scait's hiss of irritation caught Maelgrim's protest short. "Alive, Ivain-son Jaric could have been compelled to betray Keithland. Now, with his Firelord's potential lost to us, your own talent as Dark-dreamer becomes of paramount importance." The Lord of Demons paused and rubbed scaled hands together. The plan he had devised surely would wring admira-tion from even his bitterest rivals. All in the compact were aware that the wizards at Mhored Kara conscripted paranormally gifted children for training. That they culled their apprentices from families in the towns and villages of the southern kingdoms and the Free Isles' Alliance was also known fact, but what of the north? Parents there might breed equal num-bers of exceptional offspring; except in the backlands, perhaps these chil-dren passed unnoticed. With keenest anticipation, the current ruler of the compact intended to correct this oversight.

Scait extended a spurred hand toward the human crouched at the foot of the dais. "Maelgrim, by my command you will engage your powers as Dark-dreamer. Seek among men, and the children of men, for ones born with talent that any who go for training with the Vaere must possess. Find these gifted ones, and call them hither to Shadowfane. I shall reward them generously, and see that they receive instruction befitting their talents."

Maelgrim swallowed a bite of crushed fish, then licked at the oil on his fingers. Black hair veiled his eyes as he pressed his forehead to the stone before the dais. "Your will, mightiest Lord, but humbly I offer warning. The plan you suggest has flaws."

Displeased, Scait cupped his chin in flinty claws. "Name them."

"Human parents differ from those of demons." Here Maelgrim abandoned language and engaged his Dark-dreamer's skills to impart his concept intact. Humans lacked the treasures of eidetic memory; to them, the past, and the histories of the dead that were of such vital significance to demonkind, came second to the young whose future had yet to be written.

"My kind will fight the loss of their children, mighty Lord. They will send armies to claim back their young." A gleam of calculating hatred spiked Maelgrim's words of conclusion. "After the first shock of surprise, the humans will organize. They will guard the children of Keithland beyond reach of my probes and my lures, for the Vaere-trained Dreamweaver who was my sister is capable of unraveling this grand plan. She is bound to defend Keithland from the designs of demonkind, else break her oath of service to the Vaere."

Scait growled low in his throat, for Maelgrim was wiser in the ways of mankind than any demon at Shadowfane. A canny ruler must heed the human's counsel and look beyond for means to turn detriment to advantage. Scait pondered a moment, yellow eyes closed to slits. Then he straightened with a leer of satisfaction. To Maelgrim he commanded, "You shall study the ways of power, and be granted control in mind-meld with the Thienz, that you can draw force from their link to augment your own. When you have mastered these skills, come to me, and we will plot. For I think that humans might be distracted from noticing those few among their young that we summon. The Dreamweaver is only one girl. She may be lured, and captured, and perhaps forced to Sathid domination as well."

The one who had been born her brother licked lips that glistened with fish oil. He smiled and fawned on the floor in abject gratitude. Twisted in ways no human could imagine, Maelgrim relished the assignment of creating his sister's demise. Taen's downfall would be all the sweeter if the Stormwarden were to be rescued by Keithland's new Firelord, only to discover his other protégé lost in thrall to the enemy.

"Your will, mightiest Lord." Maelgrim arose with joyful, overweening malice and tossed the remains of his meal into the mirror pool. As he departed, Scait caught a last glimpse of his eyes: frost-blue, and alight with hatred like a weapon's polished edge. The boy Emien had been manipulated into absolute subservience quite satisfactorily, except that his eating habits were irritating in the extreme.

Distastefully, Scait Demon Lord regarded the half-chewed fish tail that drifted, spreading an oil slick on the surface of the water. The next rival who crossed him would find itself wading to scoop out the garbage. This settled, Scait's thoughts ranged futureward, and preoccupied speculation gave way to desire fierce as greed. The finding and enslavement of gifted human children must proceed without setbacks. Once Shadowfane had developed a collection of such changelings, they could be set loose for the destruction and the extermination of mankind. Then would Scait's sovereignty be secured beyond question. The way would be clear for the compact to reclaim Veriset-Nav from the ocean and summon rescue from their homeworlds in triumph.

Winter was all but spent on the day the peace was disturbed in Keithland. High in the tors of Imrill Kand, the sister Maelgrim Dark-dreamer plotted to ruin sat amid the cropped grass of a goat pasture, soggy skirts gathered about her knees. Her cloak was pinned tight at her neck; hair black as her brother's coiled damply over her shoulders, and her slim woman's hands twisted restlessly in her lap. Though the sleet that fell at dawn had ceased, the morning remained unbearably bleak. Fog curled off dirtied patches of snow, and last season's grass lay flattened and brown against soil still rutted with ice. Taen Dreamweaver shivered. Sick with horror, she covered her eyes and tried to subdue the grief in her heart. Always, she had known this moment would come, but never had she guessed that its impact might cut her so deeply.

Ivainson Jaric might have offered comfort. But he was beyond reach on the Isle of the Vaere, training for his final ordeal, the Cycle of Fire that had driven his father to madness. If he survived, he would emerge forever changed, and no succor would he then owe to anyone. Taen lowered her hands. She stuffed reddened fingers into the cuffs of her shirt, an oversized garment of unbleached linen and silver-tipped laces she had won in a bet with a pirate captain. The fabric was dry but offered no warmth. This day the brother lost to Shadowfane had turned his demon-inspired malice against Keithland, and though Jaric's sacrifice might someday put an end to such atrocity, the sting brought on by the loss of his company only this moment struck home. The bare, ice-rimmed tor became more than a landscape ravaged by winter; some of its bleakness turned inward and invaded Taen's spirit.

Aching and weary already from long hours of husbanding power, she forced her sorrow aside. No good could be gained from brooding. Tough as the fisherfolk who had bred and raised her, the young woman mustered her Dreamweaver's awareness once more. Shortly the call she shaped sped southeast, to the straits and the isle of Cliffhaven.

The subject of Taen's search was never a hard man to locate even when obscured by a crowd. The incisive force of his thoughts struck easily through the interference patterns cast by others in his presence. By nature, the Lord of Pirates was quick to sense change, and even swifter to act. From the instant the Dreamweaver made contact, the Kielmark disregarded the presence of the two captains he had summoned into conference in his chart room. Arrested in mid-sentence, he fell silent, the maps and the pins he had been using to discuss strategy abandoned under his huge, square-fingered hands. In less than the space of a heartbeat, he slammed back his chair.

His captains knew better than to interrupt when his moods came suddenly upon him. They sat, carefully motionless, as their master arose and tossed a cloak of maroon wool over his muscled frame. Then, without a word or a look back, the Kielmark kicked open the postern and stepped out into the sea breeze that whipped across the battlements overlooking the harbor.

Taen locked her dream-sense in and framed him there, brawny and wolf-quick on his feet, his dark, curled hair crushed flat by wind and his great fists clenched at his sides. Deftly as the Dreamweaver engaged his attention, he started like a wild animal.

"Taen?" The sovereign Lord of Cliffhaven glanced over his shoulder, at a fortress that remained deserted under gray clouds and ice. No child wearing a woman's form walked the battlements to meet him, with eyes that saw far too much, and clothes that seemed always overlarge for her slim frame. The Kielmark shed his wariness with forced deliberation. Certain now that the call had come from within, he waited with cutting impatience for the Dreamweaver's message to resume.

'Trouble has arrived, and far sooner than expected,' Taen sent. The clang of goat bells on the tor faded into distance as she centered her focus upon the ruler of Cliffhaven.

The Kielmark sprang tense. "What trouble?" Even as he spoke, Taen sensed his reflexive review of men, warships, and the current offensive capability of his island fortress.

'Maelgrim has begun to try his powers.' The Dreamweaver clarified with images gathered that morning from the northern borders of Hallowild, knowing as she spun memory into dream-form that the impact would inflame the Kielmark's caustic restlessness to action.

The Lord of Cliffhaven recoiled slightly as her dream-link embraced his mind. Strong fingers bit down on the crenellation as his view of the ocean wavered, overlaid by the crude planks of a farmsteader's cottage. Sheep grazed in the dooryard. Hedges of matted thorn enclosed a snow-bound patch of garden, but there all semblance of normality ended. Blood pooled around the base of the stump the steader used to split firewood. Sodden bundles of cloth lay sprawled to one side, and with a sickened lurch of his gut, the Kielmark saw that the lumps beneath the rags had once been human. Something had driven an honest man to dismember his wife and children with an axe, and leave the corpses steaming on the ice for scavengers to pick.

The Kielmark's hackles rose. "Kordane's Fires, why?" The alarm underlying his tension struck with the force of a whiplash.

Taen instinctively tightened her protective screens. *'Dreams, dark dreams spun by Maelgrim.'* She qualified with a memory gleaned from a tinker she had found mumbling and crazed in the gloom of the steader's root cellar.

Taen shaped no more than a fragment. Yet that one glimpse was enough to make a man shudder like an insect pinned on a needle. The Kielmark started back in horror. His skin rose into gooseflesh while his awareness danced to measures of insanity. Even thirdhand, the creeping, poisonous web Maelgrim cast over his victim's minds made the spirit curdle in despair.

Taen banished the nightmare. The Kielmark stood granite-still against the bite of the wind, his blue eyes unfocused and his thoughts turned morbidly inward; she stung him alert with facts. *'When the tinker came out and saw the corpses, he ran to the barn and slashed his wrists with a scythe.'* She paused, waiting, while the sovereign on the battlements of a fortress many leagues distant steadied his shaken nerves. *'Lord, I showed you only a fraction of the force Maelgrim has brought to bear. This evil cannot be battled from a distance. I must go to Hallowild, and quickly.'*

The Kielmark looked up. The reflexive, splintering transition into fury that so often intimidated his captains drove him to swift decision. "You'll have ships. I'll place Deison Corley in command. But you'll wait to leave until he gives you escort, am I clear?"

Taen protested. *'Folk will die while I delay!'*

The Kielmark's anger went cold. "Show me the steader who can replace your talents, girl. Wait. Corley will sail with the tide. I promise you, no captain in Keithland can wring more speed from the wind than he."

The precaution was sensible; Keithland's defenses were spread perilously thin already, with the Stormwarden still trapped within the ice. Taen conceded the Kielmark's point; she would await the arrival of Deison Corley's fleet, though the constraint of delay was a bitter one.

The Dreamweaver released contact, and sensed, through the dissolution of the link, the Kielmark's great shout that brought a familiar chestnut-haired captain bounding from the warmth of the chart room. He received his master's orders, while on another isle to the north a vista of fog-bound tors swam slowly back into focus around the Dreamweaver.

After the Kielmark's explosive vitality, the chime of the goat bells seemed strangely thin and unreal. Taen sneezed at the drop of water she found trembling on the tip of her nose. Moisture seeped through her clothing; during her interval in trance, the sky had begun to spit sleet. Yet even the hostilities of the weather could not make her return to shelter in the village beside the shore. Instead she gathered herself yet again and bent her Dreamweaver's perception southwestward. Tamlin of the Vaere must be informed of the ill tidings from Felwaithe.

Taen was unsurprised when her first attempt showed nothing but a view of white-capped sea. The fabled isle was difficult to locate, even on days when she was not depleted with exhaustion and cold. Tamlin named himself master of riddles. His powers extended across both space and time, and, seemingly at whim, he caused his isle to undergo slight shifts in location. Only when he made contact with those rare few he chose to train was he found inhabiting the present.

Taen adjusted the energy at her command and successfully completed the transition into the shadowy, altered dream-image that reflected the past. Now she perceived an islet, a crescent spit of land hammered by breakers. The shoreline was jagged and storm-whipped, jumbled with stunted trees all twisted by gales and tide. Taen laced her powers into the physical presence of the land, then shaped an image wrought of dream over all. Tumbled sands and jagged rocks became a beach of smooth and creamy white. Grasses softened the dunes. Scrub trees filled out into a forest of stately cedars, tall, green, and unbent by wind. Taen wrought change until the untidy spit of land stood transformed, a place of bewitched perfection set like a jewel on the face of the sea; for by shifting that same isle beyond reach of ocean storms and out of phase with the seasons for longer than the memory of men, the Vaere had made it so.

Taen settled her dream-sense, until soil and rock and shoreline lay in balance with her image of Tamlin's isle. Then, with delicate care, she moved her awareness futureward until land and dream-vision converged into solid reality. The spicy scent of cedars filled her nostrils. She knew sunlight as gentle as spring, and soft breezes sighing through dune grass where sand swallows dipped and cried. Yet although Taen knew she had located the true Isle of the Vaere, at once she sensed something vital amiss. Precisely what was lacking eluded her, until she sought the grove within the forest where dwelt the network of energies that comprised the presence of Tamlin. No resonance of power met her dream-sense. She encountered only dark, and space, and the soundless emptiness of void. The enchanted grove had vanished from the face of Keithland as thoroughly as if it had never existed.

Though dismayed, Taen Dreamweaver did not give way to alarm. The mysteries of the Vaere were riddles within riddles, and knowledge beyond the pale of mortal men. Though no little man in feathers and bells materialized to tell her, Taen placed only one interpretation upon the emptiness she found at the isle's center. Ivainson Jaric had begun his last trial of mastery, the Cycle of Fire itself. Tamlin of the Vaere had withdrawn to oversee his ordeal and, through the time of passage, could not be recalled by any means a mortal might command. There was no remedy for the fact that the timing could not be worse, that the guardian of mankind had withdrawn beyond reach when his guidance was needed most sorely.

Troubled, Taen released the bindings of her call. The enchanted isle faded from her dream-sense, restoring her awareness to cutting cold and the strident cries of curlews. The Dreamweaver of Imrill Kand dispelled the last of her trance and stared out over the harbor beyond the tor. With the fishing fleet out plying their nets, the waters spread gray, empty except for one derelict dory left at anchor, and the mastless hulk of a sloop. As near as a fortnight hence, the bay would echo with the crack of spars and canvas; black brigantines manned by battle-trained crews would shear around the headland, the Kielmark's red wolf banner flying from masthead and halyard. Aching with worry for Jaric, and impatient to be away, Taen could do nothing but count the minutes until she could board and sail to Felwaithe. For with Jaric irrevocably committed to the Cycle of Fire, and the Stormwarden of Elrinfaer imprisoned in ice until a firelord's mastery could free him, Taen alone remained to resist Maelgrim Dark-dreamer and the forefront of the demon assault.

Warmth came unseasonably late to the latitudes of Keithland, and the ocean tossed, coldly veiled in spindrift. Corley and the *Moonless*'s five companion vessels sailed briskly, sped by the storms that habitually raked the Corine Sea before equinox. Ice still scabbed the tors by the time the small fleet hove into view off Imrill Kand.

A young cousin ran from the fishers' wharf to the cottage off Rat's Alley with the news. He found the Dreamweaver taking leave of her mother, her meager store of clothing already bundled and waiting by the door. Taen had followed the Kielmark's brigantines by sorcery, and the time of their arrival was known to her long before the masts breasted the horizon. Though the enchantress spoke her thanks, and Marl's widow offered warm bread in return for his favor, the boy refused hospitality and left. Just before the door swung closed, Taen saw him raise crossed wrists in the timeworn sign against evils brought on by enchantment.

She turned a wry grin toward her mother. "Well, you won't be sorry to see an end to that nonsense. Do you suppose the wool seller's niece will stop sending you skeins with knots to tangle my spells?"

Marl's widow grunted and shoved another billet of wood into the stove. "Won't be mattering much then. Not with you gone to sea, and unable to keep on tearing good cloaks in the briar. Now I'll only have your uncle's socks to darn. Doubt he'd be noticing knots, anyhow, with his calluses thick enough to sole boots. Kor, but it would be a blessing if he washed his feet more than once in a fortnight. His woolens would rot less, for one thing."

Even through the chatter, Taen could sense her mother's distress. Carefully unmentioned between them hung the name of Marlson Emien, the son that Taen must sail north to oppose. Prolonging the moment she must leave for that purpose could do nothing to ease the heartache. The Dreamweaver caught her cloak from the bench and reached to gather up her bundle.

Her hand blundered into her mother's stout bulk, and the next instant she found herself buried in a smothering embrace. "Don't you go cozening any more gifts from pirate captains' mates," said the widow in a strangely altered voice.

Taen's protest emerged muffled by an apron that smelled of wood-smoke and, faintly, cleaned fish. She pulled back from her mother in affront. "Corley's nobody's mate, but a captain and an officer of the Kielmark's. A shirt won on a bet doesn't mean he's in love with me. I understand from his crew that he has a collection of very lovely ladies that he visits at carefully measured intervals. All of them take money for their charms, and none of them have hair that smells of fish!"

But today Marl's widow did not respond with the dour, barbed wit Taen had known throughout childhood. Instead she raised a careworn hand and smoothed a black strand of hair that had escaped her daughter's braid. "It's a husband you should be seeking, not some ill-turned adventure against Kor's Accursed that could leave you dead, or much worse."

Silence fell in the tiny kitchen, heavy and dense and somehow untouched by the workaday bickering of children in Rat's Alley. Taen sighed, picked up her bundle, and paused by the door.

Her mother stood with her back turned, regret for her words and her faltering courage evident in her stiff pose. Taen blinked back sudden tears. "I'll be back to marry when children can be born into Keithland without nightmares waiting to kill them."

Marl's widow nodded, reached for a pot, and banged it angrily down on the stove. "Just come back, girl," she whispered. But Taen had already gone, and latched the door silently behind her.

Winter's chill hung damp on the air, and the wind blew brisk off the sea. Once past the shelter of Rat's Alley, Taen ran, fighting the tug of her cloak, her bundle bouncing off knees still scabbed from the briars she had hiked through in her outings across the tors. Ahead, across the market square hung with the drab tents of drying fishnets, she saw the masts and sails of the brigantines, tanbark-red against cloud-silvered sky. Already, tiny forms swarmed into the rigging, crewmen sent aloft to shorten sail. As Taen reached the docks, the lead vessel rounded with mechanical precision, backed sail, and dropped anchor with a splash like a faint plume of smoke. Even as her hook bit into the harbor bed, a longboat lowered from the davits. Oarsmen clambered aboard the instant the keel kissed water, and looms flashed and bit with the trained and deadly timing that marked the Kielmark's crews; none showed better discipline than the company under the command of Deison Corley, Taen decided. The long-boat clove toward the wharf with near-uncanny speed.

Taen boarded the instant the boat reached the dock. The strong hands of the coxswain caught her bundle from her, and his call to resume stroke was obeyed with such promptness that Taen unbalanced and slammed rump first into the bow seat.

"Kor, man, be easy or ye'll bruise the goods." The nearer of the starboard oarsmen capped his complaint with a gap-toothed grin at the Dreamweaver. Without missing stroke, he added, "Welcome back, girlie. In the forecastle we've a pack o' cards that ain't too soggy yet. Got a game promised after the change in the watch."

Taen caught her cloak hood before the wind scooped it from her head. "I'll be there, but only if I can beg a stake of beans from the cook."

"No bother," said the oarsman with a wink. "Some kind soul saved yer stash."

"You?" Taen flushed in a manner that made even the roughest scoundrel in the boat draw back in appreciation. "If you saved beans at all, it was to keep the wind in your sails."

"Lively!" snapped the coxswain, as the crewman drew breath to defend his dignity. "Dress oars, you fish-brained jacks, yer captain's watching."

The looms rose dripping from the sea, and the longboat drifted smartly into the lee of the Kielmark's brigantine, *Moonless.* Taen reached out to catch the waiting rope, only to have it snatched from her hands by the oarsman she had just finished teasing. Another man caught her strongly from behind. "Goods most certainly wasn't bruised," he observed.

Taen tried to retaliate with a punch, but lost the chance as she was propelled strongly upward. Forced to abandon her reprisal and grab for the strakes, or risk a fall into the heaving sea beneath, she climbed. The next moment her bundle of belongings sailed boisterously over her shoulder, and the bearded, weather-beaten face of Deison Corley appeared at the rail.

A large man with chestnut hair only just beginning to gray, the captain caught her spare clothes. With the reflexes of a trained swordsman, he slung them aside into the grasp of a sailor. "Keep the tar on your mitts, not the dresses," he cautioned, then reached out and caught the Dreamweaver's hand, half lifting her as she clambered aboard. Taen seemed even slighter than he remembered, her eyes enormous under the patterned border of her hood. Yet the wait and the worry had not sapped her spirit.

"You look as if a bellyful of sour apples left you griped," the girl observed. "Or do you wear that dumbfounded expression because you lost your whetstone overboard?"

Corley tugged the Dreamweaver off balance into his chest, his sea-roughened hands in no way clumsy as he flipped the hood over her eyes and bundled her into his embrace. "I always pack spares." His chestnut beard split to reveal a grin. "And a lucky thing, too, for I see I may be needing my flints to blunt the edge from your tongue."

Taen pinched him blindly in the arm and pulled free. She did not resist when *Moonless*'s steward hustled her off to the dry warmth of the stern cabin. Beneath the captain's gruff humor, she had sensed the question he tactfully refrained from asking; the perception left her aching, for where Ivainson Jaric was concerned, she had no reassurance to offer at all.

CHAPTER IV

Light-Falcon

Moonless raised anchor. Accompanied by her entourage, she scudded past
Imrill Kand's headland without waiting for the tide to turn. The crossing
to the shores of Hallowild was tempestuous and prolonged by contrary
winds. Captain Corley kept to the quarterdeck except for brief intervals to
snatch rest. But for fierce bouts of cards with the sailhands, Taen remained
isolated. Daily she retired to the stern cabin and plied her talents to track
the emergence of the Dark-dreamer's influence. Her findings were unre-
mittingly bleak, a systematic destruction of lives and sanity that so far
afflicted the country folk toward the north borders of Morbrith. The
particulars Taen kept to herself, as well as the fact that Maelgrim's influence was predictably spreading southward. Corley could not drive his command any faster, and ill tidings could do nothing but blunt the spirits of
his hardworking crew.

At last, in the weeks before spring planting, the Kielmark's fleet of six
made landfall. Taen stood at the rail while the brigantines anchored in the
waters off the traders' docks that lined the banks downriver from Corlin
Town. The estuary of the Redwater was clear of ice, but a freak late snowfall stung the faces of the sailhands as they stripped the canvas from
the yards. Since all but a maintenance crew would march north as the
Dreamweaver's escort, the small fleet might remain in the harbor for weeks
yet to come.

Corley spotted Taen between rounds of inspection, her blue cloak
being the brightest color on board after weeks of gray swells. "Why not
join the supply party?" he yelled across the deck. "The outing would do
you good, and you can help the men with the bargaining."

"For horses? I'm better practiced at cleaning fish." But outraged sensibilities could not quite quell Taen's smile. Her Dreamweaver's perception
had revealed the motive behind the captain's request: he wanted a woman
along to allay the suspicion invariably aroused by companies under Cliffhaven's banner. She agreed to the plan for reasons of her own. For a short
time, the sounds and sights of a strange town might divert her, enable her
to cease brooding over the fate of Ivainson Jaric, and the cruelty of the
brother sworn over to demons.

The longboat dispatched to Corlin carried no device, and the men on
board rowed with weapons and swords bundled out of sight beneath their
cloaks. Still, Taen saw laborers and teamsters pause to stare as the boat

passed the landings and warehouses of the trade port. The oarsmen's rapacious efficiency trademarked a fighting command, and six black brigantines flying the wolf in the estuary had not escaped remark. The Duke's officer of the port questioned them tactfully upon landing. He wore gold chains by the dozen, and a cloak bordered with peacock feathers; under the weight of all his finery, he sweated more than the situation seemed to warrant.

"We're just here to buy horses," said Corley's boatswain. Hatless in the cold, his single hoop earring emphasizing the fact that he had once lost half his scalp to a sword cut, he gestured toward Taen with his elbow. "Would I be lyin' in front of a woman, sir?"

"You'd lie in front of your mother, so," grumbled the official. But he granted them leave to moor the longboat.

As the Kielmark's shore party plowed into the press before the gates, the boatswain grinned at the Dreamweaver and confided, "I think the man knew we'd've bashed his birdie brains out if he refused." The pirate officer sounded self-righteously cheerful.

But Taen proved more interested in the city than in acknowledging seaman's boasts. Corlin stood at the edge of Seitforest and the backland domains of the north. Fortified by square walls of brick, trade prospered there despite roving bands of outlaws that preyed upon passing caravans; the marketplace in the commons bustled with merchants, craft tents, beggars, and a vigilant squad of men at arms, for Corlin's Duke was a man dedicated to security. Since the streets were safe and prosperous, Corley had encouraged Taen to browse and listen for rumors from the remote frontiers of Hallowild.

A girl raised in the austere society of Imrill Kand needed little excuse to explore. By day, Corlin's central square offered a maze of temporary stalls. The Dreamweaver wandered, enthralled, past merchants selling bread and beads and cloth. She stopped to hear street minstrels and watch a dancer with a monkey that leaped to catch coins. At the mouth of Craftsman's Alley, Taen found birds in wicker cages and tools new from the forge. Jostled by a peddler selling wine, she half tripped over a drag-sleigh piled with cured pelts. The hand she thrust out for balance sank to the wrist in rare fur. Mottled black and silver, a cloak sewn of ice-otter pelts would be prized like the jewels of a duchess.

Taen clenched her fingers in silky hair, remembering: Jaric had set traps for such beasts the year he had sheltered in Seitforest.

"That's hardly a perfect specimen," said a mild-mannered voice. "Would the lady care to see a better one?"

Taen looked up. At her side stood a leather-clad forester, streaked black hair tumbled over his shoulders. His face had weathered into permanent lines of patience, but his eyes were light, intent, and fierce as a hawk's.

Slammed by recognition, Taen felt words stop in her throat. She knew this man. Here stood the forester who had remade Jaric's self-reliance, a process the Dreamweaver had shared through a winter in close rapport.

The shock of meeting Telemark in the flesh overwhelmed her. Desperately she longed to speak of Jaric, to unburden her concern upon the forester's staunch sympathy. But to reveal Ivainson's trial in the grove of the Vaere to this man would shatter a peace of mind so deep that the notion itself was a cruelty. Miserably, Taen kept her silence.

"Lady?" Strong fingers supported her shoulder. "Are you ill? Do you need help?"

The touch was sure, familiar to the point of heartbreak; for thus had Telemark steadied Jaric through a period of painful convalescence. Taen bit back an urge to weep and found herself overcome. Her mind sought after Jaric in a rush of uncontrollable need.

Power surged inside her, far too cataclysmic to bridle. Without warning, her awareness exploded across space and time. After months of empty silence, Taen achieved contact with Jaric's consciousness.

Flame raged across the link, blistering flesh with pain that had no voice and no outlet; feeding on nerve and muscle and bone, Sathid-born hatred consumed the living body of the man who suffered the Cycle of Fire. In agony, Jaric resisted. Torment stripped away his humanity, left nothing but instinct to survive. He recognized no presence beyond the enemy, and the reflexive vehemence of his defense flung the Dreamweaver's contact outward into darkness.

Reality returned with a disorienting jerk. Restored to the bustle of Corlin market, Taen found herself weeping in the sturdy arms of the forester.

Telemark shifted his grip, his trap-scarred knuckles warm through the folds of her cloak. "Girl, are you ill?"

"No." His shirt smelled of balsam and woodsmoke, just as Jaric remembered. Bravely Taen composed herself. "I'm sorry. By accident you reminded me of someone I know and love."

She disentangled herself from Telemark's embrace, then fled before he could question her further. The crowd hid her from view; but for a long while afterward Taen sensed the forester staring after her with a frown of puzzled concern.

By early afternoon the boatswain and his three henchmen had driven a milling mass of horses out of Corlin market. They made rendezvous with Corley and the main company from the ships just beyond the gates. Between the shouting and the sorting of mounts and men, Taen's silence passed unnoticed; numbed by Jaric's predicament, she mounted with little of the trepidation that riding usually inspired. Beside her, the boatswain reported to his captain.

City gossip had included no mention of Maelgrim's blighted dreams, yet the lack of news was no basis for encouragement. With roads still mired with snow-melt, word would travel slowly until caravans resumed trade to the north.

"The High Earl was imprisoned for heresy, though." The boatswain stowed his bulk with surprising grace in the saddle of a rangy chestnut.

"Oh?" Corley chose a gray that nipped at his seat as he turned to mount. Unperturbed, he slapped its muzzle and vaulted astride. "When did that happen?"

"Summer before last." The boatswain spat. "Kor's brotherhood governs Morbrith in the Earl's stead. Farmers griped over the tax shares. Claimed that bloody simpering initiates counted the oats in the sheep pats to pad out their tallies."

Corley grinned, settling easy as the gray sidled beneath his weight. "Fires. I wouldn't have wanted to be the man in charge of inspecting the grain tax, then."

The boatswain howled with laughter. "Farmers would've bagged sheep leavings, surely. But they dared not, unless they wanted to see their Earl staked out for the fire."

Corley looked thoughtful for a moment. Then he summed up his opinion of priests in an epithet, and motioned his company forward. The last men mounted, and with startling speed the stamping, snorting mass of beasts sorted out into columns. Taen reined her mare in behind the lead company of men at arms. She did not join in the laughter as the sailors' contempt of the saddle found expression in a spate of coarse jokes. While Jaric suffered in his struggle to master the Cycle of Fire, she could do nothing but go forward to defend the borders; and unless he won free very soon and came north to free Anskiere, even that effort would prove futile.

Snow shifted to cold rain as the Kielmark's contingent left the road and pressed on into the hill country north of Corlin. Here the terrain was rocky, dense with forest unrelieved by way stations or hostels; the only inhabitants were the occasional isolated farmsteader, or wandering tribes of clansmen. At night the men slung their ship's hammocks from trees, or slept on boggy soil. Bow-hunting for deer kept their marksmanship sharp, and Corley's vigilance ensured that mail stayed polished, and swordblades maintained a killing edge. That six armed companies had been dispatched to protect a single enchantress was a necessity no man questioned. The Kielmark's orders were never gainsaid, and the ways of demons could be unpredictably savage as spring storms.

Yet Maelgrim once had been human, and his actions did not entirely lack pattern. He preferred to strike at night. Taen did not try to oppose him at once, but watched, well shielded, until Corley's company had traveled close enough for her talents to have maximum effect.

Seated by lanternlight in the confines of her tent, she wiped damp palms on the cotton robe she preferred to her daytime garb of riding leathers, then bent her mind into trance. Cautiously she cast her awareness over the land. The north country of Morbrith was a patchwork of wilderness interspersed with the tilled fields and orchards of steaders. Apple branches rattled in winds still edged with winter, the buds of blossom and leaf tightly furled against the cold. Taen deepened her net. The discipline of Tamlin's teaching enabled her to sense the life force of the earth, to share awareness of every natural rhythm, from beasts in hibernation to the sleeping presence of the steaders' families. She merged with the essence of their dreams and waited with coiled patience for the first, spoiling disharmony that signaled Maelgrim's attack.

This night he chose a child, a small boy with auburn hair who slept under quilts sewn by his sister and grandmother. Taen narrowed her focus, warned as the victim twitched with the first stirrings of nightmare. He dreamed that his bedclothes came alive and pinned his small limbs helplessly to the mattress.

Only a Dreamweaver's sensitivity could perceive the unnatural lattice of energies gathered about the boy's form. Taen balanced her own resources. Before his rest could be shattered with images of blood and terror and every crawling fear that Maelgrim wrought to unhinge the spirit, the Dreamweaver shot a bar of light across the child's mind, a shield to repel intrusion.

A startled pulse of force answered her effort, daunting for its intensity. At first contact, Maelgrim's strength proved more powerful than her worst anticipation. Frightened at how sorely she might be tested, Taen Dreamweaver held firm. Strangely, the counterattack she expected did not follow. Maelgrim paused in his weaving, his web work of destruction drifting incomplete above the wards she had set to protect the little boy. Rather than batter her defenses with energies to reclaim his victim, the Darkdreamer sent words across the link. *'Sister! Have the Vaere made you timid? I had expected to encounter you sooner.'*

The message held overtones of challenge, an exuberant anticipation of battle joined that made Taen's flesh creep. She strengthened her protection about the child. Then, her own shields tightly shuttered, she extended a query into her brother's mind in an effort to explore his motives. Maelgrim sensed her touch. He responded with a crackling flare of force that stung her back, but not before she divined his intent. Shadowfane's human minion intended to draw her north, and weaken her, and afterward claim her person and her powers for exploitation by demons.

Revelation of such betrayal caused a sharp ache of sorrow; still, Taen did not lose equilibrium. This moment had been inevitable since the recovery of the Keys to Elrinfaer. That day the man she knew as her brother had been forever lost. The Dreamweaver checked to be certain the momentary disruption had left her guard over the little boy's mind intact. Then, chilled by the potency of her enemy's rejection, she forgave the Kielmark's tyrannical concern for her safety. The escort he had assigned in his obsession was no less than grave necessity. Without his men at arms to safeguard her through the hours she must spend in dream-trance, the Dreamweaver would have been forced to abandon her defense of the north.

An echo of laughter cut short her thought. *'Do you think men with steel can protect you?'*

Taen drew a shaky breath. The spite that rang through the Dark-dreamer's words pained like a wound to the heart. Yet, in another manner, the nature of his cruelties only stiffened her resolve. Some aspects of her brother's character had not changed. Behind Maelgrim's malice she detected impatience, and bitter annoyance. The men at arms were an unexpected complication. Before Maelgrim could take her, he would have to contend with swords in the hands of the most tenacious fighters in Keithland.

The Dark-dreamer returned her assessment with mockery. *'And do you think I will find killing the Kielmark's few soldiers very difficult?'*

Taen started, shocked that he could so easily broach her awareness.

Maelgrim indulged in a moment of poisonous amusement. *'There are other ways to defeat steel.'* Then, with no warning, without even the briefest pretext of contention, he ripped aside the Dreamweaver's wards and pinched out the life of the child.

'No!' Taen recoiled in horror, that defeat should happen that fast, that easily, and with such terrible, irreversible finality. The little boy's fingers remained entwined in his pillow. His hair spilled in tangles across his brow as if he still slept, but his eyes would never open to see the morning.

'I could destroy the Kielmark's men at arms as easily,' warned the Dark-dreamer; and Taen saw that he might. All along he had been feinting, toying with the lives of steaders and clansmen. Never until now had he unveiled the full extent of his strength.

Yet the arrogance that drove him to flaunt his superior power itself was his greatest weakness.

"You can try." Knowing he would read her words, Taen seized the advantage. She struck while satisfaction left him unguarded, and in one bold move sounded and discovered her adversary's link with the Thienz-demons. Their collective mind augmented Maelgrim's will, granted him means to overwhelm her wards and kill.

The loss of the child was bitter. Taen let herself weep, but refused to be trapped by despair. The Dark-dreamer might break her wards over distance this first time. Now that she knew of the demons, she could alter her tactics to compensate; the abominations of the Thienz might be deflected. Within the confines of the campsite she could safeguard the minds of Corley's men. At least while the effects of Maelgrim's early training matured, to the limit of her Vaere-trained resources she would fight.

'You do that,' the Dark-dreamer invited. Hatred rang through his words. *'Hard or easy, slowly or not, the victory at the end shall be mine.'*

Taen offered no reply. Brashly stubborn as her fisherman father, she waited without moving until the abrasive evil of her brother's presence faded and departed.

The Dreamweaver roused sluggishly from trance. Drenched with sweat, and gasping from the aftermath of tears and emotional stress, she reoriented to her surroundings with a shock like pain.

The air in the tent was close, sour with the scent of mildewed canvas. Taen's robe clung unpleasantly to her skin. She wrestled off the damp cotton and sat shivering.

This night a child under her protection had died. The loss was insufferable. The Dreamweaver unstuck a lock of hair from her forehead, hammered a fist into her thigh, and uttered the favorite obscenity of Imrill Kand's most coarse-tempered fishwife. Then, feeling not one whit better, she hurled herself into trance and lashed a stinging hedge of wards about the cottage that sheltered the murdered child. She could do nothing more for the boy. But he had parents, and the young sister and the grandmother who had sewn his quilts. If Taen kept watch, she could ensure that the child's family survived to grieve.

But the night passed without incident. No trace of Maelgrim's presence returned to try her. When at last the sunrise spilled motes of light through the trees to speckle the tent canvas, Taen dispelled her wards. She rubbed tired eyes and lay down beside the blankets that were folded, unused, by her knee. Without enthusiasm she contemplated her riding leathers and hairbrush, and the daily trial of rising to wash in a creek surrounded by ruffians who inventively sought excuses to interrupt her. Though friendly, their persistence seemed suddenly too much. Taen squeezed her eyes closed. Weariness overcame her, and she drifted into sleep across her crumpled robe.

Her peace was not to last. Half an hour later the Dreamweaver was rousted by a raucous whistle, followed immediately by the slackening of a guy line. The post that supported the ridgepole of her tent toppled unceremoniously across her knees.

"Shall we pack you in with the cooking pots, then," gibed the boisterous voice of a sailor.

Taen batted collapsing walls of canvas out of her face and returned an epithet.

"Hoo, she's alive, then," observed her tormentor. But he stilled his tongue, fast, at an irritable reprimand from Corley.

The next moment the captain himself raised the tent flap and peered through the gloom within. "Taen? It's daylight. We've got to move camp." Only when his eyes adjusted did he note the raw pain in her eyes, and the mouth set with unbreakable determination. Corley's manner turned briskly direct. "What happened?"

With the canvas propped awkwardly over her head and shoulders, Taen told him everything, not sparing Maelgrim's threats against the six companies under the captain's command.

Corley considered her keenly as she finished. "You've chosen to fight, yes?"

Taen nodded. Abruptly recalled to the fact that she had thrown off her overrobe, she flushed bright pink and groped over the ridgepole for her leathers.

The Kielmark's most trusted captain dropped the tent flap without apology for his intrusion. "You'll have our full support," he said bluntly. Taen chose not to delay as he called rapid orders to his sailhands, but burrowed in panic under slack canvas to locate her tunic and boots. Her haste proved unnecessary. No man came to tease or to pack her tent until after she emerged, fully clothed.

The company moved north, and the wind grew blustery. Flat clouds lifted to admit sunlight, and in time the warmth of an overdue spring softened the frost from the ground. But while the men became suntanned and robust, Taen grew careworn, withdrawn, and pale.

By day she dream-wove defenses, intricate patterns of energy bound into wards to protect the men at arms whose ready vigilance kept her safe from assault by demons. By night she engaged in deep trance. With painstaking care she reviewed the scattered inhabitants of Keithland's north wilderness, from newborn babes in untamed circles of clansmen, to the work-weary minds of steaders. The predations of Maelgrim Dark-dreamer continued, relentlessly. In time, through repeated failure, the Dreamweaver who opposed him came to understand his Thienz-clever tricks: traps that sprung and struck her blind, or false feints that eroded her strength. Plainly, Maelgrim intended to exhaust her, then slash around her wards and take command. But the Vaere never chose the fainthearted for the training meted out to so few. As long as resource remained, Taen fought. She gained experience, and a few victories, and snatched rest in catnaps while the men made camp and cut firewood.

Corley woke her each evening an hour after sundown, and stayed through her meal of hot barley cakes, sausage, and soup.

"You can hardly keep on like this," he remarked when for the second day she pushed her bowl aside, barely touched.

Taen looked at him. Her eyes seemed the only thing alive in her elfin face. "I must. No one in Keithland can help these people. If I stop, the peril will spread."

Corley stifled an urge to argue; the fact the girl was right did nothing to ease his frustration. Abruptly he lost enthusiasm for the contest at darts started among the men by the fireside. He stamped off instead to inspect the picket lines, while the Dreamweaver settled yet again to ply her talents through the night.

Maelgrim and his Thienz never opposed her directly. Catlike, they preferred to toy with her, harrying her resources with snares and false threats. Then, in the depths of the dark when her concentration waned from weariness, they would choose an isolated camp or farmstead, and smash the defenses so laboriously strengthened each night.

Taen always sensed the destruction of her wards. Sweating in the throes of trance, she knew an answering flare of pain as her energies unraveled into chaos. Such times she rallied what resources remained and strove to block the evil dreams that Maelgrim wove about the minds of his victims. Power ebbed and flooded, pulled like tidal surge between opposing factions. Sometimes Maelgrim fashioned nightmares for the collective presence of a family; other nights he attacked a child, or someone's cherished elder, and broke their minds like twigs before an avalanche of terror.

Taen lacked the resources to rout such nightmares directly. Maelgrim could draw endlessly upon the reserves of his Thienz; through their support, he could outlast her endurance, sour her efforts with despair. At best Taen slowed his work, blurred his focus, and dissipated the potency of his imagery; occasionally her intervention enabled his stronger victims to survive. Far more often, conflict ended with the loss of a life. Grapevines might flower with spring, and sunshine return each morning, but the backlands of northern Hallowild became cursed with terror and madness.

In the chill gray hour before dawn, Corley returned to Taen's side. Invariably he found her shivering in the extremity of exhaustion, yet never would he let her see the depth of his concern. Each morning he affirmed her faith in life with carefully tempered banter. Toward the fourth week, when the release of laughter began to fail, he gathered her up and held her until she slept like a child in the hollow of his shoulder. Then he wrapped her slack form in blankets, settled her in a horse litter, and yelled for the camp to pack up. Risk increased so near the borders of the fells. The best defense was to keep moving, that demons could engineer no ambush upon his position.

Constantly shifting camp, the company traversed the orchards of northern Morbrith. Taen's exhaustion deepened. The day came when she did not waken until the column rested at noon. Frowning, irritable, she kicked free of her blankets and waspishly upbraided Corley for not rousing her sooner.

Dismounted to loosen his gelding's girth, the captain unwisely neglected to watch his back. "Fires, witch, you didn't miss a damn thing."

"The boatswain says differently," accused the Dreamweaver.

Corley rolled his eyes. "That man lies to his soup at night. Will you let be? All we saw was a priest who groused that Cliffhaven's rabble appeared to be trampling territory belonging to Morbrith apples."

Taen's annoyance changed to interest. "What did you do to him?"

The gray snapped. Too late, Corley delivered a ringing slap on its muzzle. "Sent him galloping back to the Brotherhood with arrows sticking through his cowl. Now go eat. I don't want to answer to the Kielmark if you waste away to bones."

Taen departed, leaving the captain cursing the gray, who had inconsiderately ripped his last pair of leggings; suddenly the Dreamweaver's exhaustion became excuse enough to camp early. Irritable at the last, Corley stripped to skin and knife sheaths and tore into the baggage looking for awl and spare thongs. Men at arms gathered around him like vultures. They speculated heatedly over the number and anatomical location of the insect bites their captain was sure to suffer, and presently debate gave rise to an exchange of spirited wagers. But the betting lost impetus when the man who listed sums and odds got assigned to waxing bowstrings. Grumbling and irrepressible, the Kielmark's company settled for the night.

Taen completed her defense wards and rolled in a blanket to nap. Although her bones ached with weariness, rest eluded her. The fields of her Dreamweaver's awareness remained tuned and wary; even the chirp of spring peepers added to her restlessness. She shifted in her blankets, eyes open to the twilight that seeped through her tent flap. By nightfall, Maelgrim Dark-dreamer would choose another victim and strike. His strength grew steadily with the passage of time, while her own resources dwindled, overtaxed by exhaustion. Very soon she would be unable to cope. The day would come when nothing remained but to tell the Kielmark's stalwart captains to order a retreat to the south.

Hopes of Jaric and the Cycle of Fire only fueled her despair. Surely no man of his sensitivity could weather the agonies she had sensed in Corlin market; one bitter moment, Taen had glimpsed understanding of Ivain's crazed malice. That Keithland's need required such suffering of the son was cause for deepest grief. Weary to the heart, the Dreamweaver felt the burden of Jaric's sacrifice as a sorrow more tragic than death.

Daylight seeped from the sky. The inside of the tent darkened to blackness unrelieved by any star. Taen lay sleepless, listening to the wind. At any moment the Dark-dreamer would tumble her wards.

Yet this time the attack came with none of the usual warning. Energy slashed Taen's thoughts with the splintering force of a lightning bolt. Slammed into dirt as she flung herself clear of her blankets, the girl recoiled in defense. Barriers bristled reflexively across her mind before she realized this intrusion held no trace of Maelgrim's malice. Raw energy continued to prickle across her skin. Confused, the Dreamweaver probed with her talents.

Light stabbed her eyes. Dazzled nearly to blindness, Taen squinted. Etched in painful glare, she beheld a bird of prey ringed with fire. The image echoed the configuration of Anskiere's stormfalcon, and sudden revelation caught her breath in a sob.

"Jaric!"

Her cry opened contact. Swept into thundering torrents of power, Taen screamed aloud. Her spirit was wrenched across an abyss of time and space, to meld with another that inhabited a flaming crucible of agony. Racked by torment that burned the spirit to a febrile spark of consciousness, Taen beheld the branching nexus of choice presently confronting Ivainson Jaric on the Isle of the Vaere.

One path led to darkness and oblivion; but the death at the end was illusion. Sathid would conquer before life was extinguished. Although suffering battered his thoughts to shapes unimaginably severe, Jaric rejected self-immolation. Neither did he reason as mortal man might; as Taen shared his passage, she perceived the defense that hopeless suffering drove him to consider. Like Ivain before him, Jaric understood that life might continue if mortal emotion were canceled. Fire could be endured, pain overcome, the unthinkable ignored, *if he let himself feel nothing at all, not joy, not compassion, not love.* He would yield his humanity. But in turn the Sathid would lose all his vulnerabilities to exploit; it must surrender to his will and reward him with power beyond measure.

Thus had Ivain conquered the Cycle of Fire; pressured to the limit of endurance, Jaric fought but found no alternative. Stripped of pride and grace, at the last he appealed to the peer he cherished for forgiveness, since the madness he must inherit to survive could not help but cause her sorrow.

Taen's control crumbled away, and the falcon's graceful form splintered through a lens of tears.

"Jaric, don't!" Protest was futile. She felt Ivainson's fiery presence begin to withdraw, even as she spoke. Grief prompted her to act.

Once, when Anskiere's geas had forced Jaric to untenable suffering, Taen had used dream-sense to weave him a haven; now experience gained in conflict with Maelgrim made her adept at turning nightmares and suffering aside. Swiftly, surely, the Dreamweaver fashioned a shelter for Jaric's beleaguered mind. She shaped peace where the Sathid could not reach, numbed the hurt of burned and lacerated nerves. Her work took immediate effect. Jaric yielded gratefully to exhaustion. Punished beyond thought, he slipped into deepest sleep, while the Sathid striving for conquest hammered vainly against Taen's bastion of wards.

The Dreamweaver realized then that Jaric's humanity did not have to be lost. With her help, he might recover equilibrium, even escape the madness inherent in the Cycle of Fire. Excited to hope, Taen forgot caution. Her discipline slackened for one preoccupied instant; and the crystals paired to Jaric gathered force, then turned poisonously against the source of interference.

The attack caught Taen woefully unprepared. Her Sathid-based powers as Dreamweaver resonated in sympathetic response; in an instant, her own crystal could cross-link and join the raging conflict with Jaric. Taen knew fear like the plunge of a knife. Should such a melding occur, the combined strength of the Sathid would expand in exponential proportions; battered by a ninefold increase in force, Dreamweaver and Firelord's heir would find their wills pinched out like candle flame.

Taen struggled to restore separation and balance. Immediately she sensed she would fail. Ivainson could not help; with his matrix-based powers still in dispute, he had no control to apply. And since the dream-link that bound him to the Dreamweaver skewed through time as well as space, the energies were tenuous and difficult to maintain. No enchantress who commanded the resources of a single crystal could hope to repel attack by wild Sathid within so fragile a framework. Power stabbed Taen's defenses. She countered, barely in time. Her bond-crystal quivered, half-wakened to rebellion, as backlash deflected like sparks.

Disaster awaited if she lingered through a second such shock. No choice remained except to release contact with Jaric, cleanly and at once. But the cruelty of that expedient marred judgment. Taen hesitated, and the untamed Sathid struck again.

Energy whirled her off center. Flayed by a vortex intense as a cyclone, the Dreamweaver screamed. In desperation she collapsed the wards protecting Jaric. Fire tore him awake with a heartrending cry of agony. He all but lost his grip upon life as mingled awareness revealed the extent of Taen's peril. Overwhelmed by fear for her, he reached for the only available recourse. Only the madness of Ivain would enable him to bridle his Sathid before the Dreamweaver he loved suffered harm.

"Jaric, no!" Taen's cry crackled across widening veils of distance. "Jaric, hold firm. I will disengage. If I journey to the Isle of the Vaere, I believe I can help you with safety. Wait for me . . . fish-brains, please wait. . . ."

CHAPTER V

Deliverance

The contact dimmed and snapped. Taen roused, shuddering, and broke into stormy tears. Returned to darkness and her blankets in northern Hallowild, she blinked eyes stinging yet with the light-falcon's afterimage. No means existed to determine whether Jaric had heeded her plea. Her dream-sense roiled like current disturbed by tide, and she needed every shred of concentration to settle her half-roused Sathid. The upheaval slowly subsided. Restored to emotional balance, Taen started as mail jangled suddenly beyond the tent flap. A swordblade slashed the ties. Canvas gaped open to reveal a flood of torchlight and men at arms, with Corley in the lead in his steel cap and armor.

"What's happened?" The captain's tone held no inflection, as if he anticipated killing. With a shock Taen realized the sentry on duty had heard her outcry and gone on to muster camp in expectation of attack.

She answered quickly to disarm the tension. "I had a vision, but not from Shadowfane. Jaric struggles to master the Cycle of Fire. If I journey at once to the Isle of the Vaere, quite possibly I can spare him the madness that destroyed Ivain."

Corley passed his lantern to the nearest man at arms. His eyes gleamed hard and dark as shield studs as he sheathed his sword. "If we go, the north will be left defenseless against the Dark-dreamer."

Taen met his expression, her features white with empathy. She well understood the consequences of her suggestion, and her honesty was painful to observe. "I cannot stay Maelgrim once his command of Thienz-linked power matures."

The tent flickered into shadow as wind winnowed the lantern flame. The man holding the light shifted uneasily.

Only Corley stood like a rock, the beads of reflection on his helm so still they might have been nailed in place. "I think no option exists. Whether you misjudge or not, we risk Morbrith. But if Jaric fails, all hope is lost for Keithland."

Relief broke Taen's composure; seeming suddenly, poignantly frail, she bent and buried her face in her hands. Jolted by recollection that her chronological age did not match her maturity, Corley disbanded his swordsmen with curt orders to break camp. Speed and protection were the only comforts he could offer the Dreamweaver under his care; but for beleaguered Morbrith, dependent on priesthood and prayers, he intended a last brave gesture.

Corley stopped and gently raised Taen's chin. Tears dampened his knuckles, twisting at his heart, but still he managed a lopsided grin. "Dress for the saddle, little witch. We've a task to finish before *Moonless* strains her stays for the sake of Ivainson Firelord."

Bits chinked in the darkness, counterpointed by the grimmer chime of mail and weaponry. The Kielmark's sailhands turned soldier mounted with none of their usual cursing as they began their southward march through Morbrith. To Taen, riding behind Corley's gray, the freshening beauty of spring seemed displaced by wrongness sensed elsewhere. Here moonlight might silver the apple blossoms like lace against star-strewn skies; but northward the Dark-dreamer remained free to dismember the minds of children at will, and the man with potential to check him writhed in agonies of flame on the Isle of the Vaere to the south. Though surrounded by fresh new life, Taen could not escape her burden of care.

The company seemed to reflect her mood. Scouts rode out at the alert, as if threatened by hostile territory, and the brisk pace set by the vanguard soon mingled the pungency of horse sweat with the fragrance of the orchards. Taen sat uneasily to the rhythm of her mare's stride. Dulled by concern, she failed at first to notice that Corley's second-in-command, captain of *Shearfish*, had reined up, blocking the head of the column.

Slit-eyed and large, the man bristled with belligerence even in the best of tempers. Usually he restrained his moods enough to avoid challenging his commander, but tonight's tension appeared to have upset his judgment. "You're going to Corlin by road. Man, are you crazy?"

Corley regarded his subordinate with fixed lack of expression. "The road is the fastest route to the port. Now, if that horse isn't lame, you'd better make it trot."

The officer pressed on heedlessly. "Fires, you'd ride through Morbrith? Priests'll be onto you like wasps."

"I know." A subtle change in the captain's manner made Taen start with chills.

The officer also saw; he swore and kicked his mount into stride alongside Corley's. "Priests hate the Kielmark. You know that." Jostled as his horse ducked the teeth of the gray, the man resumed without minding his superior's warning. "You ride past Morbrith Keep, you'll start a battle. Road won't take you anywhere quick then."

"So," Corley said equably. He did nothing apparent but flick his reins. Yet his gray sidled violently and bashed the insubordinate officer's mount into a tree. Taen saw metal flash in the moonlight. There followed an abbreviated thunk; and the officer reined up short, the handle of Corley's belt knife quivering in bark beneath his chin.

For a moment the two men glared at each other, breathing hard. Then

Corley spat. "Since when has any captain of the Kielmark's taken orders from Kordane's Brotherhood? Get back into line."

Only then did Taen notice that a second knife waited, gripped in a hand held steady to throw. The officer's lips curled back from his teeth in an animal display of anger; but he spun his horse and abruptly rejoined his company.

At the head of the column, Corley twisted in his saddle. As he jerked his blade from the tree trunk, Taen glimpsed his expression; witnessed firsthand, the force of personality required to maintain discipline among a band of renegades made her gut wrench. She might have sympathized with the priests, except that the preternatural alertness of the men who rode beside her suggested danger. Very likely the officer's complaint was just. Still, the Kielmark's first captain proceeded southeast, straight for Morbrith Keep.

The company traveled through the night without incident. Moonlight yielded to pearly dawn, and the orchards thinned to farmland mantled in mist. Taen rode with her reins slackened on the mare's neck. She said nothing of the wards broken by Maelgrim, or the family of hillfolk stripped of human reason and slaughtered in her absence. Saddle-weary and wan, the Dreamweaver barely reacted when Corley's mount jostled to a halt ahead of her.

"Hold hard, Taen." The captain caught her horse's bridle and jerked it to a stop. "We've a scout coming in."

In her preoccupation Taen had not seen the horseman who approached at a gallop. He called out as soon as he reached hailing distance.

"Morbrith's mustered. Three companies march, not two miles ahead." Dirt scattered over wet grass as the scout reined in his winded mount. "They're fully armed, maybe two hundred mounted lancers, as many bowmen, and two divisions of pikemen."

Corley sat still, eyes narrowed to slits; then his fist tightened. The gray shook its head with a dissonant jangle of bit rings. "They set after us yesterday, then, and won't expect us this far south. Tell me what banners they carry."

"Stars and fireburst of the priesthood. The High Earl's standard flies underneath." The scout hesitated, then added, "If they don't expect us, they look uncommon keen."

"So." Corley sounded unimpressed. A madcap glint lit his eyes, and he turned aside to face the Dreamweaver. "Taen, would you dream-send a message to an army, if I asked you?"

Struck by suspicion, she glared at the Kielmark's captain. "You planned this! Didn't you?"

Corley grinned. "Provoked it, rather. I can't leave a domain threatened by demons to rot under incompetent leadership. If the priests wanted Morbrith, they should've burned the High Earl while they had the chance."

"That's an excuse, you bloodthirsty maniac." But the captain's spirited daring left Taen much heartened. She agreed to lend her talents to his plan.

There followed an interval through which Corley issued a rapid string of orders. The company re-formed with the ease that stamped every enterprise beneath Cliffhaven's command. Men cleared weapons from their sheaths, and faced their shields at the ready. They did not curse, but moved as machines perfectly tuned; even the clink of armor and weapons became subdued. When the flag bearer unfurled the Kielmark's red wolf standard, a whistle like the reedy call of a gull signaled the advance. The men moved silent as ghosts through thinning cobwebs of mist.

The air smelled of grass and dew and plowed earth; birdsong rang from the treetops. Riding through a world spangled gold by early sunlight, Taen felt exhilarated and uncertain all at once. She might be surrounded by the most competent fighters on Keithland, yet fact remained: an army outnumbering Cliffhaven's force four to one barred her way to the Isle of the Vaere.

Corley worked on unperturbed. He positioned his men in a copse that flanked the verge of a dirt lane. Then he, the flag bearer, and a picked team from *Moonless* arrayed themselves across the gap. Taen could see them plainly from her position at the edge of the wood. But archers stationed scarcely twenty paces off blended invisibly among the trees.

The lane stretched empty to the south, a ribbon of packed earth dividing a plowed expanse of cropland. The fields were newly turned, deep and moist, and impossibly peaceful for a site that might soon see a battle staged. Tentatively Taen extended her dream-sense. At once her sensitivity encountered overwhelming numbers of men: mounted lancers with bodies weighed down with steel; garrison soldiers well trained at arms but soft on foot, their heels sore and blistered from a march forced on them by priests; after them came archers, some still blinking sleep from their eyes. Taen sampled the mood of the men from Morbrith and found them hungry, disgruntled, and surly over the fact that their own green standard hung beneath the starfield and fireburst of Kordane's initiates. Corley's assessment of the host sent against them was dead accurate. Carefully the Dreamweaver set about shaping the call he had asked of her, even as the troops rode into view.

Lance heads splintered the morning light, tightly clumped as tatting needles jabbed through silver lace. The reason for Corley's deployment immediately became apparent. The front riders from Morbrith crowded the narrow way to avoid miring their mounts in the soft earth of the field. War-horses bunched and jostled, squeezing mailed legs and scabbards one upon another, and bumping painfully against the lighter riding horses that conveyed the commanding priests. Kor's Brotherhood protested. Like a swirl in a log-jammed current, they pressed ahead to ease their battered knees.

In the shadow of the copse, Taen saw Corley's teeth flash in a grin.

Then a leaf flicked close by; one of the Kielmark's archers knocked a shaft to his bowstring. With lethal steadiness, he drew, released, and the morning stillness became shattered by a wailing scream as a whistle arrow sprang aloft.

The lancers' destriers were war-trained, and not an animal among them flicked an ear at the head-splitting racket. But the Earl's palfreys shied and spun and reared, flapping blue robes, and spilling two priests off into freshly turned earth.

"Behold, the Great Fall," shouted Corley from the lane. The priests still in their saddles looked up. In outrage they spotted the small force awaiting them under the Kielmark's wolf banner. Then the whistle arrow bit into ground, leaving memory of the captain's mocking profanity ringing across silence.

The priests still in their saddles gesticulated like a conclave of angry puppets, while the ones who had fallen caught their horses and remounted. Someone shouted a command. The starburst standard wavered and thrust straight. Lance tips, pikes, and helms roiled as the men at arms behind gathered to charge. The actual moment of threat seemed utterly unreal. Taen swallowed, biting lips gone white as her cheeks. She shut her eyes, forced her mind to focus, and stabbed the full force of her Dreamweaver's powers straight into the gathered army.

'All men loyal to Morbrith stand firm! Desist from attack at the edge of the trees. Let Cliffhaven strike only those who usurp the rule of their High Earl.'

The call touched the men at the instant they spurred their horses. Hooves gouged the turf, gathered into the thunder of full stride. But in the act of charging, the oncoming line broke, forced to separate to avoid its disordered knot of priests. The men on the flanks trailed raggedly behind as their horses plunged off the road, to labor over the grabbing soil of plowed ground. Taen sensed answering movement around her. The Kielmark's archers nocked broadheads to their bows while the war host hammered down on their position. Posed as bait in the lane, Corley clamped his thighs to his saddle and unsheathed his blade to signal his concealed men to kill.

In panic, Taen sent to the war host again. 'For the love of your Earl, halt now!'

For a moment, nothing changed. Then somebody in Morbrith's front lines whooped like a boy and reined in. Around him, leveled rows of lance tips shuddered, and raised, and a cheer burst forth from the men. Warhorses slid on their hocks, and like drops sprayed from a pool, six blue-robed priests suddenly galloped undefended toward the wood.

"Strike your mark!" yelled Corley.

The archers in the trees released. A storm of shafts darkened the air, struck flesh with a sickening smatter of sound. Bristled like pincushions, the mounts of the priests staggered out of stride and fell screaming. Kor's initiates spilled like rags into the road. They scrambled to pick themselves up, while in disciplined silence, Corley's chosen company swooped out of cover to claim their prey.

As they closed, the head priest reached his feet. Mud-scuffed and bleeding from a scraped cheek, he straightened his silver-bordered tabard, glared at the naked steel that surrounded him, then lifted his bearded chin to meet the Kielmark's captain. Others of his order were herded into a bunch while a pair of scar-faced sailhands manhandled one who was slow to find his feet. The man cried out, possibly injured. But his captors showed him no pity.

"You commit an atrocity," accused the High Priest. Lank, almost shriveled with age, his voice carried thinly over the tumult. The boisterous noise of the Morbrith men quieted as he spoke. "Since when do armed companies of criminals trespass upon the lawful domains of Keithland? Landfast will punish your boldness."

"Fires!" Grinning as his blasphemy caused the priest to flinch, Corley resumed in a tone gone dangerously mild. "Since when have the Kielmark's captains wasted time taking heed of religion?"

From her vantage point among the trees, Taen saw two of the High Priest's companions tense. One edged closer to his master, hands fluttering nervously at his waist.

"Don't move!" snapped Corley. "D'you think the Lord of Cliffhaven gives a bent half-copper for your lives?"

Mention of the Kielmark made the High Priest blanch; he lost any inclination to speak. At present, the ships carrying temple gold from Kisburn to Landfast passed through Mainstrait untouched except for tax. But a word from the Lord of Pirates would cause those vessels to be boarded, plundered, and sunk. Much revenue might be lost.

Corley sat, reins pinched under crossed hands on his saddle horn. "Here's what you are going to do for the Kielmark," he began. "For a start—" And suddenly, without warning, he jerked straight.

Steel flickered between his fingers. A blade scribed a line through sunlight and Taen saw the nearest of the priests crumple over with a scream. He pitched to the ground, blood flooding in a stream over the fists pressed tight to his abdomen. The Dreamweaver recoiled, sickened. Corley was always accurate with his knives; without visible provocation he had struck a man down, his intent not to kill, but to torture.

Taen barely felt the arms that steadied her in the saddle. "Don't look," said *Moonless*'s steward in her ear.

But shutting her eyes did nothing to block the screams that ripped across the wood. Corley's voice rose like a scourge above the noise. "I said, *don't touch him.* Do you all want a steel decoration in your guts?"

Taen shivered, weeping. Her dream-call had brought an unarmed man to suffer. She sat stunned, as slivering cries of anguish subsided to retching whimpers no whit more bearable. Corley continued without break, his icy phrases directing his captains and Morbrith's army to the completion of his plan.

"You, muster the men from the ships *Ballad, Scythe,* and *Sea Lance.* Take this priest at sword point to the Sanctuary tower. Free the High Earl and accompany him home to defend his keep. Make the Brotherhood understand that Cliffhaven will level the temple if even one initiate attempts interference. The other two ships' companies will escort the Morbrith army back. The rest of the Brotherhood go with them, as hostages. I don't care if you slit their holy hides to achieve it, but make the temple garrison there open the gates. Since the Brotherhood's services from that time on will be unnecessary, you will all stay on and aid the Earl with his defenses."

Men shuffled, and silence fell suddenly, as the wounded man ceased outcry.

"Murderer!" shrieked the High Priest. "Fires consume your wicked flesh!"

His passion drew Taen's attention. Despite the steward's protest, she looked in time to see the High Priest's lung hammered short by the closed fist of a seaman. On the ground the wounded brother lay still, a second knife transfixed through his throat. Corley spurred his horse callously over the corpse. "*Moonless*'s company, to me. We've a crossing to complete, and quickly."

Sticks snapped as the Kielmark's first captain reined his gray through the muddle of men at arms. He entered the woods in time to see Taen pull free of the steward's arms, her face pinched white with shock.

He stared at her, taken aback. Then his eyes turned bright with anger. "Oh, Fires, get her moving," he snapped to his servant. Then he jerked his head at *Moonless*'s mate. The rest of *Moonless*'s company formed up promptly and began their brutal ride across Morbrith.

Within the hour the horses jogged lathered with sweat; breath labored in their lungs, and foam spattered from their bits. Still Corley drove onward. Taen clung to her mare until her mind swam with exhaustion. The sun shone hot on her head, adding dizziness to fatigue. Her knees rubbed raw on the saddle. Even her fingers blistered. Of Morbrith's broad fields and gray stone keep she remembered little; progress became marked by the change in the ground, hoofbeats shifting from the deadened thud of dirt to the jarring clang of packed roadway. The company stopped to change mounts at a post station. Shortly afterward a sailor caught the Dreamweaver swaying in the saddle. He said no word to his captain, but watched her without slackening pace. When her hands slipped from the reins, he reached out and caught her as she fell. Taen finished the ride half-conscious in his arms.

At noon the riders swept into the crossroads settlement of Gaire's Main. The site had once been sacred to the hill tribes, but the spring where the clansmen convened for rites now filled a brick trough for watering livestock. Sleepy stone cottages roofed in thatch lined the thoroughfare. Hens scattered squawking through the dust as the horsemen reined up in the square; doors banged and shutters slammed in the lane beyond as villagers fled hastily into their homes. Their fear made Corley grimace in annoyance; his horses all stumbled, and the men who rode them were tired, hungry, and thirsty to the point where an insult might knock them down.

The captain halted his gray in the yard before a rambling two-story tavern. He signaled the men to dismount, then crossed to the doorway in three stiff strides. The latch proved to be bolted. Out of temper, Corley whirled and caught the signboard that swung creaking from the gable. One yank snapped its rusted chain, and his follow-through battered the nearest shutter and splintered the hasp. The window crashed open. A frying pan flew out, fended off with a clang by Corley's mailed fist.

He sprang and wedged the shutter back with his sword hilt. "Kor's Fires, woman! I'm not here to rape your wenches. My men pay silver for meat and rest. But by damn, deny them, and I'll let them kick in your walls for sport!"

Chain rattled. The door creaked, then widened, and a raw-boned blonde in frowsy skirts stepped out, hands braced on her hips. She surveyed the company of men and horses crowded untidily across the spring yard.

Then, with sharp calculation, she regarded the burly captain who had dented her best piece of kitchenware. "Inside, and welcome, then. But damages will be added to your tally, starting with my busted sign and shutter."

Corley refused to haggle. Having spotted one seaman still mounted with Taen lying limp in his arms, he turned on his heel and splashed his way through the mud beside the spring. The tavern mistress watched with hard eyes as he exchanged low words with the sailhand. Then, without fuss, he lifted the girl down himself.

Black hair tumbled free of the Dreamweaver's hood as Corley strode back to the tavern. "Open your door," he said briskly.

The girl's extreme pallor convinced the woman to abandon argument. She shook out her apron, stamped across the threshold, and bawled for her daughter to fetch a flask of spirits from the cellars. Then, as the old stablemaster and his single lad ventured from their hiding place in the grain stores, she motioned Corley and his following into the tap.

Minutes later, Taen aroused to the sharp taste of plum brandy. Tired, aching, and disoriented, she opened stinging eyes and discovered that she slouched on a chair in a low-beamed room crammed with men. Someone knelt by her with a flask. Weaponry chinked as he bent closer. Shocked back to memory, Taen recognized Corley, still clad for battle in his mail and helm. The same hand that had knifed the priest reached down to help her sit straight. She cringed back reflexively.

"Kor!" Corley's blasphemy came out a whisper. He shot to his feet, and brandy spattered his wrist like blood.

Taen ached to speak, but words would not pass her lips. As she hesitated, the captain turned his back. For a moment he stood as if he would say something. Then, abruptly, he strode off.

Soon afterward, *Moonless*'s steward arrived at the Dreamweaver's side. He clutched the brandy flask anxiously against his chest, but one glance convinced him that drink would not ease the distraught girl. The servant abandoned the spirits on the nearest trestle and glanced quickly over his shoulder. Corley was not in sight.

"Step outdoors for a moment with me. The air might do you good." The steward caught Taen's shoulder, pulling her firmly to her feet. She quivered under his fingers as he steered her past the hearth, around tables of men wolfing stew, and out through the wide plank door.

Midday sun warmed the inn yard; overflow from the spring trickled soothingly over the lip of the trough. Nearby the aged stablemaster and a freckle-faced lad hustled to and fro, watering horses. The steward searched for a quiet spot and finally found a log bench against one wing of the inn. He seated Taen, then settled himself on the grass at her feet.

On shipboard he was known as a gray-haired, unimposing man, by turns appreciated for efficiency and cursed for his motherly sense of propriety. But today his fingers jabbed nervously at the grass and he spoke with hesitation. "Lady, I'm going to tell you things my captain will not. He's got pride like the devil, enough so he'd lay me across a hatch grating to be flogged if he knew I'd interfered."

"Don't." Mention of further violence caused Taen to tense in distress.

The steward reached out and caught her hand. "I must."

Taen shuddered. She pulled free in protest, but did not turn away as the steward continued.

"You couldn't see from the wood. But that priest got knifed because he disregarded the captain's warning. The Brotherhood often communicate with hand signals. Corley caught the wretch trying to provoke a plot with his fellows. Had no one cowed them, forcefully and at once, that small batch of priests could've brewed trouble clear to Landfast."

"But why? Corley tortured that man before he killed him. What could justify such brutality?" Taen chewed at a broken thumbnail, and started as she tore it to the quick.

The steward answered gently. "Ending dissent could, at the cost of one life rather than many. The road was fastest, and any delay threatens Jaric. Had you forgotten?"

"No." Taen pressed her stinging finger against her leathers and waited, sensing the steward would add more.

"Corley's mother was a Morbrith lady's handmaid. While he was a lad, a hilltribe's chief stole her away during summerfair. In bitterness the father ruined himself with drink. The High Earl saw the boy got leavings from his own board so he'd have enough to eat. The mother returned years later with a hillman's get, a girl-child who spoke clan dialect and never learned civilized words. Corley fought himself bloody, defending his sister from abuse. But one day he caught three boys at rape. The scuffle that resulted left the Morbrith heir badly cut. Rather than shame his benefactor at trial, Corley shipped out with a trader. He ended serving the Kielmark."

Here the steward paused. He checked to be certain Taen still listened. "Corley once said his High Lord was a hard man, but just. In arranging the Earl's freedom, I think our captain cleared what he saw as a debt."

Taen stared at the ground. Despite her Dreamweaver's perception, she had never probed Corley's mind throughout her time on *Moonless*. What had shocked her most that morning was the chilly calculation that inspired the man to violence; unlike the Kielmark's, this captain's temperament did not skirt the edge of madness.

"I suppose I owe him an apology." She looked up, but noticed the steward had left her. Probably he hoped she would think and forgive his captain on her own; the courtesy left her relieved. At least she would not be pressured to confront the matter at the extreme end of her resources.

Taen sighed. Too tired to move, she curled against the warm boards of the inn and slept. Afternoon passed; the shadows gradually lengthened and trees striped patches of shadow against the gray timbers of the wall. At the usual hour, the blind, senile woman who served as priestess of the well crawled from her nook in the loft. Though decades had passed since hill-folk celebrated rites at her spring, she still wore the knotted leather garments of the clans. Her shuffling step carried her past the bench where the Dreamweaver lay asleep. For a moment the woman's milky eyes turned aside. A prickle of warning stirred within her; she strained to interpret, but lost the thread of prophecy in the vagueness of advanced age. Muttering and shaking straw-tangled hair, the priestess moved on to the kitchen stoop, where the inn mistress's daughter waited with her daily mug of milk.

Taen slept until Corley's mate came to fetch her at sundown. She barely had time to eat supper before the men saddled horses in the stable-yard. The trip to Corlin resumed with stops through the night to change mounts; Corley steered himself clear of the Dreamweaver's presence throughout.

The company reached the ferry over the Redwater by dawn. With the least possible delay, the captain left the horses in the care of a drover, then bribed the bargemaster on duty with gold. Stranded caravans and merchants hollered imprecations from the bank, while the men loaded gear, and a Dreamweaver who slept soundly in blankets; they completed the trip down the estuary afloat. *Moonless* put to sea before Taen awoke. By then the shores of Hallowild had disappeared astern. The brigantine drove with the wind on her quarter, toward Jaric and the Isle of the Vaere.

CHAPTER VI

Demon Council

Lanterns shuttered with scarlet glass cast baleful, bloody light over the rock hall of Shadowfane. Demons all the sizes and shapes of nightmare stirred restlessly in the gallery, while, dark against darker shadow, a newly spawned Karas shape-changer lay puddled like slime on the floor behind the mirror pool. Presiding from the dais above, Lord Scait sat upon his throne of human trophies, spiny hands poised on stuffed knees. None in the chamber made a sound, though alliances within Shadowfane were uneasy; the sighted and the eyeless alike strained forward, attention fixed on the human who knelt at Scait's feet.

"Rise." The Lord of Shadowfane blinked, scaled lids momentarily eclipsing evil yellow eyes. "Speak the tidings you came to deliver."

The one known as Maelgrim touched his forehead to the floor. "Your will, Lord Mightiest." Wire bracelets chimed at his wrists as he straightened. Extended periods spent in mind-link with the Thienz had left him painfully thin. Black hair fell uncut to his shoulders, and a tunic of dyed linen clothed his wiry frame, belted at the hips with a sash of woven gold.

A rustle crossed the assembly, scratchy as wind through dry leaves. Maelgrim raised his face toward the throne. His eyes shone ice-pale, accentuated by bony sockets. When he spoke, he mixed images with words no human would comprehend. "She has gone, this Dreamweaver sent by the Vaere. The might of Shadowfane could have killed her easily. By your command, such was not done. Now she has sailed for the Isle of the Vaere with the ship *Moonless* and the red-haired captain of the Kielmark's." The creature who had once been human paused, his expression twisted with frustration. "Lord, by your command, two most troublesome enemies are granted liberty to escape the net I wove. Why should this be?"

This news roused consternation from the gathering. Murmurs arose, sullen in overtone, underlaid by whispers of complaint. Scait's favorites exchanged uneasy glances, while numerous cadres of rivals expectantly licked pointed teeth.

Their stirrings and rustlings caused Scait to clash his jaws, and the long hackles trembled at his neck. "Silence!" He surveyed the room, his glare baleful red in the lanternlight. As the assembly subsided to stillness, he focused once again upon Maelgrim. "Your insolence is inappropriate, spawn-of-a-mewling-human. More important matters lie at stake than the death of your sister-accursed. Listen well. Learn patience, for the Dreamweaver and her captain go free only to dance to a grander plan. Be content, Dark-dreamer. You shall have what you desire, and sooner than you presently think."

The Lord of Shadowfane croaked with a demonic equivalent of laughter, then arose from his throne of human remains. He spoke loudly that all might hear. "O my kindred, my brothers, the Kielmark's captain has divided his force. Half of them convey to Ivain's heir, Jaric, the Dreamweaver who might have unraveled my plan. The rest remain, abandoned to their fates in Morbrith domain. These ones and all they stay to defend now lie vulnerable to exploitation. Listen and know! Maelgrim's search has located human children with the talent we require. These will be taken alive and brought to Shadowfane. Once their enslavement to a Thienz-dominated Sathid is complete, their talents will be turned to the ruin of humanity. Then shall the descendants of *Corinne Dane* suffer revenge for our centuries of exile!"

Beneath the dais, Scait's circle of favorites nodded among themselves. A quiver rippled the jellylike surface of the Karas, and Thienz hummed softly in mind-meld. Here and there, dark as clotted ink between the feet of the larger demons, the furred forms of Gierjlings twitched in communal sleep. But the boldest of Scait's rivals were not satisfied.

The nearest leaped up with a guttural growl of displeasure. Swift as the lash of a whip, Scait interrupted before she could speak. *'Be still, or earn bloodshed, for I have not forgotten the Set-Nav unit from* Corinne Dane *accursed!'*

The rival bristled her short hackles. She poised on the verge of challenge, but the colleagues at her side chose not to support her defiance. They wished to hear of Scait's plot, and alone she was no match for the Lord enthroned on the dais. Left without recourse, she subsided as hushed anticipation settled over the assembly.

As if no disturbance had occurred, Scait outlined the remainder of his intentions. By the time he finished, even the most bloodthirsty rivals were forced to reluctant admiration; the plan to storm Keithland and reclaim the lost Veriset-Nav computer was a masterwork. Corley had unwittingly played straight into the Dark-dreamer's hands; and even the Kielmark's formidable discipline became a tool for Shadowfane's machinations.

Jabber arose from the packed ranks of the assembly. Young Thienz clustered about their elders to share in subtlety and speculation. Gierjlings sensed the rising excitement and stirred from sleep, their opened, reasonless eyes glowing violet in the shadows. Now only the most vicious of the rivals considered dissent. The plan for humanity's destruction seemed brilliantly conceived.

The brigantines left at Corlin might indeed be purloined. They could ply south to recover Set-Nav with no human to dispute their passage, for did not vessels under the Kielmark's banner fare at will within Keithland? No king, no councilman of the Alliance, and no priest of Kordane's Brotherhood interfered with captains who flew the red wolf banner. To risk the

Pirate Lord's displeasure was to set a stranglehold upon commerce, and humans did not place their gold in jeopardy. This every demon understood.

But snags remained: neither did the Kielmark's officers brook interference. Their loyalty was tight as old roots, impossible to bend or loosen. Memories-of-ancestors confirmed such beyond question: demons had died screaming upon Cliffhaven. To meddle with the King-wolf-pirate was to risk much, or so the rivals determined. Some of them gnashed their teeth. One female, Scait-egg-sister, went further and dared raise an objection. "Lord, your proposal is flawed-dangerous, a plan for the wise to spurn. Kielmark-accursed has a taste for mad-vengeance, and his chestnut-haired captain is like him."

Scait disdained to raise his hackles against a sibling. With a lazy hiss, he gestured toward the newly hatched shape-changer that glistened like jelly at his feet. "But we have a Karas to replace this captain," he admonished. "Through the crews left vulnerable at Morbrith, we shall gain access to *Moonless*, and through *Moonless*'s master, shape-changed to a likeness of Deison-Corley-killer-of-brethren, the Kielmark shall meet his death. So shall my grand plan triumph."

The Lord of Shadowfane waved a spurred forearm. In the corner farthest from the dais, a black knot of flesh stirred and unraveled into the separate forms of a mature circle of Gierjlings. Six sets of eyes glimmered like sparks in the gloom.

Scait turned eyes the disturbed gold of turbid oil upon the boy from Imrill Kand. "Maelgrim Dark-dreamer, at last you may claim the greatest gift of your inheritance. Accept these Gierjlings and school yourself to merge with their minds. When you are able to embrace their powers fully, you are to wreck the bondage of Shadowfane upon the souls of Morbrith and with them the Kielmark's crewmen. That is my command."

In the deepest hour of night four days after *Moonless*'s departure, the Kielmark's four captains left stationed in Hallowild left their beds, though no circumstance had arisen to waken them. In separate but simultaneous movement, they dressed, and armed, and abruptly roused their ships' companies to depart from Morbrith Keep. The men obeyed with spiritless efficiency. By torchlight they saddled and mounted. A puzzled captain of the Earl's guard watched them ride out in cheerless silence. Once past the gates, they spurred south on the road toward Corlin.

The early hours before daylight saw their arrival at the crossroads settlement of Gaire's Main. There, while villagers shrank behind locked doors, the men at arms paused to water tired horses.

Disturbed by the chink of metal, the ancient priestess of the well stirred in the loft above the stableyard. The strange, prickling sensation that accompanied her gift of clairvoyance brought her fully and instantly awake. Stiff-jointed, but clear of mind, she rose from the straw and crept to the trapdoor. Night wind carried the scents of horses and man-sweat; yet the creatures who moved among the animals below were not as they should be. The priestess blinked blind eyes. As a maiden she had undergone training and a painful initiation to gain the enhanced perception of a clan priestess. Her altered mind sensed a wrongness about these horsemen who swaggered in the stableyard below.

Troubled, the clanswoman scratched her belly through a rent in the skins that clothed her. Slowly, muttering all the while, she made her way to the ladder and crept into the shadowed darkness of the stable. None noticed as she shuffled to the doorway by the grain bins.

Close at hand, the sense of wrongness became overpowering. Horses stamped and men cursed; the company had remounted, ready to resume their ride. But over the clank of weapons, stirrups, and mail, the priestess sensed a ringing overtone that bordered the edges of pain. Never in life had she known such a presence of evil. Her duty was plain. Trembling, the crone stepped into the yard to challenge.

Her voice rang girlishly clear. "Behold! Trespassers enter Keithland. They ride as humans, yet they are shells, emptied of spirit and possessed by demons. True men, be not deceived. Know ye stand in the company of Kor's Accursed!"

"Fires!" Corley's first captain slammed his mount with his heels and jerked around to face her. "Woman, as you value life, be silent."

"Demon." The priestess stabbed a bony finger in his direction. "Death cannot change the truth!"

The captain gripped his sword hilt. "Since when do the Kielmark's officers take orders from old women?" He smiled with icy mockery; and still smiling, drew steel and cut the blind priestess down.

She fell against the water trough with a coughing cry. Blood flooded hot over her hands. Yet purpose made her fight for strength. Sinking to her knees, she groped through the mud and the run-off from the spring. Her palms touched the sacred surface of the well-stone. Energy surged from the contact. Dying, the priestess melded with the mystery within and sent warning.

South, in the underground installation on the Isle of the Vaere, a monitor light flashed on the communications panel. Circuitry activated to receive an incoming signal that twisted across time and through space; the message originated from a dying priestess in Gaire's Main. Though the culture of the hilltribes was patterned after primitive ritual magic, the clairvoyance of their priestesses in fact disguised a network of Set-Nav's comlink; thus had the remotest wilds of Keithland been watched continually for intrusion, transmissions sent by means of talisman stones no demon yet thought to examine for technological artifacts.

Even as the clan priestess breathed her last, Set-Nav merged her fragmented warning with data in the memory banks. Numbers flashed through probability equations, and the monitors glittered amber with distress lights. Keithland's existing defenses were critically inadequate to offset Shadowfane's latest offensive. Set-Nav had no means to sequence second-ary alternatives. Jaric's Firemastery lay yet in jeopardy. Although he clung stubbornly to sanity, his strength ebbed with each passing day; even if he embraced Ivain's philosophy at once, his resilience had worn to the point where the paired Sathid might still overthrow his will. The Dreamweaver perhaps could save him. But Set-Nav sorted facts, and by extrapolation perceived impending danger to Taen.

Power surged to transmit the priestess's warning. Far to the north, a century and a quarter out of phase, Taen Dreamweaver started awake in her berth aboard *Moonless*.

Jostled against the lee boards by the rising toss of the sea, the girl lay in darkness, straining to catch a silvery jangle of bells. Yet she heard only the thud and hiss of waves against the hull, and wind thrumming through the rigging. No trace remained of Tamlin of the Vaere except the warning left echoing in her mind.

Taen shivered and sat up. Her cabin seemed suddenly ominous with threat. The darkness oppressed her without remedy. The lamp in its gim-baled bracket was empty of oil, the reservoir dry since the evening before. With *Moonless* pitching uncomfortably to weather, the girl had stayed in rather than cross spray-drenched decks to find the steward.

Yet deep in her heart, Taen knew that weather was only an excuse; she had avoided the kindly old servant since leaving Gaire's Main. Her self-consciousness stemmed from the fact that she had yet to muster the nerve to make her peace with *Moonless*'s captain. While crew and brigantine drove south under straining yards of canvas, Corley kept to the quarterdeck. Storms invariably made the captain moody and unreasonable about inter-ruptions. But now the Dreamweaver had no choice. Tamlin's warning forced her to confront him without delay.

Taen slipped from her blankets into dank, chill air. More than cold raised gooseflesh on her skin as she tugged a linen shift over her head. Too hurried to fight the pitch and toss of the deck and dig out heavy clothing, she slipped the latch, then clawed her way against the elements to the quarterdeck.

Topside, the brigantine seemed frail as a sliver slammed through a black expanse of spindrift and sea. Wave crests foamed across the waist, carved into geysers by the ratlines; after each successive flooding, spray showered back in sheets between taut curves of canvas. In the puddled glow of the binnacle, two men labored to hold the brigantine on course, lanternlight glazing their fingers orange as they strained against the drag of the double-spoked wheel. The nearer one worked with his hood thrown back. Through tangled chestnut hair, Taen recognized *Moonless*'s captain. She called out and worked her way aft, over planking sleek with seawater.

Corley lifted his head. Startled to see the Dreamweaver on deck, he mistimed his pull. The wheel kicked under his hands. He lost a spoke, swore, and threw his weight against the helm as a headsail banged forward. *Moonless* heeled, overcanvassed, and unforgiving under a murderous burden of wind. Two strong men could barely maintain her course.

Corley shouted to the officer on watch. "Call the boatswain away from the pumps. He's needed on deck. And tell him to roust the second mate to replace him below."

Somewhere in the darkness, a crewman answered. With less than a minute's delay, the boatswain arrived, panting, to relieve his captain at the wheel.

Corley stepped aside, a bulking, windblown shadow with water dripping silver from his beard. He lingered over the compass. Then, satisfied *Moonless* was secure on her heading, he turned and met the Dreamweaver with eyes that were bright and inquiring and alert as a predator's.

Killer's eyes, Taen thought; she shivered involuntarily.

Corley misinterpreted. "You're chilled." Swiftly he shed his cloak. Before the Dreamweaver could decline, his hands bundled her in salt-drenched wool that soaked her own garment to the skin. Yet she endured the damp rather than suffer the captain's touch again.

Moonless tossed. Balanced on his feet with catlike ease, Corley spared her the need to speak first. "What brings you out? Not the shaggy mug of my helmsman, surely."

His humor raised no smile. "I have tidings from the Vaere," said Taen. "We are pursued out of Hallowild. I was told to warn you. Beware of the demon-possessed."

Corley frowned. He did not move, even when a shower of windblown spray plastered his shirt to his back. Suddenly he gestured with decision. "Come below. We'll talk."

Given any choice, Taen would have declined. But strained emotions did not blight her common sense; she knew the captain's request concerned the men left stationed at Morbrith. For their sake, she permitted Corley to hustle her through the hatch and into the dry comfort of his stern cabin.

A lantern burned over the starboard sea chest. In wildly flickering light, Taen observed that the sheets were turned down on Corley's berth. Evidently the steward cherished hopes that his captain would snatch time to undress and sleep. But as always, such solicitude proved futile. Corley flung off his drenched tunic and tossed it carelessly across the linen. Then he gestured for Taen to sit on the locker nearest the coal stove.

The Dreamweaver did not remove his dripping cloak. Though the spare orderliness of the captain's quarters had always before reassured her, she had lost any inclination to abandon her reserve. "The Vaere gave me no particulars. I know only what I told you on deck."

Voices in the cabin drew the steward, who ducked his head in the door. Corley dispatched the servant to the galley to fetch mulled wine, then seated himself before the streaked panes of the stern window. He scrubbed the salt from his brow with his knuckles and again looked at the Dreamweaver. "I need your help to contact my captains at Hallowild. They may be better informed of the danger we face. If not, they deserve warning. Our peril might become theirs as well."

Taen bent her head, expression hidden by a fallen veil of hair. She sat so still that Corley thought for a moment she had refused his request.

He tried gently to reason with her. "If you can't act for my men, then do so for the safety of Morbrith's folk."

But Taen did not hear. Already she had blanked her physical senses and slipped deep into trance. She extended her focus across leagues of wind-torn ocean to the far shores of Hallowild. To her dream-sense, the town of Corlin appeared as clustered sparks of light, each person a jewel shining against velvet dark. Other glimmers lay scattered across the expanse beyond: post stations, farmsteaders, and foresters plying livelihoods in solitude. Taen refined her probe, centering upon the estuary of the Redwater where five brigantines rode at anchor, commanded by the captain of Cliffhaven's vessel *Ballad*.

Although the river was jammed with the customary traders, no spark matched the abrasive presence of *Ballad*'s master. Taen hesitated, perplexed. On the chance the man was off board, perhaps enjoying a drink or a wench in one of Corlin's three taverns, she swept the harbor again, seeking the *Ballad*'s boatswain. That search failed also. Alarmed now, Taen turned north to Morbrith where the Kielmark's other companies remained to defend the keep.

The backland hills lay studded with familiar compass-ring formations that marked a clansmen's camp; northwest held only darkness. Puzzled, Taen hesitated. Beyond the sparkling cross that was Gaire's Main, the living folk of Morbrith should have glimmered like a constellation of stars. No light remained. Shadow seemed to have fallen over keep and farmstead and wildlands. Touched by fear, the Dreamweaver intensified her search. Through the lengthening days of spring she had guarded twice ten thousand people from the predations of the Dark-dreamer; surely Shadowfane could not have obliterated so many in so short a span of time!

Yet Morbrith domain stayed dark, as if a veil of mourning had been drawn across the land. Not the High Earl in his hall, nor the surly temper of Corley's first-in-command, nor a single man of Cliffhaven's defense force remained. Reckless with disbelief, the Dreamweaver delved deeper. She strained the limits of her strength seeking life, to no avail. *Nothing;* blackness absorbed her effort. Her senses sank into endless, numbing cold. Shock and grief drove her to sound that well of oblivion; but as Taen extended her senses, evil moved at its heart. She jerked back in alarm. Aware of her, the presence that occupied Morbrith Keep reached out in challenge. Though its essence was recognizably part of Maelgrim Dark-dreamer, another more alien resonance suffused the pattern of his being.

This overtone was *other,* and terrifying in a manner no word could describe. The Dreamweaver dared not delve deeper over distance. If the people of an entire domain could fall to the Dark-dreamer's strange and amplified influence, hope for Keithland now relied upon *Moonless* and Ivainson Jaric.

Taen broke contact, restored to the toss of stormy seas and the clink of mugs as the steward served spiced wine in the stern cabin. She clenched bloodless fingers in the wool that cloaked her shoulders. Feeling helpless and desperate and alone, she sought means to voice a horror that defied credibility. Shadowfane had struck. Morbrith was no more; every competent, rough-mannered seaman who had remained to defend the High Earl was now lost to the living. Taen tried to speak, but anguish and disbelief stifled the breath in her lungs.

"Taen?" Warned of something brutally wrong, Corley dismissed the steward, and said, "Girl, you look ill. What's happened?"

The Dreamweaver could do nothing at all except break the news. "Morbrith has fallen to Kor's Accursed. Not a man, woman, or child escaped." She shivered, forced herself to qualify though her voice broke. "I don't know how! But your men are gone, even *Shearfish*'s master and crew. I found no trace of the companies you stationed to aid the High Earl's defense."

An interval loud with waves and creaking timber answered her terrible words. The only movement in the cabin was the rising curl of steam from the one mug the steward had managed to pour. Jolted by the captain's profound stillness, Taen at last looked up. The blanket bunched in her trembling fingers. Where she had braced herself in expectation of curses and violence, Corley had done very little more than surge to his feet.

His face was open as few ever saw it, a naked expression of horror and pain and disbelief. As Taen watched, the creases around his eyes clenched. The grief that rocked him was deep, and private, and woundingly intense. Incongruity struck her like a slap. That a cold-handed killer could own such depth of compassion became impossible to countenance.

Unable to reconcile the emotion with the man, Taen gasped and quivered and at last gave way to tears. "Corley, they're gone, all gone. Even *Ballad*'s awful cook, who put all that pepper in the beans."

The captain's stunned moment of suspension broke. He reached her in a stride, caught her heaving shoulders in his hands, and stroked her hair. "Easy. Easy."

His control seemed restored, his shock and his loss instantly masked to master the needs of the moment; but no one with a Dreamweaver's sensitivities could ignore the truth: the man behind the facade still wept inwardly for the death of the crews under his command, as well as the mother left behind years past at Morbrith. Taen felt a hard something give inside. The distrust that had festered since the incident with the priests found release in racking sobs. The Dreamweaver buried her distress in dry linen that smelled of soap and the herbs the steward used to sweeten the sea chests. Yet horror did not abate. Deison Corley might be forgiven his cruelties; the firm play of muscles beneath her cheek might steady her, but no human comfort could ease her sorrow. Not even for the sake of Ivainson Jaric could Taen forgive herself for abandoning Morbrith to the mercy of the Dark-dreamer.

Corley shook her gently. "Ease up, little witch. You've pitched yourself alone against an enemy too great for all of us. Don't feel craven for stepping back." His tone assumed a hint of iron. "Once Jaric gains his mastery, we'll have the means to fight."

Yet the captain's confidence was forced. Morbrith had fallen, quickly, inexplicably, and finally, claiming the only relation who recognized him and five companies of the Kielmark's best men. Grimly Corley wondered when the pursuit promised by Tamlin's warning would overtake his single ship; even if he contrived to escape the fate that had befallen the High Earl, how long before Ivainson Jaric broke under agonies beyond the means of any human mind to endure?

That question would not find answer in darkness on the open sea. As soon as Taen had calmed somewhat, Corley settled her by the stove and belatedly offered mulled wine. White-faced, fighting to control her sorrow, she badly needed the restorative. Although she accepted the cup, she did not drink.

Instead she clenched her fingers as if her hands were cold. "The Kielmark will have to be told."

Corley expelled an inaudible sigh of relief. He had always known the girl had pluck. For the first time he realized how dependably he could count on her good sense. "You might want to finish your wine first."

Taen shook her head. "No." The faintest amusement brightened her tone. "Unless the Kielmark has miraculously learned temperance, I rather think I'll need the drink afterward."

She hooked her mug in a bracket to warm upon the stove, then bowed her head in dream-trance once more. Her powers answered with reluctance. Weary in a manner that had little to do with the lateness of the hour, she gathered her awareness in hand. The scent of sweet wine and spices and the salt-smell of Corley's sodden woolens faded slowly from perception as she cast her call outward, over leagues of storm-tossed ocean toward the Kielmark's stronghold on Cliffhaven.

Corley poured no wine for himself, but paced the cabin while he waited for her to rouse. He compensated without effort against the roll of the deck as *Moonless* thrashed through the swells. Gusts blew savage blasts of rain against the stern windows. Streaks of wet ran down the glass, gilt against the darkness beyond. Corley gazed into the storm with unseeing eyes and noticed very little until the steward appeared at the companionway with a quiet inquiry after Taen. The captain paused then, abruptly aware that the Dreamweaver had lingered too long in trance.

His concern transformed to alarm. The girl lay motionless by the stove, black hair drying in tangles over her shoulders. Her borrowed cloak had slipped aside, the one wrist visible beyond the edge too still to seem alive. Between one stride and the next, Corley knelt at the Dreamweaver's side.

Taen stirred almost immediately. Conscious of the captain's presence even before she had reoriented to the stern cabin aboard *Moonless*, she opened eyes gone bleak with dismay. "I couldn't get through."

Corley reined back an overpowering urge to question; his impatience could only add to the girl's alarm. Against all instinct he waited, and in her own time Taen qualified. She touched his mind directly with her dream-sense, and Corley shared firsthand the dense, almost suffocating darkness blocking her attempt to reach the Kielmark.

He spoke the instant her touch released his mind. "Do you think the event is related?"

Taen knew he referred to the disappearance of his men and the strange darkness over Morbrith. "We dare not assume otherwise." Her hands twisted the cloak's damp fabric over and over, while Corley assessed the implications of leaving the Kielmark uninformed.

But Taen already thought ahead of him on that count. "Cliffhaven must be told. With Tamlin of the Vaere unavailable for advice, no choice remains but to work through the wizards of Mhored Kara."

The girl's resilience astonished. Still on his knees, Corley started back, his hand out of habit clenched on the hilt of his most convenient knife. "You risk much," he said incredulously. "There's no love lost between the college of sorcery and the Kielmark."

"Meaning they fight like weasels." Taen was not intimidated when Corley drew his blade and tested the edge with his finger.

"One of the conjurers Anskiere destroyed at Cliffhaven was the Lord of Mhored Kara's son." The captain flipped the blade neatly and made a cutting motion in the air. "Why do you think the Kielmark's so touchy on the subject of sorcery? Aside from the upset arranged by the witch Tathagres, we've been expecting arcane retaliation in some form for the better part of a year."

"Yet your master cannot guard Mainstrait against a threat he knows nothing about." Taen reached out and with a touch stilled Corley's knife hand in the air. "Some problems can't be solved with steel. You'll have to trust my judgment."

The captain disengaged and returned the bleakest of smiles. "My boatswain says you're a crafty hand at cards. That's a fair blessing, girl. Because against the wizards of Mhored Kara, you'll need every trick you have, and a dozen others only the devil could arrange." The knife flashed once as Corley turned the blade and rammed it into the sheath at his wrist. Worry hidden behind brusqueness, he added, "Good luck, little witch. If you get through, and if the Kielmark neglects to thank you properly for the service, I'll personally thrash him at quarterstaffs the next time we dock at Cliffhaven."

Taen grinned. "You'll try." And she ducked as Corley grabbed for her. "Don't expect me to watch you get bruised."

"There's faith." The captain grimaced sourly and rose, half thrown to his feet as *Moonless* yawed over a swell. The wind had freshened. The scream of the gusts through the rigging penetrated even the cabins below decks. By now the watch would be changing. Anxious to return to his command, Corley yelled for the steward to bring his spare cloak. Then, too impatient to wait, he stamped through the companionway into the storm. Let the servant pursue him to the quarterdeck. The Kielmark's first captain had great courage, but not so much that he could stay and watch as a Dreamweaver too young for her burdens rallied her remaining resources and plunged once again into trance.

CHAPTER VII

Cycle of Fire

The settlement of Mhored Kara lay on the coast east of Elrinfaer, to the south of the merchant city of Telshire. Taen had never traveled those shores, but during off-watch hours Corley's sailhands had told her tales. The wizard's towers perched on the very tip of a peninsula, black and notched, or black and pointed like rows of soldiers' spears. The structures had few windows. On dark nights strange lights burned from slits cut in the seaward walls, sometimes green, other times red. The phenomenon was not without precedent, for Vaerish sorceries commonly generated illumination; but as described by the sailors, the spells of Mhored Kara were scintillant and hurtful to the eye.

Taen considered her task with trepidation. For centuries the conclave had provided conjurers for the courts of Felwaithe and Kisburn. Only once had the Dreamweaver encountered their work. As a child she had seen three such sorcerers set the enchanted fetters that blocked Anskiere's command of wave and weather. The strongest of the three, who once served as Grand Conjurer to Kisburn's King, had gone on to strip the Stormwarden of protection, by murdering the birds fashioned of weather wards for defense. Taen recalled the sorcerer's hands, streaked and dripping with blood as they stabbed and stabbed again with the knife. Even the memory made her feel ill.

She had been untrained then, utterly ignorant of her Dreamweaver's potential. Newly wise to the ways of power, she lacked the understanding to determine how a Vaere-trained sorcerer in the fullness of his mastery could be subdued by lesser wizards from the south. Perhaps against three, Anskiere could not save himself; far more likely he had surrendered willingly for some obscure purpose of his own. Whatever the reason, that Kisburn's conjurers had constrained his powers was a real and chilling fact. Taen gathered herself in trance, coldly aware that she courted danger.

Caution was necessary also because the location of Mhored Kara was unfamiliar to her; to find the wizards' towers she had only a compass direction plotted off Corley's charts, and imperfect images garnered from the recollections of sailors. She began quickly, lest her resolve become daunted by uncertainties.

The lash of the seas and the work and creak of *Moonless* dimmed in the Dreamweaver's ears as she unreeled her awareness over Elrinfaer. She crossed acres wasted by Mharg-demons in the generation before she was born, league upon league of desolation where life had yet to recover. Her mind traversed a landscape of treeless rock, of earth ripped by wind into sand and dust devils. Deserted cottages caught drifts of soil in the stones of tumbled chimneys. The pastures that once nourished livestock grew no fodder, but baked and cracked like desert bottomlands deprived of any shade. Not even bones remained of the folk who had once tilled fields and pruned lush acres of orchards. The sky overhead was empty of clouds or birds; beneath the golden glare of sunrise, sorrow seemed instilled in the stripped bones of the hills.

Taen pressed south and east, to the far side of the tors of Telshire. There bare earth gave way to stunted weeds, then grasses tasseled with seed. Spring was well along in the lower latitudes. Wild apple trees showed hard green knots of new fruit. Beyond rose the deep, dark pines of the Deshforest, all shadows and interlaced branches fragrant with the scent of resin. None dwelt here but wandering clans of hilltribes and the occasional isolated trapper. Farther still, the forest wilds fell behind. Taen traversed scrublands pale with reed marshes, and chains of brackish pools that smelled of kelp. As she neared the sea, the vegetation changed to saw grass and beach plum, which clothed the high dunes of the south peninsula. There at last she found the towers of Mhored Kara, dull black against dawn sky, and narrow as swords; slate roofs caught the light like silvered lead. None of the wheeling gulls that scavenged the shoreline circled near, or roosted there.

Taen damped her powers to a spark and guarded her presence under ward. The wizards might not be sensitive to the resonance of Vaerish sorcery, but only a fool would presume so. With apprehension and no small degree of misgiving, she narrowed her focus upon the tallest and slenderest of the spires and searched its salt-scoured stone for an opening.

She entered through a rune-carved arch nestling beneath the eaves. The interior beyond was dusty and dim. Her questing dream-sense encountered trestles scattered with books and the burnt-down stubs of candles. The strange paraphernalia of magic stood crammed between shelves of phials, philters, and collections of stoppered jars with faded labels. The bones of tiny animals moldered within, or birds preserved in brine. Unpleasantly reminded of Anskiere's slaughtered wards, Taen pressed on. Her awareness funneled down a spiral stairway dark with mirrors that did not reflect their surroundings. She sensed these for a trap and did not probe within; dream-sense warned her of mazes that twisted and turned in endless convolutions designed to ensnare the mind. For the first time, fear made her hesitate. What sort of intruder inspired the Mhored Karan wizards to build such cruel traps?

Yet news of the blight upon Morbrith allowed no space for faintheartedness. Taen forced herself onward. One level lower, she found storerooms filled with casks and boxes fastened with wire. The air had a musty smell, like fur locked too long in old trunks. By now aware that she had entered

by way of the attics, Taen dropped lower still. Three levels down, she
encountered gray-robed boys with shaved heads who meditated in cubicles
of silence and shadow. A moment's pause revealed these to be novices, and
not the ones she sought. Taen passed on, through a bare hall where the
wind blew through slits in the wall. From there she descended yet another
spiral stair and quite suddenly came upon the sound of voices.

In a chamber spread with wine-colored rugs, five sorcerers sat in a
circle discussing the merits of an aspirant recently arrived from Telshire.
Two wore black, two wore red, and the last, robed richly in purple and
gold, was a wiry ancient with peaked brows and bleak eyes. His cheeks
were tattooed with sigils of power, and each of his fingers, even his spatu-
late thumbs, was heavily ringed with silver. Taen extended her dream-sense.
After the shallowest of scans, she singled the elder out as one great in the
ways of power. He had an aura set into discipline like a watercourse channeled through rock, and his titles were Magelord of the Conclave, and
Master of Mhored Kara.

He sensed the presence of the Dreamweaver at once. His cold eyes
lifted, he stiffened very slightly on his cushions. At his movement the
black-robed wizard to his left murmured inquiry and was silenced by a
wave of the old one's hand. Silver rings flashed briefly by candlelight. The
gesture that followed was in some way arcane, for Taen felt a charge of
force sting the outer barrier of her wards.

She deflected the thrust without difficulty, though the energy was configured differently from anything she had previously encountered.
Whether the spell was shaped in defense or query, Taen chose not to
fathom. Rather than wait for a second attack, she manifested a detailed
illusion of her presence in the chamber at Mhored Kara.

Her form appeared between one breath and the next, robed in the
pearlescent, shimmering gray given only to a Vaere-trained Dreamweaver.
Her black hair was caught into a coil of wire, and her flesh gave off a
tangible, living warmth. Her eyes, blue and direct as sky, were focused
solely upon the Magelord of the Conclave. "Do you always greet visitors
with hostile spells, Your Eminence?"

"Only those who arrive unasked, and by sorcery." The ancient's voice
was dry as wind through dead leaves. He spoke as if to empty air, and to
Taen's astonishment, the other four sorcerers in the chamber recoiled
upon their cushions as if startled. The nearest of the red robes raised his
hands. A spindle of light bloomed between his palms, but died out immediately as his Master snapped his fingers for him to desist. The underling
subsided with a sullen look, while his Magelord answered Taen's puzzlement directly.

"My fellows of the conclave neither hear you speak nor see you." The
old one qualified with ancient, embittered malice. "My conjurers see only
what is real, Lady. Within these walls, you do not exist."

Taen absorbed this in furious thought and gained her first insight into the powers of Mhored Kara's conclave. They were unquestionably men of talent, but molded by tenets far different from those of any Vaerish master. Where the powers of Sathid bonding took inherent talent and by resonance expanded an inborn trait into something greater, the wizards of Mhored Kara learned to reach inward, to grapple and twist reality to the dictates of mortal will. Taen studied the ancient and his four confederates more closely, and concluded that such manipulation of natural order came at punishing cost. Pitiless decades of training left the wizards emaciated, humorless, and baleful as crows. Their tireless and exacting analysis of reality might strip and banish Sathid-born conjury as dream; led to extreme, these wizards might even enter the mind and sunder rapport between Sathid master and crystal. But in directly applicable force, Vaerish powers were as beyond them as sky over earth. Taen perceived the workings of how Anskiere's gifts had come to be bound by such constraints; what she might never understand was why the Stormwarden had permitted Kisburn's conjurers the opening to let his imprisonment happen.

The Magelord's manner sharpened suddenly. Perhaps he realized that Taen unraveled the secrets of his conclave in the dream-space of her silence, for he clenched his hands with a dissonant clash of rings. "Why do you send to the one place in Keithland where illusions such as yours are not welcome?"

Taen detected threat behind the words. Although in theory the Magelord's spells could not set her at risk, she chose not to test that chance. The Master of Mhored Kara certainly could be dangerous, cruel as he was within, and emotionally steeped in spite against all things he could not influence.

"I bring tidings," Taen said directly. "Keithland is imperiled." Without further opening, she translated the image of Morbrith, and all that its darkness signified, directly into the old mage's mind.

He hissed, his dark eyes wide with affront. Spindles of light snapped forth from the palms of all his underlings, the red-robed ones and the black. Taen felt a blow hammer her shields. The image she had constructed in the chamber shattered like a smashed mirror. She let it go without contention, and instead reshaped the core of her energy into a presence wrought of sound whose existence not even the underlings could deny. *'For the sake of Keithland and the reality you value, send warning and word of Morbrith's fall to the Kielmark on Cliffhaven.'*

The Magelord countered in rasping irritation. "The conclave has sworn no oath of protection to the Vaere! And the Kielmark deserves no favors. Do not forget that he once granted sanctuary to one who later killed two of our own."

Taen noticed the elder's queer reluctance to mention the Stormwarden by name. She probed on impulse, and perceived in the Magelord an apprehension that bordered upon outright fear. Anskiere's potential for redress against the wizards who had interfered with him did not sit well with the conclave at Mhored Kara. Though the idea of vengeance from the Vaere-trained was a misapprehension, Taen amplified their false belief to a cutting edge and pried at the wizards' reluctance. *'Do you wish to answer to Anskiere of Elrinfaer for release of the frostwargs? To claim injury for Kisburn's conjurers is to assume culpability for their crimes.'*

The Magelord glared at the air. His ringed hands worked as if he longed to reach out and throttle the voice wrought of dreams. "What of the ice cliffs?" he rasped. "Your Stormwarden is prisoner still."

In answer, Taen sent him an image of Jaric, whose resemblance to his father, Ivain, at times could be uncanny. *'The Firelord left an heir, Eminence. He completes his passage to mastery even now on the Isle of the Vaere.'*

Though the Master of Mhored Kara would never concede defeat, the spite reflected in his obsidian eyes assured Taen better than promises that she had won his acquiescence. The conclave would inform Cliffhaven. And wily and snappish as a wolf, the Kielmark could be depended upon to inflame the rulers of Keithland's multiple, bickering governments until each and every one of them took action.

Corley checked his cabin later, to find Taen settled and asleep beneath the steward's watchful eye. Informed by the servant that her demand upon the conclave at Mhored Kara had been successful, he returned at once to his quarterdeck. Though the wind had risen, he issued no orders to shorten sail. Instead he posted a second lookout in the crosstrees and doubled the watch on deck. All night he stood by the helmsman, strained and tense and watching for dangers he had no words to describe. When dawn broke over the ragged crests of the waves, he called all hands and broke news of the evil that had overtaken their companions in the north.

After their captain's summons, *Moonless*'s company became haunted by insecurity. The sailhands glanced over the shoulders as they went about their duties; the smallest of unusual noises made them start. Banter and swearing ceased altogether. When the gale lifted, the men toiled in the rigging without hot food to sustain them, for Corley kept the galley fire out rather than risk having smoke reveal their position to the enemy.

Moonless made fast passage, sped by the fresh winds of spring. But the fact that the weather held fair and the horizon remained empty day after day did nothing to lift the spirits of her crewmen. Gaunt and wary, and driven by a captain with hunted eyes, they finally hove the brigantine to in the empty ocean southwest of the Free Isles' Alliance.

"I sail on alone," said Taen to the Kielmark's first captain. Clad in a Dreamweaver's robes of silver-gray, she stood by the mainmast pinrail, her hands clenched as if she expected argument. "You can loan me the jolly boat."

Corley folded bare arms across his chest. The straps of his knife sheaths crisscrossed both wrists, cutting into his tanned skin. "Only you know where you're going, little witch. If you'll accept no escort to the Isle of the Vaere, at least know this. *Moonless* won't leave these waters until you and Jaric return."

Taen took a quick breath. "There's danger."

"Where is there not?" Corley grinned as if the threats of Shadowfane and the perils of the Vaere were of no consequence. "Besides, I want my jolly boat back. In one piece, mind. No chips or dings in the keel."

"Done." Taen tried valiantly to smile. The gesture made her seem poignantly vulnerable and young. "Well, do I have to launch the tub myself?"

"Maybe." The captain called two sailhands away from splicing a replacement stay and regarded the Dreamweaver intently. "You know my mate's fallen permanently in love with you. I'd bet my best dagger he'd rather take that jolly boat and scrape barnacles off *Moonless*'s rudder than see you row off without him."

"I'm flattered." The Dreamweaver pulled a sarcastic face, then ruined the effect by blushing. "Tell him to scrape barnacles anyway. If you wait for me, we all might need to leave in a panic."

Corley sobered instantly. "I'll chance that." Then, as if the sight of her caused him pain, he spun on his heel and shouted to the sailhands. "Get aft and lower that jolly boat. Lively!"

Men sprang to obey. Barely had they freed the tackles before Corley pushed the nearer sailor aside and busied both hands on the lines. His tongue turned sharp as his knives, and after the briefest possible interval the boat struck the sea with a smack. Before the ripples scattered, Taen found herself loaded and cast off. She seated herself jauntily on the jolly boat's seat, threaded oars, and glanced one last time at *Moonless*'s quarter-deck.

Corley stood with his back turned, hands braced on the binnacle. He refused to come aft to watch her off. If he glanced around once he would see how frail she looked, alone on the empty sea; then he could never bring himself to let her go.

"Keep your bearings, captain," Taen called. She turned her hands to the oars and wondered why her words made Corley flinch. Never before had she seen him uncertain; almost, she would rather have watched him killing priests.

The slanting light of afternoon touched the wave crests like chipped quartz, and flying fish scattered in shimmering arches before the bow of *Moonless*'s jolly boat. Taen rested her oars and rubbed a blistered palm on her knee. Well practiced at rowing as the daughter of a fisherman, she had made good progress in her slight craft. The brigantine had diminished astern until tanbark sails showed as a speck against flawless ocean; ahead, no life stirred but the strafing flight of shearwaters. Yet that emptiness itself was deceptive. Taen knew by her dream-sense that she neared the Isle of the Vaere.

She extended her perception, and once again the minute vibrations that could be neither seen nor felt by the flesh touched her dream-sense. The fabled isle lay very near. Careless of her blisters, the Dreamweaver lifted the oars. She rowed one stroke, two, three; a wave lifted the keel and coasted the jolly boat forward. Suddenly the vibrations peaked, the dissonance against her inner awareness clearing to a single sweet tone. Taen jabbed the oars deep, scattering spray as the wave rolled past. Before the current could drift her off location, she shaped a dream-call to alert Tamlin of her presence.

Sky, sunlight, and shearwaters vanished without transition into mist. Wind slapped the water, and wave crests frayed into sudden foam. Taen shipped the jolly boat's oars. Through a whipping tangle of hair she saw a flicker like heat lightning rend the air. A booming report followed, but the Dreamweaver did not hear. The ocean around the jolly boat underwent an abrupt change. The gale died to a breeze, and she drifted amid a roiled patch of water. Elsewhere the sea lay preternaturally calm. Slate-gray clouds extended to an empty horizon; *Moonless*'s sails no longer showed astern. But off the jolly boat's bow stretched beaches unmarred by tide wrack. No storm had ever hammered the dune line beyond, nor the cedar forests of terrible beauty that lifted majestically skyward. Taen had visited the Isle of the Vaere before, yet her breath caught in wonder all the same. The unspoiled splendor of the place could bewitch the most jaded of eyes.

Then, with a thrill of joy, the Dreamweaver noticed something less than perfect upon that enchanted shoreline. On the sands at the sea's edge rested an ungainly wooden fishing boat, the name *Callinde* carved on her thwart. Anxious for Jaric, Taen Dreamweaver slammed oars into rowlocks and hurled her craft toward shore.

Bells jangled the instant the jolly boat grounded. Taen twisted around in time to see Tamlin stride down the side of a dune. His cap lay askew, and the white beard strewn across his shoulders tangled with fringes of feathers and beads in his haste.

"You won't listen. That's trouble." The tiny creature stamped his foot in anger. Taen looked on without surprise as his boot left no impression in the sand. "You promised help to Jaric. Did you guess you risk your life, and his as well?"

Taen jammed the oars one by one beneath the jolly boat's stern seat, then stepped, barefoot, into the shallows. An ebbing wavelet chuckled over her ankles, sucking the sand from under her soles. "I had to come."

"So." Tamlin cocked his head and frowned keenly. His black eyes seemed to bore holes through her flesh; no approval showed on his shriveled, walnut features. "So," he said again, then slapped his thigh in conclusion. "You love him, yes?"

Taen caught her breath, then released a gasp. She blinked, sat on the jolly boat's thwart, and stared unseeing at her sandy toes. "I never thought of him that way." But the instant Tamlin had broached the subject, she realized she must.

Troubled by emotions she barely dared to confront, Taen turned her Dreamweaver's perception inward to reexamine the past. While the jolly boat heaved beneath her on the surge of an incoming wavelet, she recalled Jaric as she had encountered him first, tying supplies on a drag-sleigh in the snowy yard of a forester's cabin. He had been younger then, troubled and uncertain, and frightened of the future. Taen had felt pity at the time, not love. Later, she had restored the memory he had lost, used her talents to force his destiny; then she had acted upon the orders of the Vaere, for the sake of Keithland and the brother imperiled by Kor's Accursed. Taen frowned, oblivious to the sunlight that broke through the clouds and warmed her back. She had gone on to deliver Jaric to the merciless terms of Anskiere's geas. Love did not effect such betrayals.

Neither did love abandon a man to a lonely crossing in an open boat, without comfort. Taen swallowed, fighting an irrational urge to weep. Unbidden, a memory sprang complete in her mind. Once she had stood on cold stone in the Kielmark's dungeon and waited while Jaric rubbed at wrists scraped raw by steel fetters. At the time, Tamlin's directive had been clear: force Ivainson to the completion of Anskiere's geas. Yet Taen had not intervened. Instead she had left the decision to Jaric himself. Closer to him than anyone in Keithland, she had known he had the fortitude not to flee. She had cared for his integrity enough to free him; and afterward she had defied the Vaere, defending Cliffhaven from demon assault, all for the safety of Ivainson Jaric.

Taen drew an unsteady breath. She attempted to picture another man in Jaric's place, and felt misery. She tried to imagine a future without him, and could not; plainly, foolishly, she realized all along she had been think-ing as a child, not the Vaere-trained enchantress who now was a woman grown.

"Yes." Taen's reply to the Vaere was filled with wonder and discovery. "I love him." And recognizing as she spoke that Jaric might well regard the fact as a nuisance, Taen swore until she exhausted every profanity learned from Corley's sailhands and the fishwives of Imrill Kand. When next the Dreamweaver sought Tamlin, he stared stubbornly out to sea.

The jolly boat bumped and ground against the sand. Moved by habit, Taen kicked the craft into slightly deeper water. Poised uncomfortably on the thwart, she waited through a tactful interval until the Vaere spoke again.

Fey creature though he was, Tamlin understood human nature quite clearly. "For Keithland's sake, you must succeed."

Taen stood. Afraid of what her mentor might add, she heaved the jolly boat onto the beach with a coarse grating of pebbles. "Then allow me to try at once."

Bells jingled. The Vaere vanished and reappeared, standing on the bow with his head level with hers. Breeze still blew strongly off the sea, but his feathers hung motionless. His wizened features seemed wistful and sad and hopeful all at once. "Fortune speed you, child. Be brave and finish what you began."

Taen shivered. She tried to break the creature's gaze, but the Vaere spoke sharply. "Listen! Stay here. Do not enter the grove. Engage your Dreamweaver's powers in behalf of Ivainson Jaric. Then stand firm. If your man survives to win his mastery, he will return to *Callinde* and find you."

The air rippled as if disturbed by heatwaves. Then, with a faint sigh of bells, Tamlin disappeared.

Taen regarded sunlit boards where the Vaere had stood, as if she might read the riddle of his existence in the grain of the wood. The creature would not return; with growing apprehension, the Dreamweaver pondered how much had been left unsaid. Her peril was no less for Tamlin's silence.

Fear shadowed Taen's resolve. Her Sathid might easily rouse and link with the dual matrix Jaric fought to subdue. If that happened, both of them would be killed. They might die quickly, even painlessly under the merciful touch of the Vaere; but die they certainly would, for Tamlin had once revealed that no man who undertook mastery of three crystals ever escaped domination. The few attempts had turned out monsters, beings so malevolently warped that, for the safety of Keithland, the Vaere had destroyed life rather than let them survive.

Decision bore heavily upon the Dreamweaver. To act at all was to assume responsibility for a loved one's life. Each instant of deliberation extended Jaric's pain; that suffering must eventually drive him to madness became insupportable. Taen could never endure such an outcome. To watch as he lived and breathed, unable to comfort or share emotion, was to lose him in a manner more final even than death. Taen dug her toes in hot sand, but in the end she could not keep still. She abandoned the jolly boat where it lay and crossed the sand spit to *Callinde*.

The boat had not been left trim. Jaric had brailed the mainsail neatly to the yardarm, but jib and spanker lay heaped in a bow, a negligence he never would have tolerated by choice. A halyard dangled loose in the breeze. An incomplete splice marred one end; Taen rested a hand on the prow and wondered what mishap had parted so stout a line. The boat reminded her poignantly of Jaric, laughing and strong with his hair tangled from wind; together they had sailed this same craft to Cliffhaven with the Keys to Elrinfaer in hand. Taen bit back an urge to call his name aloud. Courage returned. Life or death, suddenly she realized she had no choice but share his passage to mastery. Keithland and her own heart would be as a wasteland without his presence.

Taen raised her knee over *Callinde*'s thwart. She clambered aboard. Sand from her toes pattered over floorboards soiled with swallow droppings. The dirt would have annoyed old Mathieson; grinning at recollection of the aged man's swearing, the Dreamweaver sat on the folded mass of the spanker and stared over the mast. Blue sky shone like enamel between torn streamers of cloud. For an instant she imagined she might never behold such beauty again. Then, with the sturdy self-reliance of her fisherman forbears, the girl closed her eyes and gathered her talent.

Heat and pain and searing brilliance: Taen felt herself immersed in fire. Body and mind, she shared the suffering that riddled Jaric's flesh. Strangely, his will seemed absent. Through a bottomless well of torment she searched, yet found only the echoes of contentment generated by Sathid entities that judged their conquest assured. But the conflict was not finished. Somewhere, somehow, Jaric resisted still, for pain flared and sparked over his nerves with an intensity that dismembered thought.

Taen fought to sustain her purpose. Though able to banish torment in an instant, she dared not grant Jaric the reprieve she had offered once before; should she try, his paired Sathid would recognize outside intervention and attack. This time her only chance was to work through the beleaguered consciousness of the victim himself. Though the agony inherent in the Cycle of Fire dizzied her almost to delirium, Taen shaped her presence into a call of compassion. Then, softly, tortuously, with many a hesitation and misstep, she began to trace the network comprising the mind of Ivainson Jaric.

The process caused her to know him better than ever before. Underneath the Sathid's litany of conquest, she experienced the despair of an infant deprived of mother and father. The taunts of boyhood apprentices became slights against herself; and later, on the wind-whipped deck of a fishing boat, she shared a betrayal she herself had helped complete, when the weight of a sorcerer's inheritance fell full force upon the shoulders of a boy ill equipped to cope. Pained by his suffering, Taen continued her search, through the heartbreak, and the hardship, and rare moments of happiness. She explored Jaric's growth all the way to adulthood, but still encountered no spark of the consciousness that made the man.

At a loss, Taen drew back; bereft, almost beaten, she fought to preserve hope, even as the predatory litany of Jaric's Sathid battered her dream-sense ragged. At any moment the crystals might conquer, destroy this mortal who, against the severest odds, had mustered courage to strive after powers he had never desired. Desperate to avert the inevitable, Taen ransacked memories like an eavesdropper. By accident she stumbled across a sliver of remembrance so well protected that she had overlooked it entirely until now. Jaric had sailed to the Isle of the Vaere for Keithland; *and also for love of the black-haired daughter of an Imrill Kand fisherman.*

Taen knew pain then, sharper than the physical torment of flame. Never could she endure the ruin of one who treasured her more than life itself. Heedless of discomfort, she hurled herself into the very heart of the conflagration. There she found Jaric. Like a limpet in a tide pool, he clung to the most precious memory he possessed. Once he had stood in *Moonless's* aft cabin, struck dumb by recognition and loss; now, against the insupportable anguish of the Cycle of Fire, Taen saw that he defended the last of his integrity with the memory of herself, asleep in trance against the fine-grained wood of Corley's chart table.

The discovery nearly unbalanced her. Dangerous as the bared edge of a razor, the Sathid prepared to press their final attack. No margin for error remained. Taen engaged her Dreamweaver's powers with utmost care. She did not force or possess, but blended with Jaric's awareness; tenderly she reshaped the memory he held in his inward eye. Adding dream-vision to his image, she caused the girl at the table to lift her head and smile; along with awareness of her presence, Taen gifted him with hope, and compassion, and light. She met the gaze of the boy in the dreaming mind of the man; there followed a moment of recognition as deep as the sea's depths, endlessly wide as night sky.

The Sathid felt Jaric stir with renewed life. Vengefully strong, they redoubled their onslaught of pain. But even as fires flared to unendurable torment, Taen acted. She reached through the network of Jaric's consciousness and blocked all sensation of hurt.

His relief was immediate, but exhaustion left him limp. He lacked the vitality to respond. Taen wept in dismay. The Sathid also felt Jaric falter; they chiseled at his defenses with ferocious energy. The Dreamweaver understood that the instant he broke, her presence would be discovered. The matrixes would then strike to engage her own crystal, and defeat for them both would be final. Enraged by the threat of such loss, Taen could not bring herself to retreat.

Suddenly a voice reached through her dismay. *Fishwife. Will you never learn to be patient?*

Taen smothered a flash of hope. Perhaps Jaric's passivity was feigned, a ruse intended to throw the Sathid off guard while he marshaled resources for his final step into mastery. Afraid for him, but steady, Taen watched while Jaric extended his awareness into the raging heart of the conflagration. Defended against pain, he now could merge with the living flame, unlock its structure even as he had unriddled the pebble that granted him Earthmastery. Taen sensed a stab of malevolence; Jaric and his enemy Sathid blurred into a single entity. Then, in a split-second transition, he claimed his sorcerer's heritage and tapped the force of the fire itself.

Energy raged raw across the contact. Taen felt herself savaged by a light that brightened and blistered and waxed impossible to endure. Jaric became lost to her, walled off by ringing roulades of power. No mind could encompass his presence. Taen felt her dream-sense falter. Ivainson the man burned, then blazed, then exploded into brilliance more terrible than Keithland's sun. The Sathid presence recoiled in alarm. Jaric pursued. Vengeful as sword steel, he struck. Searing illumination sundered the web of contact Taen had drawn about his person. Even as Keithland's newest sorcerer achieved the Cycle of Fire, her own awareness winnowed like blown sparks and went dark.

CHAPTER VIII

Gierj Circle

Alone in a sapphire expanse of ocean and sky, the Kielmark's brigantine *Moonless* changed tack precisely according to schedule. The helmsman turned the rudder hard alee. As the shadow of the spanker scythed across the quarterdeck, Corley paused with his hands gripped fast to the rail and gazed astern, toward the elusive Isle of the Vaere. The seas were mild, and the wind brisk. Canvas banged taut against sheet lines and boltropes. As crewmen trimmed the staysails, the brigantine lifted into a heel, the foam of her wake fanned like lace across sapphire waters; the weather was so clear that the horizon beyond seemed trimmed by a knife.

"Nor' nor'east, an' steady as she goes," called the quartermaster. *Moonless* cleaved like an axe through the swells, her crewmen trained to the keenest edge of fitness.

Still, her captain regarded the sea with brooding eyes. No pursuit had arisen yet from Shadowfane; but the slightest error in navigation might set his vessel too far south, within the influence of the fey caprice of the Vaere. Despite five days of easy sailing, the manner of Taen's departure made Corley fret. Watching through the ship's glass, he had seen *Moonless*'s jolly boat swallowed by fog arising out of nowhere. There had followed a shimmer like sheet lightning and a muffled boom; then the mist dispersed, ragged as torn gauze, with only the limitless blue of the water remaining. Corley shivered at the memory. The Dreamweaver and her tiny craft had disappeared as thoroughly as if they never existed.

Though the ocean presently showed no trace of the uncanny Isle of the Vaere, not a crewman aboard could look astern without qualms. The stress of unseen threat altered established patterns in *Moonless*'s routine. Sailors ceased grousing over the cook's mistakes in the galley; the mate took his sun sights at noon and quietly gnawed his nails down to the cuticle. Even the steward made himself scarce. All the while Corley paced the quarterdeck, his steps quick and tigerish, and his temper short.

"Deck there!" The lookout's hail from the crosstrees made the captain start at the rail. "Ships to windward!"

"How many?" Corley reached instinctively for knife and whetstone while the boatswain ordered a man aloft with a ship's glass.

"Two, sir." The lookout paused, leaned out, and caught the ship's glass from the sailor in the rigging. "Possibly more. But nothin' shows above the horizon yet but masts."

"Whose colors?" Corley sheathed his knife. With whetstone still in hand, he rocked impatiently on the balls of his toes, as if at any moment impatience might drive him to leap for the ratlines himself.

The lookout hooked a bronzed elbow around the shrouds and balanced against the lift and surge of the sea. Sunlight flashed on brass fittings as he focused his glass. Then, with a delighted whoop, he answered. "Kielmark's red wolf, cap'n! Damn me if our own *Shearfish* don't lead the lot."

Corley directed a tense glance at the compass. Then he swore with an emphasis he employed only before battle, unaware that hands in the waist left off mending canvas to stare. "Weather in their favor, and I'd bet silvers to a dog's fleas the other four sail behind her."

Headsails banged forward. Corley rounded angrily on the quartermaster, whose attention had strayed from the binnacle. "Steer small, you! Want to set us smack into the tricks o' the Vaere?" Without pause to draw breath, the captain shouted at the boatswain. "All hands on deck!"

His order tangled with another call from the lookout. "Five vessels, sir, flyin' Cliffhaven's colors. Dreamweaver steered us wrong, plain as the Fires o' judgment. Seems what ships we left in Hallowild all got clear."

Cheers arose from the men in the waist, enthusiastically repeated by newcomers rousted from the forecastle. Every man grinned in expectation of rendezvous and celebration, except Corley. He spun from the helm with an explosive snarl of annoyance.

"Caulk yer gullets!" As the shouts lost gusto and died, the captain lowered his voice. But his tone made the hair prickle at the nape of his crewmen's necks. "I want this vessel trim and armed for battle, *now*. Move sharp! This may be the last engagement *Moonless* ever fights. We're five to one, and downwind, with a wee fey isle full of snares to leeward."

The sailhands shuffled callused feet. One among them muttered an astonished protest. Corley heard, and gestured for the boatswain to cull the offender from his fellows. A mutinous silence developed as the officer carried out the command.

"D'ye think I jest?" Corley ran stiffened fingers through his hair, his manner suddenly tired. "Those ships may be ours, but not the men. Do you understand? At best, *Shearfish* and the rest are traitors, for no man loyal to the Kielmark would leave his post of duty. Morbrith fell to demons. *Any one of ours would have died beside the High Earl.*"

With his crewmen stiffly, uncomfortably attentive, Corley shrugged as if harried by stinging flies. "I don't like taking arms against our own ships. But if we don't see the battle of our lives before sunset, I'll take the whipping due the man presently in care of the boatswain. Now arm this vessel! Man the pumps and wet down all sails and rigging."

The sailhands disbursed. There followed an interval of tense activity. While the first watch splashed seawater from stem to stern and spread wet sand on the decks, the second watch rolled oil casks into the waist and wedged them beneath the pinrails. They wheeled out arbalests, stripped their covers of oiled hide, and lashed them to bolt rings in the deck. Other men fetched lint and rags from the hold. The boatswain doled out bows, fire arrows, and weaponry, while Corley directed action from the quarter-deck. The lookout reported regularly from the crosstrees, as five vessels flying the red wolf of Cliffhaven bore down upon *Moonless's* position, has-tened by following wind.

Masts, then yardarms, then hulls became visible from the deck. Corley pocketed his whetstone and snatched his ship's glass from the steward. Glued to the quarterdeck rail, he searched the approaching fleet for dis-crepancy to prove the vessels unfriendly. His effort yielded nothing. From *Shearfish* in the lead to the trailing vessel, *Ballad,* Corley found only the clean-cut seamanship indicative of Cliffhaven's finest. Even the coding of the signal ensigns was correct. Sweating, frustrated, and acutely aware of discontent among the men who strung bows and oiled weapons in the waist, Corley almost missed the change, even as he saw it: *Ballad* sailed without anchors.

A chill roughened his flesh. "Lookout! Check *Ballad* and see whether you find anything amiss with her rigging."

Corley waited, taut with nerves. *Moonless* tossed under his feet, cavort-ing like a maid in the spray as the fleet closed the distance between.

The lookout's shout began with a blasphemy. "Kor! The fittings are missing from the masts, and by damn if the martingale chains aren't made of blackened brass. I can see by the scratches, fer Fires' sake!"

Corley's apprehension transformed to outright alarm. Only once had he seen a vessel altered in such a fashion; that ship had spear-headed the assault upon Cliffhaven one year past. She had carried the witch Tathagres and her allies, a sextet of Gierj-demons whose ruinous powers of destruc-tion could be thwarted only by the presence of steel.

"By my grandmother's ass bone, we have trouble now." Corley swore, then prepared to lift his voice and inform his crew.

Words never passed his lips. A force cut into his mind, overran his intent with the trampling force of an avalanche. Air jammed in his lungs. He could not speak. Nor could he force his limbs to move, except as something alien and *other* commanded. His head whirled dizzily and his eyes lost power to see. Corley recoiled, struggling. For a second he felt the rail press solidly against his ribs. He gasped, forced a whisper past his throat. But the presence within his mind flung him back, helpless as a beetle drowning in oil. He thrashed inwardly, to no avail. Imprisoned within his own mind, Corley heard someone speak. Fearfully, horribly, he recognized the voice as his own, commanding *Moonless's* crewmen to clear the decks of weapons and sand, and run up flags to welcome Cliffhaven's fleet.

The captain fought in a frenzy of anguish. He longed for one loyal man to notice the significance of *Ballad's* missing anchors and stab a knife in his back. But the diabolical discipline of the Kielmark's command itself prevented insurrection; or else the sailhands worked under demon possession as well. Corley raged, even as the enemy smothered his awareness in darkness. The captain knew nothing more, while Maelgrim Dark-dreamer extended his hold through the borrowed powers of Gierj and claimed *Moonless* intact for Shadowfane.

Taen woke to a warmth like noon sunlight and the touch of someone's hand on her shoulder. She stirred, brushed an arm across her face, and felt the fingers withdraw from her person. Still disoriented from dream-trance, she opened her eyes to discover sundown already past. The crumpled sail where she lay was dusted silver with dew. *Callinde*'s thwart framed a starry expanse of sky, and both heat and a glow like candle flame emanated from a point just past her head. Taen frowned. The breeze off the sea blew briskly enough to extinguish anything but a shuttered lantern.

Even as the Dreamweaver raised herself on one elbow for a better look, the illumination began to fade. Before it died entirely, she glimpsed a man with hair the color of wheat at midsummer. He wore a red tunic trimmed with gold, and his eyes, dark as chestnuts, were strange and ancient as time.

"You were chilled," said Jaric out of the darkness.

Taen pushed herself to her knees, startled by cloth that fell with a slither around her calves. She touched, and felt fine velvet and silk; a Firelord's cloak had been tossed over her while she slept. The man who owned the garment sat intense and still, his presence as fathomless as sky.

Taen bit her lip. The Ivainson seated on *Callinde*'s aft sail locker both *was* and *was not* the boy she had known on board *Moonless*. Wrung by sudden uncertainty, the Dreamweaver drew a careful breath. "I thought you'd burned me like a charcoalman's sticks." She drew another breath, this one less than controlled. "Great Fall, *do you know what we've done?*"

Callinde's lines tapped the mast through a comfortless silence. Jaric did not reply. Roused to concern, Taen probed with her dream-sense. She discovered him afraid that if he reached for her, she would vanish away like the Vaere, leaving him in solitude on a desolate shore.

Her trembling transformed to laughter. "Fish-brains! You're Keithland's first sane Firelord, and still you haven't a featherweight of good sense." With that, the Dreamweaver surged forward and caught Ivainson around the neck. Half-grinning, half-weeping, she dragged him down into her nest of soggy sails.

Jaric stiffened with surprise. Then, as her cheek nestled into his shoulder and her tears fell hot on his throat, he caught her close in his arms. "Will you always arrive in time to haul me out of trouble by the heels?" But he did not wait for her answer; instead he threaded both hands in black hair, bent his head, and stopped her lips with his kiss.

The Firelord's cloak tumbled unheeded to the deck. Taen traced her fingers along the line of Jaric's collarbone. Gone to the Vaere as a child of ten, she had never known a man. Aside from the premature development that resulted from her mastery, in years and experience she was still very near to a child; but contact with elders on Imrill Kand had influenced the sensitivity that later gave rise to her Dreamweaver's powers. In some things the girl possessed an understanding far beyond her age. Taen snagged laces of braided gold and deftly began to untie them. "Did I hear you say I was cold? That's a lie."

Her reward was Jaric's quick laugh. "Shrew. I'll change that to no sense of propriety. Will you marry me on Imrill Kand?"

Taen freed the last tie and squirmed to reach his belt. "No." Hands busy, she kissed his chin. "I won't wait that long. Corley can marry us at sea." Sharply she tugged at his buckle.

Jaric twisted and caught her wrists. "Wait." He raised her and settled her comfortably against his side. "You can rush the wedding all you like, but not this. I love you. All Keithland can wait while I tell you so."

Gently he touched her face, her neck, her shoulders. Then he kissed her, softly as mist clinging to a flower. His hands moved, and he kissed her again. Taen felt the heat in his blood. In his restraint, she discovered something finer than the joyless appetites of the men from Imrill Kand. Tension, nervousness, and all fear inside her loosened. Jaric was here, now, for her, and she would never lose him. Warm fingers slipped the clothing from her shoulders. As the stars wheeled over the Isle of the Vaere, a Dreamweaver's robes of silver-gray joined the Firelord's cloak and tunic on the deck. By dawn, two lovers lay tangled asleep in the sails, heated by a tender glow of happiness.

Taen woke, this time to sunshine that was real. She lay with her head in Jaric's lap. By minute movements of his muscles, she realized he had roused ahead of her and busied himself with a chore. She opened her eyes, found him weaving a splice with his marlinspike, and promptly pinched his flank. "Haven't you anything better to do?"

"I didn't want to waken you." Jaric jammed his marlinspike through the plies in the rope and caught her teasing fingers.

But Taen's other hand remained at liberty, and with that she explored his person with provocative delight. She discovered him naked of clothing. Sitting up to admire the view, she saw that his skin had turned fair as ivory during his stay in the grove of the Vaere. "Kor's mercy, stay sitting in the sun and you'll ripen like a turnip."

"So." Jaric grinned. "You're right." He dropped the halyard he had been mending, caught her laughing in his arms, and lifted her strongly.

"Jaric!"

But Taen shouted too late. Her man stepped solidly over the rail and ran with her into the sea. They stayed there most of the morning, cradled in each other's arms amid the swell of the waves. Only when both had loved to exhaustion did Jaric remember his unmended halyard. *Callinde* could not sail to weather with no headsail; back on board in the heat of the day with duty on his mind, Jaric sought a linen shirt to protect his back from the sun. But, clad like a sea queen in nothing but a wet and extravagant fall of hair, Taen sat squarely on the locker that contained his clothes.

"You'll spoil the fun," she teased.

Jaric laughed. Soaked himself, and caked with sand to the shins, he tried to protest. "I smell like a fish."

"Not to another fish." Taen uncoiled from her perch and piled full force into his middle. Both overbalanced into a loose mass of sailcloth.

Sundown found the two of them curled beneath the patched canvas of the headsail, asleep. *Callinde*'s lines slapped gently against the mast, repaired and ready for sailing. But Keithland waited one more night for the Firelord, while Jaric told his Dreamweaver that he loved her.

When he wished to be alone, Maelgrim Dark-dreamer preferred the cavern that riddled the rock beneath Shadowfane. There, surrounded by the sullen drip of subterranean springs, he could light oil lamps, or sit in darkness as he pleased, for his demon overlords entered caves with reluctance; their influence could not pierce solid rock. Places below ground made them feel their vulnerability, but Maelgrim did not share that discomfort. Above him rose the crag of Shadowfane, with walls and fortifications enough to ensure his safety. While the passage leading to the dungeon remained open, he had solitude, and a channel through which to implement his mastery.

At present, clad in wire ornaments and a loose-fitting tunic and hose, Maelgrim sat between a pair of unlit lanterns. Darkness helped him assimilate the focus of the Gierj-demons given him by Scait. Although the creatures possessed neither intelligence nor self-awareness, a precise melding of minds enabled them to generate more raw force than a Vaere-trained enchanter. Manipulating a circle of six, Maelgrim had possessed five companies of the Kielmark's men at arms, and obliterated the inhabitants of Morbrith; with twelve, he boasted he could overrun Landfast. But Scait demanded otherwise. Cliffhaven was to be defeated first, and to that end, six Gierj had set sail on the decks of the Kielmark's brigantine *Ballad*.

From his nook in the caverns of Shadowfane, Maelgrim directed their song of power. One by one he extinguished the lives of additional crewmen captured in the south reaches of the Corine Sea. Aboard *Moonless*, their bodies lived on, but animated by an extension of Maelgrim's will made manifest by Gierj. The Dark-dreamer smiled in the shadows. Then he rested and dreamed, violent, bloody scenes of himself as Keithland's overlord.

When he woke, he resumed his trance. Far south, in the chilly hour before sunrise, Gierj stirred from sleep on the decks of *Ballad*. As the creatures opened their eyes, six sets of images inundated Maelgrim's mind: varied views of leaden swells hatched by stays and ratlines, of sanded decking, and a sky pricked by paling stars. The Gierjlings' multiple viewpoint still made him queasy. But demon masters had promised that his body would change to accommodate, over time, he would cease feeling disoriented by the impressions of separate eyes, and by vision that perceived more than a man's.

A shadow moved across *Ballad*'s waist. Secure in his cave, the Dark-dreamer translated images and identified the crewman who had once been first mate. The body might walk, talk, and act as a man, except now he was puppet to a master seated in Shadowfane.

Maelgrim shaped a mental command. Power flared through the Gierj-link like a spark touched into flame, and the mate called out to a sailor by the rail. "You there! Fetch Captain Corley on deck!"

The sailhand seemed unsurprised by an order to manhandle a superior. As stripped of spirit as *Ballad*'s officers, he hastened down the companion-way to bring the Kielmark's first captain topside.

Maelgrim waited. Taut with anticipation, malleable to his every mood, the Gierj transmitted his restlessness. Claws scraped planking on the quarterdeck, and even the man on watch at the helm tapped his fingers against the oaken spoke of the wheel.

Gierj-images showed the sailhand's return in kaleidoscopic duplication. He prodded a second man ahead of him, one whose movement seemed drugged and slow. Demon perception revealed a greenish shimmer of light surrounding his body; that aura offered the only means to distinguish the living from the dead in thrall to the Gierj-link.

In the cave, wire clinked over the ceaseless drip of spring water; Maelgrim wrapped his forearms around his knees and studied his prisoner in multiple detail. *Moonless*'s captain wore the same clothes he had at the time of his capture. But fine linen lay crumpled across his shoulders, and his tunic showed waterstains from the bilge. Ensnared by the Dark-dreamer's influence, his wide cinnamon eyes stayed fixed as polished stone. Maelgrim smiled in the darkness of his lair. Horribly, uncannily, Corley's lips echoed his overlord's expression, even as the sailor's dead hands prodded him up the companionway to the quarterdeck.

The captain stopped beside the mizzenmast. Maelgrim's view tumbled dizzily into change as, with wiry, insectlike movements, the Gierjlings surrounded their captive. The link stabilized, showing multiple views of Corley, silhouetted against a silvered predawn horizon, backed by the red glare of the binnacle lantern, and as a tall shadow with salt-matted hair looming against the mizzenmast shrouds. Maelgrim savored the moment well. Here at last stood the captain who had carried the false flag of surrender, luring Tathagres and eight demon allies into a trap of double intrigue that had foiled the compact's conquest of Cliffhaven. For that, Scait had commanded that a shape-changer impersonate *Moonless*'s master and later assassinate the Kielmark. The process would destroy the original captive. Gloating like a spider with a fly, Maelgrim Dark-dreamer vowed to see Corley die screaming.

The unimpressed shape-changer imported from Shadowfane quickly scented its victim. Slimy and featureless as a slug, it slithered from its tub in the galley and wormed across the open deck. Atop the companionway, it subsided, a grayish puddle of flesh nestled between coils of rope. Everything stood ready. Carefully, triumphantly, Maelgrim Dark-dreamer eased the constraints upon Corley's mind; awareness returned for the first time since *Moonless*'s capture.

The captain blinked, shook his head once, and frowned, for the helmsman was no crewman from his own command. Next he noticed demons ringing his feet: Gierj, lean and furtive as weasels, with eyes glowing lambent as a ghost ship's lanterns; at that moment Corley remembered. He stood, not on his own brigantine *Moonless,* but on the quarterdeck of *Ballad.* Both vessels now were prizes under Shadowfane's command. A spasm of anguish crossed the captain's face.

'*You live at my mercy,*' Maelgrim Dark-dreamer whispered through the Gierj-link.

Corley's head jerked up. He looked wildly around, but saw no speaker. He reached for the knives at his wrists, but found only empty sheaths. Belatedly he recalled that no steel could remain on his person in the presence of Gierj; then Maelgrim bound his limbs from movement. Corley fought, straining until the veins stood out on his neck. In a white heat of rage he never noticed that his enemy played him like a hooked fish. While he struggled, a Karas shape-changer's jellied mass quivered and slowly began to take from within a bight of rope to one side.

Through the Gierj-link, Maelgrim watched his victim's shirt become patched with sweat. The captain's hands locked into rigid claws, and breath escaped his throat in heaving gasps. The thing in the rope coils acquired two nostrils, and air began to sigh through them in unison. Corley heard. He attempted to turn his head, and with a sneer of contempt the Dark-dreamer allowed his captive that liberty. Maelgrim's lips parted with laughter as the captain jerked back in horror.

The Karas shape-changer now resembled a lump of softened wax, gray-white and gross except for two eyeballs of vivid, cinnamon brown. Even as Corley flinched, his reaction spurred growth. A smeared line opened beneath the creature's nostrils. Folds appeared, firmed, and shaped a recognizable pair of lips. Toothless and tongueless, the mouth was the mirror image of Corley's.

'*You see now,*' Maelgrim taunted through the link. '*You exist this moment expressly to serve Shadowfane.*'

Corley's features twisted. "Never!" But even as he protested, the thing at his feet puckered and flowed and changed. Tissue slimy as raw egg white filmed over, firmed, and developed a peppering of hair follicles. Within moments, it grew a beard textured chestnut and gray, strand for strand a counterpart of the captain's. The lips, fully fleshed, now worked; they mimed the original with chilling perfection.

'*Enjoy yourself,*' said the Dark-dreamer. '*Few men ever witness a shape-changer's metamorphosis.*'

Clued that his struggles might key the creature's alteration, Corley forced himself to relax. If he stayed passive, the loathsome creature's development might be arrested. Hope was probably in vain. Still, the captain closed his eyes. He did not think, but concentrated on sensations, from the lift of *Ballad*'s deck beneath his feet to the clean scents of sea and wet wood, overlaid by a sour tang of tarred rope. Aft, a pot clanged in the galley; as if the day were ordinary, the cook lit his fire and sliced sausage for sailhands about to come off watch. The unbroken adherence to routine raised a chill on Corley's flesh, aggravated by the step of the quartermaster, arrived to relieve the night helmsman. Sunrise brightened the east, tipping wave crests with sequin highlights; but the Kielmark's first captain felt cold to the heart. He stood still, listening to the wind, while Gierj coiled sinuously around his feet. Their limbs interwove until they resembled a ring of braided yarn, dotted with eyes glowing greenish as sparks from a drugged candle.

Corley concentrated on the immediate. *Ballad* sailed to a following breeze. An unoiled block squeaked with each roll, and one of her headsails luffed lightly. On *Moonless*, such lapses would earn the mate on watch a sharp reprimand.

'*Such is the difference between the Kielmark's senior captains, and their underlings,*' Maelgrim interjected, as if trying to prompt conversation through the Gierj-link.

Corley ignored the intrusion, following only the splash of spray off the bow. He ached; keeping still required an alarming amount of muscle tension. With his attention immersed in the rolling wash of the wake, the captain subdued the macabre need to see whether the shape-changer had evolved any further. Still, no effort of will could prevent him from noticing sounds not normal to a ship working on a broad reach. Something flopped on the deck by the pinrail, like a fish, but not.

Corley felt his skin raise into gooseflesh. He stood sweating until the Dark-dreamer jabbed through the Gierj-link and compelled him to look.

The captain opened his eyes to unmitigated horror. A half-completed replica of himself lay beyond the ring of Gierj. Hands, feet, face, and forearms, it matched his every detail, even to scars of former battles and the calluses of everyday living. But beyond wrist and neck and ankle, where clothing covered his body, the thing was formless jelly. One hand twitched and touched a deck fitting. Two fingers bent grotesquely, jointless as worm flesh, for as yet neither bone nor muscle supported the structure underneath.

Corley's stomach heaved; and even his revulsion triggered growth. The abomination quivered and firmed, its abdomen acquiring the semblance of a rib cage. Sweat traced Corley's spine. The feeling of moisture trickling over his anatomy detailed the beginnings of an indentation on the shape-changer's back, made visible as it flopped across the deck. Sickened by the mirroring twitch of his nemesis, Corley averted his face.

Maelgrim's laughter echoed across the link. *'Ah, Captain, you begin to understand the nature of Shadowfane's miracles.'* Bored with passive observation, the Dark-dreamer reached through the Gierj. He forced his victim to watch while the unfinished shape-changer scrabbled clumsily upright, then advanced on wobbling feet. It crossed inside the ring of demons and stopped at the captain's side.

Driven to tears of frustration, Corley beheld eyes, a complete face, identical to his own. "Why?" he gasped, revolted as the thing echoed with a slurred attempt at speech.

The Dark-dreamer reveled in the captain's discomfort. In reply, he had the quartermaster turn from the helm and speak in words of his choosing. "Can't you guess, my captain? The shape-changer will replace you, and sail *Moonless* to Cliffhaven. The Kielmark will never guess his first captain disguises as a demon, until too late. Your replica will run a knife through his heart."

The words struck Corley like the killing thrust of a sword. Through trust in his closest friend, the Kielmark would be betrayed. In anguish, the captain whispered, "No! Fires take you, not while I live!"

Maelgrim laughed through the mouths of *Ballad*'s crewmen, then made them chant in eerie unison. "But you won't live, my flag-bearing turncoat. Karas shape-changers devour their victims after metamorphosis to fix their final form. And through Gierj-power I shall keep you alive, while the Karas chews through your vitals one bite at a time."

Corley said nothing. White-faced, trembling with despair, he stared unseeing at the sea while the shape-changer pawed and fumbled, ineptly removing his clothing. Its touch proved corrosive; each brush of its fingers raised welts, sharp and painful as hornet stings. Try as he might, the captain could not contain his reaction. His muscles flinched and shivered in agony, each cord and tendon defined beneath his skin. As he suffered, his structure became faithfully recorded by the Karas, down to the smallest bulging vein, and the last bead of sweat.

Breeches, shirt, and knife sheaths lay in a tumbled pile on the deck when the Dark-dreamer made Corley dance. Up, down, around, he sprang in dizzying gyrations that forced the fullest range of extension from his body. The Karas followed suit, its contours molding ever closer to the brawny frame of the captain. Gasping, wretched, and sick with exhaustion and harrowed dignity, Corley knew that now not even his mother would recognize him from his demon counterpart. He wished himself dead; had the Dark-dreamer of Shadowfane relinquished control for an instant, the captain would have sought immediate means to end his life.

The Karas bent with mannerisms identical to Corley's and donned knife sheaths, then breeches and shirt. It ran its fingers through chestnut hair, adjusted a wrist strap, and laughed.

'*Once it tastes your flesh, its form becomes permanent.*' Maelgrim allowed satisfaction to seep across the link. '*Your skills, your memories, even your innermost secrets will all be inherited intact.*'

With a look of wry humor still on its face, the Karas reached for its counterpart's wrist. But the instant before contact, a burst of light shattered the horizon. The Gierj started up in alarm, eyes flaring like flame as the sun vanished into mist. Maelgrim's smile faded, and even the Karas paused. A shimmer like sheet lightning rent the sky. Thunder pealed, rattling timbers in the deck, and wind sprang out of nowhere, backwinding *Ballad*'s sails with a violence that snapped a stay.

Ballad's captain sprang half-dressed and shouting from the stern. "Quartermaster, bear up! All hands on deck to shorten sail!"

Yet the confused weather cleared before men could stumble from the forecastle. Fog dissolved into clear air, and breezes resumed from the west. South, where the horizon had bordered empty sky, an islet notched the sea. The shoreline glittered white in sunlight, sands ground fine as bleached flour, and mantled by a royal crown of cedars.

The Gierj twittered nervously. The linking bond of their attention faltered. Irritably, Maelgrim bound them tighter. Through their eyes, he beheld the elusive Isle of the Vaere where his sister had vanished after Anskiere stole her loyalty.

The Karas stared also. Its pose was an effortless replica of Corley's, but its allegiance was to Scait and Shadowfane as it murmured in excited discovery, "Set-Nav. Veriset-Nav for sure."

Suddenly a dull square of red unfurled above the beachhead. Maelgrim quivered like a hound on hot scent and focused his Gierj. Multiple images showed him the frail silhouette of a fishing craft, her crew busily setting sail. The caverns beneath Shadowfane's dungeons rang with his harsh laugh, for there sailed *Callinde*, towing *Moonless*'s jolly boat; Jaric was not at her helm. Through the perception of his Gierj, the Dark-dreamer found the sister he longed to murder sitting defenseless at the small craft's steering oar.

The Karas whirled with Corley's crisp air of authority. "Call Scait," it commanded. "We must take Set-Nav. Its powers of communication can call allies from the stars. From them, the compact shall gain weapons and machines enough to desecrate all of Keithland. Then, when vengeance is complete, our exile upon this accursed planet may come to an end."

But Maelgrim did not respond, obsessed as he was by a glimpse of black hair against the white of *Callinde*'s wake. Duty warred with emotion; and the cruel conditioning of his mastery overturned both. "First I will smash the Dreamweaver." He lashed out through the link, sending the Gierj scrambling to form a circle unencumbered by shape-changers or men. The demons coalesced like ink and began the warbling whistle that focused their full range of power.

"No!" The Karas's muscles knotted. It seized the nearest demon, jerked it from the circle, and snarled to the Gierj-master who manipulated his minions from Shadowfane, "Desist! The girl may be defended. You must call Scait!"

Yet Maelgrim would brook no interference. Taen was alone, he had checked; she had grown powerful, strangely powerful, but before his might she was helpless. *He could slay her easily with the Gierj at his command.* The Dark-dreamer engaged his will. On *Ballad*, the Gierj hissed. Fanged jaws slashed at the Karas's forearm and forced it into retreat. Only then did it notice that, with Maelgrim's attention diverted, the Kielmark's first captain had managed to throw himself halfway over the rail.

"Look to your prisoner!" shouted the shape-changer.

The Dark-dreamer disregarded its urgency. In another moment his circle of demon underlings would generate the power to strike his sister down. Nettled by the Karas's interference, Maelgrim laughed over the rising song of the Gierj. He permitted Captain Corley his leap into the sea, knowing the Karas must pursue, or forfeit the pattern of its change.

CHAPTER IX

Counterstrike

The whistle of the Gierj ascended the scale, gaining volume until the very sky seemed to ring with harmonics.

Taen tightened her hands on *Callinde*'s steering oar. The sound beat against her ears, keen and deadly as a razor's edge; the demon circle would reach pitch at any second. The instant their powers peaked, Maelgrim Dark-dreamer would crush her defenses easily as a child might mash an ant.

Wind hooked *Callinde*'s spanker. Her hull heeled and drove bucking through a swell. Foam burst off the bow like a spray of thrown diamonds, but Taen had no attention to spare for beauty. She sailed by touch, eyes clenched shut while the Gierj-whistle jabbed like a lance into her dream-sense. The note keened abruptly to a crescendo. The darkness behind Taen's eyes buckled, then shattered into sparks before an onslaught of unbearable power. The steering oar slipped from her grasp. *Callinde* rounded to weather with a shattering bang of sails, her lapstrake planking exposed broadside to the demon fleet.

Taen threw back her head and drew a shuddering breath. "Now!" she cried. Before Maelgrim broke her mind, she released the veil of conceal-ment she had cast about Ivainson Jaric.

Fire exploded from *Callinde*'s prow. The conflagration gained intensity until the waves themselves seemed aflame. A boiling, snapping inferno smothered the face of the sea. Caught like lint in a cauldron of hell, six of the Kielmark's brigantines crisped to ash in an instant. The Gierj-chant cut off as if strangled. Maelgrim's attack broke with it. Taen sagged exhausted against *Callinde*'s thwart, while her brother's thoughts echoed across the dying thread of the link that connected to him at Shadowfane. *He had lost his circle of Gierj, spoiled the chance to capture Set-Nav; now he must face Scait with ill news. Keithland had gained a new Firelord. . . .*

The contact subsided into fury, then dissolved. Taen roused to the thunder of luffing sails and a snaking mess of slacked lines. She lifted shaking arms, caught the steering oar, and muscled *Callinde* back on course, away from the Isle of the Vaere. Ahead, the horizon lay marred by smoke. Where tanbark sails had caught clean wind only moments before, charred beams wallowed amid ash-smeared waves.

"They're gone." Taen glanced to the bow where the Firelord knelt, staring fixedly at the hands held clenched against his chest.

Jaric flinched at the sound of her voice. He raised tortured eyes and said softly, "Already it begins."

Taen knew he referred to the killing, and the fact that his first use of mastery had been an act of destruction. She bit her lip, shaken herself by the swift and terrible ruin brought down upon a fleet that had included Corley's own *Moonless*. "They were all dead, puppets of demons." Cut by echoes of Jaric's pain, the Dreamweaver sounded more brisk than she intended. "To leave such men alive would be more cruel, surely!"

Jaric rose. His hair caught like fire with sunlight as he strode aft, eased the sheet lines, and took the steering oar from Taen's grasp. She trembled, uncontrollably.

Sickened himself, the son of Ivain caught her and pulled her close. "I know the burning was necessary," he murmured into her hair. He paused, while *Callinde* rocked gently under freed canvas. "But I don't have to like the violence. Otherwise, like my father, someday I might grow to enjoy such brute power too much."

Taen pressed against him, drawing comfort from his lean strength. Her eyes stung with tears not entirely due to the smoke. After a time, Jaric leaned around her, yanked mainsheets and jib taut, and swung the steering oar to restore *Callinde*'s course. His one free hand knotted fiercely in Taen's hair, then released.

"Little witch, I need you for one thing more." Ivainson sounded tired, even reluctant, to ask. "Check and make certain no demon-possessed remain. For Shadowfane must never gain access to the Isle of the Vaere."

Taen drew her knees up and curled against him on the stern seat. With her ear to Jaric's side, she heard his heartbeat and knew: he had been shocked as she, to emerge from the protection of the Vaere and discover Cliffhaven's six ships under Maelgrim's control. Neither of them could bear to mention names, or count the friends whose bodies had been consigned to flame.

Callinde drove steadily northward, into waters where splinters and burned cordage dirtied the crests of the waves. Subdued by sorrow and loss, Taen tuned her inner awareness and scanned the waters for sign of life. At first her dream-sense encountered only mindless flickers, schools of scavenging fish come to feed on remains. Then she caught something else, faint, almost missed: a remembered flash of steel by starlight.

The Dreamweaver shot upright with a gasp. "Corley!" She turned widened, hopeful eyes toward Jaric, then broke into a shout of relief. "Over there!" She pointed. "Deison Corley is alive."

The Firelord needed no urging. He sprang, whipped the sheets taut in the blocks, and threw his weight against the steering oar. The compass needle swung with maddening sluggishness, north, north-northeast, to east. *Callinde* changed tack, heeled, then settled, small as a chip on her new course. The jolly boat nosed at her stern rope like a puppy just broken to leash.

"Fetch the ship's glass from the port locker. Is the captain in pain?" At Taen's nod, Jaric continued briskly. "Then we'll need spare line. Maybe the storm sail, too, unless you think we can haul him over the jolly boat's thwart without adding to his injury."

Taen's shift flapped about her knees as she flung open lockers and delved after canvas and rope. The ship's glass she eliminated; dream-sense could locate a swimmer more efficiently than eyesight, and time counted dearly. The pattern of energy she knew as the Kielmark's first captain was dim, and failing steadily. But *Callinde* closed the distance quickly; without question, Corley was alive, and very close by.

"There!" Jaric adjusted course and pointed. Ahead, dark against the crest of a swell, a man's head broke the surface of the sea. Taen saw him clearly before a drifting pall of smoke obliterated the view.

"Take the helm." Transformed by hope, Jaric snatched rope and spare sailcloth from Taen's hands. As she took the steering oar, he caught the jolly boat's tow line and yanked it inboard with hurried jerks of his arms. "Steer upwind, and heave to, can you? As we pass, I'll cast off and pick him up."

Taen nodded. Closer, through thinning wisps of steam, she sighted Corley swimming strongly down the face of a wave. He had seen *Callinde,* and his teeth flashed a smile of welcome that did not mesh with the pattern touched by her dream-sense. Taen frowned. The captain who pulled himself through the sea with such sure overhand strokes seemed too vital for one whose skin stung with abrasions, and whose lungs labored, cramped from lack of air.

Callinde heeled under a gust.

"Steady on the helm!" shouted Jaric. He leaped into the jolly boat and whipped the towline off the cleat. Suddenly afraid for him, Taen called out, "Be careful!"

But, preoccupied with the friend in the water, Jaric seemed not to hear. He bent immediately, threaded oars, and muscled his boat stern first into the waves. The jolly boat seemed a toy skewed crazily on the shoulder of the swell; smaller still seemed the man in the sea, an insect on the face of creation. As Jaric swung alongside and shipped his looms, Taen heard him shout encouragement.

"Kor's grace, man, be quick. Knives rust to scrap in the sea, don't you remember telling me?"

Corley's laugh boomed reassuringly back across the water. "No fuss. I jettisoned the knives. Had to. Ballast would've swamped me." He caught the jolly boat's transom with wet fingers, and only then did the Dream-weaver notice the shadowy wrongness that suffused his flesh.

Premonition made her shiver. Taen had seen such a phenomenon only once before, in the form of a demon shape-changer planted in King Kisburn's court to sow discord.

She shouted, frantic, "Jaric!" But wind snatched her words. The thing that looked like the captain caught the hand of his rescuer and heaved himself, dripping, from the sea. *His wrists, his hands, his very skin was unmarked, while the pattern Taen's dream-sense knew as Corley stung with painful cuts.* "Jaric, he's Shadowfane's!"

Yet even as the Dreamweaver called warning, the fists of a Karas shape-changer clamped over Ivainson's throat. Jaric lashed out in defense. Fire flared, bristled with terrible, spitting snaps down the creature's arms.

The Karas screamed with Corley's voice. Crazed by an agony of grief, Jaric reacted in madness. Flame shot skyward. Light glared like molten metal over the waves, and the captain's form became momentarily incandescent, reduced to ash in an instant. Still the flame continued, searing the air with a shriek like hot steel hitting water.

Jaric shouted, his words a blasphemy against Kor's mercy. Then as if his knees had failed him, he folded against the jolly boat's thwart. Fire died while he wept. For a moment, Taen feared to touch him, his thoughts ranged so far beyond reason. Shaking, tearful with reaction herself, she steadied her dream-sense. The moment she tuned her powers, she encountered Corley again, reduced to a flicker, an echo, submerged beneath the waves. No time remained for finesse. Taen shaped a dream-call that bordered the edge of compulsion, and sent her find directly into Jaric's mind.

Then tears blurred her eyesight completely. She heard but did not see the splash as Ivainson dove. By the time her vision cleared, the jolly boat drifted empty, one oar canted crookedly against the bow seat. Wind puckered the swells, and *Callinde's* sails flapped. Taen steadied the steering oar and waited an interminable interval until Jaric broke the surface, burdened by something heavy and limp. He kicked awkwardly and caught the jolly boat's rope.

Taen glimpsed a snarl of chestnut hair; this time there could be no mistake. Jaric had recovered the true Corley from the sea, for this victim matched the mangled pattern picked up by her dream-sense. Demon captivity had been cruel. The captain was injured and very near death from drowning. Jaric ran rope beneath Corley's shoulders and secured him to the jolly boat's transom. As he rowed and boarded *Callinde*, Taen raced and freed a spare halyard.

With all possible speed, Dreamweaver and Firelord hoisted the helpless man aboard *Callinde*. The crisscrossed marks of his knife sheaths showed white against Corley's tan; no scrap of clothing remained to hide skin torn everywhere with abrasions and burns. Something, horribly, had gnawed off one finger at the knuckle. Blood from the stump threaded streamers through the puddled water on the deck.

"Karas," said Taen faintly. "Shape-changers eat portions of their victims to permanently maintain form."

Jaric reined in the fury her words inspired. He spoke in a deadened voice and kept to immediate needs. "There's a tin of healer's salve in the starboard locker, and we can tear my dry shirts for bandages."

But the true extent of the damage did not become apparent until Corley's hurts were dressed and he lay wrapped in blankets by the mainmast.

Taen knelt at the captain's side when his bruised brown eyes flickered open. "We're taking you back to Cliffhaven," she offered. But her words were received without comfort. All that remained of *Moonless* and her fleet of five brigantines was one man, and a jolly boat dragging astern. Corley turned his face miserably to the thwart. To him survival offered no joy but a burden nearly impossible to endure.

Taen touched the captain's shoulder and gently pressed his mind into sleep. Grief leaked through the contact, born of loss, but also something more: Corley was inwardly wounded beyond her power to console. He had prided himself for loyalty; the youthful sense of honor that drove him to leave Morbrith rather than shame the High Earl's son had matured to service and friendship now granted to the Kielmark. But on the decks of *Ballad*, Dark-dreamer and Karas had proven that faith could be corrupted into a weapon designed for murder; neither sword steel, integrity, nor death itself held power to avert a betrayal of everything Corley held dear.

Discouraged and sad, Taen rose and joined Jaric at the helm. The hope gained when Ivainson achieved his Firemastery seemed suddenly withered, blown to dust like seedlings killed in a drought. Shadowfane's reach was longer and more powerful than ever she could have imagined; Maelgrim's conquest of Morbrith and subsequent possession of Corley's command required powers that defied credibility. If his Gierj-circle was replaced, what damage might Keithland suffer before *Callinde* reached Cliffhaven to free Anskiere?

Troubled by Taen's stillness, Jaric threaded an arm around her waist and drew her close. "Don't fret, little witch. You've done enough, and more than enough."

Taen shook her head. Troubled by the memory of her brother's last thoughts, she spoke unthinkingly aloud. "Whatever did Maelgrim mean by Set-Nav, anyway?"

A wave jostled *Callinde* off course. Jaric reached to shift his grip and ended banging his knuckles against the shaft of the steering oar. "Tell me where you heard that." He turned and faced her, at once a stranger with the terrible, edged presence of a Vaere-trained Firelord.

Thrown off balance by the depths in him, Taen drew back. "When you flamed the Gierj, Maelgrim cursed the loss of a thing named Set-Nav. In some manner, his reference referred to the Isle of the Vaere. What do you think he meant?"

Jaric sat motionless. Through dream-sense, Taen determined that the term "Set-Nav" was familiar to him, and connected to a strange scrap of information found in Landfast's libraries. Then Jaric's expression turned harsh as chipped agate, and his mind became closed to her. He started to say something, paused, and instead arose to tighten the headsail halyard.

"Jaric!" Taen caught the abandoned steering oar and muscled *Callinde* back on course. "Whatever could Maelgrim mean?"

Ivainson replied with his attention trained keenly on the set of the jib. "I don't know."

He told the truth. Though Taen pressed after the reason for his unsettled response, Jaric refused to elaborate. A part of his mind would brook no interference; like the Stormwarden, Ivainson Firelord now owned mysteries even a Vaere-trained Dreamweaver could not encompass.

The sail north to Cliffhaven required six weeks. Taen soon found that the death of Maelgrim's Gierj had lifted the block preventing contact with Cliffhaven. She dream-sent only once, to ascertain that the conclave at Mhored Kara had honored her request and relayed the news of Morbrith's fall. Evidently it had, for the Kielmark was in a black temper, savagely intolerant of intrusion. Rather than exhaust herself needlessly trying to calm him enough to receive dream-image, Taen obtained her information through Captain Tamic, the Kielmark's next in command during Corley's absence.

The second captain was a burly man, given to boisterous phrases and rougher judgment. Taen he treated with respect, mostly because she had stopped his tongue with a spell the first time he tried to insult her. Forced speechlessness did not wear well with Captain Tamic. He greeted the Dreamweaver's sending from the south reaches with a curse, but related the state of affairs on Cliffhaven with the malicious abandon of a gossip.

"Oh, aye, yer tamed pack o'wizards sent word. Came in the form of a wee box carved with runes, dumped in with the tribute off a trader bark from Telshire."

'A box?' Taen queried.

She sensed Tamic's brows lift in reproof. "Aye, a box, wench. As sorcerers go, the conclave's lot aren't stupid. If the Magelord or one of his minions dared the straits, Kielmark'd dice him up like stew meat. For what his conjurers did to Anskiere, you understand and probably a bit on general principle. Hates sorcery of any sort, does the Pirate King, since it litters up his domain with powers he can't control."

'And the box?' prompted the Dreamweaver.

"Kor." Tamic paused. Carefully he excised from his reply those obscenities which might earn him the Dreamweaver's reprisal. "That box had a message in it, all wrought of spells. Bad news by my guess, because the Kielmark hammered the table with his sword and gouged up a helluva splinter. Now there's activity in the harbor like sticks astirring through bee nests."

'Morbrith fell to Shadowfane,' Taen returned, *'that's why your Lord is distressed. When he's finished yelling, tell him I sail north on* Callinde *with the newly invested Firelord. Corley's with us.'* She kept her sending terse, mostly as an excuse to end contact. Even disaster could not upset her judgment enough to deliver

word of the fleet lost to the Gierj with the Kielmark in a killing fury. As she released her dream-sense, Tamic's humor transformed from sharp concern to wonder, that the small diffident boy he had once dragged off the north shore in a storm had gone on to complete the Cycle of Fire.

Callinde sailed on through the Free Isles. Twice Jaric made landfall for supplies, at Westisle and Skane's Edge. Corley helped with the loading, but refused to show his face to the villagers. That none would know him as the Kielmark's captain, he worked muffled in Jaric's spare storm cloak despite the warmth of high summer. Only Taen understood why.

"He fears to be used as a tool against Cliffhaven," she confided to Jaric, who cursed in exasperation and worried the captain might collapse from the heat. That the Firelord's anger was rooted in grief helped nothing. Each day it seemed more certain that Maelgrim and Shadowfane had broken the spirit of a friend.

Back at sea, Jaric flung open the locker nearest the helm, retrieved *Callinde's* last rigging knife and whetstone, and presented them to the captain. "You can fashion a sheath from the leather I bought to make sandals," he offered. "Only stop moping in port like a priest losing faith at a heresy trial."

Corley accepted the gift, but did not sharpen the blade. Hour after hour his hands hung limp in his lap, except when *Callinde* required sails changed, or navigation, or repairs to worn rigging. Wind blew from the west, then the north, and slowly, shifted back due south. Following a stop at Innishari for water and food, fair weather alternated with two storms and a gale. The air grew sharp at night. Close to the first of autumn the sturdy craft neared the latitude of Cliffhaven.

Twelve leagues offshore, with the watchtower not yet visible on the horizon, Taen entered dream-trance and contacted the Kielmark for the last time before *Callinde* reached port. She had informed him long since of Morbrith's fall, and the fleet lost to Shadowfane; but not until now could she bear to reveal the ruinous change in Corley.

Seated in his library at the time, the Lord of Cliffhaven received her tidings with uncharacteristic equanimity. Taen suspected a more explosive reaction, perhaps held in check beneath his calm; but since he cut contact with more than his customary curtness she had no chance to read deeper. Though *Callinde* returned with a Firelord and hope for Anskiere, Taen roused feeling dispirited.

She retired to the bow rather than disturb Jaric, who tended *Callinde's* steering oar with apprehensive thoughts of the ice cliffs, and the fact he must soon unravel the wards there with the same powers his father had used to betray the Stormwarden's peace.

Corley leaned against the mainmast with his shirt laces open at his throat. He seemed asleep; Taen knew by her dream-sense he was not. She huddled against the prow, troubled by doubts of her own. How would

Anskiere judge her brother, when he wakened to find Morbrith lost, and Marlson Emien the cause? The Dreamweaver brooded, while the bow wave crumpled into froth beneath the keel and day wore on to afternoon.

Jaric's shout broke her reverie. *"Corley, no!"*

Taen spun in alarm, just as Ivainson sprang from the helm. He piled into the captain. *Callinde* veered sharply to weather; the shadow of the mainsail swung aft, and the Dreamweaver glimpsed a flash of sunlight on steel. Corley strove to sink the rigging knife into his chest. Only the straining hands of Ivainson Firelord prevented the blade from striking home.

"Taen, help," gasped Jaric. Corley's sweat slicked his palms, and his hold slipped. The blade dipped, quivering, and nicked into skin.

The Dreamweaver gathered power and slammed hard into the captain's mind. His limbs sagged with paralysis, and the knife tumbled, clanging, into the bilge. Jaric caught the unconscious man and eased him awkwardly to the floorboards.

"Kor's mercy!" Taen reached the captain. Corley breathed as if asleep, except that beads of crimson seeped through his shirt front. Taen bent and tugged the linen from his shoulders. Only when she proved the wound was a scratch did she start to quiver with shock. "What would make him desperate now, after all these weeks?"

Jaric did not answer. Instead he delved into an opened locker for the ship's glass, balanced himself against the roll of the swell, and scanned the eastern horizon.

Presently Taen saw his mouth flinch into a line. "Here's why." Ivainson lowered the glass with what seemed like annoyance. "There's a sloop out there on a broad reach, with one man aboard. Corley guessed who before I did. The Kielmark sails *Troessa* to meet us."

Untended, *Callinde* jibed with a thunderous bang of sails. Jaric leapt to slacken lines. Only when he had finished did Taen realize his curtness was rooted in distress. Corley lay sprawled on the floorboards, strong hands outflung and empty and his face untroubled in sleep. He might have been napping; except his friends remembered he never quite abandoned tension, even during rest.

"You did your work well, little witch." Jaric knelt, recovered the rigging knife, then wedged it out of sight behind a water cask. "He'll not wake if we move him? Then let's get him up."

Built light and lean to carry dispatches, *Troessa* raced down upon the ungainly *Callinde* with what seemed uncanny speed. Taen had barely made Corley comfortable in the bow when the small sloop rounded to weather. She drifted on *Callinde*'s windward side, sails slatting loose in the breeze. Jaric sprang and caught the line thrown by her helmsman.

The Kielmark paced with impatience while his craft was made fast to a cleat. Ebony hair ruffled against sky as, with astonishing agility for a man burdened with broadsword, boots, and crossbelts jingling with throwing knives, the sovereign Lord of Cliffhaven leapt the gap between boats. He landed sure-footedly on the thwart. *Callinde* rocked sharply, canvas flung into a jibe. Forced to duck the swing of the headsail, Taen sensed rather than saw the Kielmark check. Eyes pale as ice chips fixed on Corley's bloody shirt.

"Kor's Fires, what's happened to him?" Enormous in *Callinde's* cramped cockpit, the Kielmark reached for his steel.

"That's a scratch!" Taen supplied hastily. "Corley's alive, and well, but not stable. He tried to take his life when *Troessa* breasted the horizon." She engaged her dream-sense and tried vainly to soften the impact of the news.

The Kielmark tensed at her touch. The ruby torque flashed at his neck as he whirled around, knuckles whitened on his sword hilt. Should he follow through with his draw, he could not help but slash stays and bring down the mast; but temper left him wild enough to strike without thought for consequences. "Take *Troessa* and see to your Stormwarden, enchantress. I'll look after my captain."

The Kielmark turned on his heel. Charged with threat like a thunderhead, he reached Corley in the bow, plainly intending to move him. When Jaric hastened to help, Taen restrained him with a dream-touch.

'*Don't. His Lordship is dangerously upset.*' She caught Jaric's wrist and held on as the Kielmark lifted Corley in his massive arms. Contact seemed to reassure him; the mad edge softened from his temper as he bore his captain aft.

The King of Renegades settled Corley in the stern seat, then positioned himself by the steering oar. "How long will he sleep?" he demanded of Taen.

"Well past nightfall, unless you wish otherwise." As the Kielmark's mood eased, the Dreamweaver sensed that his temper stemmed from more than Corley's straits. The tension probably rooted in the conjurer's message concerning Morbrith, but now was a poor moment to press the issue. Again urging restraint upon Jaric, Taen waited by the mast.

The Kielmark threw off baldric and crossbelts. Stripped to boots and leggings stamped with silver, he spoke with his gaze trained on Corley's still features. "Jaric, you must free Anskiere directly. If the wind holds, *Troessa* should bear you to the ice cliffs before sundown." He paused, raked sweat-damp hair from his temples, and looked up. "Every sovereign ruler of Keithland and all the council members of the Alliance await you at Cliffhaven. Return there when you can."

"Councilmen of the Alliance!" Jaric broke in. "How did you ever pry them out of Landfast?"

The Kielmark's teeth flashed in an expression not quite a smile. "I sent ships and men at arms to collect the first two. Then one day their conjurers told them that Morbrith's citizens had dropped in their tracks like carrion. After that, their eminences came flying like sparrows chased in by a gale." Pointedly not looking at the Dreamweaver, he leaned forward, caught the trailing end of the jib sheet and hauled in the sail. "Go now. Time is critical."

Canvas filled with wind, and *Callinde* bore off. Jaric squeezed Taen's hand, released her, and stepped around the mast. He flipped *Troessa*'s line from the cleat. Tanned from seafaring, and clothed in a sailor's linen tunic, he hardly appeared the master of a Firelord's powers as he leaped lightly onto the gunwale. But when the Dreamweaver hurried to join him, he paused, poised like a cat. "You sail with *Callinde*."

Taen stiffened to argue. "Where you go, I go also."

"No," said Jaric. "Not with frostwargs unleashed." He spoke quietly. But his voice carried an edge that made the Kielmark start at the steering oar. Ivainson was a lad no longer. On *Callinde*'s rail stood a sorcerer charged with ringing nets of power. His hair might be sun-bleached, his hands worn with sailing; but fire would blaze at his command, and the ordinary brown of his eyes reflected mysteries deep as earth.

"Stay," said Ivainson Jaric to Taen. His tone gentled. "I'll return with Anskiere, and meet you at the fortress."

He sprang into *Troessa* and cast off. Taen did not try to follow, but hung on the thwart as the sloop caught the wind and bore off northeast.

The Kielmark hardened the sheets. As *Callinde* steadied on course for the harbor, he looked up and noticed the Dreamweaver's expression. "Enchantress," he called grimly from the helm, "quit fretting. I'll be sending a patrol to the north strand with horses. You can go and meet your man. But first you'll help sail this bucket to shore. Are we agreed?"

"Horses!" Taen returned a brave but weary smile. "I sail a boat with far better grace than ever I sat a saddle."

Jaric landed *Troessa* at sunset. Slanting light tipped the topmost crags of the ice cliffs with rose and gilt; below, breakers crashed and threw smoking streamers of spray, tinged ice blue in shadow. As always, Anskiere's prison overwhelmed the eye with beauty. But the Firelord charged with the Stormwarden's deliverance felt no confidence as he beached his small sloop on the strand. He had no experience battling demons, and scant knowledge of the frostwargs he must subdue; far more than a sorcerer's survival rested on his success.

The air blew chill off the heights. Jaric shivered in his thin tunic and squared his shoulders to climb. Ice and rock had contained the frostwargs since Tathagres' sorcerers had provoked their escape; presumably fire would control them. Ivainson set his hands to the rock. Contact with the land proved a revelation after lengthy weeks at sea; stone and soil seemed alive, responsive to his Earthmastery. Unlike his previous climbs, the cliff face welcomed his presence, yielding footholds and fissures to his inner awareness. Jaric smiled with self-revelation; on a whim he could mold the rock face into stairs to ease his ascent. But caution and his own reluctance to wield power caused him to climb without enchantments. Later, against the frostwargs, he might need every available resource.

Twilight dyed the sea indigo beneath a violet arch of sky. Dwarfed by cascades of ice, Jaric set foot on the uppermost tier of the ledge. With closed eyes he extended his senses and mapped the tunnels carved by Ivain to contain the frostwargs. Sealed off by the cold, the entrance angled steeply beneath the headland. Passages bored deep into rock, linked by chains of caverns and buttresses of chiseled stone. The upper levels were choked with spellbound ice; below, closed in fetid darkness, lurked the frostwargs. Though the creatures preferred live prey, they could also draw sustenance from soil and rock. They did not breathe; water could not drown them, nor would flame consume their shells. Only extreme heat could cause them temporarily to shift form.

Surrounded by the smells of sea and tide wrack and the sour cries of gulls, Jaric laced his fingers together. He honed his will to a pinpoint of force, stepped forward, and sank straight down into rock. The stone flowed around him, thick and turgid as quicksand. Though his eyes were utterly blind, his Earthmaster's vision saw vistas: quartz like jagged veins of frost, crystals, and rust-dark ores, and a thousand textures of mineral. Down Jaric plunged, past level upon level encompassed by Anskiere's wards. With his heart pounding from tension, he emerged at last on a ledge just below the ceiling in the cavern confining the frostwargs.

A strident whistle slashed his ears. Jaric's skin tightened with goose-flesh. The calls of frostwargs grew nearer, threaded by a scraping and scrabbling of claws. Then the creatures scented the presence of prey and burst into a full-throated ululation.

Sweating, Jaric snapped a flame out of air. It flickered from his finger-tips, weak red in the oxygen-poor atmosphere of the cavern. In baleful, bloody light, the Firelord sought his enemy. Ivain had floored the cave with a forest of sword-thin crystals; a thousand edges of reflection stabbed Jaric's eyes. Creatures scuttled between on segmented legs. Their carapaces were jointed like insects, ending in arched tails tipped with spikes. Eyes glowed violet in the dimness, speckling highlights over terrible, curved mandibles and razor sets of foreclaws that gnashed air with tireless feroc-ity. Stabbed by dread, Jaric saw frostwargs hurtle across the cavern and continue, *straight up rock walls toward his feet.*

He had no moment to think. The demons moved with terrifying speed. Claws snicked scant inches from his flesh, even as he set his hands to rock and transformed earth energy into fire. Light and unbearable heat exploded over the cavern. Shells clicked on rock, and whistles blended into disso-nance. Pressed against stone, Jaric struck, and struck again. Sparks flared in his hair and clothes; cinders bit into his skin but he barely noticed pain. Over and over he discharged power, until the whistles faded and died amid a roaring avalanche of flame.

At length, weak-kneed and weary, Jaric permitted the fires to dwindle.

The cavern below lay awash in golden light, details mantled under steam which drifted from the ice at the far side. Jaric searched carefully, but saw no trace of movement. Scattered amid the topaz sparkle of crystals he found black, spiny spheres, each one a dormant frostwarg. No sooner had the Firelord identified the objects, when the nearer ones began to change form. Smoky shell shifted texture, turned mottled in patterns of mustard and ink.

Appalled to discover how swiftly the horrors could recover, Jaric acted instantly. His Earthmaster's vision sounded the depths of the shaft, and encountered a circular pit at the bottom. *Ivain had not carved deep enough.* Shaping powers of fire and stone, Keithland's new Firelord shattered the roof of the cavern, then ignited the rubble and smothered the frostwargs' seed-forms in seething magma. The air shimmered with heat. Fumes roiled up, stinging his eyes. Jaric raised his hands and struck deeper. Energies crackled across rock. A chasm opened in the floor, spurting lava like a sword wound. Jaric gathered himself and struck again. Ivain's crystals melted and ran, while the base of the cavern softened, slithered, then collapsed with a roar over the brink, bearing the shells of the frostwargs deep beneath the earth. The lava would finally solidify, shackling the demons in stone until such time as the mountain itself crumbled away.

CHAPTER X

Ice Wards

The cavern of the frostwargs smoldered like a counterpart of hell. Awash in ruddy light, Jaric crouched with his head in his hands, eyes stung to tears by fumes thrown off from the magma. Coughing poisoned air, and sapped by exhaustion, he struggled unsteadily to his feet. Although he had raised heat enough to sear solid stone to vapor, the ice imprisoning Anskiere remained imperviously shrouded in fog. Without stirring from the ledge, Jaric sensed that the weather wards that preserved the barrier held firm. The Stormwarden was prisoner still.

Though confrontation with the frostwargs had left him taxed and shaken, Jaric descended through a defile. The force of his defenses had plowed the cavern floor into a tortured maze of rubble; lava puddled and spilled through the rifts, radiating sultry highlights over pinnacles and arches of slagged stone. Jaric picked his way cautiously between, his skin flushed ruddy by the fires of his handiwork. Heat charred the soles from his boots as he walked; compelled to pause and engage mastery to prevent burns, he yearned sharply for his days with the trapper and the snow-bound silence of Seitforest. But Keithland's need would not wait for daydreams. Jaric moved on, his ears tortured by the hiss of calderas and the crack and boom of settling rock. The groan of the ravaged earth inflamed his inner senses like pain. Unable to escape the proof that he had inherited the destructive stamp of his sire, the Firelord reached the mist that cloaked the ice wall. Saddened, and weary beyond thought, he stepped forward without taking precautions.

Cold shocked his flesh. Clamped in the grip of Anskiere's wards, Jaric gasped, then cried aloud as chill bit into the tissue of his lungs. He called up fire to counter. But even as warmth answered his will, a starred pulse of light canceled his effort. Weather sorcery closed like a fist mailed with winter, smothering flame into darkness. Jaric staggered backward into the red heat of the cavern. Frost spiked his hair and tunic. His hands were numb, unresponsive and whitened as bread dough. Ivainson rubbed his fingers. Shivering in discomfort as circulation returned, he contemplated the wards, and knew fear.

Never had he imagined the Stormwarden's defenses might be so strong.

Determined, Jaric called forth a tendril of flame. Without touching the mist, he teased the wards with lesser powers until their structure radiated light; glittering ribbons of energy shot through quartz-blue bastions of ice. The consummate skill of the creator made Ivainson stumble in awe, for Anskiere had laid down unimaginably potent defenses with the intricate geometry of snowflakes; the new prison for frostwargs seemed clumsy and rough by comparison.

At first Jaric despaired of finding weakness. But as he surveyed the wall, one portion of the pattern seemed dimmed, as if time and attrition had deteriorated the original spell. Ivainson refined his focus to a pinpoint, stepped up power, and rammed a cracking torrent of force against the gap.

Sparks flew. Lines of fire struck ice, and craze marks spread outward with a twang like harpstrings snapping under tension. Then vision became dazzled by a tearing burst of light. Jaric shut his eyes. He braced himself hard against the backlash, as energy shed by the wards roared like a holocaust around him. But the ordeal of Firemastery had once been as terrible; he held firm, until the last of his strength ebbed from him and exhaustion unbound his control.

Fire sputtered and died. Tear-blind and tired and swaying on his feet, Jaric surveyed the result of his effort. The disturbed glimmer of the wards revealed the barest indentation, floored with chunked ice, and churning with mist. Tentatively the Firelord extended his hand. Cold enclosed his flesh like a glove, but without its earlier, killing penetration. Anskiere's barrier was breached. But a long, arduous trail remained before help could reach the sorcerer. Stressed to the edge of collapse, Jaric set his shoulders against a warm cranny of rock. Though his heart ached and his hands stung with burns, he would rest, then try again.

The effects of the Dreamweaver's stay-spell did not release Deison Corley until well past nightfall on the day that *Callinde* made port. Bound at wrist and ankle with cord, he wakened sprawled on a moonlit expanse of carpet. Surrounded by smells of parchment, oil, and leather, and the sharper pungency of horse bridles left slung across the back of a brocade chair, he recognized the clutter of the Kielmark's personal study. The King of Pirates was absent; but the bonds, when Corley twisted, proved cruelly secure. *Moonless*'s former captain shut his eyes then, overcome by failure. He had wished to avoid a return to Cliffhaven.

An hour passed in misery, while the moon swung in the sky. The rectangle of light on the rug thinned to a sliver. Hooves clattered from the courtyard; shouts and a clangor of arms heralded the midnight change of the guard. But the clockwork routine of Cliffhaven's fortifications no longer carried the reassurance of home. Through the boisterous noise of the patrols, Corley heard the sound he dreaded most. The door latch lifted, and a soft, booted tread crossed the carpet.

Always the Kielmark moved with astonishing grace for a man of his bulk. He lit no light. Neither did he stop where Corley could see him, but spoke from behind in a voice pitched low with anger. "When a captain

under my command loses six of my ships, and every living crewman aboard
them, I expect him to return and deliver a report. *What in Keithland gave you
the idea you could act otherwise?*"

, Corley said nothing. On the carpet, the sliver of light narrowed to a
needle, then winked out as the lintel of the window eclipsed the moon.
The room plunged into dark. Listless and dead inside, the captain heard
but did not react to the incisive imprecations the Kielmark uttered against
him.

"By Kor, you're not listening," said the Lord of Pirates. He lashed out
with a kick that tumbled the captain's body across the rug. "I've killed
men for less."

Corley blinked. He lay limp as the Kielmark followed with stinging
accusations, and then blows. Pain failed to rouse the captain's attention;
but eventually he noticed that the hard, emotionless phrases were imper-
sonal no longer.

"What of the sister you lost honor defending at Morbrith?" The
Kielmark spat in the hearth. "Maybe she deserved what she got, or were
you the one whose pleasure was interrupted in the dark?"

Corley jerked against his bonds.

The Kielmark laughed, very low in his throat. "Tell me, was it *your* brat
the girl went back to the hilltribes to hide? What else could be expected
of a man who loses his command to demons, *and then runs!*"

Anger claimed Corley. He yanked, suddenly wild to free his hands. The
insults continued. The captain forgot that his tormentor was both friend
and sovereign lord. Goaded to reasonless fury, he responded to a voice
disembodied by darkness, soft footsteps that came and went, and hands
that wantonly inflicted pain. Then suddenly, Corley felt steel lick his ankle.
The restraining rope fell away. Savage with temper, he rolled to his feet.
Another tug at his wrists freed his hands.

"Come fight," invited a whisper in the dark. "We've a score to settle,
over *Moonless* and six companies of men."

Steel gleamed in shadow, then vanished. Disturbed air grazed Corley's
cheek as a knife whickered past his skin. The weapon thunked into the
settle, but the captain had already moved, springing off his toes to grapple
his enemy in the night-black confines of the room.

His hands met air, then the hard edge of the table. A fist hammered
into his side before Corley could recover balance. He staggered into a
chair. Bit rings jangled. As his attacker lunged to throw him, the captain
hooked a headstall. Harness whipped in an arc and connected; reins lashed
flesh and wound taut, snaring his opponent. Corley pounced, answered by
a grunt as he rammed solidly into muscle. Bits and buckles chinked as he
grappled for a hold, missed, and received a second chop in the ribs. Then
a hand caught his wrist and closed him in a wrestler's hold.

Corley countered with a move intentionally painful. Rewarded by a
gasp, he pressed his advantage, freed his hand, and tried a throw. But a
booted foot kicked his ankle from under him. Metal clanked faintly in

reproof as the captain twisted, caught bridle leather and shirt with both hands, and dragged his adversary down with him.

The fighters struck floor with a force that left them winded. Entwined and struggling, neither seemed ready to retire. Carpet rucked under their exertions. Locked in single-minded conflict, they rolled the length and breadth of the chamber, while furnishings careened and toppled in their wake, glass ornaments and pearl veneer dashed to splinters against the tile.

Corley panted. Bleeding from a dozen small gashes, he closed his fingers over his enemy's throat and tried to throttle his windpipe. But an animal heave of muscles hurled him up, back, and over. His shin smashed a fire iron, and a knee gouged his stomach. Breathless, dizzied, he recalled the settle, and the knife left imbedded in its oaken rail. He flung sideways, heard knuckles smack the hearthstone where his head had rested only the moment before. Then two strong legs clamped his thigh and dragged him down. Corley stretched and caught a billet of wood from the grate. He hammered until the hold loosened. His enemy snared his makeshift bludgeon and wrenched it painfully away; but not before the captain closed his hand over the knife hilt.

A curse sounded in darkness; his enemy realized he was armed. Corley showed his teeth in a savage grin of triumph; and the stakes turned from vicious to desperate. Tables crashed, and chests overturned. Broken furnishings alternately served as shield and encumbrance to a murderous thrust of steel. In time, Corley felt himself entangled in the same bridles he had hurled before in self-defense. He cut himself loose and drove forward. Darkness and luck favored his lunge. The captain's fist closed in a mat of curly hair. One lightning reaction brought the knife down. Inflamed by a reasonless lust to kill, Corley pressed steel and knuckles against the cords of his victim's throat.

Yet even as he cut, the Kielmark's ruby torque grated under his hand. Deison Corley remembered: *he fought a friend whose life was dear to him as a brother.* Horror plunged ice through his heart. Wrenched by a queer, coughing cry, the captain snatched back his hand. He flung the knife into the grate, then braced his body for retaliation that never came. The man under his hands breathed in and out, short shallow breaths of exertion; neither blows nor speech arose in retribution.

Wrung by reaction, Corley drew back, until no contact remained between himself and his lord by the hearth. Damp with sweat and the blood of minor abrasions, the captain sat and haltingly began to recount the loss of five brigantines and the flagship under his command. His voice steadied as he progressed. Helped by darkness, and the fact that the Kielmark made no attempt to interrupt, Corley finished his report with ringing bitterness.

"Lord, had Shadowfane's plot succeeded, I would have"—he paused, then forced the words—"caused your murder. Luck alone spared us both. The Dark-dreamer's powers have no equal in Keithland. At any time, Kor's

Accursed might claim my flesh as a weapon. Knowing that, did you think I'd risk Cliffhaven by coming back?"

A bit chimed in the shadows. The Kielmark stirred; he sighed under the combined effects of discomfort and amusement, then said unequivocally, "Yes. Because Cliffhaven is your home. And more than any other's in this warren of brigands, your loyalty is beyond question." The King of Pirates heaved to his feet. "Kor's grace! Have I got to stick my neck under your blade twice to convince you? In your right mind, or not, hot blood, or cold, you just proved you can't strike me down." The Kielmark ended with a snort of arrogant irony. "And if Shadowfane's demons send your husk or any shape-changed replica as assassin, they do so at their peril. Had you forgotten? *My captains never die unavenged.*"

A striker snapped in the dark. Flame rose from the candle stub in a nearby wall sconce. Shirtless, blood-streaked, and clad in ripped leggings, the Lord of Cliffhaven turned from the light and extended his hand. "Now get up. We have work ahead."

Corley noted the marks of his handiwork upon his sovereign's flesh. Then, embarrassed, he surveyed the shambled wreck of the study. "You planned this."

A grunt answered his accusation. The Kielmark bent stiffly, unlatched a chest by the far wall, and drew forth studded crossbelts and a set of beautifully crafted throwing knives. "Take these. Then find a whetstone. We have every crowned head in Keithland and the whole clutch of Alliance councilmen waiting in the great hall. That means a lot of nitpicking and a very lengthy council of war. Are you capable?"

Corley rose and accepted the gift. He drew one of the daggers and tested the blade with the finger adjacent to the stub left mangled by the Karas. "Dull," he said thoughtfully, then curled a swollen lip. "Next time I should remember that my sister's a hill chief's get. She settles her own scores, I've no doubt, with studded bracelets and weapons tempered in horse piss."

The Kielmark laughed with full-throated enthusiasm. "Fine woman. Next time you duck orders, I'll ask her to thrash you." Still smiling, he shoved Corley toward the door.

Disturbed in the depths of stasis, Anskiere dreamed, first of Elrinfaer's fair city, and then of storms and nightmare, and the terrible destruction wrought by the Mharg. Ivain's mad laughter echoed amid tumbled towers; then a fire-dance of sorcery slashed the dark. The Stormwarden's sleep thinned and broke. He had no chance to waken gradually. Roused to wet boots and a watery trickle of slush, he sensed disharmony like pain in his mind. A meddler had broached his wards. Flame had seared the patterning, torn gaping holes in a structure raised to confine frostwargs. Only one sorcerer in Keithland was capable of such feats.

"Ivain!" Anskiere's anguished whisper dissolved, pattering echoes amid the sullen drip of water. Stung by ancient pain, the Stormwarden shook melted ice from his hair. He reached for his staff, determined to mend the damage to his defenses. If frostwargs had escaped, he vowed he would silence the laughter of Elrinfaer's betrayer forever.

The tunnels that led downward were still blocked, yet the barrier had lost its glassy hardness; Anskiere touched ice gone rotten with thaw. He worked his mastery without thought for stiffened joints or muscles long unused to movement. Hair coiled damp against his shoulders. Icicles snapped beneath his tread as he cleared the passage with deft decision. Yet though he listened, he heard no whistle of frostwargs; just the whisper of his breath and the shift of frost-shackled rock. Only a thin sheet of ice sealed the entrance to the lower caverns. Keenly alert for danger, Anskiere dissolved the last barrier and looked out.

The mouth of the tunnel opened into a fiery glare of light. Squinting between drifts of fog, the Stormwarden glimpsed a cataclysmic vista of melted rock. He stepped forward, footfalls splashing through pooled water and floating shards of ice. Even in the wintry depths of the tunnel, the heat reddened his face. No frostwargs charged ravening to meet him, but their absence did not reassure. Fearful the creatures might already be released, Anskiere hurried his steps, then checked to discover a figure kneeling in his path.

The man's tunic was charred almost to rags. Spark-singed hair fringed his knuckles, which were clenched, obscuring his face; but his identity was never in question, for the skin of both wrists was abraded with the burns that were the trademarks of a Firelord's power.

Anskiere stiffened with a flash of antagonism. A halo of force flared active around the staff poised in his hands, and the slush underfoot hardened to frost with a crack like shattering crystal.

Light touched the Firelord where he knelt. With a sharp breath of surprise he raised his head to see the scarecrow figure of the Stormwarden standing over him in the passage. "Your Grace!" Startled, and showing signs of advanced exhaustion, he offered the courtesy due a prince. "I have brought you the Keys to Elrinfaer."

Anskiere stared, ambivalent, into eyes that were deep and brown, yet lucid. The brightening aura of his staff lit hair that was not red but blond as grain at high summer. Memory returned. With a gasp, the Stormwarden separated past from present. "Jaric?"

The one who had once been a scribe's apprentice rose, grown now to a man and a sorcerer. He swayed unsteadily on his feet. But perception sharpened by Sathid-bond had already caught the spasm of distrust that flawed the Stormwarden's voice. "You think me crazed as Ivain," Jaric accused.

Anskiere declined answer. "What became of the frostwargs?"

Ivainson gestured toward the sultry glow at his back. "They are bound in fire and rock. With your help, I believe they could be permanently secured."

Still the Stormwarden did not speak. Wounded by his silence, and afraid to guess at its cause, Jaric lifted a hand to his neck. He snapped the thong that hung there with a swift jerk and extended a small leather pouch. "There will never be another betrayal like Elrinfaer."

"You cannot promise that. Time is measured in ages, and blood might tell." Anskiere accepted the pouch and found it unaccountably heavy. He flicked the drawstring open. Inside lay the basalt block that secured the wards over the Mharg-demons at Elrinfaer, and also something more. With careful fingers the Stormwarden lifted two weighty, smoke-colored jewels, faceted on a six-point axis, and cold as the arctic to his touch. He knew at once what he held. Jaric had given him the Sathid crystals that were the foundation of his mastery, presumably as a token of trust.

Anskiere closed his hand. The stones clicked like dice as he flicked droplets of water from his cuffs. "Why?"

Jaric's expression revealed a flash of rare anger. "Because I'm not my father." His voice quieted almost to a whisper. "I know no other way to convince you. With my powers under your control, perhaps you'll find your peace."

Anskiere dimmed the light of his staff. Cloaked in ambiguous shadow, he studied Ivainson's profile, lined blood-red in the glare from the cavern. Though resemblance to the sire was marked, details differed; this nose was straighter, the mouth less full. Jaric stood shorter by a full three fingers. Such discrepancies gradually eased the antipathy Anskiere felt upon encountering another Firelord in the flesh. Still, he avoided revealing the depth of the uncertainties left seeded by Ivain; nor did he mention the crystals given over with the Keys to Elrinfaer. "You are more powerful than your father," the Stormwarden remarked at last.

"That I doubt." Jaric rubbed blistered wrists and grimaced. "Your ice wards were too strong for me."

"No." Anskiere twisted his staff. The looped brass top caught light like sparks on a spindle. "You lack nothing but experience. Force flows through you like a river constantly passing. If you choose, you can refine your craft, and bind what energy you don't use to an object. Such reserves can be freed at need to craft a mightier ward." Roughness eased from Anskiere's tone. "But the particulars of a sorcerer's lore can wait. Ivain's debt is canceled. At last you are free of obligation."

Jaric made a small movement in the darkness. "Free? Neither of us is free, Your Grace. Kor's Accursed grew bold in your absence. Taen's brother, Emien, has gone the way of Merya Tathagres. He is now a servant of demons. In concert with a circle of Gierj, his dark dreams have conquered Morbrith."

Anskiere bent his head. Silver hair fanned over the fingers laced around his staff. Pain inflected Jaric's statement, a bitterness akin to his own scarred memories of Elrinfaer; unhappily the Stormwarden recalled: Morbrith Keep had once been Jaric's home.

Puddled water rippled as the Firelord shifted position. "The Kielmark awaits at the fortress. He's gathered every crowned head in Keithland, and also the eminent of the Alliance for a council of war."

"We had better go, then." The Stormwarden searched the son of his former antagonist and found only solid sincerity. "Your treatment of the frostwargs must hold, temporarily. A breach in the borders won't wait."

Anskiere lifted his staff. The blue-violet radiance of his weather mastery flared over the tunnel that led to the surface as, straight-shouldered, and clad in threads of tattered velvet and gold, he began the ascent. Jaric followed. Neither sorcerer spoke of the fact that the Stormwarden retained the Sathid crystals which underlay the powers of a Firelord, as token of a trust dearly bought.

Torchlight and the pinpoint gleam of wax candles lit the great hall at Cliffhaven, though the hour was well past midnight. Clad formally in robes and myrtle circlet, Taen Dreamweaver perched on the dais to the left of the Kielmark's chair while a crowd dressed in brocades and livery milled restlessly below. Royalty, the elect of the Alliance, and an assembly of town mayors, complete with servants and attendants, squabbled over seating for the council called by the Kielmark. His unreasonable choice of timing had cut sleep and tempers short. More than one delegate examined the furnishings with displeasure, recognizing prized gifts claimed as tribute, or items pirated from vessels that had attempted to run the straits without acknowledging Cliffhaven's sovereignty.

Taen smiled as the mayor-elect of Telshire squeezed into a cushioned chair too delicate for his enormous girth. Close by, the youngest crowned head in Keithland vanished between two pages, a secretary in hot pursuit; King Kisburn's untimely death had left an heir of eight, and royal advisors had their collective hands full playing nursemaid. Fifteen council members of the Alliance clustered, stiff-backed and disapproving, before a doorway guarded by the Kielmark's sentries. Beside their weaponed presence, the dignitaries seemed palsied and gray. Never had Keithland's vulnerabilities been more evident than in the diversity of rulers gathered to formulate the defense, Taen reflected. Their bickering and disorganization might easily last until dawn.

The sovereign Lord of Cliffhaven entered, shirtless but resplendent in white breeches, sea boots, and a magnificent silver-hilted broadsword. Rubies sparkled above his bronzed and muscular chest as he strode to the dais, his senior captain in full dress uniform on his right. The buzz of conversation faltered, then renewed with a note of defiance as the Kielmark reached his leopard-hide chair. He rested crossed wrists on the back, and his voice boomed out as if he stood on a ship's deck. "Kor's grace, some of the furnishings are interesting, even familiar, I admit, but *sit down, all of you, at once.*"

As if the words were a signal, the sentries at the door dressed weapons. The sharp, metallic clang stilled the crowd in the chamber; faces turned forward with resentment.

The Kielmark surveyed the officials and the royalty gathered in his hall. "That's better." With the passionless interest of a king wolf, he sat himself; and the sentries by the doorway sheathed steel to chilly silence.

Corley took the chair to the right. Bruises from a recent fight discolored the skin over his collar. But the death wish that had troubled him earlier now seemed utterly banished; as the Kielmark opened council, his senior captain calmly took up whetstone and knife. The Dreamweaver closed her eyes with relief.

"I called you here for the purpose of defending Keithland against Kor's Accursed." The sovereign of Cliffhaven paused and fingered his sword; and immediately the Alliance representative from Skane's Edge disrupted order. Bald, middle-aged, and overdressed in a robe festooned with ribbon, the man sprang to his feet.

"Pirate! How dare you preside over honest men? Is it true a Firelord has returned to Keithland soil? Your kitchen scullion said a son of Ivain took shelter on Cliffhaven only yesterday."

Uproar swept the chamber. Ivain's cruel exploits were remembered with resentment and fear, and news of an heir to the Cycle of Fire abruptly overturned propriety.

Yet the Kielmark ruled a lawless following. Within his halls he managed insolence with strength, brutality, or wolfish cleverness, whichever suited the moment best. Neither royalty nor the august peerage of the Free Isles merited exception. Before debate could organize to rebellion, the King of Pirates unsheathed his sword and bashed the flat of the blade across his chair.

"Silence!" The effect proved sufficient to intimidate. The councilman sat swiftly, and the noise subsided. The Kielmark rested his sword point against the floor and addressed the troublemaker in tones of blistering scorn. "Do you rule by the gossip of servants, *Eminence*? The scullion you bribed suffered a whipping for his indiscretion." Aware of a few sullen murmurs, the Lord of Cliffhaven inclined his head toward the captain seated to his right. "Corley, deliver your report."

Moonless's former captain rose and, with a poise impossible an hour before, related the demise of his fleet of six. By the time he spoke of his experience with the Karas shape-changer, the assembly sat strained and disturbed. Corley ended, finally, to thick silence.

The Kielmark now had their attention. He sheathed his great weapon, and one by one called upon the rulers of Keithland to evaluate the status of their domains. Other than prowling bands of Thienz, most had little to contribute; skeptical expressions crept back until the Queen of Hallowild announced that her northern domain of Morbrith had fallen to the Darkdreamer's influence. In a voice tremulous with sorrow, she told of fields and towns littered with corpses, and of caravans that ventured through Gaire's Main never to return. The Kielmark incisively pointed out that the timing of the deaths coincided with Jaric's destruction of the Gierj.

Corley sat with his whetstone clenched in whitened knuckles; and Taen wept, for the folk she once had defended were now bones rotting in the sun. Even the irascible King of Felwaithe sat silent in his chair; his lands lay closest to Shadowfane, and only the inscrutable caprice of Kor's Accursed seemed to have spared his subjects from ruin.

The Kielmark stirred, eyes gone cold as chipped ice. "Plainly the demons challenge our borders once again. Landfast itself may be threatened. Any man who thinks our survival is not in peril may abdicate, now. Keithland has no leeway to spare for dissent."

A murmur swept the chamber, ominous as the grind of storm surf over rock. Though every ruler present bridled at the Kielmark's assumption of authority, none dared arise in complaint. Forced to alliance by a common cause, Keithland's council tallied resources and argued strategies of attack and defense until well after dawn. Taen listened in silent distress. Her Dreamweaver's perception grasped the truth: neither weapons nor the bulwark of faith in Kor's canons could match the Dark-dreamer and his circle of Gierj.

Daylight spilled cold, gray light through the arches when the clatter of hooves echoed up from the courtyard. Corley stilled his whetstone and knife. The Kielmark lifted his chin from his fist, eyes narrowed with speculation, as the great double doors burst open.

Two men entered, both of them ragged. The taller wore the remains of a blue velvet tunic; tangled silver hair streamed over the wool of a sentry's borrowed cloak. His lean features were hooked into a frown, and he carried a sorcerer's staff capped with looped brass. As he strode past the guards, a hush settled over the council. The pale eyes, sure step, and stern countenance of Anskiere of Elrinfaer were known the breadth of Keithland.

The silence grew strained at the appearance of the Stormwarden's companion, a slight, blond man in singed linen whose eyes no man could endure without discomfort. But to the woman in Dreamweaver's robes on the dais, the sight of Ivainson Firelord brought joy.

"Jaric!" Taen left her chair running. Her myrtle circlet whirled to the floor as she hurtled the length of the hall into his embrace.

Keithland's newest sorcerer spun her around. Oblivious to propriety and the presence of royalty, he kissed her; and his exuberance shattered order within the council. Kings and council members rose, some in awe, others shouting imprecations. But louder than the din rose the Kielmark's rich laughter, and the voice of the King of Felwaithe.

"Hail, Stormwarden! Hail, heir to the Firelord! Let Shadowfane rue this hour, and Keithland rejoice. For the victory!"

"For the victory!" echoed the elderly Queen of Hallowild, while, with a predatory smile, the Kielmark beckoned Stormwarden and Firelord to join him on the dais. To the right of the leopard chair, Corley smiled grimly. Plans to wrest Morbrith from the Dark-dreamer could now begin in earnest.

CHAPTER XI

Crisis

The click of beads echoed across the mirror pool at Shadowfane as the Thienz bowed obsequiously, forelimbs clutched to its chest. 'Lord-mightiest, I bring news.'

Scait regarded the creature, his eyes already slitted with annoyance; earlier he had learned that two of the human children taken captive had died in training. A third had weakened to the point where it would not survive, and the advisors had begged to open it for dissection. Scait forbade them, though they grumbled; with only five human young left to be enslaved through a cross-linked Sathid, the Demon Lord gestured irritably for the Thienz to continue.

Beads clicked; the Thienz was young, an immature adult. It squirmed with reluctance, which meant that its message would be unwelcome. 'Exalted, the watcher sends words of a discovery,' it blurted in a rush. 'Gierjlings have gathered. They have chosen a lair in the caves beneath Shadowfane. A spore to form the Morrigierj is already spawned and growing apace.'

Scait gouged spurred thumbs deep into the stuffing of his throne, while at his feet the Thienz cowered and shivered. No news could have been worse.

This setback made other difficulties pale to insignificance. The master plot to conquer Keithland hinged upon expendable human pawns to focus the Gierjlings' killing powers; but a Morrigierj was the creatures' rightful overlord. This advent of a spawning was centuries premature, and a perilous upset, for the naturally focused forces of the Gierjlings were mightier by far than the combined powers of the compact. Shadowfane itself might be threatened. Scait snarled at the Thienz. 'You are certain of this?'

The messenger bobbed, exuding a stink of nervous sweat. 'Mightiest, the Watcher-of-Gierj itself sent me.'

'I come at once.' Human hide tore beneath Scait's claws as he thrust himself abruptly to his feet.

The Thienz scrambled to complete its bow, then scuttled off like a whipped dog. Normally the Demon Lord sent underlings upon those errands to the catacombs beneath Shadowfane. But with all hopes, even continued survival, ultimately dependent upon conquest of Keithland, the possible development of a Morrigierj became a priority concern. Inwardly as distressed as the Thienz, Scait strode from the hall without pause to call a lackey to replace the rent limb of his throne arm. While the Thienz scrabbled clear of its master's feet, the Demon Lord descended the spiral stair that gave access to the lower levels of the fortress. From there he traversed a mazelike chain of corridors that altered, in subterranean depths, from pillared construction and hexagonal brick to the uneven contours of a cave. Dampness streaked walls stained rust red with mineral deposits. The enclosing confines of rock seemed suffocating, a barrier impervious to the finely developed psychic sensors of most demons. Scait hissed uneasily. He blinked glowing eyes in the gloom and chose his path with caution. At length, on the heels of the Thienz, he arrived at the chamber the Gierjlings had chosen for their lair.

The underling scrabbled aside and fled. The Demon Lord it had escorted ducked through an archway into darkness studded with the yellow-green glimmer of eyes. Gierj were there, numbering hundreds or maybe even thousands, jumbled one upon another like a mat of living fungus.

Jostled by wiry, furred bodies, Scait snapped his teeth in displeasure. The creatures eddied away with a clicking of claws and an occasional whine of protest. Presently the Demon Lord gained an unobstructed view of the spore, a stonelike sphere nested in a depression in the floor, black and dull, and protected by a shell of insurmountable hardness. Scait already knew that no force possessed by the compact was capable of destroying it; memories-of-ancestors ascertained this fact beyond doubt. The only way to kill a Morrigierj spore was to launch it into the heart of a star. Lacking ships, such remedy was impossible; but space communication and transport might not prove beyond reach, should *Corinne Dane's* Veriset navigational module be recovered.

Scait blinked, and opened his retinas to their widest aperture. Normally a spore should take a decade to mature, but past data offered no reassurance. Keithland's magnetic fields must be differently tuned from those of the home star where Gierj had evolved. Plainly, the natural rhythms of the cycle were upset. The spore that Scait regarded should not have been spawned for another two thousand years.

'Other things than nature might stir the Gierj to a spawning.' The sending originated from a hulking form that shuffled down the corridor beyond the Gierj-lair.

Scait stiffened, irritated that his guard had been breached. Only one being in Shadowfane would dare his anger; that one was very old, and far too wise to offer reckless challenge.

The Watcher-of-Gierj sent again with a note of driest acerbity. 'Your rivals will claim that misuse of the Gierjlings given over to Maelgrim served to hasten the breeding cycle. Whatever the cause, Lord-exalted, this spore in all probability will hatch prematurely.'

Scait required no warning of the Morrigierj's pending development. His eyes had fully adjusted to the dimness. Now that his sensors had acclimated to the unaccustomed restrictions of stone, he, too, felt the flare of primal awareness that stirred beneath the spore's surface. Spider-limbed Gierjlings rustled restlessly in the dark. Their zombie eyes burned balefully while the Demon Lord sorted ramifications.

"The compact is thwarted, now." The shuffling step drew nearer. Presently the nasal voice of the Watcher sounded from the doorway immediately behind. "Morrigierj will upset all plans."

Scait spun around as the creature's domed hulk crowded through the arch. Hunched and armored like a scavenger beetle, it picked at the carcass of a fish. Cartilage crunched delicately as it cleared its mandibles and qualified. "Even fully bonded-to-Sathid, your talented litter of humans dare not contest the sovereignty of the Morrigierj. Most-jealous-of-masters, its vengeance would surely be bloody."

Scait's lip curled and bared rows of sharpened teeth. "What will that matter? Take Set-Nav, and we can escape this planet. Then let the retribution of the Morrigierj fall and wreak death upon mankind."

The Watcher crunched a last bite of fish. "But Set-Nav's location is not known to us. The Sanctuary Towers at Landfast no doubt hold the key. Except they are guarded by priests, and the most secure of arcane defenses. The captive manlings bonded to Sathid will never mature in time to spearhead your assault against Keithland."

The Demon Lord shrugged with malevolent displeasure. The Watcher was the last of its kind; it had no ambition for power. If he slew it in a fit of defensive rage, its skills could not be replaced. "I will grant Maelgrim Dark-dreamer a Gierj circle of sixty, and permission to enslave all of humanity."

"Gierj power on that scale will ruin the boy's health quickly," scoffed the Watcher. "That he would be dead long before Landfast's securities could be breached is a foregone conclusion." It blinked tiny, wise eyes and waited, but its overlord whirled and strode from the chamber, kicking Gierj from his path with more than his usual viciousness. The Watcher sighed with resignation. Patiently it combed fish oil from its quills, while the Gierj closed like a living blanket around the black spheroid of their spore.

Keithland mustered for war. On Cliffhaven, where armory and warehouses were stocked with weapons for every contingency, the Kielmark ordered the forges lit to benefit those domains less well prepared. The clangor of his armorers' mallets rang night and day over the fortress, while ships came and went in the harbor, delivering dispatches and transporting men. The vessels sailed always with fair wind and full sails. Recovered from his prison of ice, Anskiere of Elrinfaer served as weather warden. Between time, he began instructing the Firelord to refine control of his mastery. The Kielmark observed Jaric's progress with narrowed eyes, then immersed himself in strategy and planning. Even the defenses of Vaere-trained sorcerers had limitations. Force of arms must not be neglected in preparation for battle against Shadowfane.

The south-shore kingdoms and the Alliance archipelagoes proved woefully underequipped; Kisburn's troops were still depleted from an ill-fated alliance with Tathagres, which left the north-shore garrisons maintained by Hallowild and Felwaithe. The Kielmark detailed captains to evaluate them; then, clad in the white breeches he had not taken time to change since the council two days past, he sent for Deison Corley.

The first captain was slow to arrive at the study. His smudged hands and tunic showed that summons had reached him at the waterfront, where he labored with the dock workers to black down the rigging of the brigantine commissioned for his command. Both sleeves bore stains at the wrists from the tanner's oil that softened a new set of knife sheaths.

The Kielmark analyzed such details at a glance; judging his captain well recovered from the incident with the Karas, he made a decision and spoke. "The sorcerers and the Dreamweaver sail for Morbrith with the turn of the tide."

Corley crossed the carpet, sat, and stared at his boot cuffs as if the leather desperately wanted mending. He showed no surprise. "Then you'll order me north to Cover's Warren, to muster the patrol fleet and guard Felwaithe?"

"No. Tamic's doing that." The Kielmark watched, muscles coiled like a snake's, as his first captain shot up straight with a screech of chair legs. For a moment blue eyes locked with ones of cinnamon brown.

Then Corley said, "Why?" A stranger would not have noticed his hurt, that his Lord had sent another, perhaps steadier man, where once he would have gone himself.

"Because I'd never trust Tamic to keep order in this den of outlaws." The Kielmark rested his fists on the table; rubies flashed like blood at his neck as he leaned forward. "We'd have mutiny and murder within the hour *Ladywolf* sailed."

Corley blinked and slowly turned white as the name of the brigantine registered. *Ladywolf* was the Kielmark's personal command. "You'll be going yourself, then, with Taen and the rest?" His brows peaked in disbelief. Through fifteen years of service he had never known the Lord of Cliffhaven to leave his island fortress.

"Who else could keep Alliance councilmen, Kor's priests, and a flighty mess of royalty in agreement enough to lead an army?" The Kielmark gestured in exasperation. "I have to go. I'm the only one who can threaten both trade and their treasuries. D'you know any better way of keeping humanity in accord?"

Corley grinned. A little color returned to his face. "You're Keithland's most likely candidate for a fine, solid citizen, right enough."

"Fires," snapped the Kielmark, for once intolerant of his first captain's sarcasm. "Slack the discipline while I'm gone, and I'll flay your hide from your heels up." As if reluctant to continue, he stopped, straightened, and twisted his jeweled torque from his neck. He cast the circlet onto the boards, and gold clanged sourly between his fist and his first captain's hand. "If any man questions your right to command, that's my token."

Corley swallowed, speechless. Light came and went like flame in the heart of the rubies as the Kielmark leaned across the window. He hooked his baldric from the marble arms of the cherub, then tossed his great sword over his back. Neither man spoke as he crossed the chamber; but both understood that the torque on the table was as close as this sovereign would come to naming a successor.

"Watch your back, friend," Corley whispered at last.

The Kielmark paused by the doorway, wary as always, but smiling. "Speak for yourself," he said roughly. Then he strode without farewell into the candleless gloom of the hall.

Ladywolf raised anchor within the hour. Jaric stood at her rail, hands laced over the cross guard of his own sword, newly reclaimed from the armory where it had lain since the last time Corley made port with *Moonless*. From the deck by his side, Taen regarded the weapon with trepidation. Traditionally, Vaere-trained sorcerers disdained to carry steel; but when Anskiere began training to refine this Firelord's talents, Ivainson claimed the blade for his focus. Neither reason nor propriety could induce him to revert to the usual staff. The newest sorcerer sworn to service by the Vaere owned an obstinacy that even a Dreamweaver who loved him dared not cross.

Taen's preoccupied silence passed unnoticed as the Kielmark shouted orders to his boatswain; feet thumped on planking, and crewmen surged up the ratlines to make sail. By itself, Jaric's dissent was a mere defiance of form; but when Stormwarden and Firelord were together, the Dreamweaver noticed each one guarded his thoughts. That uneasiness troubled her; for, to combat the demons of Shadowfane, the two sorcerers must work mind within mind, attuned in flawless rapport.

The boatswain shouted. Canvas cascaded from the yards with a crack and a slither of boltropes. Poised to work his mastery on the foredeck, the Stormwarden of Elrinfaer lifted his head, his eyes the gray of rain beneath an overcast. He wore a sailor's tunic of plain, bleached linen, knotted at the waist with a sash worked in silver. But simple clothes could never mask the magnitude of his powers. His touch with the wind seemed effortless, deft with a proficiency born through decades of experience.

Jaric watched the sails clap smartly into curves overhead, the mild, wistful expression Taen associated with admiration on his face. As the *Ladywolf* shuddered and steadied into a heel, he smiled, his hair tumbled by the eddies off the headsails. "Anskiere's control is matchless. If I tried something comparable, like lighting the galley fire with sorcery, I'd probably crisp everything to the waterline."

"You'll improve." Taen leaned hard into her man's shoulder, heartened by his enthusiasm for his new craft. But her contentment faltered as the

Stormwarden glanced aside and noticed the Firelord watching him. Dark brows lowered almost to a frown; then, without greeting or encouragement, Anskiere strode aft.

Ivainson's exhilaration withered, and Taen felt tension harden the muscles of his forearm. "What happened at the ice cliffs?" she demanded impulsively. "Why should the Prince of Elrinfaer distrust you?"

Jaric considered his sword, as if inanimate Corlin steel might answer her query for him. His eyes turned deep, uncipherably intense, and he spoke at last with bitterness. "Anskiere believes that one day I will betray my own kind as my father did." Suddenly restless, he drew back, as if the very air might burn him. Taen clung to the rail. She did not follow as Jaric left her side. The quality of the Firelord's silence suggested that he had tried his utmost, in some manner even abandoned pride; still he had failed to assure Anskiere of Elrinfaer that his inheritance included no portion of his sire's mad malice.

Night fell, cloudy and fitful with gusts, over the Corine Sea. Despite the prevailing weather, the sky above *Ladywolf*'s masthead remained star-strewn and clear; her sails curved to the steady winds of a broad reach. On deck, the Kielmark remained braced against the rail long after the gleam of Cliffhaven's light tower vanished astern. His brigantine fared alone upon the sea. The bulk of the fleet stayed behind to defend Mainstrait; except for the picked company of men on board, the campaign to recapture Morbrith depended upon garrison troops to be levied from Corlin. The Duke at least maintained proper discipline, if the proficiency of his men at arms fell short of Cliffhaven's exacting standards. The Lord of Renegades frowned at the sparkle of phosphorescence churned up by the wake. Since no action could be taken until his vessel reached shore, he brooded; stable conditions left his crewmen idle, and himself more time than he liked for thought.

One fair day melted into the next. *Ladywolf* logged league after league at a steady twelve knots, but for Jaric the crossing did not lack challenge. Striving to master the nuances of a sorcerer's craft, he secluded himself in the chart room from morning till dark with the icy weight of his sword balanced across his knees. The weapon was the gift of Telemark the forester, granted on the eve that a boy had left Seitforest for his destiny as Firelord's heir. More than once the blade had drawn blood; never had it slain, but the armorer who had done the forging well knew his trade. From keen edge to the blue-black gloss of temper, the steel was fashioned expressly to maim. Jaric strove to change its nature. Yet day after exhausting day, success eluded him. A fortnight of effort had yielded no progress at all.

The Firelord sat back against the chart locker and sighed in frustration. Sunset had long since faded. Light from the deck lantern gilded the salt-crusted panes of the stern window, and shadow swathed the corners like velvet. The wear and creak of seagoing wood seemed abnormally loud, until Jaric recalled that the sailhands would be crowded in the galley at this hour. He should have been hungry, but supper did not interest him. Although the weight of the blade bore grooves in his thighs, quitting never entered his mind. He had not chosen the weapon for its deadly potential, as Anskiere believed. To marry power with a blade designed for killing might instead remind that the heritage of a Firelord tended ever toward terror and destruction. Jaric set his hands to the sword. Determined to complete what he had started, he closed his eyes in concentration.

He tuned his Earthmaster's perception to the blade. Like stone, or soil, or the symmetrical crystals of a mineral, the metal was composed of brightness; pinpoint eddies of energy interlocked and delicately balanced. Jaric embraced the pattern with his mind. Then he drew a filament of flame from his Sathid bond. With the care of a man unraveling spider silk, he endeavored to weave that energy, warp into weft through the steel. Sweat dampened the hair at his temples. To thread dissimilar powers through a structure of such delicacy taxed every resource he possessed; each attempt since dawn had ended the same way. Strain sustained for too long marred his control. Jaric cried out in dismay, even as energies strayed, jostling the symmetry of the metal fractionally out of alignment. The blade in his lap glared red, then white, disrupted by fire that licked and twisted to break free.

The Firelord stilled his inner mind. Heat beat unpleasantly against his flesh. The stresses of confined sorcery hammered his nerves like pain. He licked dry lips, tried to push back the fear that curled through his gut. This time his spell had progressed too far for retreat. Tired, and discouraged by knowledge that Anskiere could weave storm into a feather inside a fraction of an instant, he forced himself steady. No recourse remained but to correct his mistake.

"You're nearly there," said a voice at his shoulder. Cool hands slipped over Jaric's hot ones. A presence filled his mind like wavelets soaking gently into sand. "Try this." A prompt within his awareness flicked the fire-thread in another direction.

Jaric accepted the pointer; and like water breaking silver through a log jam, his spell unsnarled, lacing scarlet ribbons of energy through the steel. The process seemed utterly natural. Ivainson marveled, wondering why he had not worked in harmony with the metal's innate pattern earlier. Excitedly he continued the configuration, until the swordblade rang along its length with stored force; Jaric joined the ends of the energy complete and looked up, to lanternlight and the still presence of Anskiere of Elrinfaer. The sorcerer's eyes were gray and clear and kindly, and he smiled.

"I think I understand now." The Firelord lifted the weapon from his lap; its reddened glow touched his upturned features, underlighting his jaw to more angular contours, and lending his brows a pronounced arch.

His gold hair gleamed copper with highlights. Through the touch still in his mind, Jaric shared the Stormwarden's viewpoint; for a split second, he beheld in himself the mirror image of his father, Ivain.

Anskiere flinched back. Sorcery answered by reflex, and his half-raised hands sparked blue. A whirlwind ripped into being, sharp with the bite of ozone. Charts flapped helter-skelter across the table, and the lantern pitched on gimbaled mounts, flame extinguished in the draft.

"No!" Bashed backward into the bulkhead, Jaric dropped the sword. "Ivain is *dead!*" His shout tangled with a belling clang as steel struck the deck at his feet.

The violence of Anskiere's reaction died away. Air winnowed, then stilled, and charts ruffled to rest. Beyond speech, the Stormwarden sat and bowed his head over sleeves of stainless white.

"I do understand." Jaric raised himself awkwardly. "Through Llondelei imaging I shared your grief at Elrinfaer's loss." His voice turned edged with anguish. "But how will we ever conquer demons? You can't trust, and I cannot be other than myself."

Anskiere looked up, a tired half smile restored to his face. "We shall manage, I think. Look." And he pointed to the sword, which lay forgotten in the dark.

Steel forged by Corlin's armorer was ordinary no longer, but shining with the orange-red halo that marked the primary ward of a Firelord's staff. Two more auras soon would accompany that foundation, one a secondary level of power, and the third a protection against tampering by strangers. Like braiding, Jaric grasped the concept; intuitively he knew he could master the remaining sorceries more easily than the first.

Yet as he lifted the weapon, he damped the light of his accomplishment like guilt. "What good is skill if you won't believe in me?"

Cloth rustled; Anskiere touched Ivainson's shoulder in darkness and sighed. "I must learn how to forget the past. For in all ways that matter, Jaric, you are son to the friend I loved like a brother, before the Cycle of Fire overturned his humanity."

Ivainson completed the defense wards on his sword in the heat of an Indian summer calm. The Corine Sea lay leaden and smooth, but Anskiere's winds held true; *Ladywolf* neared the shores of Hallowild late the following day. Trouble met her even before land appeared above the horizon.

The sun shone like a disc of tarnished gold through billowing veils of smoke. Sailhands gathered at the rail, while the King of Pirates himself climbed aloft to investigate.

Sweating in the heat, and clad in little but a sword belt and a matched pair of wristbands, the Kielmark swung down the ratlines. He passed his ship's glass to Anskiere, who waited on the deck, and said tersely, "By the heading, I'd guess Seitforest is ablaze. The weevil in the oatmeal is, why?"

Anskiere accepted the glass, but made no move to focus. "Not lightning," he said presently. "The nearest thunderhead lies three hundred leagues due north. Nor could someone's cooking fire ignite the forest by wind. The air is dead still in that region. Taen might inform you better."

The Dreamweaver was below decks, apparently asleep; the Kielmark ordered his steward to wake her, and also summon Jaric from the chart room. Then he turned cold eyes to the Stormwarden. "Make a gale and drive this vessel into Corlin. She'll blow out sails for certain, but the damned sticks'll take it."

But Taen Dreamweaver was not sleeping. When the Kielmark's steward reached the stern cabin, he found her berth empty. The enchantress was settled cross-legged on a sea chest, her eyes wide open and unseeing in the depths of a trance. As leery of sorcery as his master, the man hesitated in the companionway; the creak of a hinge betrayed him. Taen started slightly. She blinked and shivered. As if she were dazed, her gaze focused slowly upon the servant poised to enter her cabin.

The next instant she shoved to her feet, urgent with alarm. "Where's the Kielmark?" she said quickly. "Send him here, with both of the sorcerers. Peril has come to Hallowild."

The steward spun and all but collided with his master, who chafed at delay and impetuously sought Taen himself. The servant recoiled, then wisely ducked clear before the Kielmark shoved him bodily from the companionway.

"Seitforest burns," the Lord of Cliffhaven snapped directly. "Can you tell why, girl?"

Taen met the Kielmark's impatience with a poise like edged steel. "The Dark-dreamer brings us war like none fought in Keithland before." She abandoned language; the unspeakable could be explained more efficiently through her talents. Dream-image sheared into the Kielmark's mind. He recoiled with a curse and a gasp as through the influence of sorcery he beheld Shadowfane's new army. The sight carried horror beyond all imagining.

Bull-mad with outrage, the King of Pirates roared out his orders before the vision was fully spent. Though called from below decks, his crewmen heard and obeyed his commands with alacrity. The brigantine came alive as men ran full tilt up the rigging. Canvas cracked from the yardarms, snapped into curves by the winds raised by sorcery. Ladywolf sheared into a violent heel and tossed Taen headlong from the trunk. The Kielmark's great fist caught her before she slammed into him. He righted her with a brusqueness that allowed no space for apology. "Fetch the Firelord. We'll be ashore before nightfall, and both of you must be ready to land."

Sunset came smudged by smoke pall. Though waters elsewhere lay polished under calm Ladywolf sheared into the estuary of the Redwater with her stuns'ls and flying jib flogged into tatters. Anskiere's winds dispersed, leaving canvas and snarled lines hanging limp as shreds on a scarecrow. While crewmen dropped anchor, a barge bearing ranking men at arms and the Duke's first commander approached from the quayside. As the craft pulled alongside, the officer confirmed Taen's initial dream-search in a voice inflected by fear.

Morbrith's dead had risen. Half-rotted corpses from the fields and towns took up swords, then marched in grisly ranks to pillage and desecrate and wreak ruin on domains to the south. Fire might stop them. To that end, panicky farmsteaders led by a priest had set Seitforest ablaze, then prayed vainly for a breeze to arise and spare their fields.

Their faith availed nothing, the officer concluded drily. Divine fires cared nothing for farmers, and south winds never blew during droughts. The army of the dead advanced and slaughtered refugees without hindrance until the Duke's men at arms organized resistance.

The Kielmark demanded particulars, even as Firelord, Stormwarden and Dreamweaver joined him at the rail.

The weather had been still, and seasonally dry; Seitforest blazed past saving, even if every able man had not been busy defending the borderlands. Worried for the trapper who had sheltered him as a boy, Jaric interrupted. "How much woodland has burned?"

The first commander shrugged, his dress tunic darkened with sweat. "Who can say? Last messenger thought seven square leagues, but that was a guess, and hours old by now."

The Kielmark snapped a question. "How many men fight, and how many of the garrison remain in Corlin?"

"The Duke rode out with all but three companies." Stung by a frown of disapproval, the first commander qualified waspishly. "Would you leave a town threatened by siege undefended? The Dark-dreamer's army advances far south of Gaire's Main by now. Corlin could be under attack by dawn."

"Belay that!" The Kielmark called a sailhand to uncleat the barge's painter. Then, ignoring the honorific due Corlin's ranking officer, he gave orders. "Take the sorcerers ashore and find horses for them. My men will follow by longboat and muster what troops remain. There had better be horses in the town somewhere, because I intend to march every available swordsman who can ride against Maelgrim without delay."

Signaled by the boatswain, Taen started down the side battens, while a stiff-faced first commander retorted with hysterical disbelief. "What! You give me two sorcerers and an enchantress, then propose to strip Corlin defenseless? We fight an army of *corpses*, man! Weapons can't kill what's already dead."

The Kielmark folded massive forearms. His cold, angry gaze saw Jaric over the rail, then flicked back to the officer in the barge. "You fight a human aberration and a demon circle of Gierj. Shut the gates for a siege, and I tell you, everyone within will die and join the Dark-dreamer's legions."

A tense moment passed while Anskiere followed the others into the barge. The instant the Stormwarden set foot on the thwart, the King of Pirates barked an order. The sailhand who waited with the painter promptly cast off. Current swirled; caught standing as the barge wheeled downstream, the officer lost his balance. He flailed backward, tripped over the coxswain's ankles, and toppled into the laps of his oarsmen. Confusion resulted. By the time looms could be threaded into rowlocks to steady the ungainly craft, argument and decorum were irretrievably lost.

Separated by a widening expanse of water, Corlin's first commander fumed helplessly as the Kielmark dispatched crew to launch longboats. Cliffhaven's sailhands obeyed with formidable speed. Blocks squealed and lines came unlashed without fouling or wasted motion. The first boat smacked into the harbor within a minute and a half, and oarsmen scrambled aboard. Somewhere in the interim they had armed themselves for war. Their timing as they threaded looms and initiated stroke against the tide was irksomely flawless. They would reach the town docks, all of them, before the ungainly barge of state could recover headway.

The first commander of Corlin banged a frustrated fist against the stern seat, while his own rowers strained awkwardly at their benches. An officer, however senior, did not countermand his Duke; and the Queen herself had delegated authority to this pirate and his pack of trained cutthroats. Left no graceful recourse, the disgruntled first commander saw two sorcerers and an enchantress delivered to the south shore landing and speedily mounted on horses.

Though the animals were fresh, they suffered in the still air. Their coats shone dark with sweat in the torch-lit yard by the ferry dock. The jangle of bits and swords and mail made them prance as the men at arms appointed as escort prepared to ride.

"Where will you go?" demanded the first commander. He spoke through his nose, as if the air had a taint that disagreed with him.

Anskiere replied with little more courtesy than the Kielmark. "To Seitforest, and thence to the battlefield."

The officer reverted to outrage. "Kor's grace, sorcerer, are trees and squirrels of more account than the living people of Hallowild?" But his question was lost in dust and noise as the Stormwarden's party thundered away from the docks. Taen had no chance to reassure the man that Jaric and Anskiere between them had formulated a plan; her own mount bolted to keep pace with the others. Caught flat-footed by the landing, the soldiers on escort detail clambered belatedly into saddles to give chase.

CHAPTER XII

Hallowild

Night fell; hidden in darkness, the track above Corlin ferry lay soft in the hollows, gouged by livestock and caravans to ruts where puddles were slow to dry. The horses cantered through air that smelled of crushed clover and mud and river reed. Southwest, beyond the streaming flame of the outriders' torches, Seitforest stood rimmed with fire and smoke. The swirl of the Redwater bounded the trail to the north, snagged into ghost-fingered foam where current curled over submerged rocks.

Taen clung by reflex to a bay gelding, her customary distrust of horses eclipsed by dream-trance. Immersed in nets of power, her mind ranged through woodland seeking a man who in autumn should be found wearing soft leather and a jingling clip of bird snares. While Seitforest burned, no semblance of seasonal rhythms remained to guide her search. The trails where the forester normally fared were overrun by panic-stricken wildlife. Blazing thickets and smoke-smothered dells yielded no trace of human awareness. At last, on the verge of despair, Taen sampled the mind of a sparrow; through its ear she heard the sharp ring of an axe. She pinpointed the sound and immediately encountered a presence intent as a hawk's. With a cry of relief, the Dreamweaver broke trance and set heels to her horse.

The bay tossed its nose in protest, then lengthened stride to match pace with the Firelord's mount. Taen raised her voice in answer to Jaric's concern. "Telemark is unharmed. You'll find him cutting a slash in attempt to check the fire." Dream-image showed him a lantern-lit draw, thick with smoke and the scent of crushed fern; there the forester labored with shovel and axe in a solitary effort to avert disaster.

Ivainson knew the place. He also saw that the forefront of the blaze raged scarcely half a league distant. Trees exploded violently into flame, fanning deadly flurries of sparks. No mortal endeavor could spare Seitforest from ruin. Telemark worked on out of stubbornness, for the trap runs and the cabin that were all he loved in life. Obligated by friendship and a deep sense of debt, Jaric took immediate action. Trusting Taen to explain to Anskiere, he whipped up his mount and plunged toward the wood at a gallop.

An outrider reined from the column to follow. "Stay here!" commanded the Stormwarden. "You'll only get in his way."

The officer in attendance shouted protest. Anskiere of Elrinfaer did not trouble to answer, but instead woke the light in his staff.

Every horse in the company shied. Riders fought to stay astride, while the night around them grew charged with the sense of impending storm. Breezes heavily scented with rain licked the grasses, bowing their tasseled heads to the earth. The weather wards brightened steadily until Anskiere's tall form stood rinsed in violet glare. Around him, two score hard-bitten men at arms trembled in raw terror, while clouds whipped over the tree-tops, and the still, hot air of calm broke under influence of sorcery.

While other men of Hallowild battled to rout the Dark-dreamer's horde of animated human remains, the forester, Telemark, sent his axe ringing into the trunk of a silver beech. Green wood resisted, the steel rebounded with force, chewing off the thinnest of chips. Telemark blinked tear-blurred eyes. Slowed by smoke and the sting of split blisters, he hefted his axe for another stroke, then paused as a rustle disturbed the undergrowth beyond the ground cleared by his efforts.

A man emerged from the trees, well proportioned and dressed for the saddle. As he strode closer, lanternlight revealed gold hair, a tunic of imported design that had fared badly in the briars, and a very familiar face. Telemark straightened in surprise.

"Put down your axe, old friend," said Jaric. He smiled at the forester's astonishment, then crossed the expanse of stripped earth at a run.

Though stronger and broader of shoulder than the boy who had wintered in Seitforest, Jaric still moved with care, as if at any moment the soil might rise up and trip him; but a glimpse of his eyes showed that such diffidence was long outgrown. The man who returned to embrace his former mentor owned power enough to shape the very stones for his feet.

Telemark returned the greeting, then stepped clear, his axe rested helve downward in the moss. Sweat streaked his wrists like gilt in the torchlight, and black-and-white hair hung matted with ash. "The Llondelei foretold with truth," he observed, his welcome subdued by grief for his ruined wildlands. "Seitforest burns."

Jaric considered the churned dirt, the swath of razed greenery that love and desperation had accomplished. "I think I can help."

As if a weapon could achieve the impossible, he moved back and drew his sword. Telemark recognized the blade. But what once had been ordinary steel brightened with the triple halo of a Firelord's defense wards.

The forester dropped his axe in amazement. "Great Fires! *You're* the heir of Ivain?"

Jaric gave no answer. Eyes closed, sword upraised, he engaged his mastery and summoned. The fire that raged through Seitforest responded as if alive. Treetops tossed and rattled, twisted by violent drafts. Telemark braced against a beech trunk, as, whipped by terrible energies, the darkness over his head roiled and broke, transformed to a red-gold sheet of inferno.

In a magnificent display of power, the conflagration that had devastated leagues of dry woodland coalesced like a whirlpool to the Firelord's bidding. The air shimmered, tortured into heat waves by a vast wheel of incandescence.

Still the fires gathered. Flame melted into flame, until Jaric stood drowned in light. Telemark shielded his face, overawed by a reality foretold by Llondian vision nearly two years past. Pride and emotion stopped his breath. Had he known at the time whom he recovered from the predations of forest bandits, he might never have found the courage to offer the shelter that had succored the heir of Ivain.

Yet even such breadth of revelation could not eclipse Seitforest's need. Telemark squinted and bent and groped after his axe. That moment, a chilly fall of rain pattered over his shoulders. A glance at the sky did not dispel the miracle. The drought had broken; clouds blanketed a sky that only moments before had been harsh with heat haze and smoke. The forester shouted in relief. "Son of Ivain!"

"Go home and rest." Jaric's voice sounded distant through the thunderous snap of flame. "The Stormwarden of Elrinfaer will drown the last cinders and see your forest safe."

Abruptly conscious of a bone-deep ache of fatigue, Telemark straightened before the heat of the Firelord's presence. "What will you do?"

The face in the conflagration smiled. "These flames may be needed in Corlin's defense." And sensing a dry watercourse beneath the ground that sloped conveniently toward the river, Jaric stepped into earth and vanished.

The unbearable brilliance of fire went with him. Blinking in commonplace lanternlight, Telemark retrieved his axe. The sting of his blistered hands woke him as if from a dream. Grateful for solitude, he wept unabashedly while around him the rains beat drum rolls of salvation over green trees, and brush, and acres of seared earth.

The storm gained force at Anskiere's bidding. White torrents poured over the burned expanse of Seitforest, and embers extinguished into hissing plumes of ash and steam; but no rain fell on the south side of the river. Taen, the Stormwarden and Corlin's contingent of nervous cavalry continued their ride on dry ground. The horses accepted the novelty with equanimity. After the first jigging steps, they trotted willingly forward, hooves lifting spurts of chalky dust from the road. But the soldiers assigned as escort muttered and hung back from the Stormwarden's presence.

"Jaric waits for us ahead," Taen informed Anskiere. Taxed by the need to ride and ply her talents simultaneously, she gripped her reins like the life lines on a boat. "Corlin's main army is driven into retreat. The Kielmark knows. He's gone in ahead of the reserve garrison to take command. We'll meet him with the rear guard, about half a league from the Redwater."

"The enemy lines are that close?" Spurred by concern, the Stormwarden put his mount to a canter.

Light flared suddenly ahead. Leaping, distorted shadows fanned from the forms of brush and riders. Around the next bend in the trail, a figure lined in brilliance blocked the way. The Firelord sat astride his plunging, quivering mare, his sword raised over his head; above the blade towered sixty-foot sheets of flame, drawn from Seitforest, and bound by sorcery to a nexus of biddable force. Glare burnished the ground like beaten metal for yards in each direction, and the trees on either side of the trail rippled with heat waves.

As Anskiere and Taen drew rein, their trailing escort at last caught up.

"Kor!" The sergeant in command covered fear with nervous speech. "Pity the river's too deep for fording. On the other side that fire could spare some lives."

Busy murmuring encouragements to his mount, the Stormwarden flicked sweat-soaked reins. When his animal ceased trying to sidle and bolt, he said, "That's exactly what Jaric intends." He added a bitten syllable. The staff over his head flared purple. An eerie note of power thrummed on the air, followed by a crack like breaking crockery. Every soldier from Corlin cried out as the mighty span of the Redwater glazed over and froze.

"Ride!" shouted the Stormwarden. He kicked his mount to a gallop and reined headlong down the bank. The animal landed on current chilled hard as black glass. Ice chips scattered from its hooves as it slid and careened to keep balance.

Better accustomed to goats than horses, Taen grasped mane in both hands and clung as her bay scrambled after. The animal stumbled. Banged face first into its neck, she cursed, and clutched, and somehow kept her seat. Her mount skated wildly beneath her. It regained stride, only to slip again down the hardened falls of a rapids. Taen dropped the reins and grabbed saddle leather. The thrust of the horse's shoulders pinched her knuckles. Then the beast was across, and galloping up the embankment to the roadway on the far side. Bruised in places she winced to contemplate, Taen fumbled after her reins. She dared a breathless look back. Jaric followed with a frown intent as his father's, his sword point streaming like a fire beacon.

The riders sent as escort still milled in confusion on the far bank. Neither sorcerers nor enchantress paid them further heed. Thankful for the lapse, two score stalwart men at arms abandoned duty and permitted their mounts to bolt in panic toward Corlin.

A mile farther on, the Stormwarden slowed to allow the horses to breathe. Hooves clanged on the wheel-scarred slate of the roadway; that and the gusty roar of flame effectively foiled speech. Taen snatched the interval to gauge the battle's progress.

The outlook proved discouraging. Corlin's troops were hard-pressed, with the Duke forced to issue another command to withdraw. Dismayed by this development, Stormwarden and Firelord wheeled their mounts from the roadway.

They continued at a gallop across tilled fields and pastures, until the stone walls of a sheep fold obstructed the way. Anskiere launched his horse in stride and leaped over. But Jaric had not been raised a prince with the finest of blooded horses at his disposal; he summoned Earthmastery and dissolved the barrier into a spattering rain of sparks. Taen followed him through the gap, grateful because her knees galled her. The bay dropped back to a walk.

The defending ranks of Corlin's army were now overwhelmingly close, and losing ground steadily. Just beyond the next rise, shouts and the clangor of weapons tangled with the screams of maimed soldiers. A horn winded close by. The wail of a whistle arrow signaled the recall, answered by the thunder of a cavalry charge to give faltering knots of foot soldiers a second's space to regroup.

"If they get pinned against the river, they're lost," Jaric shouted.

Anskiere gestured in bleak agreement. He reached the crest of the hill, drew rein, and faced forward, stunned speechless by the vista that met his eyes.

Taen and Jaric stopped their mounts at his side, equally appalled. The sight below affronted human dignity. Fires burned, red and raw as wounds across the valley. Outlined in hellish light, two armies struggled, one composed of staunch but frightened men, and the other of bones of the dead, laced clatteringly together by dried strings of tendon. Men, women, even children had not been spared service to Shadowfane's minion. They fought through no will of their own, skeletons animated to grisly purpose. Gut and soft tissues had long since been chewed away by scavengers. The shriveled gristle of the faces exposed jawbones and teeth, and eye sockets scraped clean by beetles; but the bony hands of thousands swung weapons.

Their blows wrought tireless slaughter upon the living. Taen saw a handsome young swordsman get his skull half cloven by an axe. Blood fountained as he stumbled; yet he collapsed no farther than his knees. In horror, the Dreamweaver watched him rise, turn, and slash, killing the shield mate who fought at his side. The soldier died with a look of agonized surprise.

Men slain on the field only augmented the ranks of Maelgrim's atrocities. Taen dismounted. Devastated that such malice should be engineered by one she had known as her brother, she stumbled against Jaric's knee.

Ivainson leaned over his horse's withers and offered comfort. The heat of his fires enfolded her. Taen clung as if she might faint, but no space remained for weakness. As Anskiere called an impatient query, Jaric reluctantly touched her hair. "Little witch?"

Taen straightened with a nod that was dogged bravado; inside, she wanted badly to weep. But her talents could not be spared. Without words, she handed the reins of her gelding to Jaric. Then she settled in the damp grass and gathered her awareness into trance, to assess the strength of the Dark-dreamer whose influence they must overcome, or else surrender the kingdom of Hallowild to Lord Scait and Shadowfane.

The battlefield looked different to the inward eye. In dream-sense, the spirit glow of living flesh outshone the flash of swords and steel-headed lances. At the far flank of the fighting, the flare and sparkle of spells showed where the Duke of Corlin's conjurer bolstered the offensive with wizardry.

But if the army of defenders was visible as light, the enemy they engaged and died to obstruct was darkness, black and featureless as chaos before creation. The shadow that animated the dead arose out of Morbrith. Like tide it swirled and pressed south, tireless enough to engulf the domains of Corlin and Dunmoreland in turn. Cautiously Taen extended her awareness. She probed the edges of the Dark-dreamer's powers, and encountered the singing of Gierj.

Far above the limits of normal hearing, the note that enabled the demons to meld and generate energy dashed against her Dreamweaver's probe. Resonance pierced Taen's defenses, tore gaps in her concentration wide enough to defeat her.

She slammed back with a cry of pain. Her trance broke, awareness wrenched without transition into night and screams and the clash of thousands of weapons. Gasping and confused, she felt someone's arms encircle her from behind; the solicitude was Jaric's. Light thrown off by his fires played in patterns over her lap.

Reluctantly Taen raised her eyes. The fighting was perilously near at hand. By now the Kielmark had overtaken the rear lines; his great shout lifted above the din and exhorted panicked men to hold their shield wall. "Belly-crawling lizards, stand firm! If another of you spins and runs, by Kor, I'll have your gizzards out and bleeding on the lances of the relief garrison."

His imprecations ceased, drowned by the batter of weaponry as Maelgrim's horrors pressed the attack.

Against smoke and flame glow and night sky, Anskiere sat his horse like a stone image, his hand clenched taut on the reins. "If they stand, they're just going to die that much quicker." Sickened by the killing, the maiming, and the madness that ruined good men without letup, he turned from the battle and saw the Dreamweaver had aroused from trance. The starkness of her features caused his manner to ease just a little. "Can you tell us what we face, little witch?"

Taen shook off the discomfort that lingered from her probe. As Jaric loosened his embrace, she straightened and attempted a report. "Maelgrim directs his assault from Morbrith Keep. His source to animate the dead is drawn direct from Gierjlings. I don't know how many, except this time their numbers are too great. I cannot unbind the demons' link. Nor can

I break the Dark-dreamer's control so long as his Gierj-circle remains active."

Tortured by the need for clarity, the Dreamweaver delivered the last of her message in image. Through dream-touch, Stormwarden and Firelord understood that Maelgrim's demons generated harmonics forceful enough to strip her defenseless. Unless the meddling of his Gierjlings was disrupted, she could do nothing; and plainly Maelgrim intended no surcease until the last of Corlin's inhabitants were annihilated.

Anskiere dismounted. Grim and preoccupied, he tossed his reins over his horse's head, then glanced in apology to Jaric. "I had hoped to avoid the use of force. Now the necessity can no longer be denied."

Ivainson Firelord flinched taut in anguish. He had never wanted a sorcerer's powers. Since the day he undertook mastery, he had prayed beyond hope never to engage his Vaerish powers in the cause of war. All too easily the hurt and the hatred inspired by his father's madness might find new focus in him.

Taen sensed Jaric's conflict. Though closest to his heart, even she could not offer solace. Always Ivainson tried, yet failed, to bend the wind; his destiny inevitably was too great for any mortal to alter.

Sick with shared grief, the Dreamweaver stumbled to her feet. The man she had come to love rose at her back and bore up. Inscrutable now as his father, Jaric gathered the reins of his own mount, and the bay, and finally Anskiere's gelding. He laced the leather gently through Taen's hands, while the Stormwarden delivered instructions.

"The horses must be led clear. We've no time for niceties. The effects of raw power can't help but spook them."

His decision was in no way premature. Shadowfane's army of horrors advanced relentlessly. The cries of wounded men and the horns of the officers sounded almost at the foot of the hilltop where the Vaere-trained prepared their defense. Fighting surged like current dragged through shallows. The foremost line of defenders was spearheaded still by the Kielmark and his scythe of a broadsword. Predictable as death, he shouted insults; and as if by arcane inspiration the strongest men rallied in support.

Yet this once the Lord of Cliffhaven's ferocious penchant for command invited disaster. As the ranks on either side turned toward safety, he and his cadre of fighters were left without support. Already the vanguard of Shadowfane's corpses threatened to surround his flank.

Anskiere stepped to Jaric's side. "Act quickly. Another minute, and we'll have no choice but to slaughter some of our own with the enemy."

Taen overheard. Rein leather crushed in her sweating hands as she tuned her concentration to warn the bravest defenders of their peril. She found the Kielmark and the men he led lost utterly in the clash and chime or weaponry. Her dream-touch itself became a hazard; one careless thought, and she would deflect the fighters' concentration, or disrupt the critical timing of parry and riposte. During crisis perfect concentration proved impossible. Any attempt at precision became overturned by the terrible wail of the Gierj. The convergence of power through Maelgrim's focus frayed Taen's talent until the battlefield below became form and movement without meaning, a nightmare afflicting a mind that did not seem her own.

Stressed to distraction, she had no choice but to abandon her efforts. If she persisted, her meddling might earn the imperiled soldiers a quicker end on the swords of Maelgrim's apparitions. The horses were her assigned responsibility. Firmly Taen took them in hand, to lead them away from the tumult before the powers of Stormwarden and Firelord joined the battle. She managed a scant dozen paces before Anskiere's staff flared active at the crest of the rise.

Light stabbed forth amid chaos. Wards surged and crackled into readiness and triple purple halos scattered ghost glints amid the dew. Storm wind followed, whipping droplets like sparks into darkness.

The horses balked. Intimidated by their huge strength, Taen stroked the sweat-sheened tautness of their necks and coaxed, without success. That moment, Ivainson Firelord engaged his mastery. He built the blaze gathered from Seitforest higher and hotter, until flames ripped skyward with a roar that deafened thought.

The big gelding reared. Wrenched off her feet, Taen shouted, but could not bring it down. Her own mount and Jaric's mare wheeled together. Rather than suffer dismemberment, she let the reins burn through her fingers. The knots at the ends broke her grip with a jerk. As the horses shied and thundered wildly off into the night, Jaric and Anskiere joined forces. The combined intensity of their powers lit the heavens, and burned a baleful, fiery glow over the battlefield beneath.

Taen scarcely noticed. Tumbled in a heap on damp grass, she cursed like a fishwife and sucked skinned knuckles. Above her, the directives of two sorcerers merged. A screaming cyclone of wind wrapped itself in fire, then ripped downslope to the destruction of the risen dead.

The energy struck with the immediacy of a lightning flash. Cavalry bolted in panic. Live men broke ranks and fled before the conflagration; the Kielmark's band wheeled and fell back along with them. But the demon-possessed marched yet, blindly oblivious to ruin. Fires overtook them with a roar like storm surf.

Bones danced an instant in silhouette; whirled like sticks into tangles, thousands of corpses ignited and burned. Rickety fists clenched weapons that heated white, then splashed molten to the earth. Trees exploded into torches. Skulls bounced and rolled over the ground, eye sockets streaming cinders.

The fire seared forth, utterly without discrimination, and razed all in its path. Wounded men and disabled horses screamed and died in agony. The flames raged and cracked and licked outward until the entire valley west of the Redwater lay mantled in scarlet and gold.

Only then did the onslaught cease; between one breath and the next, the fury of sorcery died.

Flame flicked out as if snuffed by darkness. The ground where Maelgrim's atrocities had marched lay black as a pall of death. Charred weeds and bushes tasseled with embers rimmed a field veiled heavily in smoke; feathers of ash sifted earthward. At a price terrible to behold, no bones remained to rise and kill. The song of the Gierj that had animated Shadowfane's army was disrupted at last to ragged and impotent disharmony.

At the brow of the hill, Anskiere quenched his staff and glanced over his shoulder. "Now, Taen!"

Below him, the men at arms left living cheered with hysterical relief. Some banged swords on their shields, but the Dreamweaver could not share in the victory. Called to sever the Dark-dreamer's link with his Gierj, she flung herself deep into trance.

Dream-sense showed Taen a place of damp, cold stone, and a sensation of dizzy height. Chills touched her, as awareness embraced Maelgrim's lair in the watchtower at Morbrith. The sense of evil lurking inside made her quail. Torches in wrought-iron brackets licked the walls with orange light. Over dissonant eddies of Gierj-whistle she heard a clink of wire; that small sound became her guide.

The Dark-dreamer of Shadowfane leaned by the south-facing window, flicking silver bracelets with his thumb. Night sky framed a face more finely drawn than Taen recalled. Under level brows his eyes shone enormous, depthless as smoke, and entirely devoid of humanity.

"Well met, my sister." Maelgrim bowed in the high style learned in Kisburn's court. "Though I'd say your rescue of Corlin was flamboyantly overdone."

Taen ignored the jeer. A secretive attempt to read the entity that inhabited the flesh of her brother yielded a barrage of viewpoints, as if he perceived his surroundings through multiple sets of eyes. The experience left her queasy and disoriented. The task of separating the minds of demon from host lay beyond her abilities; Maelgrim's mind was *other,* transforming by Gierj contact to the point where even his thoughts were alien. But Stormwarden and Firelord had engaged desperate measures to gain this opening. For their sake, for Corlin's, and for the fact that this atrocity sent from Shadowfane had once been her sibling, Taen had to try.

"The boy you called Emien was pathetic, frightened of everyone and most of all himself." Maelgrim smiled, and the familiarity of the expression wrenched his sister's heart.

"I have no brother." Wary of his malice, Taen probed for a weakness. Maelgrim permitted her search. That in itself offered warning. Her powers were useless here; if she lingered, she risked more than her life.

"You guard the wrong front, my sister." Maelgrim lowered his arm. Bracelets jangled around the heel of his hand, and as if the gesture signaled attack, the Gierj-song's pitch leveled out.

The Dreamweaver never registered their recovery. Demon power crested too swiftly for thought, battering against her senses and threatening her identity with chaos.

Belatedly, Taen strove to rally. In the instant before retreat became necessity, she hammered her query home, and confirmed her worst suspicion. Maelgrim struck now to wound more than human soldiers. The arm and the instrument of Shadowfane, he moved to cut down the only living resource capable of marring the demons' plans of conquest. His target now was Anskiere of Elrinfaer, and after, the Firelord, Ivainson Jaric.

"No!" Taen understood her position was futile. She challenged anyway.

Maelgrim retaliated. His power lanced her mind, cast her away as an ox might shudder off an offending fly. Taen knew darkness. Hedged in by the dagger prick of her brother's desire to see her broken in defeat, she raised a stinging lattice of wards. Yet Maelgrim only toyed with her. His laughter filled her ears, and contact with Morbrith sundered in a ripping flash of pain.

Hurled to her knees on stony ground, Taen twisted to avoid a fall. A hand caught her, Jaric's, red-lit by the aura of his drawn sword. He stood alone on the hilltop, amid weeds and rocks and a windy expanse of night sky.

The Dreamweaver drew breath in alarm. "Where's Anskiere?"

"Down there." Jaric inclined his head toward the valley where, by the dying flicker of fires, men at arms converged around the tall presence of the Stormwarden. "He went to advise the troop captains."

Tiny with distance, the army looked like an array of toy figurines; except that the weapons were sharp enough to kill, and the blood on the surcoats had not been painted on for effect. "Signal the Stormwarden back." Shrill with dread, Taen qualified. "He's in danger."

Before she could finish, the Dark-dreamer struck. Taen engaged her talent to ward, but Maelgrim foiled her. His thrust was not shaped against Anskiere himself. Instead, Shadowfane's minion attacked the undefended mind of the man at the sorcerer's back.

Gierj-power overran the victim's will in an instant. Enslaved utterly by enemy compulsion, the soldier drew his dagger and lunged to stab the Stormwarden from behind.

Taen cried out. Panic constricted her talents. She closed her eyes, strove frantically to recover control enough to warn before treachery struck Anskiere down. But her attempt to establish rapport opened a buffeting channel of sensations. Savaged by a flare of cruel heat, she heard the ringing scream of a man in his final agony.

Surely the possessed man's dagger had found its mark. Crushed by grief and failure, the Dreamweaver looked to find the Stormwarden unharmed within a cordon of stupefied men at arms.

The possessed man who had attempted murder writhed in flame at Anskiere's feet, felled by Ivainson's conjuring. A senior officer sprang to end the traitor's suffering. As his sword rang from his scabbard, Taen sensed echoes of laughter through the Gierj-song. Before she could rally, the Dark-dreamer struck again.

The officer on the field completed his mercy stroke. With no break in motion, he turned his fouled blade and lunged to murder the sorcerer beside him.

On the hilltop, Jaric gasped as if he had been hit. Again he summoned fire. Dazzled by glare from the backlash, Taen perceived her brother's diabolical design. Maelgrim intended to continue, forcing one man after another to raise arms. Anyone in the field might turn assassin at his command. Taen's talents could never extend far enough to secure the minds of an entire war host. If the Stormwarden was to be saved, Jaric might be forced to massacre every living ally from Corlin.

The night seemed suddenly cold beyond bearing. Taen shivered miserably in dew-drenched weeds, arms clenched around her knees. Her spirit reeled in the throes of bleakest despair. She dared not think of the Firelord, whose distaste for violence could not be reconciled with killing, even to defend the Stormwarden's life.

Yet power rose again at Jaric's bidding. Through empathy compelled by love, Taen suffered equally as the death screams of Maelgrim's victims cut her man to the marrow; she shared guilt and the tearing effort of each successive counterstrike.

"This has to end!" Jaric cried at last.

Below, the Kielmark had perceived Anskiere's peril. Heedless of complications, the sovereign of Cliffhaven gathered his men and stormed recklessly through the ranks toward the center of conflict. His loyalty only courted tragedy; the killing intensity of his fury would make a ready tool for Maelgrim's Gierj.

Jaric closed his fists in an agony of helplessness. Hoarse with self-loathing, racked by the possibility he might be forced to cut down a friend, he appealed in desperation to his Dreamweaver. "Can't you fashion a ward that the Gierj-crazed can't pass?"

Taen lifted her head. The Firelord awaited her reply, desperate as the time he had first scaled the ice cliffs to answer Anskiere's summons. Haunted and horrified and self-betrayed, he fought to thwart the demon-possessed, while she herself had withdrawn, disheartened. Such passivity from her was wrong in a way that defied reason. Jaric regarded her with sudden clear-eyed concern. "Little witch, what's amiss?"

His words sparked revelation. Abruptly aware of outside interference, Taen perceived with damning clarity that her emotions themselves had become the tool of Maelgrim's design. Snared during her sally in the tower, she had apparently fallen victim to his control.

CHAPTER XIII

The Reaving

Before Taen could sound her inner depths to assess the extent of Mael-grim's stay-spell, Anskiere raised the powers of his staff.

In the valley, sorcery shattered darkness as the auras of his weather wards sprang active. Purple glare lit the nightmare reality of another man drawing steel under Maelgrim's influence. Anskiere slapped his attacker off balance with a gust. The man fell heavily upon his back, winded, but struggling still to raise his sword.

Jaric could no longer spare Taen his concern. Determined to avert another killing, he engaged Earthmastery from the hilltop. At his bidding the grasses whipped into rope and bound the assassin's body at feet and wrists. The measure was stopgap, an inadequate diversion that could last no more than a minute.

Struggling still to recover her initiative, Taen caught the echo of Mael-grim's amusement. His laughter mocked her efforts, and cast a veil of confusion over the disciplines of her craft. Still helpless, she felt the Dark-dreamer counter Jaric's ward by releasing control of his victim's mind.

The officer under demon influence recovered self-awareness instanta-neously. Denied any memory of his assault upon Anskiere, he discovered himself shackled by earth sorcery. The bodies of slaughtered companions smoldered in the weeds nearby. Over them loomed Anskiere of Elrinfaer, his eyes like chipped ice, and his staff charged with energy like a storm front.

The officer screamed in terror. "Kor's Fires! We're betrayed like the folk of Tierl Enneth!"

Only those men who were closest had seen the attempted assassina-tion. Blocked by the press, the ranks behind knew only that the situation seemed suddenly, dangerously wrong; already traumatized by sorcery on a scale that defied understanding, their commanders shouted orders.

The army raised weapons. Light from the Stormwarden's spells span-gled a steely hedge of swords, halberds, and axes with edges angled to charge; archers reached to string bows, and lancers took to horse.

Anskiere raised his staff. Hair whipped back from his face as he bound his waxing powers into whirlwind, to be turned in self-defense against enemies that were human.

But these men were misguided, not possessed. The Stormwarden poised to destroy could not know that his attackers acted outside the

Dark-dreamer's influence. Taen stiffened her back. Though she wrestled yet to disengage Maelgrim's restraint, more ordinary means remained to stem the rush of the army.

"Frighten them," she cried to Jaric. "They're not deprived of wits, and they'll run." The tactic might work; certainly panic would make the men at arms more difficult for Maelgrim and his Gierj to manipulate.

Yet sorcery did not answer immediately. On the ridge, the Firelord stood like rock, his face tipped toward a sky pinpricked with stars. His expression seemed strange and remote as he slowly raised his sword.

Light slashed the darkness. Dazzled by an overwhelming discharge of power, the Dreamweaver glimpsed gold-barred feathers. Above her, the light-falcon which once had summoned her to the Isle of the Vaere unfolded wings that spanned the breadth of the heavens. The bird screamed. Its crested head swiveled, eyes of burning yellow surveying the army massed to kill in the valley. Jaric spoke a word. Air hissed between spread pinions; then, with awesome and terrible grace, the focused manifestation of his power sprang aloft. It swooped down upon the ranks of Anskiere's attackers, trailing a wake of crackling flame.

Maelgrim Dark-dreamer sensed the rising flux of power. Pressed by the threat raised by Jaric, his attention shifted; and in that instant, Taen cut through his block and broke free. The crippling despair lifted from her, just as the effects of Ivainson's conjury reached the valley.

The light-falcon's flight cut the night like a blade heated red from the forge. Scaled by wind off its wings, men looked up, their shouts of alarm transformed to a chorus of terror. No weapon would avail against the unleashed projection of a Firelord's anger. Most men broke formation and fled. But maddened by the appearance of certain doom, others leveled weapons and charged vengefully upon the sorcerer who still stood vulnerable in their midst.

Yet the Stormwarden stayed his hand. Whirlwinds shrieked in check in response to Taen's plea for time to engage her dream-sense. This time Maelgrim's meddling did not cripple her. She magnified fear into a weapon, striking panic into hostile minds until, in a rush, the last men broke and ran.

Alone in the wash of light from his staff, Anskiere damped the winds of his conjuring. Wrapped in smoke and a drifting fall of ash, he bent his head in sorrow for the dead heaped grotesquely at his feet.

On the hilltop, stillness reigned. Jaric sheathed his sword. All expression erased from his face as he said, "We'd better go down."

Taen sensed the emotions he held in check, even under cover of darkness. She ached to touch him, but sympathy could not comfort. The survivors of Corlin's army might flee safely to town walls and their Duke; but the measure of Maelgrim's victory remained. Word of the sorcery that had unhinged this war host's manhood would travel the breadth of Keithland. Folk would believe that the malice of Ivain Firelord had been reborn in his heir. Hereafter, Jaric could expect locked doors, and welcome at no man's hearth.

Taen shared the chill of that rejection. She averted her face, as the sacrifices forced upon a man of gentle nature opened a wound near-impossible to bear. But sorrow, even bitterness, was a reaction too costly to indulge. The crisis was not over. Even now Maelgrim whipped up his Gierj for a second attack. Too likely this time his targeted victims would be innocents, the women, children, and elders who sheltered within Corlin's walls.

"The Dark-dreamer will be stopped," said Jaric, his voice a reflection of Taen's fear. "If we have to rip down the fortress of Morbrith to achieve it, your brother will never again wield Gierj." Hands clenched on his sword hilt, he strode forward to join Anskiere.

The Dreamweaver followed, bitterly silent. The rending of Morbrith's battlements could help nothing. Maelgrim and his demons had grown too powerful to stop by force of arms. Only sorcery remained, and there the Vaere-trained had run out of resources. A Dreamweaver's gifts by themselves were not enough, and with horses the fastest means of travel, distance prevented Stormwarden and Firelord from launching an assault in time to spare disaster.

Taen was not alone in her assessment. Ivainson reached the boundary of a farmer's pasture and paused with his hands on board fence. "What about the relief garrison from Corlin? After this, we'd be fools to order an army north to Morbrith."

The Dreamweaver tried to match his restraint, and failed. Her voice shook. "I've warned the Kielmark. The companies raised at his command already return to their Duke. But the King of Pirates insisted on coming himself." At Jaric's unspoken protest, she shrugged. "I can ward the man's mind from Maelgrim's Gierj more easily than I could stop him, I think."

Jaric caught her close. "Little witch," he murmured into her hair. "I'm sorry."

His clothing smelled of cinders and sweat. Pressed against him, Taen felt fine tremors wrack his body. Powerless to ease his distress, or the slightest bit of her own, she made a stilted effort at humor. "I'd rather be here than wait out the conflict at Cliffhaven. Do you suppose Corley's got a blade left that isn't sharpened down to a needle?"

Jaric raised her in his arms and perched her on top of the fence. "I doubt that. The Kielmark has steel enough in his armory to choke the channel through Mainstrait. And look, he's reached Anskiere before us."

Taen twisted around to see a broad-shouldered figure with blood-stained gauntlets striding toward the Stormwarden. The sovereign Lord of Cliffhaven had taken charge with his usual impetuous initiative; with reins gripped in both fists, he towed four shying horses by main force over the scorched and corpse-strewn field.

"Kor," said the Dreamweaver. Strain broke at last before laughter.

"Did he have to anticipate the possibility we wouldn't be mounted? Put me in the saddle again, and I swear by Kor's Fires, I'll die of a fall."

"Do that and I'll jump after you." The Firelord vaulted the fence and raised his hands to lift her down. "Some things are more important to me than Keithland. Now will you walk, or because there are horses, must I drag you?"

The Stormwarden paced the ravaged earth of the battlefield. Except for the Kielmark's presence, he walked alone, a dark figure against a darker expanse of seared and trampled landscape. His clothing was silted with ash, and his features were like flint from suppressing sorrow and exhaustion. "The Gierj still sing," he observed as Jaric and the Dreamweaver arrived. His voice showed all of his concern.

Enchantress and Firelord were equally weary and soiled. Jaric had thrown off his fine tunic. Clad in the singed linen of his shirt and hose, he looked haunted by the sorrows of the damned. Taen's robes were crumpled from her sitting unprotected in the dew. Her spirits seemed little better. She halted well clear of the Kielmark's horses and called answer to Anskiere over the restive stamp of hooves. "I couldn't stop the Gierj. Maelgrim has grown too strong. Perhaps if we rode to Morbrith . . ."

The Stormwarden stopped abruptly. "We dare not. With Gierjlings still active, to go closer would invite failure and Corlin's certain doom. Taen, the Firelord and I must lend your mastery support. If we can channel our powers through your gift, you must try again to break your brother's link with the Gierj."

Yet the risks of that suggestion were surely too perilous to contemplate. Had the ground not been littered everywhere with the charred bones of corpses, Taen would have gone to her knees and pleaded to be quit of the Stormwarden's request. No need in Keithland could be great enough to demand such responsibility of her. She controlled but a single Sathid crystal, where Anskiere and Jaric each held mastery of two. For the Dreamweaver to merge minds with them offered the doubled effects of an exponential increase in power. That Taen by herself should trust her lesser discipline to wield the combined might of Stormwarden and Firelord was unthinkable, a transgression of natural limits no desperation would sanction.

"I dare not," she protested.

Jaric steadied her from behind, yet he offered no further encouragement. Anskiere remained silent also, his eyes impenetrable as sheet silver. Neither Stormwarden nor Firelord would compel her to attempt this most dangerous of undertakings. Nor would the sorcerers badger her if she lacked enough courage to try.

The Kielmark had no such scruples. "Girl, you must." He stood like an anchor against the drag and plunge of the horses. "What end could be worse than conquest by Shadowfane's compact?"

"If I failed," Taen said, so softly her voice became lost in the empty landscape. Only a sorcerer bonded to Sathid might understand the consequences. The smallest mistake would bring backlash, an uncontrolled burst of power capable of unleashing cataclysm. The disasters at Tierl Enneth and Elrinfaer would seem but a pittance before the ruin courted by stakes such as these. First among thousands of casualties would be the same Vaere-trained defenders who upheld mankind's last hope of survival.

The choice was one Taen begged to avoid; could time turn backward, she would have asked her lame leg back, and her talents left latent, to unsay Anskiere's words. Not least was the anguish of chancing such unprincipled power to destroy one born as her brother.

Alone of them all, Jaric seemed to recall this; he gathered her firmly against his shoulder. "Maelgrim's death need not be on your hands, little witch. Confine his Gierj-powers under ward, and Anskiere or I will wield the sword."

"Or I," the Kielmark said quickly. "I've not forgotten the oath of debt I swore to the Dreamweaver who spared Cliffhaven from invasion."

But in the end, the support of friends and Firelord did not help. Taen was forced to decision as her brother whipped up his Gierj for renewed assault upon humanity. Even as she deliberated, demonsong resonated against her awareness, invasive enough to paralyze thought. Reflexively Taen cast wards about her dream-sense, yet this time no precaution sufficed. Maelgrim's forces built, and coiled, and beat against her mind, prying to gain entry. The horses milled against the Kielmark's restraint as if crazed, and the very earth went still as the Dark-dreamer marshaled his powers to destroy.

Compelled by a greater fear than failure, Taen slipped clear of Jaric's embrace. She encompassed both sorcerers and the Kielmark with a look that was poignant to acknowledge. In the heat of crisis, how easy it had been to overlook the fact that the Dreamweaver was younger in actual years than her body appeared.

Yet when she spoke, her voice was steady. "By Kor's divine mercy, act swiftly."

"Jaric!" Anskiere spoke sharply.

The Firelord wrested his gaze from the Dreamweaver's. Concern for Taen might inhibit an expedient that might endanger her; though he could be trusted to find his equilibrium in the face of Keithland's need, the slightest delay might cripple their chance to stop Maelgrim. Anskiere took no risk, but raised the powers of his staff at once.

The wards flared active with a crackling explosion of light. To merge with him, Jaric must match the force with conjury of equal and opposite intensity. Blank-faced, he drew his sword. Less fluid than Anskiere, but growing daily more proficient at his craft, he wove sorcery until the halos surrounding staff and sword stood configured in mirror image.

The orange-red light of Firemastery merged gradually into the blue-white glare of storm sorcery. With trepidation, Taen readied herself for what no training offered by the Vaere had prepared her for; as the auras of both sorcerers joined into a halo of incandescent brilliance, she had but a second to brace her will. Then Stormwarden and Firelord caught her into the link.

A hammer wall of force slammed Taen's mind. Utterly overwhelmed, her senses became sundered from reality as a torrent like white-heated magma coursed across her dream-sense. The channels of her awareness burned raw under the pressure. Heightened sensitivities escaped control, and she felt as if her spirit were blasted headlong into the void before creation.

Colors streamed past her inward eye. Her ears were buffeted by unidentifiable sound. Taen struggled to orient, to bridle the forces raging wild within her. Yet even the most basic discipline of her craft failed. As she reached for mastery, her awareness imploded to a pinpoint focus that threatened to pierce her very being. Power that tore with the cataclysmic force of the tides unexpectedly responded to a feather-light touch.

The irony daunted; Taen faltered, directionless in the flood. Afraid to grapple for command lest she misjudge and destroy herself, she knew if she held herself passive she would be equally lost.

"Imagine you could balance a boulder on the shaft of a needle." The voice was Jaric's, and the encouragement an observation gained from his recent initiation to the handling of shared power.

The Firelord's advice seemed simple. Taen fought to embrace the forces that ravaged her inner self, but found them too potent. Her awareness could not encompass such depths, or the dizzy breadth of vision that great power required. Brought to her knees by the scope of her own inadequacy, she struggled through other channels to grasp the subtleties that Jaric had striven to impart.

The knowledge she required was inherent in the minds of the sorcerers who shared their access to power; but the key to true partnership, the path of Jaric's new learning, lay twined through skeins of association. Taen reached forth and became entangled in memories whose vividness shattered thought.

Anskiere's past touched her first. Through him, Taen relived an earlier backlash, the result of a stolen wardspell that brought destruction upon Tierl Enneth. The Dreamweaver felt the rumble of the wave that had arisen to rip homes and men and all their children, wives, and livestock from the shores. She heard the suck and boom of the waters, the splintering of wood. Droves of people fled with their mouths opened wide with screaming.

Yet no mortal could outrace the sea. The cries of the doomed became buried amid tumbling masonry, the falling, grinding crash as an entire generation met its end by drowning. Spray fountained like jewels over the collapsing tiles of the rooftops, then cascaded into waters congested with flotsam. The terrible wave receded, dragging dark swirls of current through a city's ruined beauty; the agony afterward became unbearable. Taen recoiled in an anguish only partly the Stormwarden's: too easily, Tierl Enneth's misfortune might become Hallowild's.

She voiced an unthinking protest. *'Having failed Tierl Enneth, how could you ask this trial of me?'*

Anskiere fielded her accusation with equanimity. *'I made no choice without discretion. Should a Vaere-trained Dreamweaver be compared with a thief enslaved by demons? Merya Tathagres was driven by the greed of the compact. She had no understanding of the powers she stole and tampered with. But if I am wrong, Taen, and my judgment stands in error, better that Keithland's north shore comes to ruin through backlash than fall in malice to the Dark-dreamer. As one born and trained to rule, I say this risk is justified.'* Here the sorcerer who had once been heir to Elrinfaer's crown paused. All the years of his sorrows rang through the nets that bound three Vaere-trained minds together. *'Never did I claim to welcome such a choice.'*

Humility leached away Taen's fury. Power ripped at her senses, made her body ache for a refusal that now was too late to sanction. Jaric had risked his father's madness; Anskiere had seen Tierl Enneth destroyed and before that the ruin of his own fair kingdom of Elrinfaer. Neither man had abjured either sorcery or responsibility. Could she do less and find peace anywhere in Keithland? Cold to the heart, and ridden with doubt, Taen imagined that she balanced a boulder on the shaft of a needle. She immersed herself within the terrible nexus of powers and somehow achieved a response.

Dream-sense answered, but not in any familiar manner. Taen experienced her native talent with a scope and intensity incomprehensibly wide. Her awareness engaged fully with the powers of Stormwarden and Firelord, and the margin of safety narrowed to a thread. If her touch was too bold, she would upset the balance of the link; and if she acted too timidly, Maelgrim's attack would sweep her defenses away before any ward could be conceived to restrain him.

The Dreamweaver focused and gained a vision of Morbrith castle that dizzied in its clarity. The view lay silvered in moonlight, the stone of tower and barbican slashed with ink-deep shadow. Where normally the initial probe would encompass visuals alone, the added talents of Firelord and Stormwarden colored the result; Morbrith rang with emptiness, a queer, brooding presence like coming storm. Breezes soughed through fields overgrown with weeds. Grasses habitually grazed short by livestock waved tasseled heads in the pastures. Dream-sense blended with glimmers of an Earthmaster's perception, of soil leached by unharvested crops and unclipped hedgerows. Stone itself spoke through the link, alive with the glint of mica and the captive heat of sunlight.

Taen was in no way tempted to explore this rich influx of sensation. Her borrowed powers encompassed the city of Morbrith from flag spires to dungeons in a fraction of an instant; amid the wonders of nature and the varied invention of man, the pervasive presence of Maelgrim and his Gierj stood out like rot in the heart of a flower. Even as the Dreamweaver recognized the enemy, Shadowfane's Dark-dreamer sensed her presence.

He struck with the speed of a snake.

Taen had no time to consider consequences, but only to react as energy arose like a whirlwind to crush her. The counterward she crafted sprang up with the brilliance of lightning flash, combining the strengths of three Vaere-trained masters. Stonework seared, and the air flashed fire. Maelgrim howled curses in surprise.

He emerged unscathed. Vexed mightily, and aware that Stormwarden and Firelord had joined their talents to bring him down, he rallied his Gierj. Taen felt his hatred as a storm wind of malice and murder that threatened to smother her defense. She fought an influx of nightmare; if she succumbed, Maelgrim and his demons would rend her mind. They would take their pleasure and hideously dismember her body before she died. The Dreamweaver retained her grip against a wave of stark horror. Maelgrim was too strong. Unless she acted instantly, the combined powers of Stormwarden and Firelord would not be sufficient to thwart the evil her brother had become. Scared to defensive desperation, Taen seized the powers of the link. Heedless of peril, she wove energy into bands that crackled and burned, then forged the result into a barrier to imprison.

The walls of Morbrith defined her outer bastion. To stone and mortar and the metal of lock and drawbridge she added bindings fashioned of sorcery. As the patterns of her labors bloomed in light over postern and gate towers, she felt other forces twine with hers. Finely spun as spider silk, but stronger than drawn wire, Stormwarden and Firelord joined their own spells through the link. Anskiere's long years of experience at confining demonkind made his handiwork practiced and swift. Before Maelgrim could raise counterwards, the lattice of Taen's prison became anchored by spells wrought of air and weather. Jaric joined in, adding stay-spells rooted like knotwork through the heart rock of earth and stone.

Maelgrim immediately divined his predicament. Gierj-song shivered the air, and his counterthrust shot sparks against the shimmer of the wardspells. Yet the barrier deflected his sally in a pulse of blinding light. Morbrith Keep remained unbreached. The Dark-dreamer's cry of rage and frustration echoed among deserted towers, then diminished. Before his last hope of freedom could be sealed, Maelgrim resorted to guile.

Gierj-song breached Taen's shield. In an image keen as a knife slash, she saw her brother, cruelly exploited by demons and pleading a sister's forbearance. Let her hand turn from redress to mercy, let the smallest measure of forgiveness be granted, and Marlson Emien vowed to turn coat on his demon masters. Morbrith's fate might be shared by Shadowfane, and mankind's survival be assured.

"No!" Taen's denial echoed over towers whose occupants were dead beyond redemption. Inured to loss as were her fisherman forebears, she locked sorrow and grief in an iron heart. The boy Emien had chosen his own course; the betrayals that had brought him to his transformation at Shadowfane had revoked any right of reprieve. Yet even as Taen Dreamweaver held equilibrium, the powers of Stormwarden and Firelord faltered. In horror she saw that Maelgrim had breached the link.

The images he inflicted were personal and poisonously cruel. Anskiere of Elrinfaer saw his royal sister, who had died with her kingdom under the depredations of the Mharg. Young, alone, she sat weeping with a crown she had never wanted pressed hopelessly between her hands. Over and over she cursed her brother, for leaving his inheritance to her in his pursuit of Vaerish knowledge. For all his sorcerer's mastery, the Stormwarden was not present to intercede when creatures out of nightmare dropped from the sky and slaughtered Elrinfaer's citizens in the street.

The intensity of the princess's grief was too detailed to be anything other than real. Taen saw that demons had garnered this moment through Mharg-memory, then saved it as a weapon against just such a moment as this. The impact caused guilt enough to shatter Anskiere's poise.

'Free me,' Maelgrim begged. 'Let my powers avenge your beloved sister who died of Shadowfane's designs.'

Taen did not linger to know how the Stormwarden would resolve his grief and guilt. Worried for Jaric, she reached through the link and found him racked by his own vision of hell. This image was recent, and Maelgrim's own, and vicious enough to stun. For Jaric, Morbrith bailey danced to a bloody flare of light. There, bound with wire to a horse hitch, the master scribe who had championed his cause as a boy writhed in a pyre of flame. Fuel for Iveg's torment was a cache of books and scrolls, the scholarly achievements of a lifetime kindled to roast his flesh.

While Stormwarden and Firelord were diverted, the wards over Morbrith stood in jeopardy. The Dreamweaver acted out of reflex, driven by anger akin to madness. Across Maelgrim's dark dreaming she crafted images of her own, the separate suffering of every soul she had battled to save, and lost, through her months in the borderlands of Morbrith. Children, parents, and elders, she recounted each death distinctly; the agonies of each victim's final minutes distilled to a sorrow overpowering for its cruelty.

As the compact's minion, Maelgrim met her vision of suffering with venomous amusement. But Stormwarden and Firelord screamed with one voice. Reminded of their purpose, they rallied. Power surged back into the link. Now anguish for a tortured scribe and guilt for an abandoned sister became edges honed against a common enemy. Joined in grim purpose, the Vaere-trained of Keithland sealed the wards over Maelgrim's prison. As their combined sorceries fused complete, a shriek of defeat and frustration rang over the wail of the Gierj. The sound was savage enough to daunt the spirit. No mortal could listen, and linger.

The link-born power died out with a snap. Taen relinquished the discipline of trance. Sore to the bone, she opened tired eyes and reoriented her awareness to a battlefield long leagues to the south.

Ashes gritted under her knees. Her hair fell in tangles around her cheeks, tear-soaked, and acrid with the smell of smoke. Taen shook it back. She lifted a face pale with stress to the Stormwarden and Firelord, who stood near, shaken still from the shock of her counterdefense. Shivering herself, Taen drew a difficult breath. She did not voice what all of them already knew: Maelgrim might be mewed up within Morbrith, but his Gierj still sang. Though tired and harrowed to the heart, the three of them had no choice but ride north without delay.

Efficient in all respects, the Kielmark had selected his horseflesh with an unerring eye for the best. Though mounted on a blooded, blaze-faced mare of prized Dunmoreland stock, Taen failed to appreciate the Pirate Lord's expertise. Her knees chafed raw on a saddle intended for a large man, and the animal underneath it pulled like a steer, skinning her fingers on the reins. She cursed and tugged, and barely managed to match pace with the gelding that carried Jaric.

Anskiere rode ahead on a cream stud conscripted at swordpoint from a dandy. Its harness sparkled with a crust of silver and pearls, but threads now trailed where bells had hung from the saddlecloth; in disgust the Stormwarden had ripped the ornaments away. The Kielmark brought up the rear, on a black that snorted with each stride. He sat his saddle with an air of wolfish intensity, one hand poised on his blade.

Yet as the company set off for Morbrith, both silence and vigilance seemed wasted. No travelers fared on the road. Houses by the wayside lay deserted, and the crossroads settlement of Gaire's Main stood abandoned and dark when they stopped to breathe the horses. Spring water trickled mournfully from the stone trough, but livestock no longer drank the run-off. Neglect left holes in thatched roofs, and the inn bulked black by starlight, one door drunkenly ajar.

The Kielmark was quick to remount. Anxious to leave the deserted village, Anskiere and Jaric followed him to horse. No one seemed inclined to speak, since the ordeal of warding Morbrith. Taen swung into the saddle last. Though distracted by the need to review the security of her work, she still remained open to the sensitivities of others. Jaric had passed through Gaire's Main the time he had fled Morbrith on a stolen mount. Now the inept stablemaster who had reshod his horse was dead, along with the young girl who had offered him charity out of pity. Murdered on the brink of womanhood by Shadowfane's possessed, she had neither grave nor kin to remember her. Only chance-met travelers who had passed through Gaire's Main before Maelgrim's devastation might recall that the girl had lived at all.

Weary and sad, Taen let her mount lean into a canter. Gaire's Main fell swiftly behind. The road to Morbrith stretched northward, silver under a haze of ground mist; the mare tried restively to gallop ahead of the others. The Dreamweaver tightened raw fingers and winced as the horse shook its head. It bounced one stride in protest before responding to the rein.

· Jaric swerved his gelding to avoid being jostled. "Doesn't that mare know she should be tired by now?"

Taen shook her head. "She smells me for a fisherman's daughter and knows I hate riding."

Only, looking at her, with her brows leveled by an intent frown and her back held straight by something indefinably more than courage, Jaric reflected otherwise. Her childhood in the fishing village of Imrill Kand was behind her now; at no time in life had she ever seemed more like the Vaere-trained enchantress she had become.

Night passed, measured by drumming hoofbeats. The stars to the east paled above the rolling hills of the downs, yet dawn did not lessen the shadow of danger. Each passing league brought the riders nearer to final confrontation with Maelgrim Dark-dreamer. Threat seemed a palpable presence in the air. Unable to shake the hunch that Keithland's defenders rode toward a trap of Shadowfane's design, Taen focused her talents. Braced for the bite of Maelgrim's malice, she cast her dream-sense north to check the security of her brother's prison.

Stillness met her probe. Disturbed, Taen tried another sweep. This time she included the grounds as well as the watchtowers at Morbrith. Her effort yielded nothing. Silence deep as windless waters bound the keep's tall battlements; even the pigeons had abandoned their cotes in the falconer's yard. Unnerved by the lifeless air of the place, the Dreamweaver drew a worried breath. She rebalanced her awareness, and only then noticed the absence of the Gierj-whistle. Surprise made her cry out.

Her companions drew rein in the roadway. Stopped in their midst, the Dreamweaver exclaimed in disbelief. "I've lost Maelgrim. The Gierj-whistle's stopped, and I can't track the presence of the enemy."

Anskiere drew breath with a jerk. "The wards are intact?"

Taen started to nod, then froze as she noticed a detail that first had escaped her. A small black hole lay torn through the spells that sealed the main gate. The rift was too small to admit the body of a man, but wide enough, surely, to pass the rope-thin bodies of Gierjlings.

This news raised varied reactions in the gray gloom of dawn; both Firelord and Stormwarden had contributed to the setting of those defenses; the power required to cause a breach overturned their most dire expectation. Jaric raked back hair in need of a trim; his eyes seemed distant with exhaustion under soot-streaked lashes. The Kielmark stilled with a look of rapacious speculation.

Only Anskiere straightened with a glare like frost. His hands braced on his horse's neck, he said simply, "Track the Gierj, then. If Maelgrim's left Morbrith, through whatever means, we have no choice but follow him."

"But the breach is too narrow," Taen protested. "The Dark-dreamer couldn't escape, and he can't have vanished. He shares my blood. Surely I would know if he took his own life." She blinked away rising tears, vaguely aware of Jaric's touch on her arm. The contact failed to steady her.

The creak of the cream's harness filled silence until Jaric intervened. "Kor's grace, can't you see she's upset?"

His plea was ignored. "Taen," the Stormwarden said firmly, "if Maelgrim Dark-dreamer has left Morbrith, we'll have to know at once."

CHAPTER XIV

Morbrith

Taen drew an unsteady breath. The surrounding landscape seemed ghostly, a place halfway between dreams and waking where nightmare could transform the ordinary without warning. She disengaged from Jaric's hold. Isolated from his sympathy by the demands of her craft, she rallied and marshaled her talents to trace Maelgrim.

Morbrith's gray walls shouldered through tatters of thinning mist, sealed off by the lacework glimmer of wardspells. Beyond, the houses loomed empty, row upon row of rooftrees outlined coldly in daylight. The Dreamweaver concentrated directly on the palace. Her probe traversed empty corridors and wide, cheerless rooms with hangings moldering on the walls. She swept bedchambers with mildewed sheets, kitchens where rats chewed the handles of the cutlery. Pantry and granary had been ransacked by insects and mice, while the armory's stock of weaponry rusted in neat, military array.

Taen tried the libraries, and ached for Jaric when she found the door splintered inward. Parquet floors bore the stains of spilled ink flasks; dust layered shelves stripped of books. Burdened by sorrow, the Dreamweaver moved on, past the darkened windows of the guards' barracks and a gate sentry's box whitened with bird droppings. The stables beyond held the rotting carcasses of the manor's equine casualties, from the Earl's niece's pony to war destriers and carriage horses. Only the stair that led to the watchtower was not empty.

Taen found her brother in a windy cranny framed by stone keep and sky.

No Gierj were with him. His Dark-dreamer's presence had diminished to a lusterless spark of his former vitality. Shocked by the change in him, the Dreamweaver brushed his mind. Maelgrim flinched from the contact. Wire chinked as he raised his hands, as though to ward off a blow; the mad, lost light in his eyes bespoke thoughts that were directionless and confused.

Taen retreated without probing deeper. Keeping her awareness well guarded, she listened while wind moaned between Morbrith's empty battlements. Yet nothing untoward arose to challenge her. Maelgrim's condition apparently masked no tricks.

Daylight brightened steadily over pastures whose only yield was weed; the farmsteads beyond the walls lay deserted. The Gierj-demons who had expanded the Dark-dreamer's powers of destruction seemed nowhere to be found. Suspicious of their absence, the Dreamweaver extended her focus over bramble-ridden fields and orchards choked with mist.

If not for the scold of a jay, she might have overlooked the rustle of movement through the valley east of Morbrith. Gierj poured like spiders through the undergrowth, eyes flashing like mirrors filled with moonlight. They ran in silence. Steps coordinated in unison lent the disturbing impression that their movements were controlled by the hand of a mad puppeteer. The sight seeded growing uneasiness. The brother Taen found at Morbrith owned neither presence nor self-command, which meant the Gierj answered now to a new master, one whose summons came direct from Shadowfane.

The Dreamweaver dispelled her trance. Roused to the sting of saddle-galled knees, she stirred under the scrutiny of Stormwarden and Kielmark. Dismounted, Jaric stood at her mare's bridle. He restrained the restive creature with a patience that belied his exhaustion, while the Dreamweaver related her findings concerning Maelgrim, and the apparent desertion of his Gierj-circle.

She finished, feeling drained. Autumn winds whipped the brush by the roadside. The scratch of dry leaves filled silence as her companions considered the implications of an event no man understood.

"Hold the wards firm," said Anskiere. He then issued orders to ride. Jaric released his grip on Taen's reins and set foot in his own stirrup.

"You know this might be a trap!" the Dreamweaver warned. The Stormwarden set spurs to the cream; as his steed leaped to gallop, she shouted after him. "Gierj or no, Maelgrim is still possessed through his Sathid-link with demons. I doubt he's either vulnerable or helpless."

"Belay the talk, woman!" The Kielmark drew his sword and smacked the flat smartly across the mare's hindquarters. He qualified over the ensuing thunder of hooves as both their mounts flattened ears and ran. "We have no choice but go forward. Fool or otherwise, we can't let the Stormwarden ride into danger unsupported."

Blue, fierce eyes reminded that, like the wolf, the Kielmark's loyalties ran deeper than reason. Though few things in life frightened Taen so much as the change she sensed in her brother, she gave the mare rein and galloped.

Leaves scattered, brown and dead, in the wind swirling under the battlements. The bailey beyond lay deserted, the smell of moss and sun-warmed stone glaringly wrong for a keep once filled with the bustle of habitation. No sentry called challenge to the party who rode in with the morning. Silence and the ghost-glimmer of wardspells shrouded a fortress better accustomed to the ring of destriers' hooves, and the shouts of patrols returning from the border. Having loosed their own lathered mounts by the river, Jaric trailed Anskiere through the gates. A thin snap of sound marked his passage as he crossed the boundary of the wards. Taen came after, followed by the Kielmark, whose weapons and mail shirt jingled dissonantly with each stride.

Ivainson emerged from the far shadow of the arch and abruptly stopped.

"Not here." Taen shook off a compulsion to whisper. "We'll find Maelgrim farther on, within the Earl's hall."

But the Firelord gave no response. His first, sweeping survey of the holdfast where he had been born ended at the stone blocks used to hitch horses. Rusted loops of wire dangled from the rings, cruel testimony of a prisoner recently bound there. Breeze blew. The fetters swung, blackened by fire above a flattened circle of ash; amid the debris Taen saw charred leaves of parchment, recognizably the half-burnt remains of books.

The name of Morbrith's master archivist hovered, unuttered, on Jaric's lips. Taen sensed his deep and cutting grief. Although no bones remained, the Firelord beheld proof that his former master had died a tormented victim of demon caprice. "Kor's eternal grace!"

The vehemence of the blasphemy caused Anskiere to pause on the stair, a look of inquiry on his face. "Jaric?"

A shimmer gathered around Ivainson's still form. For a moment raw anger threatened to explode instantaneously into fire. Taen tensed in alarm. But the Kielmark stepped sharply forward and reached Jaric ahead of her.

"I'll skewer the Accursed who did this." The Lord of Cliffhaven wore an expression that chilled. Dangerously still in his silver-trimmed surcoat, he regarded the wire and the ruined parchment, as if to engrave the sight in his memory. Then, with a hand that half steadied, half pushed, he sent Jaric after the Stormwarden. As an afterthought, Taen recalled that the King of Pirates revered books; on Cliffhaven, his archivist was the only hale man not required to bear arms.

Moments later, the party entered the candleless gloom of the keep. Dream-sense overlaid impressions like echoes, as the ruins prompted remembrance of an elegance that now lay wholly desecrated. Backland in location alone, Morbrith's Earls had been gifted with longstanding admiration for the arts. Scrolled cornices above the doorframes had once held porcelain statuary. Liveried retainers and ladies clad in silk and jewels had laughed and listened to music in halls now gritty with the refuse of bats. Unswept stone, and soiled hangings, and the weaponed ring of the Kielmark's tread made that past seem a fanciful dream. Anskiere walked, haunted by memories of other ghosts from Elrinfaer. Harrowed beyond sorrow, for this keep had once been his home, Jaric did not mourn for himself. Instead he ached fiercely for Taen; somewhere within Morbrith waited an enemy who had once been her brother.

A stray shaft of sunlight silvered the Stormwarden's head as he followed the Dreamweaver's lead into a vaulted foyer. Four doors opened into chambers and a corridor swathed with spiderwebs. Dream-sense tugged left. Numbly Taen turned, through bronze portals chased with a hunting scene. The antechamber beyond lay heaped with broken furnishings and the moldered skeleton of a cat. Dampness from the floor chilled through the soles of her shoes. She shivered and kept on, barely aware of Jaric at her side.

"Ahead lies the hall of the High Earl." Echoes blurred the Firelord's words. "An entrance in back leads to the Lord's quarters. Servants used to claim there was a spy closet."

Taen nodded absently. The pressure against her mind grew insistent, and suddenly she knew. The bedchamber and suite of the Lord's quarters lay deserted. The spy closet, if any existed, was empty. Maelgrim Dark-dreamer waited beyond the shut panels of the great hall.

Taen stopped and pointed. Unable to move or speak, she watched Anskiere hook the lion-head door ring and pull. Silent on oiled hinges, the heavy double doors swung wide.

Brushed into motion, a pawn from a fallen chessboard rolled across waxed parquet; it vanished under rucked carpets and a jumble of over-turned trestles. A lark cage swung from a scrolled pedestal, the occupant a dead and musty clump of feathers. Taen blinked. Openly trembling, she started as Jaric gathered her close in his arms. The vast chamber was deserted except for the dais, where a man sprawled in the Earl's chair of state. Even before she glimpsed black hair, Taen knew. She confronted the atrocity whose name had once been Marlson Emien.

The Kielmark drew his broadsword. He crossed the threshold like a stalking predator, his step a whisper on wood, his face a mask of controlled fury. For Corley, for the dead scribe of Morbrith, and for six companies of slaughtered men, he was set to kill out of hand. Anskiere flanked him. Rarely impatient, his princely bearing never left him; except a cold glow woke in his staff. His glance carried an edge no mortal ruler could match.

Yet the Dark-dreamer stayed strangely still in his chair. Before the threat of bared steel and sorcery, he lay as if dead.

Taen disengaged from Jaric's embrace. Wide-eyed with distress, she started for the supine form on the dais.

"Don't let her touch him," Anskiere cautioned. Lest sentiment overwhelm her good sense, the Kielmark clasped her shoulder in one mailed fist. With Taen shepherded between them, Keithland's defenders skirted a fallen trestle and mounted the steps to the dais.

Morbrith Keep's chair of state jutted like a monument above the table with its seal and documents. The restored rule of the high Earl had been brief enough that he had not finished reviewing his accounts. Struck down with equal lack of warning, his conqueror sprawled with his head cradled on the emerald velvet armrest. Dark hair looped one carved post. Opened eyes shone vacant as sky above cheeks scribed with blood. More scarlet streaked from ears and nose, to pool in rusty stains at his collar. The dread Dark-dreamer of Shadowfane breathed through parted lips like a sleeper; stubble shadowed his chin. Hands that had guided a young sister to the tide pools to collect shells now rested palm upward, as if beseeching mercy. Taen caught her breath in a sob. More than ever, this man seemed the brother she recalled from Imrill Kand, but scarred in places she had not guessed, and lost in clothing too large for his underfed frame.

"When his Gierj deserted him . . ." Taen skirted the edge of breakdown, yet forced herself to qualify. "The effect wounded his mind. He feels like a vessel empty of spirit." Hesitantly she stepped closer.

"Don't touch!" warned Anskiere.

The Dreamweaver seemed not to hear. Near enough for contact, she raised a hand to her brother's shoulder. Yet even as she reached, the Kielmark's hands spun her back, into Jaric's restraining grasp. Taen cried out. Stone walls splintered her grief into echoes, deadened as Cliffhaven's sovereign pushed past. Muscles bunched in his forearm; he raised his sword over the still figure in the chair, blade angled for a mercy stroke.

Taen flinched, then buried her face in Jaric's arms. Even after the massacres at Morbrith and Corlin, and the murder of friends under Corley's command, she could not bear to watch her brother slaughtered.

The blade flashed and fell. Anskiere thrust his staff between. Steel struck brass in a dissonant jangle of sound.

The Kielmark locked eyes with the sorcerer like a wolf whose pack mate had foolishly intervened with his kill. "Are we women, faint at the thought of blood? Kor's Fires, Prince! That's not like you."

Anskiere shook his head. More than compassion tempered his reply. "No. I've not abandoned reason for mercy. For Keithland's sake, we must understand what's happened here. I very much doubt that the Dark-dreamer's collapse was anything planned by Shadowfane."

The Kielmark lowered his sword, point rested with dangerous care against the floor. "Just how will we accomplish that? Taen's not fit to sound the mind of a mouse. If you ask any more of her, I'll stop you."

Anskiere sighed with weary resignation. "I'd thought to contact the Morbrith burrow of Llondelei." The light in his staff faded slowly as he added, "Now, please, would you sheath that weapon? Gierj can't build power in the presence of steel. Between you and Jaric, we've swords enough to safeguard a garrison."

The chamber in the north spire of Shadowfane was curtained, walls and windows, with drapes of woven wool. Yet drafts still seeped through the cracks when wind swept across the fells. A swirl of chilly air teased the flame in the red-shuttered lantern. The wick guttered, thinned to a spark as Scait Demon Lord stepped through the door, into stillness and shadows.

"The Morrigierj stirs," rasped a voice from the chamber's dimmest corner. It spoke a language unknown to men, and used by demons only when contention for dominance made the sharing of thoughts an unavoidable challenge.

Scait stopped. "You say?" He narrowed sultry eyes and waited.

The voice resumed, dry over the moan of the wind beyond the drapes. "I know. Maelgrim's Gierj have deserted. The call of their true master drew them while he was engaged in mind-link. The damage caused then is irreparable. Your Dark-dreamer lies dying and Shadowfane itself is endangered."

The gust ended. Icy air mantled Scait's ankles, and the flame in the lantern brightened, throwing ruddy light over the chamber. On a reed pallet by the wall, a young Thienz with turquoise markings lay ill and gasping for air. Scait recognized the one who had bonded the Sathid that once had controlled the witch Tathagres; when Marlson Emien had stolen that matrix, the process of cross-link had inseparably paired the boy's life with that of the Thienz. The elder who attended the sick one crouched on pillows in the corner, its flesh wrinkled and hideous, and its gillflaps yellowed with age. Honor bracelets crusted all four of its limbs, badges of superior status among its fellows. As the Demon Lord crossed the chamber, the creature watched with bead-black eyes and no sign of humility.

Scait read censure in the creature's manner; short hackles prickled at his neck. "Show me."

The old Thienz delayed, implying defiance. By granting the Dark-dreamer a twelve Gierj-circle, the Demon Lord had directly jeopardized the young Thienz whose Sathid base Maelgrim shared. The old one's outrage swelled as draft eddied the lantern, and shadow dimmed the chamber once again.

Scait ruffled his hackles down, disdaining challenge. "Yes, your kind have grown few in number. But no life has passed to memory in vain. Firelord, Stormwarden, and Dreamweaver, and also the Thienz-murderer called Kielmark, are presently in Maelgrim's presence, true?"

The old Thienz pinched its lips in acquiescence.

Scait gestured. "So, then. Our control of Maelgrim will last so long as life remains. Let us work together and arrange the downfall of enemies."

The elder demon considered and grudgingly yielded. While the flame in the lantern stretched upright and brightened, it shuffled over to its ailing companion. There it crouched, eyes hooded by lashless lids. Presently the one on the pallet sighed and stirred weakly upon the cushions. Scait shifted his weight, impatient, but the old Thienz would not be hurried. It removed an honor bracelet and bent the ornament around the supine Thienz's wrist. The fact that the recipient lacked strength to acknowledge the accolade gave the Demon Lord pause; Maelgrim must be failing fast, to have drained a Thienz to the point where it abandoned indulgence of vanity.

At last the elder raised its head. 'To the death of enemies,' it sent, then passed its ludicrously tiny hand before the lantern. Awareness joined with

the underling linked to Maelgrim in Sathid-bond, and an image shimmered to visibility above the flame. The Earl's hall at Morbrith became
manifest through the distant eyes of the Dark-dreamer. . . .

Night darkened the high, arched windows there, but no stars shone.
Hedged by deep shadow, fallen trestles and furnishings bulked like the
broken bones of dragons against a solitary gleam of light, a candle shielded
behind panes of violet glass. Tinted illumination was unnatural for mankind; at least one figure gathered around the stricken form of the Dark-
dreamer was not human. From the shadowy depths of a cloak hood
gleamed the eyes of a Llondian empath.

The Kielmark stood to one side, both fists clasped to his great sword.
Distrustful as he was of strangers at the best of times, the presence of a
demon called in as ally did little to settle him. He watched with predatory
vigilance as the Llondel sat forward and laid six-fingered hands upon the
unconscious form of Maelgrim Dark-dreamer.

Taen's brother did not flinch from the touch. The tissue of his brain
had suffered massive disruption, and internal bleeding impaired what
bodily function remained. After the briefest moment of rapport, the Llondelei lifted her hands and broke contact. She turned bleak eyes upon the
humans.

'He dies the Gierj-death, this human enslaved by Shadowfane.' Her thought-
image came tinged with anger, a bitterness indefinably deep. Maelgrim's
affliction resulted directly from manipulation of a Gierj-circle. Demons at
Shadowfane well understood the consequences attached to such power;
they ensnared humans in Sathid-bond expressly for the purpose of manipulating Gierj-born forces without sacrificing one of their own. When their
victim collapsed from hemorrhage, a replacement could always be created,
until the store of stolen matrix was exhausted.

The Llondel ended with a flourish of apology and sorrow. The crystals
had come to Keithland with her kind; malicious creatures from Shadowfane had plundered the heritage of the Llondelei young expressly to engineer betrayals such as Emien's, and before him, Merya Tathagres'.

The Kielmark's grip tightened on his weapon. Taen sat with her face
in her hands; Jaric's arm tightened around her shoulder.

But the Stormwarden raised a face turned bleak as midwinter. His
voice reflected no gentleness. "Why should the Dark-dreamer's Gierj
desert, when plainly the plans of Shadowfane's demons were incomplete?"

The Llondel whistled affirmation. Her thought-image qualified, showing a smooth, spherical object that drifted at the height of a man's shoulder. Harder than rock, and defended by deadly nets of force, the thing
wakened slowly to sentience. In future time, energies sparked and flared
beneath its surface; Gierjlings that were its natural servants banded
together and invaded Keithland, to ravage and conquer. Under their rightful overlord, their power for destruction knew no limit. Even the compact

at Shadowfane feared the network of forces that Gierj might sing into being. The Llondel finished with a spoken name, Morrigierj, never before mentioned among men.

Anskiere frowned. "Then the Landfast archives are inaccurate, and the Vaere misled. No Morrigierj was ever listed among Kor's Accursed."

The Llondel whistled a minor seventh. *'Surely the records kept by men are limited. Where there are Gierj, a Morrigierj will eventually develop to focus them. But the creature takes many scores of centuries to mature. Perhaps your forebears did not know.'*

The comment met with silence. That a threat might exist more grave than the existing power of the compact was a concept that defeated hope.

Only Taen thought one step further, to a purpose that all but undid her with dread. Pale in her soiled shift, she locked gazes with the glowing eyes of the Llondel. "What if Emien wasn't the only one?" Sick inside, she reviewed Morbrith's dead, the mind of each person ruthlessly sorted before life had been pinched out with the ease of so many candle flames. Taen forced herself to speak. "Suppose Emien was expended because the demons already got what they wanted? Children with latent talent might have been stolen during his conquest of Morbrith. With no parents alive to raise outcry, who would know? Orphans might be held prisoner at Shadowfane to suffer the fate of my brother."

Air hissed over steel as the Kielmark raised his sword. He tossed the blade fiercely from right hand to left and said, "The Dreamweaver's right. And the Stormwarden deserves an apology for my words against him earlier." He gestured to the Llondel, then angled his blade toward the waxy figure of Maelgrim. "Alive, that scum might tell us for certain."

Anskiere nodded acknowledgment. Too enmeshed in concern to be astonished by a word of conciliation from the Kielmark, he spoke a phrase to the Llondel in the creature's own tongue.

The demon returned an image of stream water running uphill; but the adage perhaps held another meaning to those of her kind, for instead of rebuttal, she bent willingly and laid twig-thin fingers once more upon Maelgrim's brow. . . .

In the red-tinged gloom at Shadowfane, anger finally prevailed; the long hackles lifted at Scait's neck, and he swiped a fist through the tenuous image garnered from Maelgrim through the senses of the failing Thienz. Flattened by disturbed air, the lantern flame guttered. The vision of the Earl's hall with its gathering of men and Llondel went dark.

The Demon Lord hissed. "I've seen enough, toad. Hear my orders. Destroy the one who shares Sathid bond with Maelgrim, that the Dark-dreamer perish at once. Better they both die early than have mankind learn more of the Morrigierj and my plot to ruin Keithland."

The ancient Thienz shifted with a jingle of bracelets. It blinked eyes opaque as gimlets and responded with disarming submission. "Your will, Lord Scait."

The Demon Lord spun on his heel. Shadow swept the room as he strode between lantern and pallet, and departed. Then the outer door boomed closed, leaving the soft sigh of drafts, and the labored gasp of the injured Thienz.

The elder stroked the near-departed's gillflaps long after its master's footsteps died off down the corridor. It saw no wisdom in Scait's high-handed command, not when the Vaere-trained of Keithland had already divined the gist of Scait's intentions. Both of the Sathid-bound would be consigned to memory by morning anyway. Until then, the old Thienz chose to maintain its foothold in Maelgrim Dark-dreamer's mind.

Toward dawn, the wind stopped. The red-panel lantern burned low; the chamber at Shadowfane grew stifling with the reek of hot oil as the sickened Thienz breathed its last. Far to the south, the wracked body of Marlson Emien shuddered a final time and stilled; his wax-pale fingers loosened in death. Taen covered her face in her hands and wept.

At Shadowfane, the Thienz elder's awareness of her faded away with the essence of its departed cousin. The demon stirred stiffly from its corner. Layers of honor bracelets jingled as it rose to ungainly feet and closed the eyes of its departed. Then, with a croak of irritation mostly due to aching joints, the old one waddled out to seek Scait. It bore news of much import. Humans and Llondelei had held council during the night. Between them they had determined that demon-controlled atrocities such as Merya Tathagres and Maelgrim Dark-dreamer were a menace too grave to risk again. Even as Taen Dreamweaver mourned by the corpse of her brother, Ivainson Jaric and Kielmark Thienz-murderer mounted horses and turned east, their intent to steal Sathid from Shadowfane.

A grimace that passed for a smile cracked the old Thienz's lips. Humans might know of the Morrigierj; but Shadowfane had gained warning as well. Shortly Ivainson Firelord and the hated sovereign of Cliff-haven would be bait for the taking.

At Morbrith the night seemed to linger without end. Darkness still cloaked the high windows of the Earl's hall when the candle behind its violet glass flickered in a spent pool of wax. Taen rose from her vigil beside her brother's body. She rubbed stiffened and saddle-galled knees, then straightened her crumpled clothing. What remained of Emien, the creature that Shadowfane's demons had named Maelgrim, was gone now. The grief of his passing was not new. For a very long time, Taen had accepted the fact that she had lost a brother. During his final hour of life she had tried to take comfort from the fact that his end had come without need of an execution by the Kielmark. All that remained was to inter his body, and in that she would have the Stormwarden's help. Jaric had used Earthmastery to carve out a grave site, before he departed.

The final details of burial at least would wait till the morning. Exhausted enough that she thought she might sleep, Taen raised the lamp left by the Llondelei healer. She covered her brother's face with a tapestry, then picked her way around ruined furnishings and passed the great doors to the corridor.

Darkness closed about her, dense and musty as old velvet. Taen raised the candle to see better. The flame flickered, then died, quenched in puddled wax. Caught in the midst of a turn, Taen tripped on an edge of crumpled carpet and cursed.

That moment something beyond the keep walls chose to meddle with her wards. The Dreamweaver felt her skin prickle in the dark. She dropped the spent lantern with a crash and strove through weariness and muddled emotions to muster her talents.

Jaric and the Kielmark had ridden out more than an hour ago; unless they met trouble and turned back, no living being should remain in Morbrith to try her defenses. The alternative was daunting in the extreme, that Shadowfane's demons might already have launched an offensive. That the probe was aggressive was never in doubt. Even as Taen sent a call to warn Anskiere, the disruption came again.

She set her focus at once on the main gate. The mist there glowed silver, but not from moonlight. A robed figure stood before the arch. The glow emanated from raised hands that glittered with rings. Taen's wariness eased slightly. This was no visitor from the compact; the meddler who challenged her barrier was none other than the Magelord of Mhored Kara. Whatever cause had brought that ancient to venture from the security of his towers would not be slight. Taen guarded her relief as she dispelled trance and faced the more mundane problem posed by her spent candle.

Her powers were sorely overtaxed. The idea of using dream-sense to guide herself through the castle's darkened corridors made her head ache. Left the undignified alternative of groping, Taen resolutely trailed her fingers along the wall. After two steps she stubbed her toe roundly on a statue. She hopped, cursing irritably, then compounded her difficulties by banging her elbow against a torch bracket. Her yelp of pain drew notice.

Shadow splintered before a harsh glare of sorcery. Dazzled, Taen squinted. She managed to identify the triple halos of the Stormwarden's staff before she tripped on another rucked edge of carpet and stumbled unceremoniously to her knees.

Anskiere caught her arm in time to spare her from a fall full length upon the floor. "I was just coming to look for you." Worry shaded his tone. "Is something wrong?"

"Maybe." Taen took full advantage of the sorcerer's support and pulled herself to her feet. A wry smile bent her lips. She had to be the first to be rescued from the perils of the dark by powers better suited to harnessing storms off the Corine Sea. "We've got a visitor."

Her evident amusement gave Anskiere space to relax. He damped the intensity of his staff and rested the brass-shod end against the floor with studied care. "I gather no one dangerous."

"You'd know better than any." Taen's humor fled. "Waiting at the gate and demanding admittance is His Eminence the Magelord of Mhored Kara. Why would he come here?"

Anskiere's hand tightened upon his staff; his eyes turned icy with distance. Yet if he resented the captivity set upon him by conjurers on the isle of Imrill Kand, his words revealed no rancor. "I don't know. But if the Magelord expected to face me at the end of his road, his reasons for travel won't be pleasant."

"Well," said Taen, her most irrepressible smile creeping through, "we'd better go and meet him. The defenses won't admit him without our help, and his tampering is raising merry hell with the wards."

CHAPTER XV

Border Wilds

The wards over Morbrith Keep crackled and collapsed with a flare of intense light. Anskiere observed with his brows lifted in reproof as orange sparks trailed from the gate towers, to settle and die as they lit on the cobbles beneath.

"We didn't need protection that strong, anyway," Taen said in belated justification. "If demons send anything more against us tonight, they're going to catch me sleeping."

"Just so the work was yours, little witch." The Stormwarden shrugged his creased robe a little straighter and stepped into the bailey. "Right now I've no stomach for facing a Magelord who is capable of arranging an unbinding on that scale."

Taen gestured rudely, a hand-sign the Imrill Kand fishwives used to express withering disdain. "Was there ever any doubt the work was mine?"

"Not much." Anskiere shook his head, amused; as Taen had hoped, he relaxed his inner discipline and finished with his first smile in days.

The break in his composure was the last anyone was likely to see. Beyond the arch, His Eminence the Magelord of Mhored Kara stood with a fixed frown. His mouth gaped open in perplexity, while the incomplete spell he had intended for the purpose of breaking Taen's wards drifted aimlessly over his hands.

"Your mischief has left our visitor somewhat vexed," the Stormwarden observed. Then, discomfited himself by the unanticipated arrival of an adversary, he indulged in a rare display of power, and kindled the wards in his staff to light his steps through the arch.

Blue-violet illumination seared away the dark. Beyond the gate, the Magelord spun around as though slapped. The spell over his hands flashed out. The next instant a force slammed Taen's awareness that was vicious in its intensity. Startled off her guard, she stumbled backward and cried out.

Anskiere caught her. He guided her so that his body shielded her from harm and, with no break in motion, raised his staff. Wind rose at his bidding. It cracked across the cobbles like a living thing, making the Magelord's robes snap with whipcrack reports. The frail old conjurer could not stand upright against the force of the gale. Neither would he abandon dignity and crouch. Forced back one step, two, then three, he ended awkwardly spread-eagled against the gate tower.

Taen spoke the moment she regained her breath. "His Eminence was only testing to see whether I had sent an illusion." But Anskiere's winds snatched her words away.

His face stayed set with anger as he strode from beneath the arch. Once clear of the stone, the ward halos threw etched light across his prisoner's helpless form. The Magelord blinked in discomfort.

Yet as if pity was a stranger, the Stormwarden addressed him. "What discourtesy is this? To wield power in uncalled-for aggression is an act of rank ignorance, and to try the Vaere-trained worse folly still. Taen Dreamweaver this day spared all of Hallowild from suffering the fate of Morbrith. To subject her to truth-spells is an abuse you will answer for. Speak quickly, for my patience is spent."

The Magelord raised his chin against the confining pressure of the wind. His eyes stayed hooded, dark with ancient malice, and the sigils tattooed on pale cheeks seemed grotesque as knotted spiders. "Your Dreamweaver sent illusion to our towers. Knowing our beliefs, is that any less a discourtesy?"

Anskiere said nothing. The light from his staff shone steady as a star, but blindingly bright; only the wind relented ever so slightly.

The Magelord's purple robes settled around his thin ankles. As if the effort pained him, he pushed away from the gate tower and querulously yielded. "I have come to propose an alliance."

The Stormwarden allowed the wind to die, but not the wards. He waited without speech for the Magelord to continue, while unspoken between them rose the tension and the memory left by Anskiere's imprisonment at the hands of Kisburn's conjurers on Imrill Kand.

Taen edged out from behind the Stormwarden to better follow the exchange. The Magelord spared her a glance, but did not apologize for his aggression. Irked that Anskiere expected him to explain himself, he gripped ringed hands about the bag of amulets he wore knotted to his belt. "There have been portents." His voice turned gravelly with annoyance. "The compact at Shadowfane has brewed mischief, with worse yet to come. My seers have foreseen the wholesale destruction of Keithland."

The prescience must have been dire to induce this sour old man to abandon ceremony. Aware of nothing from him beyond bitterness for the Stormwarden's harsh treatment, Taen watched Anskiere shift unadorned hands on the wooden grip of his staff. For a while no sound intruded but the conjurer's quick breaths, and the crickets singing in the weeds beneath the gate towers.

"They could not have acted without your sanction," observed the Stormwarden of Elrinfaer at last. He did not refer to demons. Through dream-sense, Taen knew he spoke of the past, and the contention that remained unresolved since Kisburn's conjurers had tried to coerce Anskiere to free the frostwargs for the purpose of conquest and greed.

The Magelord knew also. He snapped his teeth shut in offense and squared his shoulders. "My conjurers lost their lives. Was their end not enough to redress the mistake?"

Anskiere went very still. "Have you ever seen a frostwarg disember a town?"

Aware, abruptly, that he was on trial, and that his reply would be judged, the Magelord assumed the defensive. "My successor, Hearvin, was sent to assess Kisburn's ambitions. He was a true master of the seven states of reality, and never a man to approve of rash action."

Again Anskiere said nothing.

The Magelord squinted under the painful glare of the wards; and in a moment of sharpened insight, Taen perceived what Anskiere had suspected all along; jealousy had motivated the Mhored Karan wizards in support of King Kisburn's plot. They knew well the vicious nature of the frostwargs. Secretly they had hoped to arrange Anskiere's downfall. The lengths to which spite had driven them appalled Taen to outrage. She had not guessed, when she had asked the Magelord to send her message to the Kielmark, that she had dealt in confidence with a den of serpents. In retrospect, she saw she had been fortunate to emerge without trouble.

The Magelord did not speak.

Never looking away, the Stormwarden slowly slid his hands over the staff until his knuckles met. "You never considered, did you, that Tatha-gres would use children in her attempt to force my will. Only one accepted my protection. She stands beside me, much changed, and never again a carefree girl. The brother who felt too threatened to trust me fell to Shadowfane and caused the wasting of Morbrith. Who will answer for him, Kethal? Your last offer of alliance was nothing but a misguided bid for power. The result cost Keithland dearly."

Dawn had begun to silver the mist beyond the ward light cast by Anskiere's staff. A bird twittered sleepily from a treetop, soon joined by a host of its fellows. Yet the keep behind stayed eerily silent and dark, except for the sheen of last night's dew. The Magelord regarded the Stormwarden with bleak antipathy. His ringed hands hung loosely from the gold-banded cuffs of his sleeves; yet now and again the fingers twitched, as if he longed to shape spells.

"You did not have to submit," Kethal finally accused.

And this time Anskiere bent his head. Dream-sense showed Taen his thought, that a man might misjudge many times in the course of a life-time; but for a sorcerer, mistakes claimed innocent lives. Had he not yielded his powers for Kisburn's conjurers to bind, the villagers of Imrill Kand would have attempted out of loyalty to defend him. They could only have failed. Any man who offered Anskiere protection would have been slaughtered by king's men, not cleanly, but for sport.

The Dreamweaver refused the implication, that Anskiere might be counted guilty for Emien's defection and the larger disaster at Morbrith. Their earlier melding of minds had shown the opposite. Beneath his stern exterior lay a heart incapable of cruelty; his powers and responsibilities as Stormwarden stood in ruthless conflict with his sensitivity. The deaths in his past haunted him past memory of peace, and here the Magelord's envy found endless opportunity to inflict pain.

Taen was driven to interfere. She lashed out with her dream-sense, and caught the Magelord unprepared. Behind his guard in one swift thrust, she recoiled from what she encountered; Kethal's mind was a snarl of thwarted desires and ambition. Through his years he had accumulated layer upon layer of achievement around a core of deepest mistrust. He called no man friend. Altercations with other mages were never settled until he had subjugated any who came against him. Only the Vaere-trained had balked him, and for that, they and every principle they upheld had earned his undying hatred, until now, when the conjury of Mhored Kara's master seer had placed this petty old man in stark fear of his life. More ruthless than was her wont, Taen peeled away Kethal's framework of excuses and justifications. She made of her talents a mirror and showed the Magelord of Mhored Kara the unadorned image of himself.

He quivered as the import struck him. Rings flashed as he raised his hands, but not to shape conjury. Instead the old wizard covered his face to hide shame. For the first time in life he understood the guilt borne by Anskiere of Elrinfaer.

The effect catalyzed change, marked him too deeply to shelter behind his accustomed mask of lies; no longer could he find solace in spite, or in the belief that the Vaere-trained held arrogant power that deserved to be taught humility. Forever after, even until death, the Magelord would suffer remorse for the fate of Morbrith, and for depriving Keithland, even temporarily, of her most powerful sworn defender.

Taen relented only when the aged ruler of Mhored Kara had bent his stiff back. As he fell to his knees on the dusty cobbles beneath the gate, she addressed him with uncharacteristic acerbity. "If you come here for help, Your Eminence, then ask."

The Magelord lifted a face traced silver with tears. Revealed by brightening daybreak, his purple robes were travel-creased and worn. Left only desperate rags for decorum, he seemed somehow diminished. "You demand difficult terms."

"Fair ones, I think." Anskiere's voice was only slightly unsteady; but his hands clenched white on his staff as he released his defenses. The wards snapped out with the speed of a lightning flash, leaving the gray weariness of his face exposed in the half-light. "Name me your portents, Kethal."

Without asking, Taen stepped forward and helped the ancient wizard to his feet. He spoke then, in dry, measured phrases, and described a course of ruin that made the destruction of Morbrith look petty by comparison.

"Morrigierj," Anskiere concluded when the Magelord completed his account. Neither he nor Taen need question that the conjury of Mhored Kara's seers were accurate.

"The threat is perhaps much closer than our allies the Llondelei expect." The Stormwarden's lips thinned grimly, and he nodded to Taen. "Show the old one in, little witch. There seem to be things we'll need to discuss with him after all."

While Taen, Anskiere, and the Magelord held council to negotiate terms of alliance with the wizards of Mhored Kara, mist settled silver in the hollows east of Morbrith. Jaric eased his horse over rocky ground, cautious of a misstep that might bring lameness and delay. The Kielmark rode ahead with his great sword slung crosswise over his back. The black that bore him walked with its head held low, stockinged legs buried to the hocks in fog. Both horses stumbled with fatigue; neither beasts nor riders had rested since leaving Corlin the night before. Yet the need to travel in haste could not be denied. Shadowfane held the last of the Llondelei Sathid; if children stolen from Morbrith survived to replace the Dark-dreamer, the well-being of humans and Llondelei lay in jeopardy.

Daylight brightened, catching dew like jewels in the grass beneath the horses' hooves. Jaric resisted the need to collapse in sleep on his mount's neck. His knees ached. When he freed his feet to relieve cramped muscles, his stirrups banged painfully into his ankles. That discomfort kept him alert until the Kielmark called a halt at noon. Pausing only long enough to refill the water flasks and eat journey bread and sausage from the stores in the saddlebags, pirate and Firelord rode on until shadows slanted toward late afternoon, Jaric unsaddled his horse, his only comfort the fact that Taen need not share the peril of his journey; in the company of Anskiere, she would return to Cliffhaven on board *Ladywolf*, for the straits offered the only defensible position should a Morrigierj arise and drive its minions to invade Landfast.

The horses were utterly spent; unbridled and turned loose, they grazed without inclination to wander. The Kielmark stretched out with his sword ready at hand. Nearby, cushioned by the damp wool of his saddle blanket, Jaric slept dreamlessly on the grassy verge of a stream.

The following days passed alike, landscape alternating with the reed-choked banks of an uncountable succession of fords. Orchards gave way to wilderness and the terrain grew rough. The appearance of the riders became raffish to match, as they slept in thornbrakes and thickets and once on the dank floor of a cave as rain hammered the earth in angry autumn torrents.

The Kielmark's black threw a shoe. Progress slowed for two days, until they traded fresh mounts from a remote camp of clansfolk. Dunmoreland stock was prized by the hilltribes; formal in a headdress of mules' ears, the chieftain finalized the exchange without spitting on his knife, meaning no vengeance would be exacted if the beasts proved unsound. But his less trusting wife watched the strangers off with an expression like sun-baked clay. Jaric was glad to ride briskly after that.

In forests and moonlight and cloudy dark, Firelord and Kielmark crossed the northern tracts of Hallowild. On a windy morning, they broke through the scrub to dunes, and the wide white beaches of the coast. There they dismounted and cut brush for signal fires until their palms blistered on the hafts of their daggers.

The Kielmark maintained an outpost on the isle of Northsea for provision and repair of his fleet of corsairs. Few beside his captains knew the location, which was healthiest for the peace of mind of Keithland's merchants. The sloop that answered his smoke-fire summons was lean and efficient, and bristling with armed men who easily preferred battle to bedding a wench.

The boatswain at the helm landed singing, until he noticed who waited on the strand; his stanza ended in a curse of embarrassed surprise. He mastered himself with striking aplomb. After loosing the horses to fend for themselves, Kielmark and Firelord boarded with no more than wet boots, despite the heave of strong surf.

Jaric endured a jostling crossing. After weeks in the saddle, with fire-charred fish or the stringy meat of skulk-otters for fare, the smoky shacks that comprised the Northsea garrison seemed the height of luxury. At a scarred board table in the kitchens, he dined on bread and mutton and wine, while the talk of the men swirled around him.

"Cap'n Tamic's in at Cover's Warren." The officer in charge had a broad south isles' accent, but there was nothing lazy about the way he answered the queries of his sovereign. "Shipyards there been a'slacking, and he poked in to shake things up."

The Kielmark scratched his mustache, which had grown like wire over the hard line of his mouth. Idly he retrieved the knife from his plate and began to hack at the bristles. "Does Corley know?"

"Oh, aye." The officer grinned. "Said he'd spit the foremen, one after another, if Tamic reported loose ends. Meanwhile the fleet's at sea, sweeping the bay for demon-sign, as ordered. You wantin' a boat to go across?"

The Kielmark stabbed his blade into the boards. "Tomorrow. But we won't put in at the Warren."

"Where, then?" The officer twirled his tankard, sobered and suspecting trouble.

But the Kielmark refused to reveal their destination, even to a trusted captain. Too much stood at risk should Shadowfane gain wind of his purpose. He closed the topic with a banal change of subject, and presently announced his desire to rest.

Bathed, shaved, and for once unmolested by insects, Jaric slept solidly in a bunk in the officers' shack. But respite from the rigors of travel proved brief; a sailhand shook him awake in the gray light of dawn. Feeling muzzy, the Firelord donned breeches, boots, and shirt. He hurried down to the landing by the harbor with his sword belt dangling from the crook of one elbow.

The Kielmark waited, boisterously impatient, his foot braced on the gunwale of a lean gray yawl. "There's hot bread and bacon waiting, if you're quick at setting sails."

Jaric stowed his sword in a locker, eyebrows raised in reproof. "That's no incentive. I could *make* hot bread in a blizzard."

"Oh, sure. Like charcoal," needled the Kielmark. He stepped aboard and reached to cast off docklines.

Jaric clambered into the bow and began to sort hanks on the headsail, more to keep from thinking how much he missed Taen than from any sense of urgency for Keithland. By sunrise the yawl sheered on a reach around the cliff heads of Northsea, toward the shoal-ridden islets of Wrecker's Bay. Beyond lay the borders of Keithland, and Shadowfane itself.

Clouds rolled in by noon, ragged black and swollen with rain. The sea heaved leaden and dark, knifed to leaping spray by a series of rocky promontories. Gusts hissed in from two directions, battering the yawl like fists, and tearing at Jaric's clothing as he rose to reef sail.

The Kielmark shouted over the slap of canvas. "Leave her be. There's no room to run in this pocket. We're safer on the beach if it squalls."

Jaric eased sheets for a run, then sat and braced against the mast. Outlined by storm sky, the Kielmark's profile seemed hammered out of rock. Muscles bulged under his sleeves as he manhandled the tiller to hold course toward land.

The centerboard banged up in its casing, and the yawl grounded on gravel with a lurch. Jaric freed the sheets and leaped into a boil of foam. Icy water poured into his boots. Then the sky opened, deluging rain. Half-blind in the torrent, the Kielmark wrestled the sails down. Together the two men dragged their boat onto the strand. Behind them, the channel became a smoking cauldron of spindrift as the squall struck full force.

Escarpments of broken rock offered scant protection from the fury of wind and water. Soaked already, and uninterested in standing while the Kielmark wrapped his sword steel in oiled rags, Jaric wandered the beachhead. Rain spattered the ground. Pebbles and small stones tumbled in the run-off, to be battered in turn by surf. The Firelord squinted through the storm and made out the jagged outline of a cliff face; wild and untenanted though that shoreline was, something about the place seemed familiar. As a gust momentarily parted the curtains of rain, he realized why. This was the site of Anskiere's curse against Ivain, following the destruction of Elrinfaer by the Mharg.

Jaric listened, but heard only the voice of the storm. Wind here no longer repeated the curse Anskiere had pronounced against his betrayer. Perhaps the completion of the geas's terms had unbound the spell; or maybe the words on the wind had been nothing more than a tale invented by sailors. Shivering in the cold, Jaric stepped into the lee of a ledge that jutted beyond the tide mark. Barnacles crusted the stone, white as old bone where the waves threw feathers of spray. Saw grass clung in those cracks not swept clean by weather, except in one place. Once a sorcerer had marked the cliff, to leave a message straight and bitter as vengeance. Ivainson blinked droplets from his eyes and beheld the inscription his father had left scribed in rock.

Summon me, sorcerer, and know sorrow. Be sure I will leave nothing of value for your use, even should my offspring inherit.

Jaric knew a moment of paralyzing cold. The mad malice of his father seemed to emanate from the stone, choking breath from his lungs, sapping life from his body. Wounded by hatred and spite, the son stumbled backward, into the cleansing fall of the rain. He stood for an interval, shuddering, his eyes stinging with water and tears. Then he stirred and lifted his hand. Alone in rainy twilight, he raised Earthmastery and smoothed the letters from the surface of the cliff.

Surf slammed unabated against the headland, and rain still whipped the strand. Yet somehow the squall seemed less savage, the landscape not so forsaken under the crazed onslaught of elements. Jaric made peace with the memory of his father and turned back toward the beach. He had one goal for comfort: should he and the Kielmark succeed at Shadowfane, mankind might survive to discover an answer to the threat posed by demons. Then Keithland would have no further need for sorcerers, and the agonies of the Cycle of Fire might be abandoned forever.

The crossing of the northern Corine Sea passed smoothly after Northsea, with brisk winds and fair sky seldom interrupted by squalls. The yawl sailed more handily than *Callinde*, which was well, for the waters off the coast of Felwaithe were a maze of shoals and islets that few mariners dared to navigate. Jaric learned more than he cared to know about charts and current as the yawl threaded the hazardous channels across Wrecker's Bay.

Twice their presence was challenged by corsairs flying the red wolf of Cliffhaven. The Kielmark kept the north coast under vigilant patrol, to dissuade merchant ships who thought to evade tribute by avoiding Mainstrait. Captains under his banner carried standing orders to plunder and sink any ship found bearing cargo; but often such tactics proved unnecessary. The reef-ridden channels between islands offered no sea room to fight, and many a hapless merchanter found ruin on hard rock instead. While searching the beaches for firewood, Jaric found rigging among the tide wrack, and the weather-bleached timbers of ships.

Autumn's warmth waned; the sky turned overcast and silvery as a fish's underbelly. On an afternoon that threatened rain the Kielmark beached the yawl on the farmost point of Felwaithe. Chilled in his wet boots, Jaric wondered as he stowed sails whether the two of them would survive to need the small boat again.

"My captains will spot her on the beach," the Kielmark said, as if answering the Firelord's thought. "One or another will pick her up." He did not belabor the fact that such a contingency would be necessary only if they failed to return; instead, he squinted at clouds, adjusted his sword belt, and turned his back to the sea.

Jaric followed, his fine hair stiff with salt crystals, and a knapsack of provisions slung across his shoulders. Since the fells north of Keithland sustained neither forests for cover nor forage for horses, the final leagues to Shadowfane must be crossed on foot. Kielmark and Firelord pressed forward through spiky stands of scrub pine, crosshatched patches of briar, and ravines of loose shale that crumbled and slid underfoot. By sundown, both thorns and pines thinned to isolated thickets. The soil became poor and sandy, pierced by sharp tongues of rock, and knee-high clumps of saw grass and fern. A fine drizzle began to fall. Grimly set on his purpose, the Kielmark seemed inured to the damp, though moisture matted his hair and soaked patches in the calves of his leggings.

Jaric walked alongside with less confidence. Troubled by foreboding, and yearning for Taen's company, he felt every icy drop that slipped off the pack and rolled down his collar. The warded sword at his side chafed his hip like common steel, and boots blistered his heels after weeks of barefoot comfort at sea. Still, he continued without voicing his fears. Day wore gradually into night, and fog cloaked what little visibility remained. Between one step and another, ferny hummocks gave way to stone crusted with lichen. Beyond that point, as if a knife had divided the land, wind moaned over hills unbroken by any living thing.

"We've reached the borders of Keithland." The Lord of Cliffhaven paused and rested his back against a table of black rock. "Sailors say the whole of this world is barren, except for Keithland. I've seen oceans grow strange fish away from inhabited coasts."

Jaric slung off his pack. Inside he scrounged a hardened loaf of bread, which he hacked in two with his knife; he passed half to his companion, who seemed to be listening to the wind. Explanations for Keithland's existence were many. Kor's priesthood claimed the Divine Fires had seeded lands for men to raise crops, and country folk said forests, meadows, and wildlife were the magical gifts of the Vaere. Whichever philosophy a man chose to believe, none who beheld the edge of the growing earth ever felt less than a shiver of dread.

Mist and rain overhung the rock like a shroud. The bread grew soggy in Jaric's hand; in disgust he tossed the last bit away, then dragged the pack onto tired shoulders with a muttered curse at the weather.

"Sky'll be clear before midnight." The Kielmark adjusted his sword sheath, and shook his head. "You'll wish for dirty weather then. We'll stand out on these fells like fleas on a whore's sheets, and Shadowfane's watchtowers are manned by creatures with eyes on both sides of their heads."

Jaric received this comment with skeptical expression, wasted, because of the dark. "You've been there?"

The Kielmark's teeth gleamed in a brief grin. "Never. But the fellow who told me was sober."

"My sword to a bootlace he wasn't." Jaric shook water out of his hair. "No sailor ever enters your presence who isn't full of beer to bolster his courage. You've the reputation of a shearfish, all teeth and bite."

"And a good thing that will be, if we meet Scait's four-eyed beasties in a fight." The Kielmark pushed to his feet. Spoilingly impatient, he said, "Are you ready?"

They proceeded, and the air grew colder. The breeze shifted northwest. Rain and clouds gave way to a star-spiked arch of sky. The rock of the fells extended in all directions, windswept and deserted, except for a single gleam of scarlet near the horizon. The sight raised chills on Jaric's flesh; a stronghold arose as if chiseled from a hilltop, all angled battlements, with silhouettes of spindled towers bleak and black against the indigo of the heavens.

"Shadowfane, sure's frost." Grimly the Kielmark loosed the lashing on the tip of his scabbard, that his sword might be ready for action.

Ivainson Firelord had no words for the occasion. No longer the scribe who had apprenticed at Morbrith, nor the boy who had trapped ice otter in Seitforest, he bowed his head. His hands glowed blue in the darkness as he summoned Earthmastery to sound the stone underfoot. From the images drawn from Dreamweaver and Llondelei, he knew that a chain of caverns riddled the ground beneath Shadowfane. Through them, a combination of sorcery and sailor's luck might permit entry into Shadowfane unobserved.

Far south, drizzle still cloaked a fortress under a red wolf banner. A sentry paced restlessly, his beat altered slightly to avoid a rumpled figure in Dreamweaver's robes of silver-gray. Taen sat with her head cradled on her forearms, her shoulders framed by the rough stone sill of Cliffhaven's watchtower. She had drifted into sleep while tracing Jaric's progress northward through Felwaithe, but her rest was troubled.

She dreamed of a chamber floored in dark marble where red-paned lanterns burned. There a Thienz in green beads and armbands bowed before a throne built of stuffed human limbs. "Lord-mightiest, the Firelord and his companion have crawled beneath the earth. My kind can no longer track them, but their intent is plain. They will emerge within the dungeons of Shadowfane, to the sorrow of us all."

The figure stirred on the throne, silencing the toadlike creature on the rug. Yellow eyes opened, evil and narrow and set like a snake's; razor rows of teeth gleamed in shadow as the Demon Lord responded. "No sorrow, but the humans', for Shadowfane is prepared for them. Firelord and Kielmark walk into an ambush. If we introduce a third Sathid to Ivainson's body, how long do you suppose he can maintain control? Very soon his powers shall be ours to command."

Scait added in mind-speak that through Jaric even the Morrigierj might be managed. He hissed with laughter, and his sultry gaze seemed to focus directly upon the watchtower at Cliffhaven where Taen wakened, screaming.

The sentry gripped her shoulders in mail-clad fists, vainly trying to comfort. Shivering, chilled by more than cold, Taen shook him off. "Fetch Anskiere. Tell him we must abandon the children held captive at Shadowfane. Scait has learned of our plan to steal the Sathid."

The sentry hesitated, scarred features pinched in a frown.

"Hurry!" Taen wasted no more words, but snapped her talents into focus and sent north, to warn. Her probe coursed rocky fells, windy and empty of life. The man she loved and the tempestuous King of Pirates had already entered the caverns. Since dream-search could not reach through solid stone, disaster was unavoidable. Firelord and Kielmark would walk into a demon trap ready and armed against them.

CHAPTER XVI

Stalkers

Fading enchantments lent rock walls the fleeting glimmer of faery gold; then darkness fell, in a swirl of cold air. Ivainson Jaric stepped through an archway still hot from the shaping of his Earthmastery. Sweating from the warmth thrown off by the rock, he took a deep breath. The passage he entered smelled muddy and damp. Underground springs trickled over channels worn smooth by erosion, the echoes like whispers in the dark; all else was still. No living creature inhabited the cave.

"There's still rock dividing us from Shadowfane's dungeon." Reverberation splintered the Firelord's words into multiple voices as he concluded. "This is the last sealed cavern we'll cross if you want to enter through the lowest level." He lifted his hands, and controlled flame speared the air above his fingers.

The illumination sparked mad glints in the Kielmark's eyes. Black, unruly hair bound back with a twist of linen lent Keithland's most powerful sovereign the appearance of a brute peasant. "Just so there's headroom. Can't swing a blade while grubbing along on my belly."

Metal whined in shadow as he cleared his sword from his scabbard. "On, then."

Jaric started forward, more like a scribe caught out of his element than the Vaere-trained sorcerer Keithland's survival depended upon. He fretted at the hazard presented by his companion, who might stumble on the rough footing and slice him through with three spans of unsheathed steel. But as always, the Kielmark moved like a cat. Except for his weapon, he might have been enjoying a holiday procession in Kor's temple, so blithely did he keep pace at Jaric's shoulder.

Ahead, the cavern loomed dark as a grave. Ivainson adjusted his mastery, and flames flared brighter from his fist. The passage crooked through buttresses of stone and widened into a troll forest of stalagmites, colored bone and ocher, and sleeked like slag with run-off. A black maw opened underfoot, where streams carved into the unknown deeps of the earth. Jaric jumped the crevice. His heels grated on sand as he strode to the far wall and applied his Earthmaster's touch. The fingertips of both hands flared blue as he traced an area encrusted with limestone. Sathid-born powers resonated through the cavern. Ivainson's features tightened, and the hotter fires that leaped above his knuckles suddenly extinguished.

"You play havoc with a man's night sight that way," carped the Kielmark. His boots scraped over stone as he closed the last stride by touch, disoriented only slightly by the sudden dark.

Jaric disregarded the complaint. "Beyond this barrier lies Shadowfane." Harrowed by sudden uncertainty, he lowered his arms to his sides. Anskiere's distrust, Taen's love; all that he strove to change or cherish in his life within Keithland seemed remote as the lushness of spring when snows lay deep over the land.

Air winnowed, sliced by steel as the Kielmark raised his sword. "Nothing to gain by waiting, sorcerer. Either you make spells, or I shove you aside and start chipping rock."

The ruthless arrogance in the words startled like a blow, until Jaric recalled the six companies of Cliffhaven's men who had perished with Morbrith. The Kielmark's grudges inevitably resolved in bloody vengeance; whether the offenders were human or demon made no whit of difference.

Jaric raised hands that once had penned copy for the archives of an Earl's library; those pages were ash, now, and mourned not at all, unless by the ghost of the master scribe tortured to his death in Morbrith's bailey. With more sorrow than anger, Ivainson Firelord marshaled his powers. He touched, and where his fingers passed, a livid red line seared the stone.

Fumes scoured his nostrils. Jaric directed his Earthmastery through the sheen of tear-blurred vision. Presently the line parted, frayed into light like the edge of a smoldering parchment. Draft rushed through the gap. Ivainson shielded his face behind one arm, his cheek whipped by the laces of his cuff. The Kielmark sweated impatiently; heated air sang across his swordblade as the stone dividing Shadowfane from the wild caves of the fells crumpled away under the influence of sorcery.

A corridor gaped beyond, still as old dust; the one visible wall was patterned in hexagonal brick, pierced by a lintel streaked with rust from a torch bracket. No cresset blazed in the socket. Not even water drops disturbed the quiet. Jaric's enchantment fizzled into sparks, then darkness. Firelord and Kielmark paused, unbreathing, but no outcry arose; no lantern flared to expose the presence of intruders and no sentry leaped forth to make outcry. Though all but a few demons avoided the confining properties of stone, the absence of security in the dungeons under Shadowfane came as a profound relief. Fortune perhaps had seen two humans through the vulnerable moment of entry.

Jaric shifted his weight, but found his step prevented by a crushing grip on his shoulder.

The Kielmark whispered softly as a breath in his ear. "Let me go first."

Startled by an expression of trust, Ivainson conceded. Other than Corley, he had never known the Kielmark to tolerate an armed man behind him.

"Go left, then." Jaric let his Earthmastery range a short way ahead. "You'll pass a row of cells with studded doors, then a stairway. If there's a sentry, we'll probably find him on the first landing." Distressed that he still felt unequal to whatever perils might await, the Firelord summoned a spark to guide the way into Shadowfane's deepest dungeons.

"Belay the light. I'd best go on by touch." The Kielmark pushed past, his sword a flash that vanished as the Firelord closed his fist to muffle his spell.

Jaric crossed the gap on the heels of his companion. As his boot sole scuffed blindly against brick on the far side, contact touched off an explosion of energy in his mind. Evidently the passage was warded. Jaric's hand hardened instantly on his sword hilt. He groped to restrain the Kielmark, but his companion had already passed beyond reach. To call aloud might bring demons. Left no better alternative, Ivainson Firelord crossed quickly into the passage.

The air grew palpably dense, as if shadow had somehow gained substance. Jaric strained to breathe. Left in no doubt that he had triggered defenses conjured by demons, he opened his fingers. Weakened to a dull gleam of red, the spark's thin glimmer revealed a corridor choked with mist. The Kielmark was nowhere to be seen.

Mortally afraid, his body slicked with sweat, Jaric attempted another step. Sorcery rippled around him. The fog vanished in the space of a stride, and darkness thinned to normal. The simple spell in his hand brightened like a beacon star. In the sudden splash of light, Jaric sighted the Kielmark. Vital, indomitable, the sovereign Lord of Cliffhaven poised beneath the stair with his sword raised en garde. On the landing above, rank upon rank, lurked a clawed and hideous pack of demons. The fact they carried no weapon did not reassure; like the Llondelei, their ability to manipulate the mind could be lethal.

The Kielmark reflexively back-stepped. Braced against the wall to avoid being surrounded and struck down from behind, he shouted orders. "Jaric! Leave these to me."

But retreat was already useless. Thienz were telepaths; what one saw, all demons within the fortress would share in the space of a thought. The Kielmark must know that enemy reinforcements could be expected at any moment. Jaric decided their only chance of escape lay through his powers of Earthmastery. He strode forward and drew his sword.

The wards flared active and rinsed the corridor with orange light. "Fall back!" the Firelord called to his companion. In another moment the fullness of his powers could be focused. Jaric fused his awareness with the stone, prepared to seal the passage against the enemy.

But the Kielmark paid no heed. Sword angled at the ready, he beckoned to the Thienz on the stair. "C'mon, spawn of malformed lizards. In remembrance of Corley's companies, it's time to visit the butcher."

Jaric felt the hair prickle at the nape of his neck. Demons would attack the mind before they closed with the perils of steel, and against telepathic compulsion, none but Taen Dreamweaver could offer any protection. Urgently he shouted to the Kielmark, "My Lord, stand clear."

The sovereign of Cliffhaven turned a deaf ear. Since the demons could not be provoked into rushing him, he advanced instead upon the stair.

"No!" Jaric's warning echoed the length of the corridor. The wards of his sword point flared red, available for instantaneous defense, yet all of his Vaerish training availed nothing; he could not strike with a friend blocking him from the enemy. Left no other alternative, he cursed the Kielmark's belligerence and started forward himself.

The Thienz attacked.

One instant, the Kielmark filled his lungs to bellow as he charged. The next, the Thienz invaded his mind in force and damped the fury of his assault. His great sword clanged down, the edge shearing sparks against the granite stair. His hands lost their power to grip and his body to move. As if in slow motion, Jaric saw the Kielmark's stride falter. His knees buckled. Then, snarling, the Thienz of Shadowfane fell upon him.

Running now, Jaric leveled his own sword. He loosed his mastery, and fire stabbed forth, a needle of killing force that seared the air as it passed. The nearest of the Pirate Lord's attackers flared up in a flash of flame. It recoiled and rolled over and over down the stair while its companion squalled in reaction to its pain. Jaric leaped over its dying struggles. Other demons whirled at his approach. Gimlet eyes flashed in the ward light. Frog-wide mouths gaped open and exposed wicked, back-curving fangs glistening with drops of black venom; Jaric felt the sting of Thienz hatred, still more dangerous than poison, permeate his thoughts. Already the demons centered upon his mind. In a second, he would share the Kielmark's fate, as the enemy grappled his awareness with the insane compulsion to collapse the protection of his wards.

Failure was certain. Braced against hope to resist, Jaric squinted through the glare of his sorceries. Past the struggling knot of Thienz, he stove to locate the Kielmark. Not a glimpse of clothing met his search. Through wheeling shadows and the close-packed bodies of enemies, he saw no trace of a living human.

Despair sparked an anger that knew no limit. Jaric raised his sword. He would incinerate Thienz to white ashes. Yet before he could act, a bull bellow emerged from the thick of the fray. The attacking demons heaved up, and a glistening red line cleaved their midst. A gilled head rolled and bounced down the stair, followed immediately by the flopping corpse of its owner. Another body tumbled, nearly severed in half, and then another, cleaved through shoulder and neck. Jaric heard a sailor's blasphemy. Then the struggling Thienz parted like knotwork before the stroke of the Kielmark's sword.

Jaric jumped also to avoid that singing edge. No enemy lunged to strike him. Surprise momentarily left the demons without any wits to act. Perhaps the Firelord's sorcery had distracted their concentration enough to create an opening; or maybe their victim's will had never been entirely subdued. Taen Dreamweaver had found the Kielmark's mind a chaos of unbiddable madness when he indulged in his killing rages. For the Thienz, the mistake proved fatal. The sword cut left, right, and left again, leaving a wake of carnage. In retaliation for the companies destroyed with Corley's brigantine, *Moonless,* the Kielmark was bent on slaughter. Even as the demons realized their quarry could not be managed, half their number lay fallen, bloody and dying.

The ringleader squealed in panic. It and its fellows spun to quit the stair, but Jaric blocked their retreat. From both directions, the Thienz charged headlong into a wall of living flame. Their screams deafened thought as they burned. Smoke choked the corridor, foul with the reek of charred flesh. The Firelord bent coughing over the hot white metal of his sword.

The flames died swiftly. Jaric straightened, blinking stinging eyes. Through the smoke-dimmed glimmer of his wards he saw his companion cast about for more enemies. Nothing stirred in the passage but the twitching of a dozen butchered corpses; the Kielmark's teeth flashed in a grin of satisfaction. He raised his huge sword, pinched the blade in the crook of his elbow, and drew the steel clean on his shirt sleeve.

"Damned toads." He kicked a smoking corpse from underfoot, then moved to rejoin Jaric.

The irrepressible swagger in his stride touched off overwhelming relief. The Firelord resisted a weak-kneed impulse to sit down. As his companion reached his side, he said, "You're a madman." His hands shook as he damped the wards, then rammed his own sword home in its scabbard. "No good would be gained if you got yourself killed."

The Kielmark's smile died like a doused candle. "The stinking reptiles are dead, aren't they?"

Speechless, Jaric wiped his palms. Quite wisely he chose not to belabor the point that every Thienz cousin within mind-reach would shortly descend upon Shadowfane's dungeons, maddened as a stirred swarm of wasps. Rather than precipitate trouble, he touched the Kielmark's wrist and indicated the nearest of the iron-barred doors that opened on both sides of the passage.

The Kielmark balked with a sound of contempt. "You mean to hole us up in a prison cell? That's bad strategy, sorcerer. Where do you think you'll steer us next when the head jailer shows up with the key?"

Jaric never paused, but pressed his hands to the iron face of the door lock. "I'll tunnel through rock, if I must. Have you a better suggestion?" He frowned. His fingers flared blue; there followed a click, then the grate of a tumbler turning.

The Kielmark set his shoulder to wood studded and reinforced with strips of corroded steel. "None. Unless your spell-working could conjure me a flask of spirits?"

"Spirits?" Jaric shook his head in astonishment; and the Kielmark heaved. The hinges groaned and gave with a pattering of rust flakes. The panel swung inward, tearing through dusty nets of cobweb. Jaric sneezed violently. He peered into the darkness beyond, then distastefully crossed the threshold. "You always go drinking after battles, is that it?"

The Kielmark raised his brows. Drily he said, "This time I intended the stuff for medicine."

Jaric paused, aware by earth-sense that a stairway lay ahead. It wound upward, doubled, and let onto a pillared gallery where fetters dangled over moldering heaps of bones. The Firelord's blood ran cold, not only for the human wretches who had died of Shadowfane's unnamed tortures. As his companion's laconic phrase fully registered, he said, "You didn't get yourself Thienz bitten, did you?"

"No. Just clawed and stuck like a lady's pincushion." The Kielmark pulled the door to and paused. A minute passed while both of them listened. Sounds of running feet echoed through the grille from the corridor they had just left. Already more demons came hunting.

Jaric spun around without comment. He slipped past his companion and set hands to wood, steel, and the rust-marked stone of the lintel. Faint halos traced his form as he engaged Earthmastery and sealed the doorway.

"We still might get visitors from the rear," observed the Kielmark.

"We shouldn't." Jaric batted cobwebs from his hair. "I've checked. This stairway leads to a cul-de-sac."

Blank-faced, the Lord of Cliffhaven sheathed his great sword. "I see." He blotted at a cut on his jaw. "From the fireside, and straight into the soup. We're fair put to swimming now."

Earthmastery could carve a retreat, create a passageway to any place in Shadowfane's dungeons that Jaric might choose. Yet no time remained to discuss options. A gabble arose in the corridor, most likely in lament for the slaughtered Thienz. Seconds later, illumination speared through the crack beneath the door, cast by a lantern shuttered with scarlet glass. Evidently more than Thienz came hunting. Seldom did they carry lights; with their poor eyesight, they relied more on scent to find their way.

The Kielmark held motionless by instinct, the breath stopped in his throat. Jaric waited, sweating, until the light spun away and faded. Even then he held his mind blank, and prayed his companion had insight enough to do the same. The demons of Shadowfane held advantage over human trackers; they could locate a man by his thoughts.

Minutes passed. No further disturbance arose beyond the door. Jaric touched the Kielmark's shoulder, sticky with blood that might as easily be an enemy's as discharge from an open wound. Forced by priority to defer his concern, the Firelord delivered the gentlest of tugs and started forward. Silent, wary of every movement, the fugitives retreated toward the stair. Earth-sense guided Jaric's steps; he led the Kielmark as he would the blind, picking the easiest path and directing the man's feet by touch. All the while he kept his awareness tuned on the corridor beyond the sealed door, where the faintest vibrations through stone warned that a sentry still paced. One sound, a single chance blunder in the dark, and pursuit would be upon them.

For the Kielmark, who owned no sorcerer's awareness, the ascent of the stair seemed interminable. The landings switched back, or turned in convolutions without pattern; no logic dictated the distances in between. At the top, Jaric had to tap his companion twice, to assure that no further levels remained.

At least now they might have light without risk of discovery. Jaric conjured fire and set it adrift to reveal their surroundings. They stood in a gallery. Pillars carved in the shapes of malformed animals supported a ceiling cut from the natural rock of the cavern. The walls were undressed stone, strangely in contrast to floors checkered with squares of polished agate.

"Looks like a Telshire whorehouse," observed the Kielmark. But the rusted sets of fetters robbed his remark of humor. Affixed by chains heavy enough to moor ships, each pair dangled from rings pinned immovably to the pillars. Heaped beneath lay pathetic clutters of human remains, most bearing marks of abuse. "Funny place to keep captives, I say."

The dead victims of demons had not been disturbed by rats, nor had beetles nested among the half-rotted remnants of clothing. For no reason the Firelord could name, the absence of natural scavengers made his flesh creep. He ended his survey only when doubly assured that the gallery contained no exits, or so much as a spyhole in the wall.

Jaric chose not to voice apprehension, but faced his companion, and with steady eyes assessed the wounds inflicted by the Thienz. The Kielmark's linen shirt lay in shreds, stiffened and dark with blood. Between the rents were long, shallow gashes that had barely begun to clot. Gauntlets had protected his forearms; his boots and leggings had suffered scars, but the flesh beneath was unharmed.

"No bites," Jaric concluded, relieved the damage had not been worse. "You're lucky." Once he had suffered from Thienz venom. The experience was a horror he wished he could forget.

The Kielmark shrugged somewhat stiffly and changed the subject. "Luck won't recover the advantage. What did you have in mind?"

Jaric looked down, and noticed that somewhere through the ascent of the stair he had bloodied his own knuckles. The scrape was minor; but it stung with a fierceness out of all proportion to reality just when his attention was needed for planning. The Firelord drew a forced breath. "First let me set safeguards."

He had none of Taen's ability to shield the mind directly from attack. But as Earthmaster he could fashion illusion, cloak their living presence with the ponderous essence of stone, or the still dark of soil without life. Carefully Jaric wrought wards, that demons who hunted human thoughts might sense only the empty deeps, and pass onward without pause for investigation.

Once the defenses about the gallery were stabilized, Jaric and the Kielmark attended the unfortunates who had died of demon cruelty. In wordless accord, they burned the bones, and whatever pathetic rags remained to differentiate between individuals, not because the gallery lacked warmth or light, but to restore some dignity to the dead. The smoke of the pyre stung their eyes and made them cough, but neither one offered complaint. They rinsed their mouths from the water flask in the pack, but drank sparingly, for the chamber had no amenities. After that, both sorcerer and Kielmark chose to rest before moving on. Now the demon pursuit would be hottest. Later, when Shadowfane's sentries were weary, and the hunters forced to extend their search over a wider area, the chance of stealing forth unseen might be improved.

There followed an interval in which Jaric tried to sleep, but suffered miserably from nightmares. Not far from him, the Kielmark sat with his back to a corbel, methodically heating his dagger in the mage-fire left burning for light. To prevent infection, he pressed the hot steel to one wound at a time, and in the process acquired a frown that even Corley would not have challenged. If his hand trembled by the time he finished, throughout his doctoring he had uttered no word except an imprecation against sorcerers who achieved mastery without learning to conjure spirits. "Nicer by far on the nerves, and a swallow or two goes a helluva long way toward knocking the edge off the pain."

Jaric made no reply. Having been rebuffed at dagger point earlier when he offered to cleanse the wounds with Firemastery, he pretended to doze with closed eyes. The Kielmark charred his blade clean in the fire, then spat on the steel until it cooled enough to sheath. Too uncomfortable to lie down, the sovereign Lord of Cliffhaven eventually slept where he sat, his head tipped back against stone, and his knuckles loose on his sword hilt.

The next time Jaric checked with his earth-sense, the sun had arisen over the fells. Winds made brisk by autumn frost moaned around the spires of Shadowfane, sharply in contrast to the air within the gallery, which hung still as a sealed tomb. The Firelord ignored the hunger that cramped his belly. He struggled to contain the deeper longing left by a certain Dreamweaver whose path took her leagues to the south. Love for Taen could do nothing but make him ache, with demons quartering every cranny of the dungeons for the humans who had invaded their stronghold. Earth-sense could occasionally discern the pattern of the search, here by the slap of webbed feet as a party of scouting Thienz turned a corner, and there by the boom of a grate grounding against bedrock.

The demons persisted with a thoroughness that was both alien and frightening. Unable to know how readily his awareness might be traced through the stone that he probed, Jaric used sorcery with caution. He explored only caverns and stairs that seemed empty, while, with laborious precision, the Kielmark used ash to map his findings on a square of linen shirt garnered at need from their pack.

Their makeshift floor plan of the dungeons stood barely half-complete when Jaric encountered what he sought, a cell with living prisoners whose limbs were chained to rock. Though unable to divine awareness, as Taen did, his mastery could differentiate subtleties with great detail. Steel set to use as fetters absorbed the warmth of the body, and the stone floor immediately beneath sang with the queer, crystalline resonance of Sathid in the process of bonding.

"I've found them," Jaric announced. He opened his eyes, to a look from the Kielmark that made his flesh prickle. The man sat coiled, a hairsbreadth removed from unbiddable violence. Gently the Firelord tapped the map. "Here. The children stolen by Shadowfane's compact have been closed in a cell by this vent shaft." He paused and carefully added, "There appear to be six of them. I fear we're too late for rescue."

"We can end their misery, then." Single-mindedly impatient, the Kielmark consulted his chart. "And we can be sure no others suffer the same abuse, but we have to get there first. Can you guess where demons might store the Llondelei Sathid?"

Jaric forced speech. The fetters sensed through his mastery had been fashioned for wrists that were heartbreakingly small. "On the level below the cell confining the children, there's a double-sealed door that appears to secure an apothecary. I sensed shelves of wood, and rows of things stored in stoppered glass; drugs, mostly, and minerals. But among them I found a rack woven out of vines that never grew in Keithland's soil, with sealed containers inside. That's where I'd look for the Sathid."

The Kielmark nodded. As he folded his charcoal chart, his blue eyes flicked up to meet Jaric's. "Can you get us there?"

"I'll have to." The Firelord dusted ash from his fingers and rose swiftly. Trouble was imminent. The dull sense of pain beginning at the back of his head was not the effect of fatigue. Shadowfane's demons had discovered the sealed cell. As they sounded the chamber beyond for intruders, the touch of their probe against his wards caused an ache that mounted with each passing minute.

"We have visitors." Jaric motioned the Kielmark to his feet, then strode across the gallery and placed his palms against the far wall. "Set your hands on my shoulders," he instructed. "Whatever happens, keep them there. If you lose your grip, you'll end up entombed in solid rock."

The Kielmark complied without visible hesitation. "Better thank Kor for the fact I don't get jumpy in tunnels." Yet this once his bluster hid bravado. When he took hold of the Firelord, his fingers bit deeply into fabric, and his breathing went shallow and fast.

Whether the Lord of Pirates' unease stemmed from the confinement about to be imposed by earth sorcery, or the fact that, with both hands occupied, he could carry no unsheathed sword, Jaric dared not ask. Compelled by a rising sense of urgency, he engaged his mastery at once.

The air around him seemed to shimmer. Light struck the stone wall with a flash like reflection off mirror glass. The Kielmark squinted against the glare, and felt Jaric move under his hands.

He stepped forward, braced instinctively for a collision that never came. Though his senses insisted that he walked into solid rock, no barrier obstructed his body. Pirate King and Firelord moved unimpeded into a gap fashioned spontaneously by sorcery. A blister of air moved with them, charged with dry heat like storm winds swept across desert.

The Kielmark stole a look back. Behind, the gallery had vanished, replaced by a stone face that showed neither flaw nor fissure. Veins of quartz and the flash of mica flowed together at his heels, as if at each stride the sorcerer who led him traversed through matter in the midst of a moving bubble. The effort required to achieve such a wonder belied understanding.

Newly aware of the sweat that dampened the shirt beneath his grip, the Kielmark looked nervously upon the sorcerer responsible. "You know where you're going?"

Jaric did not answer. Absorbed in the workings of his art, he moved one foot, then the next, in carefully unbroken rhythm. Light flared from his raised palms, and at his command the rock parted, smoothly, soundlessly, insubstantial as a lifting curtain.

Though the effect might seem effortless, passage through the deeps of Shadowfane did not come without cost. In time, the air grew stale. The Kielmark noticed a quiver in the flesh beneath his hands. Until now mechanically even, Jaric's steps became unsteady and slow; the rock gave way before him sluggishly as syrup thickened by cold. Still the Firelord pressed on. His skin grew clammy with exertion. The power discharged from his person grew uneven, flaring like wind-torn candles into searing spatters of sparks.

At length Jaric stopped entirely. The stone before him rippled into solidity, hard and impenetrable as always, leaving the two of them within a sealed compartment of air. He rubbed his face with his hands and, in a voice muffled through his fingers, said "You can let go."

The Kielmark allowed his hands to fall. Sweating in the closeness of the stone, he gripped his sword and grimly awaited admission of trouble. The Firelord seemed taxed more than sorcery alone should warrant.

Jaric spun around quite suddenly. "We're being flanked." By the fire glow he maintained for illumination, exhaustion lay printed like bruises beneath his lashes. His hair curled damp at his temples, and his eyes shone fever-bright. "I've found demons waiting each place I've tried to emerge. Maybe they sense the currents of my conjuring. The reason doesn't matter. Quite soon we're going to run out of air."

"Overextend your resources, and we'll be trapped." The Kielmark fingered his blade. "I'd rather go fighting than get trapped like a fossil."

Jaric closed his eyes. He pulled himself together with painfully visible effort, and did not add that the working of his Earthmastery seemed strangely difficult in this place. Whether that complication was also the work of demons, only Anskiere with his years of experience might have told. Shaking in fear of final failure, the Firelord strove for steadiness. "Getting cut to ribbons by Thienz won't spare the children, or recover the Llondelei Sathid."

"Neither will suffocating in what amounts to a bubble of rock." Vexed, and disturbed by the first warning signs of dizziness, Cliffhaven's Lord jerked his head at the stone that sealed them in. "Bring us out, and quickly. Debate will do nothing but weaken our chances."

In the eerie glow of the mage fire, the Kielmark showed spirit unblunted by regret or apprehension. His hair in its linen band hung limp with sweat. He had discarded his ruined shirt; long, scabbed gashes from yesterday's battle grooved his shoulders. Still he seemed a wolf on a fresh scent, vengeance for his slaughtered companies a thorn that needled him endlessly to action. His ice-pale eyes gleamed with an anger only killing could assuage.

Jaric regarded his hands, shaking now with weariness and nerves. Never a fighter, and a sorcerer only with reluctance, he found his own wants more complex. Taen and the Cycle of Fire had taught him the value of perseverance, and Tamlin of the Vaere had sworn him to a service not lightly put aside. He was not ready yet, to settle on a recourse that could only end in death. Though weariness dragged at his nerves, and his powers as Firelord seemed less than adequate for the task, he tuned his awareness to rock and sent forth another probe.

The cell that confined the children was guarded now; Jaric knew by the whisper of air currents that eddied over stone as demon sentries paced through their term of watch. The apothecary beneath had been rigged as a snare, for the wooden shelves there resonated like sounding boards with the queer vibrations of wardspells. In every corridor, every likely cranny his earth-sense could detect, Ivainson Firelord read movement against the earth, the restless steps of scores of prowling enemies.

Desperate, he turned downward, toward the natural caverns that riddled the strata beneath Shadowfane. Most lay too far to be of use; but deep, at the end of a narrow tunnel, he encountered stillness. There lay a grotto submerged in silence so profound he could sense the settling of dust. No trace of demon presence lurked in wait to trap them. Resolutely Jaric focused his mastery. He bade the Kielmark to set hands to his shoulders once more. Then the heir of Ivain Firelord mustered his will and bored downward into earth on the chance the two of them might reach a haven to recover strength and regroup.

CHAPTER XVII

Ambush

The stone dissolved in a rain of sparks. Too spent to arrange an entry with more finesse, Jaric stumbled into the narrow passage which sloped downward toward the grotto. A half-step on his heels came the Kielmark. Dizzy and starved for air, at first the two of them could do nothing but stoop and gasp awkwardly for breath.

No demons appeared to challenge them. The place was dark and smelled of dust, to all appearances empty. Yet as equilibrium returned, Jaric felt the hair on his arms prickle with uneasiness. He could not escape the feeling that somehow their presence had been noted.

The Kielmark's instincts were aroused also. "Kor damn me for a fool if we aren't being watched." Quiet as a threat, he eased his great sword from the scabbard and rested the point against the floor.

Jaric damped his breathing with an effort. He sounded the dark with his Earthmastery, but encountered nothing untoward. The emptiness that had seemed a promise of safety now rasped at his nerves like dissonance. A feeling that waxed more insistent by the minute urged him not to linger. "We can't stay here."

The Kielmark shifted his weight to a soft grate of steel on granite. "Are you thinking of turning tail and holing up in the wild caves? If so, your reasons better be grand, sorcerer. Backtracking sticks in my craw, and no toad-faced pack of demons is enough to sweeten cowardice."

Striving for Corley's casual exasperation, Jaric raised his brows. "Every toad-faced pack of demons between you and those captive children is hoping you'll think just that. Do you always seek thrills by dangling your hide out as bait?"

A chuckle echoed drily through the passage. "Sorcerer, until demons learn not to murder Cliffhaven's companies, I'll split lizard heads until my dying moment. By the sword my mother forged, I swear I'll have your balls before I go belly down through more rock to avoid them."

"Your *mother* made that sword?" Jaric grinned in disbelief. "My ears hurt."

"You saying I'm a liar?" But the rest of the Kielmark's rejoinder died unspoken. From the hole left by Jaric's conjuring came the sound of furtive scraping.

The Kielmark recoiled from the wall. His steel whined through air as he whirled to face the disturbance. "Mothers bedamned, sorcerer, you'd better make me a light to fight by."

Fire bloomed against blackness. Jaric raised his palm, and lit the passage in a spill of raw gold. Shadows danced grotesquely over walls of water-smoothed stone. Against the natural contours, the depression left over from their retreat by Earthmastery gleamed smooth as the inner dome of an egg.

"It's still sealed," said the Firelord.

"For how long?" The Kielmark flexed his upper arms and shoulders, and shifted to the balls of his toes.

The scraping grew louder. Like sand grains before an avalanche, part of the spell-smoothed surface crumbled away. A fissure parted in the rock.

"Back," cried the Kielmark. He slammed Jaric clear with his forearm and, in wildly wheeling light, raised his sword. "Fires alone know how, but Kor's Accursed have followed us."

"Through *stone*?" The achievement should have been impossible. Bruised from the blow that had spun him toward safety, Jaric raised Earthmastery. Even as he tried to probe the nature of the breach, more sand rattled from the crack; there followed a bouncing rain of pebbles. A claw pried through. Beyond the opening rose bloodthirsty howls of impatience.

Pressed to the wall, the Kielmark braced himself at the ready. His eyes went feral with eagerness.

Jaric felt his hackles rise. He set his mind to seal the stone, or, if that failed, to sear the opening with fire and trap the enemy inside. But this time he did not face routine sentries. The fissure widened. A demon that was narrow and spined like a lizard thrust its head through the gap. As a force more dangerous than Thienz compulsion slammed Jaric's mind, he perceived the scope of his peril. This creature he faced had somehow fathomed his mastery; while he had cut his escape portal from the gallery, the adepts of Shadowfane's compact had tapped his unguarded thoughts and managed to draw from his resources, even past the shielding properties of stone. Purloined power had enabled them to replicate earth-sense and track him.

The demons' grasp upon the principles of Vaerish sorceries was shallow, yet if they found means to build upon the rudiments of rock-shifting, they might achieve the release of both frostwargs and Mharg. Keithland's dangers now lay redoubled.

"We're in trouble," Jaric whispered.

The Kielmark acknowledged with a slight jerk of his head. Then the lead demon leered in triumph. The last of the barrier crumbled away as dust. As the creature leapt through, a murder-bent horde of followers pressed toward the breach.

Jaric dared not strike. Though he held the full command of his Firemastery coiled to engage in defense, demons had tapped his talents for their own use. Until he divined how, and took precautions, the chance existed that Shadowfane's minions might also rip power from his mind, turning his own energies against him, even as they had the earth-powers that had enabled his passage through rock.

The Kielmark understood the complications. Savage as a cornered beast, he roared out to the Firelord behind. "Go back! Close the stone as you leave!" His sword never wavered. Light splintered on the edge angled to slash the attackers who charged in waves down the corridor.

The moment held all the horror of nightmare, yet retreat offered no recourse. Jaric sounded his inner self, frantic with fear, and saw that the demons' first efforts at borrowing upon the effects of his Earthmastery were crudely managed. They had succeeded only because he had been unaware.

Guarded now, he raised a ward against invasion, then jerked enchanted steel from his scabbard. The triplicate aura of his Firelord's defenses burnished the passage with glare, far too late to escape. Even had he been willing to abandon the Kielmark to peril, in the lighted entrance to the grotto at his back lurked row upon row of glowing eyes. Jaric made out the spidery forms of Gierj, ink against darkness, and pressing slowly toward him.

Their whistle rose painfully shrill in the enclosed space. Trusting the presence of steel to foil their attack, Jaric ignored them in favor of the demons who threatened his companion.

The Kielmark jerked a knife from his boot top. "Save yourself, sorcerer! Flee!" His shoulders bunched, as demons of every shape and description launched at him from the gap.

An Earthmaster could engage power, mesh his own being inseparably with the matrix of the rock; this might foil the enemy indefinitely, but only another sorcerer capable of mind-link could partner such a course. The Kielmark would be doomed. Uncomplaisant, Jaric raised fire.

The Kielmark felt heat stripe his side as he slashed. His sword bit deep into flesh. The demon in the lead tumbled against his boot, sliced nearly in half. Blood streaked the Kielmark's leggings and splashed lurid spatters on the wall. As he kicked the floundering corpse into the press of living adversaries, a fireball screamed past his elbow. In the moment while demon flesh charred, he glanced back and saw Jaric had disregarded his instructions. He also noticed the Gierj pack, whose whistle shrilled toward the upper registers where their power normally peaked. The presence of steel no longer appeared to deter them; even if Jaric sealed off the gap, attack might continue from behind.

Anger suffused the Kielmark's features. "Kor curse your loyalty, boy! *Get clear of this!* Taen asked that I keep you safe, and I swore her an oath of debt."

In the passage, demons hurdled the bones of charred comrades. Cliffhaven's sovereign spun to meet their charge. The blades in his hands arced around and gutted the front ranks. Spiny lizard forms tumbled and

writhed in their death agonies. Those Thienz mixed among them collapsed, scrabbling webbed hands and screaming. Ones behind tried to
grapple the Kielmark's mind to keep him from killing. Their attempt tangled ineffectively in fear and rage, and crazed determination. They might
sooner stay a cyclone with threads than apply compulsion against madness.

The Kielmark glanced aside and again saw that Jaric had not fled. His
exasperated curse became lost in the snarls of enemies. In a decision that
could be neither predicted nor reversed, he abandoned the security of the
wall. He leaped the bodies of the slain like a berserker who craved death,
and plunged slashing into the horde of assailants in the passage.

Jaric shouted. "No! Kor's grace, no!" Then despair canceled speech.
To summon fire would sear friend and foe alike. Helpless, Ivainson
watched the sword rise once, then twice, steel drenched crimson with
blood. Then the black hair with its simple twist of linen disappeared,
pulled under by claws and ravening fangs.

Jaric swore. Grief could not eclipse understanding; the Kielmark had
made no pointless gesture of braggadocio. He had bought his own
destruction deliberately, his purpose to sever the Firelord's responsibility
for his life. Beyond the horrid tearing of flesh, and the resonant whistle
of the Gierj, his words seemed yet to ring through the caverns of Shadowfane: *"Taen asked that I keep you safe, and I swore her an oath of debt."*

Wild with sorrow, Jaric could not believe that the imposing vitality of
the man was quenched forever; that scarred and toughened captains would
sweat no more under the scrutiny of blue eyes whose keen perception
could measure merit and shortcomings at a glance. The Firelord raised his
powers, but not to seek refuge within earth. Instead, in a single discharge,
he unleashed the latent forces of his sword.

Sorcery screamed forth, indomitable as volcanic eruption. The hordes
of Kor's Accursed had no chance to react. Fire flashed, blinding-bright,
and blasted stone instantaneously to lava. The gap in the passage crumpled
with a roar like hurricane surf. Snared in a holocaust, the murdering horde
of demons flared incandescent as lint. Bone, flesh, and sinew, they and the
corpse of their victim became immolated within the space of a second.
Through a spill of uncontrollable tears, Jaric beheld the brief white outline
of a sword. Then the arched ceiling of the passage collapsed. Gripping the
charred twist of metal his own blade had become, he evoked mastery to
shift earth.

But no powers answered. Force lashed out of nowhere, and pinched
off his talents like so many flickering candles. Jaric spun, seeking fresh
targets. He found himself surrounded by Gierj. With a horrid, jolting
shock, he realized his steel no longer worked to inhibit their powers. In
the grotto beyond, the circle of silence he had mistaken for emptiness in
fact masked Shadowfane's ultimate peril. Too late, he perceived the stillness for what it actually was: he had stumbled unwittingly upon the
warded lair of the Morrigierj. No opportunity remained to flee before the

whistle of its Gierjlings crested and sundered thought. Mortal consciousness crumpled before a venomous onslaught of pain, and Jaric tumbled
downward into dark.

Ivainson Firelord slowly recovered awareness, to hurt and guttural syllables of speech. Too stupefied to distinguish words, he stirred. The sour
chink of fetters shocked him fully awake. Memory returned, of a passage
where the Kielmark had leaped to his death. Jaric flinched. Harrowed by
loss, he opened his eyes to a bloody wash of light.

The voice continued, echoing within stone walls. "Look you, he is
moving. Did I not say the Morrigierj and its minions struck him lightly?"

Jaric blinked, unable to distinguish the speaker from the shadows. The
bonds of his wrists were forged, not of metal, but of a substance of glassy
hardness that shimmered with wardspells. Glare prevented his pupils from
adjusting.

A hiss like a stoppered kettle sounded from the opposite side. "Foolish
toad! Only that ruined lump of sword steel spared his life. Had the Morrigierj's defense reflex killed, all plans would have been spoiled."

Jaric realized with a chill that the language was unfamiliar; comprehension arose from the demons' touch within his mind. Close proximity
apparently forced a link with his captors similar to Taen's dream-sense. At
present Ivainson had no strength to resist. His flesh stung with abrasions;
Kor's Accursed had dragged him, perhaps by the cutting edges of his
fetters, for his wrists burned unmercifully. Worse, his Firemastery would
not answer; somehow demons had impaired his powers of sorcery. A furious attempt to force the ward restricting him brought pain that stopped
his breath.

"Your manling grows restless," observed the first demon. "Best you
subdue him while he is disoriented and plaint, or he may do as his companion, and destroy his own life to keep honor."

The second demon laughed. Claws scratched lightly over stone, and a
spurred foot prodded the prone body of the Firelord. "You speak as if he
is a threat! And what harm could he do, even to himself, with his limbs
bound and his powers under ward? Still, get him up. Then summon the
Thienz pawns who will cross-link the Firelord's Sathid-bond."

Jaric recovered his wind with a hoarse cry. He made a determined
effort, and managed to prop himself on one elbow before blurred vision
overcame him. Clinging to consciousness, he heard a rattling clank of
metal. Drafts raked his body, followed by the slap of many feet on stone.
Small, tough hands grasped his tunic and hauled him upright before a
trestle topped with a marble slab.

Relieved from the blinding effects of his fetters, Jaric viewed a chamber packed with the squat forms of Thienz, and other demons whose
shapes he did not recognize. A lantern dangled from a length of chain
overhead; at the boundary of light and shadow sat the reptilian Scait,

resplendent in gems set in wire and a mantle of purple plumes. Jaric was startled by his size, for the Lord of Shadowfane rose no more than shoulder-high to a grown man. Yet he poised himself with the muscled quickness of a lizard. Hungry eyes searched his captive, while spurred fingers stroked the handle of a short, sharp knife over and over, as a lover might caress a woman.

"How very timely of you to summon fire so near the chamber that grows the Morrigierj," said Scait in the tongue of Keithland. His tone held honeyed satisfaction. The most promising talent among the human children had died that morning, too frail and too young to endure the rigors of Sathid-bond. But in Jaric the compact had acquired a better victim. The Demon Lord bared teeth, and qualified. "That made your downfall swift, and inevitable. But you were doomed long before you trespassed within Shadowfane. Like Marlson Emien, and before him Merya Tathagres, you have been chosen to serve."

Jaric searched for a response, but defeat sapped the nerve for defiance. No words came to mind; only the image of Taen weeping over the ravaged body of her brother. Dizzied, numb, and sick with weakness, he caught the trestle for support. Stone jarred his fingers. He barely felt the shove as packs of Thienz froze him upright.

Demon speech came and went in his ears. Through fragmented phrases, bits of thought-image, and ragged patches of vision, Jaric saw a Thienz hand Scait a dark chunk of crystal. He recognized the same matrix that was the foundation of a Sathid-master's powers, and suddenly divined Shadowfane's intent. Dread made him blurt his horror aloud. "You mean to impose a demon-controlled Sathid upon me, and overthrow my mastery of fire and earth?" Outrage cleared his senses; he straightened in his singed tunic, and glared at the Demon Lord's scaled visage.

Scait smiled, his plumes dancing with magenta highlights in the red-paned light of the lantern. Thienz rustled in the corners, impatient for the moment when one of their own would partner the Firelord's overthrow.

Hotly Jaric protested. "You'll never control the result. Tamlin of the Vaere already tried to train men to mastery of tripled Sathid crystals. Each time he created a monster."

Scait rasped serrated teeth and tossed the contaminated matrix from palm to palm. "Monster? If by that your mythical name for Set-Nav defined a creature dedicated to destruction, nothing less would suit the compact's purpose. Our method is assured. The human mind fares poorly in multiple bonding because it is isolated. But the Thienz whose crystal cross-links with yours can achieve dominance without harm, since thousands of Sathid-free siblings will shelter its psyche from madness."

Jaric took a firmer grip on the table. Blond hair slipped forward, veiling the fury in his eyes. He heard Scait's premise and felt cold, for his fate at the hands of demons now redoubled the threat to those children left living in captivity. If the secrets of his masteries provided the final key to their survival as demon pawns, Keithland's destruction could no longer be prevented. Eyes closed in the agony of failure, the Firelord hoped the Thienz who pressed at his sides mistook his trembling for weakness. In a useless effort to buy time, he grasped after a tangent. "Set-Nav? You claim the Vaere hides a machine?"

Scait fielded the crystal, set it gently down on marble, then laced spurred fingers over his knife. "Shortly you will verify that. But the spoils of your discovery shall benefit Shadowfane."

Mute as he considered implications, Jaric wished he had obeyed the Kielmark's directive to flee while the chance had existed. Now escape of any sort was impossible. The chamber's only entrance was secured by a studded door and a clumsy mechanism of counterweights and chain.

The Demon Lord rose. Feathers rustled like whispers as he swung the hook suspending the lantern closer to the wall. Shadows shifted to reveal shelves jammed with bottled elixirs and tins of dried herbs. Among them rested a row of flasks, filled with clear fluid and cradled in a rack of woven vine. Jaric recognized the intricate craftwork of the Llondelei; and irony stung like a thorn. The very Sathid he had entered Shadowfane to steal would engineer his doom and Keithland's final conquest. Jaric drew an angry breath and bore down on the support of the Thienz until the pair of them squealed in complaint.

"Lord-mightiest, he faints!"

Scait hissed his displeasure. "Conscious or not, hold him upright." The Demon Lord selected the nearest of the flasks and released the hook. The lantern swung in drunken circles overhead; alternately flicked by shadow and light, he set his blade to the seal and slashed. Yellow eyes flashed briefly at Jaric. Then Scait took the slave crystal from the trestle and dropped it in the flask with a click. The contents churned as if alive, and a Thienz huddled in the pack cried out.

Jaric swayed. Desperate in his weakness, he watched the liquid in the flask settle and darken to amber. The change recalled a Llondelei thought-image shared on the night he and the Kielmark had set off for Shadowfane from Morbrith: *'You will know pure matrix from that enslaved by demons, for bonding turns the color like wine.'* The matrix within the flask had now melded inseparably with the Thienz-dominated crystal. A single drop in the blood-stream would initiate cross-link, and slavery more ruinous than Emien's.

Scait dipped the dagger to the hilt in the flask and waspishly addressed his underlings. "Hold him. Misery to you all if your hold slips."

The Thienz seemed small, even laughably ungainly; but their strength proved more than a man's. They caught Jaric's fetters and pinioned his arms against the marble. The vulnerable lines of human tendon and bone stood exposed in scarlet light. The blade poised above, dripping and deadly with Sathid solution already under demon domination.

Scait struck downward to cut.

"No!" Jaric twisted; fetters flashed like sparks as he jerked aside. The dagger missed flesh by a hairsbreadth and screeched across stone. Scait cursed, even as the Firelord slammed against the trestle. The flask overturned, splashing the floor with amber liquid. Wooden bracing chattered across tile as the ponderous slabtop slid and rammed the Demon Lord's midriff against hard edges of shelving behind. Tins and crockery rocked while Scait rebounded in rage. Jaric ducked the spurred swipe of the demon's fist. He dove for the elixir untouched in the rack behind, his intent to end the misuse of the Llondelei crystals forever.

Thienz sprang to restrain. Toad fingers snatched at linen and broke the impetus of Jaric's lunge. He sprawled sideways, hand outstretched. Sickness and the interference of his captors caused him to miscalculate; instead of sweeping the flasks from the shelf, to topple and spill and maybe contaminate the Thienz whose solution already puddled the tile, the Firelord crashed headlong in their midst. Glassware shattered. Edges like razors cut deep into his hands, and wrists, and forearms. Fluid deadly with unbonded Sathid seeped into open wounds.

Jaric screamed. Tamlin's care had spared him the pain of first contact through the cycle of bonding on the Isle of the Vaere. At Shadowfane, alone, he endured an excruciating tingle of nerves as multiple Sathid coursed through his flesh. His senses blurred; smell, and sound, and light milled under by fiery agony. Jaric heard snatches of a Thienz's hysterical screech; then Scait, in cold fury, calling out, "Don't touch! He'll crosslink, you father-licking fools! The wards binding his Firemastery will give way through multiple bonding and wild Sathid could overwhelm you all."

Chain rattled, followed by the boom of a door. Jaric thrashed on cold stone. His features gleamed, sweating in the glow of enchanted fetters, while two score untamed Sathid threaded rapidly through his consciousness. He began vividly to dream.

But where the progression of Vaere-trained masteries had been orderly, a logical sequence of images as Sathid assimilated experiences from infancy to adulthood, the present experience was chaotic. Each entity had a separate will, and all sought dominance over the others; Jaric felt his mind torn to fragments as Sathid awareness ransacked memory, fighting to establish parallel consciousness with the being whose body they invaded. Scenes formed, only to splinter, overturned by a bewildering and irrational succession of images. Jaric saw snowfall in Seitforest, beeches and evergreens cloaked in mantles of purest white; in a hollow between two deadfalls, Telemark shook ice from his cape and knelt to set snares for fox. The scene had scarcely stabilized when winter vanished. Fire and wind ripped the trees without warning, and sparks blew like driven lines through darkness. The forester swung his axe; sweat and grit and tears marred features racked by grief, but there memory distorted. Telemark checked in mid-swing, breaking the precision of his stroke. His blade bit earth with a thud, and fire faded before the scent of living greenery.

"Jaric?" Cleansed of tears and filth, Telemark's face furrowed with worry. "Jaric, are you all right?"

This query was not borrowed from the past. The words echoed, as if the forester spoke in the very chamber where his former apprentice lay stricken. Even as Ivainson framed answer, the Sathid jostled his mind. Telemark's presence ripped cruelly out of reach. Gale winds screamed and slashed whitecaps into spindrift. The stormy roar of breakers filled Jaric's ears. *Callinde*'s steering oar yanked blistered hands, even as Anskiere's geas tore his heart and mind toward madness; salt spray drenched his shoulders and salt tears wet his face. Then, like glass frosted with moisture, that image also faded, overlaid by the ward-bound silence of the ice cliffs.

The Stormwarden of Elrinfaer called out of darkness, his tone terrible with command. "Ivainson Jaric! What's happened?"

But that voice became lost as a great sword rose, sheened with blood in the shadowy deeps of Shadowfane. Helplessly the Firelord watched the blade fall, never to rise again. Cliffhaven's Kielmark whispered, his anger subdued to purest sorrow. *"Taen asked that I keep you safe, and I swore her an oath of debt."*

Grief caught Jaric like a blow. He wept, and the image buckled, replaced by the smoky vista of stars once revealed by the Llondelei in dreams; but this time the velvet dark where the probe ship *Corinne Dane* had sailed was slashed by fiery lines of lettering. Words that once had been strange and meaningless now were uncannily clear: *"With the Veriset-Nav unit lost in the crash, no ship can find the way back to Starhope. . . . Will our children's children ever know their forefathers ruled the stars?"*

Jaric wondered who would leave such a message, hidden in the spine of a book for a scribe to find generations afterward; as if at his command the writing faded, replaced by the face of a man with tired eyes and close-cropped gray hair. His clothing was blue, trimmed with silver in the fashion of Kordane's priests, but cut from no cloth woven on Keithland. As Ivainson puzzled over the anomaly, the image vanished. Multiple Sathid scrambled to displace their fellows, and for a moment no entity dominated.

Jaric gasped for breath. He assimilated the reality of sweat-stung eyes and muscles knotted from contortions before dreams overwhelmed him once again. Colors swirled through his mind, overlaid by light that pooled and focused. He found himself helpless under the malevolent glare of Scait Demon Lord. A Firelord in captivity repeated a phrase he had uttered only minutes before coherency left him: *'Set-Nav? You claim the Vaere hides a machine?'*

Prone on cold tile, his cheek pressed into the hard edges of his fetters, Jaric poised on the brink of vital revelation. But the crazed turmoil of the Sathid left no interval for thought or interpretation. Drowned in a flux of memory, he stepped barefoot onto sand. Sunlight warmed his body like a lover, and the spicy scent of cedar filled the air. Ivainson blinked. Touched by awe, he recognized a place whose uncanny perfection never failed to move him.

Bells jingled, merrily at odds with a voice raised in reprimand. "Ivain-son Jaric! Firelord's heir! Stand and face me."

Shocked as if plunged in cold water, Jaric whirled and met Tamlin of the Vaere. This encounter was no memory; the clamor of the Sathid receded as cleanly as a knife pulled through cloth. Drawn into stillness beyond human understanding, Jaric lost his last hope of rescue.

The gaze of the Vaere bored into him as if fey eyes could murder. "Young Master, you've transgressed mortal limits. That's trouble. No resource of mine, nor any endowment of Corinne Dane's can spare you now."

Whipped by a shiver beyond his means to subdue, Jaric regarded his teacher across the boundaries of dream. "I had no choice."

The Vaere stamped as though vexed. Poignant sorrow touched his face, half-glimpsed as he turned away. "Then understand me, Firelord's heir. I, too, have no choice. Remember that, when you face the consequences."

The querulous, leather-clad being wavered, its origin traced by an Earthmaster's perception to a form that defied all belief. Buried beneath soil and sand, Jaric saw an angular engine crafted of metal. The structure of its surface was scarred, as if from terrible impact; and energies cycled endlessly on the inside, marked by blinking patterns of light. 'I am the master of space and time,' whispered Tamlin's voice from the past. Llondelei references aligned with other words spoken by demons, to reveal a terrible truth. Jaric identified the engine as the source of Tamlin's identity: Veriset-Nav, the lost guidance system of Corinne Dane. With a jolt of wonder and fear, he realized he had disclosed the secret of the Vaere; but so, also, had demons. The heritage of mankind stood in jeopardy as never before.

Light danced as Jaric fought his fetters. Cut by the glassy stuff of spells, his wrists bled, and he cursed. The image of the machine reshaped, became a white square of parchment upon which he practiced letters. Ink stained his knuckles. The draft through the rickety north casement raised chills on his back as, sharply attentive, Morbrith's master scribe reviewed his work.

"You know the smiths thought me too stupid to keep accounts," said a younger, more diffident boy. "Why did you take me in?"

Master Iveg peered over his spectacles, his large-knuckled hands hooked loosely over his knees. "Sure, I don't know, Jaric." He grinned, affectionate as an old hound. "Your butt's so skinny, I doubt you can even warm the bench for me, come winter. Now fix those T's. They lean like a hillman's tent poles."

The kindliness of his criticism had made Jaric smile on the day he began study under the archivist. But now, with the bonds of Shadowfane constricting his flesh, and his mind lashed to delirium by wild Sathid, he cried out. Library and copy table vanished. The old scribe's voice broke into screams of agony; aged limbs jerked against wire as demons roasted him alive in a furnace of flaming books.

Jaric thrashed, retching, his wrists pressed hard to his ears. Discrepancy pricked through his torment. He coughed, tear-blinded, and remembered: he had not been present when Iveg died. The scene he currently witnessed was drawn not from past recollection but from the altered awareness of the Sathid-link itself. Ivainson explored, and discovered his perception expanded to awesome proportions. The events of past, present, and a multiple array of futures were accessible to him simultaneously. Revelation followed, bright with new hope. Mastery of fire and earth might be shackled by demon wards, but resources acquired through bonding with two score wild crystals were not. Possibly a blow could be struck against Shadowfane before the cycle of the Sathid destroyed his will.

Jaric marshaled his stiffened body. With a gasp of tortured effort, he rolled onto his back. Sweat dripped like tears down his temples, trickled through hair to pool in his ears. Dizziness flooded his mind. Queasy and whimpering and hounded by fragments of nightmare, he glimpsed Taen's distraught and weeping face. The image of her sorrow shattered thought, just as the door to the chamber boomed open.

Footsteps and voices approached, deafeningly immediate after the dream-whirl of images.

". . . must be destroyed," hissed Scait in a monotone. Spurs grated horribly against metal. "His powers are useless to us now. Even the Watcher cannot predict what befalls when wild Sathid conquer a mind that has mastered the Cycle of Fire."

Through eyes muddled by fever, Jaric saw a sword flash red by lanternlight. Rage stung him. He would be killed with no more resistance than a beast raised for slaughter; in the moment the blade sliced downward, two score Sathid shared his perception of threat. Their competitive tumult ceased, instantaneously melded to focused and biddable force. Jaric recovered power to act, even as steel stabbed a searing line of agony through his chest.

CHAPTER XVIII

Shadowfane

Black tents clustered like clumped mushrooms upon the slopes between the town and the inner fortress of Cliffhaven. As dusk fell, lanterns flickered and swung from the twisted limbs of the almond trees, while darkrobed conjurers conferred in groups beneath. To Taen, who overlooked the scene from the harborside battlement, the gathering looked like a hilltribes' summerfair gone eerily silent without music. The arrival of the Mhored Karan wizards had been her doing, and Anskiere's; despite the fact that the conclave's differences of ability had just place in the scheme of Keithland's defense, she looked upon her accomplishment and felt no confidence.

The presence of the conjurers made itself felt in strange ways. The wards they established to enforce the reality that formed the foundation for their creed ran counter to Vaerish sorcery. Proximity to their encampment tended to inhibit the workings of dream-sense; still, Taen sensed that something, somewhere, went amiss. Against all logic, the feeling persisted. The spells of the Mhored Karan conjurers were no part of the cause, but only the foil for an apprehension Taen had no name for.

The air above Mainstrait hung unnaturally still. Over the crack of shipwrights' mallets, the Dreamweaver heard footsteps approaching from the postern. She lifted her head and saw Deison Corley stride toward her, his hair tangled with pitch and his brows leveled in an uncharacteristic frown.

"You know," he said as he drew alongside, "I'm going to get spitted on a shark gaff for this." He gestured toward the tents, and Taen understood he referred to the Kielmark's vociferous hatred of the wizards and their secretive conjury. The subject had sparked wild speculation among the men; wagers were on that Corley would lose his command, at the least, and just as likely, his head.

The Dreamweaver returned a sympathetic smile. "You speak as if you had a choice in the matter. You didn't, as I remember, unless you wanted to watch Anskiere call storm and scuttle every brigantine in the harbor."

Corley leaned on the battlement beside her. "Threats cut no cloth with the Pirate Lord." He paused, irritable, and rubbed to ease the unfamiliar weight of the torque at his neck. Below, boys in the gray robes of acolytes continued to kindle lanterns until the trees glittered like an opium eater's dream of exotic, night-blooming flowers. Yet the captain left in command at Cliffhaven found no beauty in the sight. "To the Kielmark, wizards are trouble, the sort that invariably leads to bloodshed."

His remark brought no reply. A herd of goats bleated in the shadow below the wall, and afterglow shed light as flat as beaten metal on the waters of the harbor. The sounds and the view seemed oddly, inappropriately ordinary. Taen stared unseeing into distance. As if hooked by a crosscurrent of thought, she murmured something concerning an oath of debt that was too quiet to be quite understood.

Corley's hackles prickled. "What?"

"He won't be shedding any man's blood. Not ever again." And as if slapped into waking awareness, Taen suddenly flinched. Her face drained utterly of color. "Kor's grace, it's Shadowfane. The Kielmark—" Her eyes widened in shock.

Corley caught her hard by the shoulders. "What about the Kielmark?" His fingers bit, unwittingly harsh, and wrinkled her linen robe.

Taen shivered. "He's dead." Her words seemed unreal. The event they described should have been beyond the pale of any Dreamweaver's insight. The Kielmark's demise had happened in the dungeons of Shadowfane, deep under rock where no Vaere-trained talent should reach. Chilled through, Taen knew of no natural way she could pick up echoes of the tragedy.

Yet the vision had come to her, hard-edged in its clarity. Taen had no chance to fear, that an absolute of Vaerish law had been unequivocally overturned. The immediacy of Corley's grief overwhelmed her sensitivity and canceled the contact.

The captain drew Taen close to offer comfort. The act became motion without meaning. The weight of the ruby torque bore heavily as a curse about his neck. He fumbled after words to ask what had happened, but his mind refused acceptance. Deprived the challenge of the Kielmark's explosive character, the future seemed brotherless and empty.

Below the walls, the lanterns of the wizards tossed gently in the wind. Corley shut his eyes as their lights splintered to rainbows through his tears. "Bad luck," he said thickly. "Any sailor knows. Talk about storms at sea, and they come. I should never have agreed when the man left his rubies on the table."

The captain's voice seemed almost detached, but Taen Dreamweaver heard beyond control to a core of blighting anguish. "Your Lord always intended to come back."

A man stopped the Kielmark at his peril, once his mind had been set; Deison Corley knew this, and was silent. His hands convulsed upon the cloth of Taen's shift. The wizards' lamps shone too bright beneath the walls. To escape their brilliance, the captain raised his gaze to the ships' masts in the harbor. "Just tell me one thing. For the sake of his final peace, and the lives lost at Morbrith, did the great foolish hero take any demons with him?"

Beyond speech, Taen Dreamweaver managed a nod.

Corley's fingers slackened slightly, though the tension coiled within him gave not at all. "My Lord would have cursed like a cheated whore, but after twisting the tail of the compact, he'd have to agree. Shadowfane's vengeance is bound to be brutal and swift. I was right to let wizards ashore on Cliffhaven."

Taen had nothing to add. She regarded the camp of the wizards, terrified to fathom the source that had touched her. All too likely, through some dangerous and unseen turn of events, the vision had come through the man who lay dearest to her heart. The son of Ivain Firelord would now be alone, and in immeasurable peril.

Night deepened over the harbor, and the air took on a bite that warned of winter. Deison Corley stirred, finally, and guided Taen firmly from the wall. "Let us go in out of the darkness. Anskiere will need to be told."

"He already knows." The Dreamweaver struggled to explain what should never have happened; her powers by themselves held no means to breach stone. Whatever force had lent her news of the Kielmark's end boded no good. Suddenly her body stiffened. Without warning she doubled over with a harrowing scream, her hands pressed tight to her chest.

Corley caught her. "Taen?" She gave no sign she had heard. "Taen, answer—is it Jaric?"

The Dreamweaver's eyes clenched shut with agony. Though her lungs felt transfixed by pain, she managed a tortured affirmation.

Corley cradled her against his chest, then sprang at once to a run. Foreboding lodged like sheared metal in his gut. He dispatched the nearest guard to fetch the Stormwarden to the Kielmark's study. Then, as an afterthought, he shouted back over the wall and demanded the presence of the Magelord of Mhored Kara. If that ancient and crotchety person did not hurry his old bones to share counsel, the successor to the Kielmark's command swore under his breath that he'd spit the old conjurer on a shark gaff.

Jaric screamed, a high-pitched cry of shock and despair that did not quite mask the scrape of blade against bone, nor the grate of steel on stone as the sword pierced through his flesh and jarred unyieldingly into tile. A flood of warm fluid gagged his throat. *Dying*, he thought resentfully; pain left no space for fear. Yellow eyes flared in darkness as Scait Demon Lord flexed his wrists to clear his blade.

Jaric coughed in agony. His hands spasmed in their fetters. Beyond the reflexes of mortal pain, he knew fury so focused his vision seemed seared with light. Unaffected by the wards blocking his Firemastery, the Sathid entities within him retaliated. Skeins of energy ripped up the swordblade and exploded with a terrible cracking flash. Scait was flung backward, spurred fingers clenched to his weapons. The steel pulled free with a horrible, sucking jerk. Jaric arched, mouth opened to scream. But ruined flesh framed no sound; his awareness splintered into a thousand spangles of fire. Scait collapsed on the floor beside him, cut down without chance for a death-dream.

Yet the Demon Lord's end did not satiate. The rage-roused tide of wild Sathid reached around the torment of Jaric's chest wound and ransacked his memories for facts. In a flash their awareness encompassed the massacres that had decimated Elrinfaer, Tierl Enneth, and Morbrith. Polarized to immediate revelation, the crystalline entities perceived the demon compact as a threat. Their clamorous bid for survival meshed with Jaric's own cry for vengeance, not least for the theft of human young and the entrapment that had destroyed Marlson Emien.

Even as Ivainson Jaric thrashed in the throes of dying, hysterical packs of Thienz sensed the stir of wild Sathid within his mind. They backed away from the corpse of their overlord, and stampeded in terror from the chamber. However frantically they barred the door, neither flight nor steel locks could save them. The fading spark of the Firelord's awareness charged two score Sathid to a rage like unleashed chaos. Jaric allowed the current to take him. Even as death dimmed his thoughts, power more intense than any he had initiated as Firelord surged forth. The Thienz who scuttled through the corridor were obliterated in a searing flash. No outcry marked their passing. Neither did the Sathid subside.

Instead they fused with his hatred. One terrible instant showed Jaric the passions that had twisted and ruined his father. He had discovered in full measure the lust in his desire to destroy. Capacity for power touched off a heady joy. His enemies would fear him as they perished. One breath ahead of oblivion, Jaric embraced the poisonous euphoria of vengeance. The Sathid within him responded.

Dizzied by a rush of expanded perception, Ivainson sensed the citadel of Shadowfane in its entirety, every warren and passageway and convoluted maze of stairwells; lightning-swift, cruel with excitement, the killing powers of his anger coursed outward. From deepest dungeon to the spindled eaves of the keeps, every cranny became seared with unbearable light. All that lived perished instantly. The eggs of Karas shape-changers scorched to dust in their sacs, and Thienz died wailing. The great hall of the council chamber entombed Scait's advisors, favorites and enemies alike immolated to drifts of ash; between one moment and the next, the mirror pool reflected an empty throne, and a sooty arch of vaulting.

Deep beneath the storerooms, in a grotto that opened onto a corridor of fire-slagged stone, a warded circle of stillness remained untouched. Alone of the demons of Shadowfane, the Morrigierj and its underlings escaped the Sathid's cyclone of destruction. Jaric could do nothing in remedy. Bleeding, cold, and abandoned, he had no resource left. His last thread of self-awareness slipped inexorably downward into night, as he battled, and failed, and lost consciousness. Motionless alongside a corpse whose spurred fingers clamped the grip of a bloody sword, Ivainson Firelord stopped breathing.

Yet the bindings of his spirit did not loosen.

Alien energies coursed through his body, pinching off blood flow to ease his labored heart, and mending with speed and sureness no surgeon could have matched. Being self-aware and psionic, the will of the combined Sathid could unriddle the mysteries of nature in an instant. While the damage inflicted by sword steel sapped life, their collective awareness diverted to the knitting of bone and sinew and organs.

One Sathid, two, even three could not have cheated death; but Jaric bore the seeds of two score entities. Each one constituted an exponential increase in power, the sum of which approached the infinite. The echoing clangor of the chain and counterweights that dead Thienz had used to secure his tomb had scarcely faded from hearing when his chest shuddered into motion. Breath wheezed through torn tissues. Life endured, precarious as candle flame winnowed by draft.

Hours flowed into days; Jaric drifted on the borderline of death. At times, his skin glimmered blue, as the resources of crystalline entities lent him energy to survive. Later, fever raged, and he thrashed in delirium. Dreams gave rise to nightmares as, inescapably, the cycle of bonding continued.

Days became weeks. Jaric's condition stabilized. Sathid attended the needs of his body and mind, and at length encountered the wards restraining his mastery of fire and earth. The crystals challenged, displacing the patterns of the spells. Enchanted fetters flickered on lax wrists. Dimmed as coals in ashes, the bindings of sorcery faded; and two score wild Sathid encountered the quiescent presence of their own kind. Innate obsession for dominance drove them to meld.

As their energies roused and interlocked with the crystals of Vaerish origin, the cycle granted an interval of reprieve. Jaric opened his eyes to darkness thick as felt. He shuddered and breathed, and immediately choked, overpowered by the stench of corrupted flesh. Dizzied, he wet his lips with his tongue; then he flinched, recalling Scait and the sword that should have ended his life. A frown marred his brow. He raised scabbed wrists, and by the absence of illumination recognized the collapse of the demons' wards. Though Firemastery might answer his will once more, he dared raise no light. On that point, Tamlin's teaching had been explicit. To engage Sathid-based sorcery while bonding additional crystals could only hasten disaster.

Jaric sat up. His own rasping breath and the chink of spent bonds echoed loudly in the dark as he crossed his hands on his knees. His mind seemed suspiciously lucid. Certain the passive state of the Sathid could not last, Jaric tightened the muscles of his forearms and jerked. The links connecting the cuffs of his fetters gave way with a sound like breaking glass. Grateful for even that small freedom, Ivainson rubbed his abraded skin. Then a presence touched his mind, insistent, familiar, and gentle enough to break his heart.

'Jaric?'

The Firelord stiffened. Wary and alone in his misery, he presumed the call was illusion; the chamber of his prison was still sealed, and no Vaere-trained Dreamweaver could breach the barrier of stone. Well might the Sathid indulge in such tricks to torment him. But the touch came again. Undone by longing, he surrendered himself. The reality of Taen's presence embraced him, warm and immediate as sunlight. Yet the reunion yielded little joy; wild Sathid coiled to observe, patient and deadly as a nest of adders. The Dreamweaver sensed their presence with a cry of dismay. *'Ivainson, beloved, what have they done?'*

Defenses parted. Jaric beheld a cherished face framed in black hair. He tried words. But the knotty mass of scar tissue left by Scait's sword obstructed his voice, and he barely managed to croak. "Little witch, if life were just, I should have died before you found me."

'Sathid, Jaric. Demons infected you with crystals?'

"Not exactly." He qualified with incriminating brevity. "Scait tired to place my mastery in bondage through a matrix cross-linked to a Thienz. I avoided the same fate as Emien, but only by contaminating myself to the point where Kor's Accursed dared not meddle." Ivainson swallowed painfully and finished. "Scait perished. The compact died with him, but the Llondelei should know. Their store of stolen matrix can never be recovered."

A disturbance eddied the dream-link. Taen's image diminished, and the sealed chamber at Shadowfane seemed suddenly, intolerably desolate. Jaric sensed echoes. Shivering, his eyes flooded shamelessly with tears, he waited while the Dreamweaver pleaded with someone far distant. Then, poignant with distress, she sent an abbreviated farewell, *'Jaric, I love you. Never, ever forget.'*

Her warmth faded sharply away. Savaged by loss, Jaric struggled to recover composure, even as a voice of uncompromising command snapped across the dream-link. *'Ivainson Jaric!'* Wind eddied the chamber, fresh as frost amid the miasma of decay; through discomfort and despair slashed the presence of Anskiere of Elrinfaer.

Unnerved by failure, Jaric shrank but could not evade contact. The Stormwarden appeared, straight and tall before the windswept arch of Cliffhaven's watchtower. Cloaked in cloud-gray velvet, he stood with his staff propped in the crook of one elbow; breeze off the sea ruffled his white hair. His eyes were lowered, sorrowfully regarding a pair of amber crystals in his palm. Chilled to the heart, Jaric recognized the jewels that founded his mastery of fire and earth.

Brass-shod wood grated gently on stone as the Stormwarden turned. *'You are doomed.'* He gazed into the haze of the horizon; so long had Jaric known darkness that the vision of ocean and sky and sunlight that filled his mind seemed unreal. At length Anskiere qualified. *'Tamlin of the Vaere warned you. No help and no hope remain. Have you strength enough to keep loyalty to your race, or do you need assistance?'*

The gravity of the plea overshadowed all else; for the safety of Keithland, the Stormwarden required Jaric to take his life before wild Sathid
overturned his mastery and brought disaster upon mankind. The request
was not made lightly. The crystals cupped in Anskiere's hand were no
longer coldly neutral but warmed by conflicting energies. Even as the
Stormwarden awaited answer, wild Sathid sensed threat to their numbers.
In a flash of shared awareness, they stirred their bonded counterparts
toward rebellion.

Ivainson needed no urging to perceive the gravity of his predicament.
He laced scarred fingers together, tightening his grip until his knuckles
went numb. He had effectively died once. A second time should not prove
unendurable, except that Scait's fatality thwarted all hope of simplicity.
Impeded by scars and uncertainty, Jaric strove to relate how intervention
by wild Sathid had healed a sword wound of fatal proportions. He might
take courage into his hands, run himself through with a blade, yet still
survive the result. Words would not come. The dizzy whirl of Sathid-
sickness defeated concentration, and his struggle to frame speech went
unnoticed.

Anskiere spun from the window with his brows forbiddingly lowered.
'Firelord! You swore me an oath, that day beneath the ice cliffs. Dare you break faith?'

The accusation cut like a lash. Jaric knew pain, then anger, that his
sincerity still stood in question. He ignored the suspicion that wild Sathid
tuned his emotions for their own gain, and returned a look wholly his
father's. "Do you doubt my word?"

Anskiere did not speak, but lifted his hand so Jaric could see; the
crystals he held glowed red. Provoked by the rigors of bonding, their
surface flared hot enough to blister. Yet the Stormwarden's least concern
was the pain. At any moment the structure of the matrix would collapse,
unleashing hostile energies no human could withstand. Before then, for
the safety of humanity, the man who had mastered them must die.

Sweat sprang at Jaric's temples. His anger transformed to raw desperation, for steel no longer held power to kill him. If he consented to the
grace of a mercy stroke, even one fashioned by sorcery, disaster might
follow. His executioner might provoke wild Sathid to the same defensive
reaction that had slain Scait and every demon in the compact. Ivainson
forced his ruined throat to frame speech. "Your Grace, there is danger in
my death."

'More than this?' Anskiere opened his fist. Ruby light speared the chamber; with a sudden, searing spark, the crystals burst raggedly into flame.

Powerless to bridle the blaze of his own mastery, Jaric shouted frantic
affirmation. No chance remained to explain. Wild Sathid whirled his
thoughts like wind devils. Through rising curtains of fire, he saw Anskiere
tumble both crystals of mastery across the sill. Unseen to one side, Taen
shouted a useless plea concerning conjury and the wizards of Mhored
Kara. The Stormwarden returned a look of anguish. Sorrowfully he shook

his head. No magic in Keithland could spare the life of her love. Pitiless as an autumn storm front, Anskiere of Elrinfaer caught his staff in blistered fingers. Defense wards activated with a blinding shimmer of light.

"No!" Ivainson raised his hands, as if the gesture might somehow span ocean and avert the staff's descent; by Vaerish law, the destruction of a sorcerer's matrix would kill with swift finality. The wild Sathid were aware. Jaric cried warning, not for himself, but in agonized concern for the lands and the people under the Stormwarden's protection. "Prince, you and all you defend are in danger!"

The protest emerged as a whisper that had no chance to be heard.

Isolated by brightening veils of power, Anskiere prepared to obliterate the crystals on the sill. Necessity compelled him to wall away sympathy for the boy he had called from Morbrith Keep, who had suffered the Cycle of Fire and won a Stormwarden's freedom from the ice cliffs, only to be judged and slain in the comfortless dark of Shadowfane. No sorcerer held power to change destiny or reverse the command of the Vaere. For the sake of mankind's survival, the Stormwarden repressed awareness of private tragedy, the impact of which was cruel enough to deter him. Later, when Keithland's safety was secured, the ghost of Ivainson Jaric would join the dead of Elrinfaer, and Morbrith, and Corlin, until one day the sorrows of guilt and responsibility became too heavy to endure.

Jaric screamed in a rage of futility.

And the staff struck.

A note parted the air like a slashed harpstring. Jaric suffered a blow that rocked the seat of his being. He crashed on his back, winded, paralyzed, blind, and deafened, while the fires in the crystals at Cliffhaven extinguished like water-drowned sparks. All mastery of power sundered instantly.

Yet like a curse, life endured.

"No," Jaric whispered. His body seemed a husk sucked hollow by torrents of wind as two score wild Sathid marshaled force to retaliate.

In vain he tried to resist, to smother the cataclysm of ruin that earlier had destroyed the demons. His effort was swept aside by pain that thrilled and a joy that sickened him to experience. An insatiable lust for cruelty was now permanently instilled in the Sathid's collective memory. No act of reprisal could unmake the forces his rejection of principle had created. Jaric cried out in agonized recognition. Too well he understood the downfall of Marlson Emien; too late he begged for remission. His plea might as easily have reversed the flood of the tides.

Anskiere sensed the surge as power aligned against him. Undone by memory of a second betrayal, he cried out, "Ivain! By Kor's grace, not again!" White with recognition, he angled his staff toward the window, as if some miracle wrested from the sea might save him.

No evasion could bridle the untamed Sathid's attack. Energy cracked forth, virulent as summer lightning, and hammered against the Stormwarden's defense.

For an astonishing moment, he held out. Jaric sensed a reflection of the stresses Anskiere withstood through long years of experience and a persistence born of ruthless desperation. Yet courage could not avert the inevitable. The pressure of the wild Sathid lashed sparks from the wards. The Stormwarden called warning to Taen, then slammed his staff horizontal. Energies snapped and sang. His defenses crumpled, instantaneously obliterated by a shattering explosion of light. The powers of the Sathid whirled away Jaric's view of Stormwarden, tower, and ocean in a blazing coruscation of energy no sorcerer could hope to survive.

Jaric howled denial. The enormity of the wild Sathid's retaliation inflicted a burden too terrible to bear. As the rage of crystalline entities milled the last of his reason to slivers, he thought he heard Taen weeping. The sound pierced his soul. If the cycle of destruction took her life, her Dreamweaver's intuition might never unlock understanding that he had never intended betrayal of Keithland for Shadowfane when the Sathid's powers of defense struck Anskiere down.

The backlash did not end with the Stormwarden's fall. Worse than the darkest nightmare, Sathid entities redoubled their ferocity. Utterly helpless to intervene, Jaric thrashed as surge after surge of force arose from the depths of his being. Blame could not be attributed to the crystals' willful nature. They had melded with his mind, molded their earliest awareness from him. Jaric's own passion for vengeance had schooled the Sathid to murder. That humanity might share the fate of Shadowfane's compact as a result left guilt that could never be assuaged. No ward ever raised by Tamlin's masters could thwart such fury from destruction; the heir of Ivain Firelord could do nothing but endure through the evil his weakness had created until the storm of the backlash was exhausted.

In time the riptide of cataclysm faded; like spent ripples on the surface of a pond, all settled finally to stillness. The Sathid entities retired, their focus of fearful energies centered once more upon the drive to mature and dominate.

Ivainson Jaric was left to the prison of his thoughts, and horror too grievous to escape. Firelord no longer, he raged, broken and damned by fate. Misery acquired new meaning, and its edge cut deep; still braceleted with the husks of Scait's fetters, he smashed his fists into stone. Over and over in his mind he saw his view of the Stormwarden cut off by energies no sorcerer could withstand. Hope perished also. A forester's wisdom, an old fisherman's gift of a boat, and a master scribe's kindness no longer held power to inspire. Jaric covered his face with bleeding fingers. Possessed by despair near to madness, he wept in understanding of the father he had never met.

Ivain Firelord had inflicted ruin as wanton as this. Gone to the Vaere a laughing, generous man, his hope of serving Keithland fresh as morning, he had suffered the Cycle of Fire, then yielded up integrity to survive. He also had seen all that he valued come to grief. Finally, poisoned by self-loathing, torment, and loneliness, he had died by his own hand.

Abandoned in confinement at Shadowfane, Jaric drew a shuddering breath. Like the tortured soul who had sired him, he had nothing left in Keithland to lose. Close by, the corpse of the Demon Lord lay with a sword still clenched in its fist. Jaric rolled onto his side, fingers outstretched and groping. But two score Sathid divined his intent. Secure in their bid for conquest, they lashed out collectively to prevent him.

Pain mauled his body, more intense than anything he had endured through the Cycle of Fire. Jaric convulsed, whimpering until his lungs emptied. Wretched with agony, he sought refuge within his mind. But the flare and spark of alien energies pursued him even there and denied him sanctuary. Sathid arose in force to break his spirit, swiftly, violently, and forever. No vestige of will would survive their final assault. Death itself would become irrevocably beyond reach.

Jaric reacted on reflex. Although the foundations of Fire- and Earth-mastery were destroyed, exhaustive hours of training left their mark. Experience handling Sathid forces had long since fused with primal instinct; and rage lent the strength of a beast snared in a trap. Ivainson twisted, and slashed, and boldly singled one entity from the composite mass of its fellows. The move touched off an avalanche of reaction.

In instantaneous awakening, Jaric shared every scrap of knowledge gleaned and stored by the matrix. His mind expanded, assimilating web upon web of structured information. He perceived the workings of his physical body in minute detail, comprehended a miraculous capacity to heal; perception doubled, then doubled again in the dizzy change of a moment. Beyond muscle and bone and organs, he saw the helical chains of matter that encoded the secrets of life. The web work of energies that comprised mastery and emotion stood revealed, and he saw in himself nearly limitless reserves he had never tapped.

Jarred by revelation, Jaric pushed to his knees. The Sathid possessed keys to the riddles of fire and earth, taken intact from memory. The entity that emerged supreme after bonding could re-create every aspect of his Vaere-trained talents, but with near-infinite power.

Wakened as never before to the perils of possibility, Ivainson saw in himself a potential more ruthless than any mad quirk of his father's. Anskiere's death had taught him remorse; now his matrix-born potential for evil canceled temptation to engage in a struggle no mortal could win. On the chance, however slim, that isolated humans might survive, the judgment of the Vaere must stand. Even as Sathid-force poised to smash his will to oblivion, Ivainson delved inward. Inspired by new knowledge, he seized the spark of awareness that was his life and, in defiance of the wild crystals' sovereignty, claimed the initiative to unbind the threads of his existence. Warp and weft, he found a way to negate the fabric of his spirit as thoroughly as if he had never been born.

His strike caught the Sathid unprepared. The primary mortal instincts of survival had conditioned the assumption he would not violate selfhood and seek immolation from within; no healing of the body could stave off such a death. In a flurry of desperation, the Sathid pried at his resolve. Force proved counterproductive; Jaric's grip could be loosened only by precipitating the very end he desired. Nonbeing offered defeat more final than dominance. The Sathid floundered. Incapable of jeopardizing their own survival, there remained no further option. Jaric committed his will. As the spark of his selfhood flickered, the crystals reacted. Enraged in defeat, they yielded control, utterly, finally, and with a viciousness that ceded to Jaric a burgeoning nexus of power. The influx burned his senses beyond tolerance, and broke the progression of negation he had sacrificed all to achieve.

He screamed. Ripped into chaos in the shattering space of an instant, he struggled to cope; but crosscurrents of resonance flayed body and mind to tatters. Like a swimmer battered by undertow, Jaric strove to recover his wits. His eyes stung with light. Nerves sundered from bone and muscle, agonized by forces never meant for mortal endurance. No discipline taught by the Vaere could assimilate such a flux of energy; one after another the bastions of reason gave way.

Harrowed to the brink of madness, Jaric was driven to innovate. His Sathid-born inheritance superseded every former limit. The expanded prescience of his mind sorted futures and the branching avenues of event each possibility might take. From a million projections of disaster, Ivainson Jaric found and seized the one safe recourse left open to him. He resorted, in the end, to sorcery that violated every known law of creation.

Consciousness altered by Sathid recombined the basic patterns of matter; like metal smelted and reborn in the spark-shot heat of the forge, Jaric underwent change. No longer the sickly scribe from Morbrith, nor the Firelord taken captive at Shadowfane, he wove the composite energies of two score Sathid through the living essence of his body. He himself became the instrument that gathered, contained, and warded the near-infinite energies of new mastery. The result married flesh to a legacy of unimaginable power.

Victory left him exhausted. Sapped by sorrow and grief, and aching for Taen's lost trust, Ivainson Firelord cradled his head on crossed wrists. Too beaten to examine the miracle of his accomplishment, he closed swollen eyes and slept.

CHAPTER XIX

Starhope

Jaric woke to a golden blaze of light. He gasped. Certain that Thienz with lanterns had unsealed the chamber to do him harm, he pushed in panic to his feet. Movement brought vertigo. Braced unsteadily in one corner, the Firelord blinked and sought his enemies.

The trestle where Scait had threatened him canted against shelving; boxes and flasks and spilled bundles of herbs lay jumbled in dusty disarray. The lantern hung dark on its hook. On the floor, amid an eggshell sparkle of smashed flasks, the sprawled skeleton of the Demon Lord leered in death. Spurred and bony fingers still clenched the rusted grip of a sword. The doorway beyond stood sealed, its mechanism webbed over by spiders.

Jaric shut his eyes. He forced trembling muscles to relax, then carefully traced the illumination to its source. Power discharged from his body in a steady corona of light. The patterns in the aura were similar to those of a sorcerer's staff, but brighter, more intense, and complex beyond mortal comprehension. Jarred as if bedrock had shifted under his feet, Jaric recoiled against cold stone; the surrounding brilliance slivered through a blur of anguished tears.

He had changed. Only time would determine whether he had traded humanity for survival. Unwilling to sort ramifications, and afraid above all to contemplate the fate that had befallen Taen, Jaric immersed himself in the immediate.

Measured by dust and the decomposed stage of Scait's corpse, his mastery of the wild Sathid had spanned considerable time. Yet Ivainson knew neither thirst nor hunger. He surveyed his hands, found his wrists reduced to tendon and bone within the slack husks of his fetters. A white webwork of scars marred flesh that was pale, yet supple with health. Hunger, even thirst, had not touched him. Against all odds, he had survived; he wondered whether the folk of Keithland had fared as well.

The thought provoked a surge of clairvoyance; Jaric felt his mind turn like a mirror, reflecting a dizzy succession of images. Fallow after harvest, the fields at Felwaithe showed a herringbone stubble of cut corn; hill clanswomen beat clothes in the spume of Cael's Falls, and leather-clad herders drove weanling foals to Dunmoreland pastures. Ships offloaded baled wool at Landfast harbor, rigging like ink lines against wintry skies. Enveloped by consciousness of humanity's teeming complexity, Ivainson encountered no trace of Anskiere or Taen. His loss sparked awareness of others; at Cliffhaven, Corley paced the battlements, his black cloak of mourning whipped by changeable winds; at the captain's throat nestled the ruby torque that once had been the Kielmark's. Shared grief snapped the sequence.

Sheened with sweat, Ivainson Jaric gasped for breath in the musty confines of Shadowfane. Anskiere's sacrifice had not, after all, been in vain: to all appearances, Keithland had been spared the rage of the wild Sathid.

The reprieve was unexpected. Ivainson turned his face to the wall. Relief threatened his balance, and flood after flood of tears wet his cheeks. He did not weep only for release. Though his own powers of sorcery had inspired the visions, the scope and intensity of newfound awareness unnerved him. A considerable interval passed before he regained any semblance of control. Still more time elapsed before he dared to explore the source of the miracle that had preserved his land and people from destruction.

Trembling, more than distrustful of powers that bent his thoughts like a prism into focused arrows of force, Jaric directed his sight toward the watchtower at Cliffhaven. He sought the nightmare moment in the past when Anskiere of Elrinfaer had leveled his staff against the combined retaliation of two score wild Sathid.

The scene unfolded with damning clarity. Again the light bloomed with a brightness unendurable to the eyes. Like a stab to the heart, Jaric saw the sorcerer become enveloped by a raging tide of destruction. His Stormwarden's defenses were obliterated; the rough-hewn stone of the tower reddened with heat, then glazed in an explosion of force. Jaric compelled himself to watch as the blaze of the Sathid backlash coursed outward, hungry to destroy. His willpower threatened to fail him. Yet in the moment before he broke, the current turned inward upon itself, caught and twisted in check by the shadowy circle of a wardspell.

Joined in their unfathomable chants, the wizards of Mhored Kara fenced the tower with conjury that negated all resonance of Sathid power. From without they imposed the reality of unharmed tranquility that the killing backlash could not overwhelm. The wizards' philosophy provided the framework, Jaric saw. But the energies that set peace into harmony were familiar to the point of heartbreak, unmistakably lent by the hand of Taen Dreamweaver.

Keithland had been saved, but at a cost that wounded to behold.

In the comfortless dark of Shadowfane, Jaric slammed his fist into stone. Taen had divined the scope of the backlash the Sathid might unleash. Alone, betrayed, cut where love left her vulnerable, still she had mustered courage enough to act. As Anskiere had fallen, she had reached beyond heartache and achieved the salvation of Keithland.

The consequences of her sacrifice could not be escaped. Jaric suffered remorse without reprieve as wave after wave of power broke against the wizards' wards. Some robed figures rocked under the impact, others collapsed soundlessly in death, but the singing of their colleagues never faltered. The adepts of Mhored Kara held firm through the worst onslaught of destruction ever to challenge Keithland. Never once did they break either rhythm or concentration. Their defenses held. When at last the fury of backlash became spent, the watchtower at Cliffhaven remained, a slagged and smoking shell ringed by a charred expanse of paving.

The sorcerer who accounted himself responsible watched numbly while the wizards released their wards. Haggard, singed as scarecrows, the survivors of the conclave bent and tended their fallen. Jaric saw them bind the hurts of their wounded, then wash and bury their dead.

In the town, smoke rose from the chimneys of the craftsmen's shops. Ships rocked at anchor in the quay, and the sky shone an untouched blue; flocks of gulls squabbled undisturbed at the tide mark. From Felwaithe to the Free Isles, Keithland remained whole and in sunlight, as if no disturbance had threatened the continuity of life. Yet no wizard of Mhored Kara ventured across the blasted stone that marked the boundary of their protection. They did not set foot near the tower.

Neither, for all his awesome power, could Jaric. Pain stripped away his resolve; the memory of Taen's laughter would haunt him to the end of his days. Not miracles, nor breadth of vision, could lend courage enough to search amid the ruins for her remains, or meet the accusation in her eyes if by some twist of fate she had managed to survive. Anguish of spirit could never restore the trust Ivainson had taken oath to preserve. The fate of his father had at last become his own, canceling every hope he had ever dared to foster.

Left in bitterest debt, Jaric raised his face from his hands. He longed for nothing beyond forgetfulness. That being impossible, he buried his shame, abandoning all memory of the watchtower so that he could set his killer's instincts toward preserving what Anskiere had died to keep safe.

The danger posed by demons was not ended. Recalled to the peril of the Morrigierj, the son of Ivain Firelord bent his will away from the fortress at Cliffhaven. Empty with sorrow, he began a systematic review of Felwaith's north coast, which lay closest to Shadowfane, and most vulnerable to invasion.

At first glance nothing seemed amiss: winds whipped a reed-ridden channel to whitecaps, and a cutter flying the wolf of Cliffhaven scudded with her rail buried in spray. Jaric lingered in appreciation of her captain's bold seamanship, and power bucked his control. A subliminal suggestion of ruin suffused his inward eye, as if the tranquility of the bay with its rugged chain of isles were destined not to last. Jaric shivered. Touched by a clear note of dread, he hesitated; and prescience snapped all restraint. Visions of pending devastation came upon him in a virulence of Sathidborn perception.

The wind changed key. Ivainson heard the suck and thud of breakers fouled with debris. Smoke clogged his nostrils. Stumps thrust like rotted teeth from shores where, moments earlier, stands of pine had notched clean air and sunlight. The view shifted. Sea water scalded his hands, oceans sloshed with scorched fish; neglect laced runners of briar between the bones of cattle and men. South, the land was littered like storm wrack with razed towns. Roadways lay choked with toppled wagons, traces draped like knotwork over the shriveled corpses of oxen. Clansfolk rotted amid the crumpled wreckage of their tents, and the sunken masts of fishing fleets speared through the tide pools at Murieton. Cliffhaven's proud corsairs had smashed like eggshells on shore, and silent, foggy nights blanketed a beacon tower thrown down into rubble.

Sick at heart, Jaric turned to Landfast. Spires there lay tumbled like the sticks of a bird nest abandoned to winter. Waves combed vacant beaches, and the crabbed, uprooted apple trees of Telshire moldered like arthritic skeletons in dusty beds of soil. Spurred by distress, Ivainson quartered the length and breadth of Keithland. Desolation filled his vision. Not a man, woman, or child would survive the devastation to come. He recoiled in horror, hounded by prophecy, of the failure that had shattered him hideously made real. Energy cracked in white sparks around him as he dispersed his focus.

The dusty stillness of Shadowfane seemed suddenly unbearably confining. Ivainson Jaric pressed his cheek against stone and shuddered. The shadowed, sunken sockets of Scait's skull seemed to mock him from the floor. Though the compact itself was obliterated, the Morrigierj would complete the extinction of mankind. No Vaere-trained sorcerer remained for defense; the wizards of Mhored Kara possessed mettle, but little means to ward. Keithland stood open for conquest. Whipped to frenzy by their overlord, the Gierj might ravage and murder at will.

Shadowfane's stillness abruptly acquired overtones of menace. Jaric flexed scarred hands and pushed himself off from the wall. Light flared golden around his person as he pitched the force of his mastery against his prison door. Iron glared briefly red. Wood steamed, and counterweights trembled on their moorings. Then a high-pitched whine sliced the air. Planking and chain ripped apart, solidity scattered to a drifting billow of dust. Too concerned to be unsettled by the violence of his works, Jaric strode through, into a vaulted hallway where gargoyles leered from the cornices.

The light of his presence dissolved shadows from his path. Although the demon fortress was convoluted as a maze, expanded perception lent bearings. Jaric moved through passages of checkered agate, and turnings carved with runes. Slim as a wraith, and bathed in power, he sought the uncanny circle of stillness that harbored the source of all danger.

His steps reverberated through empty halls, unchallenged. Beyond a triad of hexagonal portals, he climbed the spiral staircase that pierced the inner core of Shadowfane. No demon emerged to battle him. Jaric heard nothing but the moan of wind through bleak towers; the expanded sensitivity of his mastery detected no life but the scurry of foraging mice.

The great hall of Shadowfane rose high above the level of the fells. Ivainson Firelord strode through the entry where Marlson Emien had once been dragged by the grasping fists of Thienz. No carpet remained to soften his footfalls. Shadowless amid the natural glow of his wards, he crossed an echoing expanse of marble. The chandeliers over his head hung dark on dusty chains; lancet windows outlined an overcast sky, and cloud light gleamed cold on the floors. The silvered surface of the mirror pool reflected the soaring lines of columns and a vacant expanse of dais. Scait's throne stood tenantless, a knife blade thrust through the leather of a human wrist.

Chilled to a halt by the sight, Jaric took a moment to sort the shadow ghosts of past events and recall the present. Scait Demon Lord could threaten humanity no more. Only dust remained of the compact that had hated and plotted vengeance through the centuries since *Corinne Dane*'s luckless wreck.

Yet through the emotional afterimage left by Kor's Accursed, Jaric's heightened senses picked up resonance of something stirring, the ruthless and alien force that lingered yet in Shadowfane's halls. His mouth went dry. Humans had been pawns in the demons' bid for power, yet the Morrigierj made no distinction. For the transgressions of Emien and Tathagres, who had manipulated and abused the Gierj, the desecration of Keithland would inevitably come to pass.

The Firelord whirled. The flurry of his footsteps rebounded from rock walls as he fled urgently toward the passageway. Once he might have summoned Earthmastery and stepped through stone in his haste. Now the intensity of his powers overwhelmed him to the point where he required the ordinary for reassurance. He ran like the simplest clansman. His breath rasped through scarred lungs as he plunged through the archway leading from the great hall.

The stairway beyond lay dark. Jaric needed no torches. The diffuse glow of his presence rinsed shadows from his path and shed clear, unsettling light over carved and inlaid risers.

Ivainson had not far to descend. The eerie circle of stillness began on the level below; between the posts of the first landing massed a horde of glowing eyes. Gierj gathered like clotted ink in the gloom of the stairwell, barring the way down. Above them drifted a featureless sphere. Its surface was polished ebony, and it spun in midair with a whine like swarming bees.

Jaric jerked to a stop. Sweating, ragged, and winded, he reached reflexively for a sword that was not there. The lapse made him curse. Every principle taught him by the Vaere, every painstaking refinement gleaned from Anskiere's instruction, now failed to apply. No discipline in memory could guide him. The complexities of multiple mastery were too vast to be encompassed, and even the simplest thoughts overreached his intent. Yet against the Morrigierj he had nothing else.

Jaric braced his feet upon the stair. Humanity would perish if he hesitated. Desperately seeking redemption for the lives his illicit mastery had cost, he gathered courage and raised sorcery. The Sathid glow that surrounded him split, singing, into hard-edged halos of force.

Inscrutably spinning, the Morrigierj acknowledged his presence. Ruby light pulsed beneath its surface. The glassy outer shell maintained its rotation, but the glow, like an eye, swiveled and steadied, scanning the nature of the being who trespassed within its lair.

A tingle coursed through Jaric's mind. Warned by impressions of near-infinite force and imminent danger, he attempted a counterward. Sathid-born energy defended with a snap. The alien probe disengaged. Unbalanced by the abruptness of its withdrawal, Jaric recoiled. His heel snagged on a riser, and he stumbled, shoulders rammed against the wrought-iron scroll of the balustrade. Below, like a matched horde of puppets, the Gierj advanced with a scrabble of claws on stone.

The Firelord did not give ground, but straightened and flung tangled hair from his eyes. "Demon!" he called hoarsely. "I challenge! To ravage Keithland, you must first contend with me."

Wary within the golden blaze of his wards, Jaric awaited the nerverasping whistle that heralded attack by the Gierj. But no sound arose. The Morrigierj melded its underlings and struck with none of the preliminaries required by Maelgrim or Tathagres.

The air went suddenly brittle. Warned only by a tingle of prescience, Jaric sprang tense. Then a flash of white heat stripped his shields. Had he not owned a Firelord's trained resistance to burns, his flesh would have seared instantaneously to ash. Instead, blinded by a flux of light, he tumbled over backward into eddies of deflected energy.

Risers banged his head, then his back and shoulders. He hooked the rail to brake his fall. Backlash sizzled around him, slagging stone and jagging sparks the length of the balustrade. Cut like a whip across the palm, Jaric cried out. He curled protectively into a crouch and waited for the sally to end. But strength flowed from Gierjling to Morrigierj, there to be channeled into violence with the unassailable surge of the tides; no direct measure could stem the onslaught. The assault raged on without letup.

Driven to act, Ivainson Firelord shaped a defense from the materials nearest to hand.

Earth wisdom answered. Power roared forth with a vehemence never equaled among mortals. Stone exploded; a storm of spinning, knife-edged fragments raked the front ranks of Gierj. Howls tore from the throats of the mortally wounded. The grazed and hale alike screeched in fury, while the Morrigierj zigzagged in the air, its aggression blunted by a fraction.

Ringed by a turbulent corona of light, Jaric struck again. His sorcery wrenched at keystones and pillars, exploding them to vapor with a force that negated sound. Stone rumbled; cracks ripped across vaulted ceilings, and the central edifice of Shadowfane shuddered toward collapse. Sand showered, rattling down the stair, followed by a grinding avalanche of rock and debris.

Yet even as the stone crashed downward, Jaric understood that he would fail. His Sathid-born gift of prescience read the outcome. A split second before reality, he knew the rubble would slow and tumble in the air, arrested in place by the Morrigierj.

The event followed like a double image; Gierjlings scrabbled from beneath tons of suspended stone. As they scuttled like rats toward safety, Jaric gained an instant to regroup. He moved to steal the advantage and, with a Firelord's defensive reflex, blasted the keep to inferno.

The sorcery struck in a white flash of heat. Stone ruptured. Lava dashed airborne with the fountaining force of storm spray. The walls ran red and crumpled. Isolated on an island of stairway, lit scarlet by currents of molten stone, Jaric closed his eyes. Desperate and blistered by heat, he pitched the sum of his vision into the future. There he sorted through meshes of pattern and outcome for a reality that left Keithland safe under sunlight.

His thoughts expanded with a rush that left him dizzied. The space of an instant showed him eons, a thousand times a thousand overviews of destruction. Scoured by the grief of uncounted deaths, he saw cities swept clean of life, whole planets overcrowded and enslaved. He watched great metal ships fire bolts that exploded with eye-searing brilliance against an ocean of darkness and stars. The images spanned all, from the infinite to the infinitesimal.

Houses burned, and forests withered. Stunted, malformed humans scratched crops from dusty furrows. Men in metal armor hunted other humans with nets, then lit cookfires to roast the meat of their skinned and slaughtered quarry; in another sequence, people crawled on all fours, eating roots torn raw from the ground. Their eyes were placid and dull as cattle, and their young grew to maturity without laughter. Jaric perceived all this and a multitude of other futures instantaneously. Hard on the heels of vision, he understood that the Morrigierj itself intervened. Its presence robbed him of inspiration, pinched off all possibilities that offered untrammeled outcomes of life and success.

The Firelord's heir knew anger then, resentment deeper than any experienced by Ivain. Power amplified his emotion, and the entire spired citadel of Shadowfane exploded in a focused discharge of fury. Rock melted and glazed, and the scream of tortured elements jarred on the air like a blow.

Still the battle raged. The circle of stillness that surrounded the Morrigierj stayed unbreached, while Gierjlings danced across lava with complete and terrifying impunity.

The counterstrike came without warning.

One second, Jaric stood juggling for balance against the flux of heat and chaos whipped up by the ferocity of his attack. The next, the whine of the Morrigierj changed pitch.

Reality altered.

Hurled adrift in a dimension beyond grasp of human logic, Jaric strove to recover orientation. Sensation was lost to him. His vision seemed smothered in felt. No awareness of his body remained, and other than the golden haze of his Sathid wards, he retained no concept of self beyond a spark of conscious will.

Energies flashed, blue and violet and ruby. Uncertain how to battle the intangible, Jaric tuned his perception to search for the enemy who stalked to kill. Darkness swallowed his attempt. He blundered, lost, and his uncertainty drew immediate attack.

Malice arose, cruel as the bite of a strangler's cord, and throttled his right to exist.

"No." Jaric steadied his wards.

The Morrigierj pressed a ruthless demand for proof of his worthiness.

Jaric countered by instinct, the shield he raised the constancy of his love for Taen. Too late, he realized his mistake; what had been his innermost strength now reflected his gravest shortfall. The Morrigierj granted no quarter. With a terrible, twisting sense of vertigo, it caused the darkness around Jaric to dissolve. As a man he found himself standing naked and alone on heated stone. Before him rose the ruined watchtower at Cliffhaven.

His breath caught in his throat, then exploded in a scream of anguish. "No!"

Protest changed nothing. Between himself and the tower's seared stairway loomed weakness he could not face: the meanness of spirit that had destroyed Marlson Emien, Merya Tathagres, and, not least, the Firelord who had sired him. Behind, blocking retreat, waited the Morrigierj and the threat of humanity's downfall. Jaric must go forward and confront the wreckage of his dearest dream, or bring total devastation upon Keithland.

The conflict beggared pride, left both spirit and dignity in shreds. Having given in once to cowardice, he found the first step a hardship of unbearable proportion. Jaric threw back his head. Tears spilled from his eyes and dampened the hair at his temples. No death or threat of bodily torment seemed worse than the condemnation that loomed beyond the tower's dark entry. The reality was double-edged. Either he would discover himself guilty of Taen's murder, or, worse, he would meet stinging accusation in her eyes, the wholeness of her love poisoned to loathing. More horrible still, she might live, and be piteously maimed.

Sooner would he have endured another trial by Sathid.

No such option existed. The Morrigierj pinned him without quarter. With a cry of unmitigated despair, Jaric regarded the tower. Anskiere and Taen had already suffered for his weakness. The rest of humanity must not be left to share the brunt of the consequences; greater evil could not be imagined. The son of Ivain Firelord renounced his last vestige of pride. He gathered his screaming nerves into something that passed for resolve, and started toward the tower's bleak doorway.

His next step proved no easier than the first. Shadows at the threshold seemed to wring him with sorrow. Stone heated still from the chaos unleashed by the Sathid blistered his soles as he set his feet on the stair. Almost, that pain became welcome, a distraction to blunt the greater wound in his heart. As Jaric climbed, memories arose to haunt him, of Taen's teasing laughter, the warm weight of her as she pressed into his arms. "You worry for three people, Jaric," she had said in her berth abroad *Moonless*. "Keithland won't collapse while you smile."

Yet no joy remained to him now. If he hesitated, the existence and the memory of humanity would be obliterated.

The end of the stairway loomed ahead, wreathed in clearing smoke. Through wrung and twisted lintels lay the chamber where Anskiere of Elrinfaer had raised his staff to end the life of Ivainson Firelord. Now the place seemed to echo the boom of the sea, as seared timbers settled. Warped stone translated the aftermath of violence into a miasma of suffocating heat. Sweating, Jaric reached the doorway. Punished beyond anguish, he raised his eyes and looked through.

The floor was a slagged and buckled ruin. Off to one side, through a drift of fine dust, light from the blasted window touched the place where Anskiere had raised his wards. A smoldering parcel of cloth marked the spot. Jaric made out the prone form of the sorcerer, then the outline of one lax hand. The fingers were horribly burned. Sickened, daunted by a hammer blow of grief, he almost missed the second figure, kneeling as she was in the shadows.

Taen sensed movement in the doorway. She raised her chin. Singed hair tangled over her shoulders, framing a face smeared with soot and the tracks of uncounted tears. She was not crippled. Yet as she bent over the body of Anskiere, her blue eyes reflected level upon level of anguish.

Ivainson Firelord expelled a shuddering breath. Helplessly exposed amid haze and debris, he forced himself steady through a moment of racking self-hatred. Against the gibbering dread in his heart, he remained until Taen Dreamweaver recognized his presence.

She did not recoil. Neither did she speak in condemnation.

Instead her face went transparent with hope and disbelief. "Jaric? Jaric! Kor's grace, is it possible you survived a multiple bonding?"

She rose awkwardly, reaching for him; joyous at his recovery, even though he had found death and evil in his heart, and given them both free rein.

Shame shackled him in place like new chain.

The Dreamweaver sensed this on an intake of breath. As always, her perceptions unveiled his innermost self. The darkness there made her stop, and frown for the space of a heartbeat. Then she stamped her foot with a curse of exasperation. "Jaric! You're a man, and men make mistakes. Those with more brains than a fish get up afterward, having learned something. *Did* you learn something? Or will I have to walk barefoot across hot stones and kick you to get a kiss?"

Jaric opened his mouth. Speech would not come. Impossibly, beyond belief, love seemed great enough to overlook his transgression.

"Kor's grace, Jaric," cried Taen. Impatience drove her to a gentle fit of fury. "You only have to forgive yourself!"

At last he found strength to raise his arms. She ran then, laughing with a relief edged with grief and hysteria. Warmth, healing, an end to inner suffering lay but a single step away.

But the Morrigierj stole the moment. It wrenched away Jaric's presence with a violence that canceled thought. Cast once more into the void, he shouted in anger. Now he was offered a measure of reprieve for his wrongs, the cruelty of denial sparked rage.

The glow of his wards blazed incandescent. Granted Taen's forgiveness, he added to his shield the sacrifices of a swordsman, a forester, and an aged, arthritic fisherman. But the bastions of his defense availed nothing. The Morrigierj glibly seized another imperfection to exploit.

The chill of deepest despair rocked his being. Jaric became subjected to ruthless judgment; as a man, he stood condemned for the barbarity inherent in humanity.

The Morrigierj pressed its claim. Mankind owned no civilization. Driven by greed, habituated to murder, no end of evil shaped their deeds. Sealed and sentenced, Jaric saw Morbrith wither under the malice of Maelgrim Dark-dreamer. The townsfolk of Tierl Enneth joined the rolls of the dead, with the captains and crews of Kisburn's fleet of warships added to humanity's account. Merchants plundered by the Kielmark were compiled indiscriminately with the crimes of every felon accused by the courts and councils of Keithland.

The tally was bleakly damning. In icy superiority, the Morrigierj demanded retribution.

Jaric rebutted the verdict.

He rallied and negated oblivion with the third tenet of Kor's Law: *No man shall claim wisdom to judge another; in the absence of order, law must prevail. Yet in the absence of the divine, no law, and no man, and no expedient can equal perfection. Forgiveness maintains the balance.*

Wearied through, and pressed against the knife edge of annihilation, Ivainson awaited. If humility, mercy, and compassion defined the requirements of grace, Taen's greatness of spirit alone should have established mankind's case. But the unknowable awareness of the Morrigierj dissected the ideology of Kor's priests and found no satisfaction.

Keithland's cities would perish, seared from the face of existence along with all life seeded by the probe ship *Corinne Dane.*

Jaric knew stunned disbelief. Then anger gave rise to skepticism. The decree of Morrigierj rang strangely false. Gifted with the beginnings of wisdom, the glimmer of greater truth, he realized that the sentence of death against his kind was no verdict but a foregone conclusion from the start. Caught up and agonizing over the meanness of his flaws, he had been duped into belief that humanity's fate could be redeemed by logic. Reality outlined the converse, the essence of evil embodied. The Morrigierj was a being wedded to destruction, addicted to the euphoria of exercising superior power over the weak.

Jaric retaliated with the brute philosophy of the Kielmark: *Let strategy prevail through cleverness and force! Keithland shall go free.* Driven beyond self-preservation, the master of two score Sathid released the sum of his powers against the bodiless darkness that imprisoned him.

Energy ripped outward. A core more fiery than sun force bloomed and burst across the nethermost dark of the void. Jaric screamed. Blasted raw by the recoil, he missed the dazzling play of defense wards while the demon he opposed strove and failed to compensate. As the Morrigierj and its minions became consigned to oblivion, his own awareness overloaded. Perception dimmed to the silvered gray of twilight, and plunged inexorably into shadow. Jaric glimpsed stars like frost on velvet; then vision died. Like a mote smothered in deep-ocean silence, he knew nothing more.

Ivainson Jaric roused to the needling ice of raindrops, and darkness like winter midnight. No aura of light eased his passage to consciousness; no roof shielded him from the elements. Stiff and chilled and lone, he listened to the wail of the wind off the fells. In time, vision unaltered by Sathid-power picked out the stony crest where Shadowfane's spires once rose. Not even rubble remained of the stronghold where Gierj had dueled for the chance to exterminate humanity.

Jaric blinked run-off from his eyes. Tangled hair coiled wet against his neck. His cheeks were rough with stubble, and weariness weighted his limbs like so much water-logged wood. Though he preferred not to move, cold finally forced him to his feet. Standing, shivering, he found the past too painful to think on. The deaths of a friend and a sorcerer robbed his future of joy. Suspicious that the confrontation in the watchtower had been a dream invented by the Morrigierj to test him, Ivainson avoided memory of his Dreamweaver. He had faced her ghost, and made peace. Now duty drove him to straighten his shoulders and ascend the slippery escarpment that once had buttressed Shadowfane.

His feet slid treacherously on the incline. To prevent a wrenched ankle or a spinning fall onto rock, he shed his boots and continued barefoot, though stiff crowns of lichen abraded his naked soles.

He reached the summit in the wintry light of daybreak. Rock there had fused into glassy whorls of slag; no crevice remained for plantlife to grope and cling. Jaric knelt in the full brunt of the wind. A tattered figure with rain-soaked hair and lifeless eyes, he set scarred fingers to the stone. Then, without knowing what the outcome would be, he spoke a word.

A golden haze of light veiled his fingers; his mastery was not entirely dead. He called upon the earth, and grudgingly, tiredly, power answered. The bowl of the sky brightened as he worked. Tattered storm clouds raced south and unveiled a morning sparkling with frost. Oblivious to the length of the shadow he cast, Ivainson Jaric arose. Cradled in his arms was the melted lump that once had been the Kielmark's two-handed sword. Perhaps in the past the twisted artifact had been crafted by a mother's hands, into a weapon for a wayward and precocious son; any truth in the claim had gone with the man. The Firelord sighed. His tears were long since spent. He touched the mass with his mastery, and sunlight and sorcery flashed on silver as ruined steel reshaped, perfectly replicating the blade's original form.

Jaric ran his fingers over the hilt, then tested balance and sharpness; the edge felt keen enough to satisfy the stringent standards of its master. Carefully Ivainson removed his tunic. His body glimmered with the returning trace of an aura, and he no longer felt the cold. He wrapped the blade in wool, then bound it with lacings borrowed from his shirt. When the task was meticulously complete, the son of Ivain Firelord stripped his last ragged clothing. He drank and bathed in a rain pool.

Dripping but clean, he shook the tangles from his hair. Then he gathered together his last memories of a friend, and a sword destined for Deison Corley. Clothed in a brightening radiance of power, the onetime scribe from Morbrith turned south toward the lands of men; and his steps melted footprints in the frost.

Epilogue

Warmth lingered late in the northern hills of Felwaithe. Days of rich sunlight alternated with crisp, star-strewn nights. Farmsteaders reaped full harvests and returned content to their firesides, forever secure from the predations of demons; news traveled faster than the sorcerer responsible. Clad in a shepherd's cloak of oiled wool, he made his way south on foot. He might have journeyed more speedily; the flare and shimmer of unused power veiled his form in light. Yet he would engage no sorcery since the morning he had restored the sword that hung from the strap at his shoulder. He avoided the villages and roads; but birds and wild creatures were drawn by the brilliance of his presence. Llondelei greeted him rejoicing, for their far-seers predicted a grant of new Sathid from the Vaere. In the roughest wilds in Keithland, hillfolk waylaid him with song and wreaths of fire-lilies.

He learned, then, that Corley's translation of a priestess's prophecy had been deliberately understated. The faintest spark of amusement flashed in his eyes, the first since the fall of Anskiere.

Winter spit sleet from the sky when Ivainson Jaric reached Cliffhaven. Set ashore by a crotchety fisherman with a limp, the Firelord remembered another fisherman who had died. He paid for his passage with an unsmiling face, then delivered the burden of the Kielmark's sword into the hands of Deison Corley. Memories he could not shed stayed with him.

Corley stamped cold feet, discomforted by the brilliant but taciturn figure at his side. "Come in from the wind," he invited.

Jaric declined with a faint shake of his head. He spoke his first and only words since leaving the slagged crest of Shadowfane. "Where is Taen?"

Corley raised tired eyes. "Gone. She went south, to the Vaere, when Anskiere—"

Jaric interrupted, gently, but unarguably firm. "I know."

So formidable was his conviction that the captain did not press the fact that the wizards of Mhored Kara had not entirely succeeded in damping the backlash incurred when his Firelord's powers were revoked. Several of their adepts had died, and the Stormwarden's injuries had been severe enough to require treatment on the isle of the Vaere. Corley shifted his weight, distressed by the restless manner in which the Firelord regarded the sea. "You'll find *Callinde* warped to the south dock. My shipwrights kept her seaworthy."

Jaric nodded; but his expression proved that his thoughts strayed elsewhere. He touched the captain's hand in farewell, and turned to find his boat. Long after nightfall, the sentries in Cliffhaven's beacon tower watched the distant spark of his presence vanish beyond the horizon.

Ivainson sailed through the gales of late winter and beached on the Isle of the Vaere. Snowflakes melted in sun-bleached hair as his scarred hands furled sail. At length he looked up and met a watcher with fey black eyes. Tamlin stood on the sand with his pipe, a cloud of smoke rings for company.

Jaric drew breath, troubled by the ache of old wounds. Speech came haltingly after long weeks of silence. "Your secret is secure from demons. Men can now abandon sorcery and the Cycle of Fire."

The creature, whose form was actually the projection of a sophisticated machine, was not intimidated by crackling auras of power. Tamlin lifted his pipe from his teeth and released an irreverent smoke ring. "Firelord's son, you're ignorant. Now, as never before, the strength of your mastery is needed."

Such was the perception of Ivainson's powers, the Vaere needed no words to qualify; *Corinne Dane*'s mission at last had been realized, an effective defense for psionic aliens found in the person of the Firelord's heir. Jaric must stay, and train others with talent to multiple mastery of Sathid. After Keithland, Starhope and the other worlds enslaved by Gierj and Morrigierj waited to be set free.

Jaric bent his head. He, who had desired nothing beyond the bounds of Keithland, would reluctantly blaze the path toward the stars. The thought caused him untold sorrow, until a shower of sand struck his ankles.

"Fish-brains! Beloved, you took forever to get here." Two hands plunged through the light of his presence, to lock with fierce strength around his chest.

"Taen," Jaric murmured; he turned and buried his face in black hair. Only the Dreamweaver knew that he wept. She waited, patient in his embrace, as other footsteps approached. The presence of a second sorcerer brushed her awareness. She smiled then, but said nothing. When her Firelord looked up, he would find the Stormwarden of Elrinfaer limping across sand to meet him.

Here ends
The Cycle of Fire